Stella Gemmell has a degree in politics and is a journalist. She was married to the internationally acclaimed and best-selling fantasy novelist David Gemmell and worked with him on his three 'Troy' novels, completing the final book, *Troy: Fall of Kings*, following his death in 2006. Her first solo novel, the acclaimed *The City*, was published in 2013, and confirmed her as a major name in fantasy fiction in her own right. Stella Gemmell lives and writes in East Sussex.

Acclaim for *The City*:

'An astonishing book and all the more amazing given that it is Stella Gemmell's debut . . . combines extraordinary scope with first class characterization, devastating and visceral battles, a multi-layered plot and a tightly-focused narrative that keeps you reading, eager for the next page. *The City* is easily the best fantasy novel I've read in the last decade'
JAMES BARCLAY

'Stella Gemmell's skills as an author are immediately apparent. There's a sophistication in the story-telling as the episodic structure commands attention and engagement from the readers . . . the most satisfying, intelligent and enthralling epic fantasy I've read in many a year. It stands comparison with the finest writers currently developing and exploring the enthralling balance between realism and heroism in the epic fantasy tradition that David Gemmell pioneered'
JULIET McKENNA

'One of the best fantasy novels I've read in a long time – and I read a lot . . . the world-building is handled with incredible flair . . . a book of intrigue, a story of duplicity, of revenge and of loyalty. A story that pits love against hate, and honour against deceit with an even pace and slowly building tension . . . *The City* is utterly [illegible] fiction, an awesome example of [illegible]

'A sweeping novel of great power . . . filled with eloquent, textured prose highlighting powerful emotions and beings of great power. Stella Gemmell is a writer with an engaging voice'
TOR.COM

'A brutally visual world . . . vivid, motivated characters each with a heartbreaking history . . . thrilling and devastating . . . a true epic'
SCIFI NOW

'A plethora of well-defined, superbly-executed characters . . . I found myself absolutely hooked . . . there is an ever-growing sense of tension. Even before the final, inevitable, showdown you get the feeling that things are going to get bloody and not everyone is going to make it out of this alive . . . this is engrossing stuff that's expertly executed'
ELOQUENT PAGE

'Gemmell's volcanic imagination . . . pyrotechnics of description and unstoppable lava flows of intrigue, sweeping us along to the white-hot conclusion'
SFX

'Demands your complete and total attention . . . a gripping climax and wonderful multi dimensional characters . . . a new and very powerful voice in the world of fantasy. Highly Recommended'
PARMENION BOOKS

THE IMMORTAL THRONE

Stella Gemmell

CORGI BOOKS

TRANSWORLD PUBLISHERS
61–63 Uxbridge Road, London W5 5SA
www.penguin.co.uk

Transworld is part of the Penguin Random House group of companies
whose addresses can be found at global.penguinrandomhouse.com

First published in Great Britain in 2016 by Bantam Press
an imprint of Transworld Publishers
Corgi edition published 2017

A CIP catalogue record for this book
is available from the British Library.

ISBN
9780552168977

Typeset in 11/12.5pt Plantin Light by Falcon Oast Graphic Art Ltd.
Printed and bound by Clays Ltd, Bungay, Suffolk.

1 3 5 7 9 10 8 6 4 2

THE IMMORTAL THRONE

PETRUS
The Vorago
PLAIN
OF
GARAN-TSE
TRIBAL LANDS
Arocir
GREY
MOUNTAINS
N

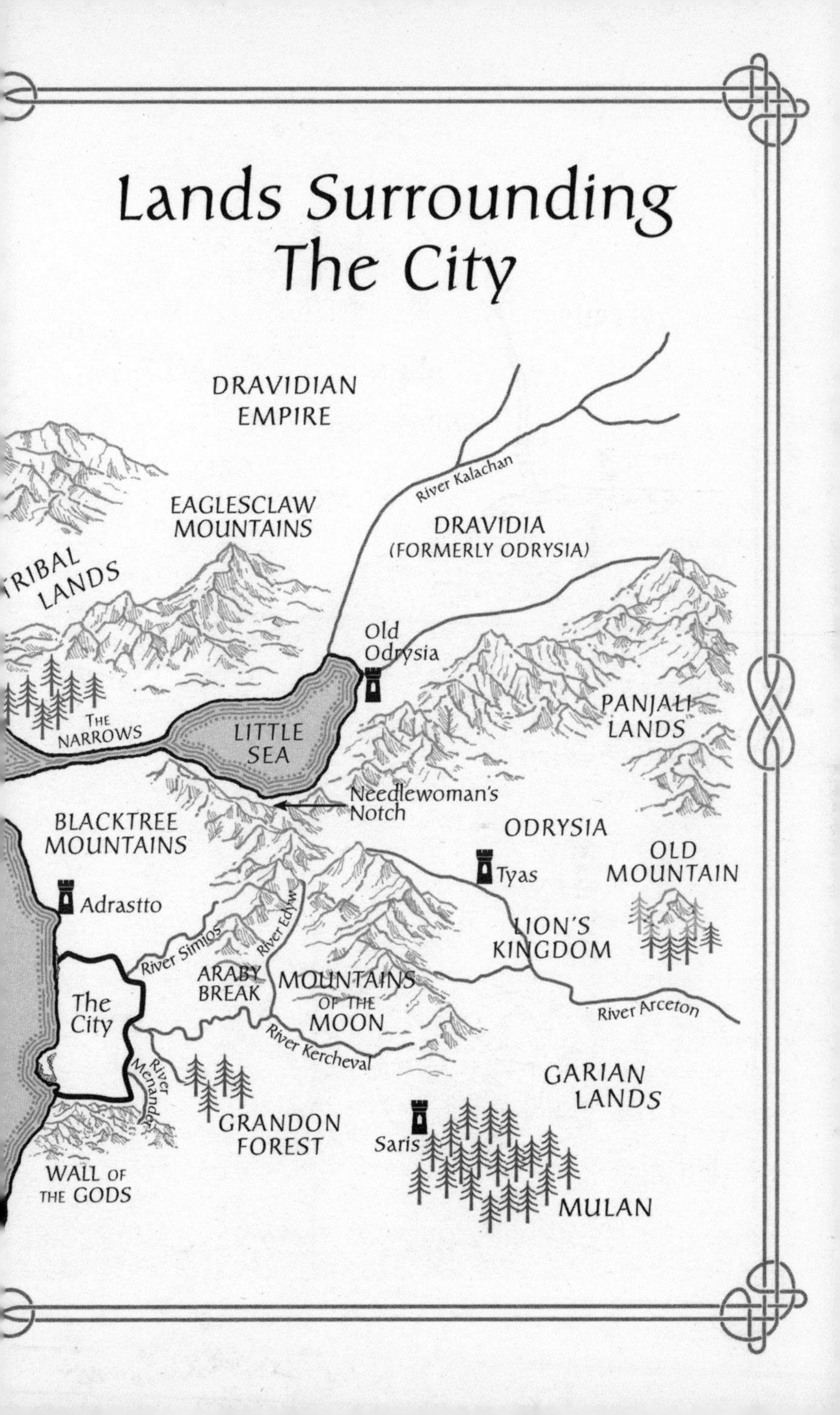
Lands Surrounding The City
DRAVIDIAN EMPIRE
River Kalachan
EAGLESCLAW MOUNTAINS
DRAVIDIA (FORMERLY ODRYSIA)
TRIBAL LANDS
Old Odrysia
PANJALI LANDS
THE NARROWS
LITTLE SEA
Needlewoman's Notch
BLACKTREE MOUNTAINS
ODRYSIA
OLD MOUNTAIN
Tyas
Adrastto
LION'S KINGDOM
River Edyw
River Simios
ARABY BREAK
MOUNTAINS OF THE MOON
River Arceton
The City
River Kercheval
River Menander
GARIAN LANDS
GRANDON FOREST
Saris
WALL OF THE GODS
MULAN

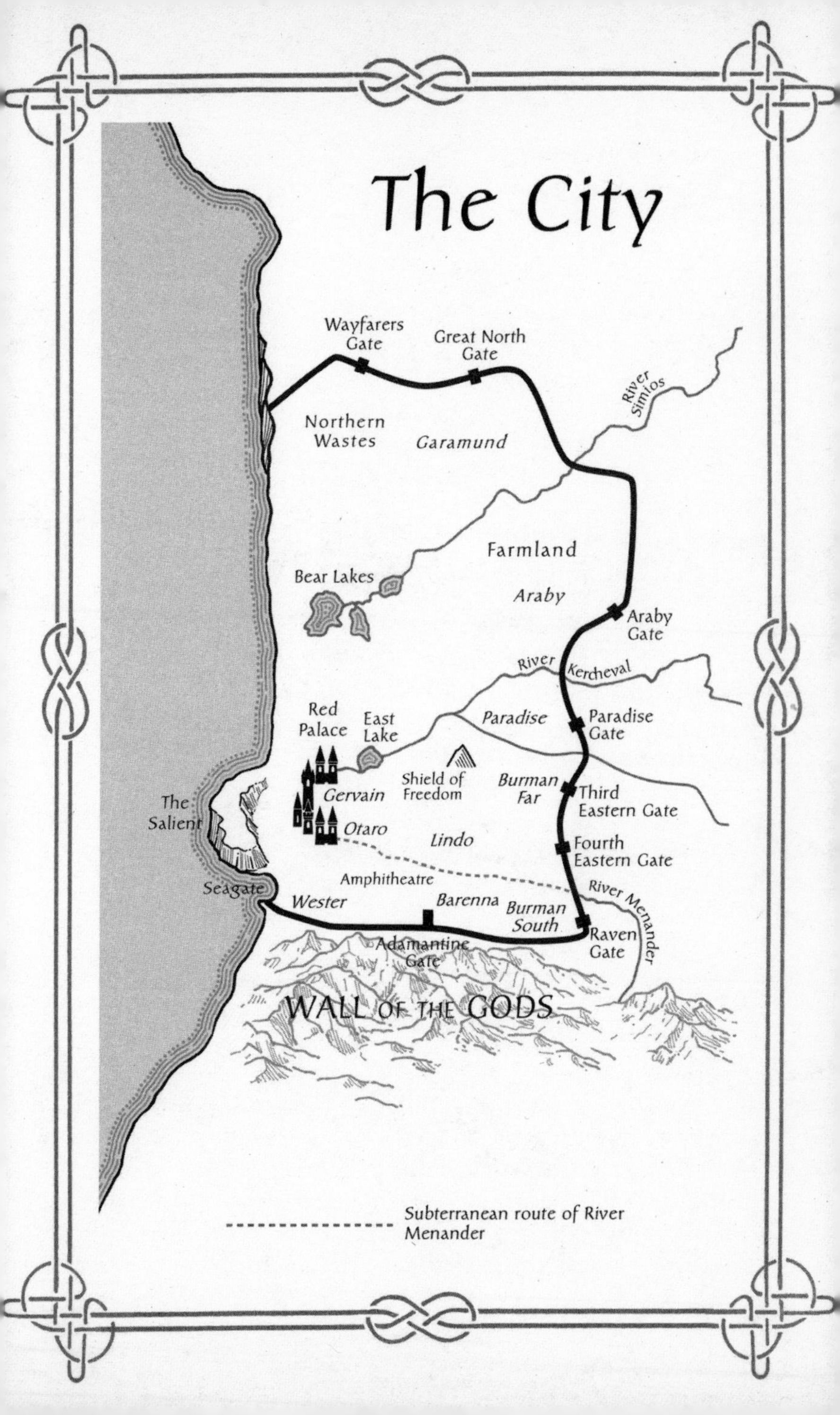
The City
Wayfarers Gate
Great North Gate
River Simios
Northern Wastes
Garamund
Farmland
Bear Lakes
Araby
Araby Gate
River Kercheval
Red Palace
East Lake
Paradise
Paradise Gate
Shield of Freedom
Burman Far
Third Eastern Gate
Gervain
The Salient
Otaro
Lindo
Fourth Eastern Gate
Amphitheatre
River Menander
Seagate
Wester
Barenna
Burman South
Raven Gate
Adamantine Gate
WALL OF THE GODS
Subterranean route of River Menander

PROLOGUE

'NO, BOY! NOT LIKE THAT!'

The old man snatched the sword from Rubin's hand and smacked him with the flat of it. 'No, you young fool!' he cried. 'Look to your sister!'

Rubbing his shoulder, Rubin turned to Indaro who, unmoved by the weapons master's fury, demonstrated the advance lunge with power and grace. Holding the stance, she was still as a statue, light as a leaf, firm as a rock. She smiled at her brother without conceit.

Suddenly dispirited, Rubin announced, 'I can't do this any more.' He felt no envy of Indaro. He adored her and was in awe of her skill. Yet although he was the younger by two years he knew he would never, even if he practised daily and lived to make old bones, make a master swordsman – or even a competent one.

Neither his sister nor weapons master Gillard moved to stop him as Rubin bounded up the steps of the sunken garden where they practised on summer days. At the top he was struck again by the chill wind off the sea. The Guillaume house, grey and four-square, stood atop the Salient, the rocky cliff piled high between the City and the sea, and it was always windy there. Rubin looked up at the house and was surprised to see their father framed in his high study window looking down at him. But then, *He's not watching me*, Rubin realized bleakly, *he's watching Indaro.*

On a whim he ran inside, along grey stone corridors, racing three at a time up the stairs to his father's study. Outside the door he skidded to a halt.

Rubin was not frightened of his father – it would be four years yet before he learned the proper meaning of fear – but he did find the man daunting. He seldom saw him, still less spoke to him, but whenever he did there seemed no bond between them, no more than existed between Reeve Kerr Guillaume and one of his servants. Rubin knocked on the door.

'Come in.'

His father still stood at the window.

'I don't want any more fencing lessons,' Rubin blurted to his back.

Reeve turned slowly, his long, ascetic face calm, as ever.

'As you wish.'

'I know I'm only twelve and it'll be four years before I join the emperor's army and I could improve in that time,' the boy went on, making an argument for his father, for it seemed Reeve would not. 'But . . .' he hesitated.

'But there is little call for fencing skills in the infantry,' his father offered.

'Yes,' Rubin went on, encouraged. 'And I think I'm holding Indaro back.'

Reeve frowned. 'Now you are lying,' he replied, but he did not sound angry with his son, or even interested. 'Indaro will not suffer for watching you stumble and fall at something she is so very good at. And you know it. You are overstating your case, boy, a case you have already won.'

Rubin shifted from foot to foot. His father regarded

him with hooded eyes, impassive. In a bid to please him, Rubin said, 'Indaro will be the greatest swordswoman in the City!'

'She already is. By the time she is sixteen she will be able to take on the best of swordsmen too. She is magnificent.'

The word hung in the air as his father sat down at his desk and bent to his work, a clear signal for Rubin to leave. But the boy loitered, gazing at the book-lined walls, wondering why any one man would need so many books.

'You won't punish Gillard, will you?'

'Whatever for?' Reeve asked, looking up.

'For striking me.'

'He's a weapons master. What do you expect?' Reeve added, 'Perhaps he hoped you would defend yourself.'

Rubin still lingered, but now he had a chance to talk to his father he struggled for something to say. The silence was broken only by the scritch-scratch of quill on thick vellum.

Finally he asked, 'Is the emperor really immortal?' This was something the boys he was tutored with talked about. The others believed the emperor would live for ever, *had* lived for ever, but Rubin argued that everything dies, even the stars, in the end.

His father did not answer for a few moments, and Rubin thought he was going to ignore the question, but at last Reeve lifted his head again and said, 'No. It is a title. He is a man like me and, like me, he will die one day.'

'Then who will be emperor?'

'Marcellus, the First Lord.'

'Why? He is not the emperor's son. The emperor is of the Family Sarkoy. Marcellus is a Vincerus.' Rubin was proud of his knowledge of the City's noble Families.

Reeve regarded him, his black eyes thoughtful. Perhaps he was in reflective mood, for his focus shifted past Rubin, through the grey stone walls and far beyond the cliffs of the Salient. He nodded to himself, a decision made.

'When the Serafim first came here . . .' he began. Rubin did not know what the Serafim were, not then, but he dared not interrupt this unlooked-for communication, '. . . there were many of them, but over time most died or travelled away, perhaps returning from whence they came. There was only a handful left of the original team and this world was harsh and perilous. Their leader Araeon decided, and the rest agreed at the time, that Marcellus should succeed him should he die. They had all been through a great deal, you see, and it was always Araeon who kept them together, kept them strong, kept them alive.'

'Did he have no sons of his own?'

'No. But a great deal changed over the long years. There were quarrels, and worse, between the Serafim, and in time some argued fiercely against Marcellus inheriting. One of them, Hammarskjald, tried to kill Araeon and wrest power. He was branded a criminal and banished from the City. Later it was rumoured he had been murdered on Araeon's orders, murdered and his body burned. Then as the City became richer and stronger Araeon started calling himself emperor, the Immortal, and stopped listening to what anyone else said. Other Serafim, including the woman who had once been his wife, conspired against him. But Araeon was wily and his reach was long and in time most of the plotters were executed or exiled. And through it all only Marcellus remained loyal, despite everything.

'Loyalty is the most important virtue of all, boy,' Reeve said, focusing on his son again, 'but you must choose the recipient of it with care. I have admired

Marcellus' faithfulness down the years, although I think he has been wrong in almost everything else.

'And now there are just three of them left – three of the First. Araeon, Marcellus, Archange. There are other Serafim, myself included, descendants of the First who form the seven noble Families of the City.'

Sarkoy, Vincerus, Khan and Kerr, Gaeta, Guillaume, Broglanh, thought Rubin. *Every child knows these names.*

'But,' his father went on, 'these three are by far the most powerful. And no one else is like them. So they are wedded to each other in a way no others can be. And when Araeon dies, for he is the oldest, then Marcellus will be his successor.'

Reeve looked troubled as he stared towards the City, as if sensing coming danger. 'This is not the subject for conversation on a pleasant summer's day,' he commented, and as he spoke the sky started to darken and within moments thunderheads began rolling in from the west. The air in the study cooled and Rubin shivered.

'When you leave this place to join the army, where I pray you will use intelligence and speed and courage to keep you alive, and not your fighting skills . . .' His father paused and Rubin saw a rare glint of amusement in his eye. '. . . I advise you to stay away from people of power. The armies of the Immortal are filled with generals who don't know a broadsword from a battle axe, and the murky corridors of the Red Palace are peopled by men, and women, whose only thought is how to stab others in the back whilst protecting their own.'

He lowered his voice. 'This is treasonous talk, Rubin, and you will not repeat it beyond these four walls. Even to your sister. Araeon is very old, older than the City itself, and is far gone into madness. But he stalks the corridors in many guises and his power is still far-reaching. His physical and moral corruption affects everyone who passes through the Red Palace.'

He paused and Rubin was captive in his father's dark gaze. 'Marcellus has always stood at his right hand and when he takes the throne people will smile and say Marcellus will be a benevolent emperor, but it is a long time since Marcellus was benevolent. He is arrogant and ruthless and he loves power and the uses of power. But,' Reeve sat back in his chair, 'he will end this war, I believe, and for that reason only I will be glad to see him succeed to the Immortal Throne.'

'He will conquer the Blues?'

Reeve smiled thinly. 'No, he cannot conquer the Blues, as you and your young friends call them. We have been at war with this alliance of Petrassi, Odrysians, Fkeni and dozens of neighbouring tribes for more than a century. We have exhausted our resources in the war, as they also have, but now the City is beleaguered as never before. You know of the blockade, boy?'

Rubin nodded. From high on the Salient you could just make out the enemy ships in the distant south guarding the Seagate, the main harbour of the City, and others in the north at the entrance to the Narrows.

'The enemy is not at our gates,' Reeve explained, 'not fighting beneath our walls, not yet, but the lands all around the City are a desert, where nothing grows and only battling armies flourish.'

He thought for a while. 'No, Marcellus will not conquer the Blues. The First Lord is a pragmatist and he has travelled far and wide while Araeon has been prowling the Red Palace. He will forge alliances, beguile enemy leaders with his charm, which is considerable, and negotiate the war's end.' He shook his head. 'The City cannot endure war for many more years.'

He bent to his desk again, writing quickly as if fired

by his own words. Rubin wandered round the room and looked out of the window where rain was starting to spit and spat on the glass. He thought about what he had heard.

'What about the emperor's wife? Is she still alive?'

When Reeve lifted his head again the boy saw his eyes were troubled. 'Archange has not been his wife for a very long time. Indeed, she left the City rather than exist in it with him. But I've heard rumours that she has returned and that cannot be a good thing.'

'Why?'

'Because Archange is perhaps the most dangerous of them all.'

PART ONE

The Third Messenger

CHAPTER ONE

THE EMPEROR EAGLE MAKES ITS EYRIE IN THE HEIGHTS of the mountains, far from the haunts of man. Though built of blood and sinew, bone and claw, like the smallest dunghill scavenger, its effortless command of the sky and all-seeing eye make it a potent symbol, in the minds of her warriors, of the mastery and might of the City.

It was not always so. For centuries the phoenix held that emblematic role, watching over the rise of the City and its fall by, variously, earthquake, war, social collapse and once, aptly, by fire. But when the emperor called Saduccuss demanded that one be captured and brought to the Red Palace for display, its mythological status proved a drawback. Saduccuss, thwarted, then decreed that the tufted pea-duck, a dramatically beautiful but stupid creature, given to panic, replace the phoenix as the City's symbol. One was netted and brought to the palace where it hid pitiably in corners, losing its feathers and its beauty until it was mercifully despatched by one of the imperial gulons.

And it was then that the emperor eagle, formerly the crimson eagle, was promoted to City symbol, having the benefit of aloofness without the disadvantage of being non-existent.

One such bird, soaring on air currents far above the topmost peaks of the Blacktree Mountains, might have looked down and wondered what the City's soldiers were doing so high in these crags at dead of winter. Time was when armies packed away their weapons and armour as the chilly weather closed in, retreating homeward like the silver bears which return to their habitual caverns at first frost to doze away the long days of ice.

Had the emperor eagle been interested, or able, to discriminate between the uniforms of the City warriors and those of their enemy, it might have thought the City embattled. True, its force was the smaller one, but it blocked the entrance to a deep, rocky valley which protected the enemy Blues – an allied army of Odrysians and Buldekki. And the City soldiers were well armed and better provisioned, whereas the Blues had been too long in the field, were short of supplies, low on weapons, far from aid.

And on this particular day, less than a year before the Fall of the City to flood and invasion, one company of Odrysians, cut off from their main army, was in a desperate plight.

The dead woman wouldn't keep quiet.

Jan Vandervarr pulled his felt cap low over his ears in a vain bid to block out her feeble cries. He was perched on a bare rocky ledge, scoured by icy wind, overlooking a mute, snow-covered valley which two days before had been a battlefield.

All the other corpses, hundreds of them, had disappeared under falls of snow and were pristine white mounds, gentle on the softened land. But the woman warmed the snow with her dying body and her uniform was a splash of black, spilled ink on white. And she moved from time to time, valiantly trying to crawl back to her lines, though she did not know the way. She would remain silent for hours, and Jan would hope she was dead, then she would moan again, or chant some City ritual. Jan wished he had the courage to descend and send her to her death gods. But he feared the long range of the heavy crossbows on the far slopes of the valley where City bowmen watched and waited.

He heard a scuffle behind him as someone emerged from the cave-mouth, and smelled the acrid odour of thick smoke and unwashed bodies pouring out on the expelled air. He and his comrades of the Odrysian Seventeenth infantry had been pinned down in this too-small cave for two nights and there was no sign they would be escaping soon. He was glad to do guard duty, to get away from the sounds and stench of forty trapped, discontented men. And there was nothing really to guard against. Nothing was moving in this silent land, except the dead woman.

'Someone should go down and finish her,' his friend Franken said, squatting beside him. The smell of smoke rolled off him.

'You go,' Jan replied.

It was a conversation they had had before.

'Rats deserve everything that's coming to them,' Franken opined.

The dunghill Rats – as the Odrysians called the City fighters – had come down on them before dusk as they trudged along the valley on their way back to the main body of their army. The skirmish had lost them a hundred or more. With darkness thickening around them they had retreated up to these caves to lick their wounds, ready to break out and hit back at the City the next day. But that night had brought heavy snowfall and the temperature had dropped like a stone. Dawn the next day had revealed a valley bright with whiteness, muffled and still.

'City sorcery,' Franken offered, sucking his teeth and spitting in the snow.

He was still talking about the woman. Jan made no reply.

Franken glanced at him. 'I wouldn't be a Rat.'

It was a common subject for discussion among the allied forces. They all knew Rats were hard to kill. They didn't know why, though there was much superstitious talk about their emperor, whom the City fighters called the Immortal, and his magics. But whatever the reason, and Jan Vandervarr didn't much care what it was, it made City warriors formidable enemies. Even the women. No one wanted to die – and yet if you had a mortal wound you prayed for a quick death or the salvation of a comrade's merciful blade. No one wanted to die like this woman, lost in the snow.

Jan sighed. His years in the Odrysian army had shown him there were no easy deaths, no easy answers. A vision of his wife Peg, dead these ten years, flashed before his eyes. He pushed it away ruthlessly. That life was long gone. This was his life now.

There was another blast of warm, noisome air from the cave-mouth, and a third soldier squatted on the ledge beside them. Jan glanced at him. It was the red-haired officer who had joined them in the autumn from a company destroyed by the City's Maritime army at Copperburn. The newcomer was young and tall and very thin, with legs like a crane's, and his fiery hair was pulled back in a wiry bunch behind his head. Jan grinned to himself. The three of them perched in a row looked like gargoyles he'd seen on the imperial palace in Old Odrysia, now lost to the Dravidian Empire.

Faint sounds drifted up from the snowy valley.

'Someone should go down and finish her,' Franken commented to the new man pointedly.

The officer nodded his agreement then stood and

stepped off the ledge into the deep snow. His skinny shanks sank into the icy crust and he nearly lost his balance.

'What are you doing?' Franken asked with alarm, grabbing the redhead's shoulder to keep him upright.

'Going down to despatch her, as you suggest,' the young officer replied, regaining his balance and taking another step.

'They'll despatch *you* before you get to her,' Franken told him, pointing to the rocky crags across the valley. 'Those bolts of theirs will skewer you like pork.'

The officer looked back and smiled. Jan saw he had the strangest violet-coloured eyes.

'No they won't,' he told Franken. 'They'll wait until I'm on my way back.'

Then he plunged forward and started forging his way through the hip-deep snow, moving his arms as if paddling a boat. It was slow going and twice he fell over, but he struggled to his feet and pressed on. As his dark figure dwindled Jan expected him to go down at any moment, felled by a crossbow bolt, but he trudged on until he reached the woman and there he stood, leaning above her like a wading bird, taking his time.

'What's he up to?' Franken asked, squinting, as if Jan might have better information than he. 'He's talking to her.' Then he added, 'Man's a fool.'

Women warriors make fools of us all, Jan thought. The Odrysians all despised the Rats, or claimed to, for including women in their ranks, but no one hesitated to kill them along with the men they stood with. In a good honest hand-to-hand battle the women were easier to kill, mutilate or disarm. But most fighting was in the scramble of a skirmish, at night, or in bad weather, or on tough terrain, and the women were often faster, presented a smaller target, and were lower to the ground, better balanced. Many of his dead comrades had learned that the hard way when hesitating to despatch a woman. Jan had no trouble killing them now, and he had learned to fear them just as much as their menfolk.

'He's coming back,' Franken announced, his finger, as always, on the pulse of the obvious.

Jan watched as the officer presented his back to the enemy and started plodding back up the treacherous hillside towards them.

'They'll take him now,' Franken said confidently, but still the young man came on, unskewered, until he was out of crossbow range and scrambling up the steep incline beneath the ledge. Jan and Franken offered a hand each and pulled. The officer's boots slid on the icy shelf, then he was beside them again. He stamped the snow off his legs and turned back towards the cave.

'Is she dead?' Jan asked him.

The young man nodded.

'What were you talking to her about?' Franken asked. But the officer moved back towards the cave-mouth, offering no reply.

'Well, what did she say?' Franken asked his back.

The officer hesitated and turned for a moment.

'She said, "Marcellus is coming."'

The red-headed officer, whom the Odrysians knew as Adolfus but whose real name was Rubin Kerr Guillaume, pushed aside the heavy groundsheet which screened the men from the worst of the cold, then ducked his head and with a sniff of distaste entered the reeking cave. There were two fires, one for the officers, one for the men, but they were poor weak things, fuelled by damp brush and twigs, pouring out more smoke than heat. The smoke lay in a thick layer in the roof of the cave. It was impossible to see through, impossible to breathe, and Rubin hurried, doubled up, stepping over injured soldiers to his billet where he sat down against the rock wall and took a cautious breath. Several junior officers watched him sourly. He was not a popular man, he knew, and if they wondered what he'd been up to they didn't ask.

Rubin, under direct orders from the City's First Lord Marcellus Vincerus, had infiltrated the Odrysian company after the Battle of Copperburn, where the City's veteran Maritime had crushed an alliance of Blues in a three-day battle of unparalleled awfulness. Rubin's command of the Odrysian tongue was pitch-perfect, and he had previously spent two years in their country, long enough to convince the keenest of inquisitors that he was a native. No, the other junior officers didn't dislike him because they suspected him of being a spy. They disliked him because they suspected him of being an arrogant, opinionated dilettante. Which was at least partly true, and which was just the way Rubin liked it.

He rummaged in his pack, pulling out some crusty old bread and leathery meat. He sniffed the meat, decided it would last a day or so more, and chewed on the bread, which wouldn't.

A dark figure emerged from the smoke, coughing. 'General wants you.'

Rubin sighed. In the scramble to find shelter after the battle two days before he had stuck closely to the senior officers and found himself in the same cave as the general. He liked to stay near the centre of things. But now it meant having to explain himself, something he didn't care for. He stood and ducked under the smoke again to where Arben Busch was encamped.

Rubin loomed awkwardly over him until the general glanced up and gestured him to sit. Busch was dark-faced and bad-tempered, but he had the reputation of a brilliant strategist, a reputation Rubin was starting to doubt now they were a hundred-odd men trapped in caves at dead of winter.

'Did you kill her?' the general asked him.

'Yes, sir.'

'Why?'

'She was affecting the men's morale, sir.'

Busch sighed, deeply pouched eyes red and weary.

'Did it occur to you that if she was affecting *our* morale she was affecting the enemy still more?'

'No it didn't, sir,' Rubin said straight-faced.

Busch snorted. 'Did you question her? What did she say?'

'She said Marcellus would come and destroy us all.'

'Marcellus is fighting in the south,' put in another officer, a loud-mouthed know-nothing called Camben.

'As far as we know,' added the general thoughtfully. Then he shook his head. 'Just words,' he concluded. 'She wields Marcellus like a bogeyman to frighten us with.'

Rubin told him: 'She was blind. She thought I was a comrade.'

'You speak the City tongue?' asked Camben suspiciously, glancing at his general to see if he was impressed by this keen deduction.

'Of course,' Rubin replied. 'Know your enemy and his ways. Don't you?' he asked in mock surprise.

'I don't succour the enemy,' replied Camben, reddening.

'Gentlemen,' Busch snapped. 'How is the terrain?' he asked.

'Hopeless,' Rubin told him. 'The snow is still waist-deep in parts. Crossing the valley would take half a day. They could pick us all off at their leisure with those hefty crossbows of theirs.'

'We don't even know if the City crossbowmen are

still there,' argued Camben. 'We haven't seen them for more than a day.'

'They're still there,' said Rubin.

Camben scowled at him, but Busch asked, 'How are you so sure?'

Rubin shrugged and flashed a smile, which was wasted on the dour general. 'I could feel their eyes on me,' he lied.

'You can take guard duty tonight.' The general cocked his head towards the cave-mouth, dismissing him.

As Rubin turned away new arrivals covered with fresh snow came in from the cold, stamping their feet, shaking themselves like wet dogs. Officers from the other caves were gathering, and Rubin would be stuck outside unable to hear what was going on. He returned to his pack, took out a thick wool scarf and a thin blanket, swallowed the last piece of bread, then went out into the icy air.

It was snowing hard now and he could see nothing but a moving white wall a few paces in front of him. It was blowing away from the cave-mouth, though, and Vandervarr and Franken had erected a small awning in the lee of a rocky outcrop. They looked quite cosy, and Rubin joined them.

'Punishment?' Vandervarr asked in his friendly way.

Rubin smiled briefly and nodded.

'Perhaps I can go back inside then,' Franken suggested hopefully.

Vandervarr grimaced. 'We may as well all go in. We're doing no bloody good out here.'

It was true. The entire City army could walk up to them and they wouldn't see it until it was a sword's length away. Rubin scrambled back until his spine was against the rock wall, then he wrapped the scarf round his head and the blanket round his shoulders. As an afterthought he pulled out his long-bladed knife and positioned it on the ground near his left hand.

'That's a pigsticker,' Franken commented.

'My father's,' Rubin replied and the two others nodded in satisfaction. This was what they expected to hear.

'Where are you from?' Jan Vandervarr asked.

'Parabel,' Rubin said, pulling out a familiar story from his mind's backpack of handy tales. 'Upper Heights. My father owned an inn there.' The mere mention of a tavern made a fighting man feel at ease, he'd discovered. 'Before the Great Catastrophe,' he added. Reference to the destruction of the winter palace and the execution of the Odrysian royal family created a bond of loss.

Franken snorted. 'You're a rich boy, then.'

Rubin shrugged. 'I bleed and die for my country like any man,' he said piously.

'Terrible old boots, though,' Franken added, staring at them.

'I've marched a long way in these boots.'

Franken snorted in derision. 'You're not old enough to have marched a long way in *any* boots.'

You've no idea what I've done, fat man, Rubin thought. But he smiled amiably.

'Married?' Jan Vandervarr asked.

Rubin could have laughed. But he shook his head as if with deep regret. 'You?'

He listened as Jan told an age-old tale of a wife slaughtered, children lost, then the three of them swapped stories of the evils of the City. Franken was a blowhard, but Rubin liked Jan, his quiet way of listening and considering. When Rubin told him a largely true story about his family's suffering at the hands of the City Rats – true in that it had happened, although not to him – the older man nodded sympathetically, and said quietly, 'Life's a funny old dog.'

As they talked the falling snow thickened and they were warmed by their companionship. Rubin found himself growing sleepy, yet it was barely starting to get dark. It was going to be a long night.

The war between the City and the allied forces City warriors called Blueskins had been going on for more than a century, fuelled, his lord Marcellus had told him, by greed and envy. The two mightiest enemies were the Odrysians and the Petrassi, whose territory abutted that of the City, but they were aided by many nations and tribes and opportunist bands of criminals from encircling lands. Here in the Blacktree Mountains an Odrysian army and hundreds of Buldekki tribesmen were holding a vital pass to the north, and the City's Fifth Imperial infantry were fighting to wrest it from them.

The fat man Franken was telling an elderly joke about a farmer, his goat and a magician's daughter when Rubin heard the subtle scrape of swords stealthily drawn. He grabbed his knife and leaped up as a dozen dark figures loomed out of the flying snow, armoured and armed with bright blades. Fear clutched his chest as he saw they were clad in the black and silver of the City's elite warriors, the Thousand.

'I am a friend!' he cried in the City tongue, raising his hands in surrender. 'My name is Rubin Kerr Guillaume!' As the silent warriors paused, swords raised, he bent and dug in the hidden pocket in his boot. He pulled out his gold insignia.

'See! I am a loyal man of the City! This was given to me by Marcellus himself!'

The leader snatched the gold square and pocketed it, then he gestured to Jan and Franken who were still frozen in place, white-faced, using hope to fend off the enemy swords.

'Prove it,' the leader said, his voice muffled under his full-faced helm.

Rubin stepped behind Franken, pulled his head back and sliced the man's throat; then as the blood sprayed he turned to Jan Vandervarr. In the instant before he pierced him in the heart, he thought he saw relief in the older man's eyes.

Life's a funny old dog, Jan.

The leader of the City soldiers nodded then cuffed Rubin across the side of the head with a heavy gauntlet. 'Bind him. Don't kill him,' Rubin heard him say as he fell dazed to the snowy ground.

In the time that followed he fell in and out of consciousness as he was shackled then dragged and manhandled up and down icy slopes to an unknown destination, sliding helplessly at times, kicked and pushed and pulled like a carcass. His two captors had been told to keep him alive, but beyond that their only interest was getting him off their hands as fast as possible. At last they reached an encampment and Rubin was shoved into a large tent among piles of provisions and armour. He fell to his knees. There was snow on the ground and it was cold as a widow's tit in there. Knowing he'd die if left bound and helpless, Rubin appealed to his guards, who were retreating, laughing and talking.

'I'll be dead within the hour if you leave me here!'

They paused and looked at each other, then left. But a short while later one returned with two blankets which he threw at Rubin. The young man stood with difficulty and pushed together two crates. He laid one blanket over them, then wrapped himself in the other and lay down. He fell asleep on the instant.

He was four years old and in his father's house on the Salient, sitting at table one sunny morning, awaiting breakfast. The little boy was always asked if he wanted one boiled egg or two. He would tell the servant one, then ask for another when he had finished the first. He sat, spoon at the ready, but no eggs appeared and no servant came to ask what he wanted. After a while he slid off his stool and trotted into the kitchens. The place was in ferment, cooks and servants, some of whom he'd never seen before, racing about shouting at each other. When his friend Dorcas, the youngest maid, spotted him she hurried over and picked him up and settled him on her hip.

'Where's my breakfast?' whined little Rubin, pulling at Dorcas' fair braids.

'Be a good boy. Sit at the table and I'll bring your eggs.'

'Where's Mama?' The boy was suddenly anxious about all the strangeness in the house. He was used to a calm, ordered routine.

'Your mother's busy. Eat your breakfast first, then we'll go and find her.'

He'd barely had time to eat his first egg when his mother came in, looking excited and pleased. She picked him up and held him close. Rubin could smell perfume which made his nose itch, and soap and, more faintly, horses.

'You must be a good boy today. This is an important day for all of us. Marcellus Vincerus is coming to visit Papa.'

'Who is he? Can I see him?'

'He is the First Lord of the City, and our greatest hero. You must be very good and stay with Dorcas and do as she tells you.'

'Where's Indaro?' He craned his neck around.

'She's at her lessons. She's being a good girl.'

All day long the boy heard whispered talk of the great lord Marcellus and, excited beyond endurance, he nagged Dorcas until the harassed girl agreed they could watch for the visitor from a first-floor balcony. They waited, as the rest of the house waited, in a state of suspended frenzy.

As night fell the sound of many hoofbeats echoed from the

distance and a group of twenty or more riders broke out from the gloom. Rubin, dozing in Dorcas' lap, threw off his tiredness and craned his neck to see past the stone balusters.

'Which one is he?' he asked the maid, disappointed that the newcomers looked like the family's troopers he saw every day. They were mostly bearded, a few clean-shaven, all wearing dark riding clothes. As they dismounted they talked cheerfully, their voices ringing in the chill air.

Impatiently Rubin pushed his head between the balusters. ''Scuse me,' he cried out in a loud whisper.

The closest rider looked up and grinned at the small boy. 'Hello,' he said.

'Are you Marcellus?' Rubin asked him.

The rider shook his head gravely. 'No, lad. That is the First Lord.' He pointed to one of the group but Rubin could not make out which.

'Who?' he whispered shrilly.

One man walked forward. 'I am Marcellus,' he said, gazing up. 'What is your name?'

'Rubin,' the boy told him in a small voice, suddenly overcome with shyness.

'Is this your house, Rubin?'

The boy thought about it. 'No, sir, it is my papa's house,' he answered seriously.

'Reeve Kerr Guillaume is your father?'

But he did not understand the question, and shook his head. The sound of the men's laughter rose up to the balcony, and he retreated behind Dorcas' skirts.

Marcellus had fair hair and black eyes and he was taller than most of the riders. He stood stiffly, a result, Rubin later learned, of an old back injury, and he reminded the little boy of a piece in his father's ancient ivory and obsidian chess set. For many years after, whenever Marcellus' name was mentioned Rubin always visualized the black king with the chipped obsidian base, surrounded by his pawns.

Rubin was awoken by loud laughter. Opening his

eyes, he found the chilly tent was alive with soldiers, ebullient with success. They'd laid straw mats and rugs on the bare ground and erected tables, and were bringing in folding camp beds and chairs. The delicious smell of roasted meat wafted in on the night air. In the centre of the tent a bay stallion with plaited tail and mane munched noisily from a nosebag. Rubin thought he looked familiar.

He sat up gingerly, hoping nothing was broken.

'Are you injured?' a well-known voice asked.

Rubin looked around. Everyone in the tent was heavily garbed, some still in blood-boltered armour, others in furs and warm wraps. Only one man was lightly dressed in clean shirt and trousers, newly shaved, fresh as a daisy.

Rubin grunted. 'It's hard to tell, under all the pain,' he answered.

Marcellus grinned at him. 'You do turn up in some odd places, young Rubin,' he said.

'The Odrysians thought you were fighting in the south,' Rubin told his lord once they were alone. He was wrapped in a warm wool blanket. He had eaten his fill of roast pig and was swigging from a cup of warmed wine. He felt a little drunk.

Marcellus *had* been fighting in the south. But that was back in the long summer, which saw the defeat of two enemy armies at the Lake of Two Geese. The onset of winter had slowed the campaigns and Marcellus, still eager for action, had struck camp and headed north with a century of the Thousand to join the City's Fifth Imperial battling to take the crucial pass to the north.

'Hmm,' Marcellus grunted, pouring wine into his cup. 'If they spent as much of their resources on intelligence as they do on these trinkets, we'd be in far more trouble than we are. Here.'

He held out a round silver object and Rubin took it in his palm. It was heavier than it looked. He turned it over curiously. It had a piece of glass inset into the metal. There were numbers under the glass. 'What is it?'

'It was found on one of their officers. It's a timepiece.'

A shudder ran through the younger man. He said sourly, 'The Blues accuse us of sorcery, yet they believe they can keep time imprisoned in a box.' He handed it back gladly.

Marcellus stared at the thing with an unreadable expression. 'Beautiful,' he whispered, then he dropped it to the floor and crushed it under his boot-heel. He wandered over to the horse, which nickered softly as he stroked its nose. Of course, Rubin remembered, it was Caravaggio, Marcellus' oldest and most valued mount, a prince among horses.

'Is the enemy destroyed?' he asked.

'Far from it,' his lord replied, turning back to him. 'The main body of Blues is still unaware of our presence, as are our Imperials. But one Odrysian company is no more and Arben Busch is in our hands. Today was a good day.'

Rubin learned that Marcellus' small force, no more than four hundred soldiers and a handful of horses, had climbed the perilous ridge called the Crags of Corenna in gathering darkness. The sounds of their approach from the east had been muffled by the thick snow and they descended on the isolated company of Odrysians like wolves in the night. Not one of the enemy was left alive except their general, who would be taken back to the City if he survived interrogation. And, of course, Rubin himself.

'Arben Busch allowed himself to be taken?' Rubin couldn't help feeling a little disappointed. You can't fight beside men for a season without some of their loyalties rubbing off.

Marcellus shrugged. 'When I arrived he was unconscious. Caught on the head, I imagine, in the skirmish. Or stood up and hit the roof of one of those damnable caves. I have no wish to kill him. He is a valuable resource.'

'But we already know everything he knows.'

'But *they* don't know that,' Marcellus replied. 'And also,' he added, '*we* only know what you have told us. Now, has your face been seen by other than the dead?'

'If you count Arben Busch among the dead,' Rubin replied cheerfully. Then he realized Marcellus' tone had hardened, and he added more seriously, 'which of course you do, lord. Then no, I have only been with the Seventeenth.'

'Good, then I have a new mission for you.'

CHAPTER TWO

MUCH LATER, DEEP IN THE NIGHT, RUBIN LEANED back in a canvas chair and gazed up at the roof of the command tent where large drops of water were gathering above his head. They reminded him of his years in the Halls, the sewers under the City. He opened his mouth to catch one, but the drops wobbled fatly, refusing to fall.

'Are we not entertaining you, young Rubin?' Marcellus asked from the head of the table.

Rubin sat up, glancing at the veteran soldiers seated around him. 'Apologies, lord.'

This gathering of senior officers was, like all Marcellus' meetings, brisk and tightly focused. Less than six hours remained until dawn when they had to be ready to attack.

The slaughter of the Odrysian company had been confined to the caves and Marcellus was confident the main body of the Blues' army, encamped two or more leagues further south-west, knew nothing of his arrival. The problem now was to link up with the City's Fifth Imperial, positioned beyond the Blues. The Imperials' general, Dragonard, also had no inkling of Marcellus' presence.

Rubin did not know why the pass named Needlewoman's Notch was so important that Marcellus had travelled for many days through enemy-haunted territory to this northern outpost. Perhaps, eventually, someone would tell him. For now they were relying on him for information about the Blues.

He told the gathered warriors, 'Our forces hold the other side of the valley. The Odrysians have been scrambling in and out of the caves in fear of their cross-bows. They might be aware of our arrival, though they would not know its significance.'

'They might have held it two days ago,' argued Leona, leader of the century of the Thousand called the Warhounds, 'but they have pulled out now, our scouts tell us.'

Rubin found it hard not to stare. He was used to women among the armed forces – after all, his sister Indaro was one. But he had not known that a woman had climbed to the top ranks of the Immortal's armies. The consensus among grunts on both sides of the war was that generals and senior officers were all wine-soaked buffoons. But Rubin knew the officers Marcellus kept close to him were all veteran fighters, proven in battle and its strategies. He would not have this woman advising him if she were not equal to the task.

Marcellus nodded. 'It would have been useful to us if they were still there. But I cannot fault their commander. Strung out along the ridge they were too vulnerable. He was correct to retreat.

'So our difficulty,' he went on, glancing at the notched candle which marked the implacable progress of time, 'is that we have less than six hours before we attack. Once the sun rises our position will likely be betrayed and battle forced upon us. We need to attack in cooperation with the Fifth Imperial, yet they do not know we are here.'

A white-haired warrior said, 'We have sent two messengers, lord.'

Marcellus shook his head. 'They are making their way round the flanks of the enemy. In this weather, at night, it is doubtful if they will get to the Imperials in time. Even if they are not killed or captured.'

There was silence, then Leona asked, 'What are your thoughts, lord?'

'My thoughts,' Marcellus replied, turning his eye on Rubin, 'are that we need a third messenger.'

Rubin's heart sank. Marcellus had told him he had a mission for him, yet he had hoped it was to be far in the future, perhaps back in the City, or at least after he had rested and enjoyed a long respite from this life of cold and fear and peril.

'This messenger,' his lord went on remorselessly, 'will be disguised as an Odrysian soldier and will present himself at the enemy lines as a survivor of the battle two days ago. He will claim to have suffered a blow to the head and barely escaped death. He will not be suspected. He will be taken in and fed. He will then, still under cover of darkness, escape the enemy ranks and find his way to the Imperials and report to General Dragonard.'

'The first part will be easy,' Rubin said, gracefully accepting the inevitable, 'for someone dressed as an Odrysian.' He looked down at the grubby Odrysian uniform he still wore. 'But he could be killed instantly once he reaches the City army.'

Marcellus leaned across the table and slid towards him the gold insignia snatched from Rubin earlier that night. 'Unlikely. He speaks the City tongue and carries the symbol of Marcellus. He will also be carrying a letter from me to General Dragonard.'

'Yes, lord. It will be an honour, lord.' Looking around, Rubin's gaze lingered on the warhorse Caravaggio, who seemed to be dozing. 'I could ride, lord?' he asked.

Marcellus frowned. 'No, boy, a survivor on a horse

will be instantly suspected. Besides, the terrain is too perilous. We lost two of the beasts on the way up here.' He too turned and looked at his mount. 'Caravaggio is sure-footed as a mountain goat, but I should not have brought him with us. This will be his last adventure.' There was sadness in his face and the atmosphere in the tent grew sombre.

The Warhound leader Leona asked, 'How will we coordinate our attacks? Dawn is a long drawn out event in these winter days.'

'I will order the Imperials to attack first,' her lord told her. 'Even at this range and in the snow we will be able to hear the commotion then make our move. In the first light the Blues won't know what's hitting them.'

Rubin's mind was idling and he stopped listening to the conversation then suddenly, rudely, interrupted his lord.

'If we each had one of the enemy's timepieces we could coordinate our attacks to the moment,' he suggested.

Marcellus scowled and there was a forbidding silence in the tent. 'I thought you feared their sorcery, boy?'

Rubin nodded. 'I do. But there could be some benefit to it if coordinating our attacks saves soldiers' lives.'

Marcellus grunted his disapproval. 'This is a pointless diversion. We do not have these timepieces.' Rubin looked at him curiously, avoiding glancing at the floor where the metal mechanism still lay, mangled and ruined. He wondered why his lord would willingly forgo using such a device to his own disadvantage.

'You will be well rewarded for this task today,' the First Lord told him briskly.

I've heard that before, Rubin thought.

Leona Farr Dulac could no longer feel her feet. As the Warhounds' commander stomped out of the tent after the meeting she peered down at her boots to see if they were encased in blocks of ice, which is how they felt. The air in the tent had been warm enough, but a penetrating cold rose from the icy ground. Marcellus had rested his feet comfortably on the table throughout the meeting, but his officers, however senior, hadn't dared.

As she stepped into the hectic torchlight of the busy encampment Leona was enveloped in a warm woollen cloak. She pulled it round her neck gratefully, and looked up into the long, gloomy face of her aide.

'How did you get it so warm?' she asked.

'I draped it over the rump of a horse.'

Doubtfully she sniffed the wool. It *did* smell of horse. She wondered if Loomis was joking. He knew she hated horses.

'Well, what's the plan?' he asked her.

'We attack at dawn,' she told him.

'Don't we always?' Loomis commented.

She looked around. Warriors were everywhere, crouched round fires, standing in groups stamping their feet, milling around laughing or griping as soldiers will. She moved away towards a quieter spot and Loomis limped after. He held a platter of bread for her and she chewed on a crust as she walked.

Beyond the flickering light of the campfires she told him, 'Marcellus is sending a messenger through the enemy lines to order the Imperials to attack.'

Loomis whistled. 'Rather him than me. Who are they sending? Valerius?'

Valerius was a veteran scout, a legend within the Immortal's armies, and he happened to be with Marcellus' small force that night. He had guided them over the treacherous Crags of Corenna.

'No. Some spy.' Leona blew into her hands, her breath visible in the icy cold.

'The skinny redhead?'

Leona frowned and her aide shrugged. 'I saw him and didn't recognize him,' he said. 'He's a brave lad. Does he know what they'll do to him if they catch him?'

She shrugged. 'We are running out of time. It seems a desperate throw, but Marcellus knows his people and if he trusts him to get this done he's probably right. He usually is. And the boy's older and more experienced than he looks.

'The scouts are out,' she added, 'but when they return Marcellus will want another meeting. Summon my captains. Do I have a tent?'

'A very small one.'

'Then we will meet here.' They were standing in a snow-free circle of ground under a spreading pine. There was a thick layer of springy needles underfoot. 'And bring me some wine. And another cloak.'

He nodded and headed back towards the campfires. Leona leaned against the tree-trunk and ate the rest of the bread, relishing the brief silence. She was still thirsty and cold and her back ached. It always hurt in cold weather, the result of a spear injury years before in the attrition of the Retreat from Araz. The surgeon at the time had predicted she would be invalided out of the army but she had fought back and returned to the Thousand. She was not as strong as she had been, though, and she made up for it by thinking her way through battles in a way she had never had to before. At last she was noticed by her commander and was promoted to his second. When the man died half a year later, in bed from a heart seizure, she had wondered who would take his place. It had not crossed her mind that she would, for she hadn't the experience or the seniority, and she wasn't the right sex. She had spent the last few years trying to keep up with the other commanders of the Thousand while maintaining an air of cool competence.

When her captains arrived she squatted down and rolled out a blank piece of parchment Loomis had brought with him. Her soldiers were used to this now, although when she first used this briefing method there was much mutinous muttering. They resented being shown pictures, like a mother's drawings for her children, and they dealt with it as men do, with jibes about her sex. But Marcellus himself used maps, many of them detailed and beautifully illustrated; she had persevered and now the captains accepted her ways.

'We do not know the fine detail of the terrain yet,' she told them. 'The scouts are still out. But Marcellus has made initial deployments.' With a piece of charcoal she quickly sketched in the enemy lines and their own, and the features of landscape they knew – the ridge, the valley and the treeline.

'Here is the body of the Imperials,' she said, drawing a circle with crosshatching, 'and here the enemy lies – between us and them. The Imperials are being ordered to attack at dawn. Then, when we hear battle engaged, we hit the Odrysians' rear. Marcellus is dividing our force into three. The division on the right, the Greenlegs, will hit the enemy's flank here. This is largely diversionary. The enemy, not knowing how numerous the attackers are, surprised in darkness, will be obliged to stretch its forces—'

'Or regroup into a defensive square. I would.'

Leona nodded, as if young Callanus was making a useful contribution. He wasn't. Marcellus had made his decision and there was no point debating it.

'Marcellus believes they are massive enough and confident enough not to immediately take a defensive stance. We then attack right of centre, chopping off their wing. For the Greens to deal with. We then forge through to our left, their centre.'

'And the third group?' Loomis asked.

'Marcellus will make that decision on the run. This part of the valley,' she indicated to the east, 'will be their escape route.'

They nodded. They all knew the value of leaving the enemy somewhere to run. A dash towards the rising sun often seemed a good idea when you were being slaughtered.

'They'll be falling over each other trying to escape,' Callanus said.

'You'd know all about that,' Loomis commented dourly and the others laughed.

Callanus grinned, unoffended. He had never turned his back on a battle, but during a recent skirmish in his hurry to get into the fight he had tripped over his sword and managed to break both thumbs. Leona liked the boy. He came from a long line of warriors. His father was one of the Immortal's generals, a man known for neither brains nor bravery. But Callanus Gaius Kerr had proved himself over and over in battle, while always remaining cheerful even when unable to wield a weapon. Leona believed she saw a future general in him – a soldier's general like Marcellus or their lost leader Shuskara – and she nurtured his skills and encouraged his ambition.

'The snowfield between here and the Blues,' Leona went on, 'is treacherous, waist-deep in some parts, scoured clear by the wind in others. Also the snow will hide many bodies, ours and theirs, from the last battle. We need speed, but most of all we need silence. No clattering of arms or armour. Hopefully all their attention will be in the other direction, towards the Imperials. Tell your people to wear their cloaks until we engage.'

There were some frowns at this. 'To muffle any sounds,' she explained.

And, she thought, to keep us warm and flexible and battle-ready, although she could not say that to these heroes, who laughed at the cold and spat in the face of discomfort. She smiled to herself.

Dismissing them, she rolled up the parchment and handed it to Loomis, then stood and looked east. No sign of dawn yet.

'What's the watchword, commander?' Loomis asked her formally.

She thought about it. 'The watchword is Rubin,' she said.

As he trudged across the snowfield, Rubin kept looking east. He knew it would be hours before the first pale fingers of light appeared, but he was acutely aware of how much he must accomplish before then.

He was as cold as he had ever been in his life. He could see the breath clouding in front of him, feel his unshaven face going numb. He was weighed down with damp, ragged blankets and his clothes were stiff with blood – not his, that of other men who had died that day. And the going was hard. At times he waded through hip-high fresh snow, at others he hurried across windswept rock impeded only by corpses. He could hear and smell the enemy encampment so he headed towards it with accuracy, but he could not see it yet. The sound of an army camp of a night was a low roar, like the sound of sea at a distance, continuous but rising and falling on the night air. It was the sound of soldiers arguing, joking, lying, complaining, farting, coughing, snoring, belching and just breathing. Even at dead of night it was impossible to keep an army of more than a few hundred quiet.

This army of Blues was stronger than most. He was

constantly surprised by how much they could do despite their reverses, despite the strength of the City forces they faced. They fought doggedly on. They were half-starved, short of supplies and sometimes deployed without arms and dependent on seizing those of the dead. They lost two casualties for every City soldier killed. Yet their armies survived and clung to their positions, sometimes even making headway.

For the City was hampered by the sheer size of the territory it was trying to defend. Immense as was the circumference of its walls – encompassing an area which made the mightiest foreign city look like a village – the length of the boundary more than trebled if one included the surrounding plains and hills and forests the emperor chose to consider the City's demesne. City warriors were constantly in the field and their supplies too were running low. The sea blockade by Blueskin ships had now lasted more than ten years and was becoming tighter with each passing season, depriving City folk of food, but also of metal ore and leather for making weapons and armour. There was hardly a soldier with a complete supply of kit: swords blunted and broke, arrows ran out, belts and straps tore, helms cracked. And the supply of young horses, now their breeding meadows had disappeared, was a major concern for Marcellus and his generals.

Rubin tried to cheer himself with an Odrysian marching song as he struggled along, but the words kept failing him, his brain frozen by cold. He had learned the tongue from Gillard the weapons master, a man of Odrysian blood who had fought on both sides in his long life. He had taught Rubin the words of the song, no doubt amused to hear a small boy mouth the ribald verses. Rubin had picked up the language quickly, his prodigious memory soaking up the alien words like a sponge. And when Marcellus discovered he spoke the language as a native, well, Rubin's future was set in stone. He ended up spending two years in the Odrysian heartlands, and in the temporary capital of the deposed king, worming his way deep into Matthus' court, sending back information to Marcellus. Then, forewarned by his lord, he had escaped the court shortly before it fell to the sharp swords of the veteran City regiment the Fourth Imperial.

At last he could make out the campfires of the Odrysians' night watch. As he hurried towards them, slipping on packed snow, he could not help but glance eastwards again. No sign of light.

'Who goes there?'

The guards were further out than he had expected. He slithered abruptly to a halt and raised his arms high in the air, shedding the blankets from his shoulders.

'Help me,' he cried, falling to his knees, his exhaustion unfeigned.

Two figures disengaged themselves from the shadows.

'Identify yourself.'

'Adolfus Cort, of the Seventeenth. Help me,' he repeated. 'I'm injured.'

The only real injury he had was a shallow cut on the forehead, but he had suffered fresh blood to be daubed on his face and neck, making it look serious enough for him to be dazed and disorientated.

The guards loomed over him, swords ready. 'Watchword?' one asked.

'I don't know,' Rubin confessed. 'But the last I knew, before the battle, was *Fortitude*.'

'What happened to the Seventeenth?'

'All dead.'

The guards exchanged a glance and one grabbed Rubin by the shoulder and roughly helped him up. The other stood back in watchful attendance.

'Papers.'

He took out the grubby scrap of forged paper. It was much folded, soaked in sweat and stained with blood, but one guard looked it over carefully and nodded. Most City soldiers were illiterate and it never ceased to surprise Rubin that so many Blues, whom City folk considered barbarians, could read and write.

He was taken into the Odrysian camp and left with a bleary-eyed sergeant who was uninterested in another ragged survivor. He told Rubin the captain of the night watch would want to speak to him, then he'd be deployed to a new unit. He offered him water but no food. Rubin stumbled through the camp, following the sergeant, watching the east. Still no sign of dawn.

At the centre of the camp he was left outside the entrance to a lighted tent while the sergeant ducked inside. Rubin peered through a gap in the tent-flap and saw the sergeant standing stiffly to attention, waiting to be acknowledged. Senior soldiers were engrossed in conversation. Time passed. Rubin looked around idly. His eyes alighted on the coloured pennants rippling over his head and it dawned on him that this was the general's command tent. He stepped closer, no longer frightened or hungry, but curious.

There were a dozen people inside. Rubin recognized the Odrysian general Yannus and was surprised to see Pieter Arendt, one of the leaders of the Petrassi, the Odrysians' main allies. This was an Odrysian engagement and he wondered what the senior Petrassi was doing here so far from his army. Rubin leaned closer, trying to hear, trying to see more. Other officers he knew by sight, but there were also two civilians. One was a fat old man dressed in the clothes of a farmer. He was red-faced and laughing. Rubin thought he looked drunk.

The other civilian was a woman. Women were seldom seen in the armies of the Blues, even as camp-followers. They did not serve in the military, for the life was considered too hard for them. This woman was tall and thin, dressed in dusty riding leathers, and she was pacing the tent as if in irritation or impatience. She looked like a warrior, but could not be. She was not old, not young, and her whole appearance was grey – grey hair and pale skin, and as she walked towards Rubin he saw she had protuberant eyes the colour of pebbles. He knew he had seen her somewhere before.

Then he caught a piece of her conversation, realizing with a shock that they were speaking the City tongue.

'We are wasting time with this nonsense,' the woman said irritably. 'If Marcus is backing this plan you can be sure it is a good one. What have you got to lose? Nothing. Ours is all the risk, yours all the benefit.'

Rubin wondered who Marcus was. It was a City name, but there were many Marcuses. He listened, avid for information he could pass to Marcellus once this battle was over. Who was she? It nagged at his memory. He knew he knew her.

One of the officers argued, 'It will be carnage. The brothers will destroy them all.'

The woman shook her head, still with her back to them, as if her face would betray her if she turned and faced them.

'I know Marcellus,' she said. 'He will not do that, not if his whore is there. And her sister. That is the crux of our plan. For all that has gone before, he still thinks of himself as a man of honour.'

She was staring out into the blackness, straight at Rubin though he was clothed in darkness. For an instant her eyes seemed to look straight into his and her gaze sharpened. He wondered if she could see him. He stepped back silently. Had she seen him? Did it matter if she had? He was just a soldier, albeit a nosy one. But he felt anxious under her pebble stare.

Then suddenly, with a surge of misgiving, he

remembered where he had seen her. It was in a meeting Marcellus had held with his palace administrators years before, a meeting to which Rubin had not been invited but which he had watched covertly, as now. Once he had placed where he had seen her he knew who she was. And he knew he was witnessing a gathering of critical importance, one around which the future of the City could turn.

And he had to warn Marcellus.

One of the senior officers in the tent became aware of the sergeant, still standing to attention as if his life depended on it, and walked over to him. The sergeant explained he had a survivor of the battle outside. The officer questioned him briefly, the sergeant shaking his head the whole time. Then he was dismissed and he rejoined Rubin. He pointed his charge at the mess tent then turned away. Rubin wandered in that direction, glancing back until the man was out of sight. Then he threw off his lacklustre demeanour and headed towards the front lines.

It was easy to slip through sentries facing outwards, watching for incoming enemies. Rubin judged his moment as the guards paced, then ran silently behind a rocky outcrop, waited, peered, then ran again. He was soon out of their sight and with a sigh of relief headed for the Imperials' camp – then he started worrying again about the dawn. He looked east for the hundredth time. Was it his imagination or was there a blur of light on the horizon, like a distant candle flame?

He hurried on, urged by this new, crucial information, and by the imminent coming of daybreak. The first indication that he had arrived with the City forces was a knife at his throat.

CHAPTER THREE

THE INSISTENT CHIRRUP OF BIRDS SPOKE OF THE coming dawn, and warriors quietly slid out their swords. Leona left hers in its scabbard. Swords were heavy, and she saw no reason to run across the treacherous snowfield wielding one until she had to. But she understood why many soldiers were unwilling to address the enemy, even at this distance, without the reassurance of a blade in hand.

She was in the centre of the front line, which faced south-west, although she was watching the rear for the order to advance. Pink rays of dawn had begun punching through dark clouds low on the horizon. There was still starlight above, although fresh snow was promised in the smell of the air. Leona dreaded a heavy snowfall. It could kill them all. It would stop them retreating to lower ground once they had beaten the Blues, and it would stop supplies from reaching them. They were already getting short of food.

She and her century were waiting in line of twenty-five, looking down on the snowfield they must cross before engaging the enemy hidden somewhere beyond. The snow was crisp and hard and she saw a small shape sprint across it and dive into an unseen burrow – a white hare or a fox in its winter coat. A light mist lay knee-deep and shimmered in the breeze from the north. It was very cold.

Leona looked to either side of her. To her right was Valla, a tall, lean warrior whom Leona had trusted with her life for the past decade. She topped Leona by half a head and her hair, white as ice, was cropped short. Valla was muttering silently to herself, but Leona guessed what she was saying: 'Bless us, Aduara, goddess of fierce women. Bless your warriors and bathe them in the blood of men. Bless your warriors and give them strength. Bless your warriors and see them safe home to your breast.'

Followers of her cult believed women were of blood and men of meat, and the meat could not act without the blood. Then there was the spark, the gift of Aduara, which animated the blood and the meat and made it human.

She saw Valla lift her face to the sky and she looked up too. It was snowing, tiny specks of ice drifting from the north. Valla grinned at her. Snow was a symbol of the spark, as was rain and the splash of water.

On Leona's other flank was Callanus. If she couldn't have Loomis at her side then Callanus was as good a fighter as any. Loomis was far behind in the ranks of the halt and lame. He had lost a lower leg five years before and walked on a carved wooden peg strapped to the stump below the knee. He could wield a sword as well as any on the front line, but City protocol meant he had to fight at the rear. Still, it was good to know he was there, watching her back.

Her soldiers' faces were stone, but their bodies betrayed them. Their fingers were constantly checking the straps of breastplates, or finding the greaves protecting their lower legs a little too tight, or too loose. These were elite warriors, the best the City had to offer, but, as such, they had seen over and over again all the many horrible varieties of injury, mutilation and death, and they would not be human if they were not nervous at this crucial moment. She was proud of them all.

'It's dawn,' Callanus muttered impatiently, rolling his shoulders. 'Time to go.'

'Quiet,' she whispered back.

But she understood his feelings. It was getting perceptibly lighter. She knew Marcellus was waiting for some indication that the messenger had achieved his mission and the Imperials were attacking. They would hear them, even with the muffling effect of the snow. She knew it would be a hard call to make. If they attacked too soon they might beat themselves to death on the main strength of the Blues. If they left it too late it could lessen the value of the two-pronged attack.

She listened hard for sounds of battle but could hear nothing. Then, on the north wind, she caught an unexpected sound and swivelled her neck to identify it. It was a faint tinkling of bells. Other warriors were looking around.

From out of the misty north dark figures emerged. More soldiers unsheathed their swords, but unspoken orders stayed their hands.

Three tiny, graceful goats, their sides thin and ridged with ribs, the bells round their necks jingling in a mockery of jollity, led a small band of refugees. After them came children holding on to their goats' leads, then two men armed only with cudgels, frightened and tight-faced, and finally women with babes in arms and the old folk trailing, struggling. Their baggage was carried by a lone old mule.

There were twelve of them, Leona counted. They were dark and small – the tallest of the men only came up to the shoulder of the shortest City warrior, and their faces were gaunt and haggard. They were clothed in rags. She guessed the beasts were the only things of value they owned. She stepped forward, hand on the hilt of her sword. They all shuffled away, gazing off, except one young woman. She wore rags like the others, but she had tied a strip of garish ribbon around her goat-hide hat. She glared up at Leona and stood her ground. Leona saw she had one useless eye, a pale opal, seeing nothing. One of the menfolk muttered to the woman, pleading, but she refused to budge. Valiant, Leona thought, but unwise.

'Where are you from?' she asked softly, aware of how sound could travel in this sterile landscape.

They said nothing. One old woman sank to her knees in the snow, overcome perhaps by fear or cold, and a child started to cry weakly.

'Where are you going?' Leona asked the young woman.

But either they didn't understand her or they were too terrified to speak.

A grizzled veteran called Aurelius came forward. 'They are Fsaan, commander,' he said. 'They won't understand you.'

'Fsaan?'

'These high valleys were once theirs. They were a mighty people once, powerful and educated. But they dwindled over the centuries, became herders. They used to pasture their goats here in summer. Then they retreated when the warriors came.'

'Where are they going?'

He shrugged. 'Anywhere away from us.'

'Let them pass,' she ordered, and stepped back. The refugees, unable to believe their fortune, hurried past, eyes down, the old woman half carried by the men. The tinkling of bells receded behind them and the City army stared forward again, waiting.

'Those goats would have made a good meal,' Callanus said regretfully.

Leona grunted. 'Among all of us? Now they can slaughter them themselves.' It might make the difference between life and death for them one night, she thought. The warm blood of the goats might keep them alive for another day or two, though there was little meat on them. How could such frail beings survive in the midst of this war? She whispered a few words to Aduara, asking her to watch over the women and girls. Then she forgot about them.

She waited for the order to advance.

For the second time that night Rubin was dragged and pushed, manhandled like a criminal, into his own army's camp. He proffered the message given to him by Marcellus but the City guards, unlettered men, regarded the written word as tantamount to witchcraft and it was all he could do to stop them trampling the paper underfoot. Desperation clawing at him, he repeated, 'Marcellus sent me!' finally convincing them not to kill him, and he was taken first to the captain of the guard then, at long last, to the Imperials' general. Meanwhile the eastern sky was lightening fast and Rubin was terrified he was too late.

General Dragonard was a small man with a sad face, receding hair and pouchy eyes. He looked, Rubin thought, more like a scribe than one of the Immortal's senior generals. When Rubin was pushed into his tent the man was seated on the edge of his camp bed, staring at the ground. He looked up wearily, as if to say *What more must I do?*

Rubin looked around. The tent was small and frayed and it contained only a bed, folding desk and chair, a small brass-bound chest and a wooden frame for armour. Everything was neat but shabby.

'Messenger, sir. From the lord Marcellus,' snapped the captain.

The general stood slowly and looked at Rubin. 'Who is this?'

'Rubin Kerr Guillaume,' volunteered Rubin urgently. 'Marcellus sent me. He has brought an army. They are waiting on the other side of the valley at the rear of the Blues. You are ordered to attack. At dawn! Now!'

The captain handed the general the message. Dragonard accepted it, but instead of reading it straight away the general did the oddest thing. From his desk he picked up a flimsy object made of two circular pieces of glass fixed to lengths of wire. He hooked the wires round his ears then balanced the whole contraption on his nose. It looked ridiculous. Hysteria rising in him, Rubin smothered a laugh. Was the man some sort of simpleton? He looked at the captain for a clue, but the man stared stolidly forward.

Peering through the glass discs, the general read the paper slowly, then read it again. Rubin shifted his feet. Finally he blurted, 'He is waiting for you to attack. At dawn! It is dawn now! Past dawn!'

The general shot a glance at the captain, who cuffed Rubin hard on the ear. He went down on his knees, his head buzzing, his heart sick.

'Marcellus wrote this?' the general asked.

'Yes, sir,' Rubin told the floor, despairing.

'And you crossed through the enemy camp to get it to me?'

'Yes, sir.'

'Then you are a brave man and you will be well rewarded.'

The general turned to the captain.

'Prepare to attack!'

Yannus, general of the Odrysians, was no fool. He expected the Rats to attack. And he expected them to attack at dawn. Both sides were low on supplies. One hope of escaping these mountains alive was to win Needlewoman's Notch, the high pass leading north to the soft hills of Varenne and the Little Sea beyond. The pass was closed by snow now but any day a sharp thaw could make it negotiable and the Rats needed to take it. It was an essential supply route for the City since the sea blockade had taken hold.

Yannus knew the Rats had no choice. But would they wait for a thaw, or would they strike now? So he kept his ragged army on constant alert, as alert as an army can be when it is frozen in one position for days. But soldiers had to rest, and they could not sleep in their armour for they would freeze to death. So they were kept on night-and-day rotations, half on guard on the perimeter of the encampment, half in the protected centre trying to sleep, although that was hard when the penetrating cold stiffened lungs and pierced men's joints with ice.

When the City's attack came it was almost a relief. Dawn was long past when the Imperials struck, coming up from the south-west, up the incline which gave the allies a fine advantage, hampered by snow and cold but with the City's expected ferocity. The Odrysians on guard sprang to meet them, blood surging, and within moments the camp was awake and in ferment. Men struggled into armour, sleep and the cold forgotten; they tore swords and axes from protective wrappings and scrambled over each other to engage the foe.

When Marcellus' forces hit them, Yannus was surprised but not alarmed. Clearly some Rats had got behind them, but it could not be more than a suicidal diversionary force. Not on this mountain, not in these conditions. Thus he diverted some of his troops, as expected and, sent his premier fighting force, the Twenty-third, to form a wedge. But orders were slow to travel. And before they could be implemented the beleaguered Odrysians were attacked from the north-east by, of all things, a century of the Thousand, the warriors his men most feared, the emperor's elite fighting force.

Leona's sword found a crack in her opponent's armour and it drove through, piercing the Blue in the belly. He fell to one knee and she plunged her knife through the eye-hole of his helm and saw blood spurt. She kicked him in the head for good measure then turned to her right. Valla was on one knee, hacking at the groin of an injured enemy soldier. He did not fall, but he offered no defence and Leona slid her sword under his armpit. As he fell she wrenched it out and spun back, but Callanus was covering her, engaging a tall Odrysian in black armour. She joined the attack and felled the man, then the three of them moved forward, holding the line.

A fresh wave of Blues came at them armed with spears. Leona ducked a spear-thrust then skewered the soldier through the privates. From the corner of her eye she saw Callanus stumble but before she could turn to help, the giant figure of Otho the axeman moved forward to cover him. A spear lunged. Otho blocked it with his axe blade then dragged a backhand cut that sheared through leather armour and flesh beneath. Otho tore the weapon clear, parried a feeble cut and hammered the axe into his opponent's face. Beside him again, Callanus blocked a sword with his shield and smoothly slid his blade into the opponent's neck. A spear grazed his thigh, but he counterthrust and his attacker fell across the growing pile of bodies. The big axeman turned and patted Callanus' shoulder with a meaty hand.

A tall warrior hurdled the wall of the enemy dead and hurtled towards Otho, sword raised. The giant's axe buried itself in his chest but the weight of the man drove the axeman back, tearing the weapon from his hands. A second enemy leaped at him, sword swinging for his neck. Otho batted aside the blade with his mailed forearm and smashed a mighty punch to the man's jaw. As he crumpled Otho twisted and wrenched his axe from the first man's body.

There was a momentary pause in the battle, a moment of calm. The Blues seemed to be giving way. Then Leona heard the familiar thrumming of shafts in the air and she yelled, 'Arrows!' and raised her shield. The percussion of three or four arrows knocked her to one knee, then she was up again, thrilling with the scent of victory. The Blues were desperate, or their orders were confused. They were loosing arrows at risk to their own front line. A second volley hammered into their ranks, then the Blues were on them again. Leona parried a thrust from a short sword then swept a double-handed blow to the Blueskin's unprotected head, caving his skull. A second man fell to her sword, then a third, and she screamed her defiance at them, her blood singing.

She stepped back, signalling a second-ranker to take her place, while she judged the progress of the battle that roared around her. It was fully light now and the Blueskins filled their sight, covering the inclined valley floor before her like army ants. The strength of the Blues was to her left, as expected. Her company's task was to drive through them, cutting off their left wing. But her own left flank was being hard hit; they were moving too far and too fast. They risked being cut off themselves.

'Hold!' she yelled. 'Hold!' She heard it repeated down the line by deeper male voices.

The order was not to stop fighting, but to hold the enemy in position, to kill as many as possible as they came at you, but not move further forward. For Leona it was a crucial and risky step. She was telling her troops to switch from an aggressive to a defensive stance. Effectively she was telling them they were no longer winning, but were at risk of defeat. Psychologically it was a nightmare. She saw Valla throw her a puzzled look then turn back to the battle. Leona shrugged to herself. If she had to defend her orders to Marcellus then she would.

It seemed the Blues had identified her as commander and two spearmen came at her, one high, one low. She flung herself to one side, rolling into the feet of the man Valla was fighting. She threw him off balance and Valla despatched him. Leona jumped up and they both turned to the spearmen. Leona batted aside one spear with her mailed gauntlet and thrust at the man's chest. Her blade slid off and lodged in the mail at his shoulder. He had a knife in the other hand and he caught her on the neck with it. She dragged the sword from his shoulder and cut into his wrist, severing the blood vessels. As red blood spurted he thrust feebly with his spear and she grabbed it and pulled him from his feet. Valla skewered the other spearman.

Leona quickly looked to her left, but as usual Callanus was protecting her flank. Yes, she thought, a good soldier and maybe a good general one day.

Another spearman came screaming up to Callanus and the young man had time to grin at Leona before dodging the weapon and gutting the wielder. Another wave of spearmen came leaping over the bodies. On Callanus' left Otho swung his axe and smashed through two as they came at him.

Callanus laughed. 'Spearmen!' he spat. 'Don't you just—'

In the blink of an eye a Blue came running fast from the left, his spear held low. He moved so swiftly his opponents seemed mired in mud. Otho was dragging his axe back, but too slowly. Callanus was turning, but too late. Before Leona could open her mouth or step forward the spear thrust past Callanus' armour deep into his side. Blood gouted from his mouth and, as she watched, helpless, his eyes went dead.

Callanus fell on his back on a pile of bodies, his throat open to the sky, his eyes staring.

With a bellow of rage Otho beheaded the killer with a single stroke of his axe. Two warriors ran at him and Otho, too close to swing, dropped his head and dived into them. One was knocked from his feet. The second came at him with sword raised but suddenly fell to the ground, Valla's dagger in his throat. The blonde warrior leaped forward and wrenched out the blade while Otho clubbed at the next opponent with his mailed fists. Valla stabbed another then was borne down by the press of enemy bodies. It was a melee. Leona waded in, piercing enemy backs, necks, any part she could reach. The Blues retreated. Valla scrambled to her feet and picked up a discarded sword.

Leona glanced back at Callanus' body and felt tears well. Then, as she had done a thousand times before, she turned her back on her dead comrade and put him from her mind.

'Advance!' she shouted and the line moved forward again.

Rubin hadn't given much thought to what would happen after he'd fulfilled his mission: he had half expected to be executed by the Odrysians before he'd got that far, and when that hadn't happened he had feared being killed by the Imperials. Once the battle started he was given dead men's armour and a sword and sent towards the enemy. Exhausted beyond reason, confused and disorientated, he barely remembered who the enemy was before they started trying to kill him.

He was not in the first line of battle, but when he saw his City comrades being slaughtered in front of him he knew his chance would come soon enough. Then a soldier went down next to him, and his sword came up and his blood rose with it, and he was into the fight.

They were battling uphill against a solid mass of Blues. The soldiers he was with, a light infantry company who called themselves Hogfodder, chanted as they fought up the slope, though two of them were falling for every enemy death. Rubin could not make out the words of the chant, but after a while he caught the rhythm of it and bellowed 'Hoooooogs!' with the rest of them at the end of each verse.

Height advantage is all very well, he thought, but it leaves a man's lower parts a soft target for piercing metal, and no one wanted that. He slammed his sword into the groin of a tall warrior, then, as the man slumped forward in agony, slashed deep into his neck for good measure. He dodged the falling body and ran up the slope to tackle the next one.

'Hoooooogs!' he shouted, blocking a thrust and slashing his enemy deep across the belly, then dodging again as the warrior collapsed and rolled past him, his entrails tangling as he rolled.

They made little headway at first, but after a time the press of Odrysians seemed to lessen and Rubin thought he heard distant horns. His comrades took no notice so he guessed the horns were giving orders to another part of the army, or Marcellus' troops, or even the enemy. He wondered if Marcellus' ploy had worked, if his desperate mission had been a success. If they were winning.

A man on Rubin's right went down and his place was taken by a tall bald-headed veteran who killed his first man with a lightning, precise sword-thrust to the neck. In. Out. Blood spurted. He looked at Rubin and grunted something. Rubin didn't catch what he said but felt reassured by the big man's presence. The two moved forward shoulder to shoulder, the bald man doing the lion's share of the work while Rubin hacked and slashed in a supporting role.

Then there was a pause in the fighting and the pair caught their breaths.

'Here,' Rubin said, snatching up an abandoned Buldekki helm, 'you need one of these.'

He spotted a flash of movement to his left and swung, sword raised – too late. He saw the spearpoint coming but did not feel it as it plunged deep into his belly.

When a battle is done and won – or at least not lost – the common soldier will check himself for previously unnoticed wounds, confirm which of his friends are still alive, then slump to the ground to sleep or complain.

For a commander that is a long-forgotten indulgence. The commander stays on his or her feet and carries on. There are friendly wounded to treat, enemy wounded to despatch or interrogate. A whole new raft of decisions needs to be made, and it is the commander who takes them. And for Leona, whose lord was Marcellus, there are meetings.

It was said by some that Marcellus never slept. This was untrue, for Leona had seen him do so. But he certainly did not need much sleep, and his energy was terrifying. After a successful battle he seemed to gain in strength and he expected his lieutenants to keep up. So he roamed the battlefield, partly to survey new ground, partly to judge the morale of the troops. And he talked and listened, discussing the battle past and the battles to come, the strategies, tactics, and those of the enemy.

But at last he retreated to his command tent with

Dragonard, and Leona was left to her own duties. She redeployed her captains then sought out Loomis. She couldn't find him. She knew he was alive for she had glimpsed him after the battle, so she guessed he was tending the wounded. A boy brought her a bowl of water and she washed the last spots of sticky blood from her hands and face. The air was bitter against her wet skin but the water revived her a little. She was exhausted but she was still waiting for that shift in her mind which would inform her that sleep was possible, so she made her way back on to the battlefield.

The battle had been a success, in that the plan had succeeded – Marcellus' group had linked up with the Fifth Imperial, cut off the enemy's wing and destroyed it, and forced the bulk of the Blues back into the valley. But the battle had been a failure, in that the enemy, though depleted, lived to fight another day. And they still held Needlewoman's Notch.

Leona looked up to where the Notch lay hidden by the curve of the valley. There would be many more hard battles before it was taken, she guessed. In addition a sharp thaw had set in and the snows were melting fast. In a matter of days, tomorrow even, the Notch would be passable and the enemy could expect to be relieved or at the very least resupplied.

Leona stood quietly amid myriad bodies, dead and dying under a weak and watery sun. All around was the sound of running water. She imagined all the gurgling streams and rivers down the valley flowing with blood. It called to her mind the little band of Fsaan refugees who were down there somewhere, perhaps looking at the flowing red water and wondering. Once more she speculated how they could possibly survive. For a moment only she thought of the children, then she hardened her heart.

She looked around. A company of the Imperials had

been charged with sorting through the bodies, distinguishing City from Blue, the living from the dead. All enemy soldiers, alive or dead, were pierced through the heart or slashed across the throat. It was a waste of time, and also unsafe, for the soldiers of the despatch party to squat down and feel for the life-force of a fallen enemy. Leona watched them move in a line slowly across the sloping field, like tall crows. A sword-thrust here, the occasional call for a stretcher-bearer there. The numbers were yet to be totted up, but Leona's long experience told her the City had lost more than five hundred that day.

A black-clad soldier stalked towards a huddled body close by where she was standing. The man glanced at her for a long moment and she thought she saw the world's hurt in his eyes. She guessed he had found few to save.

The body was clad in a filthy, blood-encrusted uniform which could have placed him in the City forces or those of the enemy. But the distinctive three-pronged helm of the Buldekki lay discarded near one hand. Blood was still flowing sluggishly from a belly wound, so the man was still alive. As the stalking soldier closed in on him, Leona saw a flash of light gleam from the dying man's outflung hand. Curious, she stepped forward. What was it he held out in her direction like an offering?

The soldier raised his sword for the death-blow.

'Stop!' she ordered, and he lowered his weapon and moved on to the next body, uncaring, incurious.

Leona knelt and took the gold square from the man's hand. With a shock she saw it showed the insignia of Marcellus, the winged horse, given only to his closest lieutenants. Its fellow was riding in her breast pocket. She peered at the wounded man's face.

She scrambled to her feet.

'Stretcher!' she yelled.

CHAPTER FOUR

IN THE GENTLE FOOTHILLS FAR BENEATH NEEDLE-woman's notch, in a temporary medical encampment which became more permanent as the weeks passed, Rubin lay close to death. And so he remained as winter gave way to spring then the days slowly warmed towards summer.

The orderlies who cared for the wounded would check his life-force each morning, expecting it to have stuttered to a halt during the long watches of the night; yet each morning they found it, weak but still detectable, and they shook their heads in wonder. The young man's body, never bulky, diminished to mere bones with a frail clothing of flesh and skin. But the blood of two Families of Serafim ran in his veins and, because he did not die immediately from the spear wound, so inevitably he would recover.

As the battle for the Notch ebbed and flowed far above, the stream of wounded soldiers passed in and out of the three large tents which housed the City's injured. Some of them glanced at the thin pale figure, never moving, barely breathing. A few heard him muttering over and over through dry and cracked lips, 'Marcellus.' But Marcellus never came.

Three days after the battle which had nearly taken

Rubin's life, the First Lord had gathered his lieutenants and three companies and departed, leaving the struggle for the Notch in the hands of the doughty Dragonard. Marcellus, it seemed, now had more important battles to fight, both against the enemy and at home in the City.

The winter thaw hit hard and fast, and spring came early that year. The mountains rang with the sounds of running water, and wildflowers blazed their bright colours from the warming soil. Grey wolves which had crept down from the ice-crusted heights in the dead of winter started returning to their mountain fastnesses to bear their pups. Within the beleaguered City, men's eyes turned to the weak sun and in hope they bent to planting crops in the fields of Garamund and the far north-east. Young foals, future cavalry mounts, ran joyfully in the water meadows.

But as the spring weather warmed the land, so new life was breathed into the battle for the City. And the City was losing.

To the south the last great Petrassi army destroyed the City's Fourteenth Serpentine in a forty-day offensive and overran the oak-covered hillsides which furnished the City with timber for its ships and buildings and wheeled vehicles and, more gravely, seized the two reservoirs which held its water supply. And the enemy fleet which had successfully blockaded the City's ports for more than a decade was buttressed by new ships from allied lands, and the blockade extended its grip southwards, so the City was effectively barricaded in by both land and sea.

Then in the east, at the height of summer, catastrophe struck. The Third Maritime, the City's premier infantry, unbeaten in the field for more than two years, was annihilated at the Battle of Salaba, surprised by a storm and ferocious flash flood. The legendary general Ren Thoring, commanding a combined Blueskin force, held an advantage of terrain when the storm struck. His army controlled a low eminence and this meagre elevation meant his troops recovered first when the waters began to subside. The City infantrymen were still floundering when the Blues hit them. More than twenty thousand City warriors were killed on the first day, and another thirty thousand in the following days of clean-up. It was the worst defeat of a City army since the Retreat from Araz. It left the City vulnerable on its long eastern side. And, for a while, the blow to the City's morale seemed mortal.

And through it all Rubin slept and dreamed.

The sewers of the City, wider than its bounds, far deeper than its heights, had been inhabited time out of mind by uncounted thousands of wretched folk who called themselves Dwellers. They named the sewers the Halls, for beneath the City were hidden marvels of architecture, built in a long-ago age when the best builders and engineers in the world were engaged to construct the largest enclosed spaces yet known to man.

The Halls were a place of danger and despair, yet they were also sanctuary to many who were fleeing the military, or the machinery of the emperor, or sometimes life itself. They were home to criminals and the unjustly accused, to deserters from the army and to sixteen-year-old girls and boys whose only other choice was to die miserably in an infantry line, but also to butchers and bakers, chandlers and spice and dye merchants whose livelihood had been ripped away as trade embargoes on the City had started to bite. They were home to the strong and, briefly, to the weak. To cannibals and their victims. To reivers. To wraiths.

And, for two long years, they had been home to Rubin Kerr Guillaume.

When he reached his majority, unlike his sister Indaro before him Rubin had not let himself be led from his home, meek and unprotesting, by agents of the City's army – to endure token training and put on dead men's armour, arm himself with their weapons and stand in an infantry line to live or die. He had certainly not, like many of his gallant young friends, marched proudly to that same grim fate.

Rather, on the night before his sixteenth birthday, Rubin had written an apologetic note to his father and slipped out of a side door of the grey house on the Salient. Dodging the guards, he had hiked the length of the cliff, avoiding the road curving down towards the City and eventually finding the hidden stairway cut into rock. A grown man would have been reluctant to attempt the steep steps in daylight, but Rubin was at the height of his youthful arrogance. He had climbed down under the light of the moon and breakfast-time found him at the stream called Goatsfoot Beck.

The City was a charnel house. Rubin could smell the blood and death from the moment he reached the edge of the Salient and looked down, unseeing in the night, on the hundreds of square leagues of brick and stone, marble and rock, wood and water which made up the oldest, the greatest city in the world. It was a place he had never entered, although he had lived within sight of it all his life.

But he was young and believed he could overcome any adversity, for he was the scion of two great Families which had wielded power in the City for generations – although not, in truth, for the last several hundred years. And when he had found the narrow culvert he'd been told about, and stepped for the first time into the darkness of the Halls, he had done so with a courage which was both natural and born of pride in his rank and upbringing. And his cruelly limited experience of life.

He lingered inside the entrance and cautiously breathed in the dark air. He coughed and spat. It was not so bad. He gazed around. The Goatsfoot, which had seemed so insignificant in the world of daylight, now thundered in a narrow man-made channel, filling his ears with sound. On one side of the waterway wide, shallow steps led down into darkness. Rubin sat on his heels and hauled out of his backpack a box of phosphorus sticks, stolen from the kitchens of his home, and lit the first of his precious torches. He knew he would have to replace them soon, but he was confident that by then he would have discovered the method of exchange among folk down here. He was confident of a great deal.

With the lighted brand held high and his long-bladed knife, a gift from his sister, at the ready he took a shallow breath and set off down.

He walked straight ahead for what seemed like hours but met no one, heard nothing but the sound of running water and the skittering of unseen rats. The smell got stronger. It was almost with relief that he saw a blur of light in the distance. He grasped his knife firmly, feeling the familiar grip of fine leather in his palm. Rubin knew he was no fighter. He had been told that by weapons master Gillard on many occasions. Rubin had never returned to the fencing lessons, though he learned some knife-fighting skills from Indaro and he knew he had speed, if only for running away.

The moving torchlight jittered closer and Rubin halted, heart hammering in his chest. Appearing out of the gloom came three men, two thin and one stout and bearded. How can a man stay well fed down here, Rubin wondered with the part of his mind which wasn't numb with fear. Perhaps this was a newcomer like himself. He put an affable smile on his face, although his chest felt as though a frightened sparrow were trapped inside and blood was pounding in his ears.

'What's your name, young fellow?' asked the stout one as they halted across his path. He held a sword casually in his right hand. It was old and looked well used.

'Adolfus,' Rubin lied promptly. 'I'm new here, good sir.'

The stout man looked around at his friends, grinning. 'We can see that,' he said. 'That's a nice blade you have there. All new and shiny.'

'Yes,' replied Rubin. 'It's shiny because I keep it so sharp, you see.'

The stout man nodded gravely. 'If you're new,' he said, 'you don't know the rules. We don't allow no weapons down here in the Halls.'

Rubin considered the array of swords, knives and cudgels the three men carried amongst them.

'You have the advantage of me,' he said. 'You know my name but I don't know yours.'

'You don't need no names, son,' said the man. 'Just give me that pigsticker and your pack. Those nice new torches are worth more than gold down here.'

Rubin stepped back a pace. 'Then I would be a fool to give them up, wouldn't I?'

He had no idea how he could survive the encounter, short of fleeing. He knew he could outrun the men, but what would he do then? Go home? Admit to his father he had run away twice within one day? Never. He raised his knife, trying to summon what he had learned about defending himself.

The stout man ran at him, his sword slashing at Rubin's head. Rubin swayed from the knees and the tip whispered past a hair's-breadth from his face. He stepped in, blade stabbing. The stout man was still moving forward and his own weight forced the knife deep into his stomach. It was a large target. The man fell to the ground, a ghastly scream dying quickly to a breathless mew. Rubin dragged the knife out and stepped towards the two others, who fled.

Elated, Rubin stood, heart pounding. It had been laughably easy. The stout man was so slow. How had such a sluggard survived down here? A sluggard and a bully must have *some* skills to survive. Rubin wondered what they were. He looked down at the man, who was panting weakly, his eyes rolling. He wondered if he should despatch him, but in the end he left him in the darkness, dying slowly.

Will every day be like this, Rubin thought, a fight just to stay alive? But he was buoyed by the encounter, and he slashed the dank air with the knife and wondered now if he should have brought a sword. He felt ready to take on anyone.

So it was with some dismay that the next people he met were a gang of seven thugs, all armed with swords, led by the two thin men, perhaps returning to avenge their friend. They emerged from the gloom like a small army, their way lighted by torches, nailed boots stomping on stone, metal and leather clanking and creaking. When they spotted Rubin they yelled and started running towards him, weapons flailing.

Rubin turned and fled.

He sprinted over wet stone, holding the torch high. He was faster than them, but not by much. He stumbled several times on the slick surface and once hit his knee so hard he feared he had broken it. The pursuers seemed more sure-footed and, glancing back, he realized they were gaining. His blazing torch was a beacon and, though he dreaded the dark, he knew he would have to ditch it. He picked his time. He recalled a side tunnel he had passed on his way inwards: he had noticed it because the more than fetid air from it had made him retch. He stole a look behind him. The men were close. Reaching the side tunnel, Rubin threw down his torch and plunged into darkness.

Dividing their resources, three of the men dived down the passage marked by the downed torch while the others ran on up the main tunnel. They made a lot of noise, grunting and cursing, shouting to each other as they searched for the boy. They found the body of their friend, now good and dead apparently, and one of the thugs spoke loudly and inventively about what he would do to Rubin when he found him.

But they didn't find him, and after a deal more cursing they marched off, leaving their dead comrade to moulder in the dark. The sound they made echoed on, and it was a long while before Rubin found the courage to emerge. In pitch blackness he dragged himself up out of the water where he had managed to lodge his body upstream of a slimy bulwark. He was amazed the thugs had not searched for him in the channel. It was some time later before he learned that, for Dwellers, falling into the stream meant only death. This was so deep-rooted that even though the water at that point was fairly fresh, having recently come from outside, the ruffians never thought to look there.

Shivering in his soaking clothes, and trembling still from the dread of being captured, Rubin hunkered down and considered his position. He still had his knife, but his pack was lost. And he was cold, hungry and in total darkness. All he could do, apart from retreating towards daylight again, was wait for someone to come along with a torch and either befriend them or follow them. His heartbeat slowly quietened, and he decided to sleep for a while. Groping along the rocky wall he found a deep niche and tried to make himself comfortable. He started to doze, his body warming a little, his fears receding.

And then the rats came. He felt something move on his arm and he twitched, brushing it away idly as he dozed. Then tiny claws caught in his bare skin and he jerked awake, leaping up shouting, brushing real or imagined animals from his clothes and body. Shuddering, he leaned back his head and screamed at the top of his voice, relieving his feelings and scattering the rats.

After that he had no choice but to keep moving inwards, fingering his way along the rocky wall, testing each footfall for crumbling steps or crevasses in his path. He was worn out but could not bear the thought of sitting down again.

Days seemed to pass and still Rubin crept along, numb with exhaustion and fear. Then he heard a faint sound and stopped, holding his breath, heart banging. It was not the skittering of rats, but neither was it the stomp of marching men. He looked around, trying to work out which direction the sound was coming from, scanning for light. Then he detected a dim blur to his right and he blinked rapidly, seeking better focus. Yes, a moving torch. He felt along the wall, trying to find somewhere to hide, but there was nowhere, just sheer rock on one side, the stream on the other. As the light moved closer he could see there was just the one flame – perhaps three people at most. He wondered if they would be friendly.

Eventually a figure emerged under the uncertain glow of a guttering torch. It was a small man edging along with a strange rolling gait. He looked harmless. His light was failing; as Rubin watched from the darkness he stopped and pulled a fresh brand from his sack, and lit it expertly from the dying one. The man was watching his feet as he crept along, moving the torch back and forth to illuminate the damp, treacherous ground in front of him.

Gripping his knife, Rubin took a deep breath and stepped into the light-pool. In the wink of an eye the small man turned and was scuttling back along the pathway for all he was worth.

'I won't hurt you!' Rubin called. 'I mean you no harm!'

The man kept running, but he was old and Rubin knew he could catch him. Besides, he thought, he could follow the light. As if in response to this thought the man threw down the torch and vanished. Rubin ran to it and gratefully snatched it up, feeling the warmth of another hand on the rough wood. He stood quietly for a moment.

The scuffling sound of running feet had stopped and there was silence. Rubin walked slowly forward, alert for sound or movement. He did not fear the old man but was, on the contrary, anxious for company.

'I mean you no harm,' he repeated to the waiting darkness. 'I'm seeking information.'

There was only silence. 'I have gold,' he lied. 'I will give some to you for information.'

The silence thickened and there was no sign the Dweller would trust him. Then from the blackness to his right the man suddenly sprang out, his spindly body hitting Rubin's, his fingers grasping frantically for the torch. Rubin pushed him off with ease and the oldster stumbled to his knees and tried to scramble away. Rubin dropped the torch and lunged at him, desperate not to be left alone. He grabbed the man's skinny neck. The Dweller was twitching and shaking, whether from fear or illness Rubin could not tell.

'I don't want to hurt you,' he assured him. 'I need help.'

The old man was clad in layers of filthy rags which felt slick with grease under Rubin's hands. His face was pale as wax. He glared at Rubin with black button eyes but appeared exhausted. He could do no more than look around, ensuring his sack was still there.

Rubin cautiously let go of him and grabbed the torch then leaned back against the rock wall, trying to look unthreatening. 'My name is Rubin,' he said.

After a while he added, 'And then, you see, you say *your* name.'

His new companion peered at him suspiciously. Then he startled Rubin by suddenly shouting, 'How're we heading, boy?'

Rubin frowned. 'I don't know,' he answered. Then, 'I was hoping you'd tell me, sir.'

The man kept looking around fretfully as if expecting an army of Rubin's comrades to come storming down the tunnel.

'I'm alone too,' Rubin said, smiling in what he hoped was a reassuring way. 'Answer me one question and I'll give you light for your torch.'

'You got bones, boy?' the old man bellowed, and Rubin realized he must be deaf. He had no idea what the man meant and, it seemed, the man could not understand him. He shook his head.

'Answer me one question,' he repeated, shouting back. 'Tell me where I can go to rest in safety.'

The old man said nothing but he climbed slowly to his feet and picked up his sack, peering into it as if he feared Rubin might have looted it. Then he beckoned Rubin to follow. They quickly left the main pathway, following a narrow crack in the rock. They came out in a new tunnel, then his companion suddenly plunged down a steep stairway and Rubin followed close behind. He was worried lest he be left alone, even though he still held the torch. The smell thickened as they descended and he vomited the meagre contents of his stomach. The old man glanced behind, then scuttled left and disappeared down a near-vertical stair, leading ever down.

Rubin paused for a breath, feeling he was at a turning-point. He could still go back and, perhaps with this old man's help, find the way out to daylight, to the comforts of home. But by now the emperor's men would have arrived at the Salient, seeking him for the army. And if they could not find him they would certainly return.

So he gritted his teeth and, saying a silent farewell to the life he'd known, he followed his new friend down into the hell of the Halls, walking beyond light and hope to a world where despair squats like a toad, eating brave boys for breakfast.

CHAPTER FIVE

THE INJURED MAN WRITHED IN AGONY, FIGHTING against his captors, bellowing his pain and fury. He was a strong man, though drained by his wounds, and it was all they could do to hold him. One soldier, a heavy-muscled veteran, sat on the man's good leg while two others bore down on his shoulders. The surgeon kept hacking relentlessly through the meat of the man's thigh. His arms and apron were covered with gore, and the stench of blood and anguish in the summer heat was sickening.

It was Valla's job to catch and hold on to the big blood vessel which snaked down the inside of the injured man's thigh, to hold it and pinch it and stop it spurting his lifeblood over them all. The thing was slippery as an eel and, like an eel, seemed to have a will of its own, but Valla held on to it conscientiously. It was not her first amputation.

The surgeon, an old man called Pindar, dropped the straight knife he was wielding and grabbed the serrated bone-saw off the ground. He started scraping it across the exposed thighbone. The patient gave an agonized screech and was suddenly still.

'Is he dead?' asked Pindar, still sawing. Sometimes the heart of the strongest man would stop at this point.

One of the helpers felt the casualty's neck. 'Swooned,' he said.

Pindar grunted. Then, with a loud curse, he threw down the saw and snatched another from the ground. Blunt, Valla thought despairingly, they're all too blunt.

Mercifully the man stayed unconscious until his leg had been hacked off and thrown on to the pile of limbs, disturbing a cloud of flies. The raw stump was slathered with hot tar. Then the other helpers picked the patient up and hauled him off to the tent where recent amputees and other soldiers whose lives hung in the balance shared a grim comradeship.

Pindar nodded his thanks to Valla, dismissing her, and she wandered out into the sunshine. She raised her face to the light. Then she crossed in front of the three tents full of wounded and set off up towards the woodland stream which had dictated where the surgeons pitch their camp. Eager to get the stench of blood and fear out of her body, she breathed in the clean air, but even this small movement of her chest sparked agony in her injured arm, on top of the deep and abiding throb of pain that always lived there. As ever, she tried to put it aside and relish the fresh scents of the mountains. Down in the City, she thought, so far to the south, summer was a wretched time. The sick and elderly and the very young died in their homes from the heat and lack of water, the whole place stank of rot and decay, and the soldiers dreaded it, garbed in their armour and leather. She hated the City in the dog-days of summer, but nevertheless she wished she were there, with the Warhounds, if that was where they were, and away from this cool, pine-clad mountain. The trees were dark green and stately, pungent with sap, and the ground beneath them thick and mattressy with millions of needles accumulated over hundreds of years. She loathed being there.

She stepped across the steep, babbling stream to the other bank then knelt and let the water wash the worst of the blood off her good arm. Then she sat back on the low bank and looked up towards Needlewoman's Notch. Today's battle had started soon after dawn, as most of them did. The breeze was from the south, so the sounds were muffled: the clash of metal, the cries of the wounded. Valla had stopped counting how many battles there had been since she first arrived there with Leona and the rest of the Warhounds half a year before, when the ground was covered with clean snow and she had been a respected member of the Thousand. Now she was just a dogsbody, dressing wounds, fetching and carrying for the injured, cleaning them up, listening to the groans and screams all day and night. Her prized black and silver armour had disappeared slowly, piece by piece, stolen or cannibalized by and for other warriors. The last to go was the helm, smaller than the common size, too small for most soldiers. But it had gone anyway one day when her back was turned.

She tried to accept her lot. She tried to be useful. But she could not do much, she thought, looking down at her useless arm.

Marcellus had left the winter war in the hands of General Dragonard and marched away, perhaps back to the City. He had left the Warhounds to buttress the general's campaign to take the Notch, which was expected to last only days. But the Blues were more resilient than Marcellus had expected. Half a year on, and high summer, and they still held the Notch, despite appalling attrition on both sides.

Valla had been injured forty or so days before in an engagement between the Hounds and the Mulanese beetles, the most feared of the Blues' heavy infantry. They were dark-skinned men encased in armour from knee to helm, all of them big as trees and twice as slow. But difficult to kill.

Valla had been caught by surprise and by arrogance. She had speared two beetles, one in the knee, one between the chest plates, and had bounded back, thrilling with triumph, unaware of a third warrior looming at her rear. He had hit her below the shoulder with the full weight of his mace, a crushing blow weighted with iron and driven by dense muscle, which had shattered her arm and felled her, helpless with shock and agony, at his boots. The beetle had raised his mace for the killing blow.

Leona had saved her. Though fighting another beetle twenty paces away, the Warhounds' commander had dodged a thrust from the warrior's broadsword, turned on her heel and flung her dagger at the mace-wielder, catching him in the neck. The blow had no depth but the beetle was distracted for a heartbeat. Leona had abandoned her own opponent and run to Valla's side. She stood over her friend and defended her, not giving a pace, until she had managed to disable the beetle then kill him.

The bones in Valla's lower arm had broken cleanly, but the upper bone was shattered. The surgeon told her he had to cut it off at the shoulder but Valla had refused, arguing feebly as she fought the drift into unconsciousness, defending her arm as Leona had defended her. As she refused to lose the arm, so she refused to pass out, hanging on grimly, for she knew the sawbones would hack it off as soon as she could no longer say no. Leona had come to her aid again, telling the surgeon to wait a few days to see if the limb started to heal. Regretfully Pindar had complied. He had reset the shattered bones as best he could, then bandaged the arm in splints, strapping it across Valla's chest. And there it stayed. It had not healed, and it pained her constantly, but Valla lived with hope and she prayed daily to Aduara to make her whole again. And each day she peered at the white waxy fingertips, peeping out from the grimy bandages like those of a corpse, willing them not to turn black.

Just days after her injury the Warhounds had received new orders and Leona and her century had marched away, leaving her behind, a crippled Hound with no home and no future.

'I can have that arm off in a heartbeat,' Pindar would tell her from time to time once she was back on her feet. 'I can call a bugler in here. In the time it takes to blow ten blasts on the bugle it will be off and you'll start healing.'

Valla knew he wished the best for her but she would not agree. There were plenty of one-armed fighters in the rear ranks of all armies, but they had usually lost the limb at the wrist or just below the elbow and could strap on a shield. She would not be able to and would be a hindrance to others. No one would trust her to fight alongside them. And if she could not fight, what would she do?

Tears welled behind her eyes. She wished now she'd had the courage to have the arm taken off. She wished it had been severed cleanly on the battlefield. Sometimes she thought of taking her sword and heading up there, to the battle at the Notch where men and women died honourably each day, to die a useful death, a valorous death with her comrades.

Sitting by the stream she heard the scuff of sandals and looked round. A soldier came climbing up towards her. He sat down on the other bank and they nodded to each other. She recognized him. He had had a mangled hand chopped off and was very nearly battle-ready again. But he could not fight in the struggle above them at the Notch, for the steep and rocky terrain made two hands essential. The man, whose name she could not remember, was to return to the City to be redeployed.

She lowered her eyes, avoiding looking at his healing stump. She felt sick with jealousy, sick that this warrior would fight again, perhaps with a hook for a hand, a leather sheath for the stub. He could use a shield and was thus considered a worthy fighter. He grinned at her across the stream and she forced her face into a grimace approximating a smile.

'How's your friend?' the soldier asked her.

'My friend?'

'The one the death gods threw back. Red.'

She nodded. 'Still alive.'

Red was a marvel to them all, a soldier who should have died back in the winter when he was gutted by an enemy spear. When he was found barely alive, his guts were stuffed back into his body and he was carried to the tent for the dying. But he did not die. A thin man already, he had become skin and bones, with no more muscle on him than a butterfly. When Valla started looking after him he had been a frail, pale thing, covered with sores, his eyes sunken, his face that of an old man. She had conscientiously fed him each day, making sure he had life-giving gravy or soup. It sometimes stopped his breathing so she would roll him over easily, light as he was, and let the food trickle out of him before trying again. His will to live became legendary.

And a few days ago he had started moving a little, his muscles twitching, his swallow reflex strengthening, eyelids moving as if he dreamed. Valla washed his thin body and talked to him, telling him of her life with the Warhounds, the battles they had fought, the valour of the City's warriors. She willed him to wake up. She did not know his name – no one did – but they called him Red because of his bright hair. Valla wondered what colour his eyes were.

She looked up. The one-handed soldier was watching

her assessingly. She sighed to herself. She knew what was coming – he was about to say something flattering. They always did once they felt new vigour rising in them.

The soldier cleared his throat and said, 'They say you used to be a fine warrior.'

Valla snorted, caught between amusement and despair. She stood up, nodded amiably enough to him and made her way back to the encampment. The day's battle was still raging above; she could hear its sounds in the clear air. There would be more casualties. She decided to check on Red before they were overwhelmed.

The medical tents were no more than flimsy tunnels, open-ended, each housing more than fifty patients. They were made of thin canvas, offering shade from the heat of the sun in summer and a poor protection from the icy northerlies in winter. The farthest tent was separate from the others and it housed those who needed the least care. It was light and airy, and well away from the sounds and smells of recent casualties and the doomed. Valla's straw mattress was at the far end, the prime position, at the lip of shelving cliffside that looked down and south towards the far-distant City. In the quiet summer evenings she would lie there and watch the eagles soar on the warm winds.

She picked her way between the beds, exchanging words with the soldiers – men and women – who lay or sat or stood around. They would, most of them, fight another day, though some had head injuries which would condemn them in the last, however well their wounds healed: some had poor balance or coordination, and a few had little idea what was going on around them. Looking at those warriors, she was reminded that Aduara had been merciful to her, though her mercy was harsh.

She had moved Red's pallet opposite hers so she could keep an eye on him. He was lying on his side, where she had placed him after feeding him at first light. She paused to watch for the small movement of his back and shoulders, the weak inhalation, barely discernible, that showed he was still alive. His red hair, grown long, had flopped over his face and she pushed it back. Her breath caught in her throat.

His eyes were open.

Valla leaned close, touching him gently on the shoulder. 'Hello,' she whispered. She wished she knew his name. 'Red,' she tried.

But his eyes closed and within moments his eyelids started flickering and she guessed he was falling deep into dreams again.

Rubin and the old Dweller who, he learned, was a former sea dog called Captain Starky, journeyed down through the sewers together for a very long time, until Rubin thought he must reach the centre of the earth, then slowly back up again. Rubin later learned that the Captain was avoiding the more dangerous parts of the Halls, where reivers walked intent on theft and murder and worse.

The path along which they climbed and scrambled was at times wet and muddy, the ringing of falling water constant in their ears, and at other times dry as dust, as though it had not seen water for a hundred years. Mostly they were travelling through tunnels carved in rock or formed by natural splits in the earth. But then Rubin would suddenly realize they were crossing an abandoned chamber, complete with cobwebbed furniture. He hurried quickly through those, feeling ghosts watching him from the blind windows.

Throughout its history the City had been sinking. As it descended, ground-floor rooms were transformed into basements, first floors into ground floors. Within a generation or two a whole house could completely disappear, descending into the Halls like a very slow cage down a mine-shaft.

While Rubin had struggled to keep up, the Captain was also watching the ground, searching for pickings. Occasionally he would dart to the side, beckoning Rubin to bring the torch, then swoop triumphantly on some piece of flotsam, bringing it close to his face, inspecting it, sniffing it. If it was valuable to him he would pop it in his sack, and Rubin saw many unidentifiable morsels go in there. If the old man rejected something he would politely offer it to Rubin before throwing it back. Rubin wondered if this was a courtesy throughout the Halls. He had refused everything he was offered, craving only fresh water and rest, and a relief from the awful smell.

Once the Captain pounced on a lump of mud and, whistling to himself, cleaned it off, revealing a dead tortoise. Miserable though he was, Rubin was intrigued to know how a tortoise, of all things, had come this far into the lower depths. The Captain ripped out the decaying flesh, sniffed it, then, wrapping the shell in a rag, turned to Rubin and shouted out the first word he'd volunteered in hours.

'Treasure!' Delight lit up his wrinkled face and Rubin couldn't help but smile.

They had been crossing one large, low Hall when Rubin realized he was being rained on. He held up the torch to illumine the ceiling of the cavern, where he could see wobbling drops forming then falling in fat explosions. Is this fresh water, he wondered, his throat parched and thick with disgust.

'Can I drink this?' he asked the Captain, who shrugged unhelpfully. Rubin threw his head back and opened his mouth until a fat drop of moisture fell into it, then he gagged and spat, his mouth twisting in a spasm of revulsion.

'Rain,' Captain Starky volunteered.

Rubin was to learn that there was weather in the Halls. There was rain, from condensation on walls and ceilings when the tunnels sweated as if with fear, and from the spray from weirs and waterfalls. Mist lay on the stream of life and sometimes crept up out of the water channels and through the tunnels. This was considered an ill omen, information which made Rubin laugh bitterly when he first heard it, for talk of bad luck in such a terrible place seemed ironic – though further experience showed there were many degrees of luck in the Halls and few of them were good.

Some areas were much cooler than others. Generally, the deeper you went the warmer it was, but it was also warmer in the centres of population, where men, rats and insects gathered. And there were air currents – both gentle breezes which cooled the skin and shifted the heavy miasma of fetid air that clotted the mind and dulled the spirit, and brisk winds that rattled down tunnels, chilling the bones in winter.

It was a place of fear and terror, but also a place of safety. Like a mother, the lower depth had a warm embrace; it was a haven from the outside world, a refuge from attack. In the darkness you cannot be seen, so the frightened and fugitive were drawn towards it. It housed men and women and rats, stray dogs and myriad scurrying insects, and the odd gulon. Cows were stabled there and spent their lives in darkness; pigs too and some mules, although horses, the most sensitive of beasts, would not enter its portals; if forced there, they would quickly sicken and die.

Among the pale creatures which never saw the light of day were white crabs which lived on human excrement, and fat ginger slugs which thrived on damp walls and which would crawl into bedding in the night as if for company. These could be eaten, if absolutely necessary. Silver eels, the only creatures to be farmed there, were kept in great cauldrons fed by fresh water in the High Halls. Giant mushrooms, as big as your head, burgeoned in the ceilings. These were edible, although they were rubbery and tasted atrocious; they would keep you alive if all other sources of food failed.

Rubin's first lessons were on the places to avoid: the haunts of evil men, the regular routes of the emperor's patrols, and the most perilous of tunnels and air-shafts, called high funnels. He learned that old graves exude essences of the dead and to unwittingly walk under a graveyard was to call on oneself a sentence of death. And the blood sewers, which lay under slaughterhouses, were best avoided, for the stench was particularly vile and, it was said, could kill you stone dead with just one breath.

But it was a long time before Rubin learned all this, for he had chosen an uncommunicative teacher.

Captain Starky had descended to the Halls after the deaths of his family in the spring plague fifty years before. He was a kindly man, though eccentric, even for a Dweller. He washed his face and hands every day, whether they needed it or not, in the fresh water other Dwellers valued only for drinking, and his long grey hair was coiled carefully into a bun, topped with a ragged green net.

When, on the day they first met, the pair finally reached the cave the Captain called home, a boy came scrambling down from a high ledge to greet them. He was much younger than Rubin and he glared at him, eyes sullen and suspicious. The old man, more at ease now, stood and looked around him as if gazing across an ocean.

'How're we heading, boy?' he shouted.

'East by north, cap,' the boy replied promptly.

'Man the capstan and get under way!'

'Ay ay, cap.'

The old man nodded, satisfied, then scrambled up a crevice in the steep rock, finding handholds Rubin could not see. From a perch a good way up he beckoned and the two boys, watching each other uneasily, followed. For the next two seasons Rubin and the Captain and the boy, whose name was Brax, shared this cave high in the wall of Jack's Tail Hall, a valuable home they defended successfully against all comers until the reivers came.

The Captain was not mad, Rubin found, but he was half-deaf and, as everyone was half-blind in the Halls, he relied on the boys to sound the alarm if they were threatened. He found comfort in familiar words from his years at sea long past. He would awaken gripped by night terrors and Brax would recite a litany of phrases he had learned from the old sailor. 'Officer of the watch, call my gig!' Or, 'Come alongside, damn your eyes.' And the Captain would calm himself and sleep again.

Starky spent much of his time carving intricate gaming pieces from odds and ends of animal bones and they were much prized by Nearsiders. Rubin had a set of six knucklebones the Captain had given him. He could feel rather than see the tiny depictions of birds and fish romping on the smooth white bone, and he wondered at the skill of an old man with crabbed hands and dim eyesight. Rubin prized them, but he was careless by nature and kept them loose in his pocket and they washed away one day when he was caught by a sudden downpour in the Little Hellespont. Once the Captain was gone he sorely regretted the loss.

It was the Captain who gave Rubin his most valuable lesson about navigating the Halls, one which saved his life more than once when he wandered far from the

Eating Gate, the great weir whose cacophony was a fixed point for a majority of Dwellers. Not long after they first met the Captain scurried up to Rubin, in his way, and yelled confidentially, 'Back against the wall, laddie, back against the wall.'

He pushed and poked Rubin until, reluctantly, the boy was leaning back against the rock wall of Jack's Tail Hall.

'See, laddie, back to the wall, that be north,' he indicated with one crabbed finger.

'North, yes,' said Rubin, nodding, trying to move away.

'Listen, laddie,' Starky said impatiently, pushing him back again, 'wind in y'ear.'

The old man's finger poked impatiently at his right ear and Rubin flinched.

'Wind in y'ear!' He stared into Rubin's face intently, fingering his own ear. Then Rubin realized what he meant: in his right ear he could feel the faintest of breezes.

'That'd be north,' the Captain explained again, in case Rubin hadn't taken his point. Rubin nodded his understanding.

Every day his wits were challenged. He avoided death a hundred times, from sickness, slips in the dark, and the evil of men. Yet he did not run away. After a year or more in the Halls he began to think he knew all there was to know about life underground. He learned how to find most things he wanted – from a cup of fresh water to a cavalry sabre to a live hedgehog to make a tasty meal. He often found himself in peril, from flash floods or the sudden poisonous miasmas in the tunnels, or from roving gangs or the emperor's patrols. But he was resourceful and quick to learn, and if a problem he met had ears then Rubin could always talk his way past it. His confidence grew and he felt himself a master of the Halls.

It was this Rubin, at the prime of his youthful pride, who met the brother and sister Elija and Emly, refugees from unknown terrors. They were too young to fend for themselves – little Em was only four and was speechless with fear – and he kept them alive and under his wing in the Hall of Blue Light for a long season. He had planned to stay with them until Elija was able to take care of them himself, or until he found another guardian for the pair.

But then came the day he heard Captain Starky was in trouble.

CHAPTER SIX

VALLA HAD NEVER SEEN ANYONE THINK SO MUCH.

She sat cross-legged on her straw mattress and watched the frail young man thinking. She had fed him thin stew, slowly and patiently, and now Red was gazing out at the late afternoon. He had not yet spoken, but had cleared his throat and coughed as if engaging long-unused sinews in his throat. And he looked around him, at the tent and the other soldiers, at her, and out to the world beyond. And he thought. She could see him thinking. She waited, eager to hear his story.

Finally, as the sun started to set in the west, he turned his face to her and, clearing his throat again, croaked a word.

'Marcellus.'

She jumped up and went to his side, kneeling down beside him. His eyes were hectic and his cheeks flushed.

'Marcellus,' he repeated. 'I must speak to him.'

'Marcellus has returned to the City long since.'

'Dragonard then. Bring him to me.'

An officer, she thought. She had predicted he would be an officer. 'Dragonard is dead. These thirty days,' she told him. The death of their popular general had hit the Imperials hard.

Red closed his eyes and was silent for a while. Then he looked out at the summer sky.

'How long have I been sick?' he asked.

'Since winter. That's half a year now. You were gravely injured. They all thought you would die.'

He stared at her, despair in his eyes. 'I had a message for Marcellus,' he told her, voice faltering, 'but it is too late now.'

Then he asked, 'What news from the City?'

She looked at him helplessly, not knowing what to say. There was no news from the City. Or, if there was, nobody told her. But Red had closed his eyes and fallen asleep again.

From behind her she heard a yell. 'Valla! You're wanted!' Casualties, she thought, and leaped to her feet.

By the next day Red's improvement was remarkable. He could not stand, for his legs were weak from disuse, but he could sit up, and Valla was amazed by the amount he could eat, as if he was making up for the time spent in sleep. She brought him clean water from high in the stream, for she believed its crystal clarity would heal his body, and a little ale for strength.

And he talked endlessly, as though making up for lost time in this too. He told her of his home on the cliffs above the City, and of his sister who was a warrior – a common infantry soldier, yet he was proud of her. When he spoke of his years in the sewers beneath the City Valla was disinclined to believe him at first, for such a life seemed implausible, but he filled his stories with a wealth of detail and tales which made her smile. And he told her of his audience with Marcellus, when he was dragged out of the sewers like a rat and stood, stinking, in front of the First Lord, and about his time as a spy with the Odrysians. The one thing he would not talk about was the vital information he needed to give to Marcellus – information which was, almost certainly, half a year too late.

When he told her his name Valla remembered the third messenger, and the watchword Rubin, and she realized he was what he said he was, and that he was a hero.

'Who is commanding our forces now?' he asked her after a meal of bread and dried meat, picking crumbs off the thin blanket which covered his frail body. She had shaved him that morning and now she saw how young he was. His gaze was alert and he was interested in everything going on around him. His eyes were violet.

'His name is Gaeta,' she replied.

He stared at her. 'Of the Family Gaeta? Which one? Saul or Jona?'

She shrugged. She had no interest in the City's ancient Families, or in generals either.

He sighed. 'You're a frustrating informant, Valla,' he said.

'I'm not here as your informant,' she told him tartly. 'I'm here to care for you.'

'No, you're not,' he retorted. 'You're a warrior and should be back in the fight, not caring for the wounded.'

She made no response, but inwardly she smiled. For she had a plan now. If Rubin could convince this new general to let him return to the City post-haste, she could go with him as bodyguard. Rubin had laboriously written a message to the man and Valla had despatched it up to the Notch in the hands of a rider she trusted. She had no doubt Rubin's words would be ignored at first. But when he was on his feet again he could speak to the general himself and she believed he would convince this Gaeta of the importance of his mission.

A man with vital information for Marcellus could not be disregarded.

Rubin was dozing again and she lay back on her pallet. The warm breeze, which often carried the sounds of battle and forewarned of casualties to come, was today blowing from the south so the afternoon was silent. Valla looked out at the hills and sky. The sky was white in the late afternoon, with small storm clouds on the horizon. There was a promise of rain in the air. She looked over at Rubin. He was asleep.

She levered herself to her feet, trying to ignore the bolt of pain through her arm, meaning to go to tend to the dying. It was not a chore she relished but, like all soldiers, she was familiar with the many and cruel processes of death. She often wondered if she would prefer to be alone when she died, or to share a small part of the agony with a sympathetic watcher. Much as she thought on it she did not know the answer. She glanced again at Rubin, resolving to bring him soup when she was finished.

On impulse she reached beneath her mattress and brought out her sword. It was a good blade. It had saved her life many times. Now it lay unused, except occasionally for killing vermin as they scurried into the tent at night to torment the helpless. Her dagger was the more useful tool for the task and she had become adept at skewering rats with it as they scampered between the shadows, but sometimes it was satisfying to swing the sword at one, to hear its bones crunch and see the blood fly. Rats were a constant nuisance, though less so than the flies in summer.

She was about to slide the sword back out of sight when, in the corner of her eye, she saw movement outside the tent. She froze. A man's helmed head was rising into sight from the scrubby bushes fringing the top of the cliff. She retreated silently into the shadows and unsheathed the blade. A welcome rush of battle-lust fizzed through her veins. She gripped the hilt and her palm welcomed the familiar feel of worn leather. She peered out to see a second soldier climbing into sight. Blues!

'Attack!' she yelled. 'We're under attack!'

She leaped at them, dodging a thrust from the first man's sword then slashing him back-handed across the neck. Her blade met stout leather, but the blow spun him to his knees and she turned and parried a blow from the second soldier. On the edge of her vision she saw the first man scramble up, then a third attacker rise from the cliff-edge.

She heard the gong begin its loud, erratic clanging which warned the camp they were under assault. Behind her in the tent she could hear shouts of alarm and curses from the casualties. Then screams and the dull thwack of metal on flesh. They were under attack from both sides! She dared not look behind her, or at Rubin who lay helpless to her right. Her back felt vulnerable, protected only by the injured.

She edged in front of Rubin, eyeing the three soldiers who were closing on her. The man she had hit on the neck was the least of them; he stumbled as if dazed. Another, brown-bearded and full-bellied, surveyed her useless arm and grinned.

'Hurt yourself, girlie?'

She smiled. Men often used words to bolster their confidence. And he could not see past her useless arm. He didn't know she was a warrior of the Thousand. She realized at that instant that she was happy. Either she would survive this and live with pride, or she would die with honour. She genuinely did not mind which.

She screamed and leaped forward, but she was out of practice and her balance was off. The bearded man parried her thrust and launched a double-handed blow to her head. *He is so slow*, she thought. Valla ducked smoothly then darted sideways, stabbing him in the groin. He clutched himself and fell keening to his knees, hampering the second attacker. Valla spun round and despatched the third with a deep slice across the throat.

She stepped back and flashed a glance behind her, impatient to get into the main battle. The injured warriors had formed a ragged defensive line, the stronger guarding the crippled. But they were dying. Valla twisted back and deflected a murderous blow from the last soldier. As he swung his short sword to gut her, she swayed and the tip of the blade slashed past her hip. She darted in and pierced him in the eye. She snatched his short sword from his hand as he fell and flung it to Rubin, who was struggling, pale-faced and sweating, to get to his feet. She ran back to join her comrades.

The one-handed man she'd met by the stream was battling valiantly, but she saw he was fighting with his wrong hand – it was his sword hand he'd lost. She stepped up beside him just as he stumbled, pierced in the thigh. She killed his attacker then launched herself at the next Blue, slashing the tip of her blade across the man's throat. She stabbed him through the back of the neck as he fell forward. She saw an enemy soldier raise his sword to kill a man lying helpless on the floor, both legs in splints. She ran over and slid her sword under the Blue's arm, seeking the heart. He dropped like a felled ox and she spun back.

But there were far too many of them and the defenders were all weak or disabled. Many of those who could fight had already been killed and the survivors were struggling to retreat towards the back of the tent, towards Rubin.

A tall swordsman, lean and fast, was leading the

attack and Valla sprang towards him, determined to defend the defenceless to her dying breath. He plunged his sword into the chest of a wounded man, then turned and saw her and nodded, accepting her challenge. She saw him note her injured arm, but she knew this man was not going to chat about it. He was happy to take his time while her comrades were dying around her so she leaped in, a darting penetrating blow to the throat. He glided back, perfectly balanced, and she realized he was a swordmaster. In times past she would have been equal to him, but not now.

She attacked again and he deflected her blade and launched a blistering riposte. She leaped back too slowly and was pierced in her injured arm. The jolt of agony made her sick and dizzy. But she managed to attack again. She had little to give and knew she had only moments before he disabled or killed her. The melee around her receded and the sounds of battle became blurred.

'Enough!' a powerful voice roared, the sound freezing her bones and making her stumble to a halt. Her opponent paused too, and both looked round, puzzled.

'Lay down your swords! This battle is over!'

Marcellus! she thought. The First Lord had returned and all would be well. She had heard he could halt a fight with the magical power of his voice. A warm breeze blew through her heart, blowing away her fear and pain.

Time seemed to slow and throughout the blood-covered tent warriors were sheathing their swords. Others just dropped them to the ground, grinning, happy to be alive. Enemies clapped one another on the back. Valla lowered her sword. What a good day it's been, she thought. What were they fighting about? She couldn't remember. Her head ached, but for the first time in days her arm was not paining her. She believed she could feel life flowing through it, warm and vital, and she knew now it would heal and she would be whole again. A bubble of laughter came to her lips.

She turned to Rubin to share her joy. He was seated on the edge of his mattress, one arm supporting himself, the other outstretched towards the laughing soldiers. His thin body was shaking with effort and sweat poured down his face. Through the muffling haze of contentment Valla slowly realized something was very wrong. She frowned and walked over to him. What was the matter with him? The battle was over. He said something to her but his voice was weak and she had to lean down to hear.

'Kill them!' he whispered. 'Kill them all!'

As she gazed at him dumbly, slowly the thrall in which she was held faded enough for her muddled mind to grasp that Marcellus was not there. Rubin had done this. He had stopped the battle somehow, given them a chance of life. She shook her head, trying to clear it, trying to force her way through the conviction that all was well. Raising her sword with uncertain fingers she turned back to the enemy. As she lost sight of Rubin her confusion returned. *What was she going to do?* It was something important, but she could not remember. She looked at the bloody bodies of her comrades lying on the hard earth, the gaping wounds on men and women who still lived, unaware of their lifeblood gouting out on to the ground. She glanced doubtfully back at Rubin.

All at once resolve rose in her and she ran back to her last opponent, the swordmaster, who was standing with a bemused expression on his face, and gutted him with two savage strokes. She plunged into the enemy ranks, hacking and slashing, throats, eyes and bellies, maiming and killing the dazed, unresisting Blues. But they were quickly coming round. There were shouts of anger and anguish, and the sliding sound of swords swiftly drawn. A clumsy swing caught Valla on her bad arm, she stumbled on a body, then she was down. And the City soldiers were still wildly outnumbered.

Then in the distance, beyond the clash and curses of the embattled soldiers, came the sound of thundering hooves. Cavalry! Reinforcements summoned from the Notch by the alarm gong. A double bugle blast rent the air and the Blues spun round to defend themselves against the newcomers.

Suddenly weak, Valla pulled herself to her feet, retreated from the battle and turned to Rubin. He lay across his mattress, pale as ice, unconscious. She saw him with new eyes and a thrill of fear ran up her spine, raising the hairs on the back of her neck. Who *was* this man? Had the battle ended merely because he wanted it to? She'd been told Marcellus could end a skirmish with the power of his voice, though she had never witnessed it. But she *had* seen him kill, wreaking terrible carnage among both enemies and friends with only his strength of will. That was a memory she would like to forget.

Yet Rubin, whatever he was, was in her charge and, as the fighting in the tent came to a bloody end, she checked he was still breathing then sat wearily beside him. Her arm was in torment. Now her battle was over the pain came roaring back and she bent over, stunned by the hurt.

The following night and day was a blood-spattered nightmare. Valla worked from dusk to dusk helping the wounded, the stench of blood and fear and agony hanging over the encampment. By nightfall the bodies of City comrades had been burned and those of the enemy thrown over the cliff. The casualties had been found places to lie down and those under sentence of death were deep in lorassium slumber.

Valla stumbled back to her tent eager to sleep, but

when she saw Rubin was awake once more she went over to him and sat beside him. In the last light of the setting sun he smiled at her.

'What happened?' she asked him. 'How did you stop the battle?'

He shook his head, looking at his hands. 'I don't know.'

But she eyed him silently and after a while he sighed and said, 'I managed to get my feet on the ground. I was trying to stand, although I knew I was too weak. I put my hand out to you – I don't know why . . . to try and help, to try to get help. I remember wanting to end the battle, to rescue us both.' He rubbed his eyes. 'Then I felt this . . . energy rising from the earth, up through me, like water rising up a flooded drain.' He shook his head. 'I've never known anything like it. It ran through my belly and chest, growing hot, then crackled along my arm like lightning. I could almost see it, blazing from my fingertips.' He shook his head. 'Then everyone stopped fighting and started putting their swords away. Everything became calm and slow.'

He looked at her and she nodded, remembering.

'Everything . . .' He stopped and Valla watched the play of emotions across his face like a shallow stream over pebbles.

He struggled for an explanation. 'For a heartbeat or two I felt this . . . exultation, that I had in my grasp a power I could wield at will. But I couldn't hold on to it. It began to fade. And then you strolled over to me, smiling like an idiot.'

'You told me to kill them all.'

'Did I? I don't remember.'

She thought about it, watching the red stain on the horizon slowly disappear.

'Do you think you can do it again?' she asked.

But Rubin was asleep.

* * *

News travelled swiftly through the Halls, and news of disaster travelled quickest. Many leagues of tunnels and caverns separated the Hall of Blue Light, where Rubin had been dwelling with Elija and Emly, and his old home, but within a day he had heard of an attack by a band of reivers on Jack's Tail Hall and had set out to try to help his friends.

When he reached Jack's Tail it was deserted save for corpses. Fearfully he examined them by flaring torchlight and found many Dwellers he knew, but not the Captain or Brax. He looked around. The habitual little piles of meagre possessions, which marked what Dwellers called home, had all gone. Nothing in Jack's Tail spoke of habitation, only death.

A sound made him turn, startled, and he saw the old man called Salty who guarded the eel-tanks and fed the creatures with the care of a mother-fish.

'Salty! Where did they all go?'

The old man flung out his withered arms and shook his head. 'All dead,' he moaned. 'Dead and dying.' He sobbed and wiped his eyes. 'All dead.'

Rubin realized he was talking about the eels. The heavy tanks had been overturned and the creatures lay in slimy piles, some still twitching.

'Where's Captain Starky? And Brax?' But old Salty just moaned and kept wiping his eyes.

'Reivers,' another voice said. Rubin saw a tiny old Dweller he thought of as the Orange Woman for he had once seen her with a whole orange, guarding it like an infant, gloating over it as it dried and grew inedible. She was leaning on a crutch, an injured leg crudely bandaged with filthy rags.

'What? Where did they go?' he asked her.

'Reivers took 'em. Others ran off.' Her eyes roamed around, searching for someone, for something.

'Captain Starky?'

She shook her head distractedly.

'Which way did they go? The reivers?'

She looked up at him. 'Down,' she said. 'Reivers live in darkest.'

Rubin prepared himself well. He raided corpses ruthlessly, found torches half used and a few vital phosphorus sticks. He recovered some dried meat from the Captain's cave and filled two water skins at the nearest well. He still had his long knife, sharpened to a fine edge, and he added two more, strapping them to his body. All the while Jack's Tail's Dwellers, the fitter ones who had fled the attack, came drifting back. None could tell what had happened to his friends.

He set off, trying to recall what he had been told about reivers. They stole people away to kill and eat them and suck the marrow from their bones. Rubin had scoffed at these stories, but he had remembered them. Reivers lived to the west, towards the sea, and down, always down. Rubin knew the geography of the Halls as far west as the Whithergo, a waterway of legendary peril, and resolved to go that way.

He found Brax almost immediately. The boy lay at the corner of two main ways, gaping wounds on his head and back; he had been slaughtered with an axe or weighted blade. But he lay alone. There was no sign of the Captain.

The reivers' trail was clear as day. They left chewed bones, broken weapons and corpses in their wake. They were moving fast and Rubin reckoned they were in a hurry to get somewhere. He saw few other Dwellers, for they stayed well clear of the reivers' path, but he met one old woman who claimed there were fifty or more in the party, though how many were captives and how many captors she could not tell.

Rubin reached the entrance to the Whithergo but the

reivers had shunned it and carried on north-west. He followed them until he came to regions he had never been in before: vast chambers with blind statuary and tiled floors, empty but for bats; deep crevices in the rock which seemed to go down for ever; and once a great waterfall which fell out of the gloom far above to some point far below, crashing in a distant cacophony, unseen. He sat for a while watching the cascading water, chewing on some dried meat, his legs splashed by the rising mists. It was fresh, the water, and he drank his fill and refilled his water skins.

When he finally caught up with the reivers he almost walked into them. They had stopped to rest and just in time he saw their torchlight reflected on a rock-face. He pulled back, cramming his own torch into a deep crevice then creeping forward in darkness. He could see little, save for the wild light of many torches, but he could hear their grunts and shouts and oaths. He had no chance to count how many there were, or see if the Captain was among them, before the band set off again. After that it was just a matter of staying out of sight.

It was hard to measure time in the Halls, but Rubin reckoned he had followed them for three or four days, judging by the wear on his body and his mind, when they finally arrived at their lair. He could hear they had stopped and he lingered, as so often before, waiting for them to move on. Slowly the sounds they made dwindled and he peered out from the hidey-hole where he was lodged in time to glimpse the last man, the last torch, vanishing into a gap in the wall he would never have otherwise seen. He waited as long as his patience could endure, then he crept forward and climbed through after them. Beyond was a vast cavern, and Rubin stopped and looked up, astonished to see it was lit by daylight. It was a poor light falling from shafts in the roof of the cave but, feeble though it was, it illuminated a small settlement on the far bank of a turgid river. The band of reivers was already crossing a decrepit bridge and people were running from the settlement, greeting them with shouts and cheers as if they were returning heroes.

Rubin looked around the enormous cavern. Daylight, he could see, was also filtering from his right. As he watched it turned pinkish and he realized he was looking towards the far mouth of the cave and the light of the setting sun outside. Comforted by its glow and the promise of daylight he found a nook in the rock wall and settled down to sleep. He woke once to cringe into the shadows when he heard raucous voices pass close by. More reivers returning home. These had enjoyed some fiery spirits, by the sound of it, and there was little chance of Rubin being spotted.

At the first thin light of the new day he hurried across the rickety bridge, staying low, to the edge of the squalid settlement. Keeping to the darkness he circled the outskirts. He found the captives' prison on the far side of the village, out of the light. It was a cage bolted to a stone floor, walled and roofed with iron bars, rusty but secure. It was only half the height of a man so its prisoners could not stand. There were thirty or more men and women inside, inert, lying as if dead. Rubin could not see the Captain, but then he could not make out anyone's face and he dared not call out. The cage was locked with a heavy padlock. He resolved to find the key.

He watched from the shadows all day. Eventually a burly man came idling from the village carrying a pailful of slop which he poured through the bars of the cage, half-filling two troughs, spilling the rest to the ground. There was movement at last in the prison as skeletal figures crawled over to the wretched food. None of them was Captain Starky. Rubin pushed himself back, leaning against the stub of a stone pillar, and fell asleep.

Clearly the reivers had no fear of intruders, for they put out no sentries, and the next day Rubin found he could make his way unnoticed around the perimeter of the settlement, hugging the darkness. He soon discovered how the captives were used. He ventured right up to a rotten wooden building close by the river. The stench from it, even this deep in the Halls, made him gag. Filled with dread and loathing he pushed open the sagging door. As his eyes adjusted to the weak light he could make out a sturdy wooden block, thick with crusted blood, an array of axes and knives and in the corner a pile of meat, alive with a cloak of flies. Overwhelmed with disgust, he fled.

Near the captives' prison there was a second cage, a smaller one. This held mostly corpses – of dogs big and small and a few cats. The only living thing was a black brute of a beast, scarred and twisted. It had the body of a boar and the jaws of a mastiff, with deformed fangs and mean little eyes. Rubin had no idea what it was and he gave the cage a wide berth. Although an idea was forming.

The next day the light from above was brighter than he had seen since he left the world of daylight. In his hideaway Rubin gazed up at the thick columns of soupy light, swirling with dust motes, and guessed it was about noon on, perhaps, a sunny summer's day. A strong yearning for fresh air arose in him, bringing painful tears to his eyes. He resolved in that moment that when he had finished his work here, whether he found the Captain or not, he would go Outside again, whatever fate it brought him.

He had been dozing lightly, his belly gripped by hunger, when he was woken by screams and cries. Dazed, he peered out. The captives were moaning and crying, swaying and clutching at the bars, more alive than he had yet seen them.

'We'll give you something to cry about,' a voice called jovially and he saw two men making their way towards them from the settlement.

Rubin shook off his exhaustion. He got to his feet and hurried, crouching low, through the darkness and into the shadows behind the beast's cage. The animal watched him, motionless. Rubin slid silently on top of its prison, the creature's eyes following his every move, and squirmed to the point above the door. He took out his long knife.

As the guards unlocked and flung open the captives' prison Rubin leaned over and, drawing a deep breath, lifted the bar across the cage door. The beast shot out as if loosed from a bow then turned towards Rubin, its tiny black eyes gleaming with malice.

But at that moment one of the guards spoke. 'C'mon, two of you today. It'll be over quick. I promise.' He laughed.

Hearing his voice the beast spun round and took off towards him. It was not a big animal but it was tough and angry. It ran up the startled guard's chest and sank its twisted fangs into the man's neck. The guard screamed and struggled, then his cry was drowned in blood and he fell to his knees, moaning. The beast braced its paws on the ground and tore his throat out. The prisoners screamed and scrambled to get away from the creature, climbing over each other to get deeper into their cage. The beast, bloody meat dripping from its jaws, looked around and, seeing the second guard running for all he was worth, took off after him.

Rubin raced over and flung himself into the cage. He grabbed the first prisoner, pulling him towards the open door. 'Quick!' he said. 'Run!'

But the man shook him off and cringed further into his prison. Rubin took another by his emaciated shoulder. 'Go, while you can!' he pleaded. But the captives, steeped in misery and apathy, shrank from him as if he were the enemy.

Rubin saw a hunched figure, a flash of green. 'Captain?' But when the head turned he realized it was a woman, her face blank, eyes unseeing.

'Come with me,' he shouted at her, frustrated by their indifference.

'Where?' she whispered colourlessly.

'Anywhere from here!' he yelled. He dragged her from the cage and pointed to the west. 'There's light there! Daylight!'

She stared for a moment then seemed to awaken. She pulled her ragged skirt round her knees and staggered off. The beast, still worrying at the body of its second victim, looked at her assessingly as she hurried by. There was a shout from the direction of the settlement and Rubin saw four more reivers, three scrawny men led by a bulky woman, charging towards them armed with cudgels. The beast put its head down and ran at them. It jumped at the woman in the lead, fangs at her throat. She fell screaming, then blood flew.

Watching, Rubin smiled grimly. 'Good boy,' he said.

CHAPTER SEVEN

'DID YOU EVER FIND CAPTAIN STARKY?' VALLA ASKED, leaning forward and poking their campfire with a branch. Dying embers flared and sparks flew upwards.

Rubin shook his head. 'Perhaps he managed to flee Jack's Tail Hall when the reivers came, then returned later. I hope so. I never went back.'

'Did you escape the sewers then, as you'd vowed?'

He nodded. His violet eyes, so exotic in the light of day, were hooded and the fluid lines of his face in shadow. Only his hair blazed as he stared into the firelight.

Valla threw a handful of sticks on to the dwindling fire. It was a warm night and they didn't need it, but it was cheerful to have a blaze and there was small chance of being spotted by the enemy. They had departed the medical encampment in the Blacktree Mountains and were riding back towards the City. They had travelled by day at first, making their slow way down through high mountain passes and steep rocky trails trampled by goats and deer. Then, as they reached the foothills and the flatter, faster land beyond, they slept by day and rode by night under the light of a waning moon. Rubin had predicted they'd be in sight of the City by morning. Valla hoped so. She had not been in the saddle for years, for the City's cavalry units did not embrace women, and she had found the riding hard.

'What did you do then?' she prompted, for he seemed to be wandering in the past.

'I don't remember really. I was at the end of my strength, my sanity perhaps. I had seen the evil men can do while I lived in the Halls. I thought I had seen it all . . .' He trailed off. Then he turned to her, anxious to convey something, and Valla saw the pain in his face. 'They lived so deep in the Halls, as deep as you could go. But at the same time they were within reach of the outside – just a day or so's walk to the west was sunlight. Yet the reivers chose to live in the dark. And their prisoners, even when they had a chance, didn't try to save themselves. I had a revelation then, standing there in that terrible place. I realized I'd been insane to choose the Halls over the world of daylight, whatever the cost. It had seemed so clear to me when I first made the choice – life in the sewers or death in the armies. But I was ignorant and foolish. I thought I knew it all, but I knew nothing.'

He gazed back at the fire and she watched him, filled with concern. She did not have to see his face to know he was haunted by memories he found hard to bear. She wanted to comfort him, but feared the slightest hint of compassion might break him.

'So why didn't you go towards the sea?' she asked briskly.

'I don't remember,' he repeated after a while, frowning as if trying to catch fleeing memories. 'I was starving by then, and crazed, I think. I must have made my way up through the Halls somehow. Eventually I was picked up by a patrol.'

'Lucky they didn't kill you outright.' To the elite warriors of the Thousand the emperor's patrols were no more than bands of unruly thugs.

'I've always been lucky,' he said, and he seemed unaware of the irony. 'They thought I was an Odrysian spy. I was speaking Odrysian for some reason.'

His face suddenly lost the haunted look and he turned to her and smiled. 'Then I met Marcellus again.'

'Again?'

'I met him as a child, briefly, in my father's house. So,' his voice took on the tones of the teller of tales she knew so well, 'the guards stood me in front of him, a stinking, demented sewer rat, leaking sewage all over his fine carpet, and he asked me my name and I told him Rubin Kerr Guillaume. I've never seen Marcellus so surprised since.' He smiled again at the cherished memory.

'I told him my story,' Rubin went on, 'and he listened.' He looked at Valla. 'Everything my father had told me made me believe Marcellus was cruel and ruthless. But he was friendly and sympathetic. He was interested in me and my life and asked me about my father and Indaro.'

'Did he ask why you were in the sewers?'

'No. But I told him everything about my time there, then he called one of his senior officers and ordered him to clear the reivers out of the Salient caves.'

'And did they?'

'I was told later that his troops slaughtered everyone in the reivers' settlement – men, women and children.'

'And the captives?'

'Everyone.' His eyes were looking inward again and Valla wished she hadn't raised the subject when he clearly needed rest. She looked up. The moon was a silver sliver in the south and the stars shone in glory. She pulled her blanket out of her pack and wrapped it round her.

'Sleep now,' she told him. 'Perhaps we will see the City in the morning.'

* * *

Rubin remembered the day vividly, for it was full of wonders.

He had never before set foot in the Red Palace. He'd spent all his first sixteen years in the house on the Salient, with its worn stone corridors, its shabby rooms overflowing with books and manuscripts on every flat surface. Perhaps he expected something similar, just bigger. But as the guards led him, shackled and filthy, towards his destiny he marvelled at the lofty ceilings and windows, the marble walls and echoing chambers, sunny courtyards awash with flowers glimpsed through carved and filigreed screens, the myriad turrets and minarets. Every few paces, it seemed, they went up or down a staircase, each one rioting with carvings and gilt and wide as a City street. The walls were hung with richly detailed tapestries, each worthy of a day's scrutiny; the floors were rich with mosaics and decorated tiles; and everywhere tall statues gazed over the throng with blank eyes.

And the palace was in ferment that day. Bands of soldiers clattered down the corridors, most of them in the uniform of the City infantry or palace guards, some in the livery of the Thousand. Those elite warriors, in their black full-face helms with silver crests, their black leather body armour with silver decoration, were a sinister company. A detail of six followed Marcellus everywhere outside his own apartments, Rubin later learned, but he never became used to their silent, faceless presence.

Once the gleaming marble walls gave way to gold-encrusted alabaster, he was told he had entered the public places of the emperor and of the Vincerii – Marcellus and his brother Rafael. He was led at last into a dark, dusty chamber lit by sunlight slanting in from high windows. The room was decorated with a thousand birds and beasts, painted on walls and lofty ceilings, sewn into embroideries and upholstery, woven into rugs, their heads mounted on walls, their stuffed bodies prowling the hard stone floor. Not that he noticed all that at first. All he saw, standing in the centre of the room, was the man he recognized from his childhood as Marcellus Vincerus, First Lord of the City, its premier general. He was tall, taller than Rubin even, dressed neither in armour nor the rich robes of a nobleman, but in the austere, dark clothes of a scholar. He watched as Rubin was shoved forward by his guards.

'What is your name?' he asked, his voice neither deep nor high, his tone neutral.

Rubin drew himself up with the tattered remnants of his strength and looked into his black eyes. 'Rubin Kerr Guillaume,' he announced, though his voice sounded cracked and feeble.

Marcellus held his gaze for a long moment. Rubin felt his scalp begin to crawl and he had the urge to look away but the eyes held him captive. He could not move; he could not even blink. He heard a door open behind him. He became desperate to turn and flee through it but he could not escape. Then Marcellus' gaze shifted and he was released.

'This is clearly not the assassin,' Marcellus said sharply to someone behind Rubin. 'For one thing, he has his tongue.' He waved the guards away.

Then he smiled and the room grew brighter. 'Well, young Rubin, we have met once before, I think, in your father's house.'

Rubin could not help but smile in response. 'Yes, lord, I remember it well.'

'But you were just a small child, staring at me from the balcony, grave as an owl.'

'We had few visitors, lord, and never before one so eminent.'

Marcellus chuckled, then he ordered Rubin bathed and shaved and dressed, and later that day sat him down with fine foods and flagons of wine and quizzed him about his life.

But his first question was, 'Tell me how you happen to speak Odrysian?'

Rubin explained about weapons master Gillard, whom Marcellus knew. This surprised Rubin at the time but he later learned his lord had a remarkable memory for faces and names and he had met very many people in his long life. He spoke admiringly of the old weapons master and Rubin, abashed, felt obliged to confess his deficiencies as a fighter. Marcellus listened without judgement. Then he spoke Odrysian himself, testing Rubin's skill with the language. And that was the first time Marcellus said the words, 'I have a mission for you, young Rubin.'

That first time he stayed in the Red Palace for ten days. Marcellus spent long hours with him, walking him round its great chambers as if he were an honoured ambassador from a foreign land, pointing out wonders of art and architecture, many of them made with skills now long forgotten. They strolled through lush gardens dressed with rare plants and Marcellus showed him the great aviary filled with brightly coloured birds from all over the world. At its centre a huge eagle, almost the height of a man, ignored them from a lofty log perch. Rubin was told it was an emperor eagle, caught as a chick and brought to the City from the Mountains of the Moon. The rare creature had been easy to trap for when hatched it had only one wing. Now it spent its days, its years, sitting immobile, eyes closed, dreaming its dreams of flight. But after dark the eagle was forced to climb gracelessly down the ladder that had been built for it and scuffle in the years-thick guano for food with lesser birds, hunting the sick and wounded and scuttling night-crawlers.

As they wandered the palace Marcellus would speak to its lords, generals, common soldiers, serving maids and horse boys, and all of them he knew by name and all he treated with a similar friendly interest. He introduced his brother Rafael, and Rubin hoped they might meet the Immortal, but was told the emperor rarely left his quarters in the Keep, deep in the heart of the Red Palace.

One day, as they made their way towards Marcellus' apartments, Rubin was startled to see a huge beast step sedately from behind a columned stairway. It was a gulon. How strange that one should walk the palace, proud as a courtier. He had seen several of the beasts in the Halls, usually sitting high and distant, staring down at the Dwellers from the top of some gate or rocky shelf. They were a bit like cats, a bit like foxes, longer-legged than both, with strangely human eyes. This was a big one, twice the size of any he'd seen before. It wore a wide golden collar round its long, almost serpentine neck.

Rubin held out his hand, making clucking noises as if it were a friendly dog. He felt no fear of it. Gulons rarely attacked men, and then only when cornered or starving. This was clearly neither. It sidled up to him crab-wise and sniffed his hand cautiously. He was about to stroke it but thought better of it. Its short fur looked oily and unclean and its smell made his gorge rise.

'This is Deidoro,' Marcellus told him. 'He is the emperor's—' He seemed to be about to add something more, but stopped.

'It has a name?' Rubin was amused.

'Horses have names,' Marcellus argued mildly.

'It is not a horse. Although it's very nearly as big as one.'

'Deidoro is very old. Perhaps the oldest living creature in this palace.' Rubin recalled those words later, when he knew more about the Serafim, and he knew then that it was a lie.

Marcellus called to the beast and it looked at him, its dark eyes gleaming. 'Be off. Go find your master,' Marcellus said softly, and it favoured them both with its disconcerting human stare before sliding behind an embroidered wall hanging. The air it left behind smelled of spoiled meat.

Though Rubin became familiar with the palace and its inhabitants, he never again met the imperial gulon Deidoro or ever saw its master. He was always welcomed by Marcellus as a valued friend, made to feel one with the rich and powerful. He looked forward to his visits to the palace, in fact he lived for them. His time spent on spying missions abroad or dwelling, disguised, in the shabbiest quarters of the beleaguered City in a bid to infiltrate the bands of the disaffected who flourished there, were just necessary chores before returning to the presence of his lord.

One day during that first stay Marcellus quizzed him closely about the Dwellers and it became clear that a raid had been planned on the High Halls beneath the Red Palace. Rubin could give him scant information. After nearly two years living down there he was an expert at finding his way through the labyrinth, but he could not relate that knowledge to the geography above ground. If Marcellus thought he was being unhelpful he gave no sign.

But he asked an odd question. 'Are there tales, rumours, of a lone woman who lives in the lower Halls, perhaps more than one?'

'Most Dwellers fear the wraiths,' Rubin told him, nodding. 'They are said to be women, tall and ghostly, who walk the lower depths and steal children.' He did not say that some Dwellers feared the wraiths more than the reivers, for at least the reivers were human, probably.

'Have you seen one such?' his lord asked.

Rubin shook his head, sceptical. 'Lone women in the lower depths? No. I don't think so. The lower depths are the haunt of reivers. If there were such women then their fate would be terrible.'

Marcellus nodded thoughtfully and changed the subject.

Valla could not sleep and, after tossing and turning for a while, she looked up to see Rubin still staring into the glow of the campfire.

She sat up and pulled her blanket round her shoulders. 'Are you kin to the Vincerii?' she asked him.

He frowned at her. 'No. I don't think so. There are seven ancient Families and Marcellus is a Vincerus and I am a Guillaume. I've no reason to think we are related, though we might share ancestors.'

'Marcellus can do what you did, end a battle, stop everyone fighting. I'm surprised you don't know, being good friends with him.' She was a little jealous. She had known Marcellus for years and he had always treated her with courtesy. But Rubin was his friend.

Rubin nodded, understanding completely. 'I have never been in battle alongside him, though I have heard soldiers gossip that he can call on sorcerous powers. I always thought it superstitious nonsense. Until now.'

Valla bit her lip. 'I have seen him win a battle against the odds by launching death on everyone around him. Friend and foe.' It had happened to her only once, in an encounter in the east with an overwhelming force of Buldekki. She had never spoken of what she'd seen, nor had her comrades who survived the day, but she found it impossible to forget.

'But I felt contentment and peace when you did it,' she went on. 'I didn't want to fight any more. Has nothing like that ever happened to you before?'

He paused, thinking. 'When I was small, maybe six or so, I found a dead bird, a plain brown thing, in the garden at the foot of the house. It had flown into something, a wall, a window, and broken its neck. I showed my father. He said, "Perhaps you can make it live again." I was only young so I thought he was probably right. I willed the creature to get up and fly away. But it just lay there cooling in my hands. Then,' he went on, 'when my mother was dying – I was fourteen – my father brought me to her bedside and told me to place my hands on her head. I remember being frightened for he was weeping. He seemed beside himself, desperate. I had never seen him show deep emotion before or since.'

'He thought you had healing hands,' Valla whispered.

'He hoped, perhaps.' He looked at her. 'But I clearly don't. For if I had I would heal your broken wing.'

The kindness in his voice threatened to overwhelm her and she rolled over, away from him, cradling her bad arm. Then she realized for the first time that it was barely hurting. Despite the jolting of the ride and the fatigue that dogged their every day, her arm was less painful than it had been since it was first injured. She looked at the fingers, but they still peeped out white and lifeless from the bandage.

'Your arm is feeling better,' Rubin said.

'You read minds too?' she asked a little snappily.

'I do not have to read your mind to see your arm is not bothering you so much.'

She thought about it, unlooked-for hope rising in her breast. 'It *has* been less painful. Perhaps you did something to help it, with . . . whatever you did.'

'Or perhaps it is healing now you are away from the presence of the dead and dying.'

Unwilling to jinx it by talking about it, Valla sought

a change of subject. 'You must tell me what your message for Marcellus is,' she said, not for the first time.

He shook his head. 'I cannot.'

'But we might be spotted by the enemy,' she argued. She had been giving this a lot of thought. 'If so, you are more likely to be killed than I am, for I am a warrior of the Thousand and you are, you tell me, an incompetent soldier.'

He raised his eyebrows, but did not argue.

'Unless you can use this . . . ability of yours at will,' she added questioningly. He shrugged. He had no idea.

'So you must tell me what is so important that Marcellus must hear it,' she urged. 'In case you die and I survive to pass the message on.'

He thought about it, eyes lowered. Then he shrugged. 'It's probably far too late. But you're right.'

He told her that before he was injured, in his role as third messenger he had infiltrated the Blues' camp in the night and was taken to the command tent.

'I stood outside in the cold,' he said, 'and listened. There were two civilians in there, a man and a woman, as well as senior soldiers, both Odrysian and Petrassi. I don't know who the man was, some fat old man who looked as though he'd dressed in the dark. But the woman took my interest. She was tall and thin, with grey hair and a clumsy, ungainly gait.'

He looked at Valla. 'You must understand how unusual it is to see a woman in an Odrysian force. They are not permitted to fight and, though there are camp-followers, they are fewer than you'd expect. So this woman caught my interest.'

Valla smiled. It came as no surprise that in the midst of a desperate mission, with time against him and far still to go, Rubin was inquisitive about this midnight meeting.

He said, 'I cudgelled my brain to remember where I had seen her before.'

He paused and, dutifully, Valla nodded to him to go on.

'I have kept this to myself,' he said. 'I've told only Saul Gaeta, and I was reluctant to do that but we needed the horses.'

'I would tell no one but Marcellus,' she promised, thinking, *Who could I tell?*

'It came to me at last. I had seen the woman in the Red Palace. She was with a group of people, including the Vincerii, at some meeting.' His eyes were anxious as he said, 'She is the City's Lord Lieutenant of the East. Her name is Saroyan. She is in charge of troop deployments in the palace and if she has turned traitor then the City is in desperate trouble!'

PART TWO

The Feast of Blood

CHAPTER EIGHT

A FEW DAYS LATER AND FAR TO THE SOUTH A CHILL wind howled through the streets of the City. It blew along the alleys and twittens, lifting tarpaper roofs from the hovels of the poor and slates from the roofs of the wealthy. It whipped round the towers and minarets of the Red Palace, sighing through its iron gates and flaying reddened leaves from trees in its parks. Rain rattled the windows, as if seeking entry, then found its way in around ill-fitting frames and through cracks in stone.

The quarter called Lindo, or the Armoury to those who remembered the old days and the old ways, was a maze of lanes and pathways, cramped squares and hidden passageways. One alley, so narrow and obscure as to be nameless, led off Dumbwoman's Lane, and at the corner of these two ways, on this rainy autumn morning, sat a gulon.

Gulons, half-fox, half-cat, half-forgotten by their original masters, had been brought to the City more than a thousand years before and, as they had been designed to, had mated with the local cats and dogs. Most of them, over the generations, had lost the identity of their bloodlines among those of the mangy mutts and malevolent mogs that thronged the City. But some retained their purity, though much diminished, and the gulon which waited that rain-soaked morning was one such. Small for its species, less than half the size of the imperial beast Deidoro, it was a patchwork of orange and white and black fur, with chewed, misshapen ears and a healthy colony of fleas.

The sideways rain dripped off its snout and formed fat pearls on its waterproof coat, but it kept its eyes fixed on the north, thick lashes half closed to protect its eyes from the rain and wind. The sun would not show itself that day until much later, but at the time when its first rays would have reached the tallest tower, the bells of the Temple of Themistos started their daily clangour. If the crash and clang of the huge iron bells caused discomfort to the beast, it merely closed its eyes a little more, as if that would help, and continued to wait.

When the tall figure, caped and hooded, strode into sight the gulon made no sign it had seen her, but as she swept past, bringing to its nose the scents of leather and horses and herbs and the faintest sting of alcohol, it fell in behind her and padded down the nameless alley, treading in her bootsteps.

The alley, narrow at its mouth, tapered further until it zigged sharply to the right, then zagged to the left, opening out again to embrace a few shabby shops – a shoe repairer, a potter, a maker of vellum – and came to an abrupt end at the rear of the temple. Only the sharpest of eyes would notice the ancient door set into the wall, beneath a wide and heavy lintel, half hidden by dusty ivy, apparently unopened for generations.

Glancing round to ensure no one was within sight, Saroyan Rae Vincerus, Lord Lieutenant of the East, pulled a large iron key from a pocket and slid it into the rusty lock. It turned as if greased, which it had been. The door opened smoothly and the woman and the gulon stepped inside. She lit a half-used torch on a bracket inside the doorway and plunged into the labyrinth which led to the Red Palace.

Saroyan had walked the lower levels of the palace all her life, for she had an affinity for the secret and the hidden. She would not descend to the Halls – in that place lay madness – but the palace dungeons and the dungeons of Gath and the myriad tunnels that connected them she knew intimately. She found serenity in the ancient stones and, although they were slowly sinking and each year that passed found fewer ways available to her, that in itself was also strangely satisfying.

As she walked she looked down at the patchwork gulon. It had dogged her footsteps inside the palace for more than a decade and she did not know why. In her more paranoid moments she wondered if it were an agent of the emperor, for the only other gulon which walked the palace was the emperor's pet Deidoro. The great beast had seen off the other gulons in its territory, and all the cats, and some of the imperial hounds too. But for some reason it tolerated the patchwork runt. Saroyan had once found herself idly wondering if it was Deidoro's get, then she reminded herself that the great gulon was merely a reflection, an undead beast created by the emperor, no more capable of siring offspring than was a three-day-dead corpse.

The lord lieutenant's office was high in the east wing where rainwater trickled down the wood-panelled walls from window frames warped and tortured by the inexorable foundering of the building.

Saroyan pulled off her wet cloak and hung it to dry, then crossed the room and gazed out through a cracked window looking east, seeing nothing but the perilous journey ahead of her. It had to be soon, well before the Day of Summoning, before the snows. The sooner she started for the Lion's Palace the better, for it meant a hard seven-day ride, yet it would be awkward to leave the City without good reason.

She had picked her six-man guard with care. She had ensured to her own satisfaction that they were scrupulously loyal – or treacherous, depending on which way you looked at it. Each soldier had more than one reason to hate the emperor and she did not doubt their intent. She just doubted their personal loyalty.

Saroyan was nobody's fool. She not only appreciated she was unpopular, she encouraged it. After all, a very long life offers a woman the opportunity for many changes of occupation and of personality and Saroyan, with her impatient, enquiring character, had tried them all. She had been martinet and coquette, harridan and mistress, floozy and fishwife, wife, dutiful granddaughter and doting mother.

She had been a soldier, more than once, and in her present role of Lord Lieutenant of the East she had pared her public persona down to that of a spare, efficient and cold administrator of, among other things, the security of the City.

And now she was a traitor.

Seating herself at her leather-topped desk with its neat piles of paperwork, she reflected that being unpopular was an uphill struggle for some. Mere callous carelessness with other people's lives was not sufficient. Marcellus, for example, cared only for himself and, perhaps, his emperor Araeon, and he proved it all the time with battle strategies which dazzled by their bravura and, sometimes, their success. But the waste of warriors' lives in the carnage went constantly overlooked or, if commented upon at all, was considered an unfortunate but necessary cost. For Marcellus was a hero. Even the bloodbath in the Little Opera House, just two nights before, when the First Lord had despatched his mistress of more than twenty years to save his own skin, had not affected his popularity in the palace.

Saroyan's part in the ill-fated mutiny of the Leopard century had been key. She had no power over the deployment of the Thousand, the emperor's elite, but she controlled the rotations of troops who guarded the walls and the daily security of the City. It had been a straightforward matter to raise a specious alert on the walls, pulling available manpower away from the palace. The emperor was nothing if not predictable, and in moments of danger he had always called on the Gulons, his favoured century of the Thousand, to safeguard him in the Keep, leaving the Leopards, the next in rotation, to be deployed to the Little Opera House to protect the brothers Marcellus and Rafael Vincerus. Tasker Mallet, leader of the Leopards, was eager to put into effect this mutiny, planned more than half a year before and only awaiting the right time, a time when the brothers were together and unarmed and effectively alone with the Leopards.

Saroyan could guess what had gone wrong, although the only witnesses left to tell the tale were the Vincerii themselves. Everyone else in the opera house – soldiers, counsellors, players, the First Lord's mistress Petalina and her young servant – had died hideously. Saroyan knew Marcellus had called on his Gift for destruction, a Gift which left only Serafim or their reflections unscathed. It was a desperate call, in the palace, in such a public place. Saroyan had been convinced Marcellus would not unleash carnage when his mistress was present. But she had woefully underestimated his self-interest.

The lord lieutenant became aware that someone was waiting in the doorway, breathing. She said, 'Yes?' without turning, aware she was buttressing the rumour that she had eyes in the back of her head.

'You wished to see me, lady?'

Saroyan felt her hackles rise. She abhorred being called 'lady', as if she were one with the painted doxies who serviced the lords of the palace.

'My name is Saroyan,' she said, turning to glare at the little engineer with the large moustache. Dar Thakker teetered on the threshold as if he were about to take flight.

'Yes . . . la— Saroyan,' he said.

Thakker was in charge of maintenance works in the palace and theoretically reported to the Lord Lieutenant of the North. As the holder of that title had not been seen in the City for over a year, having fled the wrath of the emperor over some real or imagined slight, by default Saroyan had taken on responsibility for the decrepit palace. With another hard winter facing them and no repair works completed this summer gone, she had ordered Thakker to report on the minimum works necessary to keep the building from falling around their ears.

'Tell me,' she said, eyeing with dislike the untidy pile of papers under his arm. If the palace's administrators and their minions *could* create paperwork they did so, usually in lieu of any real work. Yet it was part of Saroyan's personality to act expeditiously to deal with any paper which landed on her desk. She resolved that the man would take the pile away with him. 'Briefly,' she added.

'Well,' he said, glancing nervously at the gulon. The beast yawned, baring yellow fangs. He shifted the armful of papers and looked around for somewhere to put them. He caught Saroyan's forbidding expression and said, 'If we start at the south wing, er . . . Saroyan . . .'

'Is the water rising or is the palace sinking?' she asked briskly.

Thakker cleared his throat. 'Both, um . . . both.'

She stared at him until he ploughed on. 'I went down into the sewers, with a team of my men, hand-picked, and soldiers, of course, for . . . ahem . . . protection . . .'

She sat back in her chair and managed an encouraging nod. 'And?'

Thakker dumped the papers on the floor at his feet. It seemed to free his voice. 'You must understand that the City is built on many levels of earlier cities. Often previous buildings were flattened before new buildings were erected, but not always. And there are layers of cellars and . . . well, dungeons which were covered over and forgotten. The sewers and storm drains are very deep and are a honeycomb. And the river Menander runs through it all. And the rainfall this autumn has been unusually high.'

I know all this, she thought. 'What can be done?' she asked.

'Nothing,' Thakker said simply.

'Nothing?'

'All we can do is what generations of engineers have done before – try to keep the main riverways open and the great watergates working.'

'The Magisterium Gate. The Saduccuss Gate.'

'Yes, and others,' he nodded, warming to his subject now she had shown some understanding of the problem. He fell to his knees and started rummaging among papers. He rose triumphantly with a sheet and showed it to her. It was old and mildewed, and some of the script was water-damaged. Saroyan peered at it.

'Here,' the man pointed, 'and here, and here there are major blockages. They need to be cleared in order, the lowest first. This is very dangerous work. The workers would have to approach them from the lower side and it would be, frankly, suicide once the blockage shifts. We could, of course, use slaves or prisoners . . .'

'And that will solve the problem?'

'It will be a beginning. If the winter is not too wet, and the great watergates do not deteriorate further, this work should ensure the flooding does not get any worse.'

Saroyan turned as her aide appeared at the office door.

'Yes!' she barked, annoyed at being interrupted again.

'You are summoned,' the aide retorted briskly.

For a moment her heart missed a beat and her breathing stopped. Summoned. Only three people in the world had the authority to *summon* her. *Not Araeon!* she prayed. She had always feared and loathed the emperor, with good reason, but in recent years he had become more deranged and, yes, terrifying, and she could not be in his presence without her skin crawling with disgust.

'Summoned?' she repeated, forcing herself to breathe normally.

'By the First Lord.'

She nodded, relieved it was only Marcellus, and turned to Thakker. 'Very well,' she said, dismissing him. 'We will speak again.'

'Where is he?' she asked the aide after the engineer had departed.

'In the Black Room.'

This told her a great deal. Marcellus used the Black Room to discuss imminent military matters with the chiefs. And often to intimidate and unbalance their opponents. Saroyan knew that, and Marcellus knew she knew. He certainly viewed her as an antagonist, a fact they both implicitly accepted, but this choice of venue suggested something must have happened which required action. Had he found out about her part in the mutiny? Had Mallet, leader of the Leopards, revealed her involvement before he died? Or was it something else? Her greater mission, one which she hardly even thought about in the precincts of the palace, sidled into the back of her mind but she expelled it again briskly. Even she, knowing him as well as she did, was sometimes prey to the fear that Marcellus could read her thoughts.

'There is a message for you.'

The aide stepped forward and placed a piece of folded paper on the edge of her desk. She could tell from his reticent demeanour that he knew it to be perilous. She looked at the writing. It said *Lord Lieutenant of the East* in bold script. It was her own hand. It could only be from Evan Broglanh. She nodded and the aide left. Inside the paper there were three symbols, cryptic to anyone but her and Broglanh. They indicated a meeting at the Shining Stars Inn today at sunset. If Saroyan could not attend today, they would meet tomorrow. If neither, then there would be no meeting.

She put that too out of her mind and stood, readying herself. She wondered what the First Lord wanted. Marcellus would never move overtly against her, for he would never act against her grandmother Archange, a certainty that protected her also. The Black Room ploy was merely a nudge, not an open declaration of war. Nevertheless it was with heightened alertness that she set off for the meeting.

Marcellus' charm, a talent available to many Serafim, and which he used more than most, made him the most popular soldier in the City. It was a genetic trait, one he had honed and perfected over the centuries to the point where the slightest inflexion of his voice could make a listener bow to his will. Saroyan was largely immune to it, of course, but she still had to keep her wits about her in his presence.

She looked down at the gulon. It would not do if the beast were at her heels when she met Marcellus. He would think her weak. She stared at the creature, willing it s*tay here* in her mind. It looked back at her and she could detect no intelligence in those muddy eyes. Nevertheless it curled up and, placing its snout on a front paw, went to sleep.

Trailed by her bodyguard she walked from her apartments in the far east wing to the Black Room. It was a long walk, and she took her time. She stopped in on Dashoul, the palace security chief and the only civilian she respected in the entire building, to discuss the plans for Petalina's funeral, a grand occasion entirely inappropriate, she thought, to the woman's status as Marcellus' bed-warmer. She also took the chance to double-check the rotation of the two venerable regiments, the Second Adamantine and the Fourth Imperial, into the palace. Everyone had to be in the right place on the Day of Summoning.

Both brothers were in the Black Room, plus a motley collection of senior advisers. She had obviously been pencilled in as an afterthought to a meeting of the chiefs. She wondered, as was her habit, if this was a deliberate snub. The commanders were drifting out in that casual way which Marcellus liked to promote, as though they were all mere grunts getting together for a chat in a fit of camaraderie. She knew that, however much the First Lord invited a bar-room atmosphere, the wrong word at the wrong time from any one of them would see him slit up the middle like a sack of beans. Him or her, she amended conscientiously, seeing Leona, commander of the Warhounds, was there too.

Cousin Rafe was just leaving. He smiled and nodded to her, brushing by her as he went out. She nodded back. She had always been scrupulous to treat him with the courtesy his rank demanded, as Archange had decreed, but she could never forget that he was just a reflection, no more a living creature than the beast Deidoro. If Marcellus were to die, *when* he died – for even Marcellus Vincerus was not indestructible – then his 'brother' would expire on the instant.

'Greetings, Marcellus. My condolences on your recent loss,' she said formally.

He was dressed in his usual nondescript garb and looked less like a lord than a palace blacksmith. 'Hmm,' he snorted. 'It's hard to see how you could have put less sincerity into those words, Saroyan.'

They waited as the last of the warriors drifted out and the door snicked shut.

She shrugged. 'Whores die every day,' she replied, 'for far lesser cause than the life of their lord.' *Summon me to the Black Room, will you*, she thought. She wondered if she had overstepped the mark, for two servants were still present, but he merely nodded thoughtfully as if she had made a valid point.

'I have not seen you since your return,' she went on. 'How goes the eastern campaign?'

'Stalemate,' he told her. 'But we will prevail. How are you, cousin? You seem out of temper. I can relieve you of some of your duties if they are proving too much for you.'

'The lieutenancy is not in the gift of the First Lord,' she snapped, irritated in spite of herself.

'But I'm sure the emperor will agree with me. He has always held your interests close to his heart.'

'You wished to see me?' she asked, keen to get to the nub of the meeting.

'Always the professional, Saroyan?' He smiled and she felt the embrace of his words like a warm breeze, and returned a cool smile in acknowledgement of it.

'I have some good news,' he told her. 'It affects all of us and since I've no doubt you are in touch with Archange I would ask you to pass it on.'

Good news, she thought. Good news for whom? A goose as black as night ran over her grave.

'The Gulon Veil has been found and is now back in our hands.'

When she left Marcellus a brief time later Saroyan paused outside the door, distracted by the implications of the return of the veil, which had been stolen by an Odrysian assassin. She decided to think about it later. On a whim, she did not go back the way she had arrived, but walked instead through the anteroom where supplicants waited for audience with the First Lord. Mostly they were palace servants, courtiers or soldiers, for the exhaustive palace security processes weeded out all but the most persistent outsiders from seeking access to Marcellus and his brother.

Among them Saroyan noticed two soldiers, both young, travel-stained and weary. The woman sat on a bench, head down, clearly dozing. Her ice-blonde hair was in unkempt braids and one arm was in filthy bandages. Saroyan stared at her with distaste, wondering if the soldier realized how unwise she was to come before Marcellus looking more like a beggar than a City warrior. The other was a young man who lay on the bench with his head on the woman's thigh, sleeping the sleep of exhaustion. He was thin to the point of emaciation and as dirty as his companion. But it was his features which caught Saroyan's eye, the prominent cheekbones, sharp as a blade, the high, delicate eyebrows. She frowned. She had seen those features before. His head had been shaved, but bright red hair was growing through again and in the shafts of light from the high windows it glowed in a halo of fire. His face was peaceful.

Saroyan briefly considered finding out who they were, for she was sure they had a story to tell, but she was distracted by the news of the veil and, in a decision that sealed all their fates, she cast them from her mind.

As she walked back to her office she suddenly thought of Indaro Kerr Guillaume. With luck, she should be dead by now. Saroyan was satisfied with her oblique interference in that matter. She had ordered her agents at the Lion's Palace to ensure the woman was allowed to escape, knowing she would run towards the City. At the same time she had seen to it that the commander of the Gulon century, presently on some cryptic mission of the emperor's in the eastern hills, was warned to watch out for Wildcat deserters after the Battle of Salaba. It was not a guarantee of the woman's capture or death, but Indaro was in far more peril at the hands of the Gulons – the century the emperor favoured to execute black missions both in the City and without – than tucked away tidily in a cell at Old Mountain. The bright scarlet jacket Indaro persisted in wearing marked her as a target. It was a wonder she had not been killed long since.

Something was niggling at the back of Saroyan's mind. Something she had seen, something someone had said? She racked her brain. The news about the return of the Gulon Veil, an ancient artefact of great power, overwhelmed her thoughts, though it was of mixed significance. Without it the emperor had been less powerful but more unpredictable, thus more terrifying. But if plans went according to her wishes Araeon, and perhaps Marcellus too, was doomed to die on the Day of Summoning. Then the presence of the veil should be of little consequence – except to her grandmother Archange, the rightful successor to the throne.

Halfway back to her office she suddenly stopped, her escort halting awkwardly around her. A cold finger of fear was tickling her neck. She scratched at the skin, but the feeling would not go away. Saroyan was third-generation Serafim and had no Gifts, but their blood ran strongly in her veins and in her long life she had developed a fine-honed instinct for danger.

'Farrow,' she said to the chief of her bodyguard, 'we are leaving ahead of time.'

'Tonight?' he asked her, glancing out of a window. She knew he was thinking that the moon was waxing and would offer them good light for night travel.

She shook her head, for the fear was growing. 'Now,' she said. 'We have no time to waste. We ride immediately.'

So Valla and Rubin were still fast asleep in the anteroom, dreaming of hot food and soft beds, when Saroyan and her escort rode from the palace and headed for the Araby Gate and their last journey east.

Leona did not leave the Black Room through the same door as the lord lieutenant, so did not pass through the anteroom, and thus she missed seeing Valla. She would hear of her friend's return to the City, but she would not see her again until they battled side by side amid the carnage of the Day of Summoning.

In the following days there was a pregnant atmosphere in the Red Palace, of secrets whispered in dark corners, of plans made and remade in dusty chambers. The mutiny in the Little Opera House had unsettled them all. The Leopard century had existed since time out of mind. It had been named for a feral beast which once stalked the southern mountains, but the animals had been hunted into extinction and now the Leopards were to be expunged from the pages of the City's history. The swords of the Thousand dripped with the blood of the Thousand and the mood in the barracks and inns where elite warriors gathered was dark.

What had made Mallet and his comrades rebel against the Vincerii? It would remain a mystery to most. The Leopards were a tight-knit group and Mallet had few friends outside the century. And those who had been his friends were reluctant to admit it. Leona hardly knew the man, but his reputation was of impenetrable loyalty. For a while, until greater events rocked the City, the whispers among the elite were of little else.

The promotion of a troop of horse soldiers to the Thousand in the Leopards' place had been met with growls of disapproval. Leona knew Captain Riis, now suddenly promoted to commander of the new Nighthawk century, for they had served together briefly in the Eighteenth Serpentine, which had both cavalry and infantry wings. He was a doughty fighter, but they were all doughty fighters, and Riis had the reputation of a womanizer and a tainted background involving some long-forgotten scandal. Leona did not like the man but she respected Marcellus' judgement and was willing to work with the horseman if that was the First Lord's will.

When dawn rose five days before the Day of Summoning Leona lay in her bed for a while longer than usual looking up at the ice crystals framing the windows. Unlike some of the commanders, she chose a life of comparative austerity. Her chambers were small and spare, her aides few. But she ensured she had a feather mattress and clean sheets on the narrow bed, and this morning she felt a reluctance to leave it.

An early, heavy snowfall had left the City icebound. The crust of ice on the palace roofs was melting slowly and water dripped from tiles and beams, trickled through cracks in window frames and down walls. A thick miasma of dampness throughout the palace dulled the spirits and made strong soldiers gloomy. Far below, the waters were rising inexorably in the lower levels and had even reached the Hall of Emperors, the entrance to the Immortal's apartments.

Leona abandoned the warm bed at last and began to dress for a dull day of administration leading up to the funeral of Petalina, the First Lord's mistress, which she predicted would be an event of unparalleled hypocrisy. But they were there to do the bidding of Marcellus – and of course the emperor. She slid into thin linen shift and drawers, stout cotton trousers and shirt, then her light armour of leather kilt and jerkin. She plaited her unruly ginger hair into a single fat braid, stepped into her best boots and laced them tightly. She hesitated when it came to her sword-belt. Unlike some of the senior warriors, she saw no point in having a heavy sword clanking at her side all day, catching on table and chair legs, if she was merely to sit and talk. In a gesture towards military preparedness she slipped her old flensing knife, honed to razor sharpness and thin as a quill, into the leather sheath on the outside of her thigh. She glanced at the sword-belt again, then sighed and snatched it up and walked out of her chamber.

She was very nearly late. The Black Room was loud with the voices of senior soldiers when she got there: other commanders of the Thousand presently in the City and the Vincerii's various military counsellors including, of course, Boaz. General Boaz, taller than a tree, was formally in charge of the Thousand, though the needs of the brothers and the emperor frequently superseded those duties. Boaz was a legendary warrior, second only to Marcellus himself, but a cruel whim of the gods had now crippled his hands with a painful affliction which rendered him useless as a swordsman.

Leona nodded to the general, whom she rather liked, and caught Marcellus' eye as he spoke to his brother

Rafe. She thought the First Lord looked tired. A moment of anxiety surprised her. Could even the legendary Marcellus be growing old? Rafael looked as he always did, 'bright-eyed and bushy-tailed', as Marcellus would say. It was appropriate, for many of the warriors referred to him, behind their hands, as 'Marcellus' hound'. Leona acknowledged other colleagues and seated herself.

The meeting had already begun when the upstart commander came in and the chamber fell silent for a heartbeat. Riis had brought an aide with him, which was considered gauche by the other chiefs who liked to think of themselves as common soldiers, unaided by other than their trusty swords. Marcellus courteously accepted the younger man but greeted Riis as a friend. It was his way and it clearly charmed the horseman.

The subject was Petalina's funeral and its security problems. This scarcely affected Leona and she glanced at Riis, wondering about him. He was tall for a seasoned warrior, for the history of warfare had proved it was the shorter men and women who were most likely to survive years of fighting, other factors being equal. They were lower to the ground, better balanced, and simply less of a target for the enemy. Leona remembered Riis was not a City man; he had been born in some foreign outpost and brought to the City as a boy as hostage for his father's good behaviour. This was a tradition that had died out in recent decades, and just as well, she thought. Taking an unknown wolf cub into the house was asking for trouble when it grew strong.

'Are you suggesting we not attend the lady's funeral rites?' Marcellus was asking Fortance, now leader of the Silver Bears.

The bearded veteran replied, 'I would suggest it if I thought that would do any good, lord. No, I'm saying you should be more conscious about presenting an easy target.'

'We are soldiers. We can take care of ourselves,' said Rafael.

It was a perennial subject, yet Leona could not help but say, 'No one doubts that, lord, but Fortance is right. We are only suggesting the two of you attend scheduled events separately.'

'All our lives are scheduled, Leona,' Marcellus replied. 'But we will think on what you say.' He waved a hand to dismiss the warriors and they began to file out. Leona looked at Fortance, who shrugged. They both knew the Vincerii would take no advice on their own safety.

As they were all leaving the room Marcellus called Riis back. The new commander glanced at Leona as he turned, smiling at her with practised charm. She managed a nod in return. *I don't like you*, she thought. *And I don't trust you.*

The little girl held on fearfully to the wooden ladder and peered down into the pit. She couldn't remember how she got there, or how long she had been there, but her small hands hurt from climbing, and her bare feet were stuck with splinters. The ladder's rungs were very far apart and each one was a scramble for her, a battle which had to be won over and over. At times she got mixed up, and thought the ladder was horizontal and she was clinging to it like a bluebottle on a ceiling. She would hold on and close her eyes tight and try not to cry.

Then she was no longer on the ladder but in a dark, smelly place where the water swished around her feet and threatened to climb up her legs. She was afraid of getting her nightdress dirty, so she held it up to her knees. But her feet were filthy too and she could no longer feel them. She could see nothing around her except blackness and she called out, very quietly, 'Mummy!'

And her mummy was there, at the end of the corridor, calling back to her. The girl ran towards her, trying not to splash her nightie, but her mummy kept drifting away, backing into the darkness, one arm held out towards her. She was wearing a long, white dress too, but the girl could see the dark water was soaking the fine lace and creeping upwards, ever upwards, staining the whiteness to a dirty grey.

But then a big, white hand came out of the darkness, a white hand with a jewelled ring which glinted in the dreary light, and it snatched her mummy away, quick as a flash, like she was falling down a well.

Saroyan awoke with a start, her heart thudding in her ribcage, her mouth dry, her body slick with sweat. It was not a dream, but a memory. She had not climbed a wooden ladder, but down a steep stone staircase with high slippery steps, each of which was a challenge to a little girl. And her mother had not been snatched away but had gone of her own accord, and her fate was worse than any child could imagine.

She rolled over and sat up on the hard earth. The fire had burned low and the full moon lit the camp with its unforgiving light. She saw the soldier on watch nod to her then retreat into the moon shadows. She stretched her back, which ached from days of hard riding. They would arrive back in the City by midday tomorrow and the plans she had been harbouring for years were about to come to fruition.

At the meeting at Old Mountain they had agreed, finally and at her suggestion, on the Day of Summoning for the long-awaited coup. The Feast of Summoning was an important time in the calendar of the people who had lived in these parts for millennia, and the day itself was a significant date in the old rites and customs of the first Serafim. Religion had ceased to have meaning for them an aeon ago, but traditions were harder to slough off.

Saroyan lay back down on the cold ground. The Day of Summoning would mark a new beginning for the City, an end to the war and a new imperium. Serenity flooded her mind. She closed her eyes and slept without conscience.

CHAPTER NINE

THE MASKED FIGURE STEPPED FORWARD, HIS SWORD directed at Fiorentina's breast. She fought the urge to back away and tried to remember what she had been taught. Attack, parry, riposte. Attack, parry, redouble. She lifted her chin and answered his attack and their blades gleamed in the dawn light as they fought back and forth across the fencing mat.

They had been practising since it was still dark outside and Fiorentina was bathed in sweat; she could feel the beads of moisture trickling, tickling, down her back. She felt like a wrung-out dishrag while her husband Rafe remained, as always, cool and poised. Trying to keep her focus – on her balance, the set of her sword arm, her feet, the intricate moves and counter-moves she had committed to memory, which were now turning into a tangle in her brain – she felt her spirits start to flag. She and her sister had both been taught to fence as girls, but she had forgotten everything she once knew and was starting to regret asking her husband to teach her again.

As if he heard her thoughts, Rafe suddenly said, 'Enough!', tearing off his mask and throwing it down. 'You are improving,' he commented.

She scowled. 'Don't patronize me,' she said, more fiercely than she had intended.

He watched her for a heartbeat, and she wondered if she had gone too far. But then he smiled. 'When we began this practice you were terrible. Now, after half a year, you are merely poor. But you have natural grace and balance and speed, and now you have added some technical skill.'

He wiped his hands and neck on a towel and she was glad to see that, despite appearances, he had worked up a sweat too.

'You must remember,' he went on, wiping the blades on a cloth, 'that the average soldier – in both our army and the Blues' – has none of those things. He has learned only to stab and slash until his enemy stops moving. A finely placed sword-tip would kill him in a heartbeat. I think tomorrow we will progress to killing blows.'

Mollified, she commented, 'We have finished early today.'

He looked out at the pewter sky. 'It is the Day of Summoning, a busy time for us all, and I have to see your friend Dol Salida before my day begins.'

'Dol Salida? Why?' She wondered if it was something to do with Petalina's death. The old man, a distant cousin of Fiorentina and her sister, specialized in intelligence and gossip and might have uncovered the reasons behind the Leopards' mutiny.

'I don't know. He sought the audience. Now, to my bath.'

She smiled. Since she had known him Rafe had bathed every day, sometimes twice a day, in a palace where bathing was generally seen as a tiresome yearly ritual. It was one of the things she loved about him.

He saluted her, then placed the swords in the rack and raced up the stairs, agile as a man half his age, heading for the Calderium. Fiorentina closed the tall windows, noting that the rain seemed heavier than ever, then walked slowly back to their apartments. It was one of the pleasures of living in the Red Palace that she could walk about freely without bodyguards. This most northerly part, called the Redoubt, had once been a small fort, built centuries before the palace, and though the palace had gradually grown and spread and enveloped the old sandstone fortress, it retained its own character, and its impregnable walls.

Her apartments were on the highest floor of the Redoubt, looking towards the Salient and the distant sea to the west. They were furnished with colourful tapestries and carved panelling and comfortable chairs, their walls glittering with gold and silver picture frames and glass sconces. Her small army of maids had been in there since the moment she left, cleaning, polishing, brushing fabrics and rugs, and placing fresh flowers in the vases, for Rafe had decreed she have fresh flowers every day, though she could not imagine where they came from in this City under siege.

When she entered, her maid Miri helped her out of her fencing gear – black shirt and wide cotton skirt – clucking, as she always did, at the ugly, graceless garments. Fiorentina was bathed and clothed in a white chemise and she sat patiently while Miri combed out her long black hair then plaited it into ropes which she curled round her head and pinned. Then the maid dressed her in one of Rafe's favourite gowns, of midnight blue silk which complemented her eyes and disguised the slight swell in her belly.

'Have you told the lord yet?' the woman asked briskly.

Fiorentina shook her head. The moment never seemed quite right; the lord was always busy or distracted or was on his way somewhere. Time was when they would spend whole evenings together talking in front of an open fire, or lying lazily in bed on a warm afternoon.

'Will you wait until you are as big as a cow?' Miri scolded her. She had been with Fiorentina for ten years and allowed herself such liberties. Fiorentina didn't mind. Only someone who has never known a mother, she thought, enjoys being mothered.

'I plan to tell him tonight.' Truth to tell, she was not sure what her husband's reaction would be.

After dressing she wandered down to the kitchens to speak with the cook. Today was an important day for the Families, and there were special meals to be prepared throughout the palace. Fiorentina's cook, Alcestis, thin and harassed, looked up from gutting fish, her red hands streaked with blood and slime.

'You won't credit,' she said as if seamlessly picking up a previous conversation, 'how hard it is to get fruit. We've only these pears,' she pointed her chin at a big bowl of pink-hued pears, shiny against the rough earthenware, 'and some dried figs and a few wrinkled apples.'

The fruit sellers and other food merchants would have been at the north gate of the Redoubt long before dawn vying with each other to offer the best produce. Alcestis knew Fiorentina liked to cut up pears to soak in red wine during the day for her husband to enjoy in the evening.

'And the fish,' the cook went on. 'I wanted to get river bream but there was none to be had. Just some old collop and this reedfish.' She sniffed. 'It's small and fiddly. When I was a girl we used to feed reedfish to the cats – now we serve it in the emperor's palace. And on the Day of Summoning too.' She shook her head at the terrible fate of the nobility in times of war.

Smiling to herself Fiorentina picked up one of the pears and left the kitchen, the woman's complaints lingering in her ears, and walked to the atrium where she hoped to see her husband again before his day began. He was there, dressed formally for the events of importance, and armed, she noticed. His black jacket was being brushed down by one of his servants. His dark eyes lit up to see her in the dress he loved and he took her hand, turning it and kissing the palm.

'Lady, you are my heart's delight.'

She smiled, but his words sparked only a pang of fear. Since Petalina's death she seemed full of fears, afraid that something would happen to him or to their baby. She said, 'Be careful,' but wagged her finger teasingly, making a joke of it, for she did not want to oppress him with her thoughts, still less for her fears to manifest as the truth.

At that moment the old spymaster Dol Salida was ushered through the door, leaning heavily on his silver-topped cane. Fiorentina had known the old man for most of her life and was fond of him, but she smiled and made her exit for she knew Dol would not be able to say what he was there for if she were present.

So she blew a kiss to her husband and, resolving to tell him that evening that she was carrying their child, turned away from him for the last time.

When Leona had gone to her rest just before dawn on the Day of Summoning it was without fear or premonition. And she had slept, as ever, without dreams.

She could not remember dreaming when she was a child, a maid in her father's house, or when, not much older, she was wooed and wed by the young blacksmith, yellow-haired and handsome, who was always cheerful, who laughed and sang as he worked, and wept with joy when she gave birth to their three children, two fair-headed boys and a girl, her precious girl, with fiery hair like her own.

And she certainly did not dream after they were taken away by the plague which sprang up in the rookeries of Lindo and swept across Amphitheatre and Burman Far before subsiding as quickly as it had appeared, leaving dead more than half the population in those parts of the City.

If other soldiers recalled the tales told to them by strangers in their sleep, and asked about hers, she would shrug indifferently, and they could take that as they wished. Sometimes she believed they were just stories, rich and strange, or trivial, or ribald, created and named 'dreams' to entertain comrades, akin to the tall tales most soldiers told to embellish their deeds and sometimes to conceal their misdeeds.

But she sometimes wished she dreamed, that in her nights she could spend time with her children, for they would have been well grown now, and she could see what sort of people they might have become. Dead, still dead, she guessed. Dead on some foreign battlefield, rather than dead in their little beds. Would that have been better, had they lived to fall in love, perhaps had children of their own, before having it all snatched away?

The year women were first drafted into the Immortal's armies was the year of the great plague. Thousands of young women succumbed to the sickness and the remainder, all the sixteen-year-olds at least, were taken away to serve their City, which most of them did by dying quickly. Almost an entire generation of girls killed within a year. The City had never recovered from this blow to its future population.

Leona, already dead inside, watched this absurdity, then chose to join it. There were no rules that said a mature woman could not sign up, so Leona went through the training process, such as it was, with girls half her age, and in the end she outlived them all. It gave her a life, though not one she had planned, and a family of sorts. In time she became the most senior female soldier in the Immortal's armies. And she loved the life now, for all the bureaucracy, the pointless regulations, the petty politicking. For at the heart of it, to a man and woman, they were burnished with pride in their cause – to defend the City – and gripped by a zeal to give their lives in its service.

When she first met Valla the girl was just one of the sixteen-year-old recruits, fresh from an orphanage, tall and leggy and terrified, hiding her fear under a thick shield of insolence. She was a natural with a sword. She had speed and grace and balance. Leona had been her training officer and she marked the girl down for progress if she continued to survive. When Leona was promoted out of that hated role – training the hopeless and the desperate for a brief, panicked fight then a merciless death – she remembered the girl and dragged her after her, through infantry regiments and up the ranks. They had been parted when Leona was raised into the Thousand, then an unheard-of thing for a woman. It did not cross her mind to refuse, but she thought she would never see Valla again. But Valla had survived and grown stronger, and she came to the attention of General Boaz. The girl rescued three injured members of her company, defending them against the enemy until help arrived, in a skirmish with Fkeni tribesmen in the Mountains of the Moon. In an army where bravery and honour rarely counted for much, for once a courageous soldier was noticed in places of power. Leona suggested the girl be promoted to the Thousand. Boaz argued that she had no name. Leona pointed out that she herself had been just the daughter of a poor merchant. The two women had served side by side ever since.

Leona wondered how the girl was getting by with her crippled arm and why she had not sought her friend out. In two days' time she would be off duty and she would find Valla and perhaps they would renew their secret vows to each other, spoken before the all-seeing goddess Aduara.

'Leona! Wake up!'

Her eyes flew open and she was instantly awake. She did not need Loomis' hard hand shaking her shoulder.

'Yes?' she said, swinging her legs from the bed, trying to bludgeon her mind to alertness. She had been on duty all night. She did not have to look at the notched candle to know her sleep had been brief.

'The Vincerii want all the chiefs at the Porphyry Gate.' Her aide added unnecessarily, 'You don't want to be the last there.'

Leona dressed as quickly as she could and was still tucking her shirt into her trousers as she hurried out of her chamber after Loomis, who handed her her sword-belt.

She was not the last, not quite. The other commanders of the Thousand, at least those centuries presently in the City, were gathered in the command room in the shadow of the Porphyry Gate, one of the known entrances to the Immortal's Keep deep in the heart of the Red Palace. Also there were the generals of regiments now deployed in the City. Only the hated Nighthawk, the new man Riis, was not present.

Marcellus was glaring at the doorway. 'Where's Riis?' he demanded of the assembled officers, his face dark. Leona wondered what had happened to provoke his wrath.

'He has not been seen since early yesterday,' offered one commander, barely hiding his satisfaction that the horseman had stumbled at his first outing.

'Then get his second here!' Marcellus shouted, and an aide ran to obey.

Leona looked around. Rafael, dapper in black, was at Marcellus' side, while at the rear Boaz loomed above them all. There was the sharp smell of anxiety in the air, mixed with the scents of unwashed bodies, hunger and fatigue, and breath made foul by too much wine. Only a major crisis would bring all the chiefs here at one time. And a crisis directly affecting the City itself, not just a military setback in the field.

While waiting, Marcellus stalked up and down the room, his impatience clear to see, and he glared at the gathered warriors as if preparing to single one out for blame. At last the man sent to find Riis's second slid back in through the doorway and hurried to the First Lord, speaking quietly to him. Marcellus frowned and asked something. The young man shook his head.

Marcellus turned to the assembled soldiers. His voice was tight with controlled anger. 'We have information, pristine information, that there will be an assault on the palace today.'

Warriors looked at one another in incredulity.

'Where?' Leona asked him.

'Through the sewers.'

Leona heard grunts of disbelief and quiet murmurings of 'Impossible!'

'Who?' she asked.

Marcellus shook his head. 'Does it matter?' he spat. 'They are the enemy.'

'All we know,' Rafael put in smoothly, 'is that there will be an attack, through the sewers, at some time today. Or that one has been planned. There are a limited number of ways they can get through . . .'

'Only two I can think of,' growled Fortance, commander of the Silver Bears, 'and both are deep under water now.'

'The water levels are ever-changing,' Rafael said. 'Both upwards and down. Only yesterday, I'm told, the level of the Leaving Street cistern suddenly dropped by half, despite all the rain. It's still half-empty, so the water must be draining away somewhere new.' This was baffling news. The Leaving Street cistern, which supplied fresh water to the Armoury and parts of Burman South and Barenna, rarely dropped except in the driest conditions.

'Could it be deliberate, the work of these sewer-rats?' asked Langham Vares, general of the Twenty-second.

'I can't see why,' Marcellus retorted. 'They can scarcely be hoping to conquer the palace by drought.' He was badly out of temper.

'Our source of information is a reliable one,' explained Rafael. 'If it tells us an invasion through the sewers is being attempted, then it is so. Only a small number of soldiers can be involved, for the conditions down there must be next to impossible.' He paused, then added, 'So we must assume this is just a diversion from some greater attack.' He stared round the assembly. 'Our first duty is to guard the emperor so, in the absence of the Gulons, Fortance's Bears will take on bodyguard duty in the Keep.'

Fortance nodded briskly and Leona saw the pride in the old man's eyes. The veteran commander had been under a shadow since a foul-up that summer when one of the Immortal's proxies was almost killed in an enemy ambush. Fortance, then leader of the Emperor's Hounds, had been in command of the whole benighted operation and had been demoted, but shortly afterwards replaced the leader of the Silver Bears. Clearly he had now been completely absolved.

'Aquila,' Rafael went on, 'your Night Owls will back up Fortance. Are you still six down?'

'Yes, lord.'

Leona thought to herself, *Two centuries in the Keep? Do we really need almost two hundred elite warriors to guard a being who has shown over and over that he cannot be harmed?* She always shuddered when she thought of

Araeon. Her first duty was to the City and the emperor, but her private loyalty had been, always would be, to Marcellus. She had fought beside the First Lord for ten years and in the silent recesses of her heart looked forward to the day when he ascended the Immortal Throne. Only Marcellus could end the war, for the emperor, she was sure, was too far down the path of madness to do so. But she was a loyal daughter of the City and must, and would, guard Araeon to the death.

As Rafael ordered the deployment of the City's forces, Marcellus listened, occasionally nodding. Leona's Warhounds were to search the public rooms of the west wing, while soldiers of the Twenty-second would have the hazardous duty of exploring the lower depths, chambers and corridors abandoned to the rising waters.

When Rafael had finished Marcellus told them, 'The Great Gates are being closed until further notice.' He looked at Boaz, who nodded. 'From today it will take a direct order from the Immortal or from me to reopen any of them.'

They are taking this threat very seriously, thought Leona, and she felt a thrill at the prospect of action.

'We are lucky,' Marcellus added, 'that the Second Adamantine and the Fourth Imperial, our most illustrious of regiments, are in the City at the moment. They are respected by the people of the City and will be a calming presence should there be any disruption today.' He turned to Boaz. 'Have the Immortal's private audiences been cancelled?'

The general smiled thinly. There was a long-standing rivalry between the two men, and Marcellus sometimes amused himself by treating Boaz as a mere secretary to the emperor.

'All except for one,' the tall soldier said, agreeably enough.

'Cancel it,' Marcellus told him.

'I will convey your suggestion to the Immortal,' Boaz responded blandly. It appeared that if he was going to be treated like a secretary, then he would behave like one. Leona was impatient with such games, which she would not allow among her captains.

Perhaps feeling the same, Rafael briskly dismissed the warriors.

'One more thing,' Marcellus put in, creating some moments' disorder as armed and armoured men turned in the doorway, bumping into one another.

'Today is the Day of Summoning,' their lord said. 'A day of very special import to the Families and to the emperor. It will not be a coincidence that the enemy has chosen this day to attack. This insult, adding to the outrage felt by our loyal soldiers, might tempt them to slaughter the invaders to a man. But we must rein ourselves in. Intelligence is our lifeline, as has been proved today. See this as an opportunity to question our enemy both about this raid and about the plans and manoeuvres of the Blueskin armies in general. This might be a vital day in the history of the City, the day the tide turns in our favour once and for all.'

His words were practical, but Leona felt pride and belief swelling in her breast. With Marcellus in command the City would prevail, and this day would be the turning-point of the war. Around her men were echoing her thoughts, murmuring their trust and confidence in their lord.

Marcellus raised his voice. 'Instruct your troops to identify the leaders, be they senior officers in command or merely platoon leaders. It is vital they are kept for interrogation. The others – kill them all!'

Leona felt it in her bones before she heard the sound: fifty veteran warriors roaring their agreement and their faith. Old soldiers all, their blood rose at the prospect of battling for the life of their City and their lords.

★ ★ ★

The patchwork gulon was accustomed to waiting. Time possessed no meaning for the creature, for its ancestors had, more than a thousand years before, been bred to have no concept of its passage.

So it carried on doing what it always did. It stalked the Red Palace, through the dark ways known only to gulons and their mortal enemies the rats, gliding behind wainscots, beneath tapestries, sliding and sidling up and down stairways, squeezing through narrow byways and, if absolutely necessary, swimming in the flooded depths of past palaces. It was searching for *the woman*, not with any intensity of purpose, but relentlessly, as it had done all its life – at least, as long as it could remember. It went to all her favourite haunts, where her smell lingered most strongly, then to other places where it had discovered her in the past, where her passing was barely detectable. After a while some part of its brain realized that she was no longer in the palace. She had left many times before. She always returned.

And the gulon was accustomed to waiting.

But when the alarm gongs started to bawl their brazen warning, two things happened. First the gulon's ears folded forward into furry grooves in the creature's skull, protecting its sensitive hearing from the racket. And something deep within its simple brain shifted, telling it its mission to protect *the woman* was aborted, for *the woman* was not present to be protected. In times of emergency its mission changed. It would search for an appropriate female to guard.

It emerged from where it was waiting in the mouldy groove behind a pillar and set off for the heart of the palace. Keeping to the dark places and hidden ways, it made its way up through the levels, moving ever eastward. It saw many men on its journey, most of them running towards the Keep or away from it. A band of the black-and-silver ones with their nut-hard skins and sharp sticks raced by. The gulon looked for females among them but there were none. If it noted that this was unusual, it was not disheartened.

Eventually, in a narrow corridor close to the centre of the palace it smelled then saw a lone female. She was not what the gulon had expected, if it had expected anything. The woman had only three limbs, which was not unusual, yet with her single front claw she wielded a sharp stick like the four-limbed soldiers.

As the gulon peered from the darkness, a man stepped lightly into the corridor behind the female. He walked stealthily after her, any sound he made smothered by the bawling of the alarm gongs. The gulon, which recognized stalking when it saw it, knew the man was intent on harm. This was clearly *the woman* it sought and it had to protect her.

On silent paws it sped from the shadows. It padded up behind the man then, its needle-sharp claws finding chinks in his outer skin, ran up his back and on to his shoulder. The man had barely time to cry out before the gulon inserted its sharp snout between throat-guard and helm and tore out the two great blood vessels of the neck. The man fell, his blood gouting, his armour clattering and momentarily obliterating the clamour of the gongs.

The woman turned, saw the dead man and the gulon, and fled.

The creature paused, tempted by the man's soft eyeballs. But it did not want to lose her trail so, licking blood from its whiskers, it padded after her.

CHAPTER TEN

STERN EDASSON OF ADRASTTO STOOD ON THE Adamantine Wall on the far south of the City, facing outwards towards the mountains, which were hidden behind a wall of weather. Sleet from the north drilled into his neck then trickled under his old armour, but he was scarcely aware of the cold. He was worried.

As a child he had always been plagued by too many thoughts. His father had tried beating it out of him, his mother had sobbed and said no good would come of it. Stern had learned over the years to hide the ideas that swept through his mind, as relentless as spring plagues and no more welcome. More so since he and his brother had left home to join the City's armies. No one wanted a soldier who thought too much. But there were times, like now, when he couldn't help thinking about things that made his head ache.

Standing with his fellow guards in the gloomy morning light high above the Adamantine Gate, theoretically watching the south but seeing only grey, he wondered what in the name of the gods was going on. The rest of the platoon had been content enough with their orders, particularly his brother Benet, for they had come from General Boaz himself.

'Bar the gates,' the veteran warrior had told them that morning, riding by and only pausing his mount briefly, 'and keep them barred on pain of death. Do not open them for any reason, until Marcellus or the Immortal himself orders it.'

The general seemed in mellow humour, for he had nodded to Stern and said, 'Your emperor values your service, soldier.'

And Stern had replied, 'Thank you, lord,' as if he conversed with generals every day.

Now, standing on the wall in the watery light, he watched and wondered.

'You still worrying about it?' Quora asked, looking up at him, for he was a good head taller.

Stern shrugged. 'It makes no sense,' he argued. The other soldiers of the platoon sighed. They had heard it before. 'We were told when we were deployed here that Boaz was our direct commander, after Caranus was killed.' Caranus had been commander of the Pigstickers, a company of the Twenty-fifth infantry, largely destroyed in the battle at Salaba in the summer. Stern and his five had survived Salaba, when the Maritime Army of the West had been surprised and slaughtered by the Blues, and had returned to the City, where they found themselves rewarded with wall-walking duties until they could be reassigned to another infantry regiment. They had walked this easternmost section of the Adamantine Wall, between the Isingen Tower and the Tower of Truth, for more than six weeks now. Stern was bored beyond reason and he hated the stones of the wall with every fibre of his being. The others seemed to find the lack of excitement restful.

'So if your commander gives you an order you take it,' he went on, 'and if your commander orders you to bar the gate you do it. But if he comes back the next day and orders you to open it again then you do that.

What general gives an order he can't countermand?' he said, coming to the nub of his disquiet.

'Let's worry about it if it comes to that,' said the veteran Grey Gus, not for the first time.

And what if, Stern thought to himself – though he did not say it for it sounded like treason – both Marcellus *and* the emperor were killed in whatever emergency this is? What then? Do the Great Gates stay closed for ever, with Stern and his warriors forever defending them to the death against the City's own soldiers?

'It makes no sense,' he muttered under his breath.

'It's not our place to question,' his brother Benet sniffed. 'We're the fighting Pigstickers, finest soldiers in the City. We follow our orders and we follow them to the death.' Benet had never been troubled by too many thoughts.

They heard the sound of marching feet and Stern walked over to the inner edge of the wall and looked down.

'Who are they?' asked Benet, peering at a group of soldiers emerging from the rain. 'Can you see?'

Stern glanced at him. His brother's eyesight had been getting worse since the head wound a year before. Now Benet could scarcely recognize his own brother's face, far less the infantrymen below.

'Shovelheads,' he answered shortly.

'Muck-shovellers,' sneered his brother. He spat in their general direction. There was bitter rivalry between the Pigstickers and the Shovelheads, whose barracks lay next to theirs in the Street of Bright Dancers and who were manning the next section of wall between the Isingen Tower and the Adamantine Gate.

Benet saw his brother was still frowning. 'Boaz ordered us,' he said. 'He's our general. If he orders us to open the gates again, we have to. He's our general.' There was no contradiction there to Benet. 'And he can do us a lot of good. He said he will be grateful.'

'He said *the emperor* will be grateful. And what if *he's* dead?'

'Who, the emperor?'

'No, you moron. Boaz. What if he's killed? What if they're all killed? Do we just stand here holding the gates until we die?'

Benet screwed up his face in a parody of thought. 'Hold the gates. Hold them to the death,' he said eventually, looking round at his fellows, who nodded, glad to agree with anything which might end this conversation. Benet looked down at the marching soldiers and happily made an obscene gesture at their backs.

Stern slumped down on the stones of the battlements. His back ached and he was grateful to be off his feet for a moment. He was tired and soaked to the skin and his feet hurt. He wondered when he had last had dry boots. He wished with all his heart it was a normal day like any other. They had been on duty all night and by now he should be back in the barracks, asleep with a full stomach of corn porridge. But their turn had been doubled and they faced another day standing in the sleet and rain. His troop stood looking at him. Despite their confident words, they knew him well enough to be worried because *he* was worried.

'What's that?' sharp-eyed Quora asked, pushing back her helm and squinting into the distance. Stern got wearily to his feet again.

'What?'

She was pointing out beyond the wall, towards what seemed to be a thickening of the mist. Stern peered, yet could make no sense of it. He caught a distant rumbling, like the muffled cavalry charge of a thousand horses. His whole troop was now squinting in that direction. All any of them could see was sleet and mist, but the sound was getting louder.

A fresh worm of anxiety moved in Stern's belly. 'Into the tower!' he yelled, without knowing why. The other soldiers looked at him, surprised, but started moving towards the door in the Isingen Tower, fifty paces away.

'Lively!' he bellowed at them and they broke into a trot, Benet straggling at the rear. Stern took another look at the darkness to the south and, fear flooding his body, ran after them. They dived into the narrow doorway, one at a time, the roaring noise quickening their boots.

Stern paused fractionally, then with horror saw a grey wall of water, higher than the Adamantine Wall itself, looming over him out of the mist. In the last heartbeat before it struck he stepped into the tower, dragging the sturdy door shut behind him.

The wall of water hit home like a battering-ram of the gods. The noise, reverberating through the hollow stone tower, was deafening. As the soldiers crouched in the dark on the inner steps they felt the shock like a blow to their bodies, rattling their teeth and jolting them to the core. Stones showered down on their helms and backs and they heard the grate and creak of tortured timbers and screams of fear and pain from comrades beneath them.

The Isingen Tower, which had stood for eight hundred years, held for a few more heartbeats before the wooden roof caved in, letting in daylight and the flood of water. With an ear-shattering roar part of the tower collapsed. An avalanche of stone and timber crashed down, scouring away the lower stairs, leaving Stern and his comrades marooned near the top. The six soldiers clung to one another on the ruined stairway, sure that at any moment they would be swept off by the raging waters or by flying stonework. Stern's eyes were squeezed shut. He was holding on to Benet and he could feel someone else's arm round his shoulder. He prayed for it to end.

Then, after what seemed like an eternity, the noise slowly receded and there was an eerie stillness, the only sounds those of dripping water and the muffled cries of terrified and injured soldiers buried in the rubble.

Stern lifted his head and looked around. The section of steps where they had found refuge had miraculously stayed intact. The southern side of the tower had disappeared completely, along with the lower steps. Stern was staring through falling rain and rising dust straight towards the mountains.

Cautiously, afraid their refuge would give way under him, he stood. Aware that his legs were like wet string, he limped down the remaining steps to where they ended halfway up the tall tower. Below him was just a pile of rubble, still shifting as it settled and as the water drained away. Roof timbers were thrown about in the debris like a child's fighting sticks.

'We can climb down here,' he said, his voice ringing hollowly in his ears. 'There will be injured.' Anyone who was on the floor of the tower when it fell would be dead, he thought, but they were comrades so they must search for them anyway. He thought he could hear far-off screams of fear and panic as the flood rolled on over the City. They would do what they could to aid the injured, but they must be ready to fight, for the next people they saw might well be Blues, now the City lay wide open to the enemy.

'This ale stinks!'

The fat man slammed down his tankard, slopping dark liquid across the rough counter. 'It's dog-piss,' he added, glaring at the innkeeper of the Three Fools tavern who watched him bleakly, mopping up the ale with a grimy rag.

Rubin couldn't but agree. But it had never been his intention to drink the stuff. One sniff was enough. He sat silently in his corner of the inn, knit cap pulled down over his forehead, watching the fat man, whose name was Drusus. He had been doing this for several days and had come to the conclusion that he was wasting his time. Drusus was just a fat oaf who boasted of friends inside the palace and knowledge of the private thoughts of the generals and commanders. He was a former dungeon guard, dismissed for drunkenness, and he clearly had friends *somewhere*, for it was impossible to stay that stout on the usual City ration of cornbread and dried peas and the odd wrinkled apple. And he had connections in the palace, for certain, because he had spoken unwisely in days past of the mutiny of the Leopards. It would have been simple enough to have him killed in a dark alley, but Marcellus, when he heard of it, gave Rubin the task of following the man to see who these connections were.

It had been easy, so easy that Rubin suspected Marcellus had given him the job to keep him busy in the empty days since his return from the mountains. He didn't mind. But it was years since he had spent any time in the City and he was troubled by the changes. Supplies were badly stretched. There was little meat to be had, and fish only from time to time. Crops were grown in the farmlands to the north-east, but the recent steady rain had ruined many of them, and clearly there were no hops. Rubin had no idea what the ale on the table before him was made of and he didn't want to think about it.

The streets of the City were populated largely by the old and the very young: the old who had forgotten what their lives were for, and the young who would probably never learn. All men and women of fighting age were either in the army or dead. There were few dogs or cats now skulking in the alleys and twittens, and only the rats seemed to flourish. And you rarely saw a fat man anywhere.

So Rubin kept following Drusus out of curiosity. The man lived in Amphitheatre, a district in the south of the City, in a house which was neither mansion nor hovel. It was small, but built sturdily of stone with a slate roof, and Drusus shared it with his elderly aunt and a servant, a female child who was no more than a slave.

Each day Drusus would leave his house at the crack of mid-morning and head to the Shining Stars Inn, a good walk away, where he would sit and drink and eat and talk to his fellow barflies. There Rubin would find him. Later the man would take a meandering course home via several other taverns and eating houses, becoming more belligerent and dislikeable as the hours passed.

Rubin's height and red hair made it hard for him to follow anyone covertly, but Drusus never seemed to notice him dogging his heels or frequenting the same inns as him day after day. The man was clearly a fool and Rubin found it hard to believe he posed any threat to the palace or the emperor.

Today was the Day of Summoning, when people all over the City lit candles at dusk to greet the gods home from their long voyage round the sun. Rubin was told that in past times the whole population turned out to celebrate, and the day was spent in feasting and worship. There would be little feasting that day.

'No one can drink this slop!' the fool said again, having downed half of it.

'Clear off then!' the innkeeper cried, waving the wet rag at him.

Drusus lumbered to his feet, knocking over the tankard, and made a grab for the innkeeper, who stepped nimbly away and dragged a stout cudgel from under the counter.

'Clear off!' the man shouted again and Rubin saw his gaze rolling to appeal to two soldiers watching from a table at the far side of the inn.

'Can't sell this piss!' Drusus argued, pointing a stubby finger at him. He drew himself up like a cockerel about to crow. 'The palace will hear of this!' he threatened. 'I've got friends!'

'Go talk to your friends,' the innkeeper said with contempt. 'You'll sup no more ale in here.'

The two soldiers pushed back their chairs and came ambling over. They'd been in the tavern for some time and had drunk a good deal and their relaxed demeanour belied a need to give someone a good kicking. They laid hands on fat Drusus and dragged him outside, protesting and flailing. Rubin stood and, nodding amiably to the innkeeper, strolled after them out into the rain-drenched street.

By the time he got there Drusus was already lying in a muddy puddle trying to curl up in a ball as the two soldiers – infantrymen of the Forty-second Celestine, Rubin noted – laid into him with their boots. The sounds were of sturdy leather hitting solid flesh, and muffled groans from their victim. After a while the soldiers got bored with kicking him and wandered back into the inn, no doubt anticipating a free drink.

Rubin decided to change tack. He crouched down beside Drusus, who was moaning and crying.

'Can I help you, good sir?' he asked solicitously. 'I saw the whole thing. The soldiers attacked you for no reason. Are you injured?'

Drusus rolled over and vomited ale on to the wet earth. He groaned and sat up, rain sluicing the mud off his pudgy face.

'Let me help you,' Rubin said again. He got Drusus

to his knees, then his feet. The fat man was clutching his ribs and Rubin suspected one or more must be broken. He found it hard to summon much sympathy, but the man didn't deserve the punishment he'd suffered for criticizing the inn's disgusting ale. Not for the first time, the thought came that the City's soldiery were out of control.

'Where do you live?' he asked, setting off south towards the man's home. Drusus pointed vaguely in the direction they were going. Rubin was too tall to support him properly but he held the man's fat upper arm and tried to prop him up as best he could.

He was still feeling drained by his long ride from the north, though many days had now passed, and as the pair struggled towards Amphitheatre he thought about Valla again and wondered where she was. He had begged her to go with him to meet Marcellus – to ensure the First Lord heard of her heroism – but after their audience, in which Valla had remained stubbornly silent, she had disappeared, telling him she wanted to look for a friend. He had not seen her since and he wondered what would become of her, if anyone would employ a one-armed warrior and, if not, how she would survive.

By the time they came within sight of Drusus' house the man was recovering his ability to speak. He was mumbling about the two soldiers, the inn, its ale and the innkeeper, spewing curses and venom on them all. Rubin wondered why he was bothering to help the drunkard. He had killed more likeable men.

Then they straggled to a halt, looking around them. A dull rumbling could be heard in the distance, like thunder on a warm afternoon, and the earth under their feet seemed to vibrate. Rubin could feel it in his teeth. A trickle of dread ran through him.

They were in the district which lay between the old

Sarantine Wall and the new walls. The Sarantine was one of the most ancient in the City but had become redundant when the Adamantine Wall – higher, thicker, stronger – was built four leagues to the south. Such faith was placed in the new wall that the Sarantine's gates had been allowed to rot.

Rubin turned around, trying to work out where the ominous sound was coming from. Drusus stood with an expression of dumb incomprehension on his fat face.

The roaring became louder and the very air seemed to quiver. There were shouts and screams. 'Earthquake!' Drusus cried. Children and old people were hurrying out into the street from their homes, the able-bodied supporting the infirm. They looked around wide-eyed, wondering at the din. It wasn't an earthquake, Rubin was sure. It was something worse. He started to move back the way they had come, his eyes fixed on the Adamantine Wall.

'Come away!' he urged Drusus, but the fat man ignored him. Rubin grabbed hold of his sleeve and started to drag him away.

Then there was a booming sound, like the crash of the waves at the base of the Salient, but a thousand times louder. Rubin was stunned into stillness. He was looking straight at the Adamantine Wall, now shockingly diminished by a grey wall of water looming above. For a moment the impossible wave seemed to hang over the tiny figures patrolling the battlements, then they disappeared as if snatched away by the gods. A stretch of the great wall exploded inwards as if pulverized by a monstrous battering-ram.

'Run!' Rubin shouted. And, letting go of the fat man, he ran for his life.

At the Isingen Tower water was still pouring from the ruined roof, mixed with the relentless rain, and Stern and his troop were coughing and choking as they climbed down the pile of timber and stone. Helping each other, they slowly made their way to the base of the tower, fearful that the remaining walls would topple and crush them. It took a long time, testing each boot-step as the rubble shifted, but with cries of relief they emerged from the shadow of the tower, bruised and clothed with grey dust and mud, but miraculously unharmed.

Stern stared through the rain at what once had been an impregnable wall, an invulnerable tower. *Where did all the water come from?* He had no idea. He heard the clop of horses' hooves and turned, thinking cavalry had come to rescue the trapped and injured.

Out of the rain stepped a troop of twenty or more horsemen, heavy cavalry on armoured mounts. The horses were puffing and blowing as if from a fast ride. Steam rose from their coats and their leather harness creaked and jingled as they circled around Stern and his comrades. Then lances were lowered and the City soldiers found themselves in the centre of a ring of sharp lance-points. Stern squinted up at the horsemen. He did not recognize their uniforms, and the helms were closed, leaving them faceless and sinister. But the pennants drooping wetly from the levelled lances were green and yellow, the colours of Petrus, and he realized their good fortune at surviving the fall of the tower had ended.

Slowly he and the others raised their hands. 'We surrender,' he said.

No one could outrun the water. But with death at his heels Drusus found new energy and he ran after Rubin as the younger man raced towards the closest sanctuary, a temple of Rharata which topped a high flight of white steps. Rubin sprinted up the steps three at a time, his stride outpacing his exhaustion. He looked behind and was relieved to see the great wave had lost much of its momentum. But though it was now no more than hip-high it carried a lethal burden of tree branches and other flotsam. Rubin watched as people fleeing the wave were overtaken, disappearing into the brown wall of water, mud and debris. Two great roof timbers were sweeping towards Drusus, who had stopped after climbing the first few temple steps as if the small elevation would keep him safe. Rubin yelled out a warning and the drunkard looked round, then cringed as the beams grazed by him and smashed on the plinth of the statue of Rharata. Drusus, drenched and staggering, scrambled further up the steps. A floating barrel passed by, still churning out its freight of red wine to mix into the muddy sea lapping at the temple.

'The gods have mercy on fools and drunkards,' Rubin muttered to himself. He sat down suddenly, his limbs like lead.

He thought of all the decent men he had killed, like Jan and Franken, the two Odrysian soldiers on the Crags of Corenna, and those he had failed to rescue, like Captain Starky. And now he had saved the useless hide of a drunkard, a blowhard and perhaps a spy whose death would certainly not be mourned and might well improve the world a little.

'Thank you,' the fat man said, gazing up at him. 'I owe you my life.' Fear, it seemed, had leeched away his drunkenness and restored his manners. Rubin nodded.

'What has done this?' Drusus asked him, his face a mask of bafflement.

'The reservoirs.' Rubin had made a leap of intuition. 'I think the enemy has destroyed the dams and used our reservoirs as a weapon against us. And with the Adamantine Wall breached it is only a matter of time before they invade the City and reach the palace. You should find a place of safety, or seek out friends and family.'

Galvanized by his own words, he got to his feet. He turned towards the Red Palace, far to the north-west, but the rain met the mist rising from the surging water and hid its pile of towers and domes from view. He made his way down the temple steps, treading into the murky water, now knee-deep.

'Good luck to you, Drusus,' he said, clapping the man on his meaty shoulder. 'Go and defend your home.'

'Where are you going?' Drusus asked.

'In search of a friend,' Rubin told him.

CHAPTER ELEVEN

VALLA RACED DOWN A STEEP STONE STAIRCASE, HER boots sliding on the slick steps, chasing the shadow of the gulon.

When she had first seen the creature, tearing out the throat from some unfortunate soldier, she had fled from it in fear, but it was much faster than her and Valla quickly realized it had no ill-will towards her. Why it had attacked the man was a puzzle, as was the beast's motive. It had since stuck to her trail, gliding out of sight in the light of day, matching her pace, sometimes close to her heels like a dog, in the darker places. When she chose one of the palace's myriad empty rooms to sleep in she had shut it out, unwilling to have it with her while she lay vulnerable. But when she awoke it was sitting in a corner, watching her with yellow eyes. She guessed it followed paths unknown to man or woman. And she became used to it.

Valla had remained in the Red Palace by simply not leaving after she and Rubin had met Marcellus. She knew parts of the building well, including the scores of empty chambers in the north and east wings once dedicated to accommodating visiting dignitaries, now abandoned, covered with dust and rats' droppings. So by day she chose a dusty room to idle away the time, sleeping and daydreaming, and by night she wandered the hallways, drifting like a ghost through the midnight corridors, through the lower levels where black water lay silent and gleaming, watched only by rats. She knew she could never fight for the City again, not with her crippled arm. She could not bear the thought of losing her connection with the Thousand completely, so she remained in a state of limbo – not wanting to stay but not daring to leave.

She had been sorely tempted to go to Leona. She had not seen her friend, or any of the Warhounds, though by checking the duty rosters in Dashoul's office under cover of darkness she had found they were now stationed in the Red Palace. She could not bring herself to call on Leona's kindness, like a lost and injured pup seeking a home. For all Leona's high status they had fought together side by side as friends and comrades, and Valla could not renew their friendship on any other terms.

But now the palace's great brazen gongs were sounding an alarm and Valla moved with a purpose. She had no idea what the emergency was but she was glad to abandon the quiet, sleeping corridors and she headed, like all able-bodied soldiers, for the heart of the palace. The gulon scampered beside her boots.

She halted at the foot of a staircase. Two warriors of the Black-tailed Eagles lay there. One's throat was slit, the other's heart pierced. Valla looked around. Nothing stirred. She dragged the breastplate off one of the bodies and, cursing her useless arm, managed to put it on. Grabbing a helm, she felt more like a soldier again and she raced towards the Keep, the imperial residence. Guarding the emperor was the first duty for all members of the Thousand, but she paused when she saw its green marble walls ahead. The only entrance to the Keep she knew was the Porphyry Gate, several floors above. She lingered, unsure how to get in. Then the gulon slid around her feet and scurried into a shadow in the wall. Following it, she came to a steep stairway leading downward. The gulon paused to check she was following, then dashed down into darkness. She grabbed a torch from a wall bracket and ran after it.

At the bottom of the stairs she was still outside the Keep. Its slick green wall was to her left and crumbling, damp stone to her right. She looked for the gulon but could no longer see it. Had it led her on a quail hunt? She followed the low corridor, which was ankle-deep in stinking water, its walls dark and clammy and lit by an eerie luminescence. Finally, with something like relief, she heard the familiar noise of battle. She ran towards the clamour of voices and ringing steel and saw light ahead, and suddenly found herself in the Hall of Emperors, where the Immortal conducted his public business.

It was a slaughterhouse and, like a slaughterhouse, it stank of death. The high, cylindrical space was filled with battling warriors, and bodies already lay on the circular floor and on the high, winding stairs. The floor was awash with blood and water and the din of battle seemed magnified in the lofty, echoing chamber. The air was thick and fetid and it sank over her like a noisome blanket. Each breath she took tasted of blood and rot and she bent over and vomited on the flooded floor.

She wiped her mouth and looked around, bewildered. All the warriors, alive, injured and dead, were wearing the black and silver of the Thousand. She had no idea who was friend and who foe. And why were the centuries fighting each other?

Then Valla spotted the axeman Otho, a familiar, powerful figure with his beard bristling from under his helm, cleaving his axe into an opponent. Her heart soared. She could not see Leona, but now she could make out other Warhounds, her old comrades. Drawing her sword, she leaped up beside Otho, pushing back her visor so he could see who she was.

The axeman grinned at her, punching her on her good shoulder, and she launched herself at the enemy. They were clad as warriors of the Thousand, but bore an unfamiliar emblem, a bird in flight. Whoever they were, the Warhounds were fighting them and that was good enough. One staggered, dazed, towards her and she slid her blade under his helm and tore out his throat. She stepped forward and gutted a wounded man. A flicker of movement to her right and she ducked and swung, catching a warrior across the knees as he swung over her head. Valla laughed. She felt invincible.

Then a soldier sporting the bird emblem ran at her, helmless, his face enraged. She swerved as he struck. His sword sliced at her neck. She brought her blade up, but too late. He caught her on her ill-fitting helm, ripping it off. Disorientated, she dropped to one knee and the warrior raised his sword for the killing blow.

In that moment the patchwork gulon appeared. On bloody paws it ran up the warrior's armour and closed its jaws over his face. Even above the cacophony in the chamber Valla could hear the man's shriek of terror as he dropped his sword to claw at the beast. She leaped up and thrust her blade under his arm, unerringly into the heart. The gulon jumped down, a piece of meat in its jaws, and ran off.

Chest heaving, Valla looked around. The stench of blood and fear was as thick as mist in the air. She recognized the veteran Fortance's burly body lying on the high staircase. She still could not see Leona. Her heart sank a little, but then a warrior stepped forward and she threw herself back into the fray.

* * *

As he made his way across the flooded City Rubin pondered how to enter the Red Palace. Security had been tightened since the massacre in the Little Opera House and he was under no illusion that Marcellus' insignia would get him past the zealous gate guards.

It took him far longer than he had hoped to get there for the going was hard, the way treacherous, littered with the debris of the flood. From time to time he looked over his shoulder, expecting to see enemy cavalry at his heels. But the only living things he saw were bedraggled survivors and the occasional straying donkey or goat. The water was disappearing, ebbing away, leaving mud and debris and bodies. The mist was starting to fade and a weak sunlight filtered on to the ruined streets. It was the first sunshine for a good many days.

Well after noon the towers of the Red Palace at last loomed before him. Rubin was heading towards the Gate of Mercy, the southernmost entry to the palace, its two huge onion domes dominating the cityscape.

He paused and squinted at the right-hand dome, which seemed to have a large bite out of its rounded profile. As he watched it trembled and collapsed, the thunder of its fall muffled in mist and water. Rubin saw he would have no difficulty entering after all for the gate was subsiding also. One stone pillar was leaning drunkenly towards the other, and the massive timber doors between them slowly crumpled like cheap wood. He remembered that the lowest levels of the palace had already been drowned in water and the entire building was collapsing into the strata of ancient cities which formed the Halls. *Will this flood*, he wondered, *be the final blow which dooms the Red Palace?*

He clambered through the gap left by the collapsed gate pillar and into the courtyard beyond. There were no guards. There was nobody. Then came a terrible groan from far below and part of the stone courtyard disappeared, dropping away into depths unknown leaving a yawning chasm. Rubin turned and ran into the south wing of the palace. Once inside he stopped again and listened. There was no one about. The high-ceilinged corridors were silent, as if waiting. All he could hear was the muffled sound of running water.

He had no idea how to find Marcellus in the vast, foundering building. He knew where his lord's apartments were, but the man would hardly be there if his city was under attack. He resolved to head for the Immortal's Keep at the heart of the palace. Marcellus would protect the emperor first, and muster his troops. As he made his decision a battalion of those troops raced towards him down the corridor, appearing from nowhere, their boots and armour clattering. But in the face of such catastrophe, he imagined they were not likely to bother with one lone civilian.

He was wrong. Their commander – a cadaverous soldier with a scarred face – paused. 'Identify yourself!' he demanded as two of his soldiers stopped to grab Rubin.

'I am Rubin Kerr Guillaume,' he told them, struggling in their grip. 'I'm a friend of the First Lord!'

'Good for you,' the commander said, as one of the soldiers cuffed Rubin round the head.

'I must see Marcellus. I have vital information. Here, I have proof . . .' He tried to reach into a pocket but the soldier's hold on his arm stopped him. The man looked to his commander, who nodded, and he let Rubin pull out his insignia. The commander scanned it carefully, then stared at Rubin as if committing his face to memory. Then they let him go and ran on. After that Rubin avoided soldiers, though he saw many, all racing towards the Keep. Before long he could hear the distant clash of blades and the clamour of voices. He paused, undecided. He was curious to know what was going on, but curiosity had lured him into trouble before. It would be madness to try to join the fight: he was not in uniform and risked being despatched by some blade-happy soldier suspicious of anyone unknown. But he knew that wherever Marcellus was, so fighting would also be.

At the next stair he came to he grabbed a torch from a wall bracket and plunged downwards, following the steps down two levels. Here the palace had long been abandoned to the waiting water. It was knee-high, but he splashed forward, knowing he was unlikely to meet soldiers down there.

He was beginning to wonder if he had lost his way when, raising his torch, he recognized the bottom of the Pomegranate Stair, where west and south wings met. He was close to the Keep. As he reached the ornate stairway he heard men talking and stopped, his heart thudding. He held his breath, hardly daring believe his luck. Yes, he could hear Marcellus' voice high above. He ran up the stairs, up many levels, and at the top found his lord with a group of senior officers. At first sight Rubin thought Marcellus drenched in blood. Then he realized that, for the first time, he was seeing him in armour. It was the colour of ox-blood and shone as though freshly shed. Marcellus glanced at Rubin as he spoke with his chiefs, giving orders, listening to opinions. He nodded slightly.

Finally he commanded, 'Go to your troops, and remember the emperor's orders. No enemy will enter the Red Palace but over the bodies of our warriors!' The officers hurried off.

'Come, walk with me,' he ordered Rubin, turning and setting off at the double with his bodyguard at his heels.

'What are you doing in the palace, boy?' he snapped. Rubin saw deep lines of strain on his face. He had never seen his lord in peril and Marcellus seemed a different man from the one he knew. He could feel the power rolling off him like ocean breakers and Rubin saw, for the first time since the day they met, why Marcellus was so feared.

'I came to warn you, lord,' he cried, matching his long stride. 'The Adamantine Wall has been breached!'

Marcellus cast him a fleeting look. 'I know.'

'Has the enemy reached the palace?'

'The enemy was already within our walls. We have been attacked from beneath our feet – they have wormed their way up through the sewers, Petrassi and Tuomi and some renegade City soldiers. And the Nighthawks have mutinied.' Marcellus spat on the floor. 'A Petrassi army has entered the south of the City but they have not reached the palace. Not yet.'

'An invasion through the Halls?' How is that possible, Rubin wondered, recalling the stifling darkness, the terror. 'How many?'

Marcellus shook his head, dismissing the threat. 'A handful only. They have been despatched. But that is not my concern.' Marcellus stopped and turned to him, his black eyes gleaming eerily in his ashen face. 'This is clearly a well-executed plan. We have been betrayed, both within and without.'

CHAPTER TWELVE

IN THE HALL OF EMPERORS LEONA GUTTED AN OPPONENT then stepped back to draw breath. She could feel blood trickling down her skin from a wound in her flank. Her left hip was injured and the leg wasn't moving freely. She shook off the pain and fatigue and looked about her. Black-armoured figures were fighting on the floor of the chamber and up the stairs. It was harder than ever to tell who was who under all the blood. She tore off her helm so she could see.

Rafael Vincerus was lying dead on the stairs, a sight she thought she would never see. Like Marcellus, Rafe was believed to be indestructible. The enemy leader was also dead, lying beneath the high landing, his body broken. Somehow he had fooled the rebel Nighthawks into believing he was the hero Shuskara, but Leona could see he was just an impostor, some old man with rags sticking out from under purloined armour. Yet the Nighthawks were fighting like demons, backed by other unidentified warriors. Leona knew her task was to kill them, or at least prevent them getting to the Crystal Gateway, the entrance to the emperor's private rooms. She accepted that she would most likely die in the endeavour.

She saw a tall, rangy soldier in a red jerkin duck

beneath the wicked blood-slicked blade of Otho's axe and plunge his sword into the axeman's belly. Otho went down, his great body crumpling to the floor. The swordsman looked around for new prey, spotted Leona and turned towards her. *A Wildcat*, she thought. She'd heard they'd all died at Salaba. Yet here was one fighting alongside the treacherous Nighthawks.

Their swords clashed and Leona was forced back. In that brief moment she knew he was too skilled for her. She swayed to avoid a slicing cut to the belly and brought her blade up to pierce the warrior's armour under the arm, but he dodged at the last moment. She went after him, forcing him back in a flurry of moves, her heart surging briefly. But he rallied and sent a lightning thrust to her neck which sheared off her throat armour. She twisted and riposted, grazing his cheek as he spun away. He came back, darting his sword at her neck again and she swayed and blocked him – and his blade snapped. He leaped back, looking around for another sword among the dead and dying, but they were all broken. He stooped to snatch up a shield and drew out a long knife as Leona stepped towards him.

In that moment, 'Broglanh!' a voice screamed and a soldier on the staircase flung the swordsman a fresh blade. He stepped back gracefully and snatched it from the air by the hilt and in the same smooth movement brought it down on Leona's unprotected head. She ducked sideways but the scything blade caught her on the injured hip and she went down on one knee, paralysed by pain.

She looked up at the pale-eyed swordsman, helpless for a heartbeat. He punched her in the face with the shield then raised the sword for the kill. Dazed, she could only watch as the world slowed, and all she could hear was her own breathless panting and the blurred sounds of metal on metal, metal on flesh . . .

A slender figure appeared from her right and slashed at the swordsman's head. He deflected the blow off his shield but was caught off-balance and fell to one knee. Leona scrambled up and turned to her saviour.

Valla!

The girl was clearly exhausted, her face misted with blood, but her eyes gleamed with a hectic light. She grinned at Leona and the commander smiled back, and the two of them moved forward, side by side.

Marcellus was marching through far-flung parts of the Red Palace unknown to Rubin. Beyond the clatter of nailed boots on marble and the creak of leather, he could sometimes hear the groan of stone on stone far below, and thin cries in the distance which might be men in torment or just the screams of seabirds. As they sped along the corridors Rubin caught the occasional fleeting glimpse of the outside world from a window and saw they were moving east. Why east?

Rubin had assumed Marcellus was skirting the parts of the palace which were foundering, but as they climbed a wide flight of stairs there was a sudden roar and crash behind them and the lower section of the staircase fell away into an abyss. Rubin's heart leaped into his throat. Marcellus paused and turned, going back down the steps to the very brink. He looked down. Rubin joined him, but there was nothing to see down there save darkness. He could hear a maelstrom of crashing water, smell the sharp odour of the sewers. Rubin gazed at his lord, but the man's face was stone, eyes hooded, cryptic. Without a word, Marcellus turned and carried on.

At last they came to a carved door in a corridor lit by high windows. Sunlight lay on the floor and the still air was stifling with dust. Marcellus dismissed his guard. They backed away, reluctant at first, then turned and ran back towards the fighting. Marcellus pushed Rubin ahead of him into a circular room. The floor was an elaborate mosaic of stones – lapis lazuli, cerulean tile and blue slate – but otherwise the chamber was empty.

'The emperor is dead,' Marcellus grunted, pulling off his blood-red gauntlets and dropping them with a clatter to the floor.

Rubin stared at him in shock. The Immortal dead? It seemed an impossible contradiction. For all his father had told him about Araeon, that the man was corrupt, perhaps insane, still he had been emperor for all Rubin's life, the strong leader of a beleaguered City. And he remembered Reeve telling him Marcellus would succeed.

'How did he die?' he asked.

Marcellus shook his head. 'I only know that he is dead,' he said. 'I know it in my blood and my bones.' He gestured at the straps holding his breastplate and Rubin sprang to help, unbuckling the thick leather fastenings and lowering the armour to the floor. It lay on the mosaic like a dead soldier, bloody and broken. Rubin stood, feeling hollow and helpless, as Marcellus knelt to remove his greaves.

'Then you must withdraw, lord,' he said at last.

'I will fight to my last breath for this City,' Marcellus murmured.

'Please listen to me, lord. The palace is falling apart around us and there are already enemy troops inside it. We know there are more on the way. You must retreat now, while there is time.' Rubin struggled to find a way to convince him. 'Fighting on means certain death, or capture and torture and death. You once told me you have to choose your battles. This one is unwinnable.'

Marcellus made no reply but walked over to the windows and looked down across his City. Rubin followed. He could see nothing amiss – no troops battling on the streets, no sign of the flood. If these streets had been flooded then they had dried since under the thin sunlight. But they were silent and empty.

'You could go to the Salient,' Rubin persevered. 'My father will aid you. From there you can plan the recapture of the City. I will go with you.'

Marcellus snorted. 'Reeve and I are scarcely allies. And, like you, he is no fighter. The Guillaumes never were.'

Then, miraculously, his face brightened. 'Except your sister. She is a warrior born!'

Rubin was astonished. 'My sister? You've met Indaro?'

'A short time ago.'

'Today? She is in the palace now?' Rubin's spirits, which were in his boots, unexpectedly soared. Indaro was alive and defending her City. 'That is wonderful news, lord! No enemy can prevail against Indaro.'

A ghost of a smile lingered on Marcellus' face, then he sighed and said, 'Perhaps you are right.' Frowning, Rubin watched him, concerned at his volatile emotions. Marcellus sounded exhausted, as if all his formidable energy had swiftly drained from him. 'Perhaps I will quit the City. I'll let others organize the clear-up. Then I will return.' He turned to Rubin. 'A great king, a warrior and strategist, once said, "I will withdraw so that, like a ram, I can butt the harder." '

In a flash of insight Rubin realized this was what Marcellus had intended all along. 'I will go with you,' he offered again.

'No. I will travel alone.'

'Where will you go?'

Marcellus stared east. The great mountain, the Shield of Freedom, dominated the view. He said nothing for a moment, then, 'That is not for you to know.'

'I meant,' Rubin prevaricated, 'how will you leave

the City? There will be enemy soldiers everywhere. The Blues will have surrounded the palace before long, if they have not already.'

Marcellus grunted and shook his head. 'Hayden Weaver, the general of the Petrassi army, has no more than twenty thousand men. Twice that could not surround the palace.'

'So few?' Rubin was amazed.

'Resources on both sides have dwindled. A century ago we could field an army – just *one* army of many – of half a million. Now we can scrape together no more than a tenth of that in all. The destruction of the Maritime in the summer was a greater defeat than most people realize. It probably doomed the City.' Rubin had heard the surviving generals of the Maritime Army of the West had been crucified on Marcellus' orders. 'But in answer to your question,' the First Lord said, with something like relish, 'I will ride across the East Lake. Caravaggio will enjoy a swim.'

'It will be his last adventure,' Rubin said, echoing his lord's words on the Crags of Corenna.

'Indeed it will. And I could not leave the old boy here to be chopped up as food for the enemy.'

Rubin guessed now why they had come so far through the palace to this place – Caravaggio was no doubt saddled and waiting somewhere nearby. Though he had been urging his lord to flee the City he felt a pang of regret that he was about to do so.

Marcellus walked towards the door, idly kicking the discarded pile of blood-red armour as he passed, as if contemptuous of those who carried on fighting, and dying, for a lost cause.

'There is one thing you can do for me, Rubin,' he said.

'Name it, lord.'

'Do you know the lady Fiorentina?'

Rafael's wife was called Fiorentina, Rubin recalled. 'She is wed to your brother.'

'Yes, and she was sister to my lady Petalina.'

'Yes, lord,' Rubin replied, puzzled by the turn in the conversation.

'My brother also died today, defending the City. Fiorentina will have no one to protect her now all our troops are fighting for the palace. They have apartments in the Redoubt, in the north wing. Go, find her and conduct her to safety.'

'Yes, lord,' Rubin replied automatically. Rafael dead? He was finding it hard to take in the enormity of the day's disasters.

Marcellus added, 'Perhaps your father will give her sanctuary.' He smiled slightly.

'I'm sure he will, if you wish it, lord.' Rubin had no idea how he would find one woman, whom he had never met, in the immensity of the collapsing palace.

Marcellus' face became grave again and he gazed into Rubin's eyes. 'You will probably be told I am dead, that I was beheaded by a soldier of the City, but do not believe it.' He waited until Rubin nodded. 'There are many who want me dead, but I am hard to kill and I *will* return when the time is right. Believe it, boy.'

'I do, lord!'

'Stay safe, Rubin. Keep your head down and your opinions to yourself until I return. And above all . . .' he paused.

'Yes, lord?'

'Do not trust Archange.'

'Lord?' Rubin frowned. He had only heard that name on his father's lips. She was once the emperor's wife, he recalled, and she wanted him dead. Could she be behind today's catastrophes? An old woman?

'Stay away from her and, if you cannot do that, do not trust her. Do not trust her words or her actions. She is more dangerous than you can possibly imagine.'

With that Marcellus pulled open the door and stepped outside. Rubin hesitated, looking at the pile of armour. For one wild moment he thought of putting it on, pretending to be Marcellus, rallying the troops, saving the City. He chuckled at his foolishness, then followed his lord to the door. He looked out into the long corridor. He looked both ways.

Marcellus had gone.

Valla was drowning. Someone had a knee in her back and a hand on her head, holding her down in the muddy, bloody water on the floor of the chamber. She tried frantically to get her good arm under her, but she was held in an iron grip. Just as she felt life slipping away, her enemy grabbed a handful of her hair and pulled her head up – then rammed it back under the water again. Then the weight on her back suddenly vanished and she rolled over and sat up, expecting to see Leona. Instead she saw another familiar warrior slice the enemy's throat then nod to her, his face impassive. It was Loomis, Leona's aide. She managed to smile to him gratefully before he limped back into the melee.

It was a bloodbath in there, the last remaining warriors hacking and slashing at each other, most bearing wounds, all exhausted. A grey mist of blood and mud and water covered everyone and hung in the air, tangible, to be breathed in with gasping, desperate breaths. Valla looked among the fighters for Leona but it was hard to make out individuals. Then her gaze wandered to the piles of dead and dying. Her breathing shallowed and her heart stopped.

Leona lay on her side on a pile of bodies, eyes open, staring at the battle. Keeping her mind empty, Valla staggered over to her. As she came into her sight, her friend blinked. Valla cried out with relief. Then she saw the gaping wound in Leona's neck. It was gushing blood still, but she knew that wouldn't last. Leona moaned, then tried to say something. Valla bent down to listen. She felt a whisper of breath on her cheek.

'Go,' her commander breathed. 'Fight a new day.'

Careless of the fighting all around them, Valla sat back, taking her friend's hand and kissing it.

'I don't even know who I'm fighting for,' she said. Tears poured down her face, misting her sight.

Leona tried to swallow but blood spilled from her mouth. 'Marcellus,' she managed, 'is our . . . lodestar.'

Valla looked around at the chamber of death. Everyone was moving so slowly.

'Where is he?' she asked. 'Why isn't he here?'

It was a foolish question. Marcellus was fighting elsewhere. Who knew what was going on in other parts of the palace? But Valla was sure only Marcellus could save them this day.

'Valla,' Leona breathed, 'go.'

Valla brought her face to Leona's.

'But . . .' she said.

'Go.'

Then as Valla watched, the light and the life died in Leona's eyes.

Sobbing, she sat back, holding tightly to her friend's hand. There was no point running. She was wounded, though she had no idea where, for her whole body was in agony. *Just give me one more moment*, she thought, *and I'll—* She closed her eyes.

Something made her open them again. She looked across the blood-soaked chamber, past the slow-moving soldiers. Framed in the Crystal Gateway was the gulon. It sat neatly on its haunches and regarded the carnage, then it turned its glittering gaze on Valla and she felt the strength of its will. The two blood-covered creatures stared at one another, unblinking.

Valla kissed Leona goodbye then struggled to her feet and, limping and hurting, made her way across the chamber of death and followed the path of the gulon.

CHAPTER THIRTEEN

Rubin ran down his quarry eventually. Weary beyond words after half a day wandering the haunted palace, he had found his way to the Redoubt and stumbled through yet another doorway into a strange chamber. He stopped and looked around, unsure what he was seeing. The room was large, rectangular and very high. The lower half was tiled and the upper half boasted tall windows on three sides. Rubin was standing on a wide ledge dividing the two halves. He looked down. The floor was covered with metal artefacts: small statues, jewellery, pots and pans and a few weapons; some seemed new, most old and corrupted. And there were coins, thousands of coins. Over everything, water lay knee-deep. The atmosphere in the chamber was warm and damp, and the windows were misted and rimmed with creeping plant life.

So fascinated was he that it was a while before Rubin noticed the woman sitting motionless on the other side of the chamber, staring down into the water. He walked towards her but she seemed unaware of him. He stopped a few paces away. She did not look up so he cleared his throat, unwilling to startle her.

Slowly she turned her head. He had no doubt it was Fiorentina. She had a dark beauty which caught the breath, and her eyes were deep blue, the same colour as the rich gown she wore. Her feet were bare and dirty.

'Have you come to execute me?' she asked. Her face showed no fear. It showed nothing.

'No!' Rubin said. 'If you are the lady Fiorentina I have come to aid you.'

'You can barely stand,' she commented, looking him up and down as if he had just crawled out of a drain. 'How can you help me?'

He frowned. The conversation was not going the way he'd foreseen. 'Marcellus,' he said, once more wielding the name like a weapon, 'asked me to see you to safety.'

'Marcellus? What of my husband?'

'I don't know,' Rubin lied.

She shook her head forlornly. 'He is dead.'

'You know that, lady?'

'I feel it in my bones,' she replied, unknowingly echoing Marcellus.

Rubin had no words to reassure her. He looked around. 'What is this place?' he asked.

'It is called the Calderium,' she told him with a sigh. 'Until a while ago it was a deep pool of warm water. Then the water started leaking away. I've been watching it go down. There must be a crack in the floor.'

'What is it for?'

'For bathing. My husband would bathe here each day.'

'Why?'

'It was fed by a hot spring. The water was warm and was said to have healing powers.'

Rubin felt time at his back, urging him on. 'We must leave, lady. If the enemy takes the Red Palace you will be in peril.' He did not mention that the palace was collapsing and they were probably in more danger from that.

She held out her hand; he took it and she stood. She was as tall as him, even with bare feet. She stared at him, her face immobile, yet far from serene. He wondered what it would be like when she smiled.

'Do you know which way to go?' she asked.

'No, lady. I have never been in this part of the palace before.'

She resisted commenting on his abilities as a rescuer, but said, 'The Redoubt is only accessible through the palace or via the northern barracks gate.'

'The gate it is, then,' he said.

They walked through darkened halls, down corridors lit only by occasional torches. Fiorentina told him the Redoubt was once a fortress, thus there were no windows in the lower storeys. Far off they could hear discordant noise, the rhythmic stomp of marching soldiers, running feet and cries of fear and panic. Occasionally there would be a rumble deep below as if the earth was about to give way, and they would pause fearfully, not knowing which way to flee, until it quietened again. They passed small groups of frightened servants all heading the other way, towards the heart of the palace. Many of them eyed Fiorentina sideways, but none spoke and they neither sought nor offered aid. Rubin guessed she knew them all but the links between them of lady and servant had been severed. They were strangers now, and strangers always brought the risk of danger.

When they came to the north barracks gate there was no one there, the guards long gone. They both stared up at it, discouraged, and Rubin realized why everyone they had seen had been going the other way. The double gates, ancient and carved with cryptic runes, were wide and high and could only be shifted by the strength of many men.

'I have only ever seen them standing open,' Fiorentina said. 'We cannot move them.'

Rubin was gazing at them with interest, walking back and forth.

'They are counterbalanced,' he said at last. 'They are designed to be opened by just one or two men, once the bar is raised.' But the locking bar was a tree-trunk, stripped and polished, which spanned the entire width of the doors and rested in great brackets on massive stone posts. Rubin shoved his shoulder under one end and heaved with all his strength. The bar was unmoved.

'It would take twenty men to shift this,' he said. 'So,' he added with a cheerfulness he did not feel, 'we can either wait for twenty men to come along and hope they're friendly. Or we can go back.'

Without a word she turned and started back towards the palace, and he followed.

Inside, her soul was howling.

While her lips and teeth and breath, and a small part of her mind, occupied themselves with speaking with this strange young man – of the difficulty they were in, of the obstacles they might find, and the violence they might encounter – the rest of Fiorentina was shrivelling, dying, with loss and pain for her beloved.

She had no doubt Rafe was dead. She knew it as certainly as she knew that new life was nestled inside her. She did not hope; hope was unknown to her. There was not even the tiniest part of her consciousness that thought they might turn a corner, walk through a doorway, and he would come striding towards her, battered, bloody, but alive.

He had often told her she was prescient, and that belief was confirmed for him when she had avoided the gathering at the Little Opera House which turned into a bloodbath and killed her only sister. In fact she had been tired that evening, and a bit nauseous, not knowing then that she was with child. Her so-called prescience was just the ability to watch and listen and observe human beings and to weigh their actions in the past to judge their possible moves in the future. To her it was simple, laughably so. For all their lives together, more than forty years, she had watched and smiled as her sister Petalina was constantly startled by events, never expecting what to Fiorentina was as obvious as if it were written in black words on white paper.

She smiled, in loving memory. She saw Rubin was looking at her. He flushed a little. 'What are you thinking?' he asked.

She looked at him, pausing under the flickering light of a torch in a bracket, and she found her practical mind trying to reassert itself over the sorrow.

'Who are you?' she asked him. 'You are not a soldier though you have clearly suffered serious injury; you speak like a lord yet I have never met you before. You claim to know Marcellus but you are not one of his aides, or senior soldiers, or counsellors, for I know them all.'

'I have been away.' His eyes flicked away from her.

'And I have lived in the palace for more than twenty years. You are scarcely older than that.'

'My name is . . .' he hesitated as if it was something he was reluctant to give away. 'Rubin Kerr Guillaume.'

Guillaume was one of the seven noble Families. Fiorentina had met the Khans, brother and sister, and daughters of the Gaeta Family, but this was the first Guillaume she had encountered. She was interested in the Families and their chequered history, in spite of the fact that Rafe tried to discourage her interest, or perhaps because of it.

'Why do you—' she asked, but he put one finger to his lips.

She listened to the silence. 'What?' she asked. 'What can you hear?'

'Running water,' he said.

The sound was coming from up ahead, so they walked towards it, neither sure of what it signified. It was lighter here, as if they were coming to the end of a long tunnel, and as they hurried towards it, the light grew. Sunshine, thought Fiorentina. She remembered then that it was the Day of Summoning. *Was it really only this morning*, she thought, *when I last saw my lord?* Misery pinched at her heart.

The palace was a ruin here, and sunlight shone down through what had been the roof. Their path was blocked by piles of slates and timbers and stone. Dust was rising in clouds, as if the collapse had just happened. Rubin glanced at Fiorentina and she lifted her skirts and together they climbed over the debris. The floor had fallen in and there was a wide crack, as wide as a man could leap, partly spanned by roof debris.

They leaned forward to look over the edge. The sound of crashing waters rose from below, and with it a stench which caught in her throat.

'The sewers,' she said.

'The Halls,' Rubin said, with wonder.

She gazed at him, eyebrows raised, her hand over her mouth.

'The people in the sewers call them the Halls,' he explained.

'People live down there?'

He nodded absently, thinking. The debris shifted a little under their feet and Fiorentina stepped back quickly, but he just adjusted his balance.

'Why would they?'

'Live down there?'

'Yes.'

'Some have no choice. The City is a terrible place for many of its people.'

Something caught his attention and he leaned forward, listening.

'There's someone down there,' he said.

All she could hear was water, but she stepped up on the debris again and peered down. He was right, there were cries coming from the depths. Without hesitation Rubin scrambled part-way down into the hole, where he found a stone ledge, once part of the floor. He squinted downwards, then said, 'I think I can get down there.'

He seemed oblivious to the smell. Each time Fiorentina looked into the pit she was left gagging weakly. She stepped back, suddenly fearing the noxious fumes would harm her child.

'If you can climb down, then they can climb up,' she offered reasonably.

'Perhaps they are injured.'

'Rubin,' she told him, 'remember your mission. You are to help me to safety, not be diverted by some hopeless task.'

He thought about it for a moment, then scrambled back to her side.

'We need a rope,' he said, looking around as if expecting to find a coil to hand.

Fiorentina sighed, then helped him search. But there was no rope to be found and they could waste no more time, so Rubin crawled down into the shaft again, willingly launching himself through a portal into a place he associated only with suffering and death.

The hole in the ground was negotiable, just. Where it was steep it was also narrow, so Rubin could span it with his lanky legs and arms and crawl down like a four-limbed spider. Where it widened out it shelved into precarious and crumbling perches. Thus he made his way into darkness, peering up from time to time, seeing Fiorentina's head framed in the diminishing light.

The familiar smell became thicker as he descended. It was not like water or air. It was solid, as if you should be able to cut a hole in it to get relief. But there was no relief to be had and his thoughts darkened and he began to doubt he would ever get out again. Then he came to the rushing water and in the dim light filtering from above found four people marooned on a precarious perch above a swift river. They were two small children, a young woman and an older man. The children looked beyond fear, their faces white and drawn, eyes half-closed against the thin light. The woman's wrist was bent at an unnatural angle and she held it gingerly, her face racked with pain.

Rubin looked up at the distant sunlight, weighing his own resources, then said to the bigger child, 'You first.'

Guiding the boy's foot- and hand-holds, and pushing from below, Rubin managed to get him up the shaft into Fiorentina's waiting hands.

'How many?' she asked him as she dragged the boy to safety.

'Three more,' he replied, lowering himself back down.

The other child, a girl, was too small and too frightened to climb. Rubin squatted beside her on the narrow refuge but she squirmed away, trying to hide behind the woman's skirts. The water, he saw with alarm, was creeping higher by the moment. He felt his strength leaching away as quickly.

'There's sunlight up there,' he told the girl. 'I'll carry you up there, if you'll help me. Don't be frightened.' But the child hid her face and whimpered with terror.

'She's never seen the sun, sir,' the woman told him. 'It's *that* she's frightened of, not you.'

But she persuaded the child to climb on Rubin's back, her eyes squeezed shut. Fearing each moment that her small weight would topple him to certain death, he managed to struggle to the surface with her.

The woman, hardly more than a girl herself, was half-swooning with the anguish of her injured arm, but Rubin used his overshirt to make a sling and, when she felt able, he half-pushed, half-carried her up the crumbling side of the pit. At the top she slumped to the ground sobbing.

Without allowing himself to think, Rubin scrambled down for the final time.

The last survivor, a big brawny man with wild ginger hair in braids, had been watching silently throughout. Now he declared, 'You should not have come back, laddie. My ankle's banjaxed. I cannot climb and you're not strong enough to carry me.'

'We can try.'

'I'll not risk throwing you into the river after your valiant actions.'

Rubin sat down gratefully on the ledge and the big man sat beside him. His ankle was badly broken, canted to one side. It should have been agonizing yet the man seemed at peace.

'What will you do?' Rubin asked him.

The man pointed to a dark recess in the rock wall. 'We came through there. I will return that way.'

Rubin doubted the big man could squeeze through such a narrow opening but he nodded. 'I will throw a torch down to you,' he said.

The man nodded, but both knew it would make little difference.

The wide river, fast and lively as an animal, now rushed past just beneath their feet. Rubin looked around but in the gloom he could see little.

'They call it the Halls, laddie,' the big man offered,

watching his gaze. 'Only the poor and desperate come down here.'

'I know the Halls. But I have never seen a river like this.'

'It is the great Menander,' the man told him with satisfaction. 'For centuries it has been hidden and confined, always seeking to break out from under layers of stone. Now it has burst its restraints. There must have been a great storm up above.'

'There was indeed.' A storm of sorts, Rubin thought. 'The Red Palace is collapsing into ruin.'

'Good.' The man's freckled face lit up. 'Who builds a palace on top of a river?' he asked scornfully. 'The poor fools.'

Rubin asked him, 'Do you have family, sir? Anyone I can tell?'

'No, lad. Don't worry about me. I'll get out.' He seemed unconcerned despite the pain he must have been suffering.

There was a high-pitched cry from above and the man said to him, 'You'd best be getting back up there. Your sweetheart is calling.'

Rubin stood. He did not know how to say goodbye so he said nothing, merely nodded and started the climb back towards the light. His legs were shaking with effort, his hands numb and bruised. And his heart was filled with sorrow. He glanced down once and saw the pale blur of the man's face looking up at him. But when he looked again moments later the man had gone and all he could see was racing water.

Regaining the surface, he gathered his breath for a moment, then picked up the little girl, took the boy's hand in his and, with Fiorentina supporting the young woman, they all headed east through the broken palace, for Rubin was eager to put as much distance as possible between them and the battling armies at its heart.

It was nearly twilight by the time they reached the eastern walls. The palace appeared undamaged here; there was no evidence of flood or subsidence. The corridors and chambers were empty and silent but dust moved in the air as if recently disturbed. They came to high gates but, like the ones at the Redoubt, they were barred. Wearily Rubin looked around then led them through the nearest doorway. Across a courtyard and down some steps he found a small room with narrow beds, perhaps servants' quarters. There was no one there. As the others sank gratefully on to the beds, Rubin searched further and found kitchens and a pump. He filled a jug with clean water and they all drank their fill then lay down.

For all his exhaustion, Rubin could not sleep, the plight of the ginger-haired man gnawing at him. Getting up again and exploring further, he discovered an elegant stairway leading up to a large chamber filled with carved furniture. It was empty, abandoned, like most of the palace they had journeyed through that day. Wide windows looked east and the Shield of Freedom was a black bulk against the darkening sky. Small lights twinkled welcomingly on its heights and as night closed in the mountain looked like a place of serenity and safety.

'We should go there,' Fiorentina said from behind him.

Rubin turned. Even after their gruelling day of fear and flight, her beauty was transcendent. With dirty smudges on her cheeks and eyes red with fatigue, she still looked like a goddess.

'I was thinking that,' he agreed. 'But the City is perilous. It will be a hard journey.'

She surprised him by suggesting, 'We could go underground. There are tunnels leading all the way to the Shield. With a good map you can get from palace to mountain and never see the sun. Or so my husband once told me.' Her eyes brimmed with unshed tears.

Rubin shook his head. 'The underground ways will be flooded and broken. You've had a taste of what it's like.'

'We need sanctuary, both of us, now the Vincerii are . . . gone,' she said sadly.

'Marcellus still lives,' he answered.

She stared at him with huge, shining eyes. 'Are you certain?'

'No,' he replied, thinking of an old horse swimming across a lake. 'But it is my hope, and my belief.'

She shook her head. 'Our only hope is to throw ourselves on Archange's mercy.'

'Archange?' He frowned, remembering Marcellus' words, that he must avoid the woman at all costs. 'Why Archange?'

'Because she will be empress now.'

CHAPTER FOURTEEN

TEN DAYS PASSED AND A WINTRY SUN SHONE benevolently on the drying, dying City. The water slowly subsided, leaving the remaining buildings and the many corpses under a thin glaze of mud, leaching down through the re-formed strata under the City, carrying its freight of bodies out to the cleansing sea.

Far off the coast, beyond the enemy's blockade of ships, beyond the little island of Tessera, lay a small boat, ostensibly a fishing boat, and before dawn on the eleventh day an old woman sat in the prow watching the east.

Low in the sky the moon was full and round as a ripe white peach. *How long is it since I've seen a peach?* the woman wondered. *Smelled a peach, eaten a peach?* She tried to summon the taste of one, and could recall the soft, furry skin, the slight give as you bit through it, the gush of juice in the mouth. But, try as she would, she could not remember the taste of the fruit.

The silvery moon created a pathway of light to the boat and she imagined she could climb over the gunwales, walk across the sea and climb the stairway . . .

'Lady, it's time.'

Giulia Rae Khan started from her reverie then groaned under her breath. Her body had stiffened, sitting for hours on the wooden chair lashed to the deck for her use. She levered herself to standing, feeling the familiar pain bite into her hands. The boat's captain was looking at her expectantly.

'Very well, Lorens,' she told him. He spoke quietly to his crew.

They had been waiting off the coast for the pre-dawn, when it would be light enough for Lorens to navigate the treacherous waters to the south of the City, but still dark enough to sail unnoticed by the great ships of the enemy blockade. That was the plan, any-way. Giulia stared towards the fleet, peering, but she could see nothing apart from the great bulk of velvet black which was the land against the moonlit sky.

She brushed down her grimy peasant dress, and watched the crew go swiftly about their tasks, hauling on lines, getting the fishing boat ready for the final leg of their voyage. The black sail unfurled and the small breeze caught in it, billowing it out, and the *Linnet* moved through the water, heading south-east.

Giulia had been travelling for almost a year, first round the islands to the west, then ever on, seeking allies for the City's fight against its enemies. She had been given only empty promises and trinkets presented as great gifts.

Then, early in the year, empty-handed and close to giving up, they had turned the *Linnet* due north, to latitudes unknown to most seamen. They passed the Land of Mists, the haunt of demons and dragons, it was said, and men with two heads and women with tails for legs, where even stout sailors like Lorens would only tread under Giulia's orders. And they came to a land of snow and ice, of harsh mountains rising steeply from narrow bays of the brightest blue. They arrived in late spring and were warmly welcomed by the old leader, who called himself a king but whose kingdom was just his grim fastness carved from granite and flanked by waterfalls, and thousands of leagues of frozen tundra, the haunt of silver bears and ice foxes.

The king, called Kern, had greeted them as old friends and they spent the shortening nights in his hall, honoured guests, offered the best of the meats at table and the plumpest maidens to warm their beds. Giulia found the old man starved of company and she entertained him with tales of their travels and of the City. As the nights started to lengthen again he asked her to stay, to become his queen. Queen, she thought contemptuously, of a thousand leagues of nothing; then she remembered the City as she had last seen it, alone in a self-made desert. She was a little tempted to stay, for the land was beautiful. The high grey mountains rang with the sound of running water in the spring as the snow-melt poured off in misty waterfalls, the rivers heaved with shining fish, the green hillsides echoed with the chatter of birds. But in winter her hands were a torment to her and the prospect of long days of ice made her yearn to be back in the warmth of the City, her City.

So she had thanked the old king and told him no and he had nodded sadly and bemoaned the fact that he was no longer virile and could not give her strong sons.

Long afterwards, when she was telling her brother about this, Marcus had guffawed and said, 'He thought a bony old thing like you could still bear children?'

A little annoyed, she asked him, 'Is my hair not lustrous, is my skin not as smooth as when I was thirty?'

'Yes, my love,' he confessed, 'but your poor hands are those of a crone.'

The arthritis pained her in summer and was an agony in winter, and all their long-hoarded medicine could do little to aid her. She wondered, not for the first time, what would become of her in the long years ahead and was comforted by the pact she and Marcus had made to end the other's suffering when it came to it.

'A nice, clean beheading,' he said, with gruesome jollity, 'that'll cure anything.'

So the men of the *Linnet* had prepared to set sail for the south. Then, before they left, the old king surprised Giulia by presenting her with three chests full of gold coins, mined, he said, in the ice mountains to the east.

'Then,' she replied, 'you are as wealthy as you are generous.'

'Ay, we are a rich people,' replied Kern. 'We have plenty of gold, but it is useless to us for we have nothing to spend it on.' He laughed and Giulia thought how much she liked the old man.

'It is a handsome gift,' she said.

'It is not a gift,' Kern replied sternly. 'It is payment. We need horses. You have told me of the herds of young horses reared each year in your meadows. This will pay for three ships full of the animals.'

Now the gold lay in the depths of the fishing boat, under a shining blanket of silvery sea bream which would argue their innocence if they were stopped by the enemy. It would be enough to pay her brother's mercenaries for a year longer. Enough, perhaps, to end the City's siege.

If they could run the blockade.

The Blues' blockade tactics varied, according to who was in charge of the fleet, and who captain of each ship. Sometimes they would let a single fishing boat sail by, unbothered by a few fishermen catching food for their table. Sometimes they would stop and board, and search the boat for reasons of received intelligence, or boredom, or whim. And occasionally they would stop and board, and kill everyone and throw them to the sea gods. The ten men on the *Linnet* were aged from sixteen to sixty and could pass for an extended fishing family, with Giulia as their matriarch. But in fact they were all soldiers faithful to Marcus Rae Khan, tough as boots, and they would all die hard before losing the gold or before any harm came to their lady.

A low whistle came from the bow. One of the men, with the eagle eyes of youth, had spotted the fleet. Giulia peered again. She could see nothing. But if she could not see the enemy ships, they certainly could not see her boat, dark on a dark sea. For a while Giulia forgot about the arthritis in her hands and hips as she felt the cool breeze comb through her hair. She sniffed the dark night. She thought she could smell the City, the City of blood she loved and hated, where her brother would be waiting impatiently for her, wondering what treasures, what words, she had brought him. She would be with him soon, with luck.

Lorens said quietly, 'Tessera.'

She knew what he meant. The isle of Tessera was in sight. They had discussed this morning's tactics during the night. They had the choice of going round the island on the far side from the fleet, which would be a longer voyage but safer. Or squeezing between it and the blockade ships, hidden from the enemy by its dark bulk. Giulia nodded to her captain, confirming her decision to take the shorter route. It was the more dangerous course, but if they were spotted, Tessera would possibly offer sanctuary.

The little boat was flying like its namesake and Giulia could dimly see the white wash of the wake on the starboard side where she stood. She wondered if there were dolphins, cutting through the water, leaping and diving, keeping up with the boat. But if there were it was still too dark to see their grey shapes. She would miss them, the dolphins, for she had become used to this travelling life, away from the blood and death of the war, and the petty politicking and power struggles of the generals.

The light grew around them and the shapes of the great ships became clear even to her eyes. Then a sailor called out, 'They're launching boats!'

'Have they seen us?' she asked the captain.

'Impossible.'

Then we have been betrayed, Giulia thought, watching the little isle of Tessera growing, too slowly, on their starboard side. *But perhaps the launch of the boats is just a coincidence; they have been waiting for dawn too, but for some undertaking we know nothing of.*

That hope was dashed as the fast galleys arrowed directly to intercept their path.

Giulia leaned over the side. 'Is the water shallow here?' she asked Lorens.

'Yes, lady, we are above a rock shelf.'

She looked to the advancing galleys, the rowers leaning into their oars.

'Will they ram us?'

'I would.'

'Then prepare to scuttle.'

'Lady?' He frowned.

'Our most important mission is to keep the gold safe. If we are rammed we can open the planks and sink the *Linnet*. They will think the vessel is foundering because of their actions. We can come back at a later time and retrieve the gold, with luck.'

'And if they kill us all? Who will retrieve it then?'

'If our coming has been betrayed, they know I'm aboard. They will take me for ransom, as sister of the City's greatest general. I will get word of the gold to my brother somehow.'

'Lady Giulia, we will give our lives to stop you being captured,' the captain argued.

'I know, my friend. But that is foolishness. If I am taken you must survive and swim to the island. They will leave you alone then, a few stray sailors, not worth the trouble of hunting down.'

'General Marcus will have my balls for breakfast.'

She smiled. 'One problem at a time, Lorens.'

The advancing vessels were closing in on them at speed. It seemed one would ram the *Linnet* amidships, the other cut across her path. Lorens ordered his men to retrim the sails and he turned the tiller towards Tessera and shallower water. But the two chasing vessels merely adjusted their course and continued towards them. Giulia could see the ram on the prow of the closest boat, painted red and carved like a fist. Then suddenly, thirty paces or more from the *Linnet*, they slowed.

'What are they doing?' Giulia asked.

Lorens shook his head. 'Perhaps the fleet's surrendering to us,' he said with dry humour.

A man stepped up to the prow of the closest boat, which was coasting slowly towards them, the oars held high. He shouted across the water, 'Lady Giulia, I have a message from your brother!'

Giulia thought for a moment. They were standing off to show good faith. And she could see no advantage to be gained by pretending to have a message from Marcus. Yet they were Blueskins. They were the enemy.

'They did come from the enemy fleet?' she asked Lorens, uncertain now in her failing memory, still wondering if this was a ploy and what it could achieve.

He nodded. 'Undoubtedly, lady.'

A message from her brother via enemy hands? Her immediate thought was *What trouble has Marcus got himself into now?* But she stood straight and called out, 'Very well.'

The oarsmen eased the enemy boat forward until the man on the prow could pass a package to a sailor on the *Linnet*. It was handed on to Giulia and she awkwardly unrolled the waterproof covering to see Marcus' familiar slovenly penmanship, drips of black ink crawling down the paper. Her heart caught in her throat. How she missed him.

The message said: *Sister mine. The war is over. Trust this man Tyler. He will see you safely home.*

The man on the prow, dark-skinned and smartly clad in a Petrassi uniform, bowed his head courteously. 'I am Tyler, lady,' he told her. 'Will you be our honoured guest?'

The Seagate was in the far south of the City where the high cliffs which formed the Salient descended sharply to the sea. The huge, unnatural harbour had been dug out in the reign of the emperor Sarkoy II using the sweat and blood of tens of thousands of labourers in times when lives were easy to come by and inexpensive. It was a magnificent structure, its high walls faced with pink marble carved with sea creatures both real and imagined, and topped with statues of the seven lordly beasts. But only a few years after it was completed an earthquake off the coast caused a tidal wave which swept away part of the walls and left the harbour filled with debris. It was rebuilt, but on a less grand scale, and in the following centuries engineers fought a constant battle against the sand and shingle which tides and currents brought into the harbour. In a bid to propitiate the gods, twin temples to the deities of winds and waves were built on the harbour arms, and sacrifices made to them. But the harbour continued to fill, and the deprivations of the endless war, sucking labourers to the battlefields to shed their blood there, meant it was largely abandoned, limited as it was to a single channel through the sandbanks.

When Giulia stepped out of the Blues' galley on to her homeland she was tempted to get down on her knees and kiss the stones beneath her feet. Rather she lifted her skirts like a girl and hastened up the steps to the top of the harbour wall from where she could see the City. It lay luminous and misty in the morning light. A pain seized her heart and tears filled her eyes. She squinted but the mist hid the distant Shield from her sight. At first she thought the City unchanged, though the Wester quarter below her looked strangely quiet. Then she looked to her left, to the familiar outline of the Red Palace, and was shocked to see it much reduced, its myriad towers, cupolas and domes blunted and broken or gone altogether.

'What has happened here?' she asked Tyler. 'What has done this?'

'We destroyed the dams, unleashing your two southern reservoirs,' he told her, stone-faced. 'The flood destroyed the eastern end of the Adamantine Wall. Much of the south-east of the City was badly damaged. When the last of the flood reached the Red Palace the water poured into the lowest levels, crumbling the already weak foundations. It is largely uninhabitable now. Only rats live there.'

She looked at Tyler's calm face, trying to absorb the enormity of what he was telling her. 'What of the emperor?'

Tyler looked around them, then walked a few steps away from the gathered warriors. 'He is dead, lady.'

'You murdered Araeon?' she cried. The thought was incomprehensible and her mind stumbled around it, trying to find a way to approach it.

'Your emperor was killed by a City warrior,' Tyler told her.

'Unspeakable! By one of the Thousand?'

'No. A common soldier, I'm told.'

Araeon murdered by a soldier of the City. She shook her head. 'I don't believe you,' she snapped.

'Nevertheless, it is true.'

Giulia's legs felt unsteady. If she had been alone she would have sat down gratefully, but she could not show weakness in front of this enemy.

'Araeon was a great man,' she declared.

Tyler sniffed. 'Getting killed was the greatest thing he ever did, lady.'

Anger sparked in her and she said, 'You seem like a civilized enough man for a soldier of Petrus – do not ever speak to me like that again.' He bowed his head a fraction.

She made a deliberate decision to think about Araeon later, when she had spoken to Marcus. 'My brother lives?' she asked, still needing the reassurance.

'Yes, lady. He is waiting for you.'

'Have the Blues captured the entire City?' she asked. She was having trouble getting her thoughts in order.

'No. Only the southern part. There is a peace treaty in place and we have agreed to restrict our troops to the south. There is much for you to learn, lady. A great deal has happened in recent days. I have been asked to take you to the Khan Palace where you will have answers to all your questions. I have ordered a carriage.'

She followed his gaze, down the outer steps of the harbour wall to where a coach and four waited. She snorted derisively. 'It will take days to get to the Shield in that thing, considering the ruin you have made of the City. I will ride. Bring me a mount.'

Tyler raised an eyebrow, but he called out orders in his own tongue and a horse was brought to meet them at the bottom of the harbour steps. Giulia frowned when she saw it was a gentle mare with quiet eyes, but she said nothing and accepted a soldier's help to mount. She kicked the beast into a fast trot. It was a long time since she had been in the saddle, but she knew she was a far more experienced rider than most of the young Petrassi troopers flanking her.

The ride was a torment. Giulia had known the City for longer than most, and she had walked its streets and alleys and squares for all that time, over generations of ordinary mortals. But she found it hard to recognize parts of it as they rode past. Everything was covered in a veil of dried dust – the buildings, the trees bordering the wide avenues of Amphitheatre, the debris in the streets. The few living people they saw peered from the shelter of ruined homes, fearing no doubt that death still awaited them at the hands of the invaders.

She broke her resolve on silence to ask Tyler, 'How many died?'

He shook his head. 'I've no idea.'

She felt her blood pressure soar but forced herself to be calm. This man was just a soldier, following orders. She would ask him no more questions. It would achieve nothing and only infuriate her.

It took them all day to reach the Shield but eventually the old Khan Palace came in sight on the western side of the mountain, surrounded by venerable pines and flanked by the White Palace of the Vincerii above and the black Iron Palace of the Gaetas beneath.

To her surprise she saw a troop of City cavalry awaiting her at the bronze-gated entrance to the mountain. *The Third Imperial, still at liberty? What sort of invasion is this?* she wondered.

'I will leave you here,' Tyler said and, before she could open her mouth, he wheeled his mount and the Petrassi party took off.

Giulia called briskly to the waiting escort, 'I do not need you! You are dismissed!' She walked her mount through the gates and on to the white Shell Path which meandered lazily up the Shield, linking the Family palaces. She held her head high as she rode, enjoying the pungent smell of the pines shading the path. The air smelled fresh, like rain.

She passed the Iron Palace and wondered if Sciorra Gaeta still lived. The last she had heard, the old woman was mired in madness, her brain ageing long before her body. At least, Giulia thought gratefully, I have my wits.

Riding higher she came to the first sharp curve of the path, where the Shrine of the First stood on a small outcrop looking west, the direction of last things. It was a plain titanium plaque embedded in a material which had once been transparent but which had weathered over the centuries so its words could no longer be discerned. Not that the language could ever be read by any but a handful of people. Giulia reined in the mare and paused, remembering those who had died. She could not recall their faces, or indeed most of their names, but it had been a long time and she knew they would forgive her. For the ones who had died had been the best of them.

But she could remember the words. She knew that when she lay on her deathbed, when she had forgotten everything, perhaps even her own name, she would remember them: *We came to bring knowledge and peace. May your gods look kindly on us for our transgressions.*

At last the horse clopped noisily across the golden stones of the Khan Palace courtyard, the sound echoing off the walls. Giulia looked around. She was greeted only by stillness, by silence. Then suddenly there was an explosion of servants from doorways on every side. One ran over and held the mare's reins while another carried the wooden block for Giulia to dismount. More servants – familiar faces – brought cool water in a pitcher filled with sliced limes, while another proffered a crystal goblet on a silver tray. Maids brought soft slippers for her feet and moist cloths to cool her brow and clean her hands. This welter of obsequiousness both amused and comforted her, for in the past year she had become used to self-denial and the grudging welcome of strangers.

Then, a sight for her old eyes, across the courtyard shambled her brother, his arms open, his face wreathed in smiles. He looked, as he always did, as though he had dressed in the dark, and tears sprang to her eyes.

He flung his arms around her and wrapped her in a bear-hug which threatened to break her spine.

'Get off me, you old fool,' she said, laughing.

Then, remembering the day's grave news, she asked him quietly, 'Araeon is truly dead?'

Marcus frowned and shook his head. *Not in front of the servants*. They walked hand in hand, as they had done since they were children, into the palace and along familiar corridors. Without speaking they found their way to their favourite parlour. Giulia felt her heart ease to see it again, with its trophies of war and peace and lives lived to the fullest, her old rugs on the floor, worn and wearied by time.

'He is dead?' she asked again once they were alone.

'He is.'

She narrowed her eyes. 'Are you sure?'

Marcus snorted. 'Araeon abandoned subtlety many generations ago. No, he has not gone to ground, is not lying in wait to see what the rest of us will do. He is dead. There is no doubt.'

'When did this happen?'

'On the Day of Summoning.'

'Then who is emperor?' she asked, the question which had been on her mind since she received his message. Her brother, she feared, would never put himself forward. *I'm just an old soldier*, he'd say. 'Marcellus, I suppose?'

'Marcellus also died,' a voice said, and Giulia turned to see a woman framed in the light from the doorway. For a heartbeat she was angered. Fiorentina? What was *she* doing here? It was the strongest indication of how her world had changed, for she would never have allowed the sister of the whore Petalina to set foot in their home. Then the words entered her consciousness and her breath stopped. Giulia clutched her chest, pierced through the heart. Marcellus dead? She sank to the floor. No, it was not possible. Memories fluttered through her mind, too many, too rich for an old woman.

Fiorentina came forward, knelt and took her hand. 'I'm sorry, lady,' she said. 'That was cruel of me. I know you were once wed to him.'

'It's all right, my dear,' Giulia lied. She tried to breathe deeply but her chest was too tight. She was surprised that word of his death had hit her so hard. There had been, after all, many times when she'd wanted to kill him herself. 'That was all long ago,' she told the girl.

Then she realized that if Marcellus was dead then Rafe, his reflection, must also be. She added politely, 'You have lost your husband too. How sad.'

'You heard, lady? Both brothers killed on the same day. What a terrible day for the City.'

Giulia's head cleared a little. *What a curious thing to say*, she thought. She looked up at Marcus' anxious face, a question in her eyes. *Does she not know?* Her brother shook his head slightly. It seemed incredible to Giulia that Fiorentina, ten years married, now widowed, should not know she had been wed to a reflection, a creature that was no more than a walking corpse.

She tried to marshal her thoughts. Araeon and Marcellus both dead.

'Then who is emperor?' she asked again. She looked at Marcus, who avoided her eyes, then at Fiorentina.

With a spasm of fury, she realized what they were going to say.

PART THREE

The Vorago

CHAPTER FIFTEEN

THE EARTHWORM WAS THIN AND WRIGGLY IN THE palm of her hand. Its blunt eyeless head quested upwards towards the blue sky then down again, trying to nose between Emly's closed fingers to find the cool earth it had been snatched from. She carefully placed it out of harm's way on a recently turned piece of soil, and marvelled at the speed with which it disappeared back into its underground home.

She dug her hands into the black loam. It crumbled like moist cake, disclosing smaller worms and scuttling beetles and a long, running creature with a score of legs. It was fertile soil, Archange had told her, brought to this garden at the White Palace, on the Shield of Freedom, at great expense from somewhere in the south. Emly sniffed it. It smelled like winter fires.

She dropped the handful and brushed off the dirt clinging to her hands. She sat back on her heels and looked around with pleasure. The garden was beautiful now the summer was almost here. Roses were awash with fat buds, both the well-mannered, pruned bushes and the uncouth climbers which rioted over the flint walls and scrambled up more stately plants. There were other flowers too, ones she had planted herself, ones she had no names for but which she called blue sticks and yellow cushions and pink dancers. The air was sweet and thick with bees.

Emly and her brother Elija had been brought to the empress's mountain-top palace more than half a year before, with the City collapsing around them. As children they had been saved from a wretched life in the sewers of the City, Em by the old man Bartellus and Elija by the enemy, and they were reunited, against all hope, on the Day of Summoning, the pivotal day in the history of the City when the tyrannical emperor was killed and his stronghold, the Red Palace, destroyed by flood. Archange, who had allied with the Petrassi general to end the war, had now been empress for nearly two hundred days.

The brother and sister had spent the first weeks there huddled together, reluctant to be parted, sharing tales of their eight years apart while Elija's broken arm mended. Then, while he started exploring the library's trove of books, Emly had set out to discover the bounds of the palace.

The White Palace, which Archange called the Serafia, was built of white marble and creamy alabaster. The halls were lofty and light, the windows reaching for the sky in elegant arches. Its spaces were bare and echoing, for the only people living there were Archange's household staff and a century of soldiers, the Nighthawks.

The contrast with the Red Palace was complete. That ruined building, far to the west, with its dark, carved walls and blood-red floors, had drawn you ever down towards the waiting waters in the lower depths. The Serafia's high vaulted rooms, white walls and soaring windows always reached for the clouds. Even the kitchens and barracks, on lower levels, were light. Nothing was cramped or confined.

'Why did you abandon it?' Emly had asked Archange

one day as they sat in the old woman's summer parlour, a round room decorated with filigreed marble and inlaid flowers of carnelian and lapis lazuli.

'We did not abandon it,' the empress replied in her contrary way. 'We just stopped coming here.'

Emly had walked the corridors, up and down stairs, in and out of high doorways until she had grasped the geography of the White Palace and felt at home. It was small compared with the vast ruin she had escaped from, but it was built on many levels. There were hundreds, perhaps thousands of steps, running inside and out, connecting all the floors and fragile towers, the fairy bridges and balconies and terraces. There was no rhythm to the place that Em could detect; nothing she saw on one floor gave a clue as to what was on the floor below, or that above. It seemed a folly, built by a madman – or perhaps for one.

Then Emly found the garden. It was on the south-west side, protected from Cernunnos the north wind by the palace walls and by a grey ridge of rock which stuck out to the west. It was a meandering patch of long grass surrounded by what had once been rose beds but which had become choked by weeds. So in the grey light of early spring Emly had set about cutting down brambles, revealing struggling roses and other plants which had been fighting to survive unseen. She had asked permission to roam the Shield and the untended gardens of the other Family palaces to seek new plants. She revelled in the quiet of these gardens, unkempt and rustling with wildlife, and the great buildings with their doors and windows locked, barred and bolted against intruders. She discovered huge glasshouses, their windows all smashed, foundering beneath the weight of scrambling weeds and ivy, and wondered what they were for.

Emly stood and rubbed her hands again and walked

to the edge of the garden. On one side was a low wall, built of flints. She picked up her skirts and stepped over it, then up a short rise to where a seat had been carved into the rock wall.

She looked down on the City spread out before her. The Red Palace was a jumble of broken rock from this distance, with only the odd robust tower still standing. A river, the Menander, ran through the ruin now, flowing freely in a deep muddy channel where once had been the sewers where she and her brother lived. She turned her gaze south, where the damage was the greatest, where the flood, caused by the enemy's forces breaking the dams of the two high reservoirs, had pulverized the great walls and brought death and destruction. Here large tents had been erected, succeeded in time by wooden buildings, to house the injured: enemy and City, soldiery and hapless citizenry. These hospitals had been a source of friction between City folk and the Blueskin soldiers and there had been much blood shed over them.

With interest Emly had watched over the past days the muster of an army led by Marcus Rae Khan, now the City's premier general. Tens of thousands of men and women and horses and carts and livestock had gathered to march north to Petrus in accordance with Archange's peace agreement with the Petrassi general Hayden Weaver, to support his people's war against the northern barbarians who had flooded his country while his armies were away fighting the City. General Weaver had sent the Petrassi army back north twenty days before. The Khan army's exodus had been delayed, then delayed again. But now it had departed. The only enemy troops still left in the City were the wounded and the soldiers charged with guarding them.

From her vantage-point Emly could see nothing to report to Elija, who was not interested anyway, and she turned and climbed back over the flint wall. Then she stopped, in shock, for walking across the garden towards her, the sun at his back, was a soldier. Evan!

Yet even in that wonderful heart-soaring moment she saw the man was not Evan Broglanh at all, but another. She and her lover had not been together since before the Day of Summoning. Em saw him all the time in the palace, for he was constantly in attendance on Archange, but although they spoke occasionally it was never of private matters. She had been forced to the conclusion that he would not feature in her future, yet her heart still yearned for him.

This soldier, a discordant figure in the gentle garden in his black and silver armour, was Darius, commander of the Nighthawks, the empress's bodyguard. He was like Evan in that he was tall with light-coloured hair, but Darius was younger, his hair redder, the planes of his face harder, his eyes a brilliant blue.

She smiled, so he would not see she was disappointed.

'You're wanted in the throne room,' he told her, brief and to the point as always.

She nodded and fell into step with him as they walked back. She had nothing to say to him, nor he to her, so she was surprised when he asked, 'Are you well?'

Emly looked up and nodded again. She was still nervous of soldiers, but this man had saved her life, and that of her father Bartellus, on the Day of Summoning and she would always be grateful to him. She wondered why such an important soldier, a hero and military adviser to the empress, should be sent to summon her like a servant – or a lowly grunt, as Evan would say. Darius strode quickly and Em, who barely came up to his armoured shoulder, had to run a little to keep up with him.

The throne room was at the centre of the palace, a

light circular space under an immense dome of glass. The glass was stained with bright colours which on a sunny day sparkled in brilliant dots of blue and green and gold on the stone floor beneath. On a normal day Em would stand entranced by this wonderful demonstration of the stained-glass artist's skill. But today was not a normal day, for the chamber was crowded and Emly paused on the threshold, biting her lip. Present were many warriors – most of Darius' Nighthawks and palace guards – along with Archange's ever-hovering counsellors and servants, and other civilians unfamiliar to her. A huge warrior stood to one side with a broadsword unsheathed, something she had never before seen in the empress's presence.

Emly hated throngs of people. In her experience of the world, nothing good had ever come of them. Her happiest times had been alone with her brother, or with her father Bartellus, or Evan Broglanh. Crowds she associated with fear and flight and blood and death. She licked her lips anxiously and sought Evan's face, but he was not there.

Archange was seated on her throne, a great slab of alabaster, sumptuously cushioned in red and gold and silver. The empress, tall and stately though she was, looked tiny on it and Emly wondered why she used the throne when it diminished her. Unsmiling, Archange beckoned her forward. She looked tired, Em thought, her face more gaunt than she had seen it, her dark eyes dull.

All faces turned towards Emly as she walked across the wide floor chequered in black and white marble, her heart fluttering, her mouth dry. What were all these people here for? There was a metallic smell in the air, the odour of blood and death.

Dol Salida, Archange's first counsellor, limped forward with the aid of his silver-topped stick. As the company fell silent, he said, 'Each of us here remembers clearly the terrible events of the Day of Summoning.' He paused, stroking his wide white moustache, as if in deep thought. 'That we survived and now live at peace under the benevolent reign of our empress is due to one man. The hero Shuskara welded the loyal forces of the City together to battle for our lives and our future. Sadly he was killed, giving his life for the City he served, and we all mourn him and are indebted to him for his sacrifice.'

He paused again and gestured to the guards on the north door. The entire company swung to watch as a ragged, badly injured man was dragged in between two soldiers.

Em had seen some terribly wounded people in the days of the City's liberation, but perhaps she had since become softened, for she brought her hand to her mouth in shock. The man's face was distorted, his jaw broken and his one eye closed shut with blood. The other eye was concealed by a dirt-encrusted patch. He could not walk. Perhaps his legs were broken too for the soldiers had to hold him up. He wheezed painfully through an injured chest. He was filthy and clotted blood covered his tattered clothes.

He was dragged in front of Emly and held by the guards. She watched him with horror then looked to Archange. *Why are you showing me this poor man?*

Dol Salida went on: 'What many of you do not know is that there was an attempt on the life of General Shuskara in the summer before, an assassination bid which very nearly succeeded.'

He turned to Emly. 'Lady Emly. Is this the man,' he asked her, raising his voice and looking around at the assembly, 'who attempted to kill you and the hero Shuskara?'

This is a trial, Emly thought bleakly. She looked at

the prisoner before her and he managed to open his one eye. His pain-racked gaze hovered uncertainly on the people around him, then veered about as if he had no control over it. Em frowned, remembering the day she had tried to forget. Then, under the blood and the swollen flesh, she could make out the features of the tall assassin who had led the men who killed their servant Frayling, stabbed her father and left them to die in the blazing House of Glass. She had memorized his face with her artist's eye; she would never forget it. And she had hoped to see him brought to justice. But she felt no vindication now, only sorrow.

The man blinked his one eye and bloody tears ran down his face. He sagged in the soldiers' grip, and they hoisted him up again on his broken legs. He peered towards Emly but his eye was unfocused and she supposed he couldn't see her.

She cleared her throat and raised her voice to the assembly.

'No,' she told them firmly, 'it is not him.'

The girl is lying, thought Dol Salida.

Although his meticulous files had foundered in the wreck of the Red Palace, and many of his informants with them, as Archange's trusted counsellor Dol now had access to information backed by imperial power. It had been easy enough to discover that one of the blackened corpses in the shell of the House of Glass was a petty thief and wastrel named Ragtail, and to follow his unsavoury trail to an assassin called the Wolf. The Wolf, it transpired, was a one-eyed former infantryman of the Eighteenth Serpentine better known as Casmir.

If this were the only lead to Casmir, Dol might have accepted that a mistake had been made and the girl was speaking truly. But he had privately followed a second, more cryptic trail which had tenuously connected the Wolf to agents of the Red Palace and to Rafael Vincerus himself. Both the Vincerii – Marcellus and his brother – had reason to want the old man dead. It was not clear to Dol whether they knew Bartellus was the legendary general Shuskara. Perhaps they did not. But, either way, he was confident this Casmir was the assassin.

And so the girl was lying. He wondered why.

He watched the guards take the broken man away. Casmir would no doubt be allowed to mend, then what? Would he be tried for other crimes? Released with the palace's regrets? Quietly taken away one night and killed? That was a problem for another day.

The girl was still standing by Archange's throne, listening to the conversations. Though a child of the sewers and just seventeen, she had been witness to momentous events and knew, in Dol's mind, far too much to be trusted. The old woman was talking to the current focus of Dol's interest, Jona Lee Gaeta. He was of the enigmatic Family Gaeta, soldiers, scholars and perhaps mystics, who had clung to the Iron Palace, their home on the Shield, long after other Families had abandoned theirs. Jona and his soldier brother Saul, their mother Sciorra and numerous unexceptional sisters had kept themselves distant, remote particularly from Araeon and the Vincerii. Jona had not fought in the war, though he looked like a soldier and Dol scoffed at the notion that he was a scholar. He was said to have a private army which stayed aloof from the events of the Day of Summoning, acting against neither the Immortal nor Archange. That lady was reticent on the subject of the Gaetas, as she was about so many things. It was not Dol's duty to keep her safe – she had a small army in the palace and constant bodyguards to do that – but he worried that this inscrutable man, perhaps a Serafim, had insinuated himself so far into her confidence.

The rest of the assembly waited patiently for Archange's permission to depart. Dol found the marble floor cruel on his game leg, and he resisted the urge to pace up and down to ease it. It would not do to look impatient in the presence of the empress. Instead he craned his neck to admire the glass in the dome high above. He had little sense of the aesthetic, he was just an old soldier, but he knew skilful work when he saw it and this was magnificent. Not for the first time he wondered how many centuries the dome had been there and what power had made it so durable.

He remembered that Emly had been a glassmaker once. It was something he had forgotten, for it had no relevance to anything.

'The girl is lying,' a voice said.

Dol Salida lowered his eyes, feeling his neck creak. Jona Lee Gaeta stood at his side, smiling pleasantly. He was dark-haired, dark-eyed, and the fact that he had sidled up to Dol unnoticed seemed a clue to his character.

Dol nodded his acquiescence. He was not going to say the words out loud. The girl was under Archange's protection, and was inviolate. In addition he himself, in a moment of insanity, had vowed to her father that he would protect her. '*I will see she is safe, general. This is not her battle.*' He would keep this promise if it remained within his power. Unless, he added to himself scrupulously, she were to prove no longer an innocent and chose to take sides against him.

'Don't you find it irritating, Dol Salida, that your keen intelligence is confounded by the words of this girl?'

Dol shrugged. He genuinely didn't. He found it interesting. 'Casmir is not going anywhere,' he said.

'We can investigate the truth of this story at our leisure.'

'The lady seemed . . . irritated.' Gaeta nodded his head towards Archange.

In Dol's experience Archange could *seem* irritated by a change in the weather, a speck of dust on the hem of her skirts, or the ripe smell of one of her guards. Yet the woman had lived as a fugitive for decades, had consorted with the then enemy, and had dwelled in the City's sewers. If she chose to take on the disposition of a finicky old biddy now, well, that was her own business. And the fact that her ward would lie to her would scarcely disturb the empress. Like Dol, she might find it interesting.

But he had no intention of airing this to Gaeta. Any more than he would confide in the girl who cleaned his chambers.

He said, 'Perhaps.' Then, to be polite, he added, 'The empress has many problems on her mind. This is not the most thorny of them by any means.'

Gaeta's look was wintry. 'Yes. Now the Khan army has marched north the City looks worryingly vulnerable.'

Then bring out your own troops to man its walls, Dol Salida thought, but he merely replied, 'We still have venerable regiments to protect our people. And the Khan army, by dealing with the invasion of Petrus, is protecting the City in the north.'

In truth, he too had been a little disappointed when they marched away, for with the Khan army went the last of the Petrassi troops and their general Hayden Weaver. An old soldier, Dol had at first bristled at the suggestion of talks with the enemy, until he discovered that most of the talks, and the peace agreement, had been done and dusted long before the invasion. His task had been to deal with Weaver to bring mutual aid to the wounded of both sides and settle the day-to-day problems of the occupation. He had expected a man of intelligence and military skill, of course, but Dol found Hayden Weaver to be a kindred spirit. The Petrassi leader was witty and plain-spoken, and interested, in a way that was unheard-of among the City's generals, in the wellbeing of his men. And he had a devious, politician's mind and, Dol later found, a fund of ribald stories to which his foreign accent added a piquant flavour.

'That's one way of looking at it,' Gaeta was saying, his eyes boring into Dol's. Dol Salida saw with discomfort that Gaeta had black eyes like Archange's. 'As the empress's most valued counsellor, did you recommend the settlement with Hayden Weaver?'

Dol did not allow it to show, but he was surprised at such a direct query. It was not the way of the White Palace, under Archange's lead, to ask questions so baldly. He said, pleasantly though ambiguously, 'The empress has many senior soldiers to advise her.'

'Speaking of which,' Gaeta said, looking around, at the gathering of soldiers and counsellors and at Emly, slight and dark, standing before the empress, 'I heard some interesting intelligence today. I understand Evan Broglanh, that most *intimate* of the empress's inner circle, has left the City for parts unknown.'

Dol gazed at him, unimpressed. 'That would be more interesting if the parts were known.' This was not entirely true. Broglanh was now one of the most powerful men in the City and the empress treated him as her closest confidant, like a son or, as Gaeta implied with crashing obviousness, like a lover. Anything that soldier did was worthy of attention.

'He left two days ago, before dawn,' Gaeta told him. 'With a handful of his men. On some mission for Archange?'

'Broglanh and I do not confide in each other,' Dol said. 'But what else would it be?'

'*Against* Archange? Or just a visit to one of his many mistresses. With a bodyguard?'

Dol chuckled and, after a moment, Gaeta joined him, saying with a shrug, 'I am merely relaying what I've heard.'

Dol would not endorse this sort of nonsense, though he privately disliked Broglanh. The soldier was always at Archange's side and Dol doubted he had time for one mistress let alone many. But the last thing Dol wanted was a return to the spiteful atmosphere in Araeon's court where insinuation, lies and mischief-making were the currency and some men would do anything, betray anyone, for a moment's fleeting approval from the emperor. Too many good men had been lost then and evil held sway.

The two turned back to the throne, where Archange was gesturing briskly at the assembled throng as if irritated they were still there. Orders were barked and the soldiers started to march out, then the rest of the company drifted away. Only Emly was told to stay.

Leaving, Gaeta said to Dol, 'I wish I could be a fly on the wall for that conversation,' nodding his head at the empress and the girl.

Dol could not but agree.

The night was silent and close. The tall windows of Emly's chamber were flung wide to catch the hope of a breeze, but the air remained heavy and still, the scent of white pond flowers intense. Em lay in a tangle of bedsheets, sleepless, her skin slick with sweat, her brain jangling with unwanted thoughts. After the long, idle spring something was changing. Something was in the air.

She swung her legs out of bed and walked on to the

balcony in her nightshift. It was no cooler out there. The cloying scent of flowers was mixed with the faint odour of roasted meat rising from the kitchens. Em wrinkled her nose. The moon was a pale fingernail low in the south and she could see little, just a faint glow in the direction of the City and a directionless gleam from the white stone all around.

Archange had asked her again, after the assembly had disassembled, if she was sure the prisoner was not the man who had attacked her. Em had looked into the old woman's black eyes. For a moment she had the sensation of falling, as if from a high tower. Then she'd nodded dumbly, not trusting herself to say the word. Archange had blinked slowly, like a lizard, and the feeling went away.

'I have a gift for you,' the empress said.

'A gift?' Em was surprised into speech. Nobody had ever given her a gift before, unless you counted the gift of life, for which she owed Evan and her father and Darius, and many unknown people she could never thank.

'Tomorrow,' the old woman said. 'At first light. Be ready. I will send someone to fetch you.'

Emly had discussed it that evening with Elija in the library, but he was more interested in why she had lied about the prisoner than in her promised gift.

'I don't know,' she said, thinking about it as he frowned at her. 'It was because, I think, there was an executioner there ready to cut his head off if I said yes. Archange and Dol Salida talk about justice, a new era of justice in the City, we hear it all the time, don't we?'

Elija nodded.

'But,' she continued, 'if I had said the word they would have killed him.'

'He's an assassin who tried to murder you and

Bartellus. You could have burned to death in the House of Glass. You both would have died were it not for Broglanh. It would have been justice to execute him.'

'And he killed Frayling,' she added scrupulously. She often wondered if she was the only person alive who remembered Frayling. The crippled servant had died for her, and she kept him alive in her heart from gratitude and from duty.

'Yes. Did you doubt it was him?'

'No.'

'Then he deserves to die.'

Emly said nothing.

'If someone else in the throne room,' her brother persisted, his face flushed, 'a maidservant say, had identified him as an assassin and he had been executed, would you have thought that wrong?'

'No,' she said in a small voice.

'So you did not want to be responsible for his death?'

Elija had looked at her sternly and she felt ashamed. He thought it was cowardly of her not to stand up for the people who had been killed by the man, although he wouldn't say the words to her.

Now, on the midnight balcony, Emly peered downwards towards the lower levels of the palace. Recently there had been the noise of building down there, hammering and the cheerful shouts of working men. A western section of the lower palace had been screened off and she supposed more rooms were being built, although she did not know why for there were enough unused already in the White Palace.

She felt a little cooler and the sweat was drying on her skin. She would try to sleep and be ready for her gift in the morning. She turned and walked back into the darkness of her bedroom. And stopped. For there was a deeper darkness, a black shape standing by the door, silent and threatening. Her heart panicked in her breast. Then she smelled new leather and, riding on it, a familiar scent.

She ran across the room and cannoned into Evan Broglanh, throwing her arms around him.

'Oof,' he said, and she could hear he was smiling.

She looked up at him from chest-height but she could only see a pale oval of his face.

'You must come with me,' he said, his voice serious now.

She nodded. She would go anywhere with him. This was something she had dreamed of.

'We must be quiet and secret,' he said. 'Pack some clothes.'

She moved swiftly about the room, fetching her old cloth bag then finding random clothes and stuffing them in. She couldn't think properly. Her mind was abuzz with the knowledge that Evan wanted her, she was going to be with him.

Then she stopped suddenly. 'Elija!' she said.

'He'll get a message to say you're safe.'

He was holding out a pair of riding breeches. 'Put these on.'

She dragged her nightshift off over her head and stepped into the breeches, which were stiff and unfamiliar on her skin. She could feel his eyes on her. She pulled on a thin shirt then a thicker tunic, and stood for his approval.

'Do you have any strong shoes, or boots?' he asked, frowning at her bare feet.

She grabbed the stout boots she used for climbing around the gardens on the Shield and laced them up. And waited again for his assessment.

'Good,' he said. He slung her bag over his shoulder, took her hand and they stepped out into the corridor.

The corridors and stairwells were lit by the empress's

new lanterns but they were few and far between and the pair hurried between one patch of light and the next. Silence echoed around them and their boots were quiet on the soft stone. They hastened down several flights of stairs, Emly running to keep up with Broglanh's long stride. He led her through the kitchens, then down another flight of winding stairs which seemed to go on for ever. She had never been there before. It was pitch dark and smelled musty and she wondered where they were. They passed through storage places packed with barrels and crates, then arrived at a narrow doorway and stepped out into the night. She could smell fresh air and the pungent scent of horses and the presence of other men.

'Can you ride?' Evan asked her, leaning over her, his breath hot against her face.

She shook her head and said, 'No,' feeling useless.

He vanished from her side and she heard the clink of bridles and squeak of leather as horses shifted restlessly, puffing out their breath on the night air. Men spoke together in low voices. Then she heard the louder creak of saddles as they started to mount. Hooves clopped on cobbles. Horses huffed and snorted. She looked around, seeing only big vague shapes, moving.

'Excuse me, lady,' said a voice and two brawny hands grabbed her round the waist and pitched her up in the air. A hand grabbed her ankle and pulled on her leg and suddenly she was seated astride a horse behind Evan. She felt the beast move under her, adjusting its stance. It seemed enormously high and frighteningly strong.

'Hold on to me,' her lover told her and gladly she crept her hands round his warm leather-clad body. The big horse set off at a walk. It clopped out from the shadow of the palace walls and moonlight fell on the horsemen. She saw there were six of them in all on horses laden with weaponry and baggage. She knew none of the faces but she felt no fear, only excitement. She wondered if they were leaving the City, for she had never been outside its walls.

'Where are we going?' she whispered.

Evan turned and grinned at her, that old rakish Broglanh grin she hadn't seen since before the Day of Summoning.

'To join the army,' he told her.

CHAPTER SIXTEEN

EMLY WAS IN AGONY. THEY HAD BEEN RIDING ALL DAY, with only a brief stop for food, and her whole body was aflame.

At first she had clung tightly to Evan, excited to be close to him and scared she would fall off, for the horse was broad under her and she could not grip it with her thighs as her lover had instructed her. By the time the sun was high the sinews of her shoulders and back were screaming and she wanted to let go and fall off into blissful oblivion.

The horse jolted her about, back and forth and up and down, and she could find no way to sit that didn't jar her. After a while she felt it would cut her in two, if the pain from her shoulders did not kill her first. She found it was best when the beast was running fast. At first this terrified her, but once she no longer feared death she learned it was the best way to travel, for it was smooth and the great animal gulped up the leagues. She hoped they would reach their destination by sunset.

When they stopped at last Evan hauled her down like a bag of clothes, told her to relieve herself, and to eat and drink her fill. She instantly forgot the first two instructions but drank almost an entire water skin. She had not dared drink while mounted for fear of falling off. Then she slumped to the ground and slept for mere moments, it seemed, before she was woken and put back on the warhorse.

Hours passed but the riders did not stop again. They rode at a steady trot, relentlessly. It seemed to her that the horses would die if they rode all day. Em was soon thirsty again and she regretted she had not relieved herself when she had the chance. The need to pee became an agony so she was forced to relieve herself in the saddle. But afterwards her wet breeches chafed her skin, and her inner thighs became a torment, the rubbing of leather a constant misery. She did not know which was worst, the tiredness or the thirst or the pain of her raw thighs. She cried then, tears mingled with sweat. And still they rode on.

She must have slept somehow, clinging to Evan's back, for it was suddenly dark and cool and they were riding in fresher air. The big horse halted, puffing and shaking its head, jingling its bridle. Evan slid down then reached up for her. Em fell into his arms and when he tried to stand her upright, like a doll, her numbed legs gave way.

When she awoke the moon was high. She tried to remember how long it had been since she stood looking at it from her balcony. Her whole body was sore, but it was hungry too and she looked around. The horses were standing nearby, their heads down. There was a campfire a few paces beyond, with men around it. The scent of roast meat and herbs reached her nose, overpowering the smell of the horses, and she breathed it in, intoxicated. She moved to sit up, then cried at the pain of her raw thighs and her aching sinews. The men turned their heads at the sound but none moved.

With difficulty she got to her knees, took a breath then stood uncertainly. She walked over to the fire, trying to step normally, though her whole body was shrieking and her legs felt as though they were being controlled by someone else.

A black-bearded man wordlessly handed her a tin plate of food. She had to stand to eat it; she could not visualize ever sitting down again. It was rabbit, with chewy roots and onions and leafy herbs. She thought it was the best thing she had ever eaten. For a moment she felt exhilarated by the midnight air, the food, the presence of the horses and their riders. She smiled, wiping grease off her chin.

'Thank you,' she said to the bearded man and he nodded.

She saw Evan was wearing a new jacket, of black leather and silver, the uniform of the Thousand. For a moment she missed the ragged red jerkin she had first seen him in. The warrior looked up at her, his face expressionless.

Then he turned to the bearded man. 'This rabbit die of old age?' he asked.

The man winked at Em but said nothing. Another soldier said, 'Tastes all right to me.'

'You'd eat dog-meat if the hound was slow.'

'You can talk, Broglanh. Who was it ate a live toad on a bet?'

Evan grinned. 'Never turn down a wager,' he said, shovelling food into his mouth.

'We'll be eating worse than toads if the empress catches us,' the bearded man said, and they all fell silent.

One of the men, younger than the rest, kept casting covert glances at Emly. 'I'm not afraid to die,' he said stoutly.

'I am,' replied the bearded man, chewing on his food and swallowing. 'And if I weren't, I'd like to die for a better reason than this.' He exchanged a glance with

Evan, who turned back to his food without comment.

He finished and threw down his empty plate, then stood. He put his arm round Emly and walked her back to her blanket. 'Get some more sleep,' he told her quietly.

She knew he didn't like answering questions, but in a small voice she asked, 'Where are we going and when will we get there?'

He looked down at her, his pale lashes bright in the moonlight. 'Our journey will take thirty days or more,' he told her, and her heart plummeted to her boots. She felt she could not bear even one more day on the horse. 'But,' he added, 'once we catch up with the army you can walk if you wish. Now, get some more sleep.'

The second day was worse than the first, and better. It was worse in that the ride was more painful, if that was possible, and Em knew for certain she would be on the horse all day. But it was better now she understood what she had to do. She ate and drank and peed when the men did, and she tried not to complain.

On the third day everything started to change. Her body was getting used to the constant movement, and her aches and pains were fading. Her bare arms were darkening under the sun and she guessed her face was too. They were well clear of the City now. It was the first time in her life Emly had been outside the walls and she started looking around with interest, breathing in the crystal air. She saw big birds hovering in the blue sky above distant hills. She saw foxes or dogs darting across the grasslands the horses were traversing. Small creatures ran or hopped out of the way as the heavy hooves passed, and when she lay down to rest there were beetles and butterflies to follow with her eyes. She was always hungry and ate as much as the men did. She started to think travelling was a life she could love.

That day they crossed a wide river, so wide Emly could barely see the other bank. The big horse plunged into the water and swam gamely with her on its back, Evan in the water alongside. Emly was charmed by the adventure. She had no idea horses could swim – it seemed impossible for they were so big and heavy – and she watched the animal's great curved neck forging forward towards the far bank, felt the cool water lap around her. She asked Evan the stallion's name and he shrugged and shook his head. Either he didn't know or didn't care. It was just a mount to him.

There were only two riders now. First there had been six, then four, now it was just Evan and the bearded man. Where had the others gone? After they dismounted that evening, and Em had walked around to work her legs, she wandered over to where the bearded rider was unpacking his gear. His mount, a blue-black horse smaller than Evan's, waited stoically as all the bags were lifted from its back. Em rubbed its soft nose and it nickered into her hand.

'Why does he have to carry so much?' she asked.

The bearded man looked at her, dark eyes twinkling. 'Because he's carrying Broglanh's war gear as well as my own. Because *his* horse is carrying you both.'

Emly felt foolish. She knew the discomfort of riding had made her selfish, but she hadn't realized it had made her stupid too.

'What is his name?' she asked, fondling the horse's ears. He huffed and waggled his head.

'Blackbird,' the man told her.

She realized she didn't know the rider's name, but she couldn't ask, not after she'd asked his horse's. The bearded man grinned as if he guessed what she was thinking.

Avoiding his eyes, she commented, 'Evan's horse doesn't have a name.'

'Yes, he does,' the man told her. 'It's . . .' he hesitated as if trying to remember, 'it's Patience.'

'Is it?' she asked, frowning at the big warhorse, who stood close by watching for his nosebag. Emly feared she was being mocked, but the bearded man went on with his work straight-faced. When she later asked Evan if his stallion was really called Patience he guffawed, but he started calling the horse that, and she was pleased when he did because it made him smile.

As the sun went down Emly found she had few regrets about leaving the closed, muffled life of the palace. But she thought of her brother each day. Elija was safe at the Serafia, but she knew he would be worried about her and this seemed unfair for she was happy and she knew he was not.

Ten days into their journey she awoke well after dawn and lay contentedly in her blanket looking up at the leaves forming a pale green canopy over the little glade where they had spent the night. The morning was already warming and the air was still and thick with the sound of bees. Emly stretched luxuriously and sat up. The bearded man – whose name, she now knew, was Chancey – was stirring oatmeal in a pot over the fire. It smelled different from usual. Em turned her head, sniffing. Something else was different. The air was charged with energy, as if there was a storm coming. There was another faint smell which she couldn't identify. She rose and walked over to the fire and took the plate of oatmeal she was offered.

Emly tried to remember the words she had been rehearsing. She had wanted to speak to Evan alone, but Chancey was always there. She swallowed some oatmeal.

'Evan,' she said, and her voice sounded nervous. He looked up.

'You must tell me,' she said, trying to be firm, 'why

we left the White Palace. I don't know about horses or riding, but I am not a child to be carried around like a saddlebag.'

Chancey lowered his head and chewed his food. Evan said, a hard note in his voice, 'I'm trying to keep you safe.'

She thought, *I was safe in the palace. I was protected by an empress.* But she asked, 'Was I in danger?'

The two men looked at each other. Then Chancey spoke up. He told her, 'The empress was a threat to you, girl. And you were a threat to the City. So we brought you away. There is no better place to hide than in an army.'

'But Archange has always been kind to me.' And to Elija, she thought, wondering if her brother was in danger too.

Chancey nodded. 'The Serafim are usually kind to people who give them what they want. The empress was kind to Evan. She gave him promotion and power beyond the dreams of most men. But if he had defied her orders she would have had him executed on the spot.' He looked at Evan, who nodded.

'But how was she a threat to me? And how was I a threat to the City?'

'You know the old veil you found in the sewer?'

'My father found it. The Gulon Veil.'

'You know it is a thing of great power?'

Emly nodded. She had been told the Gulon Veil could make the old young and the dead live, and it had given the old emperor his power to create reflections, undead creatures which stalked the palace like mortal men. But to her it was just her old veil with its friendly animals in the lacework and round the edges.

Chancey opened his mouth to go on, but a distant sound silenced him. It was a bugle call, high and brassy, quivering on the morning air. Emly looked at the two men, her eyes wide. Evan grinned and pointed with his knife. Emily scrambled up and ran across the glade into the dark line of trees. Through the narrow trunks of young birches she could see bright daylight. She burst out from the trees on the lip of a high green hill.

Beneath her was a wide valley, its floor seething with a sea of men and women, horses and donkeys, livestock and carts. They filled the width of the valley and stretched forward into the distance as far as she could see. She turned the other way and there too all she could see was moving people. There were patches of colour among them, red uniforms and green uniforms, and cavalry units in grey. The sun rising hotly in the east shone on the polished helms of riders and the harness of their mounts, the sparkling points of lances and spears, and the armour of infantrymen. The sound they made was like a distant ocean, perpetual waves on an eternal beach, and the smell was like a crowded City street, of sweat and grime and ordure, of food and grass and animals and ale.

They had found the Khan army.

An army draws followers the way a fox's brush attracts fleas.

Many of them are predators, human and animal. They lurk and creep along the sides and rear of the moving mass, hiding in the day, bolder at night, hoping to pick off strays and the weak and lame, human and animal. Wild dogs and catamounts are more of a danger after dark, and bandits and scoundrels a threat at any time. Particularly in peril are the camp-followers and their children who trail behind the baggage train, sometimes leagues behind. They travel in everyone else's leavings – unwanted food, ordure, blunt and broken weapons, discarded clothes, as well as the mountainous clouds of dust raised by tens of thousands of marching boots in the height of summer. Many of them are women who follow their soldiers for years; this is their life and they want nothing else.

Any good general, and Marcus Rae Khan *was* a good general, deploys a squad of soldiers to guard the camp-followers. It is, understandably, the most popular job in the army. As well as the often riotous company of the whores and wives and their children, the warriors enjoy having a mission beyond slogging along in the centre of a moving mass of humanity. It is sometimes dangerous, but more often not. And, when they reach their destination, wherever that might be, they are already furthest away from the action.

The wives and whores had mules packed high with pots and pans, wicker baskets, clothes in rag bags, food, even furniture. The whores wore bright-coloured clothes and ribbons in their hair to indicate their profession. They were louder and more cheerful than the wives and sweethearts, and some were no more than girls, others in the first flush of old age. There were crones too, seamstresses, laundresses, some of them veterans' wives or widows. The brats ran together in packs, and more than one of the women was heavily pregnant. Stern Edasson had seen babies born on the battlefield before, and he probably would again. It seemed to him neither strange nor wrong; that babes should be born while men and women die seemed the most normal thing in the world to a man who had been a soldier most of his life.

Also lagging far behind the army was the crowd of fortune-tellers, mystics and shamans who entertained the troops in their different ways. They were mostly spindly old men or comfortable widows who reassured lonely and frightened soldiers of the love of their mothers, or of their future wealth and a houseful of devoted sons. They were at their busiest on the eve of a battle, or when the queues for the whores were long and the waiting men used some of their copper coin to boost their hopes and dreams instead.

Stern knew the Pigstickers had landed on their feet for a change. Shortly after the fall of the City and their capture by the enemy he and his comrades had been handed over in a transfer agreed between the empress and the Blues' general. Then they'd kicked their heels in a state of military limbo until, with the other surviving Pigstickers, they'd been engulfed in the new First Imperial infantry. After a long period of inactivity they were glad to be on the march. Stern's company was deployed at the rear of the Khan army, wide on the left flank, so the soldiers avoided the worst of the dust and debris. There was a cavalry unit back there with them too, so the troopers could gallop off and take a look at anything suspicious. All the Pigstickers had to do was walk in the sunshine in daytime, and take their pick of the whores after dark. They were fed and watered well enough, and after the chaos and suffering in the City it felt good to be going somewhere.

The army had been on the march for twenty days, and the main body was strung out over several leagues. From time to time the trailing edge had been ordered to catch up, and that evening when the rest of the army halted the Pigstickers were told to march on, herding their unruly charges, until they reached the baggage train. Now they had settled, and eaten and drunk their fill, food provided by the army cooks and ale from the unit's own supplies.

And Benet was standing, peering across to where the whores were getting ready for an evening's work.

'I can't see her,' he complained.

You can't see anything much, Stern thought gloomily, but he stood and looked as well.

'She's there,' he said, pointing at the yellow-haired

whore his brother had the itch for. She was no more than sixteen and was as plump and juicy as her name, which was Peach.

'Is she on her own?'

'No, she's with the others.' The whores were like a gaggle of noisy hens, always bustling and clucking, or screeching with laughter which echoed over the encampment and went straight to the loins of many of the male soldiers, as was intended.

'I mean, are there any poxy officers creeping up on her?' Benet asked anxiously.

'Not that I can see.' Stern sat down again. He was not interested in the whores tonight.

Fastidiously, Benet wiped his greasy moustache on his sleeve, then delved in his pouch to find the coins the girl would expect. He counted out five copper pente, then tallied what he had left and stared at the result with dismay. Each night his little hoard of coin diminished, and each night he was newly dismayed.

'I think I'll go see Peach myself,' said Grey Gus, getting up and hoisting his breeches comfortably. Gus was a thirty-year veteran, who had been an infantryman for time out of mind. Stern knew he was tormenting Benet, as he often did, but Benet could never see it.

His brother stared at the older man in alarm. 'She's mine!' he cried.

'No, she's not. She's a tart,' Gus told him. 'But you can go first. I'll wait,' he offered generously.

Benet hurried off, counting his coin again, casting suspicious glances back at Grey Gus, who laughed and sat back down by the campfire. Stern knew the man had suffered a lance to the privates some years back. He had trouble pissing and had no interest in women, but Benet didn't understand that. They glanced at each other and grinned.

Gus lay back against his pack and said, 'That officer's on to him.'

Stern sighed. 'I know. But what can they do?' he asked. 'Send him back home?'

'They should put him in supplies. Or with the cooks,' said Quora, rolling over on to her back and yawning up at the night sky.

'Would you want Benet's hands on your food?' Gus asked her, and she shook her head fervently, the beads in her hair rattling.

But Stern knew she was right. The four of them had fought together for more than two years and they relied on each other in the way only warriors do. Benet trusted the others to watch his blind side, but equally they had the right to trust him. And they couldn't. Benet was a threat to them all. They had covered for him until now, as comrades should, but they couldn't go on doing it.

The previous day an officer, who had been watching Benet too closely, had asked him if his eyesight was good.

'Good as yours, sir,' Benet said promptly.

He had been coached for this eventuality by Stern, and he said to the officer, 'I can see that bird over there.' He pointed to a tall pine on the ridge above.

'What bird?' the officer asked, squinting.

'The one with the missing eyelash,' Benet told him proudly, and the others laughed and the officer smiled. He walked away but he hadn't forgotten. Stern guessed he was still watching and biding his time.

Suddenly Quora jumped up, scratching at her calves. 'Ants,' she cried, dancing around. 'We've camped on an ants' nest.'

She stamped at the ground a bit, then moved her belongings to the other side of the fire, cursing under her breath. Stern watched her through half-closed eyelids, as he often did. She was small and compact, a head shorter than him, but a fearsome fighter. He wondered what would happen to her. The empress was intent on barring women from the armies, gossip said, but there had been no sign of it so far. Quora had been fighting for ten years or more. What would she do if she was no longer wanted as a soldier?

He lay back and stared at the sky. The stars were white and fat, like snowflakes, against the black. The moon was a half-coin in the west. The air was still and warm, and the dry ground under his back hard as stone.

In his dreams he went back to Adrastto, the town of his boyhood, where the air was soft with rain and waves crashed endlessly against the cliffs as they had done since the world was young. Their father had been a fisherman who pitted his frail wooden vessel against the might of the sea daily until the one time he did not return. His wife married his brother, as was the custom in their community. But it was the end of childhood for Stern, and he and his brothers left the port town to sell their swords to the City of Gold, seeking honour and fame and wealth. They had not found any of those things. His elder brother had died five years before, a slow agonizing death from a belly wound. He and Benet had survived many battles and were content enough, despite the death and pain and horrors they had seen. This was their life and they imagined no other.

He turned his head to look at Quora, who was asleep now, dream ants making her twitch a little. He could not guess what he would do if he could no longer fight, if he was blinded or if the empress told him he had to give up his sword.

When he awoke the stars had disappeared, all but the largest ones, chased away by the dawn light. Stern rolled over and sat up, old stitches in his side pulling and making him wince. His eye was caught by movement on the hillside to the north. Riders, he thought. He was about to shout 'Incoming!' when he saw the troopers on duty had spotted them and were riding to meet them.

As they came closer he saw they were two men – one tall and fair, one shorter and black-bearded – and a youngster leading a pair of horses. Papers were demanded and given up. Another trooper, an officer, rode out towards them.

Around him his comrades were rising. They were economical with their mornings. They would roll out of their blankets, relieve themselves, then hoist their packs and start marching. Each had reserved a little food from the night before, but it was eaten on the move. The first proper meal of the day would be many leagues down the road.

Stern looked to his right again, to the green hillside, but the newcomers had gone, swallowed up somewhere into the body of the army.

CHAPTER SEVENTEEN

OF THE SEVEN FAMILIES, THE BROGLANHS WERE THE least regarded, by the others if not by themselves. They were no longer Serafim, although there was a Broglanh among the original Travellers, and yet through the myriad descendants, with their muddled, tainted bloodlines and genetic accidents, and intermittent dynastic genocide, and plain old bad luck, the Broglanhs had stayed remarkably pure over the generations. Although the word 'pure' would make Evan Quin Broglanh scoff.

Perhaps only Archange could still remember the first of the name – Donal Kyle – and she visualized a twinkly-eyed pipsqueak of a man, an engineer of some sort, she thought, cheerful and resolute even when the very first enemy they met seemed to doom them all. Then he had gone out one morning and got himself mauled by a bear, or a big cat, or surprised by an earth fall. It was a long time ago, the empress had explained to Evan Broglanh irritably. But it had taken the engineer days to die, and in that time he had learned that his woman was with child, the first mother of them all, pregnant with the first child. And the child had lived, against such great odds, and he was cheerful and resolute like his father.

And it was strange, Archange told her lieutenant, that Evan Quin was so like the Broglanhs though he was no more one of them than she was.

As small boys he and his brother Conor had been despatched to the City from the Land of Mists, sons of some fierce northern queen, thin and pale and half-starved like all those raised in those lands of uncertain weather and unreliable nutrition. The queen, red-headed and savage, rode into battle, it was said, barebreasted.

Archange had snorted at this. 'Impractical,' she had judged, crossing her arms firmly across her own old bosom, 'and as distracting to her own warriors as to the enemy.' Broglanh had opened his mouth to argue that the breasts would have been pointing at the opposition, not her own troops, then he thought better of it. His leash was long with this old woman, but he took pains not to discover the full length of it.

The tribal queen, called Gruach, had birthed twelve live young – ten boys and two girls. They were raised like pups, rolling in the ashes at their mother's hearth, fighting the war hounds and each other for scraps from the table. Gruach seemed oblivious to her get, but when each of the three eldest boys reached the verge of manhood he suffered a fatal accident. A year or so on and the next pair, twins, vanished away one night – fled or dead. The girls seemed safe in their mother's hall, then one died in childbirth aged just twelve.

Gruach, scarred and leathery, must have thought herself well past the hazards of pregnancy when the last two boys were born within a year of each other. Perhaps it was her age, or perhaps she had already lost enough children, but these last, golden-haired Conor and tow-headed Evan, were raised with more attention than their siblings.

What was in Gruach's mind when she sent them

across the world into the dubious protection of the emperor Araeon would never be known. She was scarcely threatened by the City, unless she thought the emperor jealous of the isle's bounty of cold winds, rocks and icy seas. Maybe she really believed the boys would be given an education, raised like little princes, indulged by an emperor with no sons of his own. And the pair did receive an education, though a harsh one, and they suffered hardship and torment small boys should not experience. Until Conor's short, brutal life was ended by dogs and Evan caught the eye of a powerful woman.

'To no one but me,' Archange often told him, 'are you still a frightened boy running from wild dogs.'

Gruach was dead now, Broglanh had learned. Killed by poison by her remaining daughter these ten years since. She must have been a very old woman by then, battle-scarred and battle-weary. The treacherous daughter had survived her for less than a year then she too had been murdered, along with her own seven children, by the last brother.

When he thought of his mother, whom he barely remembered, Broglanh searched in his heart for feeling. But there was none to be found, just a mild and fading interest in a land which had been his home for his first four years. And when word reached him much later that his friends Fell and Indaro had found sanctuary on the isle, he commended them to the gods of ice and fire and kept the news to himself.

His brother Conor's death and the subsequent trial before the emperor had been turning-points in his young life. Afterwards Evan Quin was adopted by the Broglanhs – at the behest of Archange – and he was raised with four older brothers as Evan Quin Broglanh.

The Broglanhs had no place, no palace, on the

Shield. Instead they lived in a rambling, tumbledown stone house in the Wester quarter, close by the Seagate, far from the Red Palace and the Immortal's gaze. The boy's new father, a grizzled old bear of a man named Donal like the long-dead engineer, was seldom seen by the boy and seemed to be as indifferent to him as his own mother had been. There was no mother-figure in the house. The boys were raised by servants and tutors and later by the Family's weapons masters. The older boys sometimes bullied little Evan and sometimes doted on him. They mostly ignored him. But he adored them all and when the eldest, Taric, was dragooned into the army and killed in action he thought his heart would break.

One by one the Broglanh boys reached the age of sixteen and were sucked into the City's war. Evan was fourteen when the last – Chancey – marched away. He thought he would never see them again, for hadn't Taric died within a year, and for the second time in his young life he was bereft of brothers. He willed the next two years to pass quickly so he would be in the army too, fighting the City's enemies. He dreamed of being reunited with his three Broglanh brothers, the four of them fighting shoulder to shoulder, earning commendation and promotion, the Immortal's grateful thanks.

The night before his sixteenth birthday he had been summoned to meet his father in the high hall of the ramshackle Family house. Donal Broglanh was an old man by then, old even in the City's terms, and he seemed to have little interest in the issue of his ancient loins; he had sired many sons over the centuries, and daughters too, and some of them were given the Broglanh name but most were not.

At night the old hall in the damp stone house was swathed in shadow. The great hearth held only ashes, for it was high summer, but the chamber was stifling with its dusty wall hangings and narrow windows. Thick rushes and bundles of herbs covered the floor where the master's hounds lay with noses on paws, watchful and unmoving, among gnawed bones. It was well past midnight and the house echoed loudly with silence. Evan strode to meet his father who sat in a deep, carved chair, very much like a throne, at the far end of the hall.

'Evan?' The man grunted the question, his voice rusty. It seemed he had forgotten what his newest son looked like.

'Yes,' Evan said shortly. He was grateful to the old man, but he was not in awe of him. Besides, he would be leaving on the morrow, perhaps for good, and would probably never see him again.

'You were always a skinny runt,' Donal Broglanh said, 'but you've grown like a weed.'

Evan said nothing. There didn't seem any point replying. The observation was self-evident.

The old man stared at him, perhaps disconcerted by the boy's self-possession. 'I have two pieces of advice for you, now you're a man grown.'

'Sir?' Evan tried to seem interested although he doubted this old man could tell him anything he needed to hear.

Donal leaned forward confidentially. 'Always eat and sleep when you can, boy. A soldier never knows when he'll get his next food or rest.'

Evan was unimpressed and probably showed it. These were words he'd heard all his life, and they didn't only apply to soldiers. He wondered if the old campaigner gave the same advice to his servants.

Donal watched him, frowning, and Evan nodded seriously, as if absorbing a complex piece of information. The old man's face darkened; he knew he was being humoured. He snorted.

'And get that damnable brand cut off, if you know what's good for you.' He nodded at Evan's forearm where the S brand peeked out from the edge of his shirt-sleeve.

Seeing the boy's surprise, he grunted, 'You think I'm an old fool, but I've forgotten more than you'll ever know, young Evan.'

'Yes, sir.'

Donal growled, 'I know you think it's a mark of honour, but it's what's in a man's heart that matters, boy, not what he wears on his arm. They'll kill you, the Vincerii, if they find out about it. You and your young friends. Easy as drowning pups. It's a child's fancy, and you're a man now. I'm telling you . . .' he leaned forward again, urgently. 'I'm telling you, you'll thank me one day. Get rid of it now and save your hide.'

Evan was poised between annoyance and curiosity. How did this old man know the significance of the brand, suffered to honour his friend Sami and as a symbol of the vengeance Sami's friends had sworn against the Immortal? Evan had spoken of it to no one since it had been seared into his flesh eight years before. The rest of Sami's comrades, though emboldened by the boy's hideous death by fire at the emperor's whim, had chosen to be branded on chest or shoulder, for they were old enough to know it was something to keep secret. But Evan, the youngest, had been proud to wear the mark and at the age of eight had wanted to show it off. Later, if asked about it, he'd said it was burned by accident, in a bakery oven as he was trying to steal hot bread. Now he had taken to covering it, wearing long sleeves even in summer.

Old Donal was still glaring at him, his mouth moving soundlessly, and Evan started to back away, thinking he'd done his duty. He had urgent business with one of the kitchen maids.

'I'm not finished, you young fool. I said I have two pieces of advice!'

The boy stepped forward again, sighing to himself.

'Don't trust her, boy,' Donal told him, his deep voice falling to a growl. 'I know you think she's done well by you, and perhaps she has, saved you from wild dogs or some such. But you can't trust her. Never trust her. She's a powerful woman, ay, for good and bad, but like all the Serafim she has only her own interest in her heart, that and her get, those that are left.' He squinted at Evan, his face angry. 'Are you listening to me, boy?'

Evan nodded. He had no idea who the old man was talking about. He wondered if Donal knew either.

'I'm talking about Archange,' the man said. 'She's stripped the heart of many a youngster before you. Stay clear of her. You'll be safer against a horde of Blues than against her.' He grinned at his own words, showing rotten teeth.

Evan remembered the name Archange. She was the woman who had spoken for them at their trial eight years before. A tall old woman with white hair. Was that who Donal was warning him against? An old woman? Was she still alive even? He shrugged to himself. It didn't matter. He had listened to enough of the old man's ramblings.

He nodded again and said, 'Yes, I'll remember. Thank you.'

Donal stared at him, his mouth moving as if he had words to give but could not form them. His rheumy eyes were filled with frustration at the chasm which separated him from this boy, who bore his name but whom he scarcely knew. And in a moment of insight, Evan realized the old man was dying. His face under the scrubby grey beard was gaunt and waxy, his eyes were starting to film over and his breathing was fast and shallow.

The boy looked around him then pulled over a three-legged stool and sat down. 'Tell, me, father,' he said. 'Tell me about Archange.'

'Perilous, boy. Beautiful and perilous.'

Donal closed his eyes and sat back and for a while he was quiet. Evan wondered if he had fallen asleep and he debated creeping away. But the old man opened his eyes at last and now they were sharper, more focused.

'I was just a boy when I first met her, about the age you are now. And she was not young then, though she looked about thirteen, with long legs like a white colt. She was one of the First. She had travelled here – an extraordinary journey – and she was a light to them all, a beacon of beauty and bravery in the early days . . .'

The old man rambled on comfortably into the depths of the night. He spoke with the voice of a bard, with the rhythms of stories well known and retold often over long years. He told first of Archange and then of the Serafim. Evan could not follow much of what he was saying for Donal mused on the oldest times, when the Serafim were gods and their world was golden. Evan had heard tales of the Serafim, told by his brothers and tutors, but Donal talked as if he knew them personally. His voice grew dark when he spoke of the emperor, or emperors – Evan could not make out if he was speaking of one man or many. The Vincerii strolled into the tales again and again, Marcellus and Rafael, names Evan knew well for they were the marshals of the war, defenders of the City. But there were other names, a surfeit of them, unknown to him. The Khans, Marcus and his sister Giulia, and Reeve Guillaume and the criminal Hammarskjald. And too many people called Kerr, both villains and heroes. And always Donal returned to Archange, pulled helpless as a moth to her bright beacon.

Then the old man's mood darkened and his words

faltered. He told an age-old story of two daughters, sisters, seduced and violated. Of madness and death.

'But what could Archange do?' he asked the darkness, for surely he had forgotten Evan was there. 'Araeon had saved her life that first winter, all their lives. She had sworn undying fealty to him then. She could be ruthless with the primitives, she showed that over and over. But another Serafim? She was bound hand, foot and elbow. She couldn't raise her hand against him, though she wanted his death. Still wants it, I dare say.'

'Why could she not act against him?'

There was clarity in his father's eyes now. 'I am a very old man, but this all happened long before I was born.' He shook his head. 'But they are not like us, boy. They are as different as a dog is from the fleas on its back. And they have known each other for centuries. They have fought together and against each other, betrayed each other and conspired together. They are the last of their race as well as the first.

'To Archange Araeon had been leader and teacher, ay, and saviour. But now she wanted him dead. And if she couldn't have her way she couldn't stay. So she vanished from the City for generations. We all thought her long dead. Came back forty years ago. I couldn't believe my eyes when I saw her again. She'd allowed herself to age, you see. Always a woman of swift and binding decisions. I expect she regrets it now. It's a cruel thing being old . . .'

At times Donal fell silent and dozed, and Evan probably slept a little too. But when the grey fingers of morning found their way through the high, dusty windows the old man was still going strong and the flagon of wine at his elbow was dry. At last he fell deeply asleep and his snores echoed round the walls. Evan stood and crept away, past the silent, motionless servants who had stood all night guarding their lord, to his narrow bed for a short nap before the emperor's men came for him.

Donal Broglanh died soon after, and for a while Evan tried to store up and make sense of all the tales and tall stories, for so they must have been, that the old man had told him. Most of them drifted away from him over time, but he always remembered the story of Archange Vincerus and her two daughters and when – four years later – he first met Thekla he thought he understood.

'*Have you taken lorassium, soldier?*'

Broglanh woke with a start and vomited down the sleeve of his jacket. Panting, he looked down and wanted to puke again. A lance-head was buried deep in his chest, lodged under the ribcage. Somehow the haft had been cut off and the end was ragged wood tinged with bright red. He vomited again weakly, but there was little left to come up.

'Did you take lorassium?' the woman's voice repeated.

He nodded, feeling like a brat caught in some misdeed.

She wiped some of the vomit from his jacket and told him briskly, 'That was the worst thing you could do. You'll have to wait now.' She stood and walked away from him. Mist rolled in and Broglanh's dreams were of blood and terror.

It had not been his first battle, far from it. But it was the longest and bloodiest in four years which had already seen too much blood and death. He was just twenty by then, his unit of the Second Celestine infantry fighting a defensive action against a force of Petrassi at Dead Man's Folly in the southern mountains. They were well matched and the battle had gone on by day and night, neither side giving a pace. Finally, with the dawn, the enemy had brought up a company of lancers . . .

When he woke again someone had put a shade over him to protect him from the hot sun, and there was a cool cloth on his brow. His nose detected the whiff of something medicinal under the smell of old clothes and vomit. He wondered when it would be his turn to be treated. There were so many injured. The battle had been a horror. He wondered if they'd won.

A voice spoke. 'Here, on his forearm.' He felt a gentle touch and opened his eyes again. The same woman was kneeling beside him. 'It's the same brand,' she said, her voice warm. 'Which one is this?'

'His name's Broglanh. Evan Quin Broglanh,' another voice said.

'Evan Quin,' the first said thoughtfully. 'Archange told us that name.'

'Will he live?'

'Not without her help.'

Then there were loud voices. It was almost dark, but he could see the woman had been joined by strong soldiers. They looked down at him as she talked of pulling out the lance-head. Now would be a good time to pass out, Broglanh thought.

And, eventually, he did.

The next time he surfaced he was lying in the bottom of a jolting cart. It was night and he could see little. His body was still in agony but he managed to raise his head. The lance-head was gone and his chest was swathed with blood-soaked bandages.

'It was lodged under a rib but we managed to get it out,' the woman told him. 'I have given you something for the pain.'

'Why?' he asked her, struggling for consciousness. 'It'll rot anyway.' He'd seen plenty of these wounds. They never ended well.

'Here.' Her warm hand cradled the back of his neck and supported it as he felt a cup of water at his lips. He gulped it down gratefully. At first he thought he was going to puke again, but the water stayed down and he felt his head clearing a little. He drank some more. The pain was easing a little too.

'Thank you,' he muttered. 'Where are we going?'

'To the Adamantine Gate.'

'Where's my jacket?' he asked.

'One sleeve was covered with vomit and I cut the other one off to get it off you. The remainder's under your head.' The woman sounded amused. Her voice, he noticed, was warm and smoky.

Broglanh relaxed, strangely reassured. The jacket had been with him through a lot. He slipped then into a deep sleep. He did not expect to wake again in this world.

Afterwards he had wondered that a highly experienced battlefield surgeon, in the middle of a war, amid a sea of casualties, should pay so much attention to a lowly grunt. She sat with him in the jolting cart all the way back to the City, and when they reached the destination of the other casualty carts, the barracks of the Twenty-second, and Broglanh still lived, she stayed by him, seated in the floor of the cart, and the two continued their journey alone. Later he learned they had travelled for a covert audience with Archange, of which he remembered nothing. Then he was taken to an infirmary of the Thousand hard by the Red Palace.

At first, dazed by pain and shock, Broglanh concluded that it was his manly charms that kept the woman surgeon at his side. Then, as he recovered, common sense kicked in and he realized there was nothing very charming about an injured man puking over the sleeve of his own jacket.

The surgeon's name was Thekla. Her face was not pretty, but it had a stillness which was hard won dealing with frightened, injured men and women. Her eyes were grey and they spoke of long experience. She looked about the same age as him but he guessed early on she was older than that. Just how much older he would eventually find out.

She wore baggy, shapeless clothes of grey and brown and as she visited the other injured soldiers each day, bending to check their wounds, to discriminate the healing from the rotting, he tried to see the lines of her body, but it was impossible. It was easy to see why. She had been a surgeon for a long time and the other medics deferred to her, but many of the soldiers, the men mostly, treated her like an orderly, to tease and joke with and sometimes to try to molest. She could be harsh, and occasionally cruel, he noticed, but she was always kind with him.

Broglanh recovered from the chest wound so rapidly he wondered if the broken lance in his ribs was just a nightmare, and he kicked his heels in the infirmary until he received new orders. Meanwhile he followed his father's advice. He ate the three meals a day he was given and noted that the Thousand were very well fed. He dozed away the time, luxuriating in the fresh straw mattresses and lack of bed bugs. He found it easy to screen out the screams and mewling of the gravely wounded. He had been doing it a long time.

After Conor died little Evan had found it impossible to sleep, impossible to think without the hideous vision of his brother's agonizing death stalking his every waking moment. Then, just days afterwards, Sami had died too – Sami who had been kind to him and carried him when the other boys were too weak or indifferent to help. His death was a horror and the vision of screaming flames was almost too much for the boy's mind to tolerate. For self-protection he ran away from the memories and started building the walls which had protected him for the rest of his soldier's life. Don't think about the past. The past is gone and there is nothing you can do about it. Don't worry about the future, for you can't know what it will bring. Just stay strong and keep your sword sharp. And always be ready.

CHAPTER EIGHTEEN

EVAN BROGLANH'S PLAN TO JOIN THE KHAN ARMY DID not work out as straightforwardly as he had hoped. He and Chancey tried offering their forged papers to a young captain they found barking orders at a sullen band of infantry. But the captain, promoted beyond his competence, had no idea what to do with two stray soldiers, veterans with hard eyes and a self-assured air, and a random girl. He directed them to the front of the army, telling them to report to one of the general's aides. Evan had no intention of going within sight of Marcus Rae Khan, who would certainly recognize him, so the three moved instead towards the rear of the army where they made a place for themselves with the baggage carts, the whores and the Pigstickers, and a makeshift cavalry unit who gladly welcomed two expert riders with their own horses.

As the long summer days drifted by Emly would spend her time walking at the edge of the marching horde, leading the warhorse if Evan was with her, or a baggage pony when he was away scouting. No questions were asked, no explanations given, but the three newcomers were accepted by the ragtail army. If they believed Emly was the young sister of one of the men, then so be it, she thought. Evan had not touched her with lust in his eyes since the night above the baker's, and she might as well be his sister or his daughter, she thought ruefully. There were times when her body ached for him, but most nights, when she lay down to rest at the end of a day's march, she would fall instantly to sleep surrounded by the comforting sounds of twenty thousand men and women, most of them armed and willing to protect her.

She wondered sometimes why they were fleeing the empress and what would happen to them if the hunters found them, but her quiet existence in the White Palace seemed far away and long ago, and she was happy with this travelling life with Evan, even though she was seldom alone with him.

Often during the day she walked with the yellow-haired whore Peach, who was the same age as her but who had an entirely different experience of life. Peach was a City girl, born in Barenna. Her mother was a whore too, her father a soldier, probably. As they walked Peach gave Emly the benefit of her accumulated wisdom on the subject of men and their needs. At first Em was pleased with her new friend, for she had never had a friend before, but after a while she started to think Peach's life sad, her views entirely limited by what she could see over a man's shoulder. The whore did not dislike men, for they were her livelihood, but she had little reason to value them. Like her sisters, she welcomed some of the soldiers, the ones that were clean and respectful, and avoided others, the violent and the slovenly. But the life of a prostitute in an army was a good one, Peach believed, for there was a constant supply of customers and therefore coin, and protection which her sisters in the City did not enjoy.

'What of you, Emly?' she asked, as they marched one day in the noontime sunshine. 'You could do what

I do. You're skinny, but some men don't mind that. They like the boyish ones.'

Em shook her head. 'I have a man,' she said proudly, 'but he is far from here.' Evan and Chancey had ridden away at daybreak on some mission, so she was speaking the entire truth.

'Tell me about him,' asked Peach, and her blue eyes were wistful. 'Is he kind? Does he look after you?'

Em found herself without speech for a few moments, as she often did. The women had become used to her quietness by now, and Peach waited.

'He is a hero,' Emly said eventually. 'He is a hero of the City. He saved us all, he and his friends.'

Peach smiled. 'They're all heroes to me,' she said slyly.

Em looked up ahead. The marching horde seemed to be slowing. It was only midday, and she wondered why. At last they faltered to a stop, and she took the chance to run to the nearby stream and bring water for herself and Peach and for the little baggage pony she was leading. The girls sat down beside the trail, glad of an unscheduled rest. Em felt hot and sweaty and there was no shelter from the sun in the valley.

The army had left the flat coastal plain behind and was travelling through increasingly mountainous country. Grey peaks spotted with dark green forest stood all around. They had marched up the slow slope of the valley and were now climbing a narrow defile, a pass bounded by rock walls and shale slopes. Because of the treacherous terrain and the fear of raids security had been tightened. The women and the baggage train had been ordered to keep up. But it had been a long morning and the young girls like Em and Peach found themselves dawdling to keep pace with the older women. And now they were trailing far behind the main body of the army.

It was very still in the steep defile, but they no longer had to suffer dust flying from thousands of hooves and boots for there was hard rock underfoot. The air was fresher up here, and clearer, and Emly looked forward to climbing ever higher. She hoped soon to see all the surrounding land and, perhaps, their final destination. She asked often how much further the army would be marching, but no one appeared to know, even Evan Broglanh.

The baggage pony shied and whinnied as a loud landslip of rocks and pebbles rattled down the slope opposite. A soldier cried out and cursed when he was hit by a flying stone. Emly craned her neck but she could see nothing above them other than bare rock and a few scrubby bushes. Up ahead the army started moving again and she and Peach jumped to their feet. Em picked up the pony's rope and stroked his nose to soothe him.

Suddenly the still air was split by a woman's scream. Em's heart sprang into her throat. She and Peach turned back to where the sound had come from. There was another, lower cry – a deep, agonized moan.

'Calm down, girls,' a voice said cheerfully. A stout, red-faced woman glanced at them as she marched past, working her way back through the ranks. She was grey-haired and dressed all in sombre grey, but for an incongruous pink sun bonnet perched on her head.

'Maura,' she told them. 'She's early.'

Em knew Maura. She was a quiet, dark-faced girl, newly wed to a soldier and happily pregnant for the first time. Her condition could be seen, but it scarcely made a bulge under her dress. Emly, who knew little about such matters, wondered if an early delivery was a good thing. She thought it might be, for the babe would be small and easier to push out. Curious, she started to walk back through the marchers in the stout woman's footsteps.

'What are you doing?' Peach asked, grabbing her arm.

'I've never seen a woman give birth.'

Peach made a face – she had. 'Then you won't be any help,' she said sensibly. 'Bruenna has delivered a thousand babies. She's the one Maura needs.'

Em stood on tiptoe, looking for the pink sun bonnet, which had disappeared. Then, her mind made up, she handed the pony's rope to Peach, who stood and watched as she ran back down the slope, darting past the whores and groups of grumbling oldsters, and skipping round the hooves of ponies and donkeys and the wheels of the slow carts they drew. She found the labouring girl by following her cries. She was not far off the main trail, in a shallow depression carved out of the rock wall. She was squatting on the ground, face streaming with tears and sweat, and as Em got there she lifted her head and howled like a dog. The midwife in the pink bonnet, Bruenna, was supporting her on one side and another older woman on the other. A platoon of soldiers stood around reluctantly as if uncertain whether to stay or go.

When she saw Emly, Bruenna demanded, 'Fetch some water, girl.' Em ran to the stream and filled her water skin then rushed back to the women.

'More than that,' Bruenna snapped as she grabbed the skin.

Em looked around her, then at the lingering soldiers. 'Give me your helm,' she said to one she recognized.

The black-haired soldier merely stared at her and his comrades laughed. One veteran, grinning, said, 'Do what the little girl tells you, Stern.'

Stern unlatched and lifted off his helm and gave it to her with a wink, and she took it with a nod of thanks and ran to the stream again. Filling it with water she hurried back to the women and placed the helm carefully on the ground beside Bruenna. The midwife looked at it and nodded.

'Good girl,' she said. She turned back to the labouring woman, talking quietly to her, encouraging her.

Feeling helpless, Emly stood up and looked around. The last few heavily laden carts were driving past them, hurrying up the ravine in a loud flurry of shale and stones, the animals straining into their traces, huffing and snorting. Soon, she thought with a stab of fear, we will be left behind.

After a while Maura's pain seemed to lessen and she leaned back to rest against the rock wall. By then the final remnants of the ragtail army had passed them by and they were alone with their platoon of soldiers.

Bruenna stood up painfully and rubbed her knees with a sigh. 'We're in a pickle,' she said mildly, glancing at the sun which was just starting to fall down the sky. 'We don't want to be here come nightfall.'

'We could stop one of those carts, make them come back,' Emly suggested. 'They could carry Maura.'

Bruenna sniffed. 'They're traders, girl. If they stop it's only to make themselves a sale. And do you think they'd throw off some of their sellables to make way for a pregnant whore? Besides,' she added, 'they're in a hurry to catch up with the army.' She looked at Em. 'If you run, you'll overtake them. One of them will find room for a little thing like you.'

But Em shook her head and Bruenna sighed again and looked down at Maura.

'How long will it be?' Emly asked her.

'As long as it takes. Half a day. Tomorrow. Or it might slip out like a silverfish within moments. It happens.'

'Can I do anything?'

The woman frowned at her. 'I don't know. *Can* you do anything?'

Emly racked her brain. She could cook, she could ride a horse now, and she knew how to make coloured glass. She was learning to read and write. None of these skills seemed helpful to the labouring woman. Yet she was reluctant to leave, to run away and put their problems behind her.

The other helper, a thin, elderly woman Em had seen before, eased herself up to standing, ruefully rubbing her back with both hands. She smiled at Em.

Then, as she raised her lined face to the afternoon sun, an arrow thudded into her throat. Its black feathers thrummed slightly then it was still, as if it had always been there. In that long, silent heartbeat dark blood gushed briefly from the woman's neck and she dropped like a stone.

Em heard the swish of more arrows in the air, then a heavy blow on her back knocked her sprawling.

Stern Edasson heard the arrows' lethal flight before he saw them and he shoved the girl down on the rocky ground behind his soldiers. He raised his shield, leaned over and tipped the water from his helm and crammed it on his head.

'Arrows!' the useless officer warned, far too late, as more thudded into them, hitting only the leather of their shields, the metal of their helmets.

Riding down the shale slope opposite were two Fkeni bowmen, gripping their mounts with their knees and loosing shafts with astonishing speed. Their well-trained ponies were sitting back on their haunches, hooves sliding on the shifting shale, while their riders leaned back with them in perfect balance.

But the bowmen won no more victims and as the ponies reached the foot of the slope the Pigstickers charged. Stern lanced a spear into one bowman's side. The Fkeni's pony reared and bolted as another spear jabbed it in the chest. The rider fell forward on to its neck and he clung on as the pony galloped back down the ravine. The second pony stumbled and fell to its knees as the warriors attacked and its rider was pulled off and swiftly butchered.

Looking around, Stern saw the officer had been holding position at the rear the whole time. Once the threat was over he stepped forward.

'You,' he pointed at Stern, 'take this pony and ride to the army with all speed. Bring back a cart for the women. We need to leave here. Quickly.'

Stern sighed to himself. The man's a moron, he thought. 'Leg's broken,' he replied shortly. 'It's not going anywhere.'

The officer turned to look; the pony's slender foreleg was at an angle, the bone poking through the brown hair. He said nothing as a soldier led it limping to the threshold of the shallow shelter, then drew a razor-sharp blade. The pony shuddered and collapsed. The officer might be a fool but Stern did not have to tell him its carcass would furnish small protection against further attack. And he did not have to be told such an attack would inevitably come if the wounded Fkeni made it back to his friends.

The officer – what was his name, Carralus, Caius? – had been attached to their unit as they left the City. He was younger than most of the Pigstickers, with a pale, round face and fierce freckles. Stern had already learned that the man knew less about battle tactics than the Fkeni's dead pony, and now it seemed he was a coward too. Officers like him – usually sons or nephews of someone with influence – tended to die quickly in battle, often at the hands of the enemy. Stern knew the other soldiers would look to him now, and the burden lay heavy on his shoulders. Their situation was impossible. Even if the pregnant woman died right this moment they'd be unlikely to catch up with the army by nightfall.

He saw the girl scramble over to the woman with the arrow in her neck, but Stern knew she was dead, her rheumy eyes already filling with dust. The fat midwife was speaking gently to the girl in labour, but the whore was wide-eyed and delirious and seemed unaware of what was happening. Her face was pale as ice over water, and he could see that her dress and the cloth she lay on were drenched with dark blood.

The officer marched over to them. 'We must move this woman,' he said to the midwife. 'My troops will make a litter of their spears and carry her.'

Stern was watching his face, anxious and pale. He's not a moron, he thought, he is just frightened of making decisions, frightened they will be wrong, frightened of pain and of death.

'Don't be a fool, man,' the midwife told him. 'See all this,' she gestured at the blood soaking the ground. 'You can't move her. You'd kill her.'

'We'll all be dead if we stay here.'

The officer's words were undeniable. Stern and the other veterans watched the man with detached curiosity, wondering what he would say next.

'If we remain here, will she survive the . . . er . . . birth?' he asked, feeling his way towards a decision.

The midwife shrugged and turned her face away. The officer looked around at his soldiers who regarded him without expression. There was no help there. Stern knew they all wanted to press on and catch up with the army before sunset. If the Fkeni came back they could never survive the night. And the tribesmen had a unique way with death . . .

Yet they all thought of themselves as heroes and couldn't march off and leave the women. And the little girl with the heart-shaped face belonged to the tall

Wildcat veteran. There was no way Stern could look into his cold, pale eyes in the future if he abandoned the girl to torment and slow death. But if enough tribesmen attacked them, then that would be the fate of them all.

Still the officer said nothing so Stern took pity on him.

'We can protect this area,' he offered, and the officer turned to him with relief in his eyes. Stern jogged over to the other side of the mountain trail and looked up.

'There's nothing up above us but sheer rock,' he called. Then he walked slowly back, looking around him, collecting the Fkeni bows as he came.

'They can only come at us from front and sides. They'll come up the trail. This,' he gestured to the slaughtered pony, 'will give us some protection from their shafts.'

'We'll need a fire,' said the officer, looking around as if one might be in sight.

'The light of the fire will draw them,' Grey Gus growled at him, contempt in his voice and eyes.

'They won't need a fire to draw them,' Stern argued. 'If the injured one got back, they'll be coming. You can be sure of that. But a fire will steal our night vision. The Fkeni won't be sitting around staring into a campfire if they have a battle ahead.'

He handed the officer the two black bows. The man looked at them for a long moment. Then, 'Arrows!' he ordered. 'Collect all their arrows. Quickly now. Just the whole ones.'

Stern spoke to him quietly. 'Broken arrows can still kill,' he said.

'And the broken ones,' the officer added. 'Quickly.'

Stern sighed again. It was going to be a long bloody night.

There are seven of us, he thought. Six really. He

couldn't count Officer Quickly. For all Stern knew, the man might be a ferocious fighter but he'd seen no evidence of it. So Stern had three veterans – Benet, Gus and Quora. Once night fell, at least Benet's poor eyesight would no longer be a drawback. Quora was the steadiest. He should charge her with protecting the women, yet he was reluctant to waste such a fine warrior in the back line. He would see that the officer volunteered for that duty. The two last soldiers were young and untried. They were also brothers, Cam and Farren Cordover. They'd both attacked the Fkeni riders with gusto and without hesitation, and he hoped for much from them.

He looked up at the sky. Thin clouds were coming in from the north, which meant no stars, no light except for the thin sliver of the old moon cradling the new. He thought about it.

'Collect brushwood,' he ordered. 'Twigs, dry leaves, tumbleweed. Only the driest.' The soldiers set to with a will.

Stern looked at the back of the shallow shelter where the girl and the midwife were sitting on either side of the whore. The midwife was staring into the distance, perhaps sorting through old memories, trying to distance herself from their plight. The girl was clearly frightened, her eyes darting around, unable to settle. Stern considered giving her a weapon, but decided she'd be useless in a fight. She'd probably kill herself before she injured any of the enemy.

He sat down and rested his back against the still warm body of the pony and started to sharpen his weapons.

The sunset was turning the shale slope across the defile to bright orange. Their small encampment was in deep shadow already, and soon the sun would abandon them to darkness. Emly was as terrified as she had ever been. She hugged her knees and tried to stop trembling. Beside her Maura hovered between unconsciousness and delirium. From time to time she would awaken and try to sit up and speak; she would reach forward with her hands as if she could see someone, her eyes wide with recognition or, perhaps, pain. Then she would lapse into sleep again, the sleep of the dying. Bruenna felt her belly for movements from the babe but she could detect nothing.

Em cursed the fleeting whim that had brought her here. She thought of Evan all the time, wondering where he was and if he'd returned to the army and learned she'd gone. Or was he far away still, unaware of her predicament? Hope fluttered weakly within her. Could she really expect Evan Broglanh to rescue her a third time?

She looked up as the woman soldier, short and blonde, with brightly coloured beads woven into her hair, came over to them and knelt down.

'What's her name?' she asked, looking at the dead woman with the arrow in her throat. Em shook her head and turned to Bruenna, who shrugged. Suddenly Emly felt unutterably sad that this old woman, who had once had a life, with a mother and father and friends and, probably, children and grandchildren, should be lying dead and nameless far from home. Whatever happened this night she could not be buried, not in this unforgiving rock, and she would be abandoned to lie here alone while the creatures of mountain and sky had their fill of her.

The soldier was searching her body and found a wooden pendant attached to a thong round the woman's neck. She tore it off and handed it to Em. It was a crudely carved tree with thick trunk and wide branches. Em showed it to Bruenna and the midwife recognized it.

'It is a symbol of Vashta, guardian of the night.'

The soldier snorted. 'Perhaps if she had survived the day, Vashta would have protected her tonight. Perhaps it will protect the rest of us.' She dragged the black arrow out of the woman's throat and handed it to Emly too. For a moment the girl wondered why, then she realized: *she's giving me a weapon*.

'This won't do much good,' she grumbled, thinking a stout tree branch would be easier and more effective to wield.

'It's not for the enemy,' the warrior said.

She watched to see if Em understood, then she said fiercely, 'You must not be captured by the Fkeni. A quick death at your own hand is best.'

Then she looked at the midwife, who rummaged in a pocket of her clothing and brought out a short, sharp-looking knife. 'I'll see to it,' Bruenna told her. 'You can count on it.'

The soldier said to Emly, 'Keep the arrow. If you get the chance, it'll gouge an eye out.'

They took the officer first. And no one heard him go.

Despite all the dry twigs and brush Stern had ordered his soldiers to spread around their shelter, despite the fact that all ears were tuned to the slightest movement in the night, the Fkeni tribesmen made no sound when they captured the man and took him back to their camp. Stern guessed afterwards it had happened when a slip of stones rattled down the cliff above them, startling them all and making them curse and grumble before settling again. Or, once, they all heard a scuffling sound, then smelled the pungent odour of fox as a skinny vixen ran through their warning line of brushwood. Or perhaps the fool had just walked away to piss – Stern wouldn't have put it past him.

As it was, they only realized the officer had been

taken when Quora directed a question to the man and got no reply. Stern hissed, 'Sir?' into the darkness. He still didn't know the man's name. There was only silence. Benet, Gus and the brothers spoke up, confirming their presence. But the officer had gone.

Stern tried to tell himself the man had crept away into the dark and run up the trail, hoping to spot the army's campfires in the distance. This self-delusion only lasted until the first screams were brought to them on the night breeze, freezing their bones and chilling their souls. The first screams were of terror, of disbelief at what was to be done to him. Then they rose in pitch and desperation to an insane wailing.

'We have to go after him?' young Farren Cordover asked, fear trembling through his voice.

'Yes, we have to,' said his brother Cam, the older of the two. 'He's one of us.'

'There's nothing we can do,' Stern told them. 'That's why they're doing this. To lure us out. And out there, blundering around in the dark, we'd get no further than a few paces before they picked us off. Then we'd get the same treatment.'

The screams rose in intensity. Stern resisted the desire to hold his hands over his ears. They could hear words forming: 'Help me. Help! Gods, help me!'

'There's nothing we can do,' he repeated loudly, momentarily drowning out the sound at least to his own ears. 'Quora?'

'Yes.' Her voice was firm.

'Talk to the women.'

He heard her scrambling back to the rear of the shelter. He could not hear the words but he could hear her calm, reassuring tones, and the girl's anxious high-pitched replies. He heard nothing from the midwife, and he wondered if the pregnant one was dead. He asked Quora when she came back.

'Not yet,' she said, sitting down next to him. Then with some pride, 'City woman. She's strong.'

As the night thickened the warriors kept trying to talk, to distract themselves from the awful sounds drifting in from the darkness, but their words would always falter to a halt, overwhelmed by horror and dread. Finally the thin moon appeared from behind the clouds and each could see the others' faces, gaunt and haunted. Stern guessed he must have dozed off for a moment or two because he startled awake at a yell from the girl and suddenly the camp was alive.

The Fkeni came screaming at them out of the night, black robes flapping like the wings of the death gods. They had blackened their faces with soot and, in their tradition, they had painted white spots representing eyes above their own eyes to baffle their enemy. They carried curved blades crusted with the blood of past victims.

But the City soldiers were not dismayed. They were ready for them and they were glad of the chance to fight. They raised the tips of their spears, lying ready on the ground, stomped the haft ends into the ground with their boots, and the first few attackers were impaled on the needle-sharp points.

There were only six Pigstickers against perhaps twenty tribesmen, and the Fkeni carried with them, alongside their long curved knives, the zeal of the righteousness of their cause against the foreigners and the exhilaration of hours spent with the tortured man. But the City soldiers were well armoured and they had been fighting for years, four of them for more than a decade. They were very good at what they did.

Stern took no time to enjoy his enemy's agony as a tribesman died skewered on his spear. He tore it out of the body then drove it into a second attacker. It plunged into his throat and lodged in his spine. Stern drew his sword and slashed at a man coming at him from his right. The attacker fell back and Stern pulled the spear out of the Fkeni's throat and used it to block a scythe-blow from his left. Quora was protecting his left and, after he killed his man, he glanced around quickly. She had moved to her own left, protecting a gap in their line, stopping the tribesmen who were outflanking her to try to get to the three women. A gap in their line . . .

The Pigstickers were fighting in grim silence, apart from grunts and sighs. The Fkeni carried on screaming as they attacked, as they died. Then there was a bellowed order and the attackers retreated into the night and the silence suddenly closed around the City warriors as if it had never been breached.

'Hold!' Stern shouted, lest battle-fury tempt any of his soldiers to chase after them.

He ordered them all back behind the pony's carcass then called for names and injuries. Grey Gus had a serious wound across his shoulder, making his right arm useless. He was left-handed, though, and the injury would not slow him when lives were on the line. Benet had a chest injury, a shallow one which he was tending himself. Quora and Cam Cordover had no injuries worth reporting.

But Farren Cordover had vanished.

'Did anyone see him go?' Stern asked them.

'Go?' repeated his brother, his voice panicked. 'You think he ran away? Those dung-eaters took him. I'm going after him.'

There was a scuffle in the blackness as Benet grabbed hold of the lad. Stern said to him, 'No, I don't believe he ran away, soldier, but if you go running after him you'll be chasing certain death.'

'I can't leave him!' the young man cried. There was desperation in his voice. 'I'd never—'

'Remember why we're here,' Stern growled. 'We hold, we defend, we protect and we guard, until morning.' He looked up. 'Eyes front!'

The others, who had been watching the exchange, turned away and took their places again.

'Listen,' Stern said to Cam. 'Listen to me, soldier!' he ordered as the young man kept glancing back into the darkness as if readying himself to run off. Cam nodded, his eyes still flickering around.

Stern lowered his voice confidentially. 'If they've taken your brother they won't torment him until the officer dies. That is their way. One at a time. It increases the horror and dread for the next captive. Do you understand?' He waited until Cam took this in then nodded, his breathing calming.

'It'll be dawn soon,' Stern said to him. 'We'll stand a better chance then.'

As he turned away he caught Gus's eye and shook his head fractionally. The veteran knew the score better than most of them – he had come up against Fkeni before. Stern knew his words to Cam were vague and he didn't need anyone arguing with him. He had no intention of leaving the transient safety of this cliff to rescue the soldier, any more than he had for the officer. They'd been ordered to guard the women. They would do this before saving themselves. But he was aware that their only chance now was if the army realized they were missing and someone volunteered to come back for them. And how likely was that?

CHAPTER NINETEEN

HER MEMORIES OF CHILDHOOD WERE LIKE SCRAPS OF leaves blown about in a storm. There was the constant grumbling thunder of dread, scattered with lightning flashes of pain and alarm. Much of Emly's young life she had spent hiding, first at home – wherever that was – then down in the Halls, and she learned that silence was a virtue. She had since noticed that it was a rare commodity among men and women, its price reflecting its rarity. In silence lived calm and, to some degree, contentment.

She listened as the Pigstickers spoke together in the gathering darkness, each soldier's fear igniting alarm in the others. They could not help but speak of the captured man's torture. The words tumbled out of them as if by speaking them they would ease their own terror. Stern's repetition of 'There's nothing we can do' was intended to calm them – even Em could see that – but they could not help but speak, as if they were expelling their fear and pain by vomiting up the words for it.

Silence is the only way, Emly thought. In silence I will rise above the terror and the dread to a place where only I exist and where there is no fear, for fear lives in other people . . .

An arrow thwacked into the rock-face above her head. Bouncing off, it scored shards of loose rock which pattered down on the women. Em leaped up shouting a warning, but the warriors were already on their feet. The Fkeni tribesmen were charging at them out of the darkness. There seemed to be hundreds of them. They had to go over or round the dead pony, which gave the City warriors a heartbeat of extra time. Some of the Fkeni skewered their bodies on spears, their battle screams turning to cries of anguish.

Em looked at the broken arrow she had been gripping tightly in her hand and threw it aside.

'Give me your knife,' she said to Bruenna, but the midwife shook her head, her face pale and her expression firm. She did not have to explain: she would use it to cut Maura's throat and her own rather than hand it over to Emly.

The girl looked to the left of the line, closest to her, where Quora had speared a tribesman through the torso and stepped forward to take on another. The injured man was crawling forward, behind the line now, a curved blade in one blood-drenched hand. Em ran forward and stamped her boot on the hand as hard as she could, feeling bones crunch. She was about to snatch the knife from the man's fingers when there was a shouted order and the Fkeni vanished away again, leaving their dead and dying. Stern walked back to the injured man and cut his throat. He glared at Emly, as if wondering what she was doing, and picked up the dagger.

Em sat down again next to Bruenna, feeling useless. She was terrified by the way the enemy appeared out of darkness then vanished in a heartbeat. They seemed to be taunting the soldiers. Her stomach clenched in a pang of dread for how this night might end.

'That went well,' Stern said, raising his voice so the

women could hear. 'Chances are they'll wait until dawn now and attack en masse. Remember they'll be trying to take us alive. This will give us a great advantage.'

Em stood up. 'I need a weapon,' she said resolutely, walking over to the watching soldiers. 'Something better than a broken arrow.'

'Here, take this.' The woman Quora handed the girl her own knife, a long, wickedly sharp blade.

'No. Give it back,' ordered Stern. To Quora he explained, 'You'll do more damage with it than she will.'

'You can't leave us weaponless,' Em said to him, looking up into his dark-blue eyes. 'Give me a good knife and I'll protect Bruenna and Maura.' She found her voice was firm and level and she stared up at him unblinking.

Stern looked surprised and he hesitated.

'I will not be taken,' she assured him with perfect certainty, 'and I will ensure they are not either. Trust me. Give me a knife.'

Stern shrugged and stepped forward to hand her the dagger he'd taken from the Fkeni, but Quora moved in, took the enemy blade for herself and handed the girl her own knife. She looked at Stern, who shrugged acceptance.

Emly looked at the warrior's knife in the light of the moon. It was the length of her forearm, with a blood channel following its line. She looked up at the two soldiers and managed a smile, pleased with their confidence in her.

Stern told her, 'We're not called Pigstickers for nothing.'

Emly nodded. 'It's beautiful.' There were markings etched into the blade. She had only started learning to read, but she was fairly sure the marks were not of the

City tongue. They looked ancient and spoke to her of a land far away and, perhaps, long ago.

From behind her came a moan and a rattling sigh. She turned and saw Bruenna leaning close over Maura, listening for her breath of life. Finally the midwife shook her head. 'She's dead,' she said.

'What a pigging waste,' one of the soldiers said venomously, and Em wondered if he meant it was a waste of life, of Maura and her unborn baby, or of their own lives, thrown away on a hopeless cause.

She slumped down beside Maura, seeing the pain and fear smoothed from her face, seeing a young girl, no older than she was, with the spark of life fled.

Bruenna laid her head on the dead girl's belly and closed her eyes. Long heartbeats passed. Em watched, wondering that the midwife hadn't given up yet.

Then, 'It's still alive,' the woman said loudly, picking up the little knife. Stern gave the other soldiers a sharp order, then he and Quora both wandered over to watch.

Bruenna ripped off the rags of the dead girl's dress and expertly slit the belly. Blood oozed but did not flow. In the poor light Em wondered how much the midwife could see and she wished they had a fire. She looked up to the sky and saw clouds racing towards the moon.

Quora had seen the same thing. 'We're nearly out of light,' she commented.

Bruenna must have been working from memory and experience, for surely she could not see what she was doing, but suddenly she sat back and Em could make out something in her hands. The baby's body gleamed a little in the dim light and Bruenna shook it gently. It let out a weak squeal.

'There's a shawl in that bag,' the midwife said to Emly, who scrambled to get it. She held it out and

Bruenna thrust the babe into her arms and wrapped it quickly. Em felt its thin body move feebly against her and was startled to find tears welling.

Bruenna was briskly tying off and cutting the cord. 'Will it live?' Emly asked her.

'Babies are hardy,' the midwife said, cleaning up around Maura's body. 'They only have to do one thing – stay alive. That's what they're good at. But we need to get some milk into it.'

Stern grunted with satisfaction and the two soldiers turned back to their duty.

'It's a boy,' Bruenna told their backs, and they heard the words repeated among the remaining soldiers.

Em cuddled the baby close to her, smelling its warm body. She stilled herself and focused, and could feel its tiny heartbeat. She felt her eyes welling again and told herself sternly that tears wouldn't help the mite, only her knife and her determination. She decided then that she would die before the baby did and the thought gave her comfort as she waited for the dawn.

The sky was dark blue and she could just make out the shape of the mountains high above when the Fkeni came back. Stern was right, there were more of them this time, far more than the few soldiers could hold back.

Emly wrapped the baby up tightly in the shawl and laid it at the back of their shallow shelter. She looked at Bruenna, who nodded to her. The midwife held her sharp little knife.

Emly watched the battle anxiously, trying to learn what the soldiers were doing, but it was impossible. From her vantage point behind them it was just a frenzied battle of clashing metal and screams of pain. The soldiers were hacking at anything that moved, and the tribesmen were trying to overwhelm them with their greater numbers. There seemed to be no skill, no art such as in the sword-fights she had witnessed in the Hall of Emperors where she had watched, with terror, as Evan took on one warrior after another on the red staircase. There was nothing for her to learn here except to keep on hacking at your enemy until he was dead or disabled. I can do that, Em thought, holding the long knife so tightly her hand cramped.

And then her time came. An injured Fkeni found a momentary space between two of the soldiers and lunged through. He ran at the women, dagger raised. Em leaped forward, then ducked to one side as he plunged the blade towards her breast. She twisted and rammed her knife into his side, above the hip. It went in a short way then seemed to stick. She wrenched it out, twisting it. The man fell to one knee but kept crawling towards Bruenna. The midwife placed her large body in front of the baby's and slashed at his face with her own knife. Em plunged her blade into the Fkeni's neck. He dropped to the ground, blood pouring. Then it slowed to a trickle. She stared at him, gasping, fearful he would rise again.

'He's dead,' said Bruenna.

Em turned back to the battle. She could see the old warrior Gus battling two Fkeni and she ran forward to help. Before she could get there Gus sliced the throat of one of them. The second screamed his battle cry and swept his curved blade at Gus. Gus swayed to one side but the blade sliced his shoulder and he went down. The Fkeni caught his weapon at the top of its swing and, with graceful ease, brought it down again towards Gus's head. Emly picked up a discarded spear as she ran and thrust it at the tribesman's back. It was a weak strike and caught in his robes, but it deflected the arc of his blade and it drove into the ground. He pulled out a knife, too late. Gus was up and he ran his sword into the man's belly. The veteran glanced quickly at Em, nodded, and threw himself at the next opponent.

Then, beyond the screams and the howls, Emly heard a growing rumble, like a summer storm. Suddenly the air was thick with whirling dust and the narrow defile was crowded with horses and riders. Cavalry! City cavalry! Em found herself shaking uncontrollably. She looked eagerly for Evan but could make out no one she knew in the melee.

Then a Fkeni fighter fought free and ran at her. Em held the long knife in front of her, trembling. The dark-robed tribesman batted the knife aside with his sickle and made a grab for her. She threw herself back in terror, angling her body across where the baby lay. At that moment the mite started a thin, hungry grizzle. The Fkeni heard it and grinned at her. He stepped forward, sickle raised.

From the melee a big man emerged, ginger-headed and blood-spattered, a giant among the black-clad tribesmen. He took two rolling strides and with a mighty slash of his sword he cut the Fkeni's head half off. Gore spouted as the body dropped in the dust. The big man calmly nodded his head to Emly, then he twisted and blocked a sword-thrust from behind. He plunged his blade into the attacker's gut and the man fell screaming.

The unequal battle was soon over, all the tribesmen despatched. Emly, weak from fear and horror, looked anxiously for survivors. Of the Pigstickers only Stern and Quora still stood. The young man whose brother had been captured was dead, as was the old man Gus. The other soldier, the half-blind one, was wounded and Stern was tending him. The injury to his arm looked painful but survivable, in Emly's small experience.

She listened to the troopers talk and learned their rescuers had been out scouting far to the west and were riding hard to catch up with the army. They had found the Fkeni encampment, led by the screams of the tortured officer. The riders had slaughtered the women, who were taking turns with the victim, despatched the wretched man and released the other City soldier, who was unharmed bar a few bruises. Then they followed the tribesmen's trail.

The sun was well above the horizon by the time Em helped Bruenna on to a Fkeni pony, placed the sleeping babe in her arms, then climbed wearily on to another mount. She sat there, horses milling around her. The cavalrymen were still exhilarated by their swift, bloody victory, but she was exhausted by the night of terror.

'You all right, lass?' asked a deep, rough voice and she turned and saw the big man who had saved her life. She managed a smile for him. He wore his greying ginger hair and beard in braids, like a northlander, although he was dressed as a mercenary, in a mixture of uniform purloined from different regiments.

'Thank you, sir,' she said formally, and he grinned at her.

'You look banjaxed,' he told her. 'Can you ride?'

In answer she heeled the pony forward and it set off up the defile. The big man rode beside her, a strong, comforting presence. The movement of the pony, the fresh air in her face, made Emly's spirits lift. She had survived the night and she would see Evan again.

She turned to the northlander. 'My name is Emly,' she told him, the least she could do, she thought, for someone who had given her her life.

'Emly.' He frowned, his thick brows bristling together fiercely. 'Do you have a brother called Elija, who lives up in that high palace and has the empress for a handmaiden?'

She laughed. 'Yes, I do,' she said. 'Why? Do you know him?'

'I do, lass. And I was glad when I heard he still lived. He and I shared many an adventure together.'

He sketched a salute to her, grinned and said, 'They call me Stalker.'

CHAPTER TWENTY

CASMIR, ONCE KNOWN AS THE WOLF, NOW SPECIAL prisoner number seven, lay on the earth floor of his cell and prayed to the death gods to end his suffering. So far they had turned deaf ears to his pleas.

As a child he had broken both legs. Well, *he* had not broken them. His father had when he dropped the boy from a second-floor balcony as punishment for some childish scrape – breaking a window, or setting fire to a cat. Casmir had prayed then too, and it had made no difference. But his mother had gathered all her small savings and taken the boy to a surgeon who had straightened the bones and splinted them so that within a few days the legs had healed like new. Lying in his cell in the Dungeons of Gath, one of Casmir's many fears was that his legs would heal while still shattered, leaving him, even if he were ever freed, the choice of dragging himself about the City as a beggar or ending it any way he could manage.

In his former role as agent for Rafael Vincerus, he had often been asked to despatch one of the lord's enemies. And the victims usually prayed to the death gods for a clean ending and he had always made it so. Perhaps that was why those perverse deities failed to listen to him now, because in the past he had denied them the pleasure of many a long and lingering death. The world is full of such irony, he thought.

The pain inflicted on him since his capture had been unendurable, but he had endured it. It was such as would send a man insane, but he was not insane. He had told his torturers all they wanted to know about his mission at the House of Glass to kill the old man Bart, and other missions. When they remained unsatisfied he had started making up stories. Finally he said he had killed a dragon which emerged burning from the sewers and carried its head to the empress.

When they came for him again he cried and pleaded. He could not help himself, although he knew it would do no good. He would be picked up and placed on his feet, then his half-healed breaks would break again . . .

But this time was different. The guards brought a litter and laid it on the earth beside him and, almost with care, placed him upon it. Then they picked him up and carried him, by torchlight, on a long journey through the underground places of the City. It was still a torment and he blacked out into blissful unconsciousness a few times. But, as ever, his curiosity overcame all and eventually he started watching with something like interest as the roofs above him changed, in what became a journey from darkness into light. At last they came to a stone chamber where they set him down and produced ropes and straps. Casmir's fears came roaring back. What were they going to do to him? But all they did was tie him to the litter, then they started up a series of stairs.

At last they came out into daylight and Casmir's tears were not only from the brightness around him. The last time he had been brought into the light it was for his brief trial. Was he to be tried again or to hear his fate? The many and hideous forms of imperial execution flitted through his mind like old, ragged bats.

He was placed on a floor. A sharp voice barked, 'Not on the carpet, you oafs!'

His litter was moved and he opened his one eye and squinted around. He saw the brutal faces of his guards and, upside-down, the pale face of a woman. She walked around him until he could see her properly. She was old, with long white hair, wearing a white gown and a blue shawl. He recognized the woman who had presided at his trial. Then he realized it was the empress, and his labouring heart shrank like a dried grape. Through the pain and disorientation and fear, he readied himself to tell her exactly what she wanted.

She gestured and the faces of the guards disappeared. A small stool was placed close by him. The empress sat down and bent forward so he could see her.

'Do you know who I am?' she asked him, tilting her head and gazing into his brutalized face. He tried to speak but his broken jaw had swollen. He tried to lift his head to nod but he had not the strength.

The empress touched his face gently.

'Do you know who I am?' she asked again.

For a heartbeat he felt only the butterfly touch of her soft skin on his ravaged jaw. Then cold lightning flashed in his mind, and clotted thoughts of his stifling dark cell and pain and blood were replaced by a great hollow emptiness, full of clear light and overwhelming ennui. In a flash of images he saw a small girl, fair-haired and round-faced, smiling with her arms uplifted to him, then a crescent moon – the old moon of a tired world – and a cross on a crow-haunted hill, and the cloying scent of jasmine.

The pain drifted from his face and he opened his good eye to see the clouds that had been gathering there dispersing. He could see as well as he ever had.

He could see now that the woman was much older than he first thought. He opened his mouth to reply to her question, anxious to please, but his mouth was filled with ashes.

'Water,' she said, as if she were inside his head, and a hand brought a cup to his lips and another lifted his head with care. He drank the pure, clean water as though it was the last he would ever have.

'Do you know me?' she asked him a third time, and he swallowed and said grittily, 'Yes, lady.'

She smiled and her face became younger again. He realized she was beautiful.

'Your name is Casmir?'

'Yes, lady.'

'And you worked for Rafael Vincerus?'

'Yes.'

'And he ordered you to the House of Glass in Blue Duck Alley to kill the old man Bartellus?'

'Yes.'

'Why do you think his daughter Emly failed to recognize you at your trial?'

He thought about it, the shock and pity in the girl's eyes. 'Because she has a kind heart,' he told Archange.

The empress sat back, apparently satisfied.

'Yes, she has,' she told him, 'and, as before, that kind heart is delivering her into grave peril.'

He waited, wondering what she wanted of him, for he had nothing to give.

'Emly has been abducted,' the empress told him, 'and I want her returned in safety here to the White Palace. I believe she was taken by a soldier and that the pair are travelling with the Khan army. Retrieving renegades was once your speciality, I'm told. I'm also told you are loyal and resourceful and, above all, discreet.'

That sly goblin, hope, whispered to him from the

recesses of his mind but he tried to ignore it. He was desperate to please the empress, but could not help but say what he believed. 'General Khan can deliver them to you far more quickly than I can.'

Her black eyes flashed and she said, 'Are you questioning me?'

'No, lady. But it will take time for my legs to heal,' he said honestly, 'and time to catch up with the army. There are a thousand men better equipped for this than I.'

She leaned forward once more and touched his legs, pausing on one, then the other. There was a hideous welling of agony and the half-healed bones felt as if they were breaking again, but then he was aware of the same cool, empty feeling, and the pain ebbed. His thoughts were of fire and blackened trees. Of carriages soaring in the sky. Of a baby nestled at the breast. He felt the tears run down his cheeks and he turned his face away from her dark stare.

Time passed and nothing seemed to happen. He opened his eye again and she was still watching. He tried to sit and was astonished to find he could, though he felt feeble. His body was whole. He wondered if this was a dream, or a nightmare in which he would suddenly be crippled again, dying in agony. He was given a cup of water and he drank it all down, marvelling as the cool liquid soothed his limbs, strengthening them.

He looked around. The only others present were two warriors of the Thousand, still as statues, their helms closed.

He asked the empress, trying to sound businesslike notwithstanding his filthy body and rags, 'What about the soldier? Shall I kill him?'

'Of course,' she said.

'And bring you his head as proof?'

'I do not want his head,' the empress told him. 'Just bring me his jacket.'

'Evan.'

'Mmm.'

'Teach me to fight with a sword. Please.'

'No.'

Emly rolled over on the dry, prickly grass and hoisted herself on his bare chest.

'Please.' She batted her dark lashes, gazing down at him, and he grinned.

'You are too small to wield a sword,' he told her, 'but I will show you how to use that pigsticker Quora gave you. It is a fine gift and should be used with respect. You could disembowel a man with that in a heartbeat.'

She smiled, pleased with his words but unsure if she could do such a thing.

Gazing up at the sky, Evan added, 'Just because you are travelling with an army, it doesn't make you a warrior.'

It was five days after the nightmare in the mountain pass. Evan and Chancey had still been far away when Em returned to the bosom of the army, and when they came back the next morning and were told of her ordeal she had made little of it. 'Stern and his soldiers protected me,' she told Evan and he had nodded curtly, as if that was only what he'd expect. Then she had told him about Stalker and he immediately sought out the northlander for he recognized the name.

Now they lay in the long grass of a sunny valley half a league from the path of the army. Patience stood nearby apparently dozing. The sun beat down on them and crickets creaked in the still afternoon air.

Emly remembered the time they had spent together above the baker's before the Day of Summoning. The

Evan Broglanh she knew then was just a soldier, albeit with a major role in the insurrection. He was loyal to Archange then, and his duty was clear. Now, she understood, things were more complicated and he was unhappy in his present task, though he was following it with grim determination.

But for the moment he was in a good mood and she was eager to take advantage of it.

'You must tell me why we are fleeing Archange when she has offered me nothing but kindness,' she told him.

He looked up at her, his eyes the grey of summer seas, his lashes white in the sunlight. 'I think the empress is fond of you, in her way,' he said, 'but she has other reasons for wanting you at the palace.'

Emly waited, for she of all people knew how to use silence, and eventually he went on. 'You remember what she told us, after the scrap in the Red Palace, about the Gulon Veil.'

The Gulon Veil, an artefact of great power, Archange had told them, but to Em it was just a veil, found in a sewer by her father Bartellus and given to her as her sole and precious possession. It was a creation of gossamer thread, light as birdsong, strong as the heart of a warrior. Em had been permitted to take it to the White Palace with her but then it had vanished for it was too valuable, the empress said, for her to wear.

'My veil,' she said.

'Yours by finder's right,' Evan agreed. 'The veil was once embedded in glass and formed a cocoon, Archange told us.' He looked at Em and she nodded, remembering the evening after the Day of Summoning, the weary warriors gathered around Bartellus' dying body. 'That cocoon was broken a long time ago and now the veil is of limited use. Archange planned to exploit your skills as a glassmaker to recreate it. The veil still holds some strength, but in such a cocoon it would be powerful again, for good or evil. Or so I am told.'

'I would have gladly helped her.'

He nodded. 'I know, and that is why I had to steal you away. Others, people who know more about it than I do, believe she wanted to use it as the emperor did, for foul purposes.'

'What people? What purposes?'

When he did not answer, Emly offered, 'She said the veil can make old people young, and make the dead live.' She had been told of the reflections which once walked the corridors of the Red Palace, corpses brought to life to wear any form the emperor chose. But she had never seen one.

'The empress could not save my father,' she added.

He sighed. 'Bart was too gravely injured.'

'Surely she can find another glassmaker. There must be others in the City.'

'No, there aren't. The old ones are all dead and no new ones have been apprenticed since the war sucked all the young people into the army. There are few artists of any kind. No painters, sculptors, poets. Just soldiers.' He added, 'She will find someone eventually, perhaps from foreign lands, but for now she is thwarted. Who did you learn your craft from?'

It was the first time he had asked her anything about herself that wasn't about a fight for life. 'An old man on Leaving Street,' she told him, remembering the smell and heat of the glassworks, an angry little man with bowed legs. 'Petronicus. He was harsh and could be unkind, but he was a good artist and teacher.'

She idly stroked the scar on her lover's forearm where the old S brand had been crudely removed, then the tattoo of seven stars on his bicep. *Why do soldiers have tattoos?* she wondered. Stern had a flying fish on his shoulder, which made Em think of the last glass window she ever made, with its vibrant sea creatures. When her life was quiet and safe, before she met Archange . . .

'Do you think she's trying to find us? Archange?' she asked.

'Count on it. She'll want my balls.' Evan watched the summer sky. 'And the false trails we laid won't have misled a wily tracker like Valerius for long. But tomorrow we will cross the Vorago into the land of Petrus, then we will leave the army and you will be safe.'

'Where will we go?' Em did not like the thought of leaving her new friends behind. 'Won't we help in the war against the barbarians?'

He shook his head. 'It is not your battle. Nor mine either. We'll follow the coast to Arocir, the Petrassi city where Chancey will have a boat for us.' Chancey had ridden off the day before, leaving Blackbird for Emly and taking a fast cavalry horse.

'A boat!' Emly was thrilled by the idea. Elija had travelled by boat and had a great deal to say about its pleasures and privations.

'What's a vorago?' she asked. She was full of questions now he was so forthcoming. She thought this must be why Peach and her sisters became whores. Men were so much more agreeable when they'd had their way.

'The Vorago is a deep crack in the earth marking the border of Petrus with the tribal lands. It is said to be a thousand spans deep and for centuries was impassable, but then the Petrassi built three great bridges over it. The army will cross those bridges tomorrow. Then they will trounce these barbarians and we will go sailing.'

Emly lay back in the sunshine, holding his hand to her breast. She closed her eyes, thinking over what he'd said. Then she sat up again, frowning.

'If you wanted to stop the empress using the Gulon Veil, surely it would have made more sense to steal it instead of me?'

'Ah, you've seen through my ploy,' he replied gravely, his eyes darkening. 'Hand me my jacket.'

She reached for the jacket, which was lying a few paces away. She hauled it towards her. It was of leather, like his old Wildcat jerkin, but the leather was black and smelled new and only slightly of horses. It was heavily padded across the back and shoulders.

Evan sat up and took it from her and broke a few of the neat stitches inside the hem. He pulled back a bit of the silken lining to reveal, sewn snugly inside, shimmering, the Gulon Veil.

CHAPTER TWENTY-ONE

DAWN THE NEXT DAY FOUND THE KHAN ARMY, twenty thousand strong, plus a battalion of camp-followers and a handful of wounded, lying east of the Vorago. They had marched through the night. The army's leaders Marcus Rae Khan and, particularly, Hayden Weaver, for whom Petrus was home, had been keen to be in striking distance by morning.

Hayden, formerly general of the last Petrassi army in the field against the City, now with an ambiguous role as counsel, liaison and ambassador, sat astride his horse and stared hungrily towards the west, where the hills of Petrus were shrouded in morning mist. Their long journey was ended and soon the battles would begin.

It was his fortieth year of war, forty years of sleeping on camp beds or the good earth, of camp food and soldiers' jests and griping, years of pain and endurance and, always, the hope that one day he would be free to leave this life and spend the final years he had left in a place of peace with his wife. Anna and their three sons had found sanctuary on the isle of Chalcos, many days' sail to the west. He had last seen her nine years before, in a hurried meeting before she sailed. The two oldest boys had gone ahead and Anna, babe in arms, had been distracted, worried more for them than for the husband who was about to return to war. He had felt aggrieved at the time, and since then he had felt sorrow for her for he knew she would have later cursed her distraction.

The land of Petrus had been conquered by the City more than a century before and Hayden and his brother, though born in Petrus, were of mixed parentage and raised in the Mountains of the Moon, in the high fastnesses of once-proud tribes who had now dwindled to a few fleeing folk grubbing a transient living from unforgiving valleys. Then, nearly forty years ago, the City armies had started leaving Petrus, finally quitting for good. But the Petrassi had to fight for their land all over again, were still fighting the waves of invaders who swept down from the colder, grimmer countries of the far north, lured by the promise of green plains and rich river valleys. And one northern tribe in particular had grown in strength and ferocity in the last few years, and it was these savages Hayden had come home, with the help of the City, to confront.

When they were youngsters, just starting to be moulded into the men they would become, Hayden and his brother Mason had left the mountains and travelled to Odrysia. There they gained an education, courtesy of the enlightened king Matthus. Mason joined the Odrysian military school. He was interested in history but fascinated by warfare and he eventually, inevitably, made his way to the home of warfare, the City, which was in the end his doom. Hayden, the elder, studied architecture and philosophy, mathematics and history, but was slowly, implacably drawn to the military as well.

Although Hayden had lived most of his seventy-odd years outside his homeland, he had fought for its freedom for the greater part of his life, and now his feelings were a turmoil. This day, if God permitted, he would set foot on Petrassi soil for the first time in decades and his life would be made whole. He tried not to think further forward, of being reunited with his wife and children. This day was enough.

Atop their warhorses a short way from the Vorago, both he and Marcus Rae Khan were troubled as the mist burned away and the green hills of Petrus came in sight. Not one of the scouts sent out in the past three days had returned and they had heard no word from the Petrassi army, sent on ahead, for more than a fortnight.

The land around them sharpened into focus and the two leaders kicked their mounts forward. Orders were shouted and the great mass of men and women moved into a walk. Horses snorted and shook their reins; soldiers shouted greetings and oaths at each other; and far behind them they heard the complaints of livestock as they were cajoled and prodded into movement. And above all was the familiar sound of more than forty thousand boots on the march.

Between the army and the Vorago was a gently sloping plain but the leaders set a measured pace. They had ensured that those at the rear, the baggage train and the camp-followers, had caught up before nightfall and been enveloped in the main body of armed men and women. They wanted the crossing to be performed as quickly as possible for there were, almost certainly, enemies waiting on the other side of the bridges, enemies who had had plenty of time to prepare.

The three bridges – called in the City tongue Power, Passion and Greatness – were each wide enough to take six men walking abreast. They had been constructed five hundred years before at the behest of the Petrassi god to demonstrate the nation's willingness to seek alliances and friendships in the wider world. They were built first of timber, then of iron and stone, and were a symbol of the determination of the nation, despite all indications to the contrary, that men could move forward together for their mutual progress. They were also, of course, easily defended if it came to it.

Despite himself, Hayden urged his horse Rosteval forward, his eyes straining for a sight of the chasm and the fabled bridges. He had never seen them before. Rosteval clopped up a small eminence on the shallow plain and his rider leaned forward. He blinked and peered. His eyes were getting very poor and he fumbled his spectacles out of a pocket.

Then he slumped in his saddle, shocked by what he saw and crushed by a cold wave of sorrow and disappointment.

The bridges were gone.

He heard Marcus curse and there was a wave of oaths and despairing groans as the news spread swiftly. They had thought themselves close to their target. What now? Marcus Rae Khan heeled his horse forward and Hayden followed more slowly. They rode up to the edge of the Vorago and looked down. The tattered ends of a bridge clung to the sides of the vertiginous abyss. Pieces of tortured iron stuck out of the remaining stone piers, broken stone littered the ledges and steep rocky slopes all the way down, down to a thread of river far below. For a moment Hayden thought he saw people down there, but he blinked and realized they were just the black motes that floated in his eyes in sunlight.

The gorge stretched directly north to south across their path. He gazed longingly across the void. The central bridge's site had clearly been chosen because the abyss narrowed there. Hayden visualized a rope hurled over first, then a rope bridge strung across, then, in time, a bridge of wood, and finally one of stone. The Petrassi side was a mere stone's throw away, but it might as well have been ten leagues. Even a good horse on its best day could not leap the gap.

'What has done this?' Marcus growled.

'Black powder,' Hayden replied quietly.

Marcus looked at him, his face red with frustration and anger. 'No wonder Marcellus was long determined to outlaw it. It is a terrible weapon.'

It is, Hayden thought, a worm of fear moving in his belly. He looked to his right. 'We will have to march north, go round.'

'A good ten days' march,' Marcus sighed. He started giving orders to his commanders.

Hayden felt angered, frustrated in his ambition, yet something deeper bothered him about this move by the enemy. He was expecting a fight – that was what he was there for. Everything he had heard of the invaders who had flooded Petrus from the north indicated they were uncivilized, followers of some pagan faith who fought without battle tactics or strategy. But the demolition of the bridges was sophisticated work, beyond the knowledge of wild-eyed barbarians. Was it reckless destruction, a brutish attempt to keep the City army from the land of Petrus? Or something more calculated, a show of might, a demonstration of intent? He wondered what mind was behind this stratagem. And what of the Petrassi army sent ahead of them? Did they too stand here looking at destroyed bridges? If so, what had become of them?

He stood in the stirrups and looked to his right, along this side of the gorge. The soft plain they stood on ended abruptly a hundred paces north and for as far as he could see beyond the land was rock-strewn and tumbled, like a ruined city, barren of trees or undergrowth. The early-morning sun cast multiple deep pockets of shadow – in which an enemy could hide. Dread coiled in his belly.

'Marcus,' he barked urgently, 'look to the north!'

As they watched a dark shape appeared on the horizon, a wide blur which darkened and coalesced. The enemy had been waiting for them! Marcus bellowed to his commanders. More shapes started rising from the cluttered landscape, closer, much closer. A dull clattering started, the sound of swords battering on shields. The Khan army's captains were racing the length of the lines, shouting orders. Men and women swiftly moved into battle formations to confront the foe on their flank, clapping helms on heads and strapping on breastplates as they deployed. Cavalry units galloped towards each end of the new front line. Marcus' bodyguard, fifty veteran warriors, moved in front of the two leaders and unsheathed their swords.

'We can't attack,' rumbled Marcus with something like disappointment, 'not on that terrain. Or use the cavalry.' He turned to Hayden. 'We'll wait for them to come to us. Good enough. Who are they, d'you think?'

'The enemy we're here to fight,' Hayden said, and shrugged. 'But we weren't expecting to confront them on this side.'

The enemy line came on slowly, hampered by the landscape they'd been hiding in. Hayden could see they were dressed in a motley of furs and hides, leather and metal, and bearing swords and knives, clubs and axes. He raised his eyes, peering through his spectacles. On the horizon more enemy units were gathering. There must, he thought, be a hidden valley.

All his fears had gone now. The past year of inaction, of endless politicking and diplomacy, all drifted away. Familiar routines re-established themselves. Hayden put his eyeglasses away in their box. He muttered a prayer to his god and tightened the straps of his light armour. He rinsed his mouth with water and spat it on the ground. One of his bodyguards fitted Rosteval's thick leather chest-guard and the horse snorted. Hayden patted him on the neck. The old boy knew what was coming.

Crashing their weapons against their shields, the first few enemy fighters came clear of the rocky ground and started to run in an undisciplined charge. Some City soldiers bellowed their battle chants, but they were ordered to stay quiet. So in stony silence the first line of the City waited, shoulder to shoulder, shields up, swords ready. They knew what they were doing. They didn't have to concern themselves with who they were fighting. After weeks of marching their blood was up for the first time and they were eager for enemy heads.

The first enemy warrior crashed into the line. He was tall and fair, his face and bare arms heavily tattooed. He was armed only with a studded club. As he raised it to strike his enemy two swords drove into his chest and he was dead before he hit the ground.

A league to the south-west, the Pigstickers were back from the action and they had leisure to prepare. Emly watched them putting on armour and helms, buckling straps and tying ties. She felt helpless. A small part of her wished she could stay and fight with her friends. But Evan had told her to take the horses and go, to follow the wives and whores who were streaming away eastward under orders to put as much distance as possible between themselves and the enemy. And part of her was desperate to flee the slaughter to come.

Evan rolled out his chain mail vest and dragged it on. Em sprang forward and buckled it closed on each side, then stepped back as he knelt to tie his greaves. He reached into a pack and took out three more knives and slid them into their places on his buckler. He was not looking at her.

'Got enough blades there?' Benet asked him jovially, but Evan made no reply. He had no time for fighting beside a soldier who was half-blind, although he wouldn't say so to Stern, whom he respected.

'He thinks he's a one-man army,' Benet added to the company in general, and Evan nodded abruptly. He had no tolerance for warriors who chatted before battle either, though he understood why they did.

Emly watched Quora, who was punching the padding in her helm into shape, cursing to herself, and she wished she'd had the time to ask the warrior to teach her to fight. She admired Quora. She wasn't tiny, like Em, but she was smaller than all the men yet they treated her as an equal. Quora had no time for Benet either.

The front line was getting closer, and Em tried to shut her ears to the sounds of men and women screaming and groaning and the clash and crash of swords and shields.

Evan stopped what he was doing and turned his pale, cold gaze on her. He said nothing but she knew he was telling her to go. He and Stalker had elected to stand with the infantry and it was her task to remove the horses to safety. 'If they stay here they'll end up in the battle. Do you want that?' he'd asked when she'd argued.

He was ready to fight. He had a sword in one hand, a shield strapped to his arm and a second sword at his side. On the Day of Summoning she'd been there to witness him fighting with two swords in the Hall of Emperors, and suddenly her blood ran cold and she was desperate to get away from there, from what was coming.

She said nothing, just nodded gravely, then walked

back to where the horses were hobbled. She unroped them and tied her packs on Patience. She looked back at Evan and saw he had put the black and silver jacket back on; it had his medical kit, such as it was, in the pockets. She thought of the Gulon Veil stitched snugly into the back. She climbed up on Blackbird, holding Patience's lead, and turned to say goodbye.

But she saw he had forgotten her already. He was talking to Stern, his head down, a look of fierce concentration on his face. She turned her horse's head and headed east.

The sun was moving down the sky and the shadows were long once more, as they had been at the start of the day, the start of the battle.

Stern lay in the dirt and waited for death. In the loud heartbeats before the blade would slice his spine he realized he had been outfought, out-thought. His opponent had feinted to the right and Stern, tired and blood-weary, had followed the sword and not seen the punch coming. It had knocked him sideways, dazed, leaving his back an open target.

But the blade-thrust did not come and Stern, reprieved, rolled over and scrambled up. His opponent lay dying, split open from guts to throat. Stalker was standing over him. The big man grinned and said, 'You're welcome,' then launched back into the battle.

Stern spat out two teeth and looked around. There was a lull in the fighting, but a brief one. The enemy strategy was clear as day. The City forces were being driven back towards the chasm of the Vorago on the west and the sea-cliffs to the south. The enemy army was advancing from north and east, leaving just a narrow corridor along the high southern cliffs for the defenders to flee in the direction of the City. The more they were pushed back towards the cliff-edge, the more tempting that escape route would become. So far Stern had seen no one run. No one wanted to be the first to bolt. But it was obvious now that the enemy – whoever they were – outnumbered them at least two to one. These were odds Stern had taken before and won, but he feared the enemy had strategies left to play.

He watched as Broglanh cut down an enemy soldier, lancing him in the throat, then the warrior cast a murderous glance back at Stern who awoke from his reverie and stepped up beside him.

'We're outnumbered,' he said.

'We're always outnumbered,' Broglanh grunted as another tattooed fighter ran at him. He ducked at the last moment and drove his sword into the man's belly. 'City warriors fight best when they're outnumbered,' he said, dragging the blade out.

Stern grinned. It was something he'd heard all his soldier's life.

'Look to your brother,' Broglanh warned, dodging a blow from a cudgel and felling the man bearing it.

Stern looked to the left and saw Benet fighting in a little island of his own. He was a menace to his own comrades for he was flailing and hacking at anyone who came close. Stern moved up near him, beyond his range, and despatched an injured man, then shouted, 'Brother!'

Benet's head swung round towards him and at that moment a man came from his left, a long spear at waist level.

'Down!' Stern yelled and, though Benet hadn't seen the threat, he dropped like a stone and rolled under the spearman's feet. The man, at full pelt, stumbled and fell and Stern moved in and sliced the back of his neck under the helm, cutting through bone and gristle. He bent and tore off the bright crimson sash the man wore and tied it round his left bicep.

'I'll stand to your right,' he told Benet. 'Watch for me. Try not to kill me.'

Benet nodded, his eyes wide and full of fear.

The City warriors who'd been fighting in front of them were the Hogfodders, doughty warriors all. They had slowly been forced back by the enemy. The last few were holding their own but their comrades from other companies on either side were giving way step by step and soon the Hogfodders would be surrounded. There seemed to be no one left to give them orders so Stern bellowed for them to retreat ten paces and the veterans complied. They withdrew to line up with Stern and his warriors and for a moment there was a pause. Stern wiped the blood and sweat from his eyes.

At that moment a deep drum-note shivered across the battlefield and the enemy started to withdraw, five paces, ten. Stern looked up in the sky.

'Arrows!' he shouted and they raised their shields as one as a volley of arrows peppered their armour. A second volley followed, then Stern uncovered and looked left and right. None of his comrades had been injured.

'Cowards!' Quora spat. Bowmen were the lowest of the low. Killing from a distance was considered dishonourable work and even the City's own bowmen, though not quite despised, were not valued as warriors – they were barely equal with the stretcher-bearers in most soldiers' estimation.

Stern and his comrades had time to advance a few paces before the enemy hit them again. They mostly had fair or reddish hair, like Broglanh and Stalker, both from wild northern lands. But their faces were thickly tattooed. Few carried shields and they were throwing themselves at the line wildly as if careless of death or butchery. They were easy to kill, but there were so many of them. Inside his armour his skin crawled. *Who are they?* he thought. This army was surely the one the City and Petrassi forces had allied to fight. That was good enough for most soldiers. But not for Stern. What did they want? And, whoever they were, if they were triumphant this day and the City soldiers were left as bones and blood and flesh without life, what next? Was this a battle on which the future of the City would turn?

One of them came at him carrying a broadsword the size of a roof beam. Stern's usual ploy with such an opponent was to sway back from the heavy swing then lunge and pierce the swordsman under the exposed arm. But this giant swung his weapon low, intending to cut up and across. Stern dodged back but the swordsman took a long pace forward. The tip of the sword caught Stern under the breastplate, ripping it upwards. Stern, unbalanced, fell back and the enemy slashed again at his head. Then the man fell to his knees, pierced in the neck by Quora, his sword glancing harmlessly off Stern's armoured shoulder. Quora tipped off the man's helm as she turned back to the line. Stern leaped forward and brought his sword down on the man's unprotected head.

Spitting out blood and another tooth, Stern stepped up to cover his brother again. Benet had always been a demon in a close fight, and the fact that he was half-blind made no difference. He was hacking and slashing, leaping and charging, armed with two swords now. Stern couldn't keep up with him; he never could. He was so tired it was hard to keep his one sword raised. His jaw hurt like a bastard; he wondered if it was broken. An enemy warrior came screaming at him from his right and he blocked the man's blade and, after a short exchange of blows, pierced him through the eye. He realized he would never have spotted the idiot if he hadn't made so much noise. He tried to stay alert, stay awake.

He looked to his left where the sun was starting to sink into the horizon. Stern willed it to fall faster. Only darkness – or the mercy of the gods – could save them now. And once they were destroyed, would the City be next?

PART FOUR

Way of the Gulon

CHAPTER TWENTY-TWO

THE MOUNTAIN THEY CALLED THE SHIELD OF Freedom was not really shaped like a shield. And it had nothing at all to do with freedom.

In the earliest times, when the gods were young and the round earth was their plaything, hot and scarcely formed, a vast shard of rock had come hurtling, spinning through the roiling skies and had pierced the earth's crust like a splinter in an eyeball. As the world cooled the splinter stood out, a huge, alien object which men, when they arrived, knew with certainty to be a god. So they worshipped it and, as was their way, they sacrificed to it those things they valued – goats and bulls and hard-won horses and, of course, more than a few virgins.

Over geological ages the harsh splinter became mellowed by wind and rain, and small pockets of dust and birdshit formed on its creviced sides, and plants started to grow: first mosses and little clingy grasses and vetches, then stronger plants with insistent roots which burrowed into the rock's tiniest cracks, widening them to make way for bigger ones still. Earth built up at its base and great trees threw down roots. Men used the rock for shelter, from the remorseless sun and, in its caves and crannies, from wild beasts and other hostile tribes.

It did not take men too long to realize the upper part of the rock would make a fine military base, so the first climbers were soldiers and labourers, mostly slaves from foreign lands sent by their captors to live and die on the rock in the interest of its defence. They tunnelled out more caverns and built the first fortress and constructed, at the cost of many lives, a narrow, vertiginous pathway from base to top, and the rock suffered its first residents – ones who were not necessarily destined to die there, although most of them did.

Over the millennia men continued to burrow and build and the rock became honeycombed with tunnels. There were even wide shafts running the full height of it in which cages hung on cables could haul people to the top, but these had long since fallen into disuse, the cages hanging silent in the black air, a home to bats.

It was Marcellus Vincerus who first declared the rock looked like a shield. Ever the historian, he said it reminded him of the tall, semi-cylindrical shields whose warriors forged a mighty empire that had, or would, conquer the world.

Emly's brother Elija, languishing in the White Palace and still traumatized more than half a year after the events of the Feast of Summoning, took comfort in learning about his new home and its history, although not a great deal was set down in print. Most of what there was concerned the early history of the rock and the boy set about reading everything he could find. Perhaps he was lured by tales of tunnels and caverns, for in those he had made himself an expert, though a reluctant one.

When he was told Emly had disappeared, her brother's first impulse had been to follow her, though he did not know where she was. His second was to curl up and close himself off, for Emly was both his link to the world and his stout defence against it. And perhaps he would have taken one or other of these courses, were it not for the empress's old counsellor Dol Salida.

Elija had an enquiring mind, although outwardly he seemed timid and reticent, and Dol Salida recognized the energetic intelligence in the boy. The old man was surprised when he discovered how fluently Elija could read and write the City's script, though he had been taught by foreigners. He tried to involve the boy in his own work, but Elija had no interest in such a tedious pursuit as administration of the City. Then Dol Salida hit on the idea of introducing Elija to the game of urquat. The boy took to it with delight once he realized it was not a simple game of chance. Urquat relied on luck to some degree, but also on strategic and tactical thinking and, crucially, the capacity, hard-won by many, to embrace the concept of surrender of advantage for the prospect of future gain.

So Dol dragooned his old friend and loyal agent Sully, for urquat was a three- or five-cornered contest, and they set up a table on the west-facing balcony of the library. Each evening as the sun set they would try to winkle information from each other under the guise of a friendly game.

'Sun in three.'

Elija turned over a yellow counter and placed it on a black and white square. Dol nodded his approval and glanced at Sully, who grunted. The move was a clever one and showed sophistication for a player who'd taken up the game only days before. Yet it was the wrong move and would fix the player to a path which would inevitably end in his defeat. Elija didn't know that yet, and Dol Salida had no intention of telling him. Let him enjoy his cunning ploy for a few more moves.

'Moon in three.' Sully, small and dapper, was a conservative player, as suited his temperament.

'Hmmm.' Dol pretended to think deeply, glancing at Elija as if judging his play. In fact he was wondering how long he would have to appear to dither before the boy lost his focus on the game and started to talk about Emly again.

After only a few more heartbeats, Elija said, 'It makes no sense.'

Dol Salida smiled to himself. 'What, boy?' he asked with no indication of real interest.

'That Em would run away with Broglanh. The empress never forbade their relationship. Why would they betray her by leaving like that?'

Dol shared a glance with Sully who, he knew, shared his opinion on this. *Once a traitor, always a traitor.* It was a nagging thorn in the old counsellor's side that of all those in Archange's inner circle he was the only one who had stayed true to the City which had birthed him. Broglanh, the empress's right-hand man, had conspired to kill the emperor. Darius Hex, commander of the Nighthawks and now leader of Archange's bodyguard, had turned his troopers to side with Shuskara. Even Elija had connived with the enemy, and his sister had freed Shuskara from his well-deserved cell to lead the insurrection.

The fact that Broglanh had now betrayed the empress's trust and Emly had thrown her hospitality back in Archange's face did not surprise Dol at all. He was just amazed it had taken this long. And that Elija was baffled by his sister's betrayal.

He sat back as if undecided on his move, though he already had the next few, familiar as his two thumbs, planned.

Since Emly's flight the atmosphere in the palace had been tense. The empress was furious when she heard, from Darius, that the girl had gone. Archange had despatched scouts north, east, west and south seeking word of the fugitives. She had questioned Elija until she was convinced he knew nothing and the boy looked like a wrung-out dishclout. She had banished that night's guard, the Black-tailed Eagle century of the Thousand, from the Shield, demoted its commander and brought in the Silver Bears. Throughout all this Dol Salida had looked on with the contented contemplation of a side well chosen. He distrusted both the girl and her lover and was happy to see the back of them.

The scouts had come back with unhappy news. They had followed Broglanh's various trails without difficulty, then all had suddenly gone cold as if, said lead scout Valerius, the riders had been snatched up into the sky by eagles, horses and all. The shamefaced scouts had called for griffon hounds in a bid to pick up the scent but it was too late for their noses to detect anything useful. Dol Salida privately thought the plethora of false trails indicated the pair were probably still in the City. He had sent out his agents, so far with no success.

The really interesting thing, from Dol's point of view, was why Archange cared. What was the girl to her? Or her faithless lieutenant, for that matter? There was clearly more to this than met the eye, and he guessed that Elija, despite Archange's interrogation of him, knew more than he was telling.

'White defended,' he said, turning over his black and white counter and winning the third game in a row.

Elija was not stupid. He knew he seemed young for his age and he realized his self-absorption since the Feast of Summoning had made him appear more biddable than he really was. But he was fully aware of what the old counsellor was trying to do. And Elija hoped that in his bid to elicit information on Emly's whereabouts, Dol Salida might himself give away something the boy had not previously known.

Besides, he was enjoying learning the new game.

Waiting for the old men to reset the table after Dol's inevitable win, a lengthy task, he walked over to the stone balustrade. He leaned out over the City. He could see flickers of torchlight dotting the broken land, the sheen of moonlight on distant ruins. Level with him were the tops of trees which rose from the palace's main courtyard. He inhaled the dark air, rich with the scent of tree sap and heavy with a freight of smoke. In the terrible winter after the Feast of Summoning smoke from the funeral pyres had hung over the City like a mourning shroud. But now smoke in the air meant someone was burning debris from the many collapsed buildings, and space was being cleared for new buildings to be erected. Smoke was now a sign of hope.

Elija sighed. He still suffered a little resentment that Em had fled without telling him and he wanted to know why she had left so suddenly with her soldier, but he believed she was safe – as safe as she could be, in or out of this City. Broglanh had protected her before and Elija trusted the man to do the same again, although all the forces available to Archange were searching for them. Elija thought the pair might have followed in the bootsteps of Indaro and Fell and set out for the Land of Mists, Broglanh's birthplace, and he thought that if that proved the case, then he would eventually follow. Archange would not send out search parties if *he* left the City.

Elija sighed again, blowing his breath out into the cool night. As if in answer a frog hiccupped far to his right and another answered. A third joined in, then a fourth. The summer night was full of sounds – the creak of crickets, the flit of bats' wings close to Elija's head as they whipped invisibly past him, the cheerful song of nightingales, so out of place in the darkness. And the clatter of urquat counters, the rattle of bone pyramids at his back. Elija loved the night. He loved the darkness. Whereas Em loved the light, now she had found it.

Suddenly he thought, *frogs*? The croak of *frogs* at the top of the Shield? Frogs usually lived in rivers and swamps, wet places unlike this hot, dry mountain. Then he remembered something Darius had told him – that the night guards on the mountain, since time out of mind, had used animal and bird calls to exchange information. This had now been taken up by the Shield's newest guardians: the Nighthawks and Silver Bears.

'Are you still playing, boy?' Dol Salida asked his back and Elija turned again to the urquat table.

The boy was as transparent as water. Dol could see grief and pain flowing across his face as he sat down to resume play. He missed his sister, Dol supposed. Too bad, he thought. Most of us have lost loved ones, boy, many of them as a result of your actions.

'This is a classic move, the Hammarskjald gambit,' he explained to Elija, turning his black and red counter in an opening ploy. Dol had not lost his will to win the game, though he had been playing it for more years than he cared to remember, and he hoped he never would. But his main interest tonight was teaching the boy a little more about it, even allowing him to think he had a chance of winning, although he hadn't, and also keeping good Sully engaged. Sully, alert to the slightest stumble, could take a game or two off him if Dol allowed his concentration to lapse.

The others made their predictable moves, then Dol looked at Sully and nodded slightly.

'Where in the City were you and your sister born?' the little man asked the boy in his friendly way. 'I'm a Wester man myself.'

'Amphitheatre, me,' Dol offered, lying merely out of

habit, throwing the bone pyramids and turning over a green counter.

'I don't know,' the boy confessed, staring at the table. 'We entered the Halls when I was very young. I remember nothing before then.' He went to make a move, then stopped his hand, unsure.

'What part of the sewers did you live in?' Sully persisted as he had been schooled by Dol.

'The Halls. The Dwellers call them the Halls. Em and I lived in the Hall of Blue Light for a long time.'

'A strange name,' put in Dol. 'What was the blue light?'

Elija shrugged. 'It was just a name.'

'What part of the City was it beneath?' Sully asked. 'I understand the Halls extend to its furthest reaches.'

'I don't know,' Elija repeated. 'It wasn't important to us. You see,' he looked up, 'the Halls were all of our world and we had no interest in Outside. Just as the people on the streets have no curiosity about what goes on down there. If they even know.'

Then he thought about it, head cocked in a parody of reflection, and said, 'I have studied maps of the City since.' He paused and Dol thought, *Of course you have, boy, for your friends among the enemy.*

Then Elija said, 'I think maybe it was beneath Otaro.'

Both the older men looked at him. 'Otaro?' repeated Sully. 'Then perhaps your father was a wealthy citizen.'

Elija smiled wanly. 'I don't think so, sir. Why would I be in the Halls if he was?'

'There are many reasons to retreat into the Halls,' Dol said. 'And most of them have nothing to do with poverty.'

The boy looked surprised at these words and Dol explained gruffly, 'I have lived in the City for most of my life, boy. I know a good deal about it. And I know a good deal about the sewers, though I have never been there.'

They played silently for a while. The game was slow and Dol's thoughts, despite himself, turned back to the vexed question – why did Archange concern herself so with Emly? There was gossip that the empress intended the girl to succeed her, and that she would adopt her formally in due course. Dol thought this highly unlikely. The armies would never stand for it. But the matter of succession was a thorny one.

Archange had no direct descendants, that he knew of, now her granddaughter Saroyan was missing presumed executed. In Dol's long experience of the ways of the mighty, if one of them suddenly disappeared it was a sure sign he or she had fallen into fatal disfavour. Now the only obvious rival candidates for the Immortal Throne were Marcus Rae Khan and Reeve Guillaume, both Serafim, both men who, to varying degrees, had avoided supporting Araeon without actually acting against him. Dol snorted to himself at the thought. If Reeve were to become emperor then his daughter Indaro, a regicide, would be set to succeed him. That could not be allowed to happen. No, Marcus Rae Khan would be the best choice: a faithful subject and a good soldier. Although he had never shown interest in the machinations of power himself Giulia, his harridan of a sister, had and she might push him into it if she could convince him it was for the good of the City. Then there were the Gaetas. Saul was dead, leaving Jona, his mad mother and his multitude of sisters. *The Kerrs?* he wondered.

By not designating a successor Archange was ensuring a bloodbath when she died. But the Serafim were said to be very long-lived, and Araeon had certainly lived far longer than most men. How old was the empress? Who would dare ask?

'Moon and two,' Sully said suddenly with a grin and Dol sat back, for once defeated. *I am losing my touch*, he thought with a flare of anger, *to be fooled by such an obvious ruse*. He resolved to deny his friend any more wins that night.

'There is one thing I remember about my father,' the boy volunteered as they started to reset the table, the counters clattering against the polished wood. The two old men stared at him, waiting.

'It's just a flash of memory,' he said in his modest way, 'and probably means nothing. But I remember him wearing a red jacket. He wore it proudly as if for some feast day or celebration.' He shrugged. 'Perhaps I'm just imagining it,' he added, 'because I want to remember him.'

Elija wandered over to the balustrade again to hide his expression. Let them chew on that, he thought. His story was entirely untrue. He remembered little before the Halls. He could not recall his father's face, far less what the man wore. But it amused him to toy with these old game-players as they tried to dig out his secrets, his and Em's, under the guise of friendship. And he remembered Broglanh telling him that his old red jacket, sleeveless, worn and faded, was a remnant from his time with the Wildcats, now all gone. Dol Salida and Sully could waste their time on a quail hunt, searching through army records for long-lost Wildcats, vainly seeking his father.

He remembered Broglanh telling him Indaro had always worn a bright red jacket, shiny in its newness. But she must have lost it before she met Elija at Old Mountain, for he had never seen her in it.

Elija leaned over the balcony, his spirits high, and listened for the call of the frogs.

⋆ ⋆ ⋆

Directly beneath him, motionless against the courtyard wall, was a small, dark-haired man clothed in black. Camouflaged by the dappled moon shadows of a spreading plane tree, he had been listening to the men on the balcony, although he could make little sense of their words for the City tongue was new to him.

After a few more moments the youngster above moved away and Fin Gilshenan glided swiftly back around the courtyard. He slid in through a small window then stealthily made his way to where the two others waited with a dark lantern. The pair followed him silently. At the end of the corridor, apparently a dead-end, only a narrow, vertical black line on the wall showed where they had entered. They bent and carefully shifted the piece of wall out of place, revealing a square black hole.

One by one they slid through the hatchway and back into the echoing darkness of the lift-shaft.

It was nearing dawn when Dol Salida limped wearily back to his apartments. His leg pained him more than he could bear sometimes, and it was only when in deep contemplation of urquat that he forgot about it for a while. He had long since given up trying to sleep in a bed, and he would sit in his comfortable chair by the windows, flung open wide on these warm, heavy nights, and doze until it was time for his day to start.

So he was startled, and momentarily alarmed, when he entered his dim parlour to see his accustomed chair already occupied, a candle lit.

'Don't call the guard,' the empress ordered. 'They will not come at your command tonight.'

She leaned forward and peered at his face. 'Oh, for pity's sake, Dol Salida! I am just here to talk.'

'For a moment I feared assassins,' he said, and she watched him shrewdly in the growing light of morning.

'You have no reason to fear me, counsellor,' she told him. 'You have been a good and faithful servant, and if I harboured suspicions of you I would confront you first.'

He nodded, unconvinced. He pulled up another chair and sat down with a sigh he could not stifle.

'What can I do for you, lady?' he asked, trying not to sound as weary as he felt. 'A game of urquat, perhaps?'

'Is your wife content?' she asked unexpectedly.

Their house having been swept away in the destruction of the Feast of Summoning, Gerta and their two remaining daughters now lived in an ancient, thick-walled cottage nestled at the base of the Shield. Dol had been offered a palace, a small one, by the grateful empress, but Gerta had been unwilling to take on an army of servants. She was happy in her new home, spending the long summer tending vegetables, something she had always wanted to do. Now they were important people in the City, Dol thought with some asperity, his wife had ambitions to be a farmer. He usually stayed in his palace apartments now, the journey down the Shield being a torture to his old joints.

'She is, thank you,' he affirmed briefly, wanting Archange to get to the reason for this clandestine visit. They met every day, after all, to discuss matters of state. Secret dealings meant darker deeds afoot. He was curious, and a little uneasy.

'Has Emly been found?' he added, wondering if that was the reason for her visit.

The old woman sniffed. 'No, but she will be. She is with the Khan army, of that I am certain.'

Dol did not question her information, but he thought it unlikely. He said nothing.

'You are sceptical?' she asked.

'Hmm. Broglanh would not take the risk of being

recognized. He may be a traitor but he is not a fool.'

'He has always served in infantry regiments. If he joined the cavalry no one would know him. He could stay away from senior officers who might.'

'And the girl?'

'It is easy to lose a spare girl in an army.'

Are you guessing, he wanted to ask her, or do you have confirmation of this? His own agents had been despatched to infiltrate the army but had come up with nothing.

'And the brother?' They were also searching for Broglanh's adoptive brother Chancey, who had disappeared at about the same time.

She shook her head.

There was silence between them for a while, not uncomfortable, then the empress said, 'You were playing urquat this night? With Elija?' He was amused by the way she pretended uncertainty, for she surely knew every detail of his day.

'The boy is not saying all he knows,' he told her.

'I know that,' she snapped. 'I was hoping you could squeeze more answers from him. I'm loath to have him interrogated. He's frail, and I don't want the girl, when she returns, to find her brother dead.'

Why do you care? he wondered again. *Torture the boy for information. Drag the girl back with a rope round her neck.* The empress had never been sentimental with anyone else. Why treat these youngsters with rabbit-skin gloves?

'I have a need for new information,' she said.

At last, he thought.

'Rubin Kerr Guillaume.'

Dol thought hard. His files had been destroyed with the Red Palace, but he had an excellent memory.

'Son of Reeve, of course. Brother to Indaro – the gods curse her name,' he added formally. 'At sixteen he ran away from the Salient to escape serving in the army. Said to have fled to the Halls. Then he turned up working for Marcellus. Believed killed on the Day of Summoning.'

'But, in fact, still alive,' she told him.

He bowed his head, conceding her greater knowledge. The name Guillaume had scarcely bothered him during his many years as spymaster at the Red Palace. The old man Reeve was a dried husk, a dead-end. The two children were both deserters, perhaps both traitors.

'He worked for Marcellus,' she prompted.

He searched through his memory, summoning up his years spent studying the First Lord. He nodded as the fragments coalesced. 'Rubin served Marcellus confidentially in the last years of the Red Palace,' he concluded. 'Within palace and City and without. They were close. I believe Marcellus confided in him, trusted him in a way he could not trust many in his inner circle. And the boy – he's younger than Indaro – spent time in Odrysia on Marcellus' behalf. He spoke, speaks, the tongue fluently. Rumour at the time had it that he was instrumental in the fall of the Winter Palace.'

'A hero, then?'

Dol shrugged. 'A spy, certainly. He had no friends, apart from Marcellus, if you could call that a friendship. He probably trusts no one. It is a drawback of that line of work. He will have many acquaintances though.' He concluded, 'He is highly intelligent and, it seems, a survivor.'

'Find him for me.'

'May I ask why?'

The empress shifted a little in her seat, and it occurred to him that, like him, she was in pain. For a moment he wondered why two old folk such as they were discussing dark deeds at dawn.

'I have learned,' she said, 'that shortly before the Day

of Summoning Rubin Guillaume and a former Warhound named Valla had an audience with Marcellus at the palace, in the Black Room. I want to know what was said.'

'Was anyone else present?'

'No. Marcellus' aides were dismissed. Rubin and the woman both disappeared afterwards, believed dead in the Red Palace. But recently news reached me that Rubin has been seen. He is apparently working his way round the City's hospitals from south to north, searching for the Warhound.'

'She is injured?' Dol knew most of the Warhounds had been slaughtered in the Hall of Emperors.

'Crippled. She carries one arm strapped to her chest. But the boy believes, perhaps, that she can be found at a hospital because she tended the wounded during the campaign at Needlewoman's Notch.'

'You want her too?'

'Of course. My agents are seeking them both in the hospitals, but if your own agents are also on the hunt, their capture will no doubt come more swiftly.'

They sat for a while as light grew around them. Dol's belly rumbled and his thoughts went to breaking his fast, but he knew no servant would dare enter the room while the empress was there.

'What news of the Khan army?' he asked her at last.

'A messenger arrived last night. They will be at the Vorago by now. Marcus hopes to pacify Petrus and instal Hayden as leader by winter.'

Dol raised an eyebrow. 'I doubt it will be that easy,' he said, knowing Archange was happy to have the head of the Khan Family – and most popular soldier in the City's armies – far away. Archange had the backing of the armies and at the moment Marcus supported her. What would happen if he withdrew that support only the gods knew. Dol's fortunes were now tied inextricably with those of the empress, for good or bad, and he hoped her imperium would be long and benevolent, for when she fell then so would he, and it was a long way to fall.

CHAPTER TWENTY-THREE

THE OLD MAN TRIED TO SIT UP IN HIS BED, HIS GAZE fixed on something only he could see. He could no longer speak and his eyes passed over Rubin in their anxious search as if he could not see either. He had taken a little water earlier and his eyes had met Rubin's but there was no intelligence in them, just the simple blue gaze of a baby animal given something which makes it content. Now he turned his head away when water was offered, as if he could see only one path ahead of him and he knew he had to reach the hard end of it as soon as possible.

Rubin looked around him. This hospital, set up by the empress in alliance with Hayden Weaver's forces, was in the south-west of the City and had initially served Blues wounded in the invasion. First a small tent town, it had suffered attacks by City folk ignorant of the alliance who saw only enemies who had killed their loved ones. Dozens of citizens found guilty of attacking the hospitals, against Archange's clear orders, were put to death. The tents had in time been replaced by stout wooden huts and now, in high summer, most of the injured Blues had either died or recovered, and the hospital served sick and dying civilians such as this old man.

No one knew his name. He had been dragged here by soldiers who found him helpless in a street in Otaro. Otaro, the richest part of the City, had been hardly touched by the flood and invasion, and its citizens had no wish to see sick old men littering their streets. So he had been brought to this place where the helpless dying were fed and watered until they could no longer indicate any such need.

Rubin had come to the hospital in his continuing search for Valla and he had been sitting at the man's bedside all morning, though he didn't really know why.

When, in the early winter, he had escaped the ruins of the Red Palace with Fiorentina and the three refugees from the Halls, he had been close to despair. His lord had departed and he was in a city ruined by flood and invaded by the enemy, filled with bedraggled survivors who had lost homes and loved ones. The young woman they had rescued, whose name was Alafair, was in pain from her broken wrist, so he risked seeking sanctuary at a temple of Asklepios. The head of the temple allowed Rubin to leave the children in his care and a soldier set Alafair's wrist. After a day or two, when the wrist had started to knit, the three adults set off for the Shield of Freedom. It had taken the better part of a week to reach the mountain and when they got there they were barred from entering its boundaries by twitchy, zealous guards. For the first time since Rubin had met her Fiorentina had wielded her rank to convince the captain of the guard not to turn them away. At last an officer came down who recognized Rafael Vincerus' wife, and then they became guests of Marcus Rae Khan and his sister Giulia.

The Shield had been a strange place after the fall of the City. It seemed to Rubin that it would become the last refuge for the Families, barred and barricaded, defending itself against the unleashed violence of the invading army. Rubin had expected to be fighting in corridors, manning barricades, perhaps tending the wounded. In fact, none of these things happened, and for the first time in years he found himself getting used to feeling safe and then, surprisingly, bored.

When it became clear – initially in gossip among servants and soldiery then more formally as the City adjusted to its new status – that Archange Vincerus was now empress – as Fiorentina had predicted – Rubin was not a little worried. He remembered Marcellus' last words to him, burned into his brain in letters of fire: *Do not trust Archange. Do not trust her, do not trust her words or her actions.*

And so it was a mixture of boredom and prudence which led him to forsake the comfortable life on the Shield and go back down into the turbulent City. He knew it would come to the empress's attention, in due course, that a scion of the Guillaumes was staying in the Khan Palace and he wanted to be away before that happened. He had crossed the City and headed for the Salient and home. There was much to ask his father and much to tell him, most importantly that his sister Indaro was alive on the Day of Summoning. He had been disappointed not to see her in the aftermath but assumed she was back with her company.

Twenty days after he left the Shield he had arrived at the foot of the cliff steps he'd descended all those years before. He ruefully remembered the boy he had been, barely sixteen, armed only with a knife and overwhelming self-belief. He wondered, as he had so often, if his father would greet him as the prodigal son or a cowardly deserter. He was prepared for either, for he felt like both.

He had climbed the steep stair with difficulty, marvelling that he had once descended it under moonlight. He smiled to himself when he managed to evade the guards for a second time, then became angered that they were so incompetent – a reaction that would have been alien to his sixteen-year-old self.

It was midday and the winter sun was shining weakly when he arrived back at his father's house. His heart lifted to see its soft grey stone. There was no one in sight and he strolled up the carriageway, then stopped, shocked by the changes. The lawns, once well clipped, had become meadows, grasses waving in the cold breeze. The garden beds had run rampant, and the flowers had succumbed to the attack of brambles and ivies. The house looked much the same, but no smoke arose from the many chimneys and the shutters were all tight closed. He realized then that he had evaded the guards because there were no guards.

A figure appeared round the corner of the house, a woman bundled up against the chill breeze off the sea. She hurried over to him and he saw it was Dorcas, once his mother's maid and his friend when he was small. He realized now she was hardly older than he was, though her face was careworn, her clothes ragged.

'Rubin?' she asked, her eyes wide.

'Dorcas. Where is my father?'

'Gone, Rubin . . . sir. Gone away.'

A cold hand gripped his heart. 'Dead?'

'No, I mean, I don't know.'

She was frightened by him, he realized. He was a grown man and must look far different to her now. He softened his voice.

'Did my father die or did he leave here?'

'He left, sir.'

'When? After the fall of the Red Palace?'

She looked at him, baffled. She didn't know what he was talking about.

'After the Day of Summoning?'

She cast her eyes up, calculating. 'Yes, not long after.'

He led her to an old stone bench in the lee of a flint wall, away from the wind. 'What happened?' he asked.

'A man came to see him one day,' she told him. 'He waited at the gates but the lord would not see him. The man waited and waited, through all the snow and ice. We thought he was mad. And then the lord said he could come in. They were in his study, talking all night, the two of them. Then in the morning the visitor left. We expected the lord to come out but he never did. In the end Simion ordered the men to break down the study door but there was no one there.'

'My father was gone, but he told no one he was going?'

She nodded.

'Who was this visitor? Simion will know.' Simion was the captain of the guard.

'All the guards have gone, and most of the servants too. We keep the house shut up tight for fear of reivers.'

'Reivers? Here?'

She blinked rapidly and he saw she was on the brink of tears. 'It's been terrible these past years, sir. They say the emperor's men turfed the reivers out of their home under the Salient cliffs,' she waved her hand seaward, 'so they've been marauding all along the coast. Lots of decent folk killed or worse. Homes burned. Livestock slaughtered. The lord, your father, strengthened the doors and windows and doubled the guard.'

They both sat thinking their separate thoughts.

'The emperor's men have been here asking for the lord,' Dorcas offered. 'Then they went away again.'

'When?' Rubin asked.

The girl looked up again, her face as pale as milk. 'Five days ago,' she concluded.

So the emperor's men were, in fact, the empress's men. Why would Archange seek out Reeve Kerr Guillaume? She clearly knew nothing of his disappearance. And who was the strange visitor?

'Did he give his name, the visitor?' he asked Dorcas.

'I expect so, sir, but no one told it to me.'

'Baltazar will know.' His father's body servant for decades.

'He's gone.'

'All the men have gone?'

'Yes, sir.'

She told him the only ones left in the house were Rosa, who was simple, and Dorcas herself, who had no family and nowhere else to go.

Rubin looked towards the City, distant and dreaming in the spring afternoon. Only the Shield could be recognized at this distance, and it was merely a blur, a thumb-print. As always, answers he sought would be furnished by the rich and powerful, and in the place he had only just left. He sighed.

'Are you returned for good, sir?' the girl asked timidly.

He shook his head and stood. He took out the only coin he possessed – a gold imperial and three silvers – and gave them to her. If his father was dead, then she and Rosa were his responsibility.

'Keep the doors and windows tight locked,' he told her. 'I'll send—' What would he send? 'I will send word when I can. I will send instructions when I discover if my father lives.'

'I don't have my letters, sir,' Dorcas said, eyes cast down. 'Neither does Rosa.'

'Then I will send a message with someone I trust,' he

told her. Who this mythical someone might be he had no idea.

He smiled at her encouragingly, then, guilt plucking at his heart, left her sitting on the bench in the thin sunlight as he began his return towards the City.

Back in the hospital he was startled out of his reminiscence when a voice asked him sharply, 'Are you related to this man?'

He turned. The woman was barely shorter than him, dressed in the drab tunic of a hospital helper. Her grey eyes stared at him with distaste.

'He is dying,' Rubin said simply.

'Are you related to him?'

'No.' Rubin flashed a smile, but his normally fathomless charm had no effect. The hospital helper glared at him impatiently.

Then she said, 'These people are readying themselves to meet their gods. They are not here for your entertainment.'

Entertainment! Rubin felt anger rise. 'I was trying to help,' he said, as pleasantly as he could.

'He does not know you are here. At best, you are only confusing him. Those who really want to help clean up blood and vomit and shit, wash the floors and labour in the laundry cleaning soiled bandages and sheets. You have been here all morning, I'm told. If you are not related to the man, if you are not prepared to get your fine hands dirty, then leave this place.'

Her grey eyes were sheened with dislike. Even after all he had been through, Rubin was unused to being disliked by anyone, particularly this woman with her sharp words and hostile eyes.

'I am searching for a woman,' he said, changing tack.

'Ahh,' she said, nodding, as if that explained everything.

'An injured warrior,' he said. 'Fair-haired and—'

'I have treated a thousand injured warriors,' she interrupted briskly. 'Many of them women. Many of them fair.'

'She is skilled at tending the sick,' he ploughed on. 'I thought she might be working at a hospital.'

'I'll watch out for her. I will tell her, if I see her, that her friend is looking for her. I have little better to do with my day,' she added with heavy sarcasm.

'She has a badly injured arm,' he added.

'Injured?'

'It was hurt in battle.'

'Yes, I know what injured means,' she replied irritably, 'I'm a surgeon. It has not healed?'

'No, she carries it strapped across her chest.'

For the first time she looked at him with interest.

'Is she of the City?'

'I don't know.' He understood the point of her question. City folk healed much more quickly than foreigners. But he was lying now, eager to be away from her probing gaze, wishing he had not met this woman, cursing the whim that had brought him to this hospital.

'What is she called?' she asked, her earlier hostility vanished. Her voice was deep and smoky and could be inviting in other circumstances, he guessed.

'Dorcas,' he told her, casually purloining the servant's name. 'And you are?' he asked her, trying the smile again.

'My name is Thekla Vincerus.'

Vincerus! He wondered what relation she was to Marcellus and to the new empress. He bit down the impulse to tell her his own name. After all, Vincerus trumped Guillaume every time in this City. But he could not resist asking, 'Have you heard word of Marcellus?'

'Marcellus is dead,' she said.

They will tell you I am dead. He felt a ghostly chill as if Marcellus stood at his side once more. But not as a ghost, he amended. I know Marcellus lives.

'So they tell me, but I pray it is not true,' he said.

'His death was witnessed,' Thekla told him. He saw that, though her clothes were shapeless, they were made of good cotton, the stitches fine. She had dark curls which she pushed back impatiently with her wrist from time to time.

'By whom?' he asked, though he had heard the tale often enough.

'By the soldier who killed him.'

'Whose word can, of course, be trusted,' he replied. 'Assassins being generally trustworthy fellows.'

'Why are you interested?' she asked, but before he could answer she added, 'What is your name?'

He was about to explain himself, for he had a treacherous impulse to ingratiate himself with this woman, but he remembered Marcellus' other advice. *Keep your head down and your opinions to yourself, young Rubin.* 'I was a soldier,' he answered, ignoring her second question. 'Marcellus was my lord. *Is* my lord. I truly believe he will return.'

She looked him up and down. 'Why are you no longer a soldier? We need all the warriors we can find.'

'Yet we have sent an army to aid those who were once our sworn enemies,' he countered.

'Marcus Rae Khan's is a private army to do with as he wishes. It has always been thus. He chose to aid the Blues in their fight against the northern barbarians.'

'Leaving the City poorly defended.'

She stared at him, but she had to accept his point. Then she smiled and he felt himself relax and he smiled in return.

'Come here again at this time tomorrow,' she told him, touching his arm reassuringly. 'I will seek news of your Dorcas. I'm sure that between us we can find her.'

He nodded and smiled, as if well satisfied, and she walked away. Rubin took one last look at the old man, who was sleeping, then went out into the hot, humid afternoon, vowing to place as much distance as he could between Thekla Vincerus and himself. His resolve to find Valla, and quickly, hardened, for Thekla had only shown interest in the warrior when Rubin said she had an injured arm strapped across her body. Whatever interest the remaining Vincerus Family had in Valla was unlikely to be friendly.

CHAPTER TWENTY-FOUR

WATER WILL ALWAYS HAVE ITS WAY EVENTUALLY. After centuries of being channelled and controlled, confined and crushed by the many layers of the ancient City, anonymous and unremembered by most of its people, the great river Menander had finally burst its restraints and now flowed in a deep channel through what had once been the Red Palace. In daylight it looked like a slow-moving sea of mud, still filled with the debris of the buildings it had destroyed. But at twilight it shone like molten pewter.

Rubin sat on the river bank, on the low wall of a ruined building, and watched the sun go down through a haze of pink mist. These days mist lay on the centre of the City each evening and morning, and the remaining towers of the palace, poking above heaps of rubble, were muffled silhouettes in a murky rose-coloured world. On the river bank opposite Rubin he could just make out a broad flight of steps leading down to the muddy water. He wondered what part of the palace they had been in, for he was sure he had never seen such a wide staircase before.

Where he sat was once the barracks and stables of the Gulons, the century of the Thousand deployed primarily for the use of the emperor. The flood had washed away every wooden building, every saddle, bridle, horse, cat, rat and man in the place, leaving only the thin film of mud which enrobed most of this part of the City. First the rats had returned, and now the area was the haunt of beggars and the desperate and hopeless and the petty thieves who preyed on them. It was a dangerous place for a man alone with only a long knife to protect him, and Rubin planned to be well away before the sun touched the western horizon.

He was there to meet someone who claimed to have served with Valla. It was almost certainly a trap and Rubin had chosen an escape route and had employed a bodyguard who was sunk into the shadows of the ruins long before Rubin arrived at the meeting-point. The man was called Fenna. He was a veteran and crippled with pains in the arms and legs but he was still handy with a blade and, importantly, with a short bow. Rubin felt something bite his neck and he waved his hand to dissolve the cloud of tiny insects swirling around him. Within moments they regrouped for a new attack. Something plunked into the water at his feet, startling him, and he looked around then quickly stood as brown rats scattered. He still hated rats. Time was racing away, the sun was falling and his informant was nowhere in sight. He glanced towards where Fenna lay hidden, and shook his head.

'Adolfus?' a thin, high voice asked.

A sharp-featured child came sidling towards him along the river bank. He was in the rags of a beggar, muddy and grey, and Rubin could scarcely see him in the half-light. He stepped towards the child, who skittered away, wary as a crow. Rubin displayed empty hands.

'Yes. I am.'

'You looking for a soldier?'

'An injured Warhound called Valla. I will pay for information.'

The boy held out a grubby paw and Rubin tossed a copper pente to him. He had plenty of coin, having finally been forced to sell the insignia given to him by Marcellus. The boy caught the coin deftly and pocketed it.

'Barrabrick, 'e's yer man.'

'Who is he and where do I find him?'

Rubin held out another coin and the child sidled closer. Then the boy's eyes flicked left and Rubin spun round, knife in hand. Two thugs were racing towards him out of the mist. One fell as an arrow punched through his cheek, and he slid in a tangle of limbs on the muddy shore. The other came on. Rubin threw himself to the ground as a second arrow thrummed over him and thunked into the second man's stomach. He fell, yowling.

From his prone position Rubin managed to grab the boy's ankle before he could flee. He stood up, clutching him by his skinny neck. The boy flailed about but he was weak and scrawny and Rubin thought the only thing to fear from him was a nasty bite.

'Barrabrick? Where is he?' He shook the child in the hope of shaking information out.

'Leggo!' the boy screamed as if he was being tortured. His teeth were grey and rotten and his blast of fetid breath caught Rubin in the face. Suddenly weary, he let the boy go and the urchin took to his heels and was out of sight in a heartbeat.

'That was a waste of time,' Rubin said to Fenna, who had come out of his hole. The injured men were clearly just petty thugs. They had made no effort to get away and were stunned with pain and moaning for help. Their cries redoubled as Fenna retrieved his valuable arrows, wrenching them out of their flesh.

'We'd best be off soonest,' the veteran said, 'or the brat will return with friends. Or,' he said, looking down at the two ruffians with an old soldier's contempt, 'these dainty boys' tears will draw their mothers.'

They set off as fast as Fenna's crippled legs would allow, away from the river to the comparative safety of the Paradise border where Rubin had a room in an inn.

'Barrabrick,' Fenna said, panting a little. 'Sounds like a made-up name.'

'Boys like that lie all the time,' Rubin agreed. 'But he's unlikely to invent a name. He wouldn't have the imagination. I'll wager Barrabrick exists. I'll ask around.'

Outside the sprawling inn Rubin handed Fenna a half silver for the night's work and the promise of future help, and watched his rolling gait as the veteran ambled away.

The Bull and Bear was a respectable establishment, large and airy, and it was doing a roaring trade catering to the workers, many of them foreign, rebuilding the centre of the City. Rooms at the inn were at a premium and Rubin had paid a pretty pente for a few nights' accommodation.

He took a cup of ale and a bowl of meat stew and settled in the corner of the inn, his hood over his head though it was a warm night. He ate quickly, mopping his bowl with a stack of the golden cornbread the tavern-owner's wife made daily, then washing it down with good ale. He sat back and looked around, his anxieties subsiding a little as the food did its work. He knew most of the patrons. The central table was taken each night by the little Odrysian who was chief architect of the new buildings. His team of apprentices were well behaved and welcomed by the innkeeper.

'*Who builds a palace on a river?*' Rubin remembered the words of the man he had met in the sewers on the Day of Summoning. He had spoken to the architect and learned that the new palace would follow the line of the Menander but not intrude upon the river itself. Several new bridges had been planned – the first was nearly complete – linking north and south banks.

The future of the City seemed bright: its enemies were now its allies, and besides had left the City and marched away. Now the blockade had ended food and wine and supplies of metal and ores, coal and timber were flowing into the City. In the marketplaces you could already find oysters and spices, melons and figs, bolts of muslin and silk, cocoa and tobacco – for a price. The City had once been the centre of world trade for pearls and precious gems and, it seemed, would soon be so again. Technologies long denied its citizens were starting to filter in. The architect wore on his face a glass and wire contraption such as Rubin had first seen, to his quiet mirth, on the late General Dragonard, as did members of his team. And a welcome innovation was the glass lanterns, filled with oil and hung on the walls to give light and warmth – a huge improvement on the filthy old torches which had made a tavern like this gloomy within moments and uninhabitable soon after.

Rubin sat back in comfort, his stomach full and his mind relaxing. As he watched, three newcomers shouldered their way through the wide arched doorway, looked around as if seeking friends, then made their way to the crowded bar. Though dressed in civilian clothes they had the look of warriors, and none of them was young. Rubin hunched into the depths of his hood and scanned each face, suddenly on high alert. The first two men were unknown to him.

The third man was Arben Busch, his former commander with the Odrysian Seventeenth infantry at Needlewoman's Notch.

* * *

'Mavalla!'

Valla spun round so fast she nearly fell over. She blinked in the morning light, her head pounding.

'You're going the wrong way! Mavalla?'

She shook her head, trying to clear it, and Thorum watched her sympathetically. He was a former infantryman, a huge, freckled man with hands the size of hams and a bulky, muscled body which strained against the buttons of his jacket. His wife Wren, as small and as slender as he was stout, looked on with less patience.

One of the problems of living in an inn was that the ale was cheap and plentiful, and always there. After her duties ended each dawn she and her two comrades would make their way back to the Dragon's Child, where they had attic rooms, and break their fast with ale and bread. Sometimes too much ale.

'I'm going for a walk,' Valla told them. To clear my head, she might have said. Her stomach was threatening to rebel this morning, so after just one cup of ale she was leaving her friends, to take in the dawn air. She should have told them what she was going to do, she realized muzzily. They always had her back, as she had theirs.

The three were in the employ of the engineer responsible for rebuilding the palace on the north bank of the Menander. A huge chamber was being created – for what they had no idea – floored with glorious lapis lazuli. The walls were rising speedily, but not so speedily that thieves did not try each night to climb into the new building and hack off pieces of the precious blue stone. Valla was one of a team of ex-soldiers protecting the floor and other items of value.

Thorum nodded, though his face showed concern. His wife briskly turned and walked back into the inn and, after a pause, he followed. Valla took a breath of dawn air, foul odours scoured away by the night breezes, and headed along the river bank.

When the cadre of elite warriors, the Thousand, was created three hundred years before there was a strict rule that only warriors with three names, one a Family name, could be promoted to its ranks. This directive had been eased over the centuries, so now it could admit any soldier with a record of heroism. Valla, formerly of the Twenty-second, had saved the lives of a group of her colleagues, including Quintus Flavius Kerr, the company commander, single-handedly defending them when ambushed in a ravine in the Mountains of the Moon. Inspired by her promotion to the Thousand, she had changed her name from Mavalla to Valla, putting as much distance as possible between the common soldier who had escaped a life of grim rigour in the orphanage and the warrior in her black and silver armour. But now, in her new role of sword for hire, she had reverted to her old name.

She followed the bank of the Menander until she came to a flight of wide marble steps and climbed them, making her way through the women who came down each morning to do their washing. At the top she paused and looked out over the City. The morning mist was thinning and high above it to the west she could see the distant cliffs of the Salient and she thought, as she always did, of Rubin. She wondered if he had returned there and was living a life of ease. She turned. To the east stood the Shield of Freedom, distant but sharp-edged and clear, the sole symbol of the might and power of the City now the Red Palace was destroyed.

When she was a child, perhaps twelve, there had been a violent rainstorm one night, and from the window of the orphanage Mavalla had seen a small white dog cowering under a low wall, terrified by the fierce winds and the claps of thunder and flashing lightning. In her nightshift she had run from the building to rescue the beast. With the rain sheeting down around her she had picked it up, rewarded with a sharp nip for her pains. Splashing her way back across the mud, her feet bare, she had heard above the roar of the gale a loud *thunk*. She had stopped to see a large grey roof-tile standing upright in the ground, as if it had always been there, a pace to her right. She had looked up and realized it had been ripped from the roof by the wind, and had missed her by a fraction.

The Shield reminded her of the roof-tile. It looked as if it had been plunged into the ground from high above, or perhaps thrust up from beneath by an earth tremor. She wondered if the palace of the empress was at the top – the new empress who was, according to whom you asked, goddess or shaman or witch.

The light around her was changing. The sun was creeping above the horizon and she could hear the chirrup of early birds and the braying of donkeys. Sea birds squawked and cried. The square she was in, fronting the river, held a white temple on a high platform. It was dedicated to a god of healing. Even had she wanted to, Valla could not enter its walls. Her deity was Aduara, for good or ill, and she was a jealous god.

As she passed the temple she heard, above the random sounds of the awakening City, a stealthy footfall. She turned, sword in hand. Emerging from an alley were three men dressed like street beggars. But beggars seldom wield swords, Valla had found. Swordsmen, she thought, with a spark of interest. My speciality.

Then one flicked a glance to his left, and Valla saw two more appear, a big man armed with a club and a woman holding two daggers.

'Well,' she said calmly as she moved to her left so she could see them all, 'are there more of you, or can this game begin?' Excitement rose in her heart, though her mouth was dry. *Victorious or dead*, she thought. Either would be good.

She risked a look behind her for more assailants, and as she moved the man with the club ran in. She saw the club was too heavy for even a big man, and he had to brace to swing it properly. As he paused and swung back she darted forward and stabbed him through the heart.

She stepped lightly back, his falling body between her and the other assassins. They walked towards her, and one of them, a yellow-haired man, kicked the dying one contemptuously.

'He was a fool,' he said.

'Then you are a greater fool to bring him,' she replied.

She leaped forward, arm at full stretch, her blade seeking the yellow-head's heart. He swayed back, and a second man attacked. She twisted and parried and just managed to avoid a murderous riposte from the leader. Her blade flickered out again and she pierced the second man's upper arm, drawing a spray of blood. She leaped back and a knife hissed past her ear. She backed away, circling, trying to keep the three men between her and the knifewoman. The woman circled too, trying to find her back. The only thing Valla could do was keep moving.

She ducked and twisted, and in a blur of movement cut at the leader's knee then on up at another man's neck. She was well short, but the leader's sword came down and the second man's up. In a slashing reverse she nicked the shoulder of the second man and went for the leader's neck. The leader blocked swiftly, and Valla darted between the men, another flying knife just missing her head. But the leader was fast and in a moment he turned and was on her again, the third man with him. She parried quickly, their swords clashing loud in the quiet morning. Valla surveyed the others. The injured man was bleeding heavily but was still in the game. The knifewoman was moving again, keeping her distance.

The two uninjured men came at her in a practised ploy, going high and low. Instead of backing away she went forward into their space. Her sword flicked at the leader's neck, then she leaped and rammed the hilt into the other man's ear. He staggered and she was past. She turned like lightning but the leader was faster. She swayed to avoid a thrust to the heart, but she was too slow and he nearly caught her in the good shoulder, the blow deflected off her leather jerkin. She fell to one knee, gasping, and as she came to her feet she saw the woman with a dagger raised, her arm flicking forward.

The woman's throwing hand was chopped off in mid-throw and she screamed in agony as hand and dagger fell to the stones. A bloody sword hit the ground too, showering sparks, and Valla saw Thorum and Wren running towards them, Thorum drawing his second sword.

The big man grinned at her. 'Knife-fighters. Don't you hate them?' He stepped sideways and pierced the back of the knifewoman's neck, severing the spine.

The final encounter was brief, just three against three. When only the leader was left, Valla called a halt and stepped up to him. The swordsman was bleeding heavily from grievous wounds and was barely standing. Valla snatched up a discarded knife and thrust it under his chin.

'Who sent you?' she asked, for she was sure this was not some random attack.

He worked his mouth feebly to spit at her and Thorum smashed him in the face with his elbow. The man's head sank.

Valla glared at her friend. 'We wanted him to talk.'

Thorum shrugged and grinned at Wren. The

assassin slumped to the ground, a deep sigh escaping his mouth. Wren squatted down and felt the man's neck, then stood up.

'Dead. Good riddance.'

Valla frowned. 'Who sent them?'

Wren shrugged. 'You're alive. Who cares?'

'But why would five fighters attack a one-armed soldier? Do I look as though I carry coin?' She looked down at her old, stained clothes. No one would mistake her for a rich woman.

She became aware of early-morning spectators appearing from all around, lured by the sounds of the battle.

Thorum had been searching the bodies. 'Nothing,' he said, standing up. 'Time to go. I'm surprised the watch aren't here already.'

Leaving five dead on the stones, the three hurried back to the inn.

CHAPTER TWENTY-FIVE

RUBIN DECIDED HE NEEDED TO PUT DISTANCE BETWEEN himself and Arben Busch, a man he had last heard of in Marcellus' custody facing interrogation and death. He had no wish to confront the Odrysian general, to have his true identity unpicked and see the light of revelation and contempt in the other man's eyes. Rubin was not ashamed of his role as spy, indeed he was proud of it, but he understood why his former enemy might not feel the same.

Early the next morning he departed the Bull and Bear. His knife at his side and a small pack on his back, he set out to find the man Barrabrick. He worked his way through his network of acquaintances – soldiers and sailors, merchants and pedlars, innkeepers and brothel-keepers – but it was not until late in the day that he met a mutilated veteran who told him he had heard Barrabrick spoken of as a gangmaster. The fact that few in the area had heard of him was likely because this Barrabrick plied his trade on the north side of the river.

The north bank of the Menander was less damaged by the flood than the south and this made it a far more perilous place. Whereas in the south the palace, or the parts of it closest to the turbulent river, had collapsed, leaving only rubble and scoured streets, to the north much of the palace remained standing, though fatally undermined by the waters. The fabric was still giving way and each day there was news of some accident in which tens or scores of people, usually refugees and the poor and otherwise homeless, were killed by another building fall.

Merely crossing the Menander was dangerous. The first new bridge would be open soon, but for now the only choice was to walk all the way round, a long trip in uncertain territory. Or to chance a ferry crossing. The boatmen who offered their craft as ferries in the aftermath of the Day of Summoning were those least able to provide a safe crossing – rowing boats, barges and rafts, leaky, unseaworthy, rotten, poured into the City from along the coasts. Hundreds of people had drowned as the new ferries went down in droves in the treacherous waters.

Rubin remembered the architects. The renaissance of the palace buildings north and south was in the hands of two different teams of architects and engineers, but these men had to have some way of crossing on a regular basis. And they were important people who would not risk their lives in rotting hulks. After some thought he returned to the Bull and Bear and loitered outside as dusk drew on, finally waylaying one of the engineers. The man was drunk, drunk enough to have lost discretion, but not drunk enough to be incoherent. He was disgruntled with his employers and Rubin listened carefully, flattering the malcontent until he could buy the information he needed. The next morning he presented himself at a small but sturdy craft with papers which told the steersman he was entitled to make the crossing on the orders of the empress.

By evening he had discovered an inn in a quiet street,

paid for the room for three days and sent word to the good man Fenna of where he could be contacted. The next day he received a message from Fenna telling Rubin his room at the Bull and Bear had been invaded by cloaked and hooded men the night he left and its hapless new resident dragged away in darkness.

At that Rubin decided to move each day to a new inn. He had passed a respectable place the previous day and resolved to rest there that night. He went there at first light and paid the innkeeper two copper pente in advance. That was a mistake, for when he returned after dark, at the end of another fruitless day searching for Barrabrick, he had been run to earth.

He climbed the stairs in the back of the tavern. He could see little, for the narrow wooden staircase was lit only by starlight through a window in the roof. He walked down the creaking hallway to his room and opened the door. Then he stopped, aware of a new scent. He pulled out his knife and stepped across the threshold. Starlight bathed the bed and he smiled as he recognized the curled shape asleep on the blanket.

Valla had found him first.

'I thought,' he said to her as she tucked into the bread and cheese he had brought, 'that soldiers' senses were so highly tuned they could react to a pin dropping, even in their sleep.' In fact she slept like the dead and he'd found it next to impossible to rouse her.

Valla did her one-shouldered shrug. 'Warriors know when they are safe,' she said a little haughtily.

Rubin smiled. 'How did you find me? I've been searching for you.'

'I know you like your comfort,' she said, chewing on a crust. 'So I just went to every good inn I could find, asking for a tall, thin man with red hair.'

'But why the north bank?'

She shrugged again. 'Because that's where I was.'

While he fought with his irritation – and dismay – at being tracked down so easily, she told him about her life since they'd parted: the Day of Summoning, her battle in the Red Palace and the death of her commander.

'Did you encounter a red-haired warrior?' he asked. 'A woman, tall like me?'

'Your sister?'

He nodded.

She shook her head. 'I don't think so. It seems so long ago now. So much has happened since then.' He nodded. 'But wait. Yes. I mean, I *did* see a woman like that. She fought like a goddess, like Aduara herself. But she was fighting for the other side.' She spat contemptuously on the floor.

'Did you see the emperor?' he asked, curious, having heard whispered tales of the Immortal's death at the hands of a woman.

She shook her head again. 'It was a bloodbath. I recognized many faces, men and women I'd served with, but most of them were dead or dying. It was a bloodbath,' she repeated.

Then she told him, a little shyly, about the gulon and how it had saved her life.

'What happened to it?' he asked, smiling uncertainly, not sure whether to believe her. He had never heard of a gulon protecting someone.

'I didn't see. It disappeared after the battle. Then I got out of the palace, found a place to rest up.'

'You were lucky.'

She made no reply to that and her eyes became bleak. He knew it was her ambition to die fighting for the City, and he wondered that she hadn't.

'I was in the palace too,' he offered. Casting his mind

back, he told her about the fall of the Adamantine Wall, his last meeting with Marcellus, and about Fiorentina.

'So I spent the day fighting while you chatted with the nobility,' she said, amused.

He nodded, smiling.

She asked him, 'What happened to Marcellus? I heard gossip that he was dead, but we both know that can't be true. I've seen him in battle. Nothing can kill him. But if he's not dead why is he not emperor now? It makes no sense.'

'I don't know. But he will return, I'm certain of it. He has a plan, Marcellus always has. And we will both be ready to fight for him, if it comes to that, when he returns.'

He told her about Marcellus' last warning to him.

She looked troubled. 'I had never heard of Archange until suddenly she was empress. If Marcellus doesn't trust her then neither can we.'

'Marcellus will return,' he repeated.

'I hope so,' she said. 'I hear she plans to bar women from the military.' She snorted. 'What a nightmare that would be!'

Privately Rubin thought it wrong for women to be fighting, even gallant soldiers like Indaro and Valla, but he would never say it to his friend.

'I was starting to think you had gone north,' he told her, 'with the Khan army to fight the barbarians.'

She shook her head sadly and he cursed his own crassness. She would never see service with a regular army, not with her injured arm. To change the subject he told her about his father's disappearance.

'I'm worried about him,' he confessed. 'Where would he go? And why? He's just an old man who tends his garden. Or was,' he added, thinking of the wild meadow where there had been crisp, green lawn.

'You told me he was once a man of power.'

'A long time ago. He's no longer interested in politics.'

'Perhaps,' Valla suggested, 'politics is still interested in *him*.'

Rubin thought about it. 'You think he had business at the White Palace?'

'I don't know,' she said. 'But power always seeks power. At least,' she said, 'that's what Leona always used to say.'

'A wise woman,' he replied politely.

Then she told him about her fight in the temple square.

'I wonder,' he said, 'if there's a link to the ruffians who raided my room at the Bull and Bear. They were intent on kidnap, it seems, rather than robbery or murder. Perhaps your attackers are part of the same thing.'

'But why?' she asked.

'You've made enemies. Someone wants you dead.'

'No one knows Valla exists. Except you. I use the name Mavalla now.'

'But it wasn't a random attack. You've clearly made enemies, even if it was about something everyday, like the work you do. But if it were just some fool you've slighted at work they'd tell you about it. Silent killers point to an assassination bid.'

'I'm just a soldier,' she argued. 'I haven't upset anyone.'

She fell asleep then. She had not intended to, it seemed, but just drifted off halfway through what she was saying, a piece of bread in her hand. He pulled up a blanket and tucked it in then put his arm round her and she settled against his shoulder. He took a discreet look at the fingers of her bad arm. They were still pale and waxy, like bones dug up after a long time in the earth. But not rotten. Not yet. He was moved by pity for her, and by something like love. But everyone he had ever loved had died or walked away from him for something more important.

The candles were guttering but he made no move to light more and he sat in darkness, Valla warm against him, waiting for dawn. Her body was a bag of bones; what were curves in other women were sharp corners in her. It seemed to him that her goddess demanded too much of her, that Valla gave and gave and Aduara was unmoved. He thought it a paradox that she was tougher than him, yet at the same time more fragile. But they seemed to belong together and this meeting was as inevitable as the moon-tides.

As Valla slept Rubin pondered his conversation with Thekla, the surgeon who was of the same Family as Marcellus and Archange, and he stretched his memory back to the day at the Salient when, as a twelve-year-old, he'd spoken with his father in his study while Indaro practised fencing in the garden below. He had asked Reeve why Archange was so dangerous and Reeve's answer now seemed prescient.

'Archange's need for revenge is strong, boy, and she is very powerful. I fear a battle of wills between the three of them – Archange, Araeon and Marcellus – could end in the fall of the City.'

'Are they mighty warriors?' Rubin persisted.

His father frowned. 'Marcellus is. Why?'

'You said they are powerful.'

Reeve shook his head. 'It is a different sort of power, not strength of arms.'

'What then?'

'Araeon can make life from . . . lifelessness. And Marcellus can destroy life. But both have weakened over the years, for they are very old, far older than I am.'

'And Archange?'

'Archange has the power to preserve, and to heal.'

Rubin thought about a lot of things, lying with his arm around Valla, and by the morning he had made a decision.

'We're going to the Shield,' he told her after waking her with the dawn.

'We are?' she replied blearily, finding the piece of bread she had dropped on the floor and blowing the dust off it.

'We will seek news of my father and Indaro, and perhaps we will find out if someone's hunting us and why.'

'It's a long way,' she said, chewing, 'and it'll be perilous if someone wants us dead.'

'It'll be perilous anywhere in the City, if someone wants us dead,' he replied briskly.

'What if it's the new empress who's hunting us?'

'Then it will do no good hiding. We will be found eventually. And we have both been loyal to the City. We should have nothing to fear from the empress.' His words sounded hollow. But what was the choice? To leave the City? And go where? 'You will be my bodyguard again. We must go underground.'

Her face was calm but he saw fear in her eyes. 'Underground? You mean in the sewers, the Halls? I thought they were destroyed.'

'In the centre of the City they have been washed away, but beyond that there will still be tunnels. But I don't mean the Halls. I was told once that it was possible to walk through the heart of the City, from the Red Palace to the Shield, underground. The palace dungeons are connected to those under the mountain.'

'Are they still in use?' The emperor's dungeons had a terrifying reputation.

'I don't know. We'll find out.'
'Do you know the way?'
'No. But I know someone who does.'

CHAPTER TWENTY-SIX

IN THE KHAN PALACE ON THE SHIELD OF FREEDOM THE clank and splash of laden pails told Fiorentina Vincerus, guest of the Khans, that her bath was being readied. It had been delayed because the girls assigned to her had been snatched away at Giulia Rae Khan's whim for some kitchen task. Fiorentina snuggled into her layers of shawls and looked forward to the heat. A bath was one of the few ways of getting warm in the palace on chilly days.

The Khan Palace was one of the first built on the Shield, perhaps the very first, and it was not built for comfort. A fortress of yellow stone, it was draughty, damp and cold, even in summer. Marcus' high hall was the only chamber boasting a fire and in winter all the residents of the palace, including the Khans, bundled themselves up in coats and capes and shawls until they could scarcely move.

'Look, lady.'

Alafair, now her maid, showed her the sprigs of lavender she had found while foraging in the gardens. Fiorentina sniffed the scent.

'Wonderful!' she sighed.

'I'll put some in your bath and some under your pillow,' the girl told her. Fiorentina smiled.

There was little enough to smile about. Her pregnancy made every move uncomfortable. She could not sleep, and eating made her chest hurt. Her back ached all the time. She pined daily for her lost love Rafe yet dreaded bringing forth his child. Giulia, who had birthed numerous infants, had sniffed at her worries, but the old woman made light of any discomfort just as she scorned the comforts of bathing and decent food.

It had been a while before Fiorentina had realized the Khans were poor. All their resources seemed to have been sunk into Marcus' army, with little left for their daily existence on the Shield. Even the boatload of gold Giulia had cajoled from some northern king, intended for the war, had been handed over to the City treasury to fund rebuilding. Fiorentina guessed the Khans were poorer than many an Otaro merchant who contributed nothing to the war, or peace, apart from his criticism.

'Lady,' Alafair said, bending over her and speaking gently as if she were a sick child, 'the lady Giulia invites you to her solar.'

Fiorentina sighed. 'When?'

'Now, lady. Or,' the girl amended, 'as soon as you feel able.'

Fiorentina struggled to stand, feeling like an upturned ladybird. Alafair took both her hands and pulled her upright.

They were on the stone terrace which stretched high across the south face of the palace. The Khan Palace had no pretty balconies or peaceful gardens in which to sit, but Fiorentina's apartments gave on to the terrace and she spent a deal of time out there, for it was usually warmer than inside. The low terrace wall was thick with ivies and wild roses which billowed up over the sides and made her feel as though she was in some strange sky-garden. Fiorentina walked to the low parapet, where the terrace faced the Shell Path and a stretch of wooded slope leading down to the Gaeta palace. She wondered what Giulia wanted. She was never invited to the woman's presence for the pleasure of her company.

Looking down, she saw a movement. For a moment, a heart-stopping beat, she thought she saw her husband sauntering through the trees, up the slope. The figure disappeared then appeared again. He was dark and slender, like Rafe, dressed in black and with a sword at his hip, as she had last seen her husband. She recognized the gait. She knew it as well as she knew the lines of her face in a mirror. It was Rafe. Her breath caught in her throat.

But it could not be. He was dead. Sadly she turned away and Alafair asked, 'Are you all right, lady? You are pale.'

Fiorentina nodded, unable to speak. If he were, somehow, still alive then he would certainly have sought her out. It was not him. Over the summer she had seen other men, glimpsed in Marcus' high hall or in the palace courtyard, who she'd thought were her husband. Just for a breath.

'I had better see what Giulia wants,' she sighed.

As usual Giulia's solar managed to be both cold and stifling. It was gloomy and draped with threadbare tapestries whose ancient dust permeated the air. The dark wooden furniture and carved ceiling corbels were highly polished, though the rugs were worn and dirty. Fiorentina guessed Giulia could no longer see the grime, for her eyes were failing her, and her brother probably didn't care.

'Fiorentina,' said her hostess from the gloom. 'How are you?'

'As well as can be expected,' she replied, forcing a smile.

Giulia stepped into the light from the window and Fiorentina caught her breath. The woman had lost ten years, twenty years, since she last saw her. Giulia's hair, normally a faded yellow, was now pure gold and thick and lustrous as a girl's. Her face had shed the lines of laughter and pain and was smooth and dewy. Her eyes sparkled, and Fiorentina saw for the first time what a beauty she was. A trick of the light, she thought, feeling a little dizzy. She had been sitting in the daylight too long and the move into this shadowed place had her seeing things.

She looked around, trying to gather her emotions. She realized then that there was a strange man in the room, one dressed all in black, with dark hair. He looked nothing like Rafe.

'This is Jona Lee Gaeta,' Giulia said, touching the man's arm in a familiar way.

He bowed and, bending over, took Fiorentina's unresisting hand and pressed his lips to it. 'My lady,' he murmured.

Fiorentina was speechless. She had agreed with Giulia and Marcus that her presence in their palace be kept secret until after the birth. She had heard of this Jona, head of the Gaeta Family, but had never met him. She tried to remember what Rafe had told her about the Gaetas.

'Jona,' Giulia explained with an unreadable expression, 'is here to pay court to you.'

'She hides her feelings well,' thought Giulia. Caught between anger at the revelation of her presence in the Khan household and shock at being treated like a breeding mare, or vice versa, Fiorentina managed an expression of polite disinterest which would have done credit to any imperial counsellor.

'Cousin,' Fiorentina replied, an expression she had

never used before and one which Giulia found impertinent, 'I am quite flustered by this news.' *She looks as flustered*, thought Giulia, *as one of my gate guards*. 'But that being the case perhaps the lord's esteemed mother should also be privy to this conversation.'

Linking Giulia's status in this way with that of the mad old woman Sciorra Gaeta, with whom Giulia had long enjoyed a mutual loathing, was even more impertinent. Giulia replied stiffly, 'It is generous of you to imply kinship between us, Fiorentina, but I am here not as family chaperone but as a humble mediator, a disinterested party.'

They watched each other with hostile, smiling faces. Then Giulia sat and Fiorentina followed. Jona Lee Gaeta perched on the edge of a tapestried seat. He looked from one to the other.

Then he said smoothly, 'I realize your noble husband has only recently died, lady, and I have no ambitions to take his place in your affections. I am suggesting an alliance for political reasons between two great houses. My mother,' he said, looking at Giulia, 'concurs.'

'Which houses?' Fiorentina asked him, her voice cool. 'Archange is now head of the Family Vincerus. I am merely someone who used to be married to her brother.'

Giulia could not but admire her façade of humility, though she was wrong on every point. For one thing, Archange was never a Vincerus, though she had long since chosen to adopt the name. Only a handful of people living had ever known that, and even fewer knew why.

'I was referring to the houses of Khan and Gaeta,' Jona was saying. 'You have found sanctuary with the generous lord and lady, and I am ever seeking ways to increase the bonds between our two Families.'

'Increase them?' Fiorentina asked, her eyes narrowing. *This girl is not a fool*, thought Giulia.

Jona explained, 'We are already linked, in a way, by our mutual decision to stay aloof from the internecine struggles among the Families down the years. And we have another important bond.'

He paused, and Fiorentina asked, 'And that is?'

'The bond of geography,' Jona said. 'Between our two palaces we control the Shell Path – the entrance, and exit, to the Shield. In alliance, and with the power of our two armies, should we choose we could cut off access to the White Palace. And isolate Archange.' He smiled but his black eyes were cold as stone.

'Not that we would ever wish to do so,' Giulia felt obliged to put in.

She had been thinking about Fiorentina's pregnancy all summer. She had thought about it so hard it had worn a long groove in her mind. This child, if it were Rafael's, would be the only serious opposition to Archange's line for the throne. Archange had perhaps one daughter and one granddaughter still living, that Giulia knew of. Her get would expect to succeed.

Unless . . . unless a Vincerus son emerged. For all its original egalitarian intent, despite the fact that women fought beside men in the war, the City was wildly unequal in its treatment of the sexes. A boy child outranked a girl every time. And Giulia was as sure as she was of anything that the child in Fiorentina's belly was a boy.

But, with Marcus away, once it became known that a new heir had emerged Giulia would need allies to protect the child and to safeguard her own interests. The obvious course was to send Fiorentina away, to find her sanctuary far from Archange's reach. But Giulia could not quite bring herself to do that. To again be the hub around which great power revolves, as she had been when wed to Marcellus, was too tempting.

If the babe lives, she thought. If it is not some sort of mutant. She shuddered.

Few people now alive knew Rafael Vincerus had been a reflection. With Araeon and Marcellus dead, that just left Reeve Guillaume, who had gone from the Salient, vanished who knew where. And the Gaetas? *Does Jona know?* He always gave the impression of knowing a great deal but keeping it to himself. His mother was certainly aware of Rafael's status at one time, but Sciorra had forgotten most of what she had learned and was unlikely to have retained that piece of information in the few brain cells she had left.

As the silence stretched out, Jona said, 'You are looking very lovely today, lady Giulia.'

No one knew the effort it took her now to draw on her Gift, but it was important that Jona not underestimate her own power in these negotiations. As one of the few Serafim left on this planet, she must make best use of her resources for herself and Marcus and for the City. A Vincerus emperor with a debt of gratitude to the Khans could ensure their future for another two hundred years. But as adoptive father of the child Jona would increase the power of the Gaetas a hundredfold. Did she really want that? Fiorentina would have to marry somebody, and once the fact of her condition was known offers would come from far and wide. A new source of power was about to be born and everyone would want a piece of it. Once it was clear the child was a Vincerus, much of the power would slip from Giulia's fingers. The best way to retain it, of course, would be by Marcus marrying the woman. But, infuriatingly, he had laughed when she suggested it.

'Why would a young beauty be interested in an old goat like me?' he'd asked her.

'She wouldn't, of course, you old fool,' she'd replied.

'You're missing the point. It would keep the power in our hands.'

But he'd shaken his head and Giulia knew he would not be moved. He was just an old soldier, he'd said, not a politician.

So the only way she could retain power was by marrying the woman off to someone she would be happy to ally with, and the only obvious candidate was Jona Lee Gaeta. Relations between the Khans and Gaetas had long been cordial. Although Giulia could not tolerate the matriarch Sciorra, this seemed irrelevant now as the old woman had not been seen in public for a century and was said to be as mad as a hatter, roaming the Iron Palace like a phantom.

She bowed her head in acknowledgment of Jona's compliment. 'You are kind, sir.'

'Have you heard,' Jona said, his tone confidential, 'that the empress's ward has disappeared from the Serafia?'

'Of course,' Giulia replied, annoyed that he should think her so out of touch. She glanced at Fiorentina. It was not appropriate that Jona should gossip in front of her. She was barely better than a whore, after all.

'With Evan Broglanh,' Jona added.

Giulia could not hide that she had not known that, and her eyes sparkled with interest.

'Archange must be livid,' she said happily.

Fiorentina asked, 'Who is this ward?'

Jona explained, while Giulia sat enjoying the warm glow which came from contemplating other people's mortal follies. This was the best of news. Although no one really believed Archange wanted the child Emly to succeed her, that was now right off the table. The girl would be lucky to survive this, and as for her soldier . . . For such a betrayal Archange might well revert to her predecessor's ghastly ways with execution.

'And I understand the empress is also seeking the Guillaume heir,' Jona offered.

Giulia remembered the tall, red-headed young man, a friend of Fiorentina's, who had spent some time as a guest in her palace after the Fall. Was he being swept up and disposed of? This could also be a good thing – the more Serafim, real or potential, imprisoned or dead the better.

She commented, 'You are full of snippets of news today, my friend. Why does Archange want this boy – for execution? Perhaps he was privy to his sister Indaro's assassination plans.' She looked at Fiorentina, but the girl's face concealed any feelings she might have about this Rubin.

'Who knows why Archange does the things she does?' Jona asked blandly.

She smiled, treating the question as rhetorical, but she knew the answer. Archange was motivated by pride and by vengeance. She harboured deep wells of rancour which had destroyed Araeon, and likely Marcellus also. She had plotted the fall of the City, scheming to see it rise again under her own control.

But other people could hold a grudge too, Giulia thought, and Archange might have underestimated the hatred of those Serafim who had been absent from her world, and perhaps her consciousness, for so long.

CHAPTER TWENTY-SEVEN

IT SEEMED THAT DRUSUS THE DRUNKARD'S FLIGHT FROM the flood and invasion had not improved his personality. When Rubin and Valla tracked him down in the sixth inn they'd tried, he raised a swollen red face and glared groggily at them.

'Piss on you,' he growled.

They had walked to the ruins of Amphitheatre and found Drusus' stone house still filled with silt and debris. They had spoken to neighbours. He still lived there, they said, though his aunt was dead and his slave had run off. But Drusus had made no attempt to make the dwelling habitable since the flood and he spent his days, as before, visiting a string of taverns. Valla gazed at the house incredulously, thinking most people in the City would kill to live in such a well-built home, and she was surprised no one had taken it from the man at the point of a sword.

She was even more surprised when she met him. The former dungeon guard was not so fat as Rubin had described him, but he was wretched and dirty, the front of his shirt marking the uncertain transit of many meals and jugs of ale. He stank, the inn they were in stank, and she rested her hand on her sword-hilt and wondered if Rubin knew what he was doing.

Rubin dumped a bulging bag of coin on the scarred table in front of Drusus' bulbous nose.

'Drusus Vermilo, the empress demands your attendance.'

Ears all around the squalid inn pricked up, heads turned, eyes narrowed. Valla resisted looking at them, estimating the level of threat.

Drusus stared at the bag, then peered up into Rubin's face, and repeated, 'Piss on you, whoever you are.'

Rubin picked up the money and looked around him. 'You two,' he said briskly, gesturing to two brawny fellows, 'I have coin for you if you take this man out and dunk him in the horse trough.'

The pair leaped up willingly and grabbed Drusus by the arms, hauling him to his feet. The drunkard struggled. 'Help,' he wheezed. Several chairs were pushed back, grating across the stone floor. Valla stepped in front of Rubin and drew her sword. Its metal gleamed in the dull light and the men all sat down again.

Drusus was sobering up fast. 'The empress, you say?' he said, struggling against the pair who were trying to wrestle him through the doorway.

'We are at her command,' Rubin told him.

Once out in the daylight, blinking, Drusus complained, 'Get these thugs off me. I'll listen.' Rubin tossed the men a gold coin each and they shambled back into the inn to spend their sudden wealth.

'The name of Drusus Vermilo has come to the Immortal's notice,' Rubin told him. He leaned in confidingly. 'The Hand of Saduccuss now holds sway at the White Palace. The empress asks you to accompany us there.'

The Hand of Saduccuss, Valla knew, was one of the myriad groups of conspirators which had blossomed and died in the last years of the old emperor. It plotted self-importantly though without result and was generally thought of as a drinking-club for disaffected veterans.

'I'm your man, lord,' Drusus managed, standing upright and brushing morsels of food off his chest. He squinted at Rubin as if he might recognize him, but abandoned that and looked around. 'Where's our carriage?'

In the end Rubin had to hire a wagon, pulled by a lively donkey, to transport them across the City. During the journey, while Valla dozed and woke and dozed again, Rubin talked ceaselessly to the drunkard, building up his pride and self-belief with a mixture of flattery and palace gossip, dropping in the names of members of the Hand, until he judged Drusus was ready for the news that he had been volunteered to guide them through the tunnels to the Shield. The former dungeon guard blustered and whined, but he was an easy man to flatter and by the end of the journey Rubin had him believing the empress had personally appointed him as guide. The promise of coin helped.

Rubin knew of a portal into the dungeons via the Halls north of the former palace. But Drusus claimed there was a way to the dungeons of Gath, familiar, he claimed, only to those in the know, in Lindo. Lindo was closer to the Shield, and Rubin leaped at the suggestion.

'How do we get inside?' Valla asked, though she doubted a single word from the man's mouth was true.

Drusus winked and tapped his swollen nose. 'That's for me to know and you to find out, girlie,' he told her. Valla resolved to cut his throat once he was no longer useful.

Drusus told the carter to stop at the bottom of a shabby alley called Green Lane and watched with a frown as Rubin paid the man from the bag of coin. When he opened his mouth to speak, Rubin told him sharply, 'You will get the rest of this when we reach the mountain.' Drusus shuffled his feet and shrugged. He said no more but set off down the alley.

It quickly became narrower, then twisted sharply in a dog-leg and came out in a dusty courtyard surrounded by blank stone walls. There was an ancient well near the centre. Its high sides were crumbling and dusty, and the debris-strewn courtyard looked long abandoned. Valla guessed the well was dry.

Drusus trotted round the back of it. They followed and saw a narrow, steep flight of stone steps leading down into darkness. Valla could smell mould and decay and sewage. She took a deep breath of clean air, glancing up at the sun, before following the others as they plunged in. The spiralling steps were well worn and slippery. As the gloom rose around them Drusus paused to light a torch and Valla followed its reassuring flicker. The stench grew worse.

'This must be what the Halls smell like,' Valla said to the top of Rubin's head. He paused for a moment and looked up.

'You have no idea,' he said with feeling.

The tight spiral of steps made Valla dizzy and when they finally reached the bottom she was sweating with exertion and trepidation. The prospect of remaining underground all the way to the mountain filled her with dread.

By contrast, Drusus became quite cheerful. Perhaps he had worn off his drunken daze, and perhaps he had found a purpose in life, even for a short time. Or maybe he was buoyed by the prospect of gold. But he started talking about the dungeons and his exploits in them, talking loudly, with no concern for possible listeners. Rubin warned him to keep his voice down.

'No one to hear me here, boy,' Drusus replied airily. 'No one for leagues to come.'

Valla noted that Rubin had been demoted from 'lord' to 'boy', but he didn't seem to mind. Drusus was in his element and Rubin had reason only to encourage him.

The tunnel walls here were smooth and perfectly circular, as if bored by some monstrous machine. The surface was reddish-brown and Valla could make out the remains of murals, paintings of animals, perhaps, or gods – it was hard to tell, for they had mostly fallen away leaving small, sometimes vivid patches of colour, flecked and peeling. Drusus claimed that in the heyday of the Third Empire carriages moved regularly through this underground highway, carrying the nobility back and forth between the Red Palace and the Shield. There were empty brackets all along the walls on both sides, as if to confirm this, and a deep groove ran along the centre of the floor. Valla wondered what it was for. The floor was dry and thick with the dust of many years, although a pattern of recent bootprints ran down the centre.

After a while her dread started to dissipate. The walking was easy, a single torch lighting the way. She found herself idling along, thinking of old friends, dead friends. Then, when Drusus' droning voice quietened for a moment, she heard a sound behind her and her heartbeat quickened. She stopped, letting the others move ahead, and listened. She could hear nothing. She shrugged to herself and carried on. Again that soft sound, a pattering of footsteps. It stopped when she stopped, went on when she stepped forward. It sounded like a child.

Or an animal. She smiled.

When they paused for bread and water, sitting in a row against the tunnel wall, Rubin leaned in to Valla and said quietly, 'We are being followed.'

She marvelled that he could hear the soft sound

above Drusus' drone. 'I know,' she said. 'I think it's the gulon.'

He stared at her, eyes wide. She knew now he had disbelieved her when she told him about the beast. She shrugged. *What did I tell you?*

'Is it dangerous?' he asked her, like someone contemplating crossing a field with an angry bull in it.

She grinned at him. 'Not to me.'

When they set off again Drusus warned them to hush, for they were approaching the dungeons of Gath. Rubin and Valla exchanged an amused glance, for they had both been largely quiet thus far. Drusus spoke in a loud whisper but as the tunnel widened he fell silent. They came to a great open cavern, their passage watched by blind statues towering above. Many tunnels met here and Drusus paused as if unsure of his way. He squinted at the ancient runes carved on the walls as if he could read them, before deciding which route they should take. Soon Valla heard distant shrieks and moans and she unsheathed her sword and hefted it, comforting, in her hand. The tunnel dwindled, becoming smaller and darker. The cries became louder.

Suddenly a skinny hand darted out from the side of the tunnel and grabbed at Rubin's shoulder. He flinched and pulled away with a startled cry. Valla saw they were in a narrow corridor with cell doors on either side, each with its own barred window into perdition. Ghostly, skeletal faces appeared in the flickering torch flame, pressing themselves at the bars, their eyes closed against the light, their mouths open, howling. The corridor stretched on and on, past hundreds of such doors, and the three hurried along it, staying in the centre to avoid clutching hands, until they were past and the cacophony behind them slowly died. Their guide turned to them, his fat face livid in the torchlight, and pressed one stubby finger to his lips.

The corridor opened into another huge cavern. It too was the convergence of many tunnels, like the hub of a wheel. In the centre was seated a lone guard, his feet up on a table, fast asleep. The chamber was empty apart from the guard and his table and chair and a bag, presumably of food and drink. And a large bell on the table. This appeared to be the centre of the dungeons but there were no chains and shackles, no bunches of keys, no weapons.

Drusus silently led the way. From a pile on the floor he picked four new torches. He winked at them then crept into the next tunnel. Here the cell doors were smaller and without bars. There were no sounds in this place, no cries or howls, and the darkness pressed down like a fetid blanket. Many of the doors were marked with a painted cross. Valla suddenly felt very thirsty and she drank deeply from her water skin. She followed Drusus and Rubin, their bootsteps soft on the dusty floor, and behind them she sensed the gulon padding after.

When they had left the dungeons Drusus remained quiet and the others had no desire to start him talking, but when they stopped for a rest Rubin, ever curious, asked, 'Why just one custodian? Is he supposed to ring the bell when there's trouble? Then what?'

Drusus explained, 'There is an air-shaft above him. If he rings the bell a squad of soldiers is sent down.'

'Where from? And how long would that take? Someone could empty half those cells in a few moments.'

Drusus sneered. 'How? The doors are locked. The custodian doesn't hold the keys. The keyholder is far away, up in the fresh air.'

'What if the custodian needs to open a cell door?'

Drusus looked baffled. 'Why would he?' he asked, and Rubin had no answer to that.

'What of the doors with the crosses?' Valla asked, though she was afraid she knew.

'They call them oubliettes,' said Drusus. 'When there was some purge or mutiny and they rounded up a lot of prisoners, they'd just herd them all into one cell – sometimes fifty or more in a two-man cell. They'd have to crush them in sometimes. Then they'd lock the door and forget them. Well, we didn't forget them. We'd hear them yelling and crying for a couple of days but they soon died, from thirst or . . .' Drusus shrugged, unwilling to think what so many men forced into one small cell would die from. 'They never open the doors, those with crosses.'

He added, 'The emperor could be cruel.'

In a City where men and women were burned alive or slowly disembowelled for the entertainment of crowds, this seemed to Valla to be both obvious and appalling. She noted that Drusus admitted no part in this business, though as a dungeon guard he had doubtless been one of the men forcing the prisoners to their terrible fate.

They strode on for the better part of a day, or so Valla judged as her energy diminished, ignoring Drusus' many requests to stop. At last Rubin relented and they slept on the hard rock floor. When Valla woke, opening her eyes without moving, she spied the gulon sitting on its haunches on the edge of the light pool, watching. Their eyes met. She was unsurprised to see it, though she had no understanding of how it could be there when she had last seen it beneath the Red Palace, far away and long ago. Remembering how it had torn the throat out of her enemy, she was glad it was with her. Its golden eyes glinted in the torchlight and it was motionless until Rubin rolled over, mumbling, then it faded back into darkness.

They walked on until they saw a dull gleam in the

distance. Drusus crept forward and they followed, Valla with sword in hand. The light grew and they saw it was coming from an archway in the side of the tunnel. The way through was barred by an iron gate but, peering through its bars, they could see a lake of still water, gleaming silver, though there was no obvious light source.

'What is this?' Rubin turned to ask Drusus, to see him standing nervously on the other side of the tunnel as if he feared the silver pool.

'You're where you wanted to be,' the man said, nodding in confirmation of his own words. 'We're at the mountain. Give me my money and I'll be leaving.'

Valla stepped up, happy to get the point of her sword in a dirty crease of his neck.

Rubin told him, 'You'll be paid when we have proof we're at the Shield.'

'What do you want?' the man whined, 'a sign saying Welcome to the Shield of Freedom? I'm a man of honour. I've not played you false.'

'Valla,' Rubin said, and she willingly pressed the sword-tip against Drusus' throat. He shrank back against the rock wall.

'Kill me,' he said, his bloodshot eyes on hers, 'I'll go no further.'

Valla looked to Rubin. She would gladly slice him from ear to ear, but Rubin shook his head and she stepped back.

'What are you frightened of?' he asked the man.

'The lake,' Drusus said honestly, his eyes troubled as he stared at the shining water. 'They call it the Tears of the Dead. All the evil things that are done on the mountain leak down into it. Then, when it's disturbed they flow out again. Anyone who passes is doomed to die within the day. Or,' he added, 'that's what they say.'

'Let him go,' Rubin said briskly. 'Here.' He threw the bag of coin at Drusus, who quickly forgot his fear as he looked inside.

'Silvers!' he cried, outraged. 'You promised me gold!'

'I promised you this bag of money,' said Rubin. 'I did not say what was in it.'

But Drusus was already shambling back the way they had come, muttering to himself, fingering the coins.

'Do you think he'll raise the alarm?' Valla asked, glad to see the back of him.

Rubin shook his head. 'Those silvers will keep him in strong drink for half a year. Besides, it'll take him a while to get back to the guard station. By then we'll be long gone. Come on.'

They set off with a lighter step, knowing they were near their destination, but only moments later they were thwarted. A gate, like the one that guarded the lake, barred their way. Made of sturdy black iron, its bars were sunk deep into the walls. It was covered with the dust of ages. It was impassable.

Rubin grabbed the bars. 'Drusus was wrong,' he said. 'There is a welcome sign. This is it.'

He stood back and looked at it. The space between the bars was wide, but only a child could slip through. He took the torch from Valla and examined the gate minutely.

'Here,' he said. 'It's not dusty here.'

Valla peered at the gate. The dust lay thickly except where Rubin had laid his hands – and a section on the right where two vertical bars had been wiped clean. Rubin grabbed one and shook it. It didn't move. He grabbed the other – and it came away in his hand.

'Cut!' he said with satisfaction. He peered at the cut end, then he slithered through the gap and Valla slid after him. He set the bar back in its hidden grooves, and stared at it again. 'This is recent work,' he said, 'and clandestine. The cut end is smooth and without corrosion. Someone wanted to get in, then hide the fact that they had got in.'

'What could cut a thick iron bar like that?' she asked.

He shook his head. 'I have no idea. But now we know there are other intruders in the mountain. Besides ourselves,' he added. 'It might be useful information.'

But then they came abruptly to the end of their journey together. The tunnel they were following ended at a wide vertical shaft, which disappeared up into darkness. A sturdy ladder rose up the wall of the shaft. There was no other way.

'I can't climb that,' Valla said, her heart in her boots.

Rubin stared at her aghast. 'There must be some way—'

'There isn't,' she told him sharply. 'I cannot climb ladders. If we could see the top I might try, with one hand. But . . .' She shook her head. She had feared this might happen, that he would have to leave her at some point, but apparently it had not occurred to him. It seemed a cruel trick by the gods to bring them together then part them again so quickly. She dreaded the journey back through the tunnels alone, and busied herself divvying up the torches and lighting one for herself. She checked their water skins to see they were equally full, and that they had an equal amount of food.

'Have you seen these?' she asked him, pointing at the myriad bootprints at the base of the ladder.

He nodded. 'Whoever cut the barrier,' he said. 'I wonder who they are and what they want here.'

'I hope you find your father,' she said stiffly, torn between unwillingness to say goodbye and the need to get it over with. She placed her hand on his shoulder in a comradely gesture but he stepped forward and pulled her into a long embrace. She felt his breath against her neck as he whispered, 'Be well.'

He slung his pack on his back and she stuffed one end of a lighted torch deep in a pocket on its side. Then Rubin set his foot on the lowest rung of the ladder, nodded to her, and climbed swiftly up the shaft, not looking back. Valla watched as the blur of his torch became smaller, the sound of his feet diminishing until she could see and hear nothing more. She listened for a long time but the silence muffled her like a blanket, pressing down. She turned, raised her own torch and started back the way they had come.

Now she was alone the gulon trotted into the pool of torchlight and moved into its usual position by her heels. She looked down at it and it gazed up at her. It was more bedraggled than ever and now had a bald spot on its head in front of one of its ragged ears. She wondered where it had been, what it had been doing, since she was last underground. She had no clue. But she was glad of its company, however strange.

It occurred to her that it might know the way back better than she did. It had guided her truly in the Red Palace. She stopped and looked squarely at it. It sat on its haunches and scratched ferociously.

'Go back!' she said, pointing into the darkness. 'I'll follow.' It looked at her, its yellow eyes devoid of understanding. *It has no more intelligence than a fish*, she thought, and walked on.

Within five hundred paces she knew she was lost. There was a fork in the tunnel she did not remember passing in the darkness. She chose the widest way and kept on, trying to stay positive. She had torches and water enough for more than a day and in that time should be able to find her path back to the guard station. If necessary she would force the custodian to show her the way out.

Then she reached the meeting of four ways. She stopped, the echo of her bootsteps continuing in front of her, bouncing off walls. She cocked her head. She could hear running water. They had heard no water for their entire journey. She moved her head this way and that, trying to work out where the sound was coming from, for that was a way to avoid. She eventually chose a tunnel and hurried along it, anxiety speeding her steps. Lifting her torch she scanned the darkness. She passed two more tunnel mouths, to right and left, but kept straight on. She came to a dead-end, a rock wall. She breathed deeply, trying to calm herself.

Then she heard the distant sound of marching feet.

She hesitated for a few fatal heartbeats, then ran back down the tunnel, searching for one of the side exits. Too late. She saw a faint blur of moving torchlight in the distance and she turned and hurried back again, dousing her torch. She could only hope they had not seen the light and would take a side tunnel. She crept backwards in the darkness, fingertips against the wall, until her back was against solid rock.

The echo of heavy boots became louder, then out of the blackness loomed four warriors of the Thousand, their black and silver armour shining in the light of their torches. They blazed towards her and she drew her sword. She muttered to herself, 'Bless us, Aduara, goddess of fierce women. Bless your warriors and bathe them in the blood of men.' She heard the gulon growling in its throat beside her.

The soldiers halted and their leader stepped forward. Although he had his sword unsheathed for battle he opened his helm, a symbol of disrespect to another warrior. She did not know his face.

'Surrender to us now and you will be honourably

treated,' he told her, then paused as his words echoed off the walls, repeating over and over, diminishing. Then, 'We have orders to take you alive if possible, but dead will be acceptable.'

Valla looked down at the gulon, then smiled at the leader. 'Piss on you,' she said. And attacked.

When she came round the pain in her arm was monstrous. She lifted her head and the world lurched and she was violently sick. The effort of vomiting jarred her arm and the pain climaxed. She passed out again. When she came to a second time, barely rising above unconsciousness, a groan escaped her lips. She prayed for death but, as ever, her prayer went unanswered.

'Drink this,' a woman's voice said from a distance.

Valla opened her eyes. She was seated on a sturdy chair facing a table. On the other side of the table was an old woman. On the table was a cup. Her good arm was free and she picked up the cup and drank. It was not water. She didn't know what it was. It was both bitter and sweet at the same time. But she felt a little better afterwards as the nausea and pain receded.

She looked around. The room was small and whitewashed and there was a high window through which she could see pale sky. In the distance, strangely, she could hear music, the tender tones of a lute. Her spirits rose. At least she was out of the dungeons. She shifted in her chair and realized her legs were shackled to the floor.

The old woman asked, 'Where is Rubin Guillaume?'

'Dead,' Valla answered bitterly.

The woman waited for her to clarify, but Valla just stared at her. She had long white hair and black eyes and her face was creased with a thousand fine lines. On her breast was a crescent of silver.

'When and where did he die?' she asked patiently.

Valla peered at the ceiling in a parody of thought. 'Four days ago,' she said. 'We were attacked by a gang of thugs.' She shrugged. 'Five of them,' she added.

'Yet you were seen together,' said the woman mildly, 'no more than *three* days ago in Amphitheatre.'

Valla shook her head. 'Not true,' she said. 'I haven't been in Amphitheatre for—'

'Don't play games with me, soldier!' the woman rasped. The light in the room darkened and thickened as if something awful had passed over the sun. The floor rippled and flexed beneath Valla's chair like a great animal stretching its muscles. Pain blazed through her arm again, as if her bones were made of liquid fire. Valla moaned and silently begged Aduara for release, but her goddess would not grant her even the gift of unconsciousness.

The old woman spoke, from far in the distance, 'You are a million leagues out of your depth, girl, and still sinking, and your only way out of this room alive is to please me.'

Valla gathered her scraps of strength and opened her eyes. She said nothing.

'I see.' The air lightened and the woman sat back. 'You are seeking death. Which is why you attacked four armed men. That would have been enough to ensure your swift demise had they not been ordered to take you alive.'

Valla tried to ignore her words, seeking back through her memory, trying to work out what she could tell this woman and what she had to keep silent about for Rubin's sake. She feared torture but not, she suspected, as others did, for torment was part of her daily life.

The woman nodded to someone behind Valla and a door opened. There was a shuffle of boots, then two men came into Valla's sight carrying a bloody mess of hair. She looked at it, unsure what she was seeing, until they dumped it on the table in front of her and she saw it was the patchwork gulon. It was in a pitiful state, covered in blood, its legs broken, its head misshapen. Pus and blood oozed from it on to the table, and she guessed it was still alive, but only just. She put out her hand to touch its blood-specked muzzle. One eye opened a slit and, pathetically, it tried to lick her hand.

Fury rose in her. 'Is this a threat of what will happen to me?' she asked. 'This poor creature—'

'This *poor* creature,' barked the old woman, 'almost killed itself attacking my warriors. They had to take it alive, like you, for it is forbidden to kill a gulon.'

My warriors. Valla's befuddled, pain-racked mind finally allowed her to realize who she was facing. The empress. What have I come to, she asked herself, that I am refusing to answer questions put by the empress? For a moment her loyalty to Rubin wavered.

'How is it you have a gulon defending you?' Archange asked.

'I don't know,' Valla admitted, then she added frankly, 'It has followed me since I returned to the City. I don't know why.'

'You returned to the City before the Day of Summoning with your friend Rubin?'

Valla thought of all the people who had seen them in the Red Palace that day. 'Yes,' she said.

'And you had audience with Marcellus?'

This was something Valla could not speak of, so she stared at the woman mutely.

Archange sighed and looked at the gulon with distaste. 'This creature—' she began, but Valla interrupted her, careless that she was speaking to her empress.

'Rubin is my friend and I will not betray him, though your inquisitors reduce me to this, a sack of bones and pain,' she said, touching the gulon's ragged ear. The oozing blood had stopped and she wondered if the beast was dead.

The empress's black eyes glinted. 'You misunderstand me, Valla. I will not permit torture inside my palace. The City has seen too much of it in the past. On the contrary, I have a great gift to offer you.'

She reached out one thin, wrinkled hand and touched the gulon's back. The air burned and crackled and a new wave of agony passed through Valla's arm. She gasped. The gulon writhed, its hairy skin rippling like water. Its mouth opened and it let out a feeble whine. Its front paws scratched convulsively on the tabletop. It scrabbled with its hind legs, trying to get up. It collapsed, then got its legs under it. It looked around fearfully and jumped off the table. It scurried behind Valla's chair and she stared at it, astonished, as it peered back up at her. Then it sat down on its haunches and started to wash the blood off its paws.

Valla shifted her gaze to the empress, lost for words.

'It is strong again,' Archange told her. 'Perhaps stronger than it was before, for it is an old beast. Now,' she said, 'you have a decision to make. I can heal your arm, make it as good as new, now, this very moment. Then we will take a cup of wine together and you will tell me all you know about our friend Rubin Kerr Guillaume.

'Or,' she said, 'you and your arm will live together in agony for the rest of your life deep in my darkest dungeon.'

CHAPTER TWENTY-EIGHT

DAWN WAS A BRIGHT SPLASH OF CORAL IN A SKY OF bird's egg and navy blue, but Dol Salida did not enjoy it. It was a long time since he had last appreciated a sunrise. Once again he had played urquat far into the night until his opponents had staggered, beaten and yawning, to their beds. From then until the first chirrup of the new day he had updated his files in his meticulous, tiny hand, drawing on information gleaned by himself during the day, and by Sully, who roamed the City for him now Dol was marooned on the Shield, far from anywhere.

Time was when the old cavalryman had limped the streets of the City, disregarding the pains in his leg and hip, sucking in the fetid life-force of the alleys and lanes, the canals and culverts, markets, temples, inns and boarding houses, mansions and hovels, each day reclaiming ownership of his City for himself. He had lived and fought for it all his life and he could do no other.

But now he was caught in a two-fold trap. His new, powerful but empty position as the empress's first counsellor kept him glued to her side, for each day she needed to consult with him, on anything and everything, on troop movements among the remaining regiments, on the new embroidery for the library chairs, or on the precise meaning of a word she believed one of her military chiefs had used in a slovenly way. Archange enjoyed his company; Dol knew that. She often claimed she liked to have young people around her, but Dol didn't believe it for a heartbeat. In truth she enjoyed sharing the company of someone who understood the pains and frustrations of being old, although, he thought, he understood nothing else about the woman.

And secondly, he was trapped daily, hourly, every moment, by the pains in his leg. It had been injured fifty years before when, as a young trooper, he had been thrown from his mount during a battle, now long forgotten, against the Odrysians at the eastern frontier town of Markusia. With an old soldier's nostalgia, and flexing his new-found power in the palace, he had earlier in the year sent a troop of soldiers to investigate the town. Just dust and ruins, had been their curt report. And a few goats. Goats mean people, he had thought angrily. The townsfolk were just hiding, understandably. He was tempted to send the soldiers back, then, in a rush of common sense, had decided against it. What was the point of terrifying a handful of peasants just to satisfy a passing whim?

He had been thrown off the horse, a black mare called Darkest, but his foot had caught in the stirrup and the fool animal had dragged him half a league before stopping. The hip and knee joints had been entirely disconnected and he had spent more than ten days in misery until they healed sufficiently for him to walk again. But he never walked properly, without pain. And he had not sat a horse since.

His early-morning routine was always the same, as are, he thought to himself scrupulously, most routines. He woke, if he slept at all, in his old leather chair, an instrument of torture these days. He dragged himself to his feet, sweating and cursing, and eased out some of the agony by limping back and forth for as long as it took. His servants had learned to stay out of his sight or hearing during that time. Archange never seemed to summon him then. If she had he would have ignored her, empress or not. In truth, he would have ignored the gods of ice and fire if they had summoned him. Once his pains had settled to their regular, familiar torment, he called his servants and his day began.

But this day was different. He had levered himself from his chair, and was hanging on to the arm, feeling sluggish blood making its agonizing way through his mangled limb.

'The empress summons you, lord.' It was a soldier, one of the Nighthawks, his least favourite century.

Through gritted teeth he said, 'Tell her I am indisposed. She must wait.'

But they both knew Archange would wait for nothing and the soldier, implacable, said, 'We have brought a chair, lord.'

So it has come to this, he thought, and a flush of shame rose to his face. I am to be carted around the palace like a pile of laundry. But he had no choice. He suffered himself to be helped into the padded chair – old fool – and carried in humiliation to Archange's pretty parlour. He was surprised out of his self-absorption to see the empress was not seated in her usual place but lay on a day-bed by the window, propped up on many pillows. She looked gaunt and her eyes were dull.

She watched him without speaking as he was helped from the dratted chair and into another. A fine pair we are, he thought, to be responsible for this great City. The soldiers departed, leaving a single armed man at the door.

'Good morning, Dol Salida.'

'Morning, lady. I hope this urgent summons is worth my embarrassment?' *Let her have his head on a platter, it would be a kindness.*

She sighed and blinked slowly. 'We have had no word from Marcus in five days.'

'They will have engaged the enemy by now,' he replied sharply, still irritated. 'And Marcus and his chiefs have better things to do than write letters.'

He knew this was inadequate, a product of his discomfort. Messengers were sent daily from the City to the army and back. Marcus Rae Khan's first priority, after the execution of his mission, was to keep the empress informed.

She said with some of her former sharpness, 'Perhaps I should have left you in the torment of your own chair if that is the best you have to offer me.'

Mindful suddenly of her variable moods, he adopted a more politic tone. 'If you thought Marcus and Hayden Weaver had suffered such a setback that they could not communicate, then you would have summoned all your chiefs, not just me and my game leg.'

She smiled thinly and coughed. 'That meeting will be held later. I have called the chiefs but some will take a few hours to return.' She gazed at the ornate golden timepiece on her wall, a gift from Weaver. 'I am merely,' she sighed, 'seeking the immediate reaction of my old friend. Reassurance, if you will.'

'I have no reassurance to offer,' he said, honestly. 'There is nothing the City can do to help them if they have been overwhelmed. We do not have a few thousand spare troops to send. They are on their own.'

He had argued long and loud against sending the Khan army north to aid Weaver's forces. A third of the City's remaining troops on a fool's errand to help a man who was once, not long ago, the enemy. Vindication trumped loud in his ear, but he could take no pleasure from it.

Sharply, the empress ordered the single guard from the room. Dol looked at her enquiringly.

'I wish to discuss with you an important matter I cannot bring to the attention of my other counsellors,' she told him. As was always the case, he felt pride in the fact that she had chosen him as her foremost confidant. He regarded her closely. She seemed anxious, not an emotion he normally connected with the empress.

'Marcellus,' she said, watching his face. 'I believe he lives.'

This wasn't what Dol expected. When crossed Archange could make comments which were impulsive, outrageous even. But she was gazing at him calmly, sipping a tisane, awaiting his reaction. If it were anyone else he would have scoffed. But the empress would not have confided this concern to him unless she had good reason. He thought it through, remembering the gossip and rumour which had spread through the tortured City after the Day of Summoning. *Marcellus still lives*, people said. *He will return to rescue the City.* Superstition and nonsense, he thought. He shook his head firmly.

'We have Fell Aron Lee's testament that he executed him, severed his head and threw it from a tower of the Red Palace. We have no reason to think he was lying.'

'I do not think Fell was lying,' the empress snapped. 'When I questioned him – you were there, Dol Salida – I believe he told me the truth as he saw it. I have thought this over and over,' she sighed. 'Fell told us he killed Marcellus then made his way down to the Hall of Emperors. What did he say about that?'

Dol searched his memory. 'He said he got lost in the maze of stairs and tunnels. It took him some time to find his way back.'

'Exactly!' she cried triumphantly. 'He took some time. Yet he arrived there shortly after the death of Rafael. You verified this.'

In a moment of revelation, Dol saw what she was thinking.

'Rafael was not a mortal man,' he said.

'Indeed. He was merely a reflection of Marcellus. A remarkable one, ancient and unique, but just a reflection.'

'And a reflection cannot survive once his—?'

'Sire.'

'Once his sire is dead. Therefore, if Marcellus was indeed killed, up on the observatory tower, Rafael should have died on the instant in the Hall of Emperors.'

'Exactly so. But he didn't. You saw Rafael die.'

'I did. He was disabled by Shuskara, then executed by Indaro. The gods curse her name. Fell arrived in the Hall of Emperors shortly after. I remember wondering who he was, this tall warrior walking among the corpses.'

'Which can mean only one thing. The man Fell killed was not Marcellus.'

She sighed and set off a fit of coughing. 'It was obvious, but I could not see it, because Marcellus only created one reflection in his life, and that was his brother Rafael. He said it often and I repeated it myself and believed it, and it blinded me to the more obvious fact. That Marcellus must have made another one, perhaps more than one, in secret – he was always a secretive man – ready for just this eventuality. Araeon created any number of reflections over the years, to misguide his enemies, to guard his back. Why would Marcellus not also?'

Dol thought it through. 'Perhaps not,' he argued. 'The same facts would also apply if Rafe were not a reflection at all. Perhaps he was not. His death seemed like that of a mortal man.'

She shook her head. 'Rafael was a reflection,' she rapped. 'I know them well. I know everything about them. Marcellus was an only child, an orphan, and remained so until he was well into middle years. Then this friend, this *brother* appeared, whom Marcellus named Rafael Vincerus. Only the oldest of us knew he was no such thing. Most of the reflections that peopled the palace – there was something of a fashion for them for a century or more – were copies of their sires. They were made by Serafim using the power of the Gulon Veil. Only Araeon, who had powers far beyond the rest of us, could create reflections which were quite unlike him, at times not even human. At least, that is what we all believed.' She shuddered.

Dol sat back. He was only half listening. *Marcellus alive*, he thought. The possibility made any worries about the fate of Marcus' army fade into insignificance. If Marcellus still lived, if he had ambitions to gain the throne – and how could he not? – then all their futures looked uncertain.

'Why,' he asked, 'have you come to this conclusion now? The evidence, such as it is, has always been there for both of us. Why now?' This came perilously close to criticism, and Archange scowled.

'It is something which has bothered me for some time. But recently I had a conversation,' she said, 'with a former soldier of the Thousand. She was close to someone who knew Marcellus well, and she reminded me of something I had forgotten. She said Marcellus was a schemer, though he was at pains to hide it. He liked to appear spontaneous, impulsive. In fact all his moves were minutely calculated, like a game of urquat.'

He nodded. 'But, if that is the case, why,' he asked,

'would he stay away if his City was in trouble? And why did you not speak of your concerns before?'

She shot him an angry look. 'Why would he stay away all this time? I have no idea. And I did not speak of this before because I do not blurt out everything that is on my mind, Dol Salida. At first I was waiting for Marcellus to make a move against me, to revenge himself for the death of Araeon, and when he did not I thought he had decided to absent himself, as Serafim have done before. Or that I was merely mistaken.'

'And now?'

'Now I think he has made his move.' She coughed again and struggled to sit up. She reached out and rang the brass bell at her side.

Dol wondered what she meant for a heartbeat, then the realization was like a blow in the face. 'You think *Marcellus* is the reason we have lost contact with the army?'

Archange spoke to a soft-footed servant then waved him away. 'His troops love him,' she said, staring out of the parlour window. 'He could, if he chose, walk in and take command of the army from Weaver and Marcus. He might even be made emperor by acclamation, in the old way. He might turn the army, abort its mission to help the Petrassi, and return to the City.' She looked at him. 'And then what? The City could not stand another war, certainly not a civil war.'

Privately Dol thought that if Marcellus could seize command of the army from Marcus Rae Khan, which he doubted, then he could also turn the City's remaining forces against Archange. Not for the first time, he wondered what the relationship was between the empress and Marcellus. He had spent years secretly dogging the footsteps of the First Lord on Archange's behalf and he still had little idea. But he doubted that Marcellus, who had always been meticulously loyal to

Araeon, would be so to the empress who had snatched the throne.

But his role here this morning was reassurance. 'You are assuming too much,' he offered. 'Firstly, that Marcellus is still alive and wasn't butchered by some common soldier on his way out of the City.'

'No common soldier could kill him,' she stated, seemingly forgetting that, for a while at least, that is exactly what she had believed.

'And,' he went on as if she hadn't spoken, 'that he has reappeared hundreds of leagues away near the Petrassi border. And that he is sufficiently disloyal to his empress to act against her.'

He grunted. 'Time will tell,' he added.

'It always does,' she replied.

To Dol's satisfaction, the servant returned with something to break their fast. More tisane for the empress and watered wine for Dol Salida, and a platter full of the pastries which were the only thing Dol had ever seen Archange eat. He had always eyed them furtively but she had never offered him one. Now, however, she gestured to them and he took one. He bit into it, expecting a meat filling, but the taste in his mouth was, for a moment, strange and therefore unwholesome. Then he realized the pastry was filled with sweet fruit and honey, spiced and flavoursome. He ate it quickly then took another.

As he ate, the granddaughter glided in and spoke softly to Archange. Dol stared at her, schooling his face to show nothing. This Thekla, who had suddenly appeared at the palace ten or so days before, was an unknown quantity. She was said to be a surgeon and if this were true, Dol thought, why was she lingering on the mountain and not working down in the City where she was needed? In all his researches she had only appeared as a footnote to Archange's life. She had lived most of her years far beyond the City with her mother, for reasons unknown, at least to him. He was deeply suspicious of her and the way she had quickly, since the departure of Broglanh, made a place for herself among Archange's inner circle. He assumed she had been listening to their conversation. When she left she glanced coolly at him.

Archange was sitting up now, looking out over the City, sipping from a glass. She looked a little stronger, Dol thought.

'I have a piece of news for you,' he said, taking another pastry.

She turned her dark gaze on him, waiting.

'The lady Fiorentina has found sanctuary at the Khan Palace.'

'I don't know why you would call it *sanctuary*,' she argued, frowning. 'Are you implying she has something to fear from me?'

'Not at all,' Dol said hastily. 'But she has kept her whereabouts concealed since the Day of Summoning, as have the Khans. Perhaps she feels it is necessary.'

'I had assumed she died in the fall of the Red Palace, if I thought about her at all. Have your agents seen her, spoken to her?'

'No, and the Khan servants are fiercely loyal. But one of her former maids has been indiscreet. These people have their own network of contacts.'

She coughed. 'Scarcely conclusive. And the Khan servants may be *fiercely* loyal – they are probably too frightened of Giulia to be anything else – but I am sure the threat of interrogation will put a crack in that loyalty.'

'Perhaps. I am not sure it is that important.'

'Then why bring it to me? What do I care where the whore's sister has fetched up?'

'Just a morsel of gossip on a sunny morning,' Dol said

lightly, wishing he'd never mentioned it. Any allusion to Petalina, Marcellus' 'whore' for nigh on thirty years, however indirect, always provoked the empress.

She sat back. 'Perhaps I will call on Giulia,' she mused, 'and renew our relationship. I have not seen her since she returned from her voyage and I should express my gratitude for the foreign gold she brought to our coffers. I can mention Fiorentina and see what her face gives away. It will be informative.'

The morning passed, the sun ascended in glory, and Dol Salida found no inclination to leave the parlour. He had a full belly and his pains had died to the merest whisper.

They discussed many things, some important, many trivial. There was the matter of the Gulons, the emperor's own century of the Thousand. They had been far from the City on the Day of Summoning and had never returned. Dol had assumed the empress had ordered them rounded up and quietly despatched, like the Leopards before them. Yet apparently not, for she seemed concerned about their whereabouts and the Gulons, an elite force with, perhaps, a grudge against the empress, were a worrying loose end.

The Nighthawks were a problem for another reason. Though they had fought for the empress on the day the Red Palace fell, and she kept them close by her in the White Palace, the other centuries, and Dol himself, saw them as traitors and regicides. *Like a good dog turned bad*, he said of them to his friend Sully, *you can never trust it again*. Get rid of them, was Dol's opinion. Send them off on some hopeless mission against the Fkeni. Or split them up and mix them in with the common soldiery. Or send them north to join Marcus. Good men had died in recent clashes between the centuries and he believed Archange was reluctantly coming round to his opinion.

As the sun reached its zenith Dol realized he must leave; it would not do for the empress to think he had nothing to occupy him. He pushed himself to his feet.

'Thank you, Dol Salida,' she said as he stood, grasping his silver-topped stick. 'You have been a good servant to me.'

This sounded worryingly like a farewell and Dol was momentarily nonplussed. As if she knew what he was thinking, she added, 'And I trust you will be for many more years to come.'

'If the gods save us,' he answered gruffly.

Unexpectedly she held out her hand, something she had never done before, and Dol Salida took it awkwardly. It felt like random bones loosely wrapped in thin velvet.

'This role is not one you enjoy, is it?' she asked, looking up at him.

'It is an honour—' he started.

'Yes, yes. I know it is an honour. But?'

He thought quickly. 'I miss my wife,' he confessed, 'and my girls.' He had not made his way down the mountain since the beginning of summer so his answer was true, if incomplete.

'Then go and see them today.' She was still holding his hand and he felt a sudden warmth pass through it into him. In a heartbeat he felt his old limbs grown stronger, his brain clearer, felt blood flowing through his veins.

'I will,' he said, and he realized how much he wanted to. He left the parlour with a light heart.

Dol Salida had not lived for long on the mountain before he realized why its palaces had been largely abandoned, except for those Families either rich enough or secretive enough to endure its many inconveniences. There was only one road up the Shield, built at the cost of many lives, and it was variously narrow and steep, and frequently both. Everything – food, water, supplies of every kind – had to be hauled up by donkey or on the narrow carts specially built for the purpose. To keep the palaces, if they were all tenanted, supplied with water alone would have been an impossible task. As it was there was an endless train of beasts up and down the pathway, a permanent nuisance to anyone who wanted to descend the Shell Path by carriage. Dol was told that at one time there was a pumping system which delivered water to the top of the mountain, though he found that hard to believe.

So his journey down the path, in the late afternoon as the sun cooled in the west, was a frustrating and long drawn out business. Frustrating, that was, for the driver of his narrow carriage. Dol, basking in his pain-free condition, enjoyed the journey, slow though it was, looking kindly on the placid donkeys which plodded past them as they paused at each of many turnouts to let them by.

The afternoon meeting with the military chiefs had been frustrating, as they often were. They could not know what had happened to the Khan army, any more than Dol did, yet it was his experience that the less people knew the more vigorous they were in their opinions. There was a deal of shouting before Archange arrived, on her own two feet. It was Dol's view, and that of others, that the problem was not with the army, but the messengers. The riders must pass through Fkeni lands and once a band of tribesmen had spotted this regular daily movement through their territory it would be a simple matter to pick the lone riders off for torture or death or both. The meeting decided, predictably, that they would wait another day, until dawn, then, if no messenger returned from the north, a group of Darius' riders would set out.

When his carriage arrived at the base of the Shield, Dol was surprised and disturbed to see how much it had changed. There had always been a barracks here, for the Emperor's Rangers had guarded the mountain for time out of mind. Now, though, a new barracks had sprung up, as had myriad shacks and tents housing pedlars, sellers of foodstuffs and whores to service the soldiery, plus beggars, hangers-on and the other ne'er-do-wells such places attract. It was a small town now, stiff with soldiers but with the ragged feel of a frontier outpost. Dol resolved to speak to the empress about it when he returned.

He had chosen to walk the half league to Gerta's cottage, which nestled in the crook of the river meandering past the Shield. The day before he would not have considered such a thing, but his leg felt better than it had in years. He had heard the empress had healing hands, and gossip had it that she had recently healed a gravely injured prisoner for some reason of her own. Dol thought this improbable, for why would she choose to help a criminal before her closest adviser? But, whatever the reason, for the first time in an age he felt like taking a gentle stroll. Having shaken off the beggars who clustered when they saw his fine carriage, he set off. To the north storm clouds were gathering and a patter of light rain darkened the shoulders of his jacket.

He soon spotted the cottage and saw a thin plume of smoke arising from its fat chimney. He smiled. His wife, warned he was coming, would have been baking all afternoon, piling up the sweetmeats he loved, rich with herbs and spices. His mouth watered at the prospect.

He noticed the front door was ajar, for the late afternoon was sultry. Then he halted, his heart seeming to stop in his chest. The metallic scent of blood, unmistakable, drifted to him on the warm air. He hastened, faltering, to the door, a low moan rising in his throat. Old warrior though he was, he was terrified of what he might see.

Inside the front door he found the body of his daughter Eudice. An ex-soldier of the City, she had been caught unweaponed, and her breast had been stabbed, her heart pierced. He stumbled past her and found his other daughter, Fierro, dead in the parlour, throat slashed. Sobbing, he walked heavily to the kitchen. He knew that was where he would find her.

Gerta lay huddled in the corner in a pool of blood. Dol stood in the doorway. He knew she was dead. A knife stuck out of her throat. In his grief, he didn't see it as significant that it was still there. There was a movement; hope rose in him, and he saw his grandchild, one of them, Eudice's son. His fair head was peering out from behind Gerta's bulky body. She had protected the child to her death. Dol choked back his tears. They would not help her now.

He limped forward and picked up the child, who was white-faced and blood-covered, silent in shock. Dol pressed the boy to his chest. He had little experience of children, but he murmured, 'There, there, boy. I'll find someone to care for you.'

Dol didn't see the dark shape appear behind him in the doorway, or hear the assassin step forward on noiseless boots. But for the briefest moment he felt the hot blade of the dagger as it drove through his back and into his heart.

PART FIVE

The Lone Army

CHAPTER TWENTY-NINE

BROGLANH SAT WITH HIS BACK AGAINST A DEAD HORSE, sharpening his blades by moonlight. The landscape was bright as day and there was no need for a fire, not that any of the weary, bloodied soldiers had the will to gather tinder. He could smell the enemy's campfires in the distance, the faint musk of burning peat, the tantalizing odour of roasting meat. They had been well prepared.

Good for them, Broglanh thought. *They'll still die on our swords.*

Everything he could see was either black or silvery grey, the shadows sharp with crisp edges. He imagined it was how the deathworld would be, the place warriors of the City called the Gardens of Stone. Archange had once told him there was no such thing, and when you died your soul died too while your carcass mouldered into dust. Only simple folk believed in an afterworld, she said, and there was nothing more simple than a soldier. Eat, sleep, fight – and one day die.

Broglanh was content with that. He knew he was skilled, but he also appreciated he was lucky. He had beaten the odds an unreasonable number of times. With each warrior he came up against, be it in a momentary scrap or a gruelling contest of swords, it was kill or be killed. And each time he had killed.

And it would be the same this day. That they faced greater numbers meant nothing. That they had their backs to the wall, in a manner of speaking, meant nothing. Each fight would be a new one against a new adversary, and each would be a fight to the death.

He rolled his right shoulder, which he had wrenched sometime the previous day. It was painful but it would not hamper him. He had fought on with far worse injuries. He was hungry, but then he had been hungry since this journey started. He took a long drink from his water skin to ease the cramp in his belly. The water was vile and he spat it on the ground, trying to dislodge the taste. He used the rest to rinse his hands and face, rubbing off the sticky remnants of blood. He looked to the east. He guessed it was still long before dawn and he wondered if he could sleep for a while. Around him the Pigstickers were mostly sleeping, snoring and scratching, although some lay awake staring at the sky. Given the choice of fighting from horseback with the riders or on foot with the Pigstickers, he'd chosen to stand with the infantry. He knew them better, he knew their strengths and weaknesses – and he felt he owed them for protecting Emly from the Fkeni. Besides, too many things could go wrong on a horse; they were unreliable beasts in battle, as he'd long ago found to his cost. He had given his mount to the girl, so she could make a dash for it if everything went to ratshit.

He thought of Emly as he had last glimpsed her, holding the great warhorse's rein, ready to flee the coming battle. Her face was ashen, her eyes bright with fear. Not for herself, but for him. Broglanh felt no guilt, though he had brought her into this. He had done what he thought right at the time, right for Em and for the City. He hoped she would be safe.

He'd finished with the blades. He slipped the short

one into the groove in his boot, the two long ones in the scabbard on his baldric, and he sheathed the sword. It was a good blade, taken from a gut-skewered soldier. Some thought it bad luck to take a weapon from a dying man's hand, as if some of the ill fate could be transferred from grip to grip. Broglanh scoffed at the idea. This sword had been lucky for him; it had lasted all day without breaking or noticeably blunting. He placed the sword-belt within hand's reach, leaned back against the still-warm horse and closed his eyes.

'Have you taken lorassium?'

'No,' he lied.

'Look at me.'

It seemed a lot to ask, but he raised sluggish eyelids. It was Thekla, in a gown of midnight silk. On her breast was a crescent moon. Her blue-black hair coiled and curled, slithered and slid.

'Only the Gaetas,' she said, 'know the true power of the veil.'

He was riding in a cart again, in comfort, though it was only a rough wooden wagon with old blood-stains on the floor. It seemed to glide along as if floating in the sky. Suddenly anxious, he looked about him, but the cart was not flying. It was rolling smoothly, silently through the dark streets of the City. He saw buildings he knew well from his childhood: the trainees' barracks, the temple of Paraclites where he'd had his first real fight with some drunken roughs, the brick mausoleum of the Sarkoys. He was in Paradise.

Beside him, Thekla threw off heat like a furnace and he breathed in her scent, of silken skin and warm, mossy places. His blood started to pound through his loins. He closed his eyes and tried to think of something else.

'Have you any other injuries?' she asked him.

Injuries? Who'd been injured? He couldn't remember.

Now it was Indaro beside him. She was naked and her

mouth was red with blood. Her red hair coiled and hissed around her like blazing snakes.

'Watch your back,' she said. 'There are always more of them than you think.'

He awoke on the battlefield with a start, in a moment of pure panic. He could hear his heart's erratic thump through his ears, and his chest couldn't suck in enough breath. There were incomprehensible sounds – sharp thunderclaps and a noise like the fizz of shallow water over pebbles.

He opened his eyes. The light all around him – the air, the sky, the land – was red as blood and warriors, men and women, were rising or running or just standing frozen in shock, looking up. He looked up too.

Red stars were falling from the sky.

Rosteval was not a young horse and he had spent recent years carrying his master from the rear of one battle to the next, rarely speeding above a sedate trot. So it was with some surprise and rising excitement in his hairy breast that he felt the urgent thud of boot-heels in his sides, heard the sharp command of his rider. Rosteval lumbered into a canter.

When Hayden Weaver saw the enemy's flares he guessed the effect they would have on the troops. There is nothing more superstitious than a soldier, particularly a City soldier, and the sound and sight of the red lights would have many of them, and their mounts, fleeing in terror, fearing an attack by their ever-capricious gods. The fact that the lights were harmless devices the Petrassi had come by decades before could scarcely be explained to a panicking soldier.

The Khan army, already hemmed in to the west by the Vorago, had been pushed back southwards in the course of the day. And behind them was the sea. Now they had sheer cliffs to their backs and the gorge to their left.

As Rosteval thundered along the lines, followed doggedly by a cadre of Petrassi veterans, Hayden had no real plan. He needed to rally the City troops, but the sight of a few horsemen riding towards the enemy was unlikely to turn the soldiers, many of whom were retreating in disorder from the menace. Most were standing their ground but there is always a point when the weight of numbers fleeing turns a retreat into a rout.

Agile as a two-year-old, Rosteval dodged a pole sticking up from the ground. Hayden realized it was a City flag, stuck carelessly in the earth. He dragged it out as he passed. The flag was heavy, made to fit snugly in a holster on the flag-bearer's saddle, but he held it aloft two-handed, and it fluttered, subsided, then fluttered again in the light breeze. The City emblem was a crimson eagle on a field of gold, and as the general held it high he was aware of the irony of the situation.

'They cannot harm you!' he yelled to the wavering troops. 'They are only lights! They cannot harm you. They are a trick of the enemy.'

They did not know him. They did not know he was the general who had conquered their City. They saw only their flag, and soldiers riding towards today's enemy. Those who were hesitating, on the verge of panic, firmed their stance and looked at their fellows and grinned, if sheepishly. Those who were fleeing, creeping or running, some of them stopped and turned in the baleful light and went reluctantly back to fight alongside their comrades. They would not be deserters, at least not now.

Hayden Weaver waved the flag and the soldiers cheered and readied themselves for the order to move forward. The flares started dying away and the red light faded.

And then the cannonade started.

* * *

Stern had stood strong at first. He had seen a lot in his twenty-odd years' service and he had learned that not everything you don't understand is trying to kill you. He looked to Broglanh who stood on his right, sword in hand, gazing up at the red lights, curious but unconcerned. Stern didn't know much about this veteran who had arrived with his own private warhorse yet who chose to stand with the Pigstickers, but he was glad to have him at his side and he had learned to trust his judgement.

'Hold!' Stern warned his warriors, and he did not have to look round to know they were firm.

Then the fearful light started to fade. The cavalry horses of the Daybreakers on their left began to settle as their riders won control. Stern felt the grim resolution in advance of another day's fighting moving through the ranks.

But when a thunderous booming started it was as much as he could do not to drop his weapons and clap his hands over his ears. The sound was like a roll of thunder overhead, but the loudest he had ever heard, and it went on and on. Some soldiers fell to their knees in awe and dread, but none of them fled. *Another trick of the enemy to frighten us*, Stern thought grimly.

The first explosion came far to their left and he saw horses and their riders tossed about like rag dolls. There was a blast of hot wind and Stern, unmanned, threw himself to the ground with the rest of his troop. He pushed his face into the earth and clapped his hands over his ears, trying to block out the unearthly din, the cries of the wounded, the screams of injured horses. The earth beneath him seemed to lurch and rock, and missiles thudded around him, hitting his back and legs. There was a second explosion, then a third closer by. His ears rang with the sound and his whole body trembled. Summoning all his willpower he dragged his face out of the earth and looked about him, terrified of what he might see. All around was flying dust and smoke, as if a fire was raging nearby. Injured soldiers were staggering away from the front, some hideously wounded, limbs half-severed, blood gouting. The missiles he had felt showering him were bloody body parts: hands, feet and heads strewn all around. Another blast rocked them, the closest yet, and Stern clung to the ground and prayed to the gods of ice and fire to end the nightmare.

When he looked up again he saw Broglanh was standing and Stern scrambled up too. The noise had died down and the explosions had stopped.

'What in the name of the gods is happening?' he asked, not expecting an answer. The ringing in his ears made his voice hollow and distant. All other sounds were muffled. 'Is it sorcery?'

'No.' Broglanh shook his head, not taking his eyes from the smoke which harboured the enemy. 'But it is cowardly. No honourable warrior fights his battles this way.'

The remaining Pigstickers were battered and dazed but there were no major injuries. They started tending the wounded, relieved they had been the ones unscathed by the terrible onslaught. Stern made sure Benet and Quora were both unharmed before turning back to Broglanh, who was still watching the north, sword in hand, waiting.

'Do you think they'll come now?' Stern asked.

'I would.'

'We don't even know who we're fighting.'

'I'm fighting anyone who tries to kill me.'

Broglanh glanced briefly towards the east and Stern, catching his thought, reassured him: 'The girl'll be all right. They'll be far away now.'

* * *

The girl, five leagues away, was struggling to control her frightened horses while avoiding being trampled by donkeys and baggage ponies fleeing the terrifying sounds to the west. She scarcely had time to wonder what the distant thunder and red stars might mean. Patience and Blackbird, eyes rolling, tore away their tethers and she was scarcely able to snatch their reins before they made off. The big warhorse reared and she dodged his flailing hooves and hung on. The other women were shouting and crying and many had fallen to the ground in terror.

Emly held on grimly, talking to the horses, and the beasts, well trained, responded to her voice as she coaxed them to calmness and the lights and sounds died away.

She looked around. Most of the camp-followers were chasing their baggage animals. They had been packed and ready for a day's march – far away from the battle-field as ordered – when the enemy attack started, and they were fearful of losing their possessions. The whole encampment was stretching out, disorganized and vulnerable. Emly climbed up on to Blackbird, holding the warhorse's reins.

'We must keep together,' she called to the other women but they ignored her. She rode on, trailing Patience behind her. Most of the animals had started to calm down, to slow and to stop, lured by sweet grass, their simple minds quickly forgetting what had frightened them. Emly spotted Peach, who had found her donkey and was leading him to where her bags and baggage lay abandoned.

'We must stay together,' Em repeated despairingly, for her nights, and sometimes her days, were still haunted by fear of attack by the Fkeni.

'Let them be, girl,' a voice said. Emly turned and

saw Bruenna the midwife striding along, carrying her huge pack on her back, her pink bonnet crammed on her head and Maura's baby tucked in the crook of her arm. 'They've been doing this a lot longer than you,' she told the girl sternly. 'Once they've got their animals they'll settle all together.'

'We're too far from the army,' Em said, gazing back anxiously to the west from where distant sounds of battle floated on the breeze.

'Or, if our troops are overwhelmed, then we're not far enough away,' Bruenna argued.

'Our warriors will prevail,' Emly replied dutifully, but she knew their troops were outnumbered and her heart was full of fear for Evan.

Just as Bruenna predicted, in ones and twos the wives and whores led their animals to a copse of trees which was the only landmark in sight. Emly looked around, trying to see the land from Evan's point of view.

'We can't stay here – we can't see anyone coming if we stay among the trees,' she said to the other women. 'We should go up there.' She pointed to a long, bare slope half a league to the north, leading up to a rocky outcrop. 'We'll be able to see all around from there.'

'Who made you empress?' a sharp-faced, sharp-voiced woman called Skarritt asked her. 'There's no grazing for the animals up there, you ninny.' She halted her heavily laden donkey and started undoing his straps.

Em looked at Bruenna, who shrugged and dumped her pack on the ground. The women began to unpack again and to collect tinder to make fires. More appeared with their animals and the encampment started to settle. There seemed to be an unspoken consensus that they would go no further.

Peach came over to Emly, who remained atop Blackbird. 'Don't worry,' she said, looking up. 'No one tells them what to do, even the soldiers. You may as well unpack. We won't be going anywhere today.'

Em nodded and slid off the horse. She knew her friend was right. And if they were attacked Emly could defend herself, and maybe Peach too, with the fearsome knife Quora had given her. The Fkeni, if they came, would take the easiest targets first. It was hard but it was true.

She poured grain into the horses' nosebags then arranged her baggage – her cloth bag and Evan's spare pack – at the base of a tree and sat down. She wondered about food. She had not eaten since they had arrived at the Vorago and she knew what Evan would say – 'Eat when you can.' Like a good soldier she rummaged in her bag and brought out the last two apples of a dozen she had picked days before. They were old and wrinkled but she ate one with relish. It was juicy and sweet on her tongue. She set the other aside to share between the horses.

She needed to relieve herself, so she stood and wandered back into the shady copse. It was pretty in there, the ground dappled with light which shifted and shimmied with the movement of the leaves above. She walked into the shade and was about to lift her skirt when she realized, with sudden dread, that she was not alone. From the darkness of the trees two people emerged, a tall man holding a girl in front of him.

Peach was terrified, her eyes wide with fear above the calloused hand of the man with an eyepatch who held her tight, a long knife to her face.

'Do as I say, Emly,' the one-eyed man said. 'Go fetch those horses of yours or this one loses an eye. I'll prick it out in a heartbeat. Eyes come out very easily,' he explained to her pleasantly. 'I should know.'

Casmir had tracked the Khan army with ease. A moving mass of thousands of men and women, their chattels, livestock and hundreds of horses left a clear path of debris, cold campfires, broken weaponry, animal carcasses – and some human bodies: he could have followed if the crows had taken out both his eyes, he thought.

Unlike Broglanh, who had chosen a path far off the army's flank, chary of being noticed by scouts, Casmir had welcomed the attentions of the outriders. He had abandoned his horse, slapping it on the rump to make it run, then had walked into a scouts' camp early one morning, claiming to be a refugee from the lost Forty-seventh. He had papers, supplied by the White Palace, and was welcomed by the scouts and sent on to the main army where he was enfolded into the embrace of the infantry and deployed with the Ratcatchers. He chose the infantry because cavalrymen keep themselves aloof from the run of the army and he felt he could hunt the girl and her lover more easily from the ground.

He knew the girl was too small to be a soldier, therefore he guessed she must be with the general's party or the camp-followers. Soldiers love to gossip and a few sideways questions told him there were no courtesans travelling with Marcus Rae Khan and his chiefs. He therefore abandoned the Ratcatchers and drifted back through the throng towards the baggage train where he could watch the wives and whores from a discreet distance. Then they reached the Vorago and the battle started. Thanking the gods for the good judgement which had kept him well to the rear, he joined the press of carts and supply wagons as they retreated east from the battlefield.

He soon spotted the girl. He remembered seeing her at the House of Glass, tied to a chair, staring at him fearfully as the building went up in smoke. He often wondered how she had survived. He would ask her.

And he would ask why she had lied at his trial. There would be plenty of time for questions. Emly was leading a big warhorse – Broglanh's no doubt – and walking beside a yellow-haired whore. When the women camped he had stood in the dark of the trees and waited his chance.

Now he held the whore in front of him with ease, part of his mind still revelling in the renewed strength of his body. He grasped the girl's jaw with one hand, half lifting her from the ground, and put a knife to her soft cheek with the other. She stopped squirming when she saw the blade and hung there, sobbing and gasping.

He grinned. This was easy. Emly, soft-hearted girl that she was, would do anything he told her to save her friend.

So it was with some surprise that he saw her sit down cross-legged on the leafy grass and heard her say, 'I don't believe you, Casmir. You are a warrior, not a brute. And you will not take her eye out, for you remember the torment of it yourself.'

He opened his mouth to answer, but she added firmly, 'Besides, you owe me.'

He snorted, 'This is not a game of chance, girl. There are no debts to be owed or paid. Go get the horses or I will take her sight without hesitation or remorse.'

'And then what will you have?' she asked him reasonably. 'You will have a girl screaming and maddened by pain and I will still be sitting here. Besides,' she repeated, 'you owe me.'

Frustrated by her calm he flung the whore aside and she fell in a sobbing heap. *Why can't all girls be like that?* he thought irritably, looking at Emly who remained unmoved.

'You have come to take me back,' she said. It was not a question.

'I have. The empress charged me with killing your soldier lover and returning you to her palace. I have loyally discharged the first part of my mission. It only remains for me to take you home. There is nothing left for you here. Only death – or capture and torment and death – at the hands of the enemy.'

He saw the flicker of fear in her eyes when he lied about Broglanh, but she said, 'You have been ordered not to harm me.'

He conceded as much by saying nothing.

'Then you have a problem,' she said, rising smoothly to her feet and bringing a knife the length of a man's forearm from a sheath hidden in her skirts.

He laughed. He was back on familiar territory. 'I am a sword-master, girl. I can disarm you without scratching your pretty skin.' He unsheathed his sword and loosened his wrist.

'What happened to you, Casmir?' she asked curiously, with sympathy in her voice. 'When last I saw you you were dying.'

'You thought wrong,' he said. He smiled.

But as he raised his sword there was a yell from the direction of the camp and he turned to see a band of women running through the trees. He glanced to where the whore had lain but she must have crept away while Emly held his attention. The women, twenty or thirty of them, were bearing cudgels and knives and screaming with a shrillness which made his eye socket ache.

The Wolf turned and fled.

CHAPTER THIRTY

THE NIGHT WAS DARK, THE MOON SKULKING BEHIND slow clouds, when Emly padded across the quiet encampment, careful to avoid treading on any of the sleepers. She made her way to where the horses were tethered. She murmured a greeting to them and stroked their noses. Blackbird waggled his ears and Patience snorted softly in recognition. She had left them saddled in readiness and she tied her belongings on the big horse. She fed them the two apple halves. Then she slipped out of her skirt, abandoning it on the earth, and pulled on the leather breeches Evan had given her. She took up the horses' reins and led them away across the sleeping land.

She did not believe Casmir had killed Evan. She had thought long and hard on it and it made no sense. By far the most hazardous part of the assassin's mission would be to attack an armed soldier, a veteran, in the midst of his comrades. No, she decided, he would have planned to capture her first, then use her to lure Evan from the battlefield. Would her lover abandon his fellows in the midst of battle, even to come to her aid? She doubted it. But Casmir would not know that.

She did not fear the assassin. He could not harm her, so she was invulnerable to him. But, staying, she would put the other women in peril for Casmir would certainly make another try. And she must warn Evan if she could. He was expecting enemies to come running at him from in front, not one sneaking up from behind.

The night was cool, with the promise of autumn in the air. Emly stopped and sniffed the night scents, of earth and iron and horses, and distant corpses. She felt the power of the land rising through the soles of her boots, thrilling through her limbs. She was stronger than she had ever been, and she revelled in the freedom of the dark. She checked the long knife scabbarded at her waist. Then she climbed on to Blackbird and, with Patience on a leading rein, heeled her mount back towards the battlefield.

'Indaro would do this thing,' Broglanh said indistinctly round a mouthful of dried meat. 'She wasn't as strong as a man and couldn't behead one with a single blow. So she'd pivot . . .' he circled one finger as he swallowed, 'she'd turn on her heel and spin right round, twice sometimes, and scream and take his head off. Like you see an axeman do.'

'And her opponent would just stand there?' Stern asked sceptically. 'What would he do while he waited, burnish his weapon?'

Quora sniggered, and Broglanh grinned amiably. 'She was fast, like a whirling demon. You've no idea.'

Stalker agreed, nodding his big head sagely. 'She was a mighty warrior.'

Stern looked at the two men, both as mighty as any he'd seen, talking about this Indaro as though she were a warrior of legend.

'What happened to her?' he asked.

Broglanh shrugged, chewing, and Stalker glanced at him then said, 'She met someone.'

Stern nodded. It was a familiar enough tale. Women

could be lethal fighters. They were as tough as men, some of them, they were fast and agile and many, like Quora, were wedded to the life. But some, well, they just bided their time waiting for a man to come along, someone who'd take them out of the life and be their protector. This Indaro, admired though she was by her two comrades, sounded like one of those – flighty.

He took a bite of horsemeat. It was hard to chew, harder to swallow, but it was all they had left apart from some weevil bread. He looked around at the fifteen remaining Pigstickers, most uninjured, some with minor wounds, all of them wildly outnumbered. This day they would only live to tell the tale if the enemy suddenly decided to pack up and go home.

He wondered how Benet was. His brother had been dragged off the battlefield, a lance-head buried deep in his thigh, pouring blood, his face white and scared. It was a survivable injury, but only assuming the army itself survived to defend its wounded, and that seemed doubtful.

'Benet'll be all right,' Quora told him, guessing his thoughts. 'He's lived through worse than this.'

She was wrong. They'd never been in a pickle as bad as this. But Stern nodded. He looked at her across the campfire. Quora was propped on one elbow, gazing at him. His eyes travelled over the curve of her hip, the swell of her breasts. She watched him watching her and her dark eyes shone in the firelight. He thought he had never seen anyone so beautiful. Warmth moved in his loins and he casually rolled over on to his belly.

Stalker was looking at him, picking gristle from his teeth. 'Your brother is he?'

Stern nodded.

'Blind as a mole,' the northlander said. 'I wouldn't trust him.'

'He wasn't blind when we started out,' Stern retorted, stung by the criticism. 'We didn't ask for this.'

'Didn't you? You chose soldiering as a life, lad. You're not from the City, but you both chose to fight for her.'

Her. Stern had never heard the City spoken of as a female before. Stalker was watching him, his eyes the colour of fog on water.

'Why do you suppose I'm not of the City?' Stern asked. *I'm as loyal as any of its sons*, he thought.

Stalker shrugged. 'You have the look of sea folk.'

Stern wondered who had told him. 'My father was a City soldier.'

'I thought your father was a fisherman,' Quora put in.

'He was,' he told her, a tad annoyed. 'But originally he came from the City. Barenna.' He did not want to explain to these veterans that his father had left the army after ten years' service, back in the day when it was possible for a soldier to quit while he was still alive and relatively uninjured.

'What was his name?' Stalker asked.

'Why do you want to know?'

The northlander shrugged. 'No reason.' He lay back, arranged his ginger braids in a knot to form a pillow, and closed his eyes. Within moments he was snoring.

Stalker was a bit of a mystery. A refugee from some mercenary unit demolished by the Blues, he'd joined the Wildcats the year before and survived the massacre of the Maritime at Salaba, then somehow found himself in the Red Palace on the Day of Summoning. He'd survived that too, then turned up here with a bunch of riders and, like Broglanh, he'd abandoned the doubtful safety of a horse to stand with the grunts. He and Broglanh had not met before, but they had friends in common and in the last two days of fighting they'd bonded like brothers. Stern was glad to have them both standing with him, but he was still suspicious of the northlander. He seemed to have miraculously survived when thousands died. Not once, but over and over. In Stern's experience, that pointed to a soldier who ducked out of the worst of the fighting, emerging again once it was over. But could that be true of Stalker, who threw himself into each battle with gusto? He was certainly not a coward – but what was he?

Suddenly Broglanh dropped the horse jerky he was eating and rolled on his hip and cocked his head, listening. Then he jumped up, grabbing his helm and sword-belt, and kicked Stalker into wakefulness.

'They're coming!' he roared.

There were no red lights and explosions this day; perhaps the enemy thought they were no longer necessary. The noise Broglanh could hear was like waves crashing on a pebble beach: the sound of thousands of warriors marching. In moments they advanced out of the fog, their banners of red and gold catching the rays of the rising sun. The drums rolled and as one they started chanting, 'Death! Death! Death!', crashing their swords against their shields as they advanced.

They filled the sight, they filled the heart and mind. All the City's soldiers could think was, *How can there still be so many? We have killed and killed and killed, yet still they come.* On and on the chant went, shredding the warriors' nerves as they hastily adjusted armour, hefted swords and spears, tried to spit the dryness from their mouths.

When the barbarians were fifty paces away Stalker let out a roar and ran at them, his great broadsword in one hand, a Pigsticker spear in the other. In a heartbeat the others leaped after him. With Broglanh at his left shoulder, Stern on his right, the big northlander smashed into the enemy ranks, impaling one warrior on the spear and crushing a man's throat with the broadsword. The rest of the City forces surged forward bellowing their battle cries, then war cries gave way to the screams of the wounded.

Stern gutted one warrior, then he parried a blow from a second, backhanding his shield into the man's face. Quora sliced the man's throat.

'Stalker's gone mad!' she yelled.

Stalker was cleaving deep into the enemy ranks, cutting and stabbing, careless of a lethal vacuum building behind him. Stern and Quora hurled themselves into the breach and, for a moment, the barbarians fell back. Then a huge man in a bronze helm came running at Stalker, sword raised. The northlander parried the blow and reversed a cut to the man's neck. The great blade hammered against the mail vest and snapped. Dropping the hilt, Stalker grabbed the enemy's mail shirt and pulled him forward, butting him savagely then crashing his fist into the man's face. Broglanh, fighting to his right, threw him a sword. Stalker caught it and the blade sliced through the back of his enemy's neck.

As the battle raged there were no more battle cries from the front lines, only the groans of the dying and the grim determination of the living to survive. The City warriors were being forced back, but the barbarians had to climb a wall of their own dead, slippery with blood and brains and entrails, to get at them.

Stern staggered as an axe-blade smashed his shield. Pigging axemen, he hated them. They needed room to swing, else they were more lethal to their comrades than to the enemy. But once they had you in their eyeline . . . Stern would rather have faced two swordsmen together. He pulled out his long knife. The axeman swung again, missing Stern but pulverizing his sword. Agony speared through his arm, but he feinted with the knife then dodged to his left and crashed his fist into the man's throat. The axeman staggered, gasping for breath, and in the same moment Broglanh sliced his sword under the man's helm and into the back of the spine.

Stern nodded his thanks to Broglanh, then picked up an abandoned sword and hurled himself back into the melee.

As the sun moved on to the west the remaining City soldiers formed a wall, shields aligned against the next onslaught. Stalker had predicted the enemy would not use cannon, for those weapons would kill as many of their own in close combat and, besides, they'd not need them.

There was no bird song, no cooling whisper of breeze, only the creak of armour and the painful breathing of the wounded. As the men and women lined up snatches of prayers were muttered to the gods of ice and fire: 'Guardians of valour, make a place for me in the Gardens of Stone if you judge my death to be honourable.'

Then the day suddenly came alive again. Screaming men ran into sight, hammering swords upon shields, roaring battle cries promising death and ruin. A wave of panic rippled through the last warriors of the City.

Broglanh, who was standing front and centre, told himself there was a solid wall behind him, a wall of iron and stone, and the only way was ahead. As the first barbarian reached him he flung himself forward, clouting the man's sword aside with his shield, and pierced the enemy's throat to the backbone. He hacked at the man to his right, diverting a hammer-blow aimed at Quora, then ducked behind his shield as a sword slashed at him from the left.

He cut, thrust and slashed at the oncoming soldiers,

his focus on eyes and throats. On his right a City axe-man hammered men into bloody ruin with his heavy weapon, his non-stop attack forming a heap of the dead before him. But they came on endlessly, pouring from the north and east, the men at the back jostling to get into the fray. Broglanh could hear their screams of frustration. *One at a time*, he muttered, *don't be so keen to die.*

The front line of the enemy slipped and slithered over blood-covered bodies only to be cut down by the dwindling band of defenders. Time and again they swarmed forward, only to die on the swords of the City. But the City warriors' strength was fading fast; they were leaden-legged and there would soon come a time when they would break . . . The mood swept among the barbarians and their battle cries rose again.

Slowly the shield wall was forced back towards the abyss; even Broglanh lost a pace, then two then three. For each of their dead there were two or more of the enemy, but they knew they could not last. Yet there were no deserters.

Broglanh looked around. The last City warriors had forgotten all their fears. Hardened veterans, they fought with cold eyes, giving each of their lives hard. To his left Stern had discarded his shield and was fighting with sword and long knife. Blood ran from a wound in his scalp, but his face was set. Broglanh realized he could no longer see Stalker. He had not seen him die or seen his body, but the northlander had disappeared, his place taken by a lanky woman with blood smeared across her face who screamed her battle cry as she demolished each opponent.

The day wore on and the shield wall collapsed slowly in on itself, its dwindling band of soldiers protected by the wall of the dead. Through swollen eyes Broglanh saw the battle in glimpses, bright flashes of red: Quora darting and stabbing like a gladiator, tireless; Stern, one arm useless and tucked into his belt, battling on with a blunted sword.

Pace by bloody pace they were pushed back, and thoughts of aid were far from his mind. In truth, Broglanh no longer cared. This was to be his last battle, the final and ultimate truth for any warrior – facing death with a blade drenched in the blood of his enemies. Time stopped, and fatigue was just a memory.

Finally there were ten of them, then five. Quora fell, hit by a savage blow to her helm. Stern went down. The enemy paused and waited.

Broglanh stood gasping, his body and face drenched in gore, holding two dripping swords at the ready. He looked around. He stood alone. He looked down at himself and saw some of the blood was his own. Quite a lot of it.

He knew it was the end, and he felt only satisfaction. He thought of his mother, her braids streaming behind her as she rode to face the enemy. She would have fought to the last, however the end came. He hoped she would have been proud of him.

He stared at the enemy. They stood waiting. He wondered what they were waiting for. He heard the bark of orders, the murmuring of anger in their ranks. He felt a spark of anger too. He was ready. What were they waiting for?

'C'mon, you pussies!' he roared in frustration.

There were shouts from among the enemy, but no one moved.

Then he heard the thunder of hooves, and saw the eyes of the men opposing him drift beyond him. He turned and saw, galloping along the very edge of the cliff, two horses heading straight for him.

He stared for a moment, dumbfounded. Fatigue and blood-loss made his brain slow. *But I'm ready*, he argued with his fate. *I can die now with honour. It's my time.*

'Evan!' Emly yelled, and in that heartbeat he grasped the chance of life. He staggered towards them, his strength gone, his legs lead.

Wrapping the reins in her fist, Emly dragged the heaving gelding to a halt. She slid off and, glancing fearfully over her shoulder at the enemy army, helped Broglanh up on to the warhorse. Patience snorted and set straight off, back the way he'd come as if under orders. Emly mounted quickly and raced after them, low in the saddle, fearing enemy arrows.

After a few moments she turned and looked back. The enemy had not moved.

To get to the battlefield she had followed the line of the cliff, trying to stay furthest from the fighting. She could always tell where it was by the clouds of carrion birds circling. Now she followed the same path back, along the line of the abyss, vaguely aware that there might be a shorter way but feeling safest with what she knew.

She glanced anxiously at Evan. He was conscious, holding the reins, leaning on the pommel, bowed over as if in great pain. It had started to rain lightly and she saw the blanket under the warhorse's saddle was gradually darkening with a mixture of rain and blood. Her heart in her mouth, she urged Blackbird closer to Patience, ready to halt both horses if he looked like falling.

On her ride to the battlefield she had noted a possible hiding-place, a spot where the cliff-edge dipped into a grassy hollow edged by wind-hardy brush. She watched out for it anxiously, scanning the way ahead, trying to remember where it was, glancing at Evan, wondering if he could hold on much longer. At last, when she had convinced herself she had passed the place and missed it, her eyes alighted on it, or rather the contorted, leafless bushes which fringed it. She reined in Blackbird and called to Patience who dropped into a trot then circled obediently back to her. She slid off her mount and grabbed the other's reins, then walked them down into the grassy hollow. There the air was still and warm, and suddenly very quiet after the thrumming of hooves and the whistling of wind.

She hauled Evan off his horse and he collapsed at her feet. She helped him lie back on the grass. His face was a mask of blood on one side and she wiped some of it away to reveal a deep angry gash in his forehead, down to his left cheekbone, the skin so purpled and swollen that his eye had sunk out of view.

'Where else are you injured?' she whispered, for his clothes were ripped in many places and seemed dipped in blood.

He grasped his side and she lifted his shirt and saw the deep, bloody furrow where a lance had ripped through his flesh. A hand's width over and he'd have been disembowelled. The wound was leaking steadily and she hoped the flow would cease once he was lying down. There were plenty of other cuts on his arms and chest and a bruise the size of her head across his stomach, but the only other deep wound was on the outside of his right thigh. This was pouring blood and she thought it was the first she should bandage.

She looked up to check if he was conscious and saw one pale eye watching her.

'Are we safe?' he murmured.

She nodded vehemently. 'Safe as a general,' she told him, his own expression.

'My pack.'

She stood to unhitch his pack from the horse and brought it to him. With bloody fingers he struggled with a strap.

'Let me.' She undid it. 'What is it you want?'

'Bag,' he whispered, lying back, hardly capable of speech.

'This?' She showed him a soft leather bag tied with twine. In it was Broglanh's medical gear: old bandages and needles and a coil of grimy thread.

'Pills,' he said.

In the bottom of the bag was a waterproof package. She opened it and found some black pills, like rabbit pellets, she thought, covered in grey dust. She looked at him doubtfully.

'One,' he said.

She gave him one and he swallowed it. She found her last remaining water skin and made him drink, then he laid his head back and was instantly asleep.

She dressed his worst wounds as best she could, relieved to see the flows of blood had slowed. Then she tethered the horses at a spot where they could crop from tussocks of thick grass. She regretted she could not unsaddle them, but they all might have to flee at any moment. Lying down by Evan's side, she felt his warmth against her, and pulled her thin blanket over them both. She prayed that the gods of ice and fire, merciless deities, would overlook their little nest, just two small people when tens of thousands were dead and dying on the battlefield that night. For a long while she lay tensed in the darkness, listening for sinister sounds, the threat of evil men moving in the land. She could hear nothing but the horses placidly munching, and finally she fell asleep.

Hammarskjald, lord of the barbarian army called the Hratana, stood at the lip of the hollow and stared down on the sleeping girl. It had astonished him when he had first seen her, how like her brother she was. He had wondered if they were twins. And he wondered who their ascendants were, which of the first Serafim had that heart-shaped face which confronted the world down the generations through a pure bloodline. He could no longer remember. How many generations had it been?

He had allowed himself to grow fond of Elija last year against his best intentions, and now little Emly had crept in, like a thief in the night, and taken his heart too. He would see they both remained safe, if it was within his control and if everything went according to plan.

The soldier, though . . . Broglanh was an extra-ordinary warrior and Hammarskjald had been content to fight by his side. But if the man survived this day, he knew with certainty he would have to kill him.

CHAPTER THIRTY-ONE

When Emly awoke it was night and the moon cast long shadows on the quiet land. Her first thought was to check Broglanh was still breathing. She stilled herself, and at last felt the slow rise and fall of his ribs. Then she noticed a strange smell – the smell of cooking. She sat up with a jerk, her heart hammering, and saw the outline of a figure squatting over a small campfire, stirring something in a pot. She grasped the long knife at her waist, hand trembling.

'Be still, girl. It's only me.'

'Stalker!' She was so relieved she felt giddy. 'How did you find us?' she whispered loudly, crawling across to join him.

He waved a spoon at Patience. 'That big beast of yours has hoofprints a blind man could follow.'

'But how did you escape the battle?'

'I must have been knocked on the head,' he said sheepishly, avoiding her eyes. 'When I awoke I was under a pile of cadavers and I could see you and your man riding off.'

'What of the others, Stern and Quora?'

He shook his head. 'All dead, lass. They were badly outnumbered. How's Broglanh?'

'I don't know,' she said, the concern in his voice

stabbing her heart. Tears welled painfully in her eyes. 'He has many injuries. I fear he's gravely hurt.'

'I'll have a look when we've eaten. Don't worry yourself. He's strong.'

'What is that?' In the moonlight she could not see what he was stirring in the small pot, but it smelled vile.

'Oatmeal,' he said. 'Good for you, and for him if he can eat. There's some burnt in it,' he admitted, peering at it.

There was a lot of burnt in it, but Emly felt the virtue of the oats fill her belly and soothe her mind. Stalker had brought water and she drank her fill, marvelling at his resourcefulness, alone and horseless in enemy territory. She was so relieved to be with him; she felt there was nothing this big man could not do.

After they had eaten he examined Evan's wounds, sniffing them as soldiers will while Em watched and worried. He sloshed water over Evan's bruised face so he could properly see his damaged eye, and he felt the bones of his head.

'He's deeply asleep,' he said, frowning.

'He ate one of these.' Em scrambled to find the black pellets and showed them to the northlander.

Stalker squinted at them then snorted. 'He'll sleep all day on one of those. Two would have killed him.' He beetled his thick brows, then shrugged. 'He did the right thing, I suppose,' he said and Em felt reassured.

Then he told her, 'Get some sleep, girl. We might have to make a run for it come the morning and we want you fresh.'

But when dawn came it seemed like a dark omen. The skyline was bright orange and red, barred with lowering black clouds like a striped cat. It seemed threatening and Stalker frowned at it.

'The weather's going to break,' he said. 'That might favour us. Stay here. I'll scout about.'

He set off on Patience but within moments, it seemed, returned with news that they could move east once Broglanh awoke. The enemy were all to the west, and for a moment nothing was moving.

'We should warn the camp-followers,' Em said.

'They'll've already moved on,' Stalker assured her. 'They know which way the wind's blowing. None of their menfolk came back after the battle, so they'll be making for home. You'll be off after them.'

'Evan wanted me away from the City,' she told him. 'He said it wasn't safe.'

'I guessed that, lass, but I don't know why.' Stalker was searching through Broglanh's pack, looking for something.

Evan had sworn her to secrecy about their reasons for fleeing, but Emly was tempted to tell Stalker, who had saved her life. She hesitated.

'Is this all your goods?' he asked and she nodded. He shook his head. 'Your needles are blunt as corks. We'll search the first carcasses we see.'

'Evan wanted to take me along the coast of Petrus to Arocir,' she told him. The big man paused what he was doing and gazed into her face, watching the hesitation there. Finally she added, 'But that way is barred to us. And he cannot return to the City.'

'Ay, you're caught between the anvil and the hammer,' Stalker said, climbing up to the edge of the hollow and looking around. He seemed full of energy despite being in a terrible battle only the day before.

'I just want to keep him safe,' she sighed, close to sobs.

'We need to stay clear of that army,' he said, staring down at her. 'That's for today. Broglanh, if he lives, can decide another day where you'll go.'

She nodded fervently, trying to stop the brimming tears. She felt more terrified than she had in the ravine when attacked by the Fkeni, for now she had Evan to worry about as well as herself. She was adrift in a foreign land, far from home, and she had no idea who was trying to kill her or why.

'Who are they?' she asked Stalker, gazing up at him. 'Evan says they're not Blues. Are they northlanders, like you?' she asked shyly, afraid of offending him.

He laughed, and the merry sound lifted her spirits a little. 'Ay, they're northlanders. But the Blues, as you call them, are also northlanders. Every foreigner is a northlander to City folk. The City is as far south as most people live. To the south of her are high mountains and a bit of hot coast then fiery deserts where neither man nor beast can survive. All that's left is north.'

'Are they allies of the Blues?'

He grabbed a water skin and emptied it into a pan for the horses to drink from. 'They're not. The Petrassi have fought them for generations. They thought they'd seen them off, but these fellows were just biding their time, building up their forces while the Petrassi had their backs turned fighting the City.'

'What happened to the Petrassi army, the one which returned before General Khan's army rode north?'

'Destroyed, lass. They had no idea what hit them. And,' he added, nodding his head southwards, 'your empress has a nasty shock coming.' He grinned, seeming unworried, indeed entertained by the idea.

Emly trembled and she wrapped her arms around herself. She had not thought beyond this day. 'You mean,' she asked, 'they'll attack the City?'

'I would,' he told her. 'Low on manpower, defences down, full of sick and wounded. I would,' he repeated and his eyes were twinkling.

Emly felt hollow inside. She was afraid of returning to the City, but even more afraid that she could never return. What would she do? And what would she do if Evan died? She bit hard on her lip, bringing blood.

As if he heard her thoughts, he said calmly, 'I'll see you get to safety.'

She tried to smile, to show gratitude for his kindness, though Stalker seemed scarcely to take their plight seriously. He was just one man, however strong, and Evan said the mightiest of men could be brought low by a big enough enemy, or by one stray arrow.

'Who are they, this army?' she asked again. 'What are they called?'

'Hratana, or Free Men in your tongue. They have no possessions, except what they carry as they march, and they hate you City folk. They believe the City is a rotting midden and despise her people for their soft ways and profane beliefs. And they are lured by promises of its treasure.'

'Treasure?'

'It is named the City of Gold in most foreign lands. Many believe its palaces are made of pure gold and its people walk the streets clad in gems. The Hratana's leaders encourage that belief.'

Emly thought of the people of the City, the desperate and the hungry, the Dwellers in the Halls and the sick and poor old folk in the rookeries of Lindo.

Stalker added, 'They are a terrible enemy. They will roll over the City, killing and burning. The empress has not the might or the will to stop them.'

'But the walls . . . ?' Em said, horrified.

He snorted. 'The walls! The walls travel for hundreds of leagues, enclosing City streets and farmland, even the empty lands of the north. They are a folly, built by a fool. But they are high and broad and built with a skill that is lost now. The Hratana will not bother with the walls. They will attack the Great Gates, for there the City is weakest. They will not last long. The Hratana can destroy them, blasting them to smithereens with a power of which the City knows nothing.'

'But Evan said they were barbarians. Many of them don't even have swords, he said.'

Stalker grunted. 'The Hratana are barbarians. Your man is right. But their leaders aren't.' His eyes gleamed as he said it and she thought she saw satisfaction in his face.

He wandered over to check Evan's wounds. Em wondered once again how Stalker knew all he did, about an enemy no one else from the City seemed to know about. Evan had said he was a mercenary. She assumed he had travelled widely and fought with and against many peoples. She had heard him say that everywhere he went he was a foreigner.

It was only later in the day, once Evan had woken and they'd got him on to a horse and started slowly moving east, that Em remembered the Gulon Veil. Evan's new jacket had disappeared somewhere on the battlefield, the veil within it. Not for the first time, she wondered about its healing gift. If she had it she could try to mend Evan's wounds. But it was gone. She put it behind her and for a long while forgot about it altogether.

Among their endless array of deities, City people respect the death gods above all. They are many and various, including the seven gods of ice and fire who mark the seven stages of death and dying for a soldier. And there is Aduara, who watches over the death of women in childbirth, and Vashta, goddess of night, who brings down darkness to comfort the dying. Only Elenchus, the god who guards the way to the Gardens of Stone, is in any way a benevolent deity for, two-faced, he chooses the virtuous over the sinner, in the terms of the warrior's creed, and welcomes the hero while turning his grim face to cowards and deserters.

Stern Edasson was a pious man. As he lay waiting for death he spoke to Elenchus and appealed to him to welcome him into the Gardens of Stone and to find a place also for his brother and for Quora. Stern had no doubt Benet was dead for the battle had been lost, and they were far from home, and by now the victorious enemy would have overrun the casualty stations and would soon see off all the injured, including Stern himself. He lay trapped in a tangle of dead warriors, many of whom he'd known, and could not move. He was bathed in gore and his whole body hurt, but he could not even lift his head to see what was wrong with him. Besides, it hardly mattered now. He could not pray for a swift death, for that would mean death at enemy hands, and he could not wish for that: it was heretical, however grim the alternative.

What Stern did not know was that this new army, this unsuspected, overwhelming force whom the City warriors called barbarians, had different customs from those of either City or Blues. Once the battle was won they left the field, leaving behind their own wounded to fend for themselves and taking no time to despatch enemy injured. Their generals were in a hurry, it was true, but it was also part of their religion, for they too had a death god and this god required the agonized song of a lingering death.

When he heard the sound of approaching boots above the groans of the dying Stern guessed his time had come and he closed his eyes, hoping to see his brother when he had passed beyond the bonds of mortality. And when he heard Benet calling he believed his death had been swift and merciful.

'Stern! Brother!'

Benet's voice was raw and gravelly as though he had worn it out shouting. Stern opened his eyes again, unwilling to trust his luck. He cried, 'Benet! I'm here! Here!'

There was a scuffle of bootsteps and Benet shouted again and Stern answered urgently. He struggled to move under the pile of corpses, fear suddenly lancing through him, fear that his brother would go past him, not see him, and Stern would be left to die and rot among the rotting dead.

Then Benet was beside him, dragging bodies off, freeing Stern's legs then his arms. His chest rose and he sucked in a chestful of stinking air and tried to sit up, desperate to be free of the cadavers. Suddenly his body was in agony and the corpses around him misted and blurred.

'You all right?' Benet asked anxiously.

Stern breathed slowly and the pain started to pass. 'Too soon to tell,' he answered.

'Where are you hurt?' Benet said, his brow furrowed. 'Your head, it's all bloody.' He pushed back Stern's hair, looking for a wound.

Stern tried to lift his right hand to feel his head himself then was reminded, painfully, that the shoulder had been dislocated in the final battle.

'Shoulder,' he said.

As Benet twisted his arm to jerk it into place, Stern looked at him, trying to hold on to consciousness. His brother was covered with gore, like all of them, with a muddy bandage over the lance-wound in his thigh, but he seemed strong.

'What happened?' Benet asked.

'We need to get away from here,' Stern said, as his brother tore a dead man's shirt to make a sling. 'They'll be coming soon.'

'They've gone,' Benet told him.

'Gone?'

'After the battle. They marched off. All of them. I saw them go. They're in a hurry.'

'How did you survive?'

'The surgeon pulled the lance out, that was a horror, stitched my leg. I was told to rest but I was about to come back when the enemy overran the casualty station. They were busy killing the helpless, so I got away.'

He was grinning at his escape, careless of the slaughter of others. 'We're City men,' he said. 'We're strong.'

Not so strong in the head, Stern thought.

'They saw me but didn't bother to chase me, just one soldier,' Benet went on. 'I climbed down the cliff, into the . . . you know . . . the gorge. I was afraid all the time I'd slip, hanging on to roots and plants. Others tried too. I saw them fall. It's a long way to fall, screaming all the way.' He shook his head. 'Then I never thought I'd be able to climb back up again. But I did. And the enemy were marching away. I could see the rear, the baggage carts. They left their dying and ours. I found food and water. They were in a great hurry.'

Stern got to his feet shakily and looked around. In three directions was a sea of dead and dying men and women. The familiar stench of blood and burst entrails hung on the air. To the west, just twenty paces away, was the edge of the Vorago.

'What do we do now?' asked Benet, happy to have his brother make the decisions.

'See if there's any more like us, walking wounded.' Stern coughed and spat. 'And find some water.'

'There's a barrelful the enemy left. It's leaking but not much.'

Stern shook his head in wonder. 'Any horses?' he asked hopefully.

Benet frowned. 'I don't think so.'

Stern clapped him on the shoulder. 'Can you see all right?'

'Well enough.'

'Then we'll split up. You search over there,' he pointed to the north and east, 'and I'll go over here.'

'What are we looking for?'

'Friends, comrades. Quora, Stalker, Broglanh. Injured or dead. Anyone who can walk and hold a sword.'

'And if they can't?'

'You know.'

'And enemy wounded?'

'Let them rot.'

There is always a time, between the slipping away from the agony of mortal wounds and the coming of the enfolding wings of death, a time of clarity, when one's life can be seen for what it was and, sometimes cruelly, for what it might have been.

Marcus Rae Khan was a powerful man, with all the strength and endurance of a second-generation Serafim, but even his body could not survive the deep cuts and gouges of the flesh which were leaking his lifeblood, slowly but inexorably, into the churned earth of this foreign field. He was struggling to breathe and he tried to draw in a deep draught, but agony stabbed through him and he thought he screamed, though all he heard was a feeble cry. He opened his eyes to see the hilt of the sword which drove through his chest and into the earth below. He took little sips of breath, feeling the blade grate against his ribs. He rolled his head, trying to see the enemy, but he could find none but the dead. Something moved in his chest, giving way, and he knew he was a heartbeat from death.

But in that last brief instant he was content with his life. He had had sons – and daughters, his schooled mind added obediently – and grandsons and descendants too numerous to know or, indeed, care about. Perhaps, he thought with a brief flaring of curiosity, it was one of those who had dealt the fatal blow, whichever that was.

He thought back to the earliest years, as he often did, when their initial trials were over and their enemies vanquished and their first, magnificent palace built and they were gods among men. *Golden lads . . . golden lads* . . . his mind stuttered, the cells dying, the synapses failing to snap. *Golden lads and girls all must, as chimney-sweepers come to dust.* Golden dust, he amended, visualizing his mortal remains flung to the four winds, a last golden sparkle of defiance in the dark. He could not remember whose the quote was. Giulia would know.

He hoped he had been right to back Araeon, among all those golden lads and girls so long ago. He and Marcellus backing Araeon to the hilt, always faithful, always true down the long years. Well, until the last few years. Among all of them, all now dead. He had always been a simple fellow, but he still thought Araeon had been largely right, even though it ended so badly.

It had been a trap, of course, this Battle of the Vorago. Long in the making, young Weaver reckoned. Longer, much longer than he knew. Thousands dead. Tens of thousands, perhaps hundreds of thousands. What had happened to the Petrassi army that marched back after the Day of Summoning? Were they all dead? Who had laid this plan, what mind, what force of ill-will, had laid this plan and for what end? Marcellus? No, this long pre-dated the Day of Summoning. There was only one he could think of, Hammarskjald, but he was long dead.

They'd seen him die, then saw his body burn on a pyre. *Good riddance*, Giulia had said that day. He could still see her now, her face lit by the funeral flames, eyes shining with pleasure.

Marcus had had wives aplenty, all dead, some mouldering for centuries now. None of them came close to his sister. She was the strongest person he had ever known, the most beautiful, and he hoped he would see her again. But his faith had dwindled over the centuries and he feared it unlikely. Their father Sikander Khan was a man of strong belief in the One God and he raised his two children as such, but a thousand years is a long time to nurture a faith and Marcus' had faltered and died a long time past. And yet, if anyone could hold a lingering belief in immortality it must be a Serafim.

Dying, Marcus feared they had all gone to dust and ashes, his father and mother and all the best of those who had come to this world to give it the gift of their knowledge and ingenuity and had brought it . . . what?

In that moment Giulia was sitting on the balcony of her solar in the balmy afternoon. She sat in her habitual comfy chair, watching the north and west, watching the route she knew her brother would take back home to her once his duty was done.

And she was wondering, as ever, about Fiorentina. The woman's pregnancy was news of the greatest magnitude. *No one knew reflections could sire or bear children.* It was thought impossible. It had never happened, that she knew of, in a millennium. And if it *were* possible it could change the balance of power in the City, in the world. But with Araeon and Marcellus both dead, there remained only a handful of them who could raise reflections. Neither she nor Marcus had the power. Never had. Reeve did, though he had not done so, so far as she knew, for more than five hundred years. His children, Rubin and Indaro? Impossible to know. The Gaetas, Sciorra and her brood? Sometimes the talent skipped a generation. Archange's descendants were, as ever, an unknown quantity.

Giulia's first thought when she'd heard, the most obvious one, was that the foetus growing in the girl's belly was not Rafael's. Fiorentina had not the reputation of a whore, like her sister, but neither was she a shrinking flower. She had flaunted herself, danced and partied, always on her husband's arm, with a smile for everyone. What was more likely, Giulia thought: that a common party girl had deceived her husband, or that the lore laid down by the Serafim for a thousand years was . . . just plain wrong? So she had summoned Rafe Vincerus' servants, those who had survived the Day of Summoning, and questioned them. Fiorentina was faithful, they all said, and they all believed it, for one of Giulia's Gifts, poor and vestigial though it was, was to discern the truth in the hearts of men and women.

And, she wondered, her thoughts darting around like summer swallows, what would such a child be like, the child of a living woman and a walking corpse? Would it even survive to birth?

Squinting, she could discern a blur on the horizon. She blinked, then rubbed her eyes. Was it a small cloud, or something wrong with her sight? The blur quickly grew. She expected to hear thunder, as if it were racing towards the Shield at the speed of sound. Then she felt a sharp pain in her breast and she bent forward and closed her eyes. When she looked up again the sky to the north was dark and ominous, heavy with fate. In a moment of prescience she knew her world was ending: her brother was dying. The pain in her chest blossomed and she cried out. Grasping the arms of the chair she tried to stand.

She was aware of the door flying open and servants rushing in as she fell blindly to the floor.

CHAPTER THIRTY-TWO

ON THE EDGE OF THE VORAGO BATTLEFIELD HAYDEN Weaver lay as if dead, protected to the last by his old friend Rosteval, who had died on an enemy lance which pierced his mighty heart. The warhorse had fallen on the instant, pitching Hayden on to a pile of City corpses. Dazed, he had crawled back to the beast and, finding him dead, had passed out, exhausted and heartsick.

Slowly Hayden raised himself to sitting, checked his arms and legs for breaks or major wounds, then, leaning on the cooling body of Rosteval, he levered himself to his feet and looked around. He could see poorly and he fumbled in his jacket for his spectacles. Inside their sturdy box they were broken, the glass shattered. He sighed. There was no help for it. He would have to make do without them. He rubbed the blood from his eyes.

The first thing he saw was the body of Marcus Rae Khan. He had been hacked and torn by many wounds, any one of them fatal to an ordinary man. Hayden had known Marcus for nigh on thirty years. As opposing generals they had sat through many a night conference, seeking ways to end carnage, always failing. And in the last few years he had come to know him as a fellow-conspirator in the taking of the City, and lastly as a friend and comrade-in-arms. In all those years Marcus had not changed an iota, and Hayden had come to believe the tales about the long lives and tough constitutions of City soldiers.

Now thousands of those soldiers, however tough, were dead on a field of battle that stretched across twenty leagues or more on the east of the chasm. The Fourth Battle of the Vorago in the chronology of the City, he thought. Will anyone, but for the enemy, be able to tell its story to the City's historians? He was surrounded by corpses and the dying as far as the eye could see, and a few injured men and women staggering around looking for friends.

Hayden struggled to remember how the City dealt with its dead.

'You,' he asked a passing soldier, a tall, skinny fellow with red eyes which wanted to look both ways at once. 'Do you bury your heroes or burn them?'

The soldier seemed as bemused as he was, and just stared at him, open-mouthed, then at the dead man at his feet.

'Is that the general?' he asked.

'It is Marcus Rae Khan, dead in the service of the City.'

'General Marcus! Oh gods, what will become of us?' the man asked, shaking his head.

Irritated, Hayden said, 'You will gather together and march back to your city in good order. But first,' he added, 'you will send your general on with the respect he deserves. Is burning the respectful way to honour your hero?'

The man nodded uncertainly, staring at the body, while more soldiers came wandering up, bandaged and bloody.

'Who are you then?' one of them asked suspiciously,

hearing the question and looking the Petrassi general up and down.

They were right to be wary. 'My name is Hayden,' he replied, 'an old comrade of the general's.'

Another said, 'Lost your horse, didn't you?'

Hayden nodded. 'Now,' he told them briskly, 'find wood. There's a copse over there. We will build a pyre. For a great man died today.'

'Who are you to give us orders?' asked the suspicious one, but the other survivors started trailing away, glad of orders, any orders.

Hayden sat down beside Marcus, overcome by exhaustion and, possibly, blood-loss. In the last year he had allowed himself to hope – to hope his country would be restored, that he would be with his family again and he could retire to enjoy the remainder of his life in peace. Now, in the wink of an eye, he had lost his country, his family, his army and his comrade-in-arms. He knew that whatever future he had left lay with the City, for good or ill.

'I am responsible for this,' he told Marcus, leaning in to make his confession. 'In every way possible I have condemned the City. I left Petrus to be pillaged by barbarians. Then I did exactly the same to the City. And I walked into a simple trap. And,' he admitted, 'you were right, my friend. You were right all along. I thought we were dealing with barbarians from the savage north, barbarians in furs waving cudgels. We would sweep them from our lands by the year's end. That was,' he defended himself, 'what I was told. Messages from Petrus spoke of yellow-headed savages. But you were right, these might be savages, but they are not under the orders of some barbarian chief. They have better technology than ours, and cannon and gunpowder. And now they are heading for the City and will trample over it. And it's completely vulnerable, thanks to me.'

Wearily he levered himself up again, thinking, *I must warn them. I must warn Archange.*

'Horsemen!' he shouted to some soldiers listlessly piling branches. 'I need horsemen! I have messages to send!' They stared at him indifferently, helpless to follow his orders. For there were no horsemen. No horses. They were all dead.

By the late afternoon, Stern and his brother had gathered thirty or more survivors, among them Quora who but for her helm would be dead from a blow to the head. She could barely see for the pain, and Stern watched her anxiously, knowing head injuries could often end in sudden death. She lay by their scrappy campfire, her eyes closed, her face pale as water.

'Thirty-two,' Benet announced. 'All with wounds. Sixteen walking, if you include Quora. The others,' he wagged his head in a display of uncertainty, 'might be able to march in a few days.'

'Officers?'

'No chance.' Benet sniffed contemptuously. He had no time for officers who, he believed, quite rightly, had it in for him.

'Well, we can't go anywhere tonight,' Stern told him. 'Have you found any food?'

'Some. Most of it dried. Some of it . . . well, I don't know what it is. Foreign muck.' Benet spat on the ground.

'As long as it doesn't poison us. Tell everyone to eat their fill. We'll have to head out first thing,' Stern said, thinking that the myriad corpses would soon start ripening. 'Tell them they march at sunrise or stay here alone.'

'If we stay here we might find more wounded,' Benet suggested.

We don't want to find more wounded, Stern thought.

We want to find more warriors fit to fight. The fate of the injured men and women was weighing on him. It was a proud boast of the Pigstickers that they never left a comrade behind, although in reality they were forced to often enough. He thought of the officer whose agonized death at the hands of the Fkeni their ears had witnessed. Rescuing him would have doomed them all, and struggling now to carry wounded comrades who could not walk, and who would probably die anyway, would condemn Stern and the other survivors. It was harsh but true. If they could not keep up, they would be left behind.

He watched the survivors moving around, some of them limping, seeking food and water and rifling corpses for medical kit – clean bandages, salves and needles. From time to time a knife would be drawn and a weak grasp on life ended.

Between conflicts there were plenty of volunteers for the prestige of leadership. Soldiers were happy to tell their peers when to eat or sleep, who should watch at the top of the wall and who sleep at its base. But at times of mortal peril, when each decision could mean life and death, fewer hands were raised to claim the role. Soldiers were, by definition, followers. They had been trained to follow orders. Promotion, Stern thought, brought you nothing but trouble. None of the generals he knew of were promoted from the ranks; they were all rich and powerful men who chose to lead an army. Even Marcus Rae Khan, who was admired by his troops, had a choice between serving his City on the battlefield or sitting in some golden palace with a battalion of concubines at his beck and call. The highest promotion a common soldier could get was company commander, and no one wanted that, stuck between the grunts on the ground and the generals, half warrior, half politician.

'What are you thinking about?'

He looked round. Quora was watching him from her cocoon of dirty blankets.

'Tomorrow,' he told her. 'How's your head?'

'Better,' she said, her eyes shifting away, and he knew she was lying. She did not want to be left behind.

'What are you going to do when this is over?' Quora asked him. This was a safe haven for conversation when times were hard.

'I'm going back to Adrastto,' he told her. 'Now it's no longer in enemy hands.'

'To your mother?'

'Yes. If she lives. I'll give up soldiering and go home.' He had lost count of the number of times he had said that over the years. But now he no longer knew what he was fighting for, or who their enemies were, perhaps it would prove true.

'Benet can't fight any more,' she said quietly.

A stab of fear caught Stern in the belly. Quora had said what he'd been aware of: his brother was nearly blind now. He did not know even his friends' faces. He was trying to hide it, but it was clear to them all. He was unlikely to survive another battle, had only survived this one by a fluke.

'I have no one to go back to,' Quora said sadly. He knew that too. That was why she feared the empress's threat to bar women from the armies. She had nowhere else to go.

'Come with me,' he said suddenly.

'To Adrastto?' There was eagerness in her voice.

Stern was idly casting his eye over his small troop, a ragtag army of the walking wounded. He frowned and stood up.

'You.' He pointed at a ginger-haired soldier crouched over a campfire, his shoulders wrapped in a black and silver jacket. 'Where did you get that jacket?'

The man looked up at him and it was all Stern could do not to flinch. He had seldom seen a worse facial wound on a living man. The soldier had been chopped across the face, perhaps by an axe, some years before, and the skin had been torn off then roughly reattached. One eye was gone, and the nose, and his mouth was set in a permanent sneer showing gaping gums. There was a dent the size of a fist in his forehead.

'Off a corpse. What's it to you?' the man snarled.

'City corpse?'

The man nodded. 'But he won't need it.'

'What did he look like?'

The man stared at the fire again. 'Don't remember,' he muttered.

Stern strode over to him and dragged him to his feet. The soldier was half a head taller than him but skinny. His eyes a hand's width from the nightmare face, Stern roared, 'Tell me what he looked like, you bastard, or I'll drag you round this pigging battlefield till we find him!'

'Grey-beard,' the soldier remembered. 'Veteran.'

Stern let him go and the man stood there angrily, debating whether to get into it. Then all the fight suddenly went out of him and he sat down again. Stern walked back to Quora, who had been watching.

'That's Broglanh's jacket,' he said, sitting down again.

'He's probably dead,' she replied quietly. 'It would be a miracle if he'd survived.'

'We'd have found his body. And Stalker's,' Stern argued. 'They were fighting right beside us.'

Quora shook her head. 'Benet could have walked past them. Anyway, sometimes it's hard to recognize, you know, one of your friends.' Chopped up like meat on a butcher's slab, she meant.

'I can't believe Stalker's dead.'

'He disappeared early in the battle,' she said. 'Perhaps he ran off.' She rolled on her back, wincing. 'Where are we heading tomorrow?'

'Home, to the City.'

'Do you know the way?'

'East.' He pointed with a confidence he didn't feel. 'Over those mountains. Then south-east to the big river.'

'We came through that mountain pass,' she said. 'Where the Fkeni were. Can you find it again from this side?'

He looked east where thick haze obscured the mountains they had crossed. Could he even see them from here? He couldn't remember. Everything before the battle was tiny and distant. Suddenly the task ahead of him seemed impossible.

He shook his head sheepishly. 'I'm hoping we meet someone who *does* know the way,' he confessed. 'There'll be other survivors, plenty of them, all going the same way. Officers.'

'You don't like officers.'

'I do if they can get us home.'

One of the soldiers stood and Stern glared at him. It was the one with Broglanh's jacket and the scrambled face. He was pointing west.

'Look! Fire!' he said.

'We've got a fire,' Quora replied tiredly, but Stern turned to look.

'That's a *big* fire,' he said.

By sun-up the next day more than one hundred and ninety City warriors had gathered at Hayden's encampment, drawn by the beacon of the funeral pyre. Some would go no further and their future was bleak. Most were strong enough to march, though their progress would be slow. And a handful appeared to have been nowhere near a fight. Hayden suspected that some were runners who had seen the pyre and decided to come back now it was safe, others who had hidden, perhaps in the Vorago, perhaps just playing dead until the battle was ended. He did not judge them, but it would be useful to know who they were.

For himself, he was in an awkward position. He could not lie about his identity. None of the survivors here knew who he was but it was likely, as they made their way back to the City, they would meet others who did. He was trusting that the soldiers' lack of curiosity would be his ally. So far they had succumbed automatically to his manner of command. If those present considered him their general, others they met were likely to fall into line.

He stood at the edge of the Vorago, looking out over the chasm to his homeland. In truth, he knew the lands of the City far better than he did Petrus. When he turned his back on it, he knew it would be for the last time. His latest letter to Anna had been despatched five days before. A few more missed days and she would think him dead. A great feeling of loss came over him. If Anna thought him dead, then might he not as well be?

He thought of Rosteval. He had debated taking the old boy's saddle with him, for it was of skilled and ancient work, built by Tanaree craftsmen of fine leathers and carved wood, depicting the totems of the people, who were born in the saddle, it was said, who drank blood and crucified their enemies. He had first laid it on Rosteval's back twenty years before when the horse was a fiery young stallion. But it was heavy and to take it along would be considered sentimental by warriors who owned nothing they could not carry themselves. So, with a sigh and a convulsive heave, he had thrown the saddle on Marcus' funeral pyre. The old gods demanded the deaths of his horses when a great leader died. Hayden could not offer Marcus that, so the saddle was symbolic. Afterwards his burden, both physical and spiritual, felt a little eased.

'Sir?'

Hayden took a deep breath and turned, putting Petrus behind him. A black-haired soldier was looking at him questioningly. Hayden searched for the man's name and remembered it was Stern. He had brought thirty men and women to the pyre the night before. He was big and well-muscled, with a veteran's steely gaze and a natural way of command. Hayden already had him pegged as his second.

'Ready?' he asked.

'Yes, sir,' said Stern. 'One hundred and seventy-seven ready to march.'

'And the others?'

'We can leave them food and water, and weapons.' He shook his head in amazement. City soldiers never left food behind, he'd said.

Hayden had briefly considered leaving a platoon of relatively able soldiers to guard the wounded, but had decided against it. If the enemy army were to come back there was nothing a handful of warriors could do. And the battlefield would become intolerable in a day or so as the thousands of corpses started to rot. Even now the rats were gathering. Where do they come from, he thought, in the middle of nowhere, leagues from human habitation? Any guards would be forced to leave this place soon, as would anyone who could stagger or crawl. It would be a waste of resources. His priority was the City. He knew now he would end his life in her service. What would Mason think of that, he wondered?

Hayden strode over to the waiting soldiers, most of whom were standing by their packs ready to march. He eyed the few who remained seated.

'My name is Hayden,' he told them. 'I fought with your general Marcus Rae Khan. I believe that the reason the enemy left so quickly is that they intend to march on the City.' He looked around but no one expressed any surprise. 'Therefore we must travel with all speed. Anyone who cannot keep up will be left behind.' He had already noted in his mind which ones he reckoned would fall by the wayside, but then again, he thought, you never can tell.

'I know the general's first priority,' he went on, 'would be to get a message back to the City, for we cannot expect to arrive there before the vanguard of the enemy army. So we must watch out for horses. There will be fugitive mounts, uninjured, somewhere around. They might have run away in fear, but eventually they will return to us. Are we carrying horse feed, Stern?'

'Yes, sir.'

'This might be the single most important thing one of you does in his life. Just one horse – one rider, one message – getting through could make the difference between the City surviving and being overrun by the enemy.'

My tongue should shrivel in my mouth, he thought with grim humour, recalling his many years of planning and campaigning to destroy that City.

He looked around at them, men and women, all blood-stained, most with bandages, some with splinted limbs. In his heyday he had led armies of a hundred thousand men, soldiers long dead in the service of Petrus. This ragtag band, this remnant of an army, had the strength and courage and endurance of any Petrassi force more than twice its size – he could admit that to himself now. And they were looking to him to lead them back to their City, to fight their way through hostile territory and, perhaps, confront the barbarians again which would surely result in their deaths.

He thought back to the last thing Marcus had ever said to him and drew his sword.

Holding it high, 'May the gods of ice and fire see our valour and make us victorious!' he roared.

CHAPTER THIRTY-THREE

THE NEXT MORNING EMLY WAS ALARMED TO DISCOVER Stalker was leading them westward, back towards the battlefield. He told her the enemy lay east and north of them and they would have to lie low and wait for the army to depart before they too struck out east. She knew she had no choice to trust the northlander but she was filled with misgivings.

They followed the coast, skirting the field of battle with its piled corpses, until they were heading north, along the line of the Vorago. But by the time the sun was high and hot they were forced to stop, for Evan had fallen into unconsciousness again.

Stalker picked a spot to rest in the shadows of an ancient tree, its grey bulk teetering on the lip of the abyss, throwing out old, dry roots into the warm, still air above the chasm. Stalker walked back and forth along the brink, staring down, squinting.

Despite their setback he seemed in good humour and, as she sat pulling dried meat and drier cornbread from their packs, Emly asked him, 'Stalker, will you teach me to fight?'

He snorted. 'You're no warrior. You should keep his bed warm for your man,' he said, nodding at Evan, 'and make his food.'

'I've been lucky so far,' she argued, considering her rescue from a series of mortal perils by strong men. 'But there might come a time, there *will* come a time,' she amended, trying to sound resolute, 'when I need to defend myself and there are no soldiers like you to protect me.' Then she told him about Casmir and his trial and his bid to kidnap her. Stalker listened closely, his ginger head cocked.

'You're small,' he said at last, looking her over with a warrior's eye, 'and light. You've no mass, no muscle. You've no swordmaster handy to teach you, like Indaro . . .'

'I have you,' she said shyly.

He snorted again and spat on the ground. 'I'm just big and heavy. Everything you're not. And I'm no swordmaster.'

He pulled at his braids, thinking about it. 'Go, get your blade,' he said at last.

She scrambled up eagerly and Stalker retreated from the cliff-edge to a flat spot of ground far from Evan's sleeping body. She saw his bad ankle was no longer bothering him. Sometimes he limped heavily, she'd noticed, at others you'd believe there was nothing wrong with it.

'Come at me,' he said, beckoning. 'Kill me.'

Emly pulled out Quora's pigsticker and, pushing off her heels, ran full tilt at him. He watched her, crouching slightly, his broadsword ready. He seemed about to engage his blade with hers but at the last moment he twisted, batting her weapon away with the back of his gauntleted hand. She ploughed into him. It was like hitting a building, and she fell to the ground, dropping the knife. He picked it up.

'Where did you get this?' he asked.

'From a soldier.'

'It's a handsome gift,' he said. 'What was he called, this generous soldier?'

'She. Quora,' Em answered. 'Why?'

'Where was she from?'

'I don't know.'

He shook his head. 'This is a venerable weapon,' he told her. 'We'll make a warrior of you yet, girl.'

'Will you teach me?'

'If I get the chance.' He sat down again at their fire. 'And once we've got this blade sharpened. Have you been slicing turnips with it?'

She nodded, embarrassed.

'Once it's sharp it'll cut through leather and the boiled wool those soldiers wear for armour. Even some metals.'

He squinted at her as a stonemason might at a poorly built wall. 'You have to pick your scraps,' he said. 'You're small and you're quick. You offer a small target. You need to seek out the soft points. Eyes, throat, groin. In, out. Quick as a pixie.'

She nodded. Evan and Stern had both told her the same. 'And to defend myself?'

'You have no defence. Just turn and run as fast as you can. You'll easily outrun any man weighed down by armour and weapons.'

Emly was disappointed and her face must have shown it, because, 'I'll show you a few moves,' Stalker said at last, scratching his beard. 'Once we've a little time, and a place of safety.'

But there was no time, no place of safety. Stalker lifted his head like an old dog scenting the breeze, and Em listened too. She could hear nothing but the soughing of the wind over dry grass, the stealthy rustle of a wild animal. She closed her eyes. In the far distance she could just hear a faint sound.

'Hooves,' said Stalker. He stood up and, with an agility belying his size and age, he ran to Blackbird and mounted. The startled horse reared and Stalker pulled roughly on his reins.

'Stay here,' he ordered Em. 'Get your man ready to travel.'

Then he thundered off, heading north-east. In a moment he was out of sight.

Emly felt a chill breeze course through her, for all the warmth of the sun. She shivered. A moment ago she had been happily talking to Stalker, safe under his protection. Now she was alone again, the sole guardian of her wounded lover. For a fleeting moment she wondered if Stalker had planned to abandon them, then she squared her shoulders. Whatever happened, she would be ready. She packed their bags and strapped them on the warhorse. Patience fidgeted as if keen to be off. Then Em knelt beside her man.

'Evan.' She laid her hand on his heart, where there were no wounds. 'Evan, you must wake up.'

His eyes opened slowly, the thick blond lashes sweeping up like a curtain. His face was unnaturally calm, almost slack, as if some vital sinews had been cut; but his eyes focused and his voice, when it came, was slow but clear.

'Time to go?'

'Stalker says we must be ready.'

She helped him sit, kneeling behind him and supporting him. It was more than a day now since he had been injured and she'd expected him to be stronger. Deep in her mind a treacherous thought fluttered and bumped like a wet-winged moth. *What if he never recovers? What if, this time, his wounds are too severe?*

'Thekla?' he asked suddenly, his voice sharp as a blade. He was staring at something she could not see. She wondered who Thekla was. She stroked his hair and willed Stalker to return. But time seemed to limp by slowly, and the sun had moved across the sky before Patience raised his head and pricked his ears. Emly heard galloping hoofbeats the moment before Stalker reappeared at the top of their hideout. He flung himself off the lathered horse and knelt beside her.

'We're trapped,' he told her. 'The army's all around us, and they're scouring the cliff-edge for survivors. They'll find you in a heartbeat.'

Appalled, she stared up into his face. 'Then we'll die here together.' She put her arms round Evan.

'No need for that, lass. There's a path down the cliff under that tree, I saw it earlier. It's a goat path, but if you hide down there they won't bother to follow. They've bigger fish to catch.'

'Where?' She stood and looked where he was pointing. She peered down into the chasm. All she could see was steep, unforgiving rock, almost vertical, sprinkled with a few scrawny plants. She shook her head. 'I can't see it.'

He grabbed her by the shoulders and moved her a pace to the right. 'There.'

He was right. But it was no goat path. Someone had carved shallow steps into the cliff-face. You could only see them if you stood in exactly the right place. She marvelled that Stalker had spotted them.

'Can we get Evan down there?' she asked doubtfully.

'Not us, lassie. You.'

'What about you?'

'I'll make a run for it through their lines. They won't be expecting a lone horseman. I'll come back for you if I can. Quick now, you haven't much time.'

He helped her get Evan to standing. The soldier could stay on his feet, if supported, but he seemed to have no idea of how to move forward. He was looking round, his face pale as death, his eyes flickering constantly. Em placed his arm round her shoulders, then her arm round his waist.

They managed the first step down the cliff path,

then Stalker grabbed Patience's reins and climbed on to Blackbird.

'You're taking both of them?' Em asked him. Her heart was pounding and Evan was leaning against her.

'If I leave one it'll point straight to where you are,' Stalker said, then, without another word, taking their packs with their food and water, he turned the gelding and rode away. Em listened. The sound of hooves drifted off and there was stillness.

She blinked back her tears. 'Come,' she said to Evan, 'we must go this way. We'll be safe then.'

She pulled and pushed him one step down, then two, talking encouragingly. She tried not to think of the aching abyss on their right, the crumbling, dry rock under her feet, the placing of his boots, one at a time.

'One more step,' she kept saying. Evan was leaning on her heavily and she feared he might topple them over.

But they made it to the shelter of the old tree. Its swirling, searching roots hid a deep recess where it was shadowy and cool and a little damp. Emly helped Evan inside, where he lay unconscious again. She scrambled back out into the light and climbed a little way to check if they could be seen from above, then ducked back under the spreading roots and sat beside him, her heart heavy. Why had Stalker taken their food and water? How long would they last without it? He'd said he'd come back, but would he?

She woke with a start and wondered how long she had been sleeping. Evan slept deeply beside her and she thought that, if she could only find water, this would be as good a place as any for him to recover. In the gloom under the roots she could see his eyelids flickering as if he were dreaming. She hoped they were dreams and not nightmares, for she believed good thoughts as he slept would aid his healing. He repeated the word

Thekla and Em wondered again what it meant. She was thirsty and thought that if she searched the battlefield she might find discarded water skins. But the prospect filled her with dread and she made no move.

Then her heart leaped as she heard a sound outside, a gentle breathing, then a sharp huffing noise. It was so dark in the root cave and so bright outside that she could see nothing. She wondered nervously if it might be a wolf or wildcat, or a bear angered by intruders in its den. Knife in hand, she crawled out into the daylight.

A large brown goat stood regarding her with dark eyes. It wagged its head and huffed again. She smiled at it, wondering if she could kill it for food. Then she saw it was wearing a collar.

She heard footfalls and raised her knife. A figure clad in grey appeared, rising swiftly from the Vorago. It was a young woman, slender and fair, bearing a stout stick to aid her climb. Her robes were cut off below the knee and on her feet she wore thick rope sandals. She stopped when she saw Em. Then she spotted the blade and stepped back a pace, glancing behind her, ready to run. Em quickly laid the pigsticker on the ground and spread her hands.

'Can I help you?' the woman asked in the City tongue.

It was one of the hardest things Stern had ever had to do. Just half a day into their march in pursuit of the enemy army, injured soldiers began dropping by the wayside, and one of them was Quora.

For an old boy, Hayden had set a punishing pace. Despite his years he was whipcord thin and tough as his boots, his faded blue eyes fixed on the horizon, his lean face dark with intent. Unlike any general Stern had ever known – though such acquaintance was largely anecdotal – Hayden carried his own pack, a battered, ancient thing with his breastplate and helm strapped atop, and he ate with his troops.

But the man was relentless, determined that within days they would catch up with the weakest soldiers, the sick and injured, at the rear of the enemy army. To do that he would abandon his own wounded men and women.

'We have a long journey,' Stern pointed out to him as they marched together on the first morning. 'Do we need to catch them so soon?'

'We want them to know we're here,' Hayden replied, his eyes fixed ahead. 'If we start to pick them off they will have to consider us, make plans to deal with us. It will be something extra for them to do, something their generals don't need. We'll make them change their plans. That can only be a good thing.'

'They'll send a division back after us,' Stern predicted. 'They'd wipe us out.'

'Ay, perhaps.'

'We are fewer than two hundred,' Stern argued. 'If they come at night, there will be only our carcasses left come sunrise.' But he was wasting his breath. Hayden was the man in charge and he was not to be argued with.

When, late that morning, two men sank to their knees, unable to march on, Hayden called a brief halt. Stern was watching Quora, saw her stumble to the ground, lying where she fell. He went over and knelt beside her. She was barely conscious. He looked into her face, filled with misgiving. She was pale as sour milk, her skin clammy, eyes sunken. She rolled over and vomited a little on the ground.

'How's your head?' he asked her. 'Here, have some water.'

She made no reply, and he grabbed her shoulder. 'Quora. Answer me.'

One eye opened a slit. 'I'll be well in the morning,' she mumbled. 'Just let me sleep.'

'It's still before noon, soldier. We have far to go.' But she made no reply.

Benet came over. 'Those two are done for. One's got a broken knee. The other's sick as a dog. I'm surprised they got this far. We'll have to leave them. How is she?'

'She can't go on.' As he said it Stern saw the last wisp of hope for future happiness drift from his life.

Benet frowned. 'She's a City woman,' he said staunchly. 'Tomorrow she'll be better. Or dead. One or the other. That's for sure.'

For once he was right and there was nothing Stern could do about it. He looked around despairingly. They were crossing the wide plain between the Vorago and the mountains, and would be for some time. There were few places to hide, or to shelter from sun and rain and scavenging animals. He saw a pile of rocks, once perhaps part of a building, or a cairn broken by the years, which would offer some protection from the weather. He lifted Quora and carried her to the meagre shade of the rocks. She was lighter than Stern's backpack. He signalled his comrades to bring the others. One could not walk but could defend the other two. The second was delirious and shivering with fever, his skin hot to the touch. Stern left a water skin at Quora's side and made sure she had food. He unsheathed her knife and put it in her hand. Her fingers clutched around it, though she was unconscious now. He held her hand for a little longer than he had to. In the years they had known each other he had barely touched her.

'We're off,' Benet said, and Stern saw the ragtag army was on its feet again.

He stood and his brother gazed at him sympathetically. 'You can't save them all,' he said. Stern thought of all the men and women they had lost, comrades who had fought and died beside them. The Battle of the Vorago had taken the last of them, and now he and his brother were the only Pigstickers left. He got to his feet, turning his face from Quora, trying to think only of the living. He clapped Benet on the shoulder. 'Let's march,' he said.

By the end of the first day four more had fallen by the wayside, three felled by sickness. 'If we go on like this there won't be any of us left,' Benet commented gloomily, but Stern believed he was wrong. One more night's sleep would finally sort out the strong from the weak. He predicted losing a few more the next day, then those who were still on their feet would stay there – until they caught up with the enemy army.

Travelling in its detritus was enlightening, for it soon became clear they too had abandoned their wounded. Hayden would pause briefly when they came to each enemy body, looking at armour, visible tattoos, broken weapons. The almost-dead were despatched economically. Some living soldiers, fighting fit but for broken legs or backs, glared at the City men, spat at them and cursed in their foreign tongue. There was no questioning these, for their language was utterly strange. Stern found deep inside him a spark of kinship with these fierce warriors who had marched to their doom in a foreign country. Hayden would not let his soldiers torment them, which raised the man in Stern's judgement. They were despatched mercifully, throats cut.

Once Hayden paused and said, 'Bowmen.' A torn and battered quiver lay on the ground, trampled by many booted feet. Stern picked it up.

'Some riders can loose arrows at terrifying speed,' Hayden said. 'They are a force to be reckoned with. See the men all have shields.'

Stern grunted. 'We met some Fkeni riders on the

way here.' He threw the ruined quiver to the ground. As it hit something fell out, an object which shone in the sun.

'Stop!' Hayden shouted, and he said to Stern, 'Don't touch it!'

He crouched by the object and Stern joined him. The other soldiers watched, glad of a break. It was a small round box of beaten gold with a hinged lid, decorated with tiny fighting figures. Hayden took his gauntlets from his belt and put them on before awkwardly picking it up.

'This is an ominous thing,' he said, and his face was grim.

'What is it?'

'A poison cup. The bowmen smear the tips of their arrows with poison. The slightest scratch from them ends in madness and death. They are works of evil. We must treat these bowmen and their arrows with great caution.'

He stood for a moment in thought, then swung his arm and threw the thing far out across the plain. It glittered as it caught the sunlight then it was gone. Hayden set off again and his soldiers followed. As they marched he pointed out the ruts where the enemy's carts had travelled over rough ground.

'They are deep,' he said; 'some of their wagons are heavily loaded. With cannon, I've no doubt. It will slow them down. They can only travel at the speed of their slowest wagon. This is good news.'

It seemed like mixed news to Stern. Hayden had explained to him about cannon, the great iron pipes the enemy had used to spit fire and flame and destruction at the Vorago. Stern was unwilling to face such evil again.

He asked, 'What sort of poison do the bowmen use?'

'Snake venom,' Hayden told him. 'They live in parts

where such serpents are common. Their people, even children, become skilled at drawing the venom from living snakes. Then they mix it with a substance which makes the liquid venom easier to handle.'

'What substance?'

'They usually use their own shit. Then, if the venom does not kill you you die from infection in the wounds.'

He went on, 'It's likely we will meet these bowmen and their accursed arrows. You must instruct your troops to handle them safely. Avoid touching them and if some poor soul is wounded by such an arrow, it must be pulled out quickly with a gloved hand and the flesh around the wound cut away. Speed is vital.'

'Will that save him?'

'Probably not. In which case a clean death is preferable.'

They marched on in silence. Stern's thoughts were grim. This new world of weaponry was a terrible place. True warriors fought face to face with swords, and the better won and the lesser died with honour. Poison was a craven thing, a woman's weapon. And bowmen had always been scorned, even those of the City.

'Did your troops use these arrows?' he asked hesitantly, for the fact that Hayden was Petrassi was not something that had passed between them.

Hayden shook his head. 'No. They are dishonourable, and they are indiscriminate killers. The tribesmen who use these are much hated, even by their own allies. Their arrows can as soon be picked up by friends as by enemies. The poison is hard to contain, for the gold cups are seen and coveted. A tiny vessel like that, passed hand to hand, will kill a dozen men, two dozen.'

'I will warn our troops. Why are they made of gold – for their value to the wielder?'

'No. Gold is impervious to venom. I will speak to the men when we make camp.'

'With respect, sir,' Stern argued, 'it might be best if I spoke to them.' Hayden listened, his pale eyes showing only interest.

'They don't take well to anything new,' Stern said quietly. 'If *you* tell them about something strange and foreign they will dismiss it, for they don't understand it. If I tell them about the poison arrows they will accept it from me, because they know me, many of them.'

'I am their leader,' Hayden argued mildly. 'They have followed me so far.'

'They believe you can get them home. When the battles start, well, we'll see if they'll follow you then.'

CHAPTER THIRTY-FOUR

THE SOUND OF SPADE AND HOE DIGGING DRY SOIL WAS the only noise in the hot, arid land apart from the trickle of the river and the distant, complicated call of a bird high in the sky. The sun was scorching on Emly's back and on the young plants which lay wilting in their muddy pools.

She stood and stretched, gazing around at the grey-clad women working alongside her in the narrow field planting winter crops. Above them loomed the massive cliff of the Vorago. The shadow of the opposing cliff, sharp-edged, was coming quickly towards them as the sun moved across the sky.

Em had been in the valley for days – eight, ten? She was not sure how long for she awoke each morning feeling muddled, perhaps because she was sleeping deeply for the first time since she left the City. Their journey down the cliff had been gruelling. The woman who had found them, whose name was Cora, had left her at first then later in the day returned with another woman and a stretcher. It had taken them half the day to make their way down the rock-face, but at the bottom the women had transferred Evan to a donkey cart. They travelled swiftly after that and soon arrived at the women's citadel home.

Emly gazed at it, an ancient building carved into a layer of red rock tucked under a ridge of grey granite which hid the place from above. It was first built as a fortress, she was told, but now its walls were pocked with rounded windows and doors, its interior riddled with connecting rooms and passages. Em was given a small cell and Evan was next door. The women washed his body and tended his wounds but when asked if he would get better they shook their heads. They could not say. They asked her no questions and she gratefully fell back into silence, her old friend.

Her first day was spent sleeping and eating their good food and tending Evan, willing him to recover. Then she asked if she could help in the fields, for she had watched the women working and wanted to show her gratitude.

She bent to her task again, grabbing the next drooping plant.

'Randomly,' a curt voice reminded her.

She looked up. The woman's name was Selene. She was very tall and thin, with iron-grey hair cut like a soldier's, and, like most of them, was wearing grey cotton trousers and a green sleeveless shirt. Her skin was nut-brown and her eyes grey crystal.

Em smiled apologetically. She had been told not to set the plants in rows, for people looking down from on high might discern a pattern.

'Can they not see us?' Em had asked, looking up at the cliff.

'Only as dots,' a woman had told her. 'We are very far down. We could be goats, or a flock of crows. The heat haze confuses the eye from above.'

Em decided where to put the next plant then moved a pace to the left. She looked at Selene, who nodded. She dug a hole and sloshed water into it from a bucket then put the plant in and enclosed its roots in mud then firmed it down. Then she moved to the next one, randomly.

She had been in the field all day, apart from a break when the sun was high, when, hidden in the shade of an outcrop of rock, she had eaten fresh bread and cheese. The smell and texture of the food were intoxicating after a long season on soldiers' rations. She wondered if Stalker had survived his dash through the lines. It had seemed reckless, but Stalker had a knack for survival and she liked to think he had. She cleared her mind of soldiers and armies and concentrated on the planting, digging each hole deep, treating the roots gently, watering thoroughly.

She started as a hand touched her shoulder and Selene's voice said, 'You can stop now.'

Em looked up. She saw the others streaming back towards their home, their buckets and boxes and tools packed on donkeys. The sun had dropped behind the cliff and she had not even noticed.

'You're a hard worker,' the woman said as she helped load the last donkey.

Em stroked the beast's soft nose and thought of Patience and Blackbird. 'I am grateful,' she answered simply.

Together they walked back towards the rock citadel. Selene said, 'You have asked us nothing about this place or those who live here.'

'It is a sanctuary,' Em replied. 'And I do not need to ask why women need sanctuary in time of war.'

When they came closer to the citadel Selene started to point things out: the barns which held winter grain, the mill which turned the grain to flour, the stables for the few donkeys. Chickens, fat and noisy, clucked and fussed around their feet.

'What are they?' Em asked, pointing at a row of wooden boxes on stilts set high above the river.

'Beehives,' the woman said. She saw Emly did not understand. 'Bees make honey,' she explained. 'We use the honey they make.'

'Can I see?' Emly asked. She'd had no idea honey came from bees. It seemed very unlikely and she wanted to see for herself.

'You need special clothes to protect you from their stings. Some other time.'

'Why is that one over there?' Em pointed across the river to a lone hive.

'You have sharp eyes. The honey made in that hive is poisonous.'

'Poisonous?'

'Bees sip the liquid essence of particular flowers. For example, these bees feed on the clover that grows over these low banks. The honey is good to eat. You can have some tonight if you wish. More importantly, this virtuous honey heals wounds. But the bees on the other side of the river feed from a plant called sheep-bane which only grows there. It is not poisonous to the insects, but their honey is fatal for people to eat.'

'Then why keep them?'

'Poisons can be useful. You said your soldier ate a black pellet which helped him sleep and heal. If it is what I think it is, the essence of a blue flower, then two of those would have killed him. Sometimes there is a narrow line between that which heals and that which kills.'

'How soon will he recover?' It was a question she was afraid of asking.

Selene's face was grave. 'Do not hope for too much. He is strong but his wounds are serious and he has unseen injuries. If they heal he will live. If not, he will die.'

* * *

'Who is Thekla?' she asked him.

Evan looked up from where he was gutting a rabbit, his thick lashes bright in the moonlight.

'Where did you hear that name?' he replied coldly.

'You spoke it in your delirium.'

She watched him construct his reply, then the question she could no longer keep within her burst out. 'Is she your love?'

Emly thought he was not going to answer. Then she wished he hadn't, because he said, 'She has my heart.'

Her insides felt as if they had been scraped out with a spoon. She had to force herself to keep breathing, sucking the air in, pushing it out. 'But who is she?' she persisted, hating the whine in her voice.

'She is Archange's granddaughter,' Evan told her.

She stared at him, speechless.

'Thekla is a healer and a surgeon. She took a lance-head out of my ribs,' he said, bending to his task again.

'That was how you met? She healed you?'

'Archange healed me. But Thekla brought me to her.'

'When was this?'

He shrugged. 'Years ago.'

'Then,' she choked, trying not to cry, 'why are you here with me rather than with her?'

'Because my first loyalty is to the City. You had to be sent away.'

'You could have had me abducted and sent away. Or killed,' she added bitterly.

'That's the way of the old regime. And I made a promise to your father to keep you safe.'

She sat down suddenly, tears in her eyes.

'But you are acting against the empress, stealing the veil, stealing me.'

'Again,' he said reasonably, threading the rabbit on the string with the others, 'that is the way of the old regime. I'm acting against Archange, but for the City and with Thekla's blessing.'

Emly looked up. 'She knows about us, our journey? Your love?' She spat out the word.

'It was her idea.'

When Em woke she was sluggish, and exhausted by the vivid dreams which had plagued her since she arrived in the valley. Feeling fretful, she could not separate them from reality. Was Thekla a real woman? The thought made her tremble. Or was she just a dream phantom, summoned because she'd heard Evan say the name? If Thekla was real, why had she never heard of her? What else was being kept from her?

She washed her face and hands and dressed but she still felt anxious, fearing that events were happening which she knew nothing about. She picked up the cup she had been given the night before, full of warm milk to help her sleep. She peered inside then poured the dregs into her palm. There was something granular in it. She stood thinking for a long while.

Then she went next door. One of the women was at Evan's bedside redressing the wound in his thigh. She looked up. Em had seen her before, struggling around the citadel. Both her legs were cruelly injured and she walked with two sticks and in evident pain.

'His breathing is good,' the woman said, and she got up with difficulty and left.

Emly sat on the stool and looked into the face of the man she loved. His eyes were closed, the thick fringe of his lashes lying on his cheek. The cuts and grazes on his face were healed. Em thought this a good omen for those injuries that could not be seen. She placed her hand on his chest, felt the slow beat of his heart and the barely discernible rise and fall as he breathed.

She spoke softly to him. 'Evan, I must leave you now. I'm going back to the City.'

Was there a slight hitch in his breathing, a flicker of

his eyelids? No, she was imagining it. He could not hear her. But she still felt the need to explain.

'Someone has to go back and warn Archange. I know you want to hide me away from her but this is too important. Everything is changed now. Stalker says the enemy army is marching on the City and if I don't raise the alarm then who will?'

She paused, half hoping he would awaken and argue with her. But he slept on.

'Believe me, I don't want to go. But there is . . . I know you will think this foolish, but there is the assassin Casmir. He will be looking for me, if he lives. If he finds me, or if I find him, he will take me back to the City. It is his job to take me back unharmed. Then I can warn Archange. These women will take care of you and . . .' She found tears rolling down her cheeks, '. . . we will meet again, I know.'

She remembered another phrase he used. 'If not here, then on the other side.'

She dried her tears and left him. She found a woman and asked to speak to whoever was in charge. Eventually she was guided to a high room, small, like all of them, but with a large round window overlooking fields and river. Selene was standing at the window. She turned as Emly came in.

'Was a few days in the fields enough for you?' she asked. Em couldn't tell if she was being criticized or mocked.

'You put something in my milk,' she accused.

Selene smiled thinly but there was a brittle coldness in her eyes. 'Merely a light sleeping draught. You were exhausted when you arrived. Do you not feel stronger?'

'I am returning to the City.'

Selene frowned and her eyes glinted. 'Are you sure? It is perilous up there. You can stay as long as you like here. We need hard workers.'

'I must go back and tell them, warn the empress what is coming. There is an army marching on the City and someone must tell them.'

'You are already far behind the enemy. You cannot possibly get to the City before they do.'

'How many days have I been here?' Emly tried to remember.

'How many days do you think you've been here?' Selene retorted, and Em was reminded of Archange's cryptic answers to questions.

'Eight?'

'Well then. They are marching fast and you have no mount. This is dangerous country. There are wandering tribes of Fkeni who would make your death hard.'

Em bit her lip. It was as though the woman knew exactly what she most feared.

'There will be other survivors from the battle,' Selene argued. 'There always are. Let them take up the burden of warning the City. Stay with us.'

'I must do it, for I can't be sure anyone else will.'

'Perhaps that is arrogance speaking, Emly.' Selene's voice was hard now.

Why is she so anxious for me to stay? Em thought. *And how can she know about the enemy's movements when these women lead such secluded lives?*

She shook her head, her decision set in stone. 'I know my weaknesses. I have never been outside the City before and I am ignorant of many things. I am not a warrior . . .'

'If you stay,' Selene offered, 'we will teach you to fight. There are many veterans from the war here. Then you can go back and battle for the City. Together with your soldier.'

Em's resolution was under attack. But she said, 'I don't know much about you all and I don't know what brought you here. But I know you are hiding, and that is often the only choice a woman has in this world. But I'm not ready to hide yet. I have friends in the City and my brother is there and if he is in danger I will go and fight for him with what weapons I have.' It was the longest speech she'd ever made.

The woman nodded. 'As you wish,' she said briskly. 'And the soldier?'

'I ask you to care for him until he is well or until I return. I would leave a message for him, though I cannot write well. Perhaps someone could help me.'

Selene looked out of the window. 'Someone will help you with your letter, and a guide will take you back to where we found you. If you are set on this.' Turning, she asked, 'How old are you, Emly?'

'Seventeen or eighteen, I think.'

'Then do not judge us. Although you have seen and experienced a great deal for one so young, yet I'd hazard a guess that you have been protected by powerful people.'

Em frowned. *How could she know that?*

'Most women, and men, have nothing but their strength and wits and sometimes that is not enough,' Selene went on. 'Often the urge to run and hide is a better one than the impulse to make a hasty, foolhardy gesture which can only end in torment and death.'

The words were reasonable, but Emly saw a hectic light flashing in her eyes. Was it just anger? Suddenly she was worried the woman might force her to stay.

'I am sorry,' she said truthfully. 'I did not wish to offend.'

The woman lowered her eyes for a heartbeat and when she looked up again the strange light had gone. 'I am a good deal older than you,' Selene said. 'A few harsh words from a thoughtless girl do not have the power to offend me. If you insist on leaving I will not stop you. Go pack your things.' She turned her back.

By mid-morning Em was ready. She was given a guide, Cora again, and a donkey to aid them on the climb. Selene came out to bid her farewell. She proffered a small jar of honey, full of pale light.

'This is the clover honey which is nutritious and good for healing wounds,' she said.

'Thank you,' Em said, embarrassed by her generosity, for she felt she had done nothing to deserve it.

After a few paces Emly looked back at the rosy citadel, the women working in the quiet fields, the tall figure of Selene watching her. She wondered if she was doing the right thing. Was she being prideful to think she could make a difference? Was Selene right? Could she be trusted? Em tried to think what Evan would say and do, but thoughts of him filled her heart with loss. And she tried to suppress the stab of misgiving which told her she should not leave him, helpless, with these women.

She had hoped to reach the top of the cliff by nightfall, where she would spend the night in the hole under the tree roots. Beyond that she had no plan. But they made fast progress and the sun was still high in the sky when Cora halted.

'This is as far as I go,' she said.

Em looked up. They still had a distance to climb but the path was clear. They were on one side of a deep ravine Emly had barely noticed on their way down. Narrow but sheer-sided, it cut across the goat path they were following. It was crossed by a sturdy rope and plank bridge.

'The bridge is closed except when we greet visitors,' Cora explained.

'Closed?'

'It swings on a pivot, see? It is finely balanced. Once it is drawn to this side the rift cannot be crossed.'

'The gap is not very wide,' Em said doubtfully, thinking she could probably jump across.

'No, but there is a steep climb on each side. No man, or horse, could cross it because he could not run at it. It is the only way into the valley except from the sea. It keeps us safe. And there is a guard-post here.' She pointed to a small hut, half-hidden in the shadow of the cliff. 'Years ago tribesmen tried to invade the valley. They used hooks to get ropes across but we were waiting and simply tossed them back. They gave up in the end. That was long ago. No one has tried since.'

She added, her eyes kindly, 'If things go badly for you, you can always return, Emly. Just shout when you get here. Someone will hear.'

Em stepped across the bridge. The heavy ropes creaked, but it was the only sound in the still afternoon air. Beneath her feet she could see goats grazing peacefully on the steep sides of the ravine, and huge birds wheeled and swooped silently above. On the other side she turned and watched as Cora hauled on a rope and the bridge pivoted creakily and settled against the cliff-side. Emly hesitated, knowing she was taking the harder path, then she started climbing. Within a short while she could see the ancient tree on the lip of the cliff, its roots waving to her.

As she clambered up to the root cave she heard the soft snort of a horse nearby and, startled, her heart panicked in her chest. The Fkeni – those malevolent bats which flittered through her nightmares – came screaming into her mind. She dropped to a crouch and glanced back down the pathway. It would be easy to run and shout for Cora, to return to the safety of the hidden citadel.

She listened for a long time but could hear no voices, no sound at all apart from the slight breeze riffling her hair. She could not do nothing. Holding her courage tightly, she climbed the last few steps up the cliff, keeping her head low. Then she peered cautiously over the top.

Patience stood there, munching grass. He snorted when he spied her and fidgeted his great hindquarters. She looked around but there was no one in sight. She scrambled over the cliff-edge and ran to him, putting her arms round his neck.

'What are you doing here, boy?' she asked, bemused. Stalker must have brought him back, but he could not have known she would return. Perhaps the horse had got loose and wandered back on his own. Emly shook her head, clearing it of questions she could find no answers for. For the first time since she'd descended into the valley she felt she had done the right thing.

The warhorse was saddled and bore two bulging water skins, along with Evan's pack and her cloth bag. Em unhobbled him, then scrambled on to his broad back. Turning away from the Vorago, she pulled the stallion's head towards the City and they set off at a gallop.

Selene watched the two girls and the donkey until they were out of sight and went back into the shaded citadel.

Hilly struggled up on her crutches. 'Mother Selene, what shall I do about the soldier?'

'Leave him to me.'

She went to the cell where he lay. She stood beside him, mulling over what she would do. Perhaps she should wait a day. The girl might come back. She should have stayed here, not be wandering the world of men, a victim ripe for rape and torture. But she had abandoned the soldier and Selene had no doubt what to do with him.

She took a small pot of dark honey from a pocket and opened the lid. Its fragrance filled the small cell.

So deceptive, she thought. Evil masquerading as virtue, as in so many things. She looked down at the soldier. She waited, indecisive. She put the pot away again. It seemed a waste.

She went to the window, feeling the crispness of autumn in the air. She looked along the valley to the north. The girls had gone. Emly would not be back.

She returned to the bed and took out the honey once more. She scooped out a small amount and mixed it with water in a cup until it had dissolved. Then she lifted the soldier's unresisting head and put the cup to his lips. His swallow reflex was good. He was definitely improving. But not for much longer once the poison began its work.

She would tell the girls to throw the carcass into the river.

CHAPTER THIRTY-FIVE

SINCE THE DAY THE LANCE WAS DRIVEN INTO HIS CHEST at Dead Man's Fall, Evan Broglanh had complacently believed he possessed miraculous powers of healing. All his soldier's life he'd heard his comrades – those born in the City – boast of their toughness, their endurance and will to live compared with foreigners. Hard to kill, they'd say. He was sick of hearing the words. As a foreigner himself he knew he was just as hard to kill, and without a speck of City blood in him so far as he knew. His recovery from the lance-wound, he thought, had proved that.

And it was some years before he discovered he had been entirely wrong.

It was the summer before the fateful Day of Summoning and he was serving with the Wildcats – the company linking the chain of his destiny with Indaro Kerr Guillaume and Fell Aron Lee – and he had been sent, with Indaro, to guard the emperor on some unexplained mission. *Protect the Immortal* had been the order from his company commander, but Broglanh had known Fell was giving him the chance to get close to Araeon and kill him if he could.

But his plans had been thwarted when a band of Blues ambushed the convoy. An explosion injured the emperor and killed most of his guard. Broglanh, who had been riding behind the imperial carriage, was unhorsed and thrown against a pile of rock. His right arm was broken, both bones of the forearm snapped at an angle, the bloody white points of bone erupting from torn flesh.

The pain had been monstrous, the nausea intolerable. Broglanh had cradled his right arm with his left and prayed for death. A friend gave him lorassium and he passed in and out of consciousness as the sun crossed the sky, waiting his turn for medical aid. Then a shadow loomed over him and he opened his eyes.

'Thekla!' he slurred, unwilling to believe his fortune.

The woman sniffed. 'No, but I'd like to know why you think so, soldier. What is your name?'

He blinked, trying to focus. No, it was not Thekla. This face was hard and gaunt, the eyes cold. Why did he think it was her?

'Your name, soldier?' she snapped. She had a voice like a corncrake.

'Broglanh.'

'Which one?'

'Evan Quin.' He'd closed his eyes. Perhaps she would leave him alone now.

'Good,' she said. 'We've been looking for you.'

This was his first meeting with Saroyan. She had spotted his name on the list of wounded and he was taken back to the City in a strange re-enactment of his injury a few years before. He was greeted joyfully at Thekla's home in Otaro, where she straightened his arm and splinted it. The house was cool and quiet and had a small, sunny courtyard where he dozed away the time of healing. He waited impatiently for the arm to mend, but was frustrated when after three days it remained broken.

'You fool,' Thekla told him fondly when he complained. 'I thought you realized it was Archange who healed you of the lance-wound. You were valuable to her, for some reason I can't fathom,' she smiled. 'You are strong, my love, but even you could not have survived that.'

When a visitor arrived at Thekla's home the next day he wasn't surprised to see it was Archange. She was dressed as usual in blue – a dark blue gown with a robe the colour of cornflowers over it. He struggled to stand but she waved him back to his chair.

'Give me your hand,' she snapped and he extended the splinted arm.

She had taken his hand in one of hers and run the other up and down the forearm. He felt the pain intensify until it was hard not to cry out, then the agony slowly dissolved, until all he could feel was warmth and peace. Visions of a calm, slow river filled his head, the snow on a mountain. Thekla removed the bandage and splint and the arm was good as new except for a vivid scar where the bone had broken through. For the rest of the day he had felt light-headed, his arm tingling to the touch, his body surging with strength.

'I have a mission for you,' Archange told him, and how could he deny her anything?

Nonetheless he'd said, 'I should return to the Wildcats.' He hadn't missed the horrors of battle, the hard ground beneath him as he slept, the dreadful food. But he wanted to be with his comrades – Indaro and Garret and Doon and the others.

'Saroyan has arranged for you to be invalided out of the Maritime.' Archange's voice had brooked no opposition. 'I need you to guard an important man.'

Broglanh opened his mouth to argue.

'This man,' Archange continued remorselessly, 'escaped the dungeons and is in hiding under a false name. He is old and his memory is fading. I believe he has a cancer which will soon end his life. But he is tough and ready for his last battle. Our plans are all in place. We only need Fell now. If anyone can kill the emperor it is Fell Aron Lee.'

'I can kill him!' Broglanh told her, feeling insulted. 'You don't need Fell!'

Her lips thinned. 'You might not be fully fit by then.'

'And Fell might be dead!'

'We will keep him safe. It is strange,' she mused, 'how foreign soldiers like yourself, brought to the City as poor, abused boys, have been so unshakeably loyal to the City which gave them so little and took so much.'

'Who is this man I must guard?' Broglanh asked.

'He is Shuskara.' The name silenced Broglanh. Shuskara was a legendary general, believed long dead at the hands of the emperor. 'Although that name must never pass your lips outside this house. He calls himself Bartellus now and he lives at the House of Glass in Blue Duck Alley.'

When the old woman had left Broglanh grabbed Thekla's hand and pulled her to him. He put his good arm round her hips and buried his face in the folds of her skirts.

'I must go,' she said, and he could hear she was smiling.

'Stay,' he said, his voice muffled. His body, newly strong, surged with desire for her.

'There are sick and injured people who need my help more than you do.'

'It's not your help I want,' he told her. 'Stay.'

'And your arm is not fully healed.'

'Stay.'

So she stayed.

* * *

Broglanh awoke in a place full of light. He felt it pressing on his closed eyelids. His head was full of dreams of Thekla, as ever, but the last thing he remembered in this life was Emly saving him from the battlefield, the warhorse galloping under him.

He opened his eyes and saw he was in a small room. It was cool and the air was fresh. He rolled his head and the movement made his stomach lurch. He turned and vomited on the floor. He felt a little better and looked up at a barred window with a patch of sky beyond. He tried to sit but his muscles shrieked their dissent. He tried again, anxious to check his injuries. He tore the clean bandage off the thigh wound and found neat stitches and a cut healed without rot. He looked at the wounds on his arms and chest. Ten days of healing, he calculated. Ten days since the battle.

He wondered where he was.

After a while he tried to stand. He was weak but hungry. There was a jug of water by his bedside and he drank it down, feeling its virtue course through him. His clothes, washed and mended, lay in a corner. It took him a long time to pull them on, and he had to sit down afterwards. He kept looking at the patch of sky. Finally he stood again. He had not the strength to pull on his boots and he walked slowly, barefoot, to the door. To his surprise it opened at his touch. He stepped out.

He was on a wide, grassy slope above a river bank. He gazed along the river. To his right he could see distant figures. The enemy? No, they were too few. He raised his eyes and saw he was in a deep valley flanked by high rock walls. Behind him dwellings were hacked out of the red rock. The air was eerily still and he could hear nothing. He wondered if he was dead after all. He put one hand to his heart and closed his eyes, feeling the slow beat. He felt breath suck in and out of his chest. Not dead, he thought. Not yet.

Taking a deep draught of clean air he walked slowly to the river's edge. There was a man seated on the bank. It was Stalker. His ginger braids were dripping and his clothes were sticking to his body as if he had just been in the river.

'Where are we?' Broglanh asked him, lowering himself down beside his comrade. The water was cool on his feet. 'Are we dead?'

Stalker looked at him and laughed. 'I know *I'm* not.'

'Did we win?' Broglanh asked. He remembered nothing about the battle, except that there was one.

'Depends who you mean by "we".' Stalker grinned. 'The City army, Marcus Rae Khan's army, was trounced, leaving just a few poor souls to stumble their way home.'

Broglanh felt he was in a dream and Stalker's words only enhanced the feeling. 'Where are we, man? And how did we get here?'

'Your girl brought you. You're in the valley of the Vorago.'

'Emly? Where is she?'

'On her way back to the City on your big horse. She thinks she can save them, but nothing can do that now. Their fate was fixed a long time ago.' He nodded his satisfaction at his own words.

'She's alone?'

'Ay, but she's tougher than she knows.' The big man turned towards him and looked into his eyes. 'Where's the Gulon Veil?'

Fear flooded Broglanh as he realized at last that this was not his friend Stalker. He wondered if he was still dreaming. 'Who are you?' he asked.

'My name is Hammarskjald,' the man said, getting to his feet. Broglanh felt the power radiating from him like a northerly wind in winter. 'Mention it among the rich and powerful and see them quiver.'

He stared down, his face stone. 'You're a fine fighter, Broglanh. I'd give you a castle or three or half my realm if you'd battle at my side. But I know you'd refuse. Now, tell me what you did with the veil.'

Broglanh felt powerless before him and he believed absolutely that the man could kill him with a thought or gesture. And he was incapable of lying, for Hammarskjald's eyes held him fixed in an iron grip and nothing but the truth could force its way from his mouth.

He said, 'I don't know.' Then, 'What do you know of the Gulon Veil?'

Hammarskjald grunted. 'I know everything about it. It was created to heal the sick and the wounded, but Araeon corrupted it – as he did all things – and made it a toy for his private pleasure. He used its virtue to create a thousand reflections all designed to service his foul needs.' He spat on the ground. 'It was better lost deep in the sewers. And now it is mislaid again.' He shook his head with a sardonic smile. 'Archange has been careless with it.' The smile dropped away and his voice thickened with fury. 'She deserves all that's coming to her. Where did you hide it?' he demanded of Broglanh. 'It was not with you or the girl.'

'It was in my jacket, stitched into it,' Broglanh confessed.

The big man snorted. 'Of course! You wore it. And where is the jacket now?'

Broglanh shook his head. 'I don't know. I must have left it on the battlefield. It'll be deep among corpses.' He thought of Stern and Quora and all the others. He wondered if any had survived.

Hammarskjald nodded thoughtfully, then he raised his ginger head and whistled and Broglanh heard thundering hooves. From down-river a horse came galloping. It was a huge dappled grey, saddled and ready for war. Hammarskjald swung easily into the saddle. Broglanh felt he should do something to stop him but he was powerless against the man.

'It'll take you a long time to get back to the City,' Hammarskjald told him, gathering the reins, 'and by then it'll be long over. I'll keep Emly safe if I can, and her brother. The rest will die.'

He turned the horse's head to the north but held it back as it snorted and fidgeted, keen to be away.

'Selene wanted you dead,' Hammarskjald told Broglanh, 'but then she wants most men dead. I've given you your life today, son, for I'll not see a warrior like you slain by a woman's poison. But next time I see you I'll kill you.'

As the sound of horse's hooves faded into the distance, Broglanh lay back on the grassy bank and thought through the conversation. He had heard the name Hammarskjald only once in his life, in Donal Broglanh's high hall when the old man spoke of times long past. Was this a descendant of the man Donal called a criminal – or was it the same man?

When he felt stronger Broglanh checked his wounds again. The scars had faded from pink to white, the stitches gone. Hammarskjald had not only saved him from poison, he had healed his wounds. As with everything he did not understand he put it from his mind. He needed food. And a horse.

He got slowly to his feet and walked back to the rock dwelling. A tall grey woman stood in his path, arms folded. His old boots lay at her feet.

'Begone,' she told him. 'You're not wanted here.' Her face looked familiar.

Broglanh felt red rage swirling up through his chest, the fury that had kept him alive through all his years of battle. He would not be thwarted by this peasant.

'I could snap your neck like a twig, woman,' he told

her. He chose not to but the thought satisfied him.

She sneered, eyes gleaming. 'Just try it, soldier. Hammarskjald is not the only one in this place with power. I have promised him I'll let you live, but he would not fault me if you were killed in an attempt on my life.'

Confusion whirled his emotions like leaves in a gust of wind. He was suddenly tired of it all, of the deceits, the stratagems and lies which had been his life in the year since the fall of the Red Palace. He longed to be back with soldiers again, with the Wildcats – all dead or gone now – or with Stern and his Pigstickers, honest soldiers fighting for a clear cause worthy of the struggle.

So he said to her, 'Thank you for your hospitality.' He could afford to be polite now he had his strength again.

'Don't thank me,' she snapped. 'You'd be a corpse floating out to sea if I'd had my way.'

'What is my offence, that you want me dead?'

'You don't know who I am, do you?' she asked, wonderingly. 'I am Selene Vincerus.'

He was startled by the answer, though he did not show it. Selene was Thekla's mother, Archange's daughter, and he had been told variously that she was dead or insane or both. But he did not know what her relationship with Hammarskjald was or why she had tried to kill him. Her grey eyes were like shiny pebbles, flecked with gold, and insanity crouched there.

He shrugged as if he had no interest in her name. 'And Hammarskjald?'

Her mouth twisted into a smile and she spoke with glee. 'He is the leader of the Hratana, the great army which crushed yours. They are marching south now, far beyond your reach. He plans to scour the City away, to unleash a plague upon it which will kill every man, woman and child within its walls.'

'A plague?' He visualized the vast army sweeping across the City like beetles on a corpse, thousands dead in the streets. 'Is sending an army against it not enough?'

The woman grinned. 'Death is not enough. The City will be swept from the pages of history if Hammarskjald has his way. The only thing that could possibly save it now is the veil and you lost that, you fool, on the battlefield.'

'Why does he hate the City so?' he asked, wondering how the veil could save it.

'Because it does not belong in this world. It is a pustulent sore which must be cleansed in pain before humankind can go forward into its intended future.'

The rantings of a lunatic, Broglanh thought. He had never suffered from regrets. He would not dwell on the veil or its whereabouts, lost in a sea of rotting bodies. It was gone and that was that. His mind was already voyaging into the future. He looked south, towards the blue sea sparkling on the edge of his vision. He visualized the map of the known world, brown and faded, on the wall of Archange's library.

'Begone,' Selene repeated, waving one arm as if at a bee. 'You can take these.' She flung the old boots at him. 'You have a long road ahead.'

He bent to pick them up. 'I'm not going by road,' he said to himself.

PART SIX

Under Siege

CHAPTER THIRTY-SIX

As DOL SALIDA FELL TO HIS KNEES, HIS LIFEBLOOD pooling on the floor, his assassin stepped forward and gently lifted the child from his arms. He stood holding it, wondering what to do with it. It was mute and its eyes were glazed, in shock, he guessed. He did not kill children unless ordered. In the end he put it on the floor and left it with the corpses. Someone would find it eventually.

He took no pleasure in killing women, or old men either. But the women would die when the Plague-Bringers got there, so perhaps this was a mercy. And Dol Salida was one of Archange's close confidants. His lord had been clear on this. *Take out her inner circle first. Then those that rush in to take their places. Leave her vulnerable, isolated.*

Fin Gilshenan did not know why he had been given these orders. Nor did he care. He and his men had been sent ahead to infiltrate the mountain called the Shield of Freedom through its long-abandoned tunnels and shafts, following intricate diagrams drawn by his lord himself. They had broken through iron gates built long ago then forgotten. They had built and erected many lengths of ladder to replace those in the shafts which had rotted and fallen. And now they were ready. At dawn after the dark of the moon they had been ordered to enter the White Palace and execute the security chief Dashoul, the military commander Darius Hex, General Eufara of the Emperor's Rangers and, of course, Dol Salida. The old counsellor had surprised them, the day before his doom was destined, by suddenly visiting his wife. With time to spare, Fin Gilshenan had chosen to do this deed himself. It was the first link in a chain of events and he wanted to see it went perfectly.

He left the cottage, pushing closed the front door. The bodies might not be discovered for a couple of days, by which time the mountain would be in ferment. Even if they were found quickly it would not matter. The deaths would be put down to a passing scoundrel, or gang of them, for the mountain's base town attracted many of that sort.

He hurried back along the river bank. Rain was coming down hard. He reached the southern cliff-face at dusk. The cliff was considered unclimbable so it was not guarded. Sloppy. He found the rope he had climbed down earlier and swarmed back up it. At its top he was greeted by his second, Makenna.

The man raised his eyebrows and Fin reported, 'All dead.' Then he added, 'But for a child.'

Makenna would have been watching from a prudent distance lest some inconvenient troop of soldiers passed. Not that he would have interfered; it was crucial that Dol Salida's death be not perceived as part of a greater plot, for today. Tomorrow would not matter. If the mission had gone badly, and Fin had been killed or dragged off for questioning, Makenna would have returned to tell the others and to take Fin's place. They had no fear of torture. None but Fin could speak a word of the City tongue and no one on the mountain, or within a thousand leagues of it, could speak theirs.

Makenna pulled the rope up and the two entered a

hole disguised by broken branches, careful to replace fresh foliage behind them. It was a tight squeeze, but inside it opened out into one of the main routes through the mountain. They lit a lantern and when they reached the chosen shaft Fin started to climb, the lantern hanging from his belt. It was not the quickest route – that would be via the great shaft through the centre of the mount, connecting its base with the White Palace at its summit. But by unspoken consensus they never went that way. Climbing more than half a league on one continuous ladder was brutal on the muscles but even harder on the mind. After a while the repetitive movement, and the darkness beyond the lantern pool, and consciousness of the terrifying drop below made the mind start to play tricks. A man could believe he was crawling across a ceiling like a blowfly, or that the ladder would never end, or that the silence around him hid flying things with teeth and claws intent on tearing him off the ladder to fall, flailing, forever in darkness.

When they reached the top they crossed to the north side through an access tunnel built by and for long-ago workers, then climbed a second shaft to their adopted quarters.

It was odd to think of a palace on a mountain-top having dungeons, but that was what they were – small cells, dozens of them, long abandoned and with corroded shackles hanging from the walls. They had chosen one each, careless of the cold, the dark, the damp, for they were on a hero's path. There was a disused guardroom with an air-shaft out on to the sheer mountain beneath an outer wall of the White Palace. The air-shaft allowed them to make a fire and occasionally cook food. Yesterday they had slaughtered a wild pig, slaughtered it, butchered it, and tonight would feast on it – perhaps the last feast some of them would enjoy.

Fin reported his success and there were satisfied

nods from his men, but some looks of envy. They had a long night still to wait, then they would sally forth. Fin and Makenna would despatch the Nighthawks' leader. Darius Hex was a warrior, young and strong, but he had not seen battle recently and he had grown soft, talking to the empress each day, eating her good food. The only problem, as it would be for all of them, was to do the job in silence and leave no trace.

Fin smiled to himself. Killing an old man and some women had been no challenge. But at dawn their work truly began.

As the ten black-clad men sat quietly talking, the fumes from their fire and the rich scent of roast pig wafted along the tunnel between the cells and into a crevice where Rubin Guillaume stood, still as a carved statue, listening.

When he first discovered the intruders he had been lucky and had spotted their distant lights before they saw his. He had quickly doused his torch and followed them, intrigued to find other secret trespassers. He guessed they were the ones who had breached the barred gate at the root of the mountain through which he and Valla had entered. Over several days and nights now he had spied on them, keeping his distance, staying in darkness, watching their lanterns as they moved through tunnels and shafts. Sometimes he followed them when they crept out into the palace at dead of night, but he always made sure to be back in his hiding place before they returned.

Though they clearly had some evil intent, Rubin was reluctant to raise the alarm. Since his time in the Halls he had been attracted by the secret and hidden, and he would never find out what they were up to if they were arrested. He listened to their foreign speech and understood not a word, and he suspected no one else in the palace would either. But now he had concluded, after some soul-searching, that he must alert the captain of the guard. Above all, he considered himself loyal to his City and he could hardly go on doing so if he continued to keep this dangerous information to himself.

Leaving the intruders feasting, Rubin crept back to one of their hidden ways into the palace, feeling his way, quiet as a spider. He found the panel in the wall and pushed it open. It swung silently on oiled hinges and he climbed out, closed it behind him and, with a sigh of relief, set off through the midnight palace.

There was a wild storm outside. Heavy rain lashed the windows and he could hear the sounds of water everywhere, drumming on roofs and balconies, running down pipes, splashing leaves and tree canopies and courtyard flags. He loved the rain and on any other night would be out in it, revelling in its power. But now he was thinking hard, wondering how to reveal himself and his information without being killed by the empress's soldiers, hoping he could use his knowledge of the intruders as leverage when he found out why, and if, Archange had been hunting him.

He headed towards the western redoubt, where the captain of the watch was based. He had learned a great deal about the palace as he watched the watchers. He remained unchallenged. He saw no one. He came to a stairway, its stone steps gleaming in reflected torchlight, and ran lightly down three levels. As he passed a doorway deep in a wall he glimpsed sudden movement on the edge of his vision. Something hard struck him on the side of the head and he went down.

Dazed, he heard shouts and the sound of running boots, then his arms and legs were grabbed and he found himself spreadeagled, facing the floor, unable to move. He heard the alarm begin, a deep brazen clanging which echoed down the corridors and was taken up by more distant alarms. *No!* he thought. *That will only alert them!* He tried to raise his head to speak, but someone grabbed his hair and slammed his face into the stone. Pain seared through his head. He felt blood trickle from his nose and he choked, trying to breathe.

'Let him go,' a commanding voice ordered.

He was hauled to his feet and found himself face to face with an officer. He had reddish-fair hair and penetrating blue eyes and wore the uniform of a commander of the Thousand. He stood relaxed, hands behind his back, gazing at Rubin expressionlessly.

'Your name?' he asked.

'Rubin Kerr Guillaume. I have a message for the empress.'

The soldier raised his eyebrows, glancing at Rubin's red hair.

'You are Indaro's brother?'

'Yes!' cried Rubin, relief washing over him that this man knew his name, knew Indaro's.

'Then you must know that she has been banished from the City and her name is cursed in this place,' the officer said. His tone was unemphatic and it was impossible to tell what he thought of this.

Rubin stared at him, disbelieving, wondering that the officer could say such a thing. 'That isn't true!' he blurted. 'Indaro is loyal to the City. She is its most loyal warrior!'

'I am Darius Hex, commander of the Nighthawks, and I do not lie,' the soldier replied. 'Indaro killed the emperor.' He was watching Rubin closely.

Rubin shook his head. The words made no sense. 'But she is loyal,' he repeated. 'This is a mistake!' Then, with dread coiling in his belly, 'What happened to her?'

Darius Hex repeated, 'She was banished from the City. Now, what message have you for the empress? Quickly, boy!'

Rubin stared at the floor, trying to take in what he had been told. But Indaro fought to save the Red Palace, he argued to himself. Marcellus told me so.

Darius' voice cracked like a whip. 'Your message!'

Rubin looked up. With effort he swallowed his fear for Indaro and considered his own safety.

'My message is for Archange's ears,' he stated. The commander's face hardened and he unsheathed the thin blade at his belt. Rubin added quickly, 'The empress has been seeking me! I have come here to comply with her wishes.'

Darius looked out of a window, where the storm had abated and the grey light of dawn was chasing away the last rags of storm clouds. 'I will speak to her,' he said.

Rubin was escorted through the palace, up and up through its multiple floors, until they reached immense carved doors decorated with antelope and birds in chased silver. Darius entered and was inside for a long time. Rubin thought again of Indaro. Where had she fled to? Not to the Salient, that was certain. Then it occurred to him that his father might have fled the family home because of Indaro. He thought back to Reeve's long-ago words, that the Red Palace was steeped in corruption and duplicity. Perhaps Indaro had been a victim, a pawn used to justify a political move against the Guillaumes? After all, he thought, what was more likely – that Indaro would murder her emperor or that the death of the Immortal at whosever hands would be used as an excuse for a spate of score-settling? He found little comfort in the theory.

At last a servant opened the great doors and Rubin was led into the empress's receiving room, a circular chamber filled with grey light. Tall windows faced east where the sun still hid behind rain clouds. The high walls were painted with strange scenes of tall buildings, elegant as palm-fronds, and people in winged carriages floating in cloud-laden skies. There were thick rugs on the floor and what seemed like a thousand lighted candles on tables and wall sconces. Black and silver warriors were stationed round the curved walls, and Darius Hex and another soldier flanked Archange at the end of a gold carpet.

The empress was seated on a carved, cushioned chair. She looked ancient, her long white hair loosely bound at her neck, white robes clothing a gaunt body. But as he walked towards her she rose gracefully and Rubin realized she was not as old as he had first thought. She was taller than most of her soldiers and her face, he saw, was beautiful and serene.

'You are Rubin Kerr Guillaume?' she asked. Her voice was deep, for a woman, and warm. Rubin's fears drifted away. He realized why Archange should be empress of the City – her beauty and wisdom were overpowering. He wondered why he had feared meeting her. Someone had warned him against her but he could not remember who.

With a start he realized he was expected to answer. 'Yes, empress.'

'Darius tells me you have a message for me?' She smiled, and it was like cool water on a parched tongue. He could not help but smile back, although it seemed impertinent and he lowered his eyes. Briefly he told her of the ten men infiltrating the tunnels. As he spoke, staring at the floor, the thrall in which she held him dissipated and he saw it for what it was. He had often seen Marcellus use his dark gaze to bend others to his will. Only when he had finished his tale did he look up.

The empress frowned at Darius, who strode from the room.

'And why were *you* skulking in the depths of my mountain, Rubin?' Archange asked the question mildly but he reminded himself of Marcellus' warning: '*Do not trust her, do not trust her words or her actions.*'

He told her a partial truth. 'I was seeking my father.'

'Reeve?' For a heartbeat she looked startled, then her eyes narrowed. 'Why would Reeve be here?'

'He left the Salient, at night and alone, last winter. No one knows where he went. He has not been seen since.'

'So why,' she asked, coldness flooding her voice, 'did you not simply come to the gates of the Shield and seek audience? I could have told you he would never come here. I have not seen Reeve for—' she sighed, 'a very long time.'

He bowed his head in a show of humility, but in truth to avoid her eyes. 'I was told the Guillaumes were not welcome here, lady.'

'You thought,' she replied, her voice icing over, 'that your father would be locked away in my dungeons for his daughter's crime?'

'Indaro did not do what they say!' he cried. 'There has been a mistake—'

She caught his gaze and he forgot what he was saying.

'You came to the Shield alone?' she asked.

'Yes, empress.'

'Or with your friend Valla?'

The name filled him with dismay. What did the empress know of Valla? Had she been captured, killed? He struggled to stay calm. 'No, lady. I came alone.'

'Your friend Valla,' she repeated. 'Here.'

For a moment Rubin didn't understand what she was saying, as she turned to the tall soldier standing still and silent beside her. Then his heart leaped in his chest. Clad in the livery of the Thousand again, her face blank, Valla looked like any of the warriors on the

Shield. She stared into the distance as if oblivious to their exchange. Rubin's eyes moved to her left arm. It was no longer in a sling but was encased in leather. The fingers of that hand, though still corpse-white, were drumming nervously against her thigh, or perhaps signalling to him her restoration.

The air hardened and crackled and Rubin felt his gaze being dragged, unwilling, to the empress again. She seemed to have grown taller and her black eyes blazed with anger. She did not look beautiful now.

'You think,' she said in a voice which echoed off the walls to vibrate through flesh and blood and bone, 'to come here and lie to me, to follow your sister and creep through the tunnels like a rat on the scent of spoiled meat? Bad blood always flows true and the Guillaumes will ever be a contagion on this City. We should have had you both smothered at birth, you and your wretched sister!'

Rubin staggered under the force of her anger, like a blast of heat from a furnace-mouth. It was all he could do to stay upright. He felt his body was being wrenched apart by unseen claws. He cried out then sank to his knees. All the candles in the chamber blew out.

The empress loomed over him. 'Saroyan,' she said, her voice like thunder and lightning. 'What part did you play in my granddaughter's death, boy?'

His tongue was a dry stick in his mouth as fire raged about him. Each word was a torment but each had to be the truth. 'Saroyan conspired with the enemy,' he croaked. 'I saw her in the Odrysian camp. Two winters ago. In the stand-off at Needlewoman's Notch. I saw her with Odrysians and Petrassi. I believed they were talking—' he paused to suck in hot air and felt his throat burn and blister, '—talking treason,' he choked. 'I told my lord Marcellus.'

'When?' she asked him, her voice borne to him on waves of heat.

'Just before the Day of Summoning,' he gasped.

The heat about him intensified and he began to suffocate. He sank to the floor and rolled on to his back, trying to suck in breath. Archange stood over him. Shadowy wings seemed to rise from her shoulders and beat the hot air. He put out one hand to ward her off and, unbidden, he felt power rise in him from deep beneath the stone, up through his body and out from his reaching hand. The sudden surge of energy rocked Archange on her feet. The whole palace seemed to shake and he heard soldiers shout out. Through half-closed eyes he saw Valla step slowly, agonizingly, in front of her empress.

Then suddenly all was calm. Archange sank back into her seat. Rubin lowered his hand. Valla was standing, trembling, in front of him, her sword halfway from its sheath. The chamber was filled with smoke and an eerie greenish light. Rubin struggled to his feet coughing and stepped away from Valla, his arms raised, surrendering. He was seized by soldiers, his head pulled back, his throat exposed for the killing blade. Valla turned to the empress for orders.

Archange's voice was thin and tired. 'It seems you have a little power, boy. It will avail you nothing. You will be punished for your deeds. Saroyan, my daughter's daughter, died far from home and far from aid. Her body was found at the Araby Breaks after the spring thaw. She had been felled with a lance-thrust in the back and died in the snow. You are responsible for that. Your words to Marcellus signed her death warrant.'

She turned to Valla. 'Kill him,' she ordered.

Valla looked into his eyes. In hers he saw anguish and remorse. She sheathed her sword and took out a long sharp knife. She stepped towards him and raised the blade. She pulled her eyes from his and focused on the point on his throat where the knife would enter, to slash across from one side to the other, slicing through flesh and muscle and blood vessels.

Then there were running bootsteps outside and Darius burst back in through the doors, bringing a gust of cold, fresh air. His gaze took in the scene and his sword leaped to his hand.

Archange barked, 'Wait.' Valla paused and her eyes returned to Rubin's. They stood frozen, gazing at each other, as the empress asked her commander, 'Have you dealt with them?'

Darius replied, 'They have vanished, empress, but we will find them.' He looked at Rubin and Valla, still as statues.

'Send me Dol Salida and Dashoul.'

Darius hesitated. 'Dol Salida has gone down the mountain, lady,' he reminded her.

She clucked her tongue and shook her head, just an old woman with a failing memory. 'I had forgotten. Dashoul then.'

'Dashoul is missing.'

'Missing?'

'He did not arrive at his office this morning. His people thought it was due to the storm, yet he cannot be found. But there is graver news, empress.'

'Well?' she rapped out.

'The last riders we sent out have returned. They report there is an army on the other side of the Narrows waiting to cross.'

'Marcus?' she breathed.

'No, empress, a foreign army. One our riders have never seen before. And they are coming this way.'

The rain had stopped long since but stormwater was still rolling off the mountain, sluicing in great sheets off the cliffs, roiling and bubbling down forested slopes, moving through the decades-thick blankets of pine needles. Steep tracts of soil held in place only by myriad roots of brambles and ivies wrenched themselves free and the landslips moved down the Shield, tearing down trees and shifting crumbling rocks. In two places the Shell Path was washed away. In the White Palace guttering snapped and a torrent of rainwater flooded the armoury and kitchens and invaded the soldiers' quarters, leaving its inhabitants drenched and sleepless.

In the Khan Palace, further down the Shield, the old sandstone walls had been built into the side of the mountain and the stormwater found fewer places for entry. When its people awoke that morning they gazed out on to a fresh landscape, its colours clarified by the cleansing rain.

Fiorentina Vincerus stood on the stone terrace looking out at the bright morning and sighed.

'Bring me my perfume bottle.' She turned her head, it being an effort to turn her whole body. 'No, not that one. The green one. This is a green morning.'

Alafair brought her the perfume and lifted her lady's long dark tresses to spray her neck, already damp with sweat.

Fiorentina sighed again. 'Everything hurts,' she complained.

'I know, lady. But the baby will come soon.'

Fiorentina bit her lip, looking down at her belly. She was torn between wanting the baby to arrive quickly and fearing the birth. In the meantime she had no idea what to do with herself. She was uncomfortable sitting or lying and she could only stand for a short while without her legs hurting too. And she felt trapped in the Khan Palace. The Khans had made her welcome, in their way, but it was a comfortless place, its chambers cold and bleak, its stone walls undecorated, its furnishings old and shabby. Quite unlike her old home at the top of the Redoubt, light and airy, filled with fresh flowers on her lord's orders. She yearned for that life again and feared what the future held for her and her baby.

'I must go out,' she said to Alafair. 'I'm dying here.'

The girl combed her hair and said quietly, 'Once the baby is born you can go anywhere you like. You must be patient.'

But Fiorentina knew she was wrong. Her baby was a Vincerus, a son, something not seen in many years, for Rafe and his brother had been the last in their line. This half-life, this benevolent imprisonment, was probably as free as any she would have in the future. If, she thought, gazing at her swollen belly, she even survived the birth.

Alafair cried out.

Fiorentina looked up to see two men clad in black clambering up on to the terrace. The first grabbed Alafair, closing a hand over her mouth to silence her. Fiorentina turned to the other and drew herself up to her full height. 'I am the lady—'

He punched her on the jaw and caught her as she fell, unconscious.

Valla would have executed Rubin, for her empress had commanded it, but she could not have lived afterwards. Silently thanking Aduara for the goddess's intercession, she looked down at her trembling sword hand, and stilled it. And in a flash of insight, she realized that killing her friend Rubin would have been her punishment for her part in Saroyan's death.

When interrogated by the empress after her capture Valla had told Archange all she knew about Rubin. The old woman seemed already aware of most of it, and much was trivial, the day-to-day doings of a young man who had led a full life and spoken of it at length.

Valla had sworn to Rubin's loyalty to the City and his love for Marcellus. She had given a complete account of their meeting with the First Lord at the Red Palace. She had not known then that Saroyan was Archange's granddaughter, but it would have made no difference if she had. And under the empress's questioning, when she could no longer avoid it, she had spoken of her and Rubin's underground journey to the mountain.

'Why here?' Archange had asked her.

Valla confessed, 'I don't know. He said he was seeking his father—' Archange had sniffed at that, '—but I don't really know – he said he needed answers.'

Everything she told Archange was true, if inadequate, and Valla had wondered then – and wondered now – why Rubin was of such interest to the empress. Archange was as good as her word, though no doubt frustrated that the information gleaned had been of such little value. When ordered, Valla had unwrapped her grimy bandages, ashamed of the withered, pale stick that was her arm, and the old woman had peered at it with a moue of distaste. Then she held her hand out and Valla felt a golden warmth, killing the pain instantly and suffusing the arm with lightness. Then she had been taken to a prison cell, where she lay and worried about Rubin, and watched her arm with trepidation. At first the limb had still been useless, a piece of meat hanging from her shoulder, but over the course of a day it had filled out and she began to detect sensation in it. By dawn of the next day it had gained strength and she had laughed with delight and amazement as the fingers became nimble again.

Valla's attention was jolted back to Archange's receiving room when Eufara, general of the Emperor's Rangers, stomped into the chamber loudly cursing the storm. In a few curt words the empress informed him about the threatening army.

'Send the Tenth Adamantine to the Great North Gate,' she ordered Darius. 'And your Rangers can go with them,' she told Eufara.

The Emperor's Rangers, badly named, had not left the Shield in generations. Valla believed most of them had never even been in a fight beyond a bar-room scuffle, and she wondered disdainfully how they would fare when faced with an armed enemy.

The general bowed his head. 'Yes, lady.'

'But send your second. I want you here,' she added and the old man nodded again, perhaps relieved.

Archange turned back to Darius. 'I want Vares here with all haste. Where is he?'

'The Twenty-second is in the south, manning the broken walls,' the commander told her. 'General Vares is with them.'

There was a moment of silence which Rubin, still held in the grip of two guards, broke. 'Send me north with the Rangers,' he asked the empress, and Valla's breath caught in her throat. Why could he never keep his mouth shut?

Archange turned slowly towards him and narrowed her eyes. Anger gathered again like black blood welling into a wound. 'You are presuming this grave news has released you from the death sentence. It has not. And I am told you are no warrior.'

'No,' Rubin persisted, heedless of her threatening tone. 'But my skill is to infiltrate foreign and enemy forces.'

'Do *you* know where this new army has come from?'

'No, empress, but I can find out,' he replied with calm certainty. 'And if you still suspect my motives here on the mountain, sending me north would be a sure way to get rid of me.'

'Or I could be sending information of the security on the Shield into enemy hands.'

Rubin retorted, 'It seems the security of the Shield is fatally compromised already, empress.'

She scowled at him. 'You walk on thin ice, Rubin Guillaume, when already under the weight of a death sentence. When did you last see your friend Marcellus?'

Rubin frowned at the sudden change of tack, but answered, 'On the Day of Summoning last.'

Then he gasped, as if realizing the implication of her question. 'You don't think Marcellus is behind this foreign army?' he asked, eyes wide.

Valla trembled for him. He spoke to the empress with a familiarity which bordered on insolence. But Eufara intervened.

'What nonsense is this, boy?' the old general growled. 'The First Lord was murdered. It is an undisputable fact. The Immortal spoke to the assassin herself.' He turned to her. 'Marcellus *is* dead, empress.' But it sounded more like a question than a statement of certainty.

'*When* on the Day of Summoning?' she asked Rubin as if the general had not spoken.

'Late in the afternoon.' He closed his eyes, as if thinking back. 'The shadows were long. We were in the far east wing of the Red Palace.'

'What passed between you?'

'He told me the City and the Red Palace had been invaded and the emperor was dead.'

'And?'

'He planned to leave.'

'Did he say where he was going?'

'No, he would not tell me. Only that he would ride across the East Lake.'

'Are you certain it was Marcellus?'

It seemed a strange question and Rubin clearly thought so too, for he frowned. 'Yes, lady. I spoke to him for some time. I know him well.'

'And if I told you he was beheaded at around noon that day?'

Rubin's mouth curled. 'Then I would say you are misinformed, lady. I saw him much later and he was certainly alive and well then.'

'What were his last words to you?'

Rubin hesitated, then said, 'He warned me against you, empress.' Valla heard gasps from around the room. Such insolence to Araeon would have brought inevitable, agonizing death. But Archange merely stared at the floor, her brow furrowed.

'No,' she said at last, looking up. 'You cannot go north. You will stay here and suffer punishment for your crime. We will find out soon enough where this army has come from and what its leaders want.'

'It is an army, empress,' Darius offered calmly. 'They want to kill us all.'

'But I will defer your death sentence,' Archange told Rubin. 'You are of the Families and deserve better than summary execution. As Saroyan did. You will die in twenty days' time.' She turned to Darius. 'The execution will be held in the Circle of Combat at the Amphitheatre and will be announced daily at the Great Gates, in the old way.'

CHAPTER THIRTY-SEVEN

MANY LEAGUES TO THE NORTH, HIGH IN THE foothills of the Eaglesclaw Mountains, Benet Edasson peered at the plain below and cried, 'I can see them!'

'You can't see them,' Stern told him impatiently. 'You can barely see your hand in front of your face.' His brother continually commented on what he could see in a bid to fool his comrades, when in truth he was just drawing attention to his blindness.

Stern pointed south-east. 'There's a smudge on the horizon. It must be the enemy army at the Narrows, waiting for the tide.'

'You sure they're still on this side?' Benet asked, squinting.

'I've been watching for a while and they haven't moved,' Stern said. He was speaking for Hayden's benefit for he suspected the general too was hard of seeing. Hayden and Brel, a Petrassi captain, and he and Benet had walked up to the top of a sandstone outcrop while the rest of the troops, exhausted by the forced march, rested at its base. 'Why would they be still in one place otherwise?'

Taking silence as assent, Stern went on: 'They're a day or so ahead of us. The men and horses will cross easily enough, once the tide is right, but they've got weapons and baggage. Getting all that over will take many rafts. How many carts do you reckon they have, Benet?'

Benet, who was the only soldier to admit having seen the retreating rear of the enemy army, guessed. 'Two hundred or more?'

'They may be able to use some of the rafts we abandoned on the north shore after our crossing in this direction,' said Brel. 'But it's been weeks now and they will likely have all been stolen.'

'Perhaps they'll send their soldiers on ahead, leaving the wagons to cross later,' offered Benet. 'I would.'

The general shook his head. 'I don't think so. By sending only their soldiers against the north walls they will be warning the City of their presence, to no advantage. They'll want to bring up the heavy weaponry for their first assaults.' He looked at Benet. 'I would.'

He explained: 'Remember the great explosions at the Vorago?' The brothers nodded fervently. How could they not? Stern thought that if he lived to make old bones he would never forget the terrifying crash of the cannon, the rain of bloody gouts of flesh, the screams of men and horses, and the gut-twisting fear that had left him helpless as a child.

'Those weapons, if used properly,' said the general, 'could bring down a gate, perhaps even a great wall like those of the City. But the cannon are heavy and will be difficult to transport over the water.'

'They need boats,' Brel said. 'And strong ones.'

'They do indeed. They have been marching hard and have not been delayed by weather or military action. Perhaps that's what they're waiting for: boats. I think we have a chance of catching them in a day or two.'

'Then what?' asked Benet, eyes wide. 'What good will we do, two hundred of us?'

The general looked thoughtful. 'There is a great deal two hundred can do.'

Their little army had grown as they marched south. First had limped in more wounded, refugees and deserters; these were all welcomed as comrades, for it was impossible to discriminate between those who had fled and those left for dead. They were all heroes now. They were joined by stragglers from the Petrassi army, two dozen or so who had chosen to throw in their lot with the City forces. It was then that Hayden had been forced to identify himself to Stern and his fellows as a past general of Petrus. This had been treated with little surprise, indeed little interest. In these desperate times the City warriors chose to follow the age-old adage, 'The enemy of my enemy is my friend.'

Now they followed him without complaint, at least to his face. The real test would come, as Stern had predicted, when they engaged in battle.

Three days after leaving the Vorago battlefield they had come to the place where the fleeing womenfolk had been overtaken by the forces of the enemy. It was a grim sight, but it seemed the women had been lucky, in a situation where even bad luck has different degrees. The enemy army was marching hard and its warriors had done no more than slaughter the women as efficiently as possible, take their pack animals and march on. Benet searched among the bloody corpses for Peach but could not find her. Stern had been tempted to look for Emly, for he felt in a strange way responsible for her, having kept her safe against the Fkeni in the siege in the high pass. But in the end he chose not to. He did not want to see the girl's corpse, and if he could not find her it would mean nothing.

Then the next morning the soldiers had come across a small group of women and children, including the young whore Peach and the midwife Bruenna bearing

Maura's infant, who had successfully evaded the enemy. They had six donkeys piled with food and water, cooking gear and blankets. This morsel of good luck raised the spirits of Hayden's army.

Now, within sight of their quarry, they spent the day descending the southern slopes of the Eaglesclaw foothills until, by sunset, they were on the wide flat plain which would lead them to the Narrows and eventually, for the City folk, to home.

Stern lay staring up at the moon. His belly was full of roasted horse, his mind full of thoughts. Around him soldiers talked quietly, sometimes jesting and laughing. It was all so familiar to Stern and he could easily imagine he was in the midst of a horde of twenty or thirty thousand, as so often in the past, rather than their small, bedraggled force.

There was a great deal he did not understand and he was anxious to talk to Hayden. He glanced over to where the general sat by the campfire, but he was surrounded by his Petrassi comrades. Perhaps they were talking about their lost land. They all looked sombre.

Stern thought about Quora, imagined her lying on the other side of the campfire listening to Benet complaining, or Grey Gus yarning, as she had done so often over their years together, glancing at him from time to time, smiling in the firelight. And he daydreamed that she would walk into the campsite one evening, strong and fit, having recovered from her head wound and finally caught up with them. Any delay in their progress made his hopes rise that he would see her again. And they would certainly be delayed at the Narrows.

'General wants you,' a voice interrupted, strongly accented, and Stern lifted his eyes to see one of the Petrassi, who jerked his head towards Hayden then wandered off. Stern scrambled up and went over. Hayden looked up.

'Stern. Sit. We need to talk about tomorrow.'

Stern hunkered down beside him. 'Can I ask a question first?'

'Of course, soldier.' Hayden poked the fire with a stick and the flaring light fell on his face, revealing dark shadows under weary eyes.

'The weapons you spoke of, the cannon they used against us,' asked Stern. 'You already knew of them?'

Hayden bent his head so his face fell into shade. 'I did. Though I had no reason to believe they would be turned against us.'

Stern nodded his acceptance of that. After all, there were many Petrassi bodies among the dead at the Vorago. 'Then why didn't the Blues, your forces, use them against the City?' he asked. 'You say these weapons can tear down a wall. But you used the reservoirs instead.'

The older man was silent, collecting his thoughts. Stern had noticed Hayden seldom spoke swiftly, but examined each word before he would allow it from his mouth. Perhaps, the soldier thought, it is because he is speaking words which are foreign to him. Some of Stern's comrades believed the Blues spoke a strange tongue because they were too stupid to learn that of the City. Stern knew this was not true; still, he marvelled that a man could speak words that were not native to him with such ease. He sat back comfortably, happy to wait, inhaling the familiar scents of charred wood and meat and sweat, listening to the low voices of the soldiers and, nearby, the liquid song of a night bird.

Hayden leaned forward and prodded the fire again, then looked up. He said, 'Towards the end of the war I met a group of allied officers, Odrysians, Buldekki, others. We were intent on a final push against the City.

The Odrysians gave a demonstration of the flares – the flying red lights – and explained how they were made. This was known to us, for the Petrassi, even far from home and dispersed throughout the world as we were, had devices the City was barely aware of. Timepieces, lanterns.'

He paused and Stern frowned. From his jacket pocket the general drew a long chain with a round metal object on the end. He showed it to Stern, who took it in his hand and examined it in the flickering light. A circle of glass was embedded in the front and underneath the glass were symbols. Stern was unlettered and had no understanding of their meaning.

'This is a timepiece,' Hayden explained. 'These hands, these . . . points, go round at a fixed speed and tell the holder what hour of the day it is. Like a sundial.'

'But there is no sun,' said Stern, baffled. 'And I do not need this pretty thing to tell me what time of day it is.'

Hayden gave a rare smile. 'It has a mechanism inside which turns the hands whether there is sun or not, so it shows the hour, even at night.'

Stern shook his head. He didn't like to appear a fool, but it smacked of witchcraft to him. 'What use is it?' he asked sceptically.

'For an army it can be very useful. If you and I, for instance, were attacking an enemy from two sides. If we each had one of these we could coordinate our attacks to the moment.'

Stern nodded his understanding, though he doubted he would ever trust such a thing. 'Do you *have* another one?'

'No,' the general admitted. 'And this one is broken. But it is one of several devices other nations use which are unknown in the City, despite its past military might.

My brother Mason, who knew a good deal more about the City than I, told me the ruling faction – the old emperor Araeon and the Vincerii – forbade the use of such things and suppressed similar inventions. They relied on the strength of the City and its soldiers. All the world knows warriors of the City are hard to kill.'

Stern grinned. It had been proved time and again to his own satisfaction. But it was good to know all the world knew it too.

'At that meeting,' Hayden went on, 'an elderly Odrysian engineer, who had travelled far in foreign lands, said a nation in the far north-east, a barbaric and cruel people, had found a new, terrible use for the black powder.' He paused and, as he was expected to do, Stern said, 'Black powder?'

'It is a substance which, when set alight, burns with great power and heat. The flares the enemy used at the Vorago were of black powder. They gave light and heat but were of little use as weapons, except to frighten. But this Odrysian said the barbarians had found a way to contain the force of the powder in a cast-iron pipe and use it to propel a ball of stone or iron great distances to kill their enemies. That is what this army is using. But such devices would be heavy and difficult to transport. And the powder must be kept dry. That is perhaps why we have caught up with them – crossing the Narrows will be a hurdle for them.'

Stern looked south to where the enemy army was still on this side of the water. He smiled as he realized what the general was saying.

'So our mission,' Hayden went on, 'is to thwart them by sabotaging these weapons before they get to the City.'

'We can do that,' said Stern, grinning. It was good to have a purpose again.

'Good,' said the general. 'Can you swim?'

* * *

Hoham Shoko was a warrior, son of a warrior and grandson of a warrior. He wore a vest of man-skin and a necklet made of the teeth of women. He had fought in desert and mountain and forest and plain and no man had bested him, and the great Lord of the Hratana himself knew his name.

But Hoham was afraid of water. He thought he had seen everything in his years of war, but he had never seen such a wide stretch of water before and his bowels quaked at the prospect of crossing it.

The Lord's Army had waited on the north side of the wide river for two days now. They did not know why they were waiting, but the rest was good after many days of hard marching. Perhaps there will be another way round, Hoham thought hopefully, and the leaders are discussing the new path. He watched and waited, cursing the shifty gods of the rivers who first raised the waters then lowered them in a way that was both unnatural and menacing. Where did all the water come from? Where did it all go?

Lesser men, slaves and foreign labourers, were building boats and rafts, flimsy craft to cross such a terrible water. These vessels would carry the army's weapons, heavy armour, the great fire-pipes, and supplies. The cavalry would rely on their mounts to get them over. But the infantry would have to swim, half-naked and vulnerable.

Hoham had crossed rivers before. He could stay afloat after a fashion and always found something to cling to: a raft, a piece of debris, sometimes, in humiliation, a trooper's stirrup. But none of them had been as wide as this. You could barely see the other side.

Now it was late afternoon and the water level had sunk to its lowest ebb. And the order came to advance.

Hoham's division would be the last to cross, for they were guarding the rear – not that they had seen anything to guard it against. He waited with his comrades of the seventh infantry, anxiety rising in his mouth as the leaders and the cavalry led the plunge into the water, followed by the fourth division guarding the boats loaded with barrels of black powder. Then the sixth was ordered out, leading the pack animals. Before long all the width of the water was churning with men and animals and vessels, all dwindling southwards in the darkening light. The wait was interminable and Hoham felt sick to his stomach.

The carts bearing the great fire-pipes had been dragged up on to the sturdiest rafts and strapped on securely. The rafts were pushed off.

Only one of the six fire-pipes remained. Its cart had shed a wheel and Hoham's division had been ordered to carry the black iron weapon on to the raft and rope it down. Six of his comrades, the lucky ones, were deployed on to the raft to safeguard it, but Hoham and his fellows would have to swim behind.

As the last raft bumped away from the shore Hoham took a deep breath and marched into the water. He felt it cling to his limbs in its unwholesome way, and he pushed himself forward until he was chest-deep, trying to keep up with the raft. But though it was being paddled slowly, Hoham was even slower and when his feet left the floor of the river he tried to quell his panic, surging forward with his arms, keeping his head high, trying to stop the filthy water entering his body. He was watching the rear of the raft move beyond his grasp when he saw a dark shape rise from the water behind the paddlers. It resolved itself into a man's head and as it turned towards him, Hoham could see the gleam of a knife between its teeth.

'Enemy!' he shouted, pausing in his floundering to

point at the raft. But he sank like a stone anchor and water surged into his mouth and closed over his head. He flailed desperately with his arms until he regained the surface, thrashing and gasping. When he had regained his bearings and could see the raft again, the knifeman had gone. So had Hoham's comrades who were already swimming far ahead. He looked behind him. There was no one left. He was the last to cross.

Then a black shape rose out of the river in front of him, strong hands closed around his throat and he was dragged down into the pitiless water. He struggled and fought but the cold hands were like iron.

Stern swam under the raft in darkness. The water, churned by thousands of men and horses, was thick and muddy and he felt his way through the murk, tracing with his fingertips the ropes which lashed the vessel together. He took the knife from his teeth and sawed through one of them. To no effect. He felt along the length of the log and cut another rope. Nothing happened. The raft was well made. He was forced to rise up at the rear of the raft, avoiding the flailing paddles, and take a deep breath. He glanced swiftly behind. A few of the enemy infantrymen remained on the shore but as he watched they marched down into the water.

He sucked air into his chest and swam back under the raft. He had cut through two more of the ropes before he felt the logs shift against each other. He sawed through one more, his lungs burning. Suddenly the loosened logs started to roll, the cut ropes flailing through the water like whips. Stern dived down to the river bed then kicked himself upstream as far as he could before he was forced to emerge, gasping for air. He turned back to watch.

The raft was foundering, listing to one side as the

logs came apart. The men on board were frantically trying to stop the cannon rolling into the water. But it was too heavy and was at an angle, its big mouth pointing down into the river. The alarm had been raised and more men were swimming to help as the raft foundered. Four soldiers on board tried to hold on to the cannon but they were sinking as timber shifted under them. There was nothing they could do.

Stern lay on his back in the water, paddling gently with hands and feet, unseen in the darkness. He listened to the enemy's shouts and curses and watched the raft sink until there was nothing but blackness.

Benet suddenly emerged from the water beside him, laughing, and grabbed him round the shoulders and bore him down in the water. Stern struggled free and rose spluttering, then tried to dunk his brother just as they did when they were boys in the sea at Adrastto. They were both elated, triumphant at their victory. The only enemy soldier to spot them had been the fat oaf struggling along at the back of the army. Benet was doing him a kindness when he'd throttled him. He'd never have made it to the south shore anyway.

They swam upstream and when they waded up out of the water, eager hands reached to help them.

'Well done, men,' said Hayden, his face unsmiling but his eyes warm. 'You have given them something to think about. They will place stronger guards on their weapons now they know they are being followed. This will be a setback to their plans, and their pride.'

'They'll send scouts,' predicted Stern, rubbing himself down with a hairy blanket.

'I hope so,' Hayden said. 'If I were their general I would send out the best, and that is who we will capture. It's time we found out something about our enemy.'

'Your orders, sir?'

'We march through the night. We follow the shore

eastwards – as many leagues as we can traverse in one night – then we cross at dawn. They will be waiting for us to cross here.'

He smiled then and lifted his voice to address the rest of the army. 'We have won our first victory, comrades. The loss of one of their cannon will be a blow to them, to their plans and to their pride. We could not have done better if we had killed one hundred of their soldiers. They will feel the defeat keenly and will be seeking revenge. They will probably send a force against us tomorrow. If so, what will we do?'

The soldiers raised their voices as one. 'Kill them all!' they roared.

CHAPTER THIRTY-EIGHT

SCOUTS HAVE A VULNERABLE ROLE IN ANY ARMY. THEY travel alone through enemy territory and their fate, if captured, is grim. Nevertheless, Hayden had found, working alone appeals to a certain type of soldier and volunteers are usually easy to find.

So the general was taken aback when he asked for two volunteers and the reaction was one of shifty silence. He looked expectantly at his small army. None of them looked back.

'General,' said Stern, at his side, 'City soldiers are not given to volunteering.'

'Why?' Hayden snapped, angered beyond reason. 'They all know the value of scouting the terrain ahead. Each of their lives was certainly saved at some time by scouts.'

'In the City army,' Stern explained quietly while the soldiers muttered and grumbled among themselves, 'no one is asked to volunteer. They are ordered.'

In the end two men raised their hands. One was the soldier with the badly injured face, known to his comrades as Shivers, for even in the balmiest of days he trembled with cold. The other was a one-eyed soldier who had joined them just before the Narrows. His name was Casmir and he was a City veteran with an air of independence which marked him in the general's mind as a possible leader of men, or a troublemaker. The fact that he had only one eye was not ideal for a scout, but Hayden was content that at least he had not had to order men on this perilous mission.

They had crossed the Narrows without casualties, except for one old donkey which had drowned. The City soldiers muttered that this was a bad omen. A lot of things were considered bad luck among City troops, the general had learned in recent days. A snake in your path was a bad omen, though in the Petrassi army it was a portent of great good fortune. Bafflingly, mice were also thought to bring ill luck, but as the creatures were not seen far from the City this had scarcely been a problem.

Casmir and Shivers set out at dawn. Hayden had ordered them to take a circuitous route, avoiding enemy troops who might still be on the south bank of the Narrows waiting for them to cross. The pair were charged with locating the army, assessing its direction of march – now scarcely in doubt – and its number and complement.

The two scouts returned separately the next day. Shivers, though he had the reputation of a surly bastard, according to Stern, arrived at dawn full of news. The enemy generals had split the army in two. One part, including most of the cavalry, was heading due south, the other marching straight for the north wall of the City and probably the Great North Gate. He guessed the latter number at forty thousand men. Most of the wagons were also going that way, including the remaining cannon. Their intent was clear: to attack the north of the City and, probably, the breach in the Adamantine Wall to the south.

It was late in the day when Casmir returned, mounted on a piebald gelding, grinning with success. He had been trailing the enemy force southward. They were travelling fast, he said, but had taken time to obliterate three villages in their path, small villages struggling to recover since the end of the previous war. He had found only corpses: men, women and children. More than a hundred in all. The horse he had ridden back had wandered in during the night and when the sun rose that morning had been cropping grass nearby. Casmir saw it as a good sign and Hayden could not but agree.

'How much ground are they covering each day?' he asked.

Fifty leagues, the two scouts agreed after a brief discussion. Casmir added, 'The southern army is staying far to the east of the walls, out of sight of the City.'

'Very well,' said Hayden, 'then I need another volunteer.'

This time several of the warriors showed their hands and the general chose Casmir, who had already shown good judgement and had brought them a horse.

'Are you a fast rider, Casmir?'

'Yes, lord.'

'Then I want you to ride to the City and take a vital message to the empress.'

The one-eyed man gave the ghost of a smile.

The general told him, 'I will write a message and you will take it to— which gate, Stern?' Although Hayden knew the geography of the City better than most of its soldiers.

'The Paradise Gate is closest to the Shield,' said Stern.

'Then head for the Paradise Gate, soldier. We must get information to the White Palace on our position and number, and ask the empress to send help, reinforcements if possible, and weapons. Take this,' he struggled to pull a heavy carnelian ring from his finger, 'and the empress will recognize you have come from me.'

Casmir took the ring and put it in his pouch. Then he stood waiting, his single dark eye expressionless. Hayden was suddenly unsure he could trust this man, but the decision had been made and he rarely went back on a decision made. That was one of the things the general considered bad luck.

He squatted down and dug out paper and a quill from deep in his pack, unwrapping them from their waterproof bindings. In the last light of the westering sun he wrote a few words informing Archange of the number of the enemy force and its probable intent. He warned of the cannon, and told of his plan to stay in the rear of the army and harry it with his small force. He rolled up the paper and put it in a wooden message cylinder. Casmir was eating and drinking and the horse was being fed and watered. By nightfall he was ready, now clad in a black jacket decorated with silver which shone in the light of the campfire.

'Good luck to you, soldier,' Hayden said, handing him the cylinder. 'Your mission is vital. The Immortal will be eternally grateful to you.'

He watched as the one-eyed soldier rode out of sight, filled with misgivings.

As Casmir rode slowly south on the long leagues of undulating grasslands that stretched between the Narrows and the north walls of the City, he marvelled at the varied hands fate had dealt him, both glorious and appalling. He had plumbed the depths in torment and degradation more than once, and pleaded to the death gods for release. Yet, just as he had struggled, maimed and traumatized, back to the City twenty years ago after losing his eye, then forged a brilliant career as agent to one of the City's great lords, so this time he had survived the cruellest torture and been chosen by the empress for vital work.

And, although that did not work out, here he was, a free man with a horse, with food and water and the liberty to go anywhere he wished – as long as it was away from the battling armies.

Yet he carried on riding towards the Paradise Gate.

He took out the general's ring and looked at it in the starlight. It was clearly valuable. He put it on. He had been tempted to throw the message away as soon as he was out of sight of the camp yet the cautious part of his nature got the better of him and he kept the wooden cylinder nestled in the breast of his jacket. It was always good to keep your options open. He could certainly never go near the empress – he was not only a messenger of bad tidings, always a perilous role, but he would have to admit failing in his duty to abduct a helpless girl. The empress would have him executed or, worse, return him to the pitiable state in which she had found him. He was not sure she could do this but he was not willing to risk it.

For all he had done, Casmir thought of himself as a man of honour. Any deaths he had caused, by his own hand or those of his agents, had been in the service of the City, its generals and lords. He did not kill lightly and he did not kill women. In fact he had no interest in women at all, another result from the terrible events which had cost him his eye. He had always enjoyed the company of soldiers. And he had been surprised and, perhaps, a little moved when the unfortunate Shivers, in a fit of comradeship, had given him his own jacket before he set off.

Neither of the two scouts had told the general the full detail of their adventures. They had merely reported their findings in the laconic way expected of them. Shivers would no doubt be regaling his fellows with tales of his heroism while they sat round the campfire that night. Casmir regretted a little that he was not there.

The pair had stayed together at first. They had been unlucky to meet an enemy scout almost immediately – or rather, it had been the scout's ill luck. They had slit his throat and moved on and as they neared the foreign army they were surprised by two more of the enemy. It was a gallant, if short skirmish. Shivers proved a ferocious fighter fuelled, Casmir guessed, by long-held rage. But at one point the disfigured man had dropped his sword, his arm briefly paralysed by a blow to the bicep. Casmir had spotted his predicament and, stepping back briefly from his own fight, had thrown his knife at the other opponent's head. It was a poor throw – he was out of practice – but it rattled the enemy's helm and gave Shivers a heartbeat in which to grab his sword from the ground and bring it up to gut the man. Casmir, distracted, had nearly lost his arm to a vicious sword-thrust, but he had swerved at the last moment and the sword had ripped through his jacket, tearing off the sleeve.

Hence – Casmir guessed, for Shivers had said not a word – the gift. It was a splendid jacket of black leather and silver, much like the uniform of the Thousand. It had clearly been in battle and had suffered a clean sword-cut to one arm and a tear on the shoulder, but someone had rubbed off the worst of the blood. Casmir suspected Shivers had stolen it from a cadaver, which in no way lessened its value. It fitted Casmir perfectly, far better than his old one, and would also fit his future status as a man of wealth and power. He would return to the City, sell the general's ring, and retrieve his savings from his banker in Otaro. Then he would assume a new name, buy a house and perhaps marry a woman of breeding. He would give up the sword and live a life of ease.

But still he carried on riding towards the Paradise Gate.

He had decided that he would fulfil his mission – he was a man of honour after all. But first, he thought, he must find a way to hand over the message without being escorted to the palace for questioning.

Casmir halted when the night became too dark to see his way. There was a cold breeze from the north but he found the new jacket well padded across the shoulders and he turned his back to the chill and slept as deeply as a child.

By the next night Hayden's warriors were camped five leagues north of the enemy, itself less than a league from the Great North Gate. The enemy was within sight of the walls, and by now the City would be aware of the approaching force and the watchers on the walls would be waiting. For Stern and his comrades the anticipation of seeing the City again, perhaps the next day, was almost unbearable. But because the enemy army now knew they were there, the possibility of attack was high and Hayden had sentries out as far as he dared. For one reason or another, he and his force would be getting no sleep that night.

Hayden was as weary as an old man can be who has walked all night and day. He lay back against his pack and closed his eyes, but he had no hope that sleep would claim him. He had slept less and less over the years, and not entirely due to the hard earth under his back. If asked, he would say simply that old men need less sleep than the young, but in truth it was because he fretted more. As a young general he would make his plans then lay his head down and sleep the sleep of the resolute. These days he picked and worried at his tactics, casting and recasting them in his head until his weary brain gave up and he fell into a brief, enervating slumber haunted by dreams of death.

The enemy might have little idea of the size of the

army that was dogging its bootsteps, but its generals would be expecting an attack on their powder wagons and they would expect it at dawn in the time-honoured way. So Hayden kept his band at a safe distance, far back on the rolling grasslands, for any outright assault now on the heavily guarded black powder would be suicide and, besides, doomed to failure. Instead they would wait and see what the enemy did. Would they launch an all-out attack on the gate or the walls? Would they hold back the heavy cannon or bring them up to begin the assault?

The only way Hayden's fighters could reach the powder wagons was by stealth, but stealth is difficult to achieve when your opponent is bristling with expectation. They were not only heavily guarded, the scouts reported, and taken into the very heart of the army, but they were protected from fire arrows by hastily built wooden screens. Opportunity might come once the enemy became engaged. The first action after a long and largely uneventful march would raise the blood, and excited soldiers were unobservant soldiers. Then would be the best time to infiltrate the enemy ranks.

Stern had volunteered for the covert mission, as Hayden knew he would, but the general refused him. Stern was proving too useful, not only in keeping his own men in order, but as a wise lieutenant. Hayden would not risk him on this perilous venture. Instead he chose one of his Petrassi, the infantryman Pieter Bly, and the City soldier Torix, a thin-faced, dour veteran. Each would follow a wide path round the foreign army then try to ease into its flanks, Bly on the left, Torix on the right. The enemy soldiers dug no latrines, like civilized troops, so it was common to see men leaving and joining the camp at will throughout the day. It was ill-disciplined, shambolic even, Hayden thought, and it would work to his advantage.

Hayden's men had taken uniforms from enemy bodies they had found on their journey. Black ash mixed with water would be drawn on the infiltrators' faces to mimic tattoos. Still they would scarcely survive the most cursory glance. They knew nothing of the enemy's symbols and insignia, their passwords or codes – if they used such things – and, of course, they could speak no word of the foreign tongue. It was frustrating, Hayden pondered, that they knew so little about the enemy though they had tracked them for many days.

Dawn arrived in a glory of scarlet and gold, signalling not only a new day but the start of the slow slide into winter. Taking a deep breath Hayden levered himself to his feet, knees complaining, back stiff. He stretched his spine, looking round at the ragged band of men and women who were rolling to their feet, griping, checking wounds and weapons and drinking from water skins, then he wandered over to where Stern and his brother were camped. Stern jumped up when Hayden approached.

'Walk with me,' the general said, beckoning two of his Petrassi officers to join them. What his own countrymen thought of Stern's presence at the general's meetings, and the fact that they were forced to speak the City tongue for that reason, Hayden could only guess. Adamus Brel and Josef Menier were professional men and Hayden wanted their experience and judgement. But he needed Stern.

'The wounded?' he asked, always his first question of the day, as the four men strolled out into the grasslands, the tall dry stalks whispering as their boots brushed by. Stern reported that the last few wounded were well on the mend after another night's rest. 'But five sick,' he added.

'Five?' asked Hayden, and Brel could not resist adding, 'I thought you City warriors never fell sick?'

Hayden frowned, feeling a worm of dread deep in his gut. This sickness, which had felled two men the previous day, was sudden and vicious, like nothing he had ever seen. The worst thing that could happen would be for it to spread.

Stern, ignoring Brel's barb, went on, 'Ague from the crossing, I expect. Or the enemy's food we've been eating.'

'The night scouts are back,' Brel told his general. 'Nothing to report. The army hasn't moved.'

Hayden was not surprised. On every day of their journey so far the enemy had been on the march before dawn. They were in a hurry. But now they would have to stop and plan. No amount of long-distance reports could make up for their first view of their target – the City walls.

'See that Bly and Torix are ready,' he ordered, 'although their wait may be long. There will come an opportunity, but we must be patient.' He felt little confidence when he said it.

'We could do with a diversion,' offered Stern.

Hayden nodded his agreement. 'I have several ideas in mind, but first we must find out what they are planning.' He did not share with them his fear that the three powder wagons might themselves be a diversion. Perhaps the barrels of powder had already been unloaded and distributed within the army. In which case the wagons they were watching and targeting were a distraction – and a trap.

It was a long, frustrating day. The enemy made no move. Hayden's army stayed in a state of anxious readiness. His scouts reported the enemy troops were breaking up the rafts and boats, laboriously carried from the Narrows, to build ladders. Hayden greeted that as excellent news. If they planned to use siege-ladders that meant they would not use cannon, at least not yet.

It was not long before dusk when Shivers returned from scouting with word that the enemy army was, at long last, preparing to move. The manoeuvre was a familiar one to Hayden. The army would creep forward under cover of darkness and at dawn the defenders on the walls would see forty thousand enemy soldiers spread out before them. It would startle briefly, but that was all. It was a dramatic gesture and Hayden wondered anew whose mind was behind it.

The two volunteers, Bly and Torix, petitioned the general to let them make a bid for the powder. Hayden thought long and hard. He would give them a better chance with a swift, simultaneous lightning attack on the rear of the enemy. He could send his fifty fleetest men, armed with knives. The enemy had no cavalry to speak of; they had all been sent south. How many infantrymen would the enemy generals waste chasing down fifty soldiers when the City walls were within sight? By midnight he had decided. The black powder was crucial to the enemy's plans. If he could destroy it all it was worth the lives of every one of his soldiers, if it came to that. He called his three lieutenants and explained his thinking. They nodded gravely. They knew it was a suicide mission, but none dissented.

'Where do we attack?' asked Stern. 'Our diversionary force.'

'The guards in charge of the cannon,' Hayden told them. 'The cannon cannot be harmed or, realistically, stolen. They are too heavy. And they are useless without the black powder. So they will leave their least able warriors to guard them – the fat and the slow and the stupid.'

'We cannot be certain of that, general,' Brel put in, looking worried.

'No, but we need a plausible target for our attack. We don't want it to *look* like a diversion. An attack on the cannon would indeed be foolish, but they don't know who we are, remember. We could indeed be fools.'

And he wondered privately if they were.

Stern was leading the diversionary attack. He had persuaded the general there was no other choice. The City soldiers would follow him and respect his orders. He could say that of no other warrior among them.

Benet had to stay behind. To Stern and the others the reason was obvious, but not to Benet.

'You cannot see,' Stern told his brother for the hundredth time. And at last, when he was sick of arguing, 'You'll condemn us all,' he said brutally. 'You'll be a liability. We can't look after you.'

'I don't need looking after,' Benet responded sulkily. 'I backed you up in that river, didn't I? I killed that fat oaf.'

'This is different. We need to be able to see well today.'

'I *can* see.' Benet looked around, ready to point out, yet again, what he could see. He pointed across the plain. 'I can see that bird, the one with the missing eyelash.'

Stern smiled dutifully, though the joke had long since lost any savour. He put his hand on his brother's shoulder.

'We'll both get through this,' he said. 'We'll both go home after it's over. Don't worry, you'll have your part to play. I'll see to it. But not today.'

'I don't want to stay back with the women,' Benet argued peevishly, but Stern saw that in his heart he'd admitted defeat.

'It's not just the women. Most of us are staying behind,' he explained. 'It's only the fastest that are going. And the bowmen.' Benet knew all this. He'd been told it over and over.

'Pigging bowmen,' he grumbled, as Stern had known he would.

He was dismayed when his brother suddenly threw his arms round him. His whiskers tickled Stern's ear as he whispered, 'Don't leave me, brother. You're right, I can't see. I'm almost blind.' His voice was rough with emotion.

Stern, filled with pity, assured him, 'Just this once. We'll stick together after this. You'll be all right, I promise.' Although it was a promise they both knew he could not give.

Now, as the first fingers of dawn reached across the plain, Stern waited, crouched in the long grass, which sighed in the stiff northerly breeze. He was dressed in light armour, just leather breastplate, kilt and cap, and he bore only two daggers, no sword. They would need to be nimble. He thought of the two infiltrators, Torix and Pieter Bly, now creeping towards the enemy flanks, and he brought his hand to his heart in invocation, praying that the gods of ice and fire would allow these heroes into the Gardens of Stone if it came to that. He had no idea what gods Bly or the other men of Petrus worshipped, but a hero was a hero in any country. He looked at the Petrassi captain, Brel, who knelt at his side. Brel gazed back, his brown eyes gleaming. Stern could see he wanted to make this a race – who could get to the enemy first. Brel acted as if he was in competition with Stern, though all the reward that awaited them, probably, was torment and death.

Stern's mind drifted to the timepiece Hayden had shown him days before. That would be useful now, his practical side thought, to coordinate our movements, though his superstitious side still shied away from its magic.

Again Brel glanced at him impatiently, silently urging him to give the order. Stern chose to wait a little – fifty more heartbeats, he thought, to give the two men time.

But the decision was made for him. He heard orders shouted in a foreign tongue, then a loud drumming and the thunder of thousands of boots running as the enemy army surged forward, banging their swords on their shields, chanting their chant of 'Death! Death! Death!' Stern arose silently from the whispering grass, signalled to his men and started running as fast and as quietly as possible towards the enemy rear. At first all he could see in front of him was shoulder-high grass, then an enemy flag, waving blackly in the breeze, then the shapes of wagons. Beyond he could make out, for the first time, the north wall of the City. Stern felt his heart lift, but he turned his eyes to his target.

The guards on the cannon were not the tattooed savages they had seen so far. They were well armoured but slow. Either Hayden was right or they were too busy watching the advance. The City men hit them hard. Stern slammed his blade in the neck of a man standing gawping in the other direction and dragged it out as he fell. Two others turned sluggishly. Stern slashed the throat of one and Brel drove his knife into the other's eye.

There were no more than twenty guards on the cannon and Stern's men overcame them in a matter of moments. But the alarm, a deep, resonating horn blast, sounded out and they knew then they were done for. Stern dived among the wagons, heart pounding, looking frantically for something to rob them of, something to sabotage – something that would make a difference. Surrounded by the clash of weapons on shields and armour, the grunt and cry of fighting men, he found the cannon. He stared at them helplessly, realizing he knew nothing about them. He tried lifting the end of one. Perhaps three or four men could steal it, if they had all the time in the world and no one was trying to kill them. Was there some way he could damage it? He could see none. They were just metal pipes, open at one end. Stern forgot them and climbed into the next wagon. Here he found the balls of iron and stone. Each was heavy but he could pick it up, and then what?

He heard the crunch of a boot and a shadow flickered on the edge of his sight. He ducked as a sword splintered the wood beside his head. He turned and smashed the cannon ball in the guard's face. Another man rose and he elbowed him in the jaw then crashed the cannon ball down on his helm. The man went down. A swordsman leaped up on to the cart, but Stern jumped down the other side and rolled under it then squirmed under the next one. When he came up again he was alone and he leaped on another wagon to see what was going on. All around him his comrades were outnumbered by a company of infantry, but the enemy were hampered by their armour and the closely marshalled wagons which snagged their swords. His men relied on speed and agility and sharp knives. Stern looked south towards the City.

He paused, his heart thumping loud in his ears, as he saw the grey walls rising out of the churning sea of armed men. The clamour around him seemed to fade and for a long heartbeat he could feel the familiar stones of the City under his feet, taste its air on his tongue, hear the din of the crowds, smell the stink of the streets – the shit and corruption and death, but also the bread baking and the good ale and the perfume of women. In that moment he knew he would never return. He turned his back.

Their job of distraction was done, he decided. Those enemy eyes not on the wall would be turned to Stern and his comrades and not, hopefully, on the powder wagons. They had given Torix and Bly the best they could offer without all dying in the cause. He bellowed 'Back!' and jumped off the wagon. 'Back! Back! Back!' he yelled. His men took off, those who were still able, and ran for their lives. Stern felt the wind in his face, his chest heaving. Any moment he expected to feel an arrow, or a sword, smash into his spine. He glanced back. They were making headway, opening the gap with the chasing enemy. They came to the first marker, a sword stuck in the ground with a helm on it, and he shouted, 'Down!' Every man dropped like a stone, and the twenty bowmen rose up from the grass in front of them to shoot at the chasing men. *One, two, three, four, five*, Stern counted then he was off running again. 'Back! Back! Back!' he yelled and his men ran with him, the bowmen too. He came to the second marker and he yelled, 'Bowmen!' He and his men carried on running and the archers turned and peppered the advancing enemy with five more volleys of arrows. Then they ran again.

He could see the third marker up ahead. Stern's chest was heaving painfully. He wasn't used to running and his legs seemed huge and heavy. As he reached the marker he slowed gratefully and turned to face the remaining enemy. Then the rest of Hayden's army, the camp-followers and the lame and sick, rose from the grasses on either side and ran screaming to attack the enemy flanks with whatever weapons they had. Stern felt a sword-hilt thrust into his hand and he raced back, fatigue forgotten. He gutted one man and slit the throat of a second. As the enemy's blood sprayed, Stern's fizzed in his veins.

It was a short fight. The chasing soldiers outnumbered them, barely, but they were exhausted by running in armour and were no match for the City warriors, full of blood-lust and out for vengeance.

When it was over and the enemy survivors started

backing, then running, to the safety of their army, Hayden took a lighted brand from the fire they'd built and thrust it into the long grass. The wind from the north was brisk and the dry grasses quickly caught, and the roaring flames raced towards the enemy horde.

Under the cover of smoke Hayden and his ragtag army set off north-east, the able supporting the injured. By nightfall they came to the campsite their scouts had picked out the previous day. They slumped down, tired but jubilant. As they tended the wounded, Brel reported that they had lost only fourteen to the enemy's estimated one hundred-odd. A good day's work, but Hayden would only consider the action a success when they heard the powder wagons explode. They waited and listened. As time passed jubilation turned to anxiety, then fear for their two comrades.

That night a storm came in from the west, rough winds and sheeting rain. Hayden and his officers sat crouched under a makeshift shelter and watched the south, waiting for Torix and Pieter Bly to return. But they never came.

CHAPTER THIRTY-NINE

THE PATCHWORK GULON SAT IN THE CORNER OF A palace storeroom dismantling a pigeon. The bird's dry, dusty feathers made the creature cough and it looked at Valla each time it did so, as if in apology.

It was the gulon which had forced Valla to sleep with the stores. Although she was not a member of any of the centuries she still wore the black and silver armour, and the leader of the Silver Bears grudgingly allowed her to use their barracks. But the presence of the gulon, in the short time each day Valla left the empress to sleep, was repugnant to the other soldiers. They had heard the tale of its revival from near-death and, rather than valuing it as Valla thought they might, they glared at it suspiciously and made protective signs against evil when it was near. They did not mistreat it, they did not dare, but in the end Valla moved her straw mattress into a storeroom behind the palace kitchens so she would not have to endure their superstition and resentment.

The creature had recovered from its ordeal and now, Valla thought, the bald patch on its head seemed smaller and its ears less ragged. Was it younger? Was *she*? She was ready to believe it now she had experienced the empress's power to heal. She had already seen Marcellus' gift of destruction and she was in awe of the Serafim and content to believe they were gods, if earthly ones.

News came daily to the White Palace and each day it was worse. First the enemy had laid siege to the Great North Gate, then a second force attacked the Paradise Gate. And it was feared that a third army was marching on the Adamantine Breach, which still lay open and vulnerable almost a year since the flood which had destroyed the wall and the south of the City.

And the blackest rumours whispered that plague – that most terrifying of enemies – had broken out among the defenders of the two Great Gates.

People were fleeing the City. Roads in the south were crowded with the carriages of the rich and merchants' carts, and the poor with their goods piled on donkeys or their own backs, all trying to get to the Seagate to escape by boat. 'Cowards!' Archange would cry when she heard this, and those around her agreed, but Valla kept her own counsel, thinking it was all well and good to be defiant of war and pestilence when it was so far away from this monotonous life on the mountain.

Valla thrilled at the prospect of marching into battle again. She hoped she could win permission to leave the old woman's side, to use her old skills in the service of the City, but knew it would not be allowed. Archange had made it clear when she permitted her to don the black and silver livery again: Valla was to be the empress's body servant. It was a position of great honour, but Valla was already chafing against its bonds.

She could only stand guarding the empress and watch, with some contempt, the trivialities the old woman must endure. People were always seeking audience with Archange – warriors, counsellors, merchants and common folk. And even in time of war a part of the empress's day was spent discussing drainage, or imports of stone and timber, or the celebration of the many and various festivals. This morning she was required to slaughter ten white doves to please the goddess Vashta as her reign of long nights approached.

And as the days crawled by Valla began to fear for Archange herself, for she saw her at those times when few others did, when she awoke from a doze, confused and disorientated, or when drained by a day of endless duties. And now, as the days drew in, the empress seemed to sicken. She looked older and smaller. She walked, if she stood at all, leaning on one of her guards or servants. Her eyes were dull, without vitality or depth. Her granddaughter Thekla was now resident in the palace and the pair spent long hours together, when even Valla was excluded.

Valla learned that the old counsellor Dol Salida had taken on much of the empress's routine work, but the man was dead now, murdered, it was believed, by the same intruders who had killed the security chief. Archange's other close confidant Evan Broglanh had gone missing back in the summer, no one knew where. The only people Archange confided in these days were the granddaughter and a black-eyed lord called Jona Lee Gaeta who had slithered into Dol Salida's place. This Jona was silent of foot and quiet of voice and he had a stillness about him – like a black cat guarding a mousehole – which Valla found disquieting. Scuttlebutt among the soldiers said the Gaetas had mystical powers, and she had seen invocations to the gods of ice and fire made behind Jona's back. The Iron Palace, the Gaeta home on the south-west face of the Shield, was a place where, it was said, few went in and even fewer came out.

Meanwhile Rubin languished in the cells under sentence of death. As the days trickled by, Valla found it increasingly hard to believe that, with the City under such dire threat, Archange would fulfil her intention of having him dragged down the mountain to Amphitheatre for formal butchery. A treacherous thought stole into her mind, that on the day before the execution, if Archange had still not relented, Valla could somehow free him herself. The very idea made her sweat, not because she feared the empress's wrath, though she did, but because every moment of her life since she had first donned armour had been devoted to the City and its ruler. If she defied that ruler's orders now, then what meaning did her life have?

In the time that was left to him, there was little she could do but ensure Rubin got enough to eat. She was not permitted to see him.

'Valla!' a soldier yelled. The empress was awake and Valla's day began. She rose and buckled on her sword-belt and snatched up her helm. She glanced at the gulon, which had paused in its meal to look up at her, then she left.

Archange would normally tolerate only one armed guard while she was alone, and then only when she was awake and in her day rooms, although a dozen were always on alert close by. When Valla was given the role she had been filled with pride, but as the days passed pride had swiftly been subsumed beneath frustration. Now the City was under threat and the very air seemed thick with dread, Valla wanted to be close to the heart of the action as she had been as a Warhound.

The night guards had nothing to report as they went off duty. Valla found Archange in her parlour, lying on her couch by the window. She seemed half-asleep. Thekla was with her and as Valla entered she looked up. 'Soldier, help me get the empress to her bed.'

Valla, feeling a little awkward laying hands on her, slid one arm under the old woman's shoulders and one under her knees and lifted her carefully. It was like carrying a bag of bones and Valla was fearful of damaging her. Archange seemed scarcely conscious, her eyes narrow slits, her breathing shallow. She was as cold as death.

'She must have been up all night,' Thekla said softly. 'She is exhausted.'

Valla carried the empress to her bedroom and laid her gently on the huge bed. Thekla covered her with rich quilts. Then Valla took her place by the door.

In the harsh light of dawn Archange's face was gaunt, her eyes set in shadow. She was muttering to herself and Valla made out the words, 'The veil. Bring me the veil.'

'I cannot get it for you,' Thekla whispered to her. 'It is gone.'

'I need it.' The old woman struggled feebly to sit up and her granddaughter gently pushed her down. 'Here, take a healing tisane.' She proffered a cup.

But Archange, in a surge of anger and of strength, smashed it from her hand. 'Where is the veil?' she demanded.

Thekla lowered her voice and murmured words Valla could not hear. They seemed to calm the old woman and she lay back and drifted off. Thekla picked up the broken pieces, then she sat down again, watching her grandmother.

Valla wondered what ailed the empress. Was it just old age or was she ill? She wondered why Archange did not heal herself as she had healed others. Perhaps she could not, for why use her power to heal a humble beast rather than herself?

'Soldier?' Thekla was looking at her.

'Yes, lady?'

'What is your name? You are always here.'

'Valla, lady.'

'Valla, do not speak of anything you see or hear.'

'No, lady. But . . .'

'Yes?'

'May I get this veil for her? I will, if it is within my power.'

'No, it is lost.'

'Then can another be made?'

Thekla shook her dark curls. 'It is not a simple thing. The Gulon Veil is an ancient artefact of great power used down the centuries to heal and to preserve. It cannot be remade or replaced, like this broken cup.' She watched the old woman. 'Without it the empress can heal but it takes a toll on her. You would not understand.'

Annoyed at the slight, Valla bit her tongue then said respectfully, 'I know of the Immortal's power, lady. She healed me of a grievous injury. I owe her my strength and my life. I would help her if I could.'

Thekla turned to her, her grey eyes piercing. 'She healed you?'

'Yes, lady. And the gulon.' She flushed. The woman would think her a fool. But Thekla just nodded.

'Yes, she told me about it. I thought she was wrong to save the creature at the expense of her own strength. But Archange can be . . . sentimental. The gulon is an ancient beast.'

Valla thought Archange as sentimental as a stone wolf, but she asked, 'You know the creature?'

'I know of it. I believe it is the gulon which once pursued my cousin Saroyan, to her great annoyance.' She smiled slightly.

Valla asked, 'Why did it follow her?'

Thekla shrugged. 'Who knows what is in such a beast's mind? But the empress was fond of Saroyan and perhaps she healed it for that reason. Or,' she added, 'perhaps because it is the only thing in the palace as old as she.'

Valla looked at the empress, who now slept quietly.

'Will she die?' she asked softly.

Thekla looked up at her. 'That is a question many people would like the answer to.'

Giulia Rae Khan had not died. Much as she had wished it. After the heart seizure sparked by her brother's death she had lain close to death herself for days but eventually her scarred heart had assumed its proper rhythm, her rich Serafim blood flowed more powerfully through her veins, and she accepted that she must live a while longer.

As she lay propped up in her bed watching the road to the north, she had hoped there had been some fearful mistake, or mischief by the enemy, and that one day Marcus would come riding back. She had been parted from him often enough before, during her short, bitter marriage to Marcellus and Marcus' own wretched liaisons, and while he was away fighting and during her year-long voyage. But they had always been together in their hearts, and they always knew they would be reunited because each of them was more precious to the other than any short-lived spasm of the heart or loins.

Now she had admitted she must go on living, Giulia decided she would act the part, so one bright morning she ordered a hearty breakfast and turned her face to the world again.

When told Fiorentina had been abducted her first reaction had been 'good riddance'. But she quickly resumed her normal way of approaching life and decided this offence against her could not stand. She demanded to see Jona Lee Gaeta but was informed he was in attendance on the empress. Giulia had told no one else of the girl's pregnancy, and Jona would have no advantage in kidnapping her himself, so her eye turned, as ever, to Archange as the mover behind this outrage.

She told her servants she was leaving the palace and ordered her favourite horse saddled. This provoked an outbreak of anxiety among her old retainers, but eventually she was dressed in warm riding clothes and mounted on her favourite gelding.

She looked around with interest as the horse clopped up the Shell Path trailed by her guard of six. Labourers hard at work mending storm damage pulled off their caps and bowed their heads as she rode past. Old men most of them, they knew her and treated her with the respect she was due. She gazed out over the City as the gelding climbed higher and, for the first time since Marcus' death, she smiled. She had been told of the vast army at the northern gates but this did not trouble her. She did not fear death. Perhaps these foreign invaders, whoever they were, would bring Archange to account for her crimes. An emperor's murder, much as Giulia had disliked Araeon, should not go unpunished.

When the Serafia came into sight she halted, a variety of emotions churning through her heart. It was beautiful, perhaps the most beautiful creation of them all. It seemed to float on its mountain-top, its multitude of white spires narrowing to needle-points which appeared to pierce the dome of the sky. Some towers were connected to the rest of the palace by fragile, fairy bridges which seemed to fly across under some mysterious power of their own. A pair of eagles soared among the towers, their wings tipping to catch the thermals.

When Giulia rode up the gates were closed, all was quiet. She could see no one on the walls. The only movement was the eagles high above. She gestured to Amylas, the leader of her guard, and he dismounted and pounded on the gates with his mailed fist. In response there was only silence. Irritably she nodded to the soldier and he hammered again, long and hard. They waited.

Finally the silence was broken by the sound of shifting timbers and the gates shivered. A crack appeared in the centre and one gate opened enough for a man to sidle through. It was a common soldier, who regarded them silently.

'I am the lady Giulia Rae Khan,' she told him, thinking him a rough oaf who would not recognize her. 'I wish to see the empress.'

'The empress is seeing no one,' he replied.

He began to retreat and she rapped out, 'The empress will speak to me, soldier. Tell her I'm here.'

The soldier ducked back behind the gate, which closed. They waited in silence, Giulia fuming. Then at last the gate opened again. This soldier was tall and fair and was a commander of the Thousand, Giulia noted with approval.

'My regrets, lady Giulia, but the empress is seeing no one.'

'Where is the child!' she burst out, containing her anger no longer. 'Tell Archange I know she has stolen the baby.'

He frowned. 'There is no baby in the White Palace,' he told her, a picture of calm indifference. 'I can vouch for that. Would you like me to deliver a message to the Immortal?'

The use of this title infuriated Giulia.

'The Immortal!' she spat, losing her temper entirely. 'I knew Archange when she was nobody, a slut who'd spread her legs for any man to further her ambition. She's a malevolent, scheming bitch. Always has been. That's the message you can deliver to her, soldier!'

Then she threw her head back. 'Where's the baby, Archange?' she yelled as loud as her old lungs could manage. 'Where's the whore's sister? Have you killed them both already?' Her screams bounced off the walls and echoed round the towers and came back to them like the cries of distant gulls.

The soldier retreated and the white gates closed again and all was silent.

Giulia clutched her hammering heart. 'Bitch,' she spat, turning the horse's head for home.

Even Fiorentina did not know where she was. Unconscious, she had been brought to this prison room and left. She and Alafair had been there for many days, with no explanation and no visitors apart from the silent thug of a guard who brought their food. It was decent food, but she found it hard to eat. She had long since lost any appetite for putting food into her already crowded body. Fiorentina had demanded the guard bring her his superior, but he had ignored her and she wondered if he could even speak. She had once been told, perhaps by Rafe, that the guards in the dungeons of Gath had their tongues ripped out to stop them conspiring with prisoners. Her thoughts dwelled constantly on such atrocities.

Fiorentina assumed she had been kidnapped and was being kept alive for the baby she carried – she could see no other reason. Thus she would remain unharmed until the birth. After all, if her captors had wanted the child dead they could have killed them both at the Khans' palace. But once the boy was born, would they need her? The thought of death did not worry her – her days were a lifeless void without her husband and anyone could bring up the baby. But she wanted at least to see the boy born, to look into his small face, to see her lord made flesh again. Then she would die content.

In her mind she constantly counted and recounted the days since the child's conception. She knew she was long overdue. Alafair guessed it too; Fiorentina saw the fear in the girl's eyes when she contemplated her distended belly. Alafair was worried about helping the baby into the world, for it was something she had never done before, and she had confided her anxiety to her mistress. But there was something more. As the pregnancy stretched on and on, unnaturally, a disquiet grew between them that they never discussed.

One night she awoke, her heart racing in her breast.

Moonlight flooded the room and in its silvery path, at the end of her bed, stood a small, wizened woman with wild white hair. She was tiny but her eyes were huge in her lined face and they spoke of an indomitable will. She grinned toothily and scuttled to the side of the bed. She reached out long, curved nails like knives and touched Fiorentina's belly. Fiorentina, bloated and helpless in her final days of pregnancy, could only cry out feebly but Alafair, curled up on the couch, slept on.

The old crone whispered, 'Is he like his father? Is he dead in there, girl?' Fiorentina cringed away from the sharp talons.

Then the woman was gone, and only the bright moonlight marching through the casement was left to disturb her.

But as she turned over awkwardly before drifting off again, Fiorentina saw a man's face looking at her through the bars in the door. Believing she was still dreaming, she slept. But when she awoke the next morning Fiorentina was convinced the watcher had been Marcellus.

CHAPTER FORTY

THE END OF SUMMER CAME QUICKLY AND WHEN IT arrived there was barely time for autumn. The long hot days had seemed endless, but when they stopped and the cold and rain swept in, well, that soon seemed endless too.

The invading armies, camped outside two of the Great Gates, celebrated the rain, for their leaders had found it difficult to keep eighty thousand men watered on their long journey south. The lands they came from were cold as charity and the winds that howled across the steppes were seen as a manifestation of their warriors' strength and relentless endurance.

The City troops defending the Great North Gate were sheltered from the worst of the storms and the biting cold made little difference to their days, which were spent manning the battlements, dodging enemy arrows as they dislodged the invaders' flimsy ladders, and building up defensive walls behind the gate should the enemy break through. They had been warned of the threat of cannon, though the common soldier was inclined to disbelieve a threat he had never seen and could not imagine; he thought the towering gate, built of reinforced timbers as thick as a man's thigh, was impregnable.

The forces defending the Paradise Gate, facing east, were less fortunate. The wind and rain from the north whipped through them by day, as they worked tirelessly to move giant blocks of stone, dismantling buildings, reinforcing the gate and creating a killing field behind it, and at night as they tried vainly to sleep, hunkered down behind any shelter they could find.

In the far south of the City, at the ruined Adamantine Wall, work went on feverishly long into the night regardless of weather. Rebuilding was impossible to achieve quickly. A long stretch of the wall from the Raven Tower to beyond the Isingen Tower had been demolished by the unleashing of the reservoirs and would take years to reconstruct. So a decision had been made to excavate a defensive ditch in front of the ruins. This work moved quickly but the ditch kept filling with water, for the land was low-lying, and engineers were brought in from the suspended work on the site of the Red Palace to design drainage pipes and canals to the nearby river.

Trees were still in full leaf when rain-heavy winds started battering in from the west, and the last trees in the City which had not already been chopped up for firewood or building succumbed to the gales and were brought south for the vital work on the defences.

Rubin learned all this as he languished in his prison cell in the White Palace, high above the City. He spent his time staring out of the small window at the relentless rain and the grey sky. His food was brought by an old soldier, a stout man, one-eyed and garrulous, who enjoyed nothing more than relaying the rumours he had heard of the invading army's moves and the plans of the defenders. Rubin listened to everything he was told and tried to sort out fact from gossip. The guard, whose name was Gallan, claimed thousands of people were leaving the City – those who were able – and heading west across the sea. The rich, he said scornfully, were the first to go, then mothers and children of the merchant class, sent abroad in numbers never seen throughout the long war.

Rubin still hoped the invading army was Marcellus' work and he daydreamed that one day his cell door would fly open and his lord would be standing there, chiding Rubin for falling foul of Archange despite his best advice. Rubin's faith that Marcellus lived was strong but the best part of a year had passed now since his lord had departed the City and Rubin wondered if he still planned to return and, if so, what he was waiting for. And in his secret heart he doubted that even Marcellus could have raised such an army in that time.

What bothered him above all was why Marcellus, or any invader come to that, would not march directly south and enter the City by the Adamantine Breach? Why hammer on the front and side doors when the back door is lying open?

He had been in the cell for ten days and was fast asleep when the door opened. Rubin bolted awake, heart pounding. Was this to be a covert, midnight execution? Had the empress changed her mind? He scrambled up, looking around in the gloom for something to defend himself with, but there was nothing.

'Rubin?' a voice asked. A tall thin man stood in the doorway, face lit vividly by the lantern he held up. Rubin, squinting, was sure he knew him, but he couldn't remember from where. He sounded hesitant, unthreatening, and Rubin's heartbeat slowed a tad.

'It's me . . . Elija,' said the visitor, stepping one pace into the cell.

Rubin peered at him, scarcely able to believe it was his friend from so long ago in the Halls. Then he grinned in relief and recognition and Elija smiled back.

He was carrying a pile of books under one arm and he looked around then dumped them on the floor.

'What are you doing here?' Rubin asked, clapping his old friend on the shoulder. It seemed a miracle. He had never expected to see Elija or his sister again. In truth, he'd thought them long dead. Neither seemed to possess the strength or resilience to survive long in the Halls. Yet the boy was just as he remembered him, still watchful and anxious, though taller and better fed.

Elija lowered his eyes, looking sheepish. 'I live here now. With Emly.'

This was so unexpected that Rubin was startled into silence for a moment. Then, 'You live here in the White Palace?' he repeated, amazed. 'Are you servants?'

Elija laughed, and Rubin could see the character the years had drawn on his face.

'No. We are . . . I don't know what we are,' Elija confessed, shaking his head. 'We were adopted by Archange, I suppose.'

Rubin could only stare. 'Why?' What strange turn of fate could have brought the pair from the very depths of the City to its dizzy heights?

Elija grinned, perhaps sharing his friend's puzzlement. Then he told Rubin of their life, his and Emly's, after they left the Halls, and how Em's fortunes had become enmeshed with those of the empress. 'But Archange cares little for me,' he said.

Rubin listened, first with fascination then mounting impatience. 'Can you tell me,' he interrupted, 'about Indaro? They say she killed the emperor.'

Elija told him about the events of the Day of Summoning. 'I did not see her do it – I was not there – but I know many who did. It is true, Rubin, but—'

Rubin sank down on the bed, his mind in uproar. 'I thought,' he said bleakly, 'my sister fought *for* the City.'

'She *did*,' Elija said earnestly. 'She *saved* the City.'

Rubin snorted. 'Does it look saved to you? Do you ever go down there?'

Elija argued stoutly, 'But the war ended because of them, Indaro and Fell and their friends. The Blues have all marched away. Indaro was a hero. You should be proud of her.'

'She murdered the emperor yet you call her a hero,' Rubin said scornfully. Elija did not argue but he turned away as if about to leave.

Rubin did not want to fall out with his old friend. He asked, 'How did you know I was here?'

Elija slid his back down the wall and sat on the floor. 'No one tells me anything, but eventually I get to hear most of the gossip. I heard soldiers talking, then I spoke to Gallan, your guard. It was Gallan who let me in here. I told him we were old friends. He's a good man.'

Then he asked, 'What were *you* doing, sneaking around the palace?'

Rubin told Elija his own story. 'I came here to find my father,' he finished. 'And here I am, under sentence of death.' The retelling of the tale had made him miserable. Why had he come here? If he hadn't, he would never have heard of Indaro's treachery. And he would not be about to die.

'I will ask the empress to reprieve you,' Elija said, but the words sounded tentative and Rubin was sceptical. 'You say she cares little for you,' he retorted. 'Why would she pay any attention?'

Elija face fell. 'I can try,' he said. He looked up at the window. 'It's nearly morning. I must go. I don't want to get Gallan into trouble. I will come back if I can.'

After he had left Rubin stared glumly at the pile of books. He didn't have the heart to pick them up. The news about Indaro had crushed him. He had clung to the hope that he had been lied to, but there was no reason for Elija to lie and Rubin was forced to accept it was the truth. As the day of his death loomed, he tried to contemplate it with acceptance, hoping only that it would happen quickly.

Nevertheless, the night before his dawn execution he lay sleepless, black thoughts fluttering tirelessly round his mind. When he heard the soft sound of boots in the corridor outside a gut-wrenching panic seized hold. He could not breathe. He could not move. The cell door opened and a soldier stood in the doorway lit by a lantern.

'Rubin, come with me,' he commanded.

Rubin stayed frozen in place, and the soldier said more gently, 'I mean you no harm. Come quickly.'

Rubin saw it was Darius Hex. Curiosity forced its way past his terror, and he wondered if the palace's senior commander would fetch him to his execution. He felt around on the floor for his boots, hope flickering weakly. Darius, unarmoured and clad in riding leathers, seemed to be alone. 'Be silent,' he said, handing him the lantern. This simple gesture – giving him a potential weapon – reassured Rubin more than words.

The soldier led him at a swift pace through the labyrinth of the palace until they emerged suddenly into open air and Rubin saw they were in the great courtyard. It was seething with men and their mounts and lit by the hectic light of torches. Voices were hushed and horses reined in, but Rubin felt a barely suppressed charge. The men of the First Adamantine, the Nighthawks, had been confined in the palace for too long and their excitement was tangible as they made ready to ride. The air was icy cold and smoky with the breath of horses. Dawn gleamed pinkly in the east.

At the sight of Darius the riders' elation grew and

there were brief bursts of laughter, quickly stifled. Horses shifted and snorted, eager to be off. Darius' mount was brought up, saddled and packed with war gear. A second beast was led before Rubin, and he was handed a leather jerkin and a thick cloak which he pulled on gratefully. He speculated, not without concern, where he was being taken, though the morning chill and the prospect of riding were energizing. He took a deep breath of free air, redolent with the scent of horses and leather.

'Where are we going?' he asked as he mounted. As his foot met the stirrup the horse stood stock still, shifting its weight slightly once Rubin was aboard. The Nighthawks boasted that their horses were the best trained among the City's cavalry.

'The Nighthawks are riding to the Paradise Gate,' Darius informed him, climbing into the saddle. He pulled on his gauntlets and looked around at the milling horses and riders with pride. The remaining men mounted and there was a moment of stillness, of thrilling anticipation.

'Has the empress reprieved me?' Rubin persisted, wondering if Elija's petition on his behalf had won his freedom.

'No,' the commander replied shortly, then he signalled his men and the Nighthawks started to stream out of the palace gates.

They rode slowly down the Shell Path. It was perilous at the best of times and the violent storms had washed away long stretches. The riders passed teams of labourers, working by the light of blazing torches, who stood aside and watched them, leaning on their shovels. The Nighthawks clattered by and some of the workmen shouted to them, whether curses or cheers Rubin could not tell.

At the base of the Shield they had to wait while

Darius' second spoke to the gatekeepers, then the great bronze gates cranked slowly open. Rubin looked around him, revelling in the prospect of freedom. He wondered if the Nighthawks' commander was being sent to fight as punishment for the breach in the White Palace's security.

'Did you chase down all the intruders?' he asked him.

'One of them escaped. We are still searching for him,' Darius replied, watching the gates. 'Seven died, two captured.'

'Did you get anything out of them?'

Darius shook his head. 'We questioned them but they just cursed us in their own tongue. In the end we took them to the top of the highest shaft.' He shrugged. 'The threat was clear, whether they spoke the City tongue or not: they would be thrown down the shaft if they did not give us information by any means possible. One was stalwart,' he said, kicking his horse into a walk once the gates were open, 'and was cast down. The other,' he looked around as they trotted side by side through the base town, 'he cried and grovelled when he saw his friend's fate, but he could not speak to us, or would not. So he was thrown down too.'

Rubin, who had climbed one of the interminable shafts, his body trembling with fatigue and fear, shuddered. 'It is a terrible fate. Did Archange approve it?'

'The empress was present throughout,' Darius said, glancing at him coldly in the dawn light.

Not far down the road the commander reined in his horse beside an old man trudging along alone, away from the mountain. When the man looked up Rubin saw it was his guard Gallan. Darius leaned down from the saddle and handed him a money pouch. The guard nodded and thanked him. He nodded to Rubin too as he rode past and Rubin saluted him. It was dawning on him for the first time that he had not been released. The guard must have been paid to get to a place of safety before Archange realized her prisoner had gone.

'Why have you brought me with you?' he asked Darius. 'Am I being taken to die on the walls?'

'Elija spoke to me,' the commander answered, his eyes on the road ahead. 'He told me you saved his and Emly's lives when they were young. And were it not for them, Archange would not now be sitting on the Immortal Throne.'

Rubin waited but that seemed to be all he was going to say, so he asked, 'Does the empress know I'm gone?'

But Darius ignored the question. He was standing in the stirrups, shouting to his troopers. Rubin could only assume he had been snatched away from under Archange's nose. Had the Nighthawks also left the palace without her knowledge or permission? If so, it seemed Darius Hex was no longer in fear of the empress. Perhaps, Rubin thought, the soldier did not expect to survive to face her wrath.

There was a stiff breeze coming from the east. Soon after they left the Shield they could make out the distant din of battle, although the Paradise Gate was a half-day's ride away. Rubin had not been in battle since the lance-thrust had nearly taken his life at Needlewoman's Notch, and the far-off sounds, the cries and clash of war, made his stomach clench. By midday the horses were closing on the gate and anticipation rose among the riders. Unlike Rubin, they relished the prospect of a fight. The atmosphere now became dense with the sounds of battle; the very air seemed blood-drenched. As the Great Gate came in sight they could see the frenzied activity around it. The gate still held and teams of men and women were hauling building blocks into place, forming a vast ring of stone inside the gate in expectation of the enemy breaking through.

The Nighthawks pushed their mounts through the crowds, people falling back as the cavalry passed. At the base of the wall Darius dismounted and ran up the long flight of stone steps to the top – low, wide steps designed for horses to climb if needed. Rubin slid off his mount and followed, for he had not been ordered not to. At the top he found the wide battlements were crowded with armoured men and women, some slumped to the stones, weary from fighting, some still fresh and unbloodied. Children, boys and girls, were running among them bringing them water, fresh weapons and bandages, and collecting spent arrows for reuse.

He and Darius walked over to the parapet and looked out, then both ducked as a flight of arrows hissed low over their heads. Warily Rubin peered through the crenellations. He was shocked by what he saw. The enemy army sprawled like a stain over the eastern plain. It seemed to go on for ever and the sound it made was like the ocean breakers pounding the base of the Salient. Dotted among its ranks were tall wooden constructions, half-built siege towers. An arrow struck the stone close to Rubin's head, striking sparks, and he dodged back. Looking around, he snatched up a discarded helm and put it on then leaned over again and looked down. Beneath him ladders were being thrown up – ten, eleven at a time, he counted – and a seemingly endless stream of attackers swarmed up them. The defenders were using heavy hooks to catch the tops of the ladders and push them off or drag them sideways with their burden of enemy soldiers. Rubin saw they waited until the last moment, when each ladder was full of men, before shoving it off.

Further along the wall a band of enemy fighters had managed to clamber over and a pitched battle was going on. More defenders were racing to join in and the invaders were soon outnumbered; even as Rubin watched, the last was slaughtered or maimed, stripped of his weapons then thrown back over the wall on to his comrades below.

'Darius!' a deep voice bellowed over the clamour. Rubin turned to see a burly veteran with thick, grizzled hair and a heavy moustache. His arm was in a blood-stained sling and his face was pale and sweating with pain.

'General Kerr!' Darius shouted. 'We're here to help.'

The general nodded. 'Come with me.'

He led the way into the Paradise Tower, into a dusty chamber lit only by arrow slits. The sounds of battle were muted inside the thick walls. There were piles of armour and weapons on the floor, and the only furniture was a flimsy table with a jug and cup on it and a sturdy chair, into which the general slumped. *So this is Constant Kerr*, Rubin thought, *leader of the revered Fourth Imperial.*

The old man poured himself half a cup of wine, knocked it back, then glared at Rubin, looking him up and down. 'Who's this?' he barked.

'My aide,' Darius replied smoothly. 'How can we help?'

Kerr coughed long and hard, then spat on the floor. 'They are building siege engines, as you can see. My troops are doing a good job keeping their soldiers off the walls, and their casualties must be enormous, but if they can deploy towers taller than the wall they will have free rein to use their bowmen against us. We need to destroy those towers.'

'Fire arrows,' offered Darius.

Kerr nodded. 'Indeed. We are bringing up catapults to hurl oil against them. The fire arrows should do the rest and the Fourth Imperial has the best bowmen in the City. But we are running out of oil. And I have heard,' he snorted, 'that the supplies I demanded have been diverted to the Adamantine Breach.'

Darius nodded. 'The situation there is grave.'

Kerr's face reddened and his voice was raw with anger. 'The situation *here* is grave! We are facing twenty, perhaps thirty thousand men. When they break through the gate – and they will do, you can be sure of that – this is where history will say the City falls. At the Paradise Gate. Under my watch! The enemy are not threatening the Breach yet. They have not even reached it. Ours is the greater need! We need oil, arrows and medical supplies. And we are fast running out of food. And water. If you truly want to help, go tell the empress our need is the greatest!'

Darius was silent and Rubin looked at him. The muscles on his jaw were clenched with anger, but his voice was soft when he spoke.

'I am not here as a messenger boy, general. I am here to fight for my City. And I will not go running to the empress asking for help at the Paradise Gate when the Great North Gate has been under siege for longer. And it still holds.'

Constant Kerr swore and stood up. He clutched his bloody arm and his face grew pale. 'We will hold!' he spat. 'But I will go myself and beg the empress, on bended knee if that's what's needed, for more aid.'

'You will be wasting your time and your breath, Kerr. Do you think Aquila in the north and Vares in the south are not begging the White Palace for aid too?'

The old man sighed and fell back in his chair. Rubin could see that, beneath the bluster, he was exhausted.

'If the oil we need does not arrive before they finish their siege engines,' he said, his voice bitter, 'then we will use it for our funeral pyres.'

Neither man spoke for a moment, then the general

said, 'I hear there is plague in the north too.' He gazed at Darius, his eyes red-rimmed.

Darius nodded.

The old man shook his head. 'This is terrible news. We already have more than twenty dead and a hundred-odd sick. The sickness is swift and merciless and if it sweeps through our defenders the gate might as well be opened for their army to march through.' He lowered his shaggy head as if defeated.

Rubin and Darius glanced at each other. Rubin was wondering if the old general had the heart to lead the defence of the gate, but just then a soldier came clattering into the room. Kerr looked up.

'General!' the man cried. 'A cartful of oil barrels is on its way from the Araby Gate. The commander there learned of our need and has sent all they have.'

'Good man!' Kerr sprang up, rejuvenated. 'Let's get those catapults up here and we'll destroy their siege towers before sundown!'

'But what if the enemy attack the Araby Gate?' asked Rubin.

The general almost smiled. 'Then they will be sent oil by the next gate in line. The City works together best when it is in peril.'

He clapped Darius on the back. 'Will you join us, you and your troopers? Will you defend the Paradise Gate with us?'

The commander shook his head. 'No, general, the Nighthawks cannot fight behind a wall. We will ride south, for the Adamantine Breach – there the cavalry will make a difference.'

'Very well,' Kerr said, nodding. 'I respect your choice. And if you see the empress . . .'

'Yes, general?'

'Tell her we will defend the Paradise Gate to the last warrior.'

Darius and Rubin left the tower and stepped out into the din and chaos on top of the wall. They hurried back down the steps to where the Nighthawks waited. The commander took his mount's reins and turned his blue gaze on Rubin.

'The Adamantine Breach will soon be the most perilous place in the City,' he said. 'Come with us if you dare!'

CHAPTER FORTY-ONE

The white palace was a strange place to be as the first gales blew in. Icy winds swirling round the lofty minarets and balconies made it unpleasant to venture outside and Elija confined himself more and more to the library where he listened to the hooting of wind in chimneys and the patter of rain on windows. He was overcome by sadness. Now Emly had gone and Dol Salida was dead, he had no one left he could talk to. Rubin was awaiting execution, and all Elija could do for his friend was to ensure he had books to read.

Then one night two things happened. Rubin escaped his cell and disappeared and Darius Hex vanished with the Nighthawks. The atmosphere in the palace changed. The Nighthawks had walked the palace corridors since Elija had lived there, but the warriors who stalked the halls now were strangers who stared at him with hard eyes as if to tell him he had no place there. He knew of the invasion from the north, the attacks on two of the Great Gates, but it seemed to have nothing to do with the quiet, routine world of the White Palace.

The empress was seldom seen and her public duties were performed by her granddaughter and by Jona Lee Gaeta. Grey-eyed Thekla treated Elija as the soldiery did, as if he were an intruder. He thought she was probably right. He had been brought to the palace only because he was Emly's brother. He was of no use to Archange and the empress had always seemed barely aware of him. He watched Thekla furtively, as did most of the soldiers, for she was a woman of transcendent beauty in a place where there were few women and most of those crones.

Jona was amiable enough, though his black Serafim eyes made his gaze as disquieting as Archange's. When he spoke to Elija, which he did rarely, it was always to ask questions – about Emly and Broglanh, of course, and about Rubin. Once he'd asked if Elija was loyal to Marcellus, like his friend Rubin. 'I never met Marcellus and I was told he had been killed,' was all Elija could say, and Jona looked at him as though he'd given the wrong answer.

It was inevitable Elija be drawn to the complex of tunnels inside the mountain. Once these had been opened up and searched, the entrances were sealed again. The gate at the base of the Shield where the black-clad killers had broken in had been barricaded. Those now in charge of the security of the palace were confident it was impregnable. Elija was unconvinced and, as an intellectual exercise as much as anything, he took it on himself to test its weaknesses. The entrance to the top of one of the great shafts had been locked, not walled up like the others, and Elija knew where the key was kept.

So each night, lantern in hand, he set out to investigate the maze of tunnels, and each day he spent drawing maps of the inner highways of the Shield. At first he was fearful, for Darius had told him one of the intruders was still at large, but after a while he forgot to be scared except when he stood on the lip of one of the high funnels, as he thought of them, staring down into the abyss, attracted there each night despite himself.

He made and remade his maps, increasing their range every day.

One night he roved further than usual, heading ever north, eager to find the bounds of a particular tunnel. It finally came to a halt at the top of a high funnel. There was no way on except by ladder and, although he calculated that dawn was hastening, Elija found himself compelled by the hunt and he set foot cautiously on the first rung. It seemed secure enough, and he told himself he would climb down no more than fifty rungs; then, if he had found no way out, he would return. And at the last but one rung of the fifty he felt a change in the air flow which told him he was coming to a horizontal tunnel. He stepped off the ladder and hurried along the passage, which got smaller and smaller, the roof lowering until he was crouching then crawling on his belly. Just as he started to fear he would be forced to back out he found brickwork in his path, broken and crumbled. He thrust one arm through the gap and, feeling around, found the way opened up beyond. The lantern in front of him, he squeezed through. Beyond was a grey wall, grainy to the touch. When he pushed it it moved, disconcertingly, until it dawned on him that it was the back of a tapestry, rotting with age. He crawled round it into an empty room, dank and sour-smelling. He listened but could hear nothing.

He put down the lantern and opened the room's door, which creaked alarmingly on corroded hinges, and peered out. He could see a huge chamber, gloomily lit by high windows. It was a library, he thought, surely the biggest library in the world. Its shelves ran far into the distance in both directions and the thousands of shelves were stacked all the way to the high roof. The place was thick with dust, the books and rolled parchments laden with it. Everything was still. Elija crossed the room, aware of the trail of bootprints he left in the dust, and climbed up to one of the windows. It was filthy but he rubbed away some of the grime with his fist and looked through. It was well after dawn and he could see down into a great courtyard, deserted and desolate, and beyond its far wall part of the City. There was no mistaking the great river Menander crawling sluggishly across the ruined land, and the pale shapes of new buildings on its banks. Elija knew he had found his way to one of the abandoned palaces on the Shield, but which one? He had no idea. Still, Archange would be interested to hear it was possible to get from her palace to another – and vice versa – through the tunnels.

He determined to go straight back and report to her. Glad of a reason to leave this dreary place, he turned to go.

An anguished scream rent the stillness. He stood unmoving, barely breathing, as the scream rose to a peak then died away. It was the voice of a woman in torment. Chills crept down his spine and he shivered. Elija lived in daily fear of torture. Since Emly had fled the palace a hobgoblin of dread regularly whispered in the back of his mind that one day he would be questioned by the palace inquisitors. Dol Salida had clearly believed Elija knew more about his sister's whereabouts than he was saying, hence the urquat games. And he had listened with revulsion as soldiers spoke with relish of the agony inflicted on the intruders they had captured.

The woman screamed again, the sound echoing through empty spaces, and he forced himself to move. Frightened but fascinated, he hurried across the library into another vast chamber and looked around in the dim light. Steps ran up to higher levels at both ends. He heard another scream and ran across the room and through an open door. He raced through corridor after corridor, all empty, devoid of life. Then the cries stopped and he stopped too, despairing. This palace was larger, even, than the Serafia and it would take days to search it. But he could not leave if the woman needed help. He resolved to work his way downwards for, he thought bleakly, that is where dungeons lie.

He was creeping along a low, dismal corridor, his thoughts dark, when he heard a soft sound to his right. It was a stealthy movement, a sucking, moist sound of flesh on flesh. Elija stopped, the hairs on the back of his neck standing up, gooseflesh crawling up his arms. He stood frozen. Infinitely slowly he turned his head and there, sunk into the wall, was a low wooden door.

Gathering his courage and as stealthily as a cat, Elija stepped up to it and put his ear to the wood. Again that same wet, clotted noise. Holding his breath he leaned on the door and it creaked open slightly. The stench which rolled out made his belly rebel, but he peered in, breathing through his mouth. It was dim inside, lit by small, dirty windows. He could see nothing so he slipped over the threshold and stood waiting for his eyes to adjust. Slowly the chamber came into view. He was standing at the top of wet stone steps, the floor far below him. There was movement down there but he could not make it out. The smell was repellent, of stagnant water and mould and rotted bodies. What was that on the floor? He craned to see, one hand on the door handle, ready to flee.

Something soft touched his fingers and he whirled round, flailing at it, crying out in fear.

A small old woman, pale and wrinkled, with wild white hair and clad in a filthy shift, leered at him from the doorway. She grinned up at him, delightedly pawing at his chest and shoulders, her touch disgusting, her black eyes huge, insane. Frantic with panic, he tried to push her aside and get out of that terrible room, but she clung to his arm, her flesh clammy and cold. She was quicker than him and stronger, for all her great age. The only way he could go was into the room and he backed away and tried to slam the door on her, trapping her arm, careless of hurting her. She screeched, high and grating, and dragged the arm out. Elija leaned on the door and closed the latch with shaking fingers. There was no lock or bar, nothing to stop her getting in. He willed it to stay shut, watching the handle, waiting for it to move. He thought he would go mad if it did.

After a while his breathing started to deepen, his heartbeat stopped its wild knocking. What to do now? He dared not go out. He had trapped himself.

He turned around and looked down again. His gaze penetrated the darkness. The floor was covered by a film of thick liquid, liquid which shimmered and rippled as if alive. He stared into the corner where he had seen movement. Just rats, he hoped. He drew his knife, something he had been too panicked to do as the creature clung to him. He stepped gingerly away from the door, fearful it would fly open, but it remained shut. Holding the knife in front of him he crept down the steps, looking back over his shoulder every few heartbeats. As he reached the last step he stopped.

In the corner of the chamber, twisting in the moving water, he could see a decaying body, naked and sheened with cloying trails of mucus. The body of a wizened old woman with white hair. Dead, surely. But as he watched the pitiful figure lifted wrinkled hands to him, imploring. Elija stumbled back on the slimy steps, his legs failing him, stomach rebelling. Surely this creature was the same as the one that had pawed at him in the doorway. How could it be?

She raised the top half of her body, as if trying to sit, and water and slime poured out of her mouth. She struggled to speak, stickily, before sinking back.

Elija turned and fled back up the steps, his boots sliding on the slick surface. Careless of what was waiting behind it, he dragged open the door and ran out into the corridor. Panic-stricken, he looked wildly about him. There was no one in sight, just a wet trail leading away through the dust on the stone floor. Elija leaned his hands on his knees and vomited over and over until his stomach was dry. Afterwards, exhausted, his legs shaking, he wiped his mouth and looked up and down the corridor once more, wondering which way to go.

Then he heard the same woman's scream. Much closer. It was a human sound, however terrifying, a sound of sanity and he raced towards it. Reckless now, he called out, 'Hello!' as he ran. Then, at the far end of yet another empty chamber, he saw a pale hand reaching out from a dark recess in the wall. He stopped. A woman's voice called, 'Help us, please!'

He ran over. There was a sturdy wooden door with a barred opening. Through the bars he could see a fair young woman, her face red and tearful. When she saw him she gasped and pleaded, 'Help us! Please, sir!'

'What can I do?' he asked, thinking he was in no fit state to help anybody.

'My lady is in labour. It's going badly and I don't know what to do.' She chewed her lip, holding back tears. 'We're prisoners. Can you free us?'

Elija looked past her. Unlike the rest of the palace, dirty and deserted but for the terrible old woman, this room was furnished, with rugs on the floor, and he could see a window out to bright daylight. On a narrow bed lay a dark-haired woman. She was moaning in distress, the sheets beneath her bloody. As he watched she cried out again, more weakly.

But the door was locked. Elija looked around for a key, above the door, beside it, but there was none. He looked over his shoulder, terrified he might see the old woman again.

'Where are we?' he asked the servant, who was gazing impatiently at him, waiting for him to do something.

She frowned. 'What do you mean, *where are we?* Don't you know, boy?'

He shook his head. 'No. But I will find out. I will fetch someone,' he promised her. 'I will tell the empress of your plight.'

There was an agonized cry from inside and the servant turned back to the bed. She spoke to the woman in labour then returned and told Elija urgently, 'No, not the empress! Whatever you do, please don't tell the empress. Tell Giulia Rae Khan. Tell her Fiorentina needs her.'

It seemed to take Elija for ever to find his way out of the haunted palace and, with the exception of a burly, shabbily dressed man who lay snoring in a chair, a cudgel and an empty beer barrel beside him, Elija saw no one. He guessed this was the women's guard.

At last he arrived outside. He looked around, sucking in the fresh air. He was in the palace courtyard he had seen from above. It was deserted like everywhere else. Weeds grew long at the base of huge black iron gates. The gates were heavily barred.

Conscious of time pressing, Elija followed the palace wall, eventually coming to a tall tower. There, in the niche between wall and tower, he found a short passageway, a dog-leg, leading to a timber door set deep into the darkness of the wall. It was barred but not locked and he set his shoulder to the bar and, heaving with all his might, lifted it off its brackets. He pushed the door open. Light flooded in and he peered through, his heart in his mouth, to find he was outside the palace.

He sighed, weak with relief, and looked around. The palace, clad in black stone, loomed above, and above that was the bulk of the Shield of Freedom. In front of him a wide path made of crushed white shells wound up the mountain. He followed it upwards, relieved to be out yet anxious for the woman in labour. He saw no one but very soon came to another gateway flanked by heavy sandstone pillars. These gates were open. Elija crept in, nervous of what he might find. He saw a wide courtyard paved with golden stones, and beyond it a sandstone fortress squatting on the flank of the mountain. An armed soldier stepped into his path, sword drawn.

'I need help,' Elija told him.

The man snorted. 'You'll find no help here, lad. Be on your way.'

'Is this the Khan palace? I need to speak to Giulia Rae Khan.'

The man hesitated then said, 'Be off with you. The lady does not grant audience with anyone who asks.'

'But I have a message from the lady Fiorentina. She needs help.'

Within moments, Elija was escorted into the palace, a cold and gloomy place inside. Flanked by guards he was taken into a huge hall, smoky and damp, with a mean fire in the great hearth at one end. Seated before it was a sharp-featured woman in a dark gown, her iron-grey hair piled randomly on her head. She peered at him short-sightedly.

'Well, boy!' she rapped. 'Where's Fiorentina? What do you know?'

She listened impatiently, her mouth moving, as Elija told her briefly what had happened to him.

'Where is this place?' she demanded, frowning ferociously. 'Speak plainly, boy!'

'Down the white path,' he explained. 'The black building.'

Her eyes gleamed. 'The Iron Palace?'

Elija shook his head. 'I don't know its name.'

'Amylas!' she ordered. 'Go to the Iron Palace immediately. Find Fiorentina!'

A sturdy, black-bearded warrior nodded, but said, 'Yes, lady Giulia, but it will take days to break in. We do not have the men or the equipment.'

Elija spoke up. He told Giulia, 'They don't have to break in, lady. I left a door open.'

It does my old heart good, thought Giulia contentedly. Not only had the boy told her where Fiorentina was being kept, but he could tell her something of what went on behind the black gates of the Iron Palace. She was listening with only half an ear, the rest of her mind busy calculating what advantage she could gain from this.

'But who are you, boy, and what were you doing there?' she snapped, interrupting whatever he was saying.

'My name is Elija,' he said. *Had he already told her that? He seemed very nervous. So he should be.* 'I live in the White Palace with my sister Emly. She is—'

'I know who Emly is,' Giulia retorted. Why did everyone think her so out of touch? She peered at him, searching his face for duplicity. 'Do *you* know where she has fled to?'

'No, lady,' he said with the appearance of honesty. 'Emly did not confide in me. That would have been foolish if she was determined never to be found.'

'Of course it would,' she agreed briskly. 'And Archange is a fool if she ever believed it.'

Giulia ordered that the boy be fed and watered then she questioned him over the long afternoon as they waited for word from her men. He told her about their life, his and his sister's, and about his journey that day. The longer she listened, the more surprised she was that so frail a boy had survived such a strange and perilous existence.

When she quizzed him about the White Palace and the empress he prevaricated for the first time and she was pleased, in a way, for she disapproved of disloyalty, however well deserved.

'Loyalty is a rare beast on this mountain,' she told him, 'but I know it when I see it. Your name will not come up, I promise you.'

Elija asked, 'Will she be all right? Fiorentina?'

It was a ridiculous question, and one she could not answer, and she snapped, 'Children are born every day in this City. Thousands born every day in the world. It is as natural as breathing. It can be painful,' she conceded, 'but the girl is probably just making a fuss. She's a soft thing, though she thinks not.'

She questioned him closely about the Iron Palace and, presumably feeling loyalty to no one there, he told her all he could remember. She nodded as he spoke, suppressing a smile. That the home of the Gaetas was abandoned did not surprise her. Jona's brother Saul was believed dead in battle, and their sisters had not been seen for many years. And Giulia had always suspected that the Family's fabulous private army was just that, a fable.

Elija's words faltered when he told her of an old woman he had seen, and a creature in a flooded room. Perhaps he thought Giulia would disbelieve him, but she had the Gift of clear perception and she knew he told the truth as he had seen it.

'Who were they?' he asked her hesitantly, as if reluctant to know. 'They looked the same, like sisters, though one was half-drowned, the other—' he shuddered, 'she was terrifying, small and very old but much stronger than me, and her eyes, round and staring, insane.' He gazed at Giulia, seeking rational answers to soothe the nightmare.

'Sciorra Gaeta,' she told him briskly. 'Head of the Gaeta Family. She has lived in the Iron Palace since it was first built but she has not been seen for more than a century. The other creature was one of her abominable reflections,' she added, thinking he could not understand, but Elija nodded as if what she said made sense.

For the first time in years she found some sympathy in her heart for Sciorra. Although ancient and demented the woman, it seemed, was still trying to do what she had done with ease when she was young – people her world with reflections who would love her and serve her, and be a family to her now her own were gone. How many twisted reflections had been birthed and died over the centuries in that dreadful place, she wondered?

'It is a terrible thing to be so very old,' she told the boy.

She wanted to return to the subject of Archange but Elija had little to tell, except that the empress had been ill but now seemed recovered. There was no doubt now in Giulia's mind that Archange was responsible for abducting the pregnant girl, and that Jona had conspired with her. But why maroon her in the Iron Palace? Why not whisk mother and child straight to the Serafia? There Archange could deal with them as she chose. Kill them or let them live.

She conceded to herself, grudgingly, that she had been wrong to confide in Jona about the baby. But with Marcus dead she needed allies wherever she could find them. And Jona had seemed the best candidate out of a limited set of choices, given the available information.

But now Giulia would have the advantage again, if the babe was birthed successfully. She pondered how she might keep the child out of Archange's malevolent clutches, and her scarred heart thrilled at the challenge.

'Who is she, lady? This Fiorentina? Why was she imprisoned?'

Giulia, startled, stared at the boy. For a moment she had forgotten he was there.

'She is no one,' she told him briskly. 'But her son will be a lodestar for all of us, if he lives. He is the son of . . . a Serafim. Do you know what that is, boy?' She was surprised when he nodded. *This boy might be useful*, she thought.

'Offspring of Serafim are rare. We were beginning to believe that the Guillaume children, Indaro and—' She frowned. *What was his name?* 'Rubin,' the boy told her. 'Yes, Rubin,' she said. 'They were the last, and they were a disappointment. Gifts often skip a generation. Their father Reeve is, was, very powerful. Perhaps their own get . . . Do they have children, boy?'

'Rubin or Indaro? Not that I know of,' he told her.

'But a Vincerus son! That will be a wonder.' *If it lives*, she thought.

'Why, lady?'

'Because the Vincerus Family was always the most powerful among us. A Vincerus son will always be the first contender for the Immortal Throne.'

Elija frowned. 'But Archange is a Vincerus.'

Giulia snorted. 'Never! She has used the name for many centuries to hide her shame and most people have forgotten. But I haven't. I know her best. And I know she is no more a Vincerus than you are.'

Fiorentina believed she was dying. She thought no one could endure so much pain and live. The sun had set and risen twice as she laboured, and now it was going down again and still the baby had not emerged. When it came out, if it ever did, she was sure it would be dead. She recalled the fearful dream of the old woman. *Is it dead in there?* She was certain now it was.

Alafair was useless. She had never delivered a baby before and knew nothing. Fiorentina had screamed at the girl, spat at her and cursed her with every filthy word she could muster and, in the end, she had even cursed her lord for leaving her like this. Then she had sobbed and appealed to Alafair for help, weeping into the girl's skirts as she held her and crooned reassuring words which meant nothing. What had happened to the young man who said he would help them? Fiorentina asked it over and over but Alafair had no answer.

Now she felt her life slipping away, for she had no more strength and the sheets beneath her were drenched with her lifeblood. She drifted off, daydreaming of her years with her lord, a rich life, content and happy. Daily she had pondered how and when he had died, but there was no one to tell her, for everyone, almost everyone, who fought in the Red Palace that day was now dead.

As she would soon be.

'Lady, there is a woman!' Alafair told her, whispering loudly into her ear.

'What woman?' Fiorentina had no interest and she wondered why the girl was bothering her. Then, in a flash of hope, she asked, 'Is she a midwife?'

'I don't think so,' Alafair told her, her face ashen. 'She is very old and . . . terrible. She is outside the door trying to get in.'

Fiorentina sank back. Why was she being bothered with this?

The door rattled and the timbers creaked. Alafair stared fixedly at the door but she stayed by Fiorentina's side, clutching tightly to her hand. Through her daze of pain Fiorentina realized the girl was petrified. She looked at the door but she could see nothing through the bars.

'Nothing there,' she muttered.

Alafair crept over to the door and nervously peered through. Then she jumped back. 'She *is* there, lady.' She was trembling. 'Does she have a key?'

Fiorentina thought again of the malevolent old woman of her dream. Her heart shrivelled and she felt a wave of dread rolling over her, muffling her in its folds, stopping her breath. She tried to scream but all that emerged was a thin wail.

Then came the sound of running boots and the creak of armour. 'Lady Fiorentina!' a deep, male voice called. 'Lady Fiorentina!'

Alafair ran back to the door. She called out. A moment later Fiorentina heard the sound of heavy armour hitting strong timber, and the door crashed in. Then the room was full of soldiers.

Crying with pain and relief, she looked up into the bearded face of Giulia's captain.

'Help me!' she sobbed.

CHAPTER FORTY-TWO

THE DEFENCE OF THE CITY WAS FALTERING. AT THE White Palace there was bad news each day, each hour, then worse. A hundred times Valla had considered creeping away in the night, abandoning the empress and the frustrations of her duty, and making her way to the Adamantine Breach where defenders were desperately few and where the enemy horde were expected to march into sight at any time.

Since the departure of the Nighthawks, the palace was defended by only the Silver Bears and a company of infantry. Jona Lee Gaeta hovered constantly around the empress. He was privy to every conversation, every meeting, every plan made and remade. Even the old general Eufara, now Archange's premier military adviser, was in the throne room less often. Thekla had left her grandmother to go down the mountain again, for what reason Valla knew not.

The only good news to reach Valla's ears was that Rubin had somehow escaped his prison cell. Archange's reaction, when the news was broken to her, had been to flick a look to Valla as if she suspected her bodyguard was responsible. Valla kept her face impassive, as ever, but inside she exulted. And when it transpired that an old soldier charged with guarding Rubin had also fled, then the empress's suspicions of her faded.

This day the throne room was quiet. Apart from her personal guard, twelve men stationed round the walls and another dozen outside in the ante-chamber, Archange's only companions were Jona and a dapper little man called Sully. This Sully had presented himself to the empress after the death of Dol Salida. He claimed to be a friend and colleague of the counsellor and had offered, perhaps in tribute to him, to apprise the empress of Dol Salida's recent work. Gossip told Valla that before Dol Salida became Archange's counsellor he had been a spymaster of renown in the Red Palace. Each day now the empress met the little man, sometimes in the public arena of the throne room, sometimes in the quiet of her parlour. Valla thought she detected some irritation in Jona Lee Gaeta's manner when Sully's name was mentioned. She smiled to herself. She trusted neither of them.

Now the empress and Jona, and two quartermasters, were discussing conveying rations to the beleaguered defenders at the Great Gates. The days of peace after the fall of the Red Palace and the ending of the blockade had allowed much-needed food to pour into the City from abroad, and the harvest in the farmlands to the north-east had promised to be bountiful. But when the new terror struck from the north most of the field workers had downed spades and fled with their families towards the south and west of the City, away from the threatened gates. Yet there was no help for them there, and the western quarters were soon bursting with refugees, the Seagate under siege by people desperate to get away. And now famine had broken out among the poorest.

Valla listened to the conversation with growing alarm. Families were dying of hunger in the west while in the farmlands fruit withered on trees and grain lay unharvested in fields. With all able-bodied defenders at the gates and the Adamantine Breach, no one was left to supply food.

Suddenly, in the distance, she heard a cry, then the sound of running boots in far corridors. Then more cries and shouts, coming closer. She looked at the captain of the guard and at his word soldiers sprang to close the gold-embossed doors into the ante-chamber, where warriors of the outer guard had already drawn their swords. There was no other way into the throne room, but her warriors lined up before the empress, who surveyed them with a frown of annoyance. Valla remained at her side, sword in hand.

'Gaius!' the empress cried. 'What's happening?'

The captain was listening, head cocked. 'I fear an attack, lady.' He gestured and four of his men slid the iron locking bar across the golden doors. 'But you are safe here, empress.' He ordered Jona Lee Gaeta to retreat behind the rank of soldiers.

Archange sniffed. She listened, brow furrowed, then she lifted her head as if scenting danger. Valla felt the air in the room crackle. A grey worm of dread coiled in her belly and the hairs stood up on her neck.

The screams were getting closer. The sound was chilling, the squeal and shriek of animals being slaughtered. Valla realized her fingers were trembling. *This is what you've been hoping for*, she told herself sternly. *A chance of action!* But her body betrayed her, shaking with fear, and it was all she could do to grip her sword.

Wild shrieking from the ante-chamber tore the air and Valla could feel blood gushing through her head, pounding in time with her heartbeat. There was a frenzied, irregular banging on the golden doors. Valla could see them shudder as blows rained upon them, the locking bar rocking. The screaming rose to a deafening peak, piercing her ears like knives.

The doors bowed inward then suddenly crashed open, cracking the locking bar like a dry branch, flinging its two halves across the room. Valla's heart seemed to stop in her chest.

The ante-chamber was awash with blood. It fell like rain from the ceiling and ran down the walls and pooled on the floor and on the piles of rent flesh and sliding body parts which were all that remained of the twelve guards. A sick chill flushed through Valla and she felt her stomach rebel, the bile and fear rising in her gorge.

Out of the slaughterhouse stepped a solitary figure, clothed in blood.

Archange rose slowly to her feet. 'Marcellus!' she breathed.

He walked through the throne room, his boots squelching a bloody track across the pristine stone. He wore a gore-drenched uniform of the Thousand, and his face and hair and beard dripped blood. He carried no weapon. Valla watched him come towards her with horror. With each step he took she could feel the power building in the throne room. It crackled across her skin and sank deep into her bones. She heard herself moan with fear.

She had loyally kept the faith, repeating the words Rubin wanted to hear: *Marcellus is our lodestar. He will return*. But as his mysterious disappearance had drifted into the past, so her belief had failed. But now here he was, back from the dead, and her only reaction was terror.

Archange stood waiting, her eyes black as tar. She raised her hand to her remaining warriors. 'Hold,' she told them as Marcellus came on, though none had moved.

'How dare you!' she cried as he stopped a few paces

from her, looking round balefully, challenging any to move against him. 'How dare you slaughter *my* warriors in *my* palace!'

'They *dared* to try and stop me,' he told her and his voice was thick with anger and, perhaps, blood-lust. 'I built this palace, woman! I will not tolerate any man's hand raised against me here!'

He glared at the soldiers in front of him, his eyes lighting on Valla for a heartbeat. There was silence except for the drip of blood. The stench of the charnel house filled the room. Then all of them heard the distant tread of marching boots, coming quickly closer.

'Call them off, Archange!' Marcellus warned, his voice taut. 'You know well that I can kill every soldier in the palace!'

The empress nodded to Gaius. The captain of the guard strode past Marcellus, his eyes fixed to him, then he hesitated a moment before stepping through the piles of oozing flesh and hair and torn clothes and broken armour to the outside doors. Valla heard him bark out orders, then he returned. Archange's eyes flicked to him then back to Marcellus.

He was watching her closely. 'I could kill you where you stand, Archange. You have more than given me cause. Don't tempt me.'

She laughed then, and her voice was full of contempt. 'At one time, perhaps, little man. But I have conserved my power over the years while you wasted it on bloody spectacles like this.' She waved her hand towards the gory ante-chamber. 'Kill me? You couldn't even bruise me.' She seemed to grow taller until she dwarfed the soldiers guarding her. The air around her thickened and the illusion of wings appeared at her shoulders. Valla blinked, unsure what she was seeing. The room was vibrating with power and she dreaded what was about to happen.

The two glared at each other – blood-soaked demon and fierce angel – and the light around them wavered and crackled. The great dome above began to vibrate, resonating, sighing like a monstrous bell in a thunderstorm. Both looked up and Valla's gaze followed. They could see the glass shimmering, its colours darting, flashing all around the great throne room. The sound grew, beating on their ears, the dome visibly flexing and stretching as if in a furnace. It seemed on the verge of falling and Valla fought the urge to flee.

Suddenly the power dropped away. Valla found she could breathe normally again. Archange reseated herself, pulling her shawl around her.

'What took you so long, Marcellus?' she snapped. 'I'd thought you'd emerge from your bolthole sooner than this. We were told you were killed, though for myself I never believed it.'

He grunted. 'Well, Archange,' he said, 'I'm sorry you missed my company. It must be thirty years.'

'What do you want, Marcellus? Apart from killing warriors who have never been other than loyal to their City?'

'I could not help but notice,' he said in the old, affable way Valla remembered so well, 'that the enemy is at your gates and you no longer have the troops to defend the City, thanks to your treacherous alliance with Hayden Weaver.'

She watched him, unblinking. 'Say what you have to,' she told him briskly, 'then leave this place.'

He drew off his gauntlets and dropped them to the floor where they lay oozing blood. He wore a jewelled ring which threw out coloured splashes of light under the dome. He wiped one hand across his face then looked up again.

'I'm surprised it's still there,' he said, his expression

thoughtful. 'I'd have thought it would have crashed long before this.'

She looked up too, then conceded, 'It was well made.'

'Yes,' he said, 'we knew how to do things in those days.'

She nodded and suddenly the air in the chamber became calmer and warriors relaxed their stance. Valla had seen Marcellus' moods change before, from friendly affability to savage brutality in a heartbeat. And back again. But still she was amazed that the two mortal enemies should speak together so casually. She wondered which of them was the more powerful, and whether the palace would be destroyed before anyone found out.

Marcellus sighed, 'For all our past . . . differences, I have come to offer my help to defend the people of the City against this cruel and brutal army. I have two thousand heavy infantry even now crossing the Zarros. They are yours to command, if you wish it.'

Her eyes narrowed but she said nothing. Perhaps she was thinking, as Valla was, that until that moment she had suspected that Marcellus himself was behind the army.

'I am informed they are less than two days' march from the Adamantine Breach,' he added. 'Together with your motley crew of the old and the lame – and your new defensive ditch – we can hold off the part of the barbarian horde moving south. Your enemy here is my enemy. Even you are not too stiff-necked to recognize that.'

'In return for what?' she demanded.

'Only your love and affection, Archange,' he said, smiling for the first time. 'As ever. And, of course, the Gulon Veil. Oh,' he added, as if it were an afterthought, 'and young Rubin Guillaume who is, I understand, languishing in the cells.'

'You are welcome to the boy,' she said, waving a hand dismissively. 'I don't want him. But you cannot have the veil. You know that. You knew that when you stepped into this place, when you left whatever fastness you have made your home.'

He shook his head, a look of sorrow on his face. 'Even now the enemy's cannon is pounding on the Great North Gate. Cannon, Archange! Whatever next? And they are within days of breaching the Paradise Gate. If you allow even a handful of them past the ruins of the Adamantine Wall they will merely stroll across the City and open all the gates from the inside. Is possession of the veil really so important to you?'

'Is it so important to you that you will stand back and watch, without aiding the City you profess to love?'

He stepped forward and Valla raised her sword. He swung his gaze on her and searing agony sliced through her arm and she cried out. The blade clattered to the floor.

'Valla,' Marcellus snarled, and chill air rolled over her. 'Warrior of the Warhounds. You have chosen the wrong side. What would our lost, loved Leona say about that, I wonder.' His black gaze held her in its iron grip and she clearly heard Leona's dying words, '*Marcellus is our lodestar.*'

She wrenched her eyes from his and looked to her empress, who nodded as if she knew what Valla would say.

'I fought in the Hall of Emperors on the Day of Summoning,' Valla told Marcellus and she was surprised to hear her voice was firm. 'I fought *for* the Immortal then, and I will fight for her now. My side has never changed.'

Marcellus grunted in what could have been amusement, then turned back to Archange.

'When we meet again, lady, we can sit and discuss the old days when you were free of this corrosive bitterness and the City was still a dream of liberty and splendour. And we can debate just who it was who fled the City and who perpetrated the worst crimes in her name. But now is the time to put away our squabbles and act together for the future of the City, to ensure it has a future. By the way,' he added, 'I heard reports of Marcus' death. Is it true? I do hope not.'

She nodded. 'It is. A great loss to the City.'

'He was the best of us,' Marcellus added formally.

She nodded, but her voice was frosty as she said, 'You never cared for Marcus, or for anyone. You always thought *you* were the best of us. You still think it, for all your centuries of deception and treachery, of war and slaughter. I reject your offer today not because I don't need warriors but because you cannot be trusted. You never could. I would not trust a cup of water from your hands.'

He lowered his head in a show of thought, then said, 'As you wish. Despite your reckless decision, I will grant you one gift today. If you wish to hear it, I will tell you the name behind this northern army.'

Archange could not, it seemed, bring herself to say yes, but she did not refuse his offer.

He smiled and said one word. 'Hammarskjald.'

Valla was watching the empress and saw her eyes darken. 'Impossible!' she hissed.

'I have no reason to lie to you,' Marcellus said, shrugging.

'You have every reason,' she retorted. 'But he died,' she added, though her voice held no conviction. 'Araeon ensnared him and killed him with his own hands. Then burned the body. You were there.'

He smiled. 'Now, Archange, we both know,' he said

jovially, 'that being dead is no obstacle to ambitions of conquest.'

'He despised us all, Marcellus, but he despised the City more. You will remember as well as I do his pious monologues about the corruption of power. And, just supposing Hammarskjald does still live, why would he want to take the City when he loathed it so?'

'Perhaps he doesn't want to take it. Perhaps he wants to destroy it, to sow the ground with salt. His grievances go back a thousand years, and old sins throw long shadows, as we both have reason to know.'

She thought for a while and Valla wondered if she believed him. There was silence in the chamber. Even the steady drip of blood from Marcellus' clothes had stopped.

Then the empress raised her head and asked softly, 'Why now?'

'Because the City lies open for him like a bride on her wedding night.'

She shook her head. 'If it is Hammarskjald, which I doubt, then he must want something besides conquest. What is it, Marcellus? What are you keeping to yourself?'

Jona Lee Gaeta stepped forward for the first time. 'Marcellus, I have only heard the word Hammarskjald as a dark name from the past. But tell us all you know, if indeed you know anything, of his ambition.'

Marcellus swivelled to look at the man as if just now recognizing him. 'Gaeta!' he cried. 'I wondered who was giving Archange such bad advice. Are you actually working for the enemy or were you just born a fool?'

Gaeta flushed. 'I am proud to serve my empress and my City,' he said.

'And your mother, does she still live?'

'Yes, lord.'

'I was always fond of Sciorra, though she never

seemed to like me. Ask *her* about Hammarskjald. She knows as much about him as anyone.'

'Marcellus,' Archange said, and he turned to her courteously.

'I accept your offer,' she told him. 'Your two thousand men-at-arms for the Gulon Veil. I cannot give you the Guillaume boy. He has escaped.'

Marcellus barked his laughter. 'Of course he has. I should have known. Never underestimate that one, Archange. Very well,' he said, 'we have an agreement. Give me the veil.'

Valla wondered what the empress would do. She wondered if she was the only one in the room who knew Archange didn't have the veil to give him.

Archange nodded thoughtfully. 'If your two thousand can defend the Adamantine Breach as you say, and keep it closed to the enemy, then I will gladly hand the veil over to you. You have my word on it.'

He sighed. 'So I walk away with nothing but a promise. It is an indication of my unswerving goodwill towards you that I'm prepared to accept that, cousin.'

'If your warriors stand firm, I will be as good as my word, *cousin*.'

But Marcellus lingered, looking pensive. 'We have a fall-back position, you know, Archange,' he said softly. 'It takes five Families to wield the veil. We can attempt to put a shield over the City, as was once intended. We are old and we are dwindling, but we still have Giulia and Sciorra and Reeve. It should be enough.'

The empress narrowed her eyes. 'Use the veil as a shield!' she repeated disdainfully. 'Surely you cannot believe that?'

'Araeon believed it.'

'Araeon!' Her voice cracked like a whip. 'Then why didn't he use it to stop the invasion on the Day of Summoning?' She glared at him.

He spread his hands in a conciliatory gesture. 'Perhaps because he was murdered before he knew of the invasion.' He went on, his tone persuasive: 'The Gaetas know about such things. Sciorra was ever considered a witch.' He looked at Jona, who made no response.

'You're starting to believe our own fables,' the empress told him briskly. 'Besides, Reeve has vanished. I'm surprised you haven't heard. He disappeared from the Salient at the turn of the year and has not been seen since. My agents are searching for him, but he is probably dead.'

'His son then? Rubin?'

She admitted, 'The son has a little power.' Valla smiled to herself at that. She knew this 'little power' was enough to challenge the empress. 'But he is no longer here. Besides,' Archange added, 'even if it were possible, which I strongly doubt, it is an outrageous idea. We might destroy more than we save. I realize you are profligate with human life,' she gestured towards the ante-chamber oozing blood, 'but that is not my way, nor will it ever be.'

'Do you appreciate, woman, that Hammarskjald is using *cannon*?' Marcellus emphasized. To Valla his concern seemed genuine. 'That's what tipped me off to his hand behind this. No one else has sufficient knowledge.'

Then, despite everything, he chuckled. He said to Archange, quite conversationally, 'Trust Hammarskjald to bring cannon to a sword-fight!'

The veil again, thought Valla, watching Marcellus stride out through the blood-soaked ante-room, trailed by Archange's guards. Why is it so important? She resolved to ask Elija about the thing when she found a chance. The boy seemed to know a good deal about the empress and her past.

Archange turned to her captain. 'See that Langham Vares knows Marcellus and his army are on their way to the Adamantine Breach. We don't want fighting to break out even before the enemy gets there. I want Marcellus followed,' she told Gaeta. 'And reports on everything he does, who he meets, their conversations, the steps of every messenger he sends. I am still not convinced he is not the moving force behind this enemy army. He must not be permitted to slide away from our scrutiny again.' She thought for a few moments. 'And I want the guard stepped up on your own palace and on the Khans'. We must keep Giulia and Sciorra safe.'

'The Iron Palace is a fortress,' Gaeta assured her, 'but I will ensure lady Giulia is protected.' He lowered his voice. '*Will* you give him the veil?'

'Do you doubt my word?' she enquired, eyes narrowed.

'No, lady, but a mere two thousand—'

'I don't care a jot for his two thousand,' she snapped. 'It is Marcellus I want—' she paused as if suddenly aware of her own words, then she said softly, 'God help me.'

The old general Eufara hurried into the throne room, his face haggard with shock as he saw the dismembered bodies in the ante-room. He struggled down on his knees before Archange.

'Empress,' he cried, his voice hoarse and thick with emotion, 'he slaughtered my soldiers . . . They were helpless against him! What demon was this, in the shape of a man?'

'Get up, general,' she snapped. 'How many dead?'

'More than a hundred, lady.' He shook his head, his old eyes full of horror. 'Every soldier who came near him. They were helpless . . .' he repeated.

'You are not to blame,' she said more gently. 'And it

was no demon. No warrior can stand against Marcellus when—'

'But Marcellus was dead . . .' he muttered, his face puzzled, careless of interrupting the empress. Valla thought he seemed broken.

Gaius, captain of the guard, returned with a young rider dressed in the grey of a City messenger. The boy lingered in the ante-room, eyes wide, hand over his mouth.

'Yes?' Archange barked.

Gaius told her, 'A messenger from the Great North Gate, empress. I thought you should hear what he has to say.' He waved him forward.

Archange turned her gaze on the youngster and he quailed beneath it. He was hardly more than a boy, his clothes were torn and blood-stained, and he was limping heavily from an injury to the thigh. Valla saw he was weaving with exhaustion.

'What message do you have for me?' the empress asked, her voice suddenly gentle.

'The general gave me a paper,' he stuttered, his eyes darting round nervously. 'But I was attacked and I lost it. I lost my horse too. I had to walk back.'

The captain said impatiently, 'Tell the Immortal what you told me.'

The messenger bobbed his head. 'The gate will fall before the night of the new moon,' he recited. 'That'll be tomorrow night now. The general said that to me.'

Archange sat back on her throne and sighed. Marcellus' presence had seemed to energize her but now she looked drained and weary. 'We expected this,' she told Eufara. 'It was just a matter of time. The internal defences will hold.'

'Yes, empress.' The general seemed to have regained his composure. 'It will give our warriors the chance they want to get at the enemy.'

Gaius put in, 'There is a further message, lady.' He glared at the messenger.

'Well?' Archange snapped.

'There is plague, my empress,' the rider told her, blinking, 'within the gate. Our soldiers are falling sick, they're dying.' His voice cracked and the general gestured him impatiently to go on. 'These invaders, we call them Plaguers, because they're giving us their sickness. They've been throwing the heads of their own dead soldiers over the wall with their catapults. Everyone thought it was some foreign ritual at first, witchcraft, so we sent them flying back . . .'

'Plague,' Archange repeated. There was dismayed silence in the throne room. Valla, appalled, wondered how much more bad news there could be. The guards all stared ahead, but she felt hopelessness had entered their hearts. The rider looked at the floor, his job done.

The empress asked Eufara, 'Have we heard any more from Hayden's army?'

He shook his head. 'No lady, not for days now.'

They looked at each other bleakly, no doubt wondering the same thing: if plague had taken Hayden Weaver's ragged band of survivors as well.

'Send the Bears,' she told him.

Valla's heart sank. The Silver Bears were the last century of the Thousand on the mountain. Without them she would be the only warrior in black and silver protecting Archange.

Eufara protested, 'But that will leave barely two hundred soldiers to guard the palace, to guard you, empress.'

'Yes, general. I know the numbers. It will have to be enough. If the City falls then this palace, and I, will be irrelevant.'

Archange turned to Valla. 'I will rest now.'

Valla nodded to Gaius and the soldiers started marching from the chamber. When the throne room was empty Archange's chair was brought for her. It was a wooden contraption on wheels. She hated using it and, even more, hated being seen in it. So the corridors to her private quarters were cleared and Valla pushed her along, not speaking, trying to be detached and unseeing, her heart full of sympathy for the old woman.

When Archange was safely in her parlour, Valla gathered her courage and begged her, 'Let me go with the Bears, lady. I am a warrior. It is what I'm good at. You have healed me so I can fight again, but now I . . .' she trailed off, not daring to say what was in her heart.

'You were a warrior born but now you are just a nursemaid to an old woman,' Archange said for her. 'No,' she said and her voice was granite. 'One defender will make little difference at the gates.'

Valla knew that one could make all the difference. But she asked, 'Then send me to fetch the veil for you, lady! I will find it and bring it to you! If you value it so.'

'What do you know of the veil?' the empress asked her wearily, eyes closed.

'You spoke of it in your sleep, empress. And I asked the lady Thekla . . .'

'And she told you?' Archange opened her eyes.

'She told me nothing about it, only that it was a valuable thing which was lost. Has it now been found?'

The empress shook her head. 'No, but when it needs to be found, it will be.'

Curious at her words, Valla asked, 'Is it a thing of magic, lady?'

'In a way it is,' the empress replied. 'It is an ancient

artefact which has the capacity to heal, and to regenerate. To most people that is magic. But what I mean, soldier, is that the Gulon Veil came back to us once before in a peculiar, circuitous way, and perhaps, in this time of great danger, it is fated to do so again.'

PART SEVEN

The Gulon Veil

CHAPTER FORTY-THREE

When Stern Edasson and his brother were boys – not big enough to do useful work but old enough to fend for themselves – they would ramble the rocky beaches near Adrastto, poking sticks into rock pools, chasing crabs, wading out into the silvery waves until they became scared and splashed back to the shore. They would pick up flotsam and drag it home: driftwood for fires, the odd ruined artefact, storm-battered and unrecognizable, dried seaweed and coloured clays they would take to the healers and medicine women in the hope of payment.

One day they had found a dead dolphin lodged on rocks after a winter storm. Benet wanted to carry it home to eat, but Stern stayed his brother's hand. It was a beautiful thing, sleek and shining, its pearly skin just starting to fade and dry in the sharp wind. It was perfect, with no marks of predation or disease. Stern had seen, on his rare, precious voyages in his father's boat, the creatures frolicking just out of reach, leaping and diving for no other reason that the boy could see than for the fun of it. He squatted beside the beast and looked into its dead eye, wondering where its life had gone to and if somewhere it was still playing with its friends. His mother told him dolphins mate for life, and when one dies the survivor swims their world, singing its mate's song in every place they had travelled together. Then it would beach itself on the unforgiving, alien land and die there, drowned by the air, though no one knew why.

But in the end Stern had submitted to his younger brother's insistence and they dragged the creature, stinking, back home. Their father beat them both as reward, for dolphins are friends to fishermen, and he forced the boys to eat the bland, chewy flesh and both were sick as dogs.

Stern often thought about the dolphin, though he had not seen another since he left Adrastto so long ago. And when he realized his brother was dying, from the sickness they called mouse fever, he remembered the dolphin. For years after he had seen it he had remembered the creature as a stiff corpse, but a few years ago he started thinking of it as a living beast again, leaping and diving for the joy of it. And now, watching his brother die, he wondered how long it would be before he remembered Benet as the young warrior he once was, strong and vigorous, and not this bewildered, bright-eyed husk far down the path of his final journey.

He held his brother's hand and hoped he would die soon.

Hayden Weaver's diminished army was camped far north of the Great North Gate, in a basin in the grasslands where, the general trusted, the searching enemy bands would not find them. If they did then they would all be slaughtered, for they had neither the numbers nor strength to fend off an attack. Almost a third had already died of mouse fever and many of the rest were too weak: recovering or dying. For some did recover, as many as one in three. Some were not touched by the illness at all, not Stern or the midwife Bruenna, who had worked tirelessly tending the sick and dying. Neither Hayden nor any of the Petrassi soldiers had been affected.

They had continued their campaign of harassment against the enemy: raiding by night the vulnerable fringes of the army, routinely hunting down scouts, and mounting occasional bold, swift attacks on a wing. They had carried on until the fever had felled so many they could no longer muster a fighting unit. And still they had not managed to quiet the cannon, whose thunderous roar went on daily. The enemy were winning. They had not won possession of the walls, Hayden's scouts reported, but slowly the Great Gate was being battered to pieces. It might last no more than a day. And there was nothing Hayden and his troops could do about it. City warriors with families behind the walls dreaded their breach and the terror which would be unleashed there by the barbarian army, but Stern privately hoped the gate would fall soon, for then the struggle would become a familiar one – City warriors battling an enemy army on equal terms. But in the dark watches of the night he wondered if mouse fever had hit the warriors defending the wall. If so, then the City was surely doomed.

Benet had been silent all that day, breathing shallowly, eyes closed, his face like milk, but now he said clearly, through crusted lips, 'I'm feeling better now, brother. I want to see Peach.'

'She's not here,' Stern said gently, for the yellow-haired whore had succumbed to the fever a day or two before.

'So pretty,' Benet mumbled. 'Do you think . . .' Then his throat seized up and he could say no more.

Stern felt a presence at his side and he turned to see Bruenna. She squatted beside him and looked critically at Benet.

'Not long now,' she told Stern.

As a midwife she knew less about battlefield wounds than most of the soldiers, but when the mouse fever came they turned to her for aid – though she could do nothing but offer sips of water and a rough kindness which made the men think of their mothers and sometimes weep.

'He'll be in the Gardens of Stone soon,' she said, for most warriors liked to hear that.

But Stern was full of doubts. The Gardens of Stone seemed a terrible place to him, a bleak wasteland where soldiers fought and never won, nor lost either, just a continuous battle without wounds, without tiredness, without end. Perhaps all creatures died as they lived, he thought, and if a dolphin spent its life, and thus its death, frolicking with its friends, so a man could not expect to enjoy a gentle afterlife if his days under the sun had not been blameless.

'General,' Bruenna warned him, standing, and Stern stood too.

Hayden looked down at Benet's emaciated body. He did not ask how he was. It was obvious.

'Brel and Petronicus have just got back,' he told Stern. The scouts had been out all night. 'They say the gate is about to fall. We must be prepared. When they crash through and on to the killing ground beyond we must be ready to attack their rear. We'll move tonight.'

Stern nodded absently, his mind still on his brother.

'What about the sick?' Bruenna asked, planting her big body in front of the general, her hands on her hips. 'We can't just leave them.'

'The camp-followers will stay here with them,' Hayden told her stiffly. 'With entry to the City within their grasp the enemy will waste no more soldiers chasing us. Those who are on the road to recovery will come with us. This is why we need to move soon. Those who aren't,' he looked down at Benet, 'we leave here. I'm sorry.'

Stern knew Benet would be dead before nightfall. Even so, the prospect of leaving him, dead or alive, was distressing. A decent burning in the company of other warriors was the best a soldier could expect, but that seldom happened. Sometimes they were put in shallow graves but Hayden's soldiers did not have a shovel between them and the rolling land on which they camped was rock-hard. More often a dead warrior received the solace of neither grave nor fire, but was abandoned to fill the bellies of animals and birds.

'The mouse fever—' Bruenna began.

Stern was watching Hayden's face and he saw tension snap into place around his eyes. The general disliked dealing with Bruenna, who seemed to offer nothing but complaint, but her women trusted her and they had been vital in nursing the sick. Not only that, Hayden detested the name 'mouse fever'. The soldiers had started seeing black mice scampering through the camp a few days before the sickness struck. They held the mice responsible for they feared them. The general, on the other hand, believed the plague was caused by a miasma from the damp ground and he insisted on breaking camp regularly to outpace it. Hayden despised superstition and an argument with the men over the demonic status of mice was the only time Stern had seen him lose his temper.

'This is not a subject for discussion, woman,' the general told Bruenna, as he often did. 'It is a military decision. Every move we make must be with a military purpose. We will break camp—' Stern watched him briefly fumble for his timepiece before remembering once again that it was broken, 'at dusk.'

He walked away and Stern knelt, and found Benet

had died while they were talking. As he closed his brother's eyes he felt only relief.

Casmir lay on his belly at the lip of a slight incline a hundred paces from the rear of the enemy army. A tall cairn beside him, the Cairn of Ashes, marked the site of the last attack on the Great North Gate more than thirty years before. The assassin's dead eye-socket itched from the dust and he kept raising his patch to scratch at it. From his right Stern muttered to him, 'Be still.'

Casmir had returned to Hayden's army despite his best intention. When he reached the Araby Gate, north of the Paradise Gate, he had handed the general's message to the guards. He was left to stew in a locked room until the guards' leader came in. He was a seasoned soldier, young but experienced, and he recognized a veteran when he saw one. He listened to Casmir's story of the lone army battling for the City from the enemy's rear and he vowed the vital message would reach the empress. He told Casmir frankly, 'I wish I could come with you, friend. The City is under siege yet we are doing nothing to help.'

'You'll get your chance,' Casmir said, seeing the lust for battle in the young man's eyes. He had felt it himself once.

Then he was back on his horse and heading out of the City, going north again. He had decided he would not desert Shivers and his comrades. He had been abandoned himself, twenty years before when his fellows had left him for dead after the skirmish at Plakos, and he knew how it felt. The torment he suffered then had left him reluctant to trust comrades again. But he was an honourable man, though others were not. He would add his sword to Hayden's ragtag army, for he knew a single blade often made the difference between victory and defeat. He was fairly young, he mused, and his life of wealth and ease could wait a little longer, until after this emergency was over.

Now they were lying as close as they dared to the enemy's baggage train, separated from the tattooed horde by a stretch of earth and a few wagons. All the foreign army's attention was on the Great North Gate. It had been battered daily by cannon balls – although in the last days the pace of the cannonade had diminished – and it was still standing only because it had been shored up behind with piles of rock and stones from demolished buildings. Since the general's message had got through there was occasional communication between Hayden and the White Palace, and the general had been told a killing field, a hundred paces deep, had been readied inside the gate. It was inevitable the Great North Gate would fall. But when the enemy broke through they would have to climb over the ruins then cross cleared ground through a blizzard of arrows and crossbow bolts to reach a stretch of newly built defences on which the City soldiers – the Second Adamantine, veterans all – waited with bright swords. Hayden's fighters were desperate to join that battle.

And now everyone – enemy, defenders and Hayden's company – was waiting for the gate to fall.

It was a perilous place to be, so close to the enemy. A pall of acrid smoke lay over them from the pyres which burned day and night. The cries and groans of wounded men drifted from a nearby casualty station – one of their first targets once they were on the move. Killing the wounded would do nothing militarily but it would anger the enemy warriors – or so they hoped, for they still knew little about them, though they had walked for more than thirty days and nights in their shadow.

Casmir turned to Shivers who was lying at his other side and asked, 'All right?'

Shivers nodded. He had sickened with mouse fever and for three days had been close to death. Now he was on his feet again, weakened but anxious not to stay back with the women and the dying. His mangled face looked worse than ever but Casmir hardly noticed it any more. He still wore Shivers' jacket and his friend wore a heavy wool coat, scavenged from the enemy, with a chain mail vest beneath. Casmir had never had a friend before, and it was a strange experience to be concerned with another's wellbeing.

They were eager to get the battle under way and impatient whispering began. Warriors fingered the edges of their shields, which lay beside them, and the hilts of their swords, sheathed at Hayden's order. The general wanted no clattering metal to betray them. Then the word came down the line, 'Be still. Be quiet,' and they all settled.

Only sixty-seven warriors, Casmir thought, to face many thousands. Most would be slain, but Casmir had no intention of being there when that happened. He would kill and kill as they moved forward, but the moment they began to fall back he planned to turn and run for his life. His mouth was dry, his hands slick with sweat. He laid his long dagger on the earth and wiped his hands on his flanks, then grasped the blade again. The wall could fall any time . . .

Then it happened, suddenly, quietly. The Great North Gate, distant to Casmir's eye, simply crumpled. It seemed strong, unconquerable, standing proud as it always had, then the top half vanished in a silent explosion of dust. The enemy hordes roared their triumph, stamping their feet, clashing swords on shields, the clamour deafening. The drums rolled, then their entire army moved forward, running at the front, marching at the rear. The rumble they created was like night thunder.

Casmir, waiting, looked impatiently to his right where the order to advance would come from. Time crawled by. He looked ahead again. He could not see that far with his one eye, but he imagined the enemy soldiers climbing over the gate's ruins unhindered. Then, although he had heard no order, his comrades began stumbling to their feet, clambering over the crest of earth, running towards the vast, dark bulk of the enemy army. Casmir snatched up his shield and ran with them, Shivers half a pace behind. It was hard to see for all the dust and smoke, hard to breathe. Then shapes loomed ahead and he saw they had reached the baggage wagons. But there were no guards to detain them and they swept through. Now it was becoming a foot-race. Casmir saw Stern sprinting ahead and he redoubled his efforts to keep up. Their prize was the first enemy death.

When a wall of unarmoured backs appeared out of the murk the City soldiers were on them with shouts of triumph. Casmir hacked at one neck, then another, then a third. For a few long heartbeats he felt invincible. Then enemy warriors were turning swiftly, swinging their shields, disordered briefly by the stealthy attack. One great oaf lunged at him with a broadsword and Casmir neatly skewered him between his belly plates. The man fell howling to all fours and Casmir slashed him across the spine to finish him.

The enemy were enraged by the attack. They were forced to turn and defend their rear when all they wanted was to charge the broken gate. They were ferocious but undisciplined. One group of a dozen or more attacked haphazardly and found themselves isolated, in a trap of their own making, and were slaughtered by Hayden's fighters. Commands were bellowed by enemy leaders and some order restored.

Casmir saw Stern go down unhelmed, knocked sideways by a glancing blow from a mace. Brel, the Petrassi captain, noticed too, and he and Casmir stood over their comrade until Stern managed to get to all fours and crawl away. Brel was a swordmaster, like Casmir, but this was no place for their superior skills. They cut and hacked with sword and knife, gouging and punching and head-butting where they could, forcing the enemy back, forcing their generals to commit more men to defend their rear.

Casmir parried a thrust from a short sword. He swept a two-handed blow to a man's unprotected head which caved in his skull. Another ran forward, helmed and clad in leather armour. Casmir's blade flashed out. The enemy parried, then ducked beneath a swing to stab at Casmir's groin. Casmir leaped sideways, his weapon swinging downward in a vicious arc. The man blocked the blow but staggered, slashing wildly. Casmir spun on his heel to hammer his elbow into his face. The man fell to one knee then screamed as a blade was thrust deep into his side by Hayden Weaver. Casmir grinned at the general and Hayden nodded, dragging his sword out.

As the battle went on Casmir was wounded, cut in several places, his blood flowing freely, yet still he stood strong, Shivers on his left, Hayden on his right. But their numbers were fast dwindling.

Then came a welcome reprieve. The defenders on the walls must have realized there was a battle going on outside and crossbowmen were brought up. The first Casmir knew of it was when the man he was fighting, a soldier with tattoos so thick and black he looked burned, suddenly collapsed, felled by a crossbow bolt through the back of his skull. Casmir looked up at the battlements then retreated quickly, yelling to the others to do the same, making a clear division between the enemy and themselves. Ten of the tattooed warriors, then twenty, fell to the black-feathered bolts. They didn't know which way to turn. Hayden's force attacked them again, trusting the accuracy of the bowmen. Some of the enemy infantrymen, under attack from both sides, started retreating in disorder, heading east. Six were cut off by Hayden's soldiers and killed.

Casmir took the chance of a lull in the fighting to suck in some deep breaths, looking around. Stern was back in the battle, his head roughly bandaged. Hayden was standing on a corpse's back, surrounded by the dead and dying, gauging the battle. The general shouted to them to retreat. Some, their blood up, argued angrily. But Casmir knew Hayden was right. They'd forced the enemy leaders to rethink and they would attack in force next, a force big enough to destroy them.

Brel, limping heavily, repeated the order to retreat and Shivers and Casmir went with him, pushing and dragging some of their friends who were reluctant to leave. They ran and stumbled, heading back towards the crest of land they'd left at dawn. But it was too late.

From the south, detaching itself from the body of the enemy army, came a company of light infantry, more than two hundred men armed with long spears and tall shields. These were not the tattooed horde, Casmir could tell. They were disciplined, elite warriors, no doubt intent on finishing them off for good.

Hayden shouted to his remaining warriors to form a defensive circle protecting the injured. Their position was hopeless, but he had always known it would come to this. They were too far from the walls for the bowmen to help them now. Looking about him he saw they were back at the tall cairn where they had started the day. Now, though, there were scarcely twenty of his soldiers still on their feet, and their opponents looked fresh, well armed and intent on revenge. A dark shadow fell over him and he looked up. Storm clouds were massing overhead.

Blood ran from a head-wound and he could feel it trickling down his neck. His back was on fire and when he moved he could feel a broken sword-tip lodged beneath his shoulder-blade, gouging into muscle and flesh. It made raising his shield impossible and Hayden had long since abandoned it, relying on sword and long dagger.

A flicker of lightning flashed to his right, closely followed by a roll of thunder. Then the rain came down in torrents. Lightning overhead lit up the immense enemy army and the wall teeming with attackers. And, nearly on top of them now, the infantry sent to wipe out Hayden and his survivors. He could see the hatred in their eyes, the blood on their teeth. He thought of his Anna for the last time. All pain faded away.

A spear lunged towards him. Blocking it with his sword he dragged a back-handed cut that sheared through leather and through the flesh beneath. He parried another thrust and hammered his sword into the man's face. A blade sliced through Hayden's thigh but he scarcely felt it.

A tall warrior ran at him using all the weight of his heavily muscled shoulder and length of his arm to hurl a spear at Hayden. With no shield, the general desperately threw himself to one side. The spear caught him on the edge of his breastplate and veered off, but the weight of the blow spun him round and he fell to his knees. He pushed himself to his feet but another man ran at him. Desperately he turned aside the thrusting spear with his mailed gauntlet then punched the man in the jaw. The enemy warrior paused, befuddled, then Stern appeared out of the rain and hacked at his neck, severing the great blood vessels in a fountain of gore.

They could not stand for long. It was slaughter. His heartbeat seemed to slow and Hayden, cruelly, had plenty of time to watch as the enemy overwhelmed them. He saw Casmir, badly injured, go to Shivers' aid as he fought off an attack by three men. Both of them went down. He saw Stern brought to his knees by a kick in the stomach. Before he could move to help his lieutenant a spearman drove his weapon deep into Stern's back.

Hayden stood, chest heaving, blood and rain sluicing off him. It had been a gallant effort. His little band of survivors had been scarcely more than a fleabite to the enemy army but they had done their valiant best, and had made some restitution for their terrible losses at the Vorago. They had fought to the last man – no warrior could ask more. Looking round again, he realized he was that last man.

He saw the spear coming towards him but, weakened by blood-loss, he knew there was little he could do about it. As the point drove into his chest he grabbed the wielder's arm and slashed his knife towards the man's neck. He never saw if the blade landed.

CHAPTER FORTY-FOUR

THE NIGHTHAWKS RODE SOUTH BENEATH THE POURING rain. They kept the City walls in distant sight to their right, alert for enemy attack, but the soft eastern plain remained quiet. To their left was the Grandon Forest, a gloomy, secret place of dark trees closely ranked. They saw deer watching them from its shadows, but Darius refused his troopers' petition to hunt them. *We are riding to battle. It is for lesser men to bring food*, he told them.

After a long night in the saddle Rubin was relieved to see the great bulk of the south-east bastion, the Raven Tower, rising in their path by mid-morning. The square tower marked the transition from the eastern wall to that of the south, and was the tallest structure for many leagues around. It was their destination, the headquarters of the southern defence.

Darius was familiar to soldiers throughout the City, and when they saw him the guards raced to open the Raven Gate and admit the Nighthawks. Their mounts barely slowed, clattering across cobbles, through the cool of the tunnel, and out into the odorous tumult of the City. There the troopers reined in and Rubin slid off his mount, sinews screaming. He prayed to the gods that he might never have to sit on a horse again.

Darius ran up the steps of the tower and Rubin followed more slowly. But when the commander stopped at a lower floor and disappeared into darkness Rubin, lured by the tower's heights, carried on climbing the spiral steps. By the time he reached the top he was breathless. On the wind-blown battlements were four guards, one in each corner of the immense wooden floor, staring outward, unmoving. It was silent up there, apart from the buffeting of the easterly wind in Rubin's ear. He stepped over to the western side of the tower and looked down. He gripped the stones, astonished by what he saw.

He knew from his old guard Gallan that there had been a frantic attempt to reinforce the ruins of the Adamantine Wall and to dig a defensive ditch, but he had thought it hopeless. A ditch? A bank of earth? How could they keep out the enemy horde? But now he could see what the City could achieve when the need was dire.

A stump of the wall, from the Raven Tower westward, still stood, but it ended abruptly after one hundred paces or so. Beyond, into the far distance, he could see only jumbled stone with just the odd tower still standing. In front of the ruins an enormous ditch had been excavated, twenty or more paces wide. It was impossible to judge how deep it was for this end of it was half flooded. From the muddy waters bristled the tops of thousands of sharpened stakes. Behind the moat a gigantic earthwork, half the height of the Raven Tower, had been thrown up over the ruins of the Adamantine Wall. Thousands of workers, mostly women and children it seemed, were swarming over the giant fortification like beetles, teams shifting stones from the broken wall and convoys of ox-wagons bringing supplies of gravel and earth. He could hear bellowing oxen, the cries of the labourers and the rattle of spades on gravel but they seemed distant, whipped away by the stiff breeze which fluttered the pennants on the tower.

The new defence looked impossible to cross. In his mind's eye Rubin saw enemy troops throw flimsy bridges across the ditch, scramble over them, the defenders hurling down rocks, loosing arrows, the attackers falling, impaled on the stakes – it was a satisfying image.

The rain had stopped at last and weak sunlight touched his face. Rubin turned slowly northward, his eye passing over the City's southernmost districts of Barenna and Burman South, and beyond them the Shield of Freedom. Clouds brooded above the mountain; it was still raining there. His gaze alighted on the City's east wall leading northward to the Paradise Gate, too far away to discern. Beyond it the wall continued, leading ever north. A strong horse in its prime would take a good day, Rubin knew, to gallop from where he was in the south to the furthest northern point, the Great North Gate. From this height, and in sunlight, it was hard to believe a vast army was besieging the City. Except it wasn't a siege. Even an army ten times the size could not hope to attack the whole of the City's hundreds of leagues of wall. No, they had picked the vulnerable points, two of the Great Gates and here, this woeful breach.

Hearing voices approaching, Rubin turned to see Darius and two other soldiers climb into sight on to the tower's wooden roof. One was tall and thin, not old, wearing eyeglasses. The other was— Rubin's words of greeting caught in his throat.

Marcellus!

'Lord!' Rubin ran over to him and fell to his knees. He looked up, scarcely believing. Marcellus was full-bearded now and wore cavalry leathers like a common trooper. The beard made him look older but as always he diminished any man near him with the force of his presence.

'Well, young Rubin,' his lord said warmly. 'You do turn up in the oddest of places.' He smiled.

Rubin was beyond words, but he could have said the same. He had always hoped against hope that he would see Marcellus again, but he had never expected to meet him here, in the heart of Archange's defences.

His lord clapped him on the shoulder. 'Get up, you fool,' he whispered. Close up, Rubin thought the intervening year had been hard on him. His eyes were pouchy, his face thinner, more lined.

Rubin scrambled to his feet and glanced between Marcellus and Darius, perplexed. Elija had told him the Nighthawks had fought for the emperor on the Day of Summoning. Marcellus and Darius should be enemies yet Darius was smiling.

As if hearing his thoughts, Marcellus explained, 'I have been to the Serafia and spoken to Archange. I have agreed to join my troops with hers against this common enemy.'

Marcellus turned to the man in eyeglasses. 'You have performed miracles here, Vares,' he said, indicating the work below. 'But we are still woefully short of defenders. They are sending thirty to forty thousand against us in the south, my intelligence tells me.' He started pacing up and down the wooden floor, his prodigious energy barely contained.

'We have sixteen thousand men at arms,' said Langham Vares, general of the Twenty-second, following Marcellus with his eyes, 'including your two thousand, plus a militia of more than ten thousand. We have two hundred bowmen. But the Nighthawks are our only cavalry.'

'These militia you speak of – you mean the people labouring on the defences?' Marcellus asked, pausing at the west side of the tower, looking down. 'Women and children, and old men?'

Vares sighed, taking off his eyeglasses and cleaning them on his sleeve. He looked weary and discouraged. 'The time will come when they will be fighting for their lives, lord.'

'Or running for their lives,' Marcellus muttered. 'The enemy forces are marching hard from the north. We can expect them here by dawn. But we have another problem, and a grave one.'

'Lord?'

Marcellus lowered his voice so the sentries on the tower could not hear. 'Plague has broken out among the defenders at both the Great North Gate and the Paradise Gate.' Vares groaned, dismayed. 'We must assume it has been brought by the enemy army,' Marcellus went on. 'It can be controlled to some degree while there is a wall between attackers and defenders. But here there will be hand-to-hand combat.' He said no more.

'But if the plague is rife among the enemy they will be weakened,' Vares offered, clutching at faint hope. 'Perhaps they will not get this far south—'

'If they were to lose one in three to the plague we would still be badly outnumbered,' Marcellus cut in impatiently. 'And they have shown no sign of it. Their leader is a man called Hammarskjald. I know him well from the past. He is a ruthless enemy and I suspect his hand behind this infection.'

'Will you tell the defenders about the plague, lord?' asked Rubin.

Marcellus turned to him. 'Why would I?' he asked, raising an eyebrow.

'It might make our people fight more ferociously to stop them entering the City, or . . .' Rubin trailed off as he saw where his argument was going.

'It might make them flee in fear,' Marcellus finished. 'What do you think?'

Rubin had never suffered from a lack of confidence

but he felt daunted as the three veteran warriors watched him, awaiting his answer. His mind was still bemused as he tried to absorb the knowledge not only that Marcellus lived, but that he had brought warriors to defend the City.

'It is a matter of morale,' he managed at last. 'As in a battle, when one, or two, or a dozen flee, then others will leave in droves. But if their friends stand firm, then they will too, be they soldiers or townsfolk.' He shrugged. It seemed obvious.

'Then we must make our presence felt, you and I,' Marcellus said to Vares and Darius. 'If we stand firm, then so will our army.'

Marcellus spent the rest of the day reviewing the components of the defence; he walked the ditch and earthwork, speaking to labourers and soldiers, flanked by Darius and Vares. As night fell he summoned Vares' officers, to gauge their competence and resolve. Rubin was at his side throughout, exhilarated that his lord had not only returned but had apparently discarded his grievances with Archange to ally against their mutual enemy.

It was midnight before Marcellus sent his officers to their rest and then sat down with Rubin in a chilly chamber in the Raven Tower. It was damp and smoky in there, lit only by the flicker of torches and a poor fire. Wind gusted down the chimney sending up showers of sparks from the embers in the hearth. Rubin slumped into a chair with a groan and pulled his cloak around his shoulders. A servant brought a flagon of warmed wine.

'We are badly outnumbered,' Marcellus reiterated, savouring the wine with a sigh. He seemed to notice neither the cold nor the fumes. 'But I would not be here if we were not.'

'The ditch will be full of water by morning,' offered Rubin, who had been watching the engineers filling it. 'It will hide the stakes.'

Marcellus sniffed. 'Any enemy commander worth his salt will predict they'll be there. But they will still have to go over them. It will slow them a little. The problem,' he went on, 'is that the ditch will quickly become clotted with bodies, both theirs and ours. Once that happens the enemy will use them as a bridge to get to us.'

Rubin shuddered as hideous images of the broken and trodden dead crowded into his mind. He had resolved to stand beside his lord when the enemy struck and to stay beside him until the end, in whatever manner that came, but the prospect filled him with dread.

'Who is Hammarskjald?' he asked, to vanquish the images of death and mutilation. 'I have heard the name before, from my father, but I thought him long dead.'

Marcellus leaned back and put his feet on the table. He took a deep draught of wine. He seemed content to talk into the night.

'He was one of us,' he replied, his eyes unfocused as he looked into the past. 'A Serafim, one of the First. He was our doctor, a brilliant surgeon and a skilled physician. He was always confrontational and opinionated, and was much disliked from the outset.

'Almost immediately we arrived here he disagreed with our leader's plans, and their battles – of words – were volcanic. Eventually he departed, taking his people with him; we were short of medical aid and that callous act nearly doomed us all. That was in our very first year in this land. When he tried to return, many years later, his comrades all dead, Araeon banished him and swore he would be executed if he came back. We all believed he was condemning Hammarskjald to death for this was a perilous place for a man alone. But he survived and prospered.'

He swigged the wine, draining the cup. 'After that he was a painful thorn in our side. He'd sabotage our plans and spread disaffection. He made alliances then reneged on them. And worse. He murdered some of our best. Araeon tried to have him killed, but Hammarskjald was clever, both brilliant and devious. And as the City grew so did his hatred of us.'

Marcellus refilled his cup and called to his servant for more wine. 'Hammarskjald threatened he would destroy the City. I thought he meant it at the time, but over the years it became easier to forget him, or think him dead. I for one underestimated him. I had no idea he possessed this much patience.' He sighed and added, 'I always rather liked him.'

There was a comfortable silence in the stuffy room and Rubin found his fears dissolving in the warmth of the wine. Marcellus was rolling his empty cup between his palms, staring into the past.

Rubin asked, 'How did you raise an army of two thousand, lord? Where from?'

Marcellus' face darkened. 'It was not difficult. Many of the City's faithful warriors were angered by the machinations which brought Archange to power, and the deaths of those loyal to the emperor. Many who survived the carnage of the Day of Summoning departed the City. Eventually they ended up under my command again.'

Too many questions jostled for attention in Rubin's mind, but he asked the one that had bothered him most. 'Where have you been for the past year, lord?'

Marcellus shook his head. 'Do not ask me that, boy. Who knows who will be in power when this war is done? You might end up on the wrong side. The less you know about some matters the better.'

Gazing directly at Rubin, he said, 'I hear you have discovered a Gift of the Serafim. I always predicted you would. Tell me.'

Rubin wondered how he had heard. Only a handful of people knew of the extraordinary power he could wield and he wondered, not for the first time, if Marcellus had agents in the White Palace. His lord was watching him, waiting, and he cast his mind back to that bloody day two winters before and told Marcellus about the Odrysian attack on the City's wounded at the medical camp below Needlewoman's Notch.

'I was still feeble from my injury,' he explained. 'I could not lift a sword. I could barely lift my hand. But Valla was there.' He looked at Marcellus, who nodded. Marcellus' command of the names of all his soldiers was legendary. 'She was battling them single-handed – one-handed.' He smiled briefly.

'I remember reaching out to her. I think I wanted to save her. Or make her retreat and save herself. I don't know. But as I stretched out I felt,' he paused, trying to remember the feeling, 'an energy – like a surge of lightning – run through me. It seemed to come up from the ground and sear through me and out through my fingers.' He shivered at the memory and pulled his cloak up around his neck.

'Did you kill them all?' Marcellus asked, leaning forward, his black eyes gleaming.

'It wasn't like that.' Rubin shook his head. 'I wasn't trying to kill them. I wanted to stop the killing. All the combatants, ours and the Blues, laid down their arms. They forgot what they were doing. Only Valla realized what was happening, then she attacked them.'

Marcellus nodded. 'A strong-minded woman.'

'I know you possess such power,' Rubin said hesitantly, for the subject had never arisen between them, 'and Archange also. Much greater than mine,' he added.

'But I do not understand what it is or where it comes from.'

Marcellus stood to stretch his back. 'It is called *einai*,' the lord said. 'It is a perilous thing, both gift and curse. But I'm glad it has revealed itself in you. I always predicted you would be exceptional. You or your sister, or both. There were some among us, including Araeon, who thought you should both be despatched at birth. Your father, you see, was perhaps the only man he feared. I argued we should wait until you had reached adulthood, which is when the *einai* reveals itself. It seems Araeon was right, though, for it was Indaro who killed him in the end.'

Rubin was silent and a sliver of fear trickled down his spine. He had been dismayed when first told of his sister's treachery but thought it known only to a few. Now, it appeared, Marcellus had known all along. He was struggling to find words when the servant returned with more wine, and bread and meat. Marcellus sat down and took some bread.

'Why does it emerge then?' Rubin asked, to direct the subject away from Indaro. He helped himself to roast meat, greasy and warm.

'It was designed that way. After all, such power should not be placed in the hands of children.'

Rubin wondered if such power should be in the hands of anyone. 'Designed by whom?' he asked. 'By you?'

Marcellus laughed and the frigid air in the tower room grew warmer. 'No, boy, not by me. I have been many things in my long life – soldier, politician, historian – but I was never a man of science.'

Outside they heard men shouting and Marcellus paused, alert. Then the shouts dissolved into laughter and he spoke on.

'We waited with much anticipation. It was the first

time in generations that Serafim had produced offspring. And you and Indaro were the children of *two* Families – the Kerrs and Guillaumes. So we watched Indaro closely, but she showed no outstanding talent except as a swordswoman, and she had been trained from an early age by the very best. And then there was you.' He smiled. 'Again, you showed no special talents. Some believed the Gifts had passed over your generation and would reveal themselves in your children. Some thought the Gifts had ended with Reeve as they did with the Khans.'

Rubin frowned. 'So they were passed down through my mother, through her line?' He felt uncomfortable speaking of his parents as though they were breeding cattle.

Marcellus smiled and shrugged. 'These things are impossible to chart with certainty. Gifts inherited through the female line are always considered pure, because a mother's proof of parenthood is there to be seen. It is different for the father. Perhaps it was not Reeve who started that line which ended with you. That was the thinking at the time. But now we know that was wrong. You are both the son and the descendant of a Family line. You have proved it to my satisfaction. You will learn to manage it, enhance it, in due course.'

'Someone told me once,' Rubin said, the wine making him bold, 'that you and Giulia Rae Khan were once wed.'

He wanted to ask if they had offspring but Marcellus ignored the comment, so Rubin reverted to their earlier conversation. 'Do you really believe Hammarskjald is responsible for the plague? How is that possible?'

Marcellus looked up from his food and his black gaze was cold in the torchlight. 'He has the skills and he has the malign will.' He nodded slowly. 'Yes,' he concluded, 'I think it entirely likely.'

'But he would kill his own soldiers as well as ours!'

'Maybe. Maybe not. We shall see. One thing we can be sure of: Hammarskjald is prepared to throw his all into this wager. He has thought about it long and hard. And he will certainly have more pieces to play. We must be ready for anything.'

Soldiers always say the waiting is the worst. And in Rubin's experience of battle, it was true that the dry mouth and sweaty hands, full bladder, trembling and dread running through every nerve and sinew were bad. But they were as nothing compared with the gut-wrenching terror of actually being in battle – the panicked hacking and lunging at anything moving in front of you, the constant fear that a sharp blade will slice into your body from somewhere out of sight as you struggle to see from inside an echoing, stuffy helm. And the stench and blood and the agony-filled shrieks of the dead and dying.

So, as he stood waiting at his lord's shoulder at daybreak, he tried not to think.

They were standing at the top of the new earthwork, separated from an army of forty thousand enemy infantry by the water-filled ditch and a few paces of rocky ground. The soldiers facing them had no cannon, just sharp weaponry driven by muscle and bone and seething hatred. They bellowed and chanted, clashed their weapons and screamed taunts and curses and battle cries. Those in the front line were tattooed and dressed in hides and leather armour. Some carried cudgels but most held blades. These did not glint and gleam in the morning light as did those of the City soldiers, and Rubin realized with a roiling of his guts that their knives and swords were clotted with the dried blood of past opponents. Dawn was long gone and the morning slowly passing and still the enemy commanders held their army in check.

The City warriors were motionless as statues, silent, as they had been trained.

Marcellus stood with his two thousand, clad in armour of ox-blood red. Rubin, in borrowed armour, was now junior aide to his lord. As such it was his duty to fight in a supporting role, to spot threats unnoticed by Marcellus, to deflect stray arrows, to offer his lord water if needed and to tend his wounds if it came to that. It was an honourable position, and Rubin kept telling himself that.

When the drums finally rolled the enemy sprang forward like a rabid dog loosed from a leash. The tattooed fighters raced for the City lines, throwing themselves into the ditch yelling their battle cries, many then screaming in agony as they impaled themselves on the hidden stakes. But within heartbeats, it seemed, the front line of soldiers had surged across, reckless of their own dead and dying, and they were soon scrambling up the steep earthwork, knives between their teeth.

As the first reached the top Marcellus, long cavalry sword in hand, strode forward and swung, chopping the man's head off with one mighty blow. Blood sprayed. There was a pause, almost too brief to notice, and the horde fell on the City's defenders.

For a long time the front line held firm and the second-rankers had little to do but wait their turn. But then City soldiers began to fall before the onslaught. Rubin saw a tattooed face coming at him from his right and sprang to meet it. He parried a slashing blow to his neck, dodged left and skewered the man under his chest armour. His opponent kept coming for an instant, then collapsed. Rubin darted back to cover Marcellus, heart pounding, looking wildly around for the next attacker.

He came from the left, a bear of a man with a broadsword. In the long, slow moment before the fighter reached him Rubin saw he wore a necklace of scalps and a headband of finger bones. He grinned toothlessly at Rubin and swung the great sword at his belly. Rubin swayed away then forward, expecting the giant to be slow, but the broadsword swung back faster than he'd calculated. He dodged it by a flea's breadth then darted in and stabbed at the man's face. He missed and the giant's riposte caught him on the shoulder-plate. It clanged like a death-knell and Rubin felt it jar through his body. But it was a glancing blow and Rubin came back with a lunge to the man's bare head. The man avoided it easily, grinning, but he didn't see Rubin's long knife held at his belly and he charged into it. He stared down at his ripped flesh as the blood spurted. Rubin waited for him to fall. Then Marcellus swerved away from his own fight and, in a lightning thrust, lanced his sword deep into the giant's spine. He fell like a pole-axed ox. Marcellus nodded at Rubin then turned back to the fray.

As the battle raged throughout the day the City troops were slowly forced back and more and more of the tattooed army crossed the corpse-choked moat and scaled the earthwork. The City line held, but Rubin knew that was not enough – they had to push the enemy back over the ditch by the end of the day or the hard work of labourers and defenders would be for nothing and the City was done for.

As the sun started to set in a menacing twilight of dark purple clouds split by vivid orange slashes, Marcellus' voice suddenly rose above the clamour of battle. 'Retreat!' he bellowed. The order was repeated down the line.

Rubin slashed his sword through an enemy soldier's throat then stepped back unwillingly, staring at his lord in bewilderment. He couldn't believe it! There was no reason to pull back! They were still strong, though they had lost ground, and they had killed far more of the enemy – who seemed to throw themselves uncaring on the City blades – than they had lost of their own. Rubin himself was uninjured bar a deep gouge across his upper chest and a few bruises and scrapes.

But City warriors were backing away in good order. 'Come on, you fool!' one man growled, grabbing Rubin by the arm.

'But Marcellus?' he shouted, struggling to get free, for his lord stood alone, showing no sign of retreating. He was fighting like a demon, his two swords flashing faster than eye could follow or the mind comprehend. Still the enemy came at him and still they died.

'Marcellus can take care of himself,' the soldier grunted. He was a dark and dour veteran who had fought beside Rubin for much of the day. He was limping heavily as he dragged Rubin away.

Marcellus fought on, a colossus in blood-red armour, his opponents falling to his blades which flickered like flames. Then slowly the fighting around him began to falter. Orders were bellowed from deep within the enemy ranks and those surrounding Marcellus looked around, seeming undecided, confused. Some started to back away. A strange, ominous silence spread through the two armies under the lowering sky.

Rubin was being dragged back, still struggling, when he felt a crippling pain skewer the base of his skull. Within moments he was barely able to see and he stopped resisting and stumbled to join his comrades retreating north. As he moved away the agony in his head faded. Finally his companion halted and Rubin turned to watch.

Around Marcellus enemy warriors were falling to the ground, clutching their heads and screeching. Others were throwing themselves back into the bloody ditch, frantic to escape. Marcellus stood tall among them, weaponless now. He had thrust his two swords into the earth and was standing, gauntleted hands raised, facing the enemy.

Rubin watched with awe and horror as blood began gouting from the eyes and mouths of those closest to his lord. The blood did not fall but swirled through the air, its droplets forming a whirling vortex with Marcellus as its centre. Then, to his disgust, an enemy soldier's head exploded like overripe fruit. Another's chest was torn apart as if by unseen talons, gouts of flesh flying through the air. Marcellus disappeared within the spinning maelstrom of blood and flesh and shattered bone.

The tattooed warriors were fighting each other to get away, trampling over the bodies of their fellows, alive or dead, fleeing as fast as they were able. Some City warriors cheered but Rubin felt only revulsion.

The bloody vortex collapsed, drenching the ground, and Marcellus was revealed, armour dripping, surrounded by piles of dead bodies and butchered body parts. Rivers of gore were flooding into the corpse-laden ditch. Marcellus tore off his helm then turned and looked back at his warriors, triumphant. Released, they raced forward, back to the lip of the ditch where they had begun the day, slipping and sliding in the grisly remains.

Rubin followed more slowly. An invisible miasma of blood and guts hung in the air. He could feel it coating his eyeballs, invading his nose and mouth, sucked in with every weary breath. His head spun and nausea rose suddenly. He leaned forward and vomited on to the mud and blood. He wiped his mouth, then, straightening up, saw his lord waving him over, grinning.

Marcellus' teeth shone in the wet crimson of his face, his obsidian eyes glittered. He was elated, drunk with victory. Rubin remembered the first time he had seen his lord in his ox-blood armour, standing in the Red

Palace at the top of the Pomegranate Stair. Then he had briefly thought him dipped in gore, and now that seemed prescient, a forecast of today's slaughter.

Marcellus drew off dripping gauntlets and dropped them. With unsuppressed glee, he thumped Rubin on the back. '*That* is the power *I* can wield, boy!'

Rubin nodded, struggling to smile. He could not share Marcellus' joy at the carnage. He busied himself retrieving his lord's swords and wiping them, his mind still in turmoil.

But Marcellus grabbed him by the arm and pulled him in close. 'Tomorrow we will discover if *you* can do the same!' he hissed.

Rubin felt the unwholesome heat of him, smelled the night wine heavy on his breath and the stench of blood and guts rolling off his armour. It was all he could do not to back away in disgust.

He spent a restless, enervating night, his fleeting dreams stalked by horrors. He dreamed of Marcellus as a giant in golden armour trampling across the City. He raised his shining arms and legs high and placed his feet heavily like some huge mechanical monster. Around him men, women and children disappeared in a whirlwind of carnage, though not a drop of blood stained the monster's golden body.

When he awoke Rubin felt more weary than when he had lain down a few brief hours before. His body ached and the wounds he'd thought of yesterday as minor started their clamour. He sat up, groaning, and shook his head to free himself of the cling of nightmare. On the cold ground around him dog-tired soldiers slept and snored. Above them the waxen moon appeared then vanished behind scudding clouds.

He had killed many men, too many to count. Archange's slight, *I am told you are not a warrior*, no longer held true. Yet, for all the lives that had been ended by his blade, still Rubin was repelled by his lord's feat of slaughter and by his drunken, boastful glee. Dread washed through him at the thought that he might share Marcellus' power to destroy. *What is he?* he wondered. *And what am I?* Tentatively he felt for the power he knew lay curled within him, waiting, but could detect nothing but an empty stomach and full bladder and the pains of any mortal man after a savage battle. The *einai*, as Marcellus had called it, had previously arisen in him unsummoned. He had been its victim, its unwilling puppet. Under the random moonlight he vowed to himself that if the power emerged again he would wrest it to his own will.

That morning the battle started in much the same way as the day before, except, Rubin thought, the enemy fighters looked a little less eager. They had lost, Vares' captains calculated, as many as two thousand warriors. A triumph for the City, but not nearly enough to turn the tide. Marcellus' rout of the enemy was barely mentioned, except when soldiers predicted they would walk in dread of him in future. On the contrary, Rubin feared, his lord would be the prime target now.

He lined up beside the same dour veteran who had dragged him away the previous day. Loomis, he learned, had once been a Warhound of the Thousand, and word of the century made Rubin think of Valla and her unconquerable faith in Marcellus and in the City. He smiled fondly. For all the enemy's superior numbers, their new weaponry, and the dread plague, Valla would have no doubt the City would prevail. The thought encouraged him. He hoped she was still safe in the White Palace and not in the front line somewhere.

As the drums rolled and the enemy horde charged Rubin put aside all his misgivings about Marcellus and resolved to protect his lord to his last breath. What else, otherwise, was he there for?

A City soldier fell in front of him, leaving a gap in the line. Two swordsmen came storming through. Rubin swerved to his right and ducked a swinging blade, then speared the first man. Then he darted left and parried a mighty blow from the second warrior which forced him to one knee. He drove his knife blade into the man's groin. As the man sagged, blood spouting, he leaped up and finished him with a throat cut. He looked around for Marcellus, then stepped over a body to cover his lord's back again.

Next to him Loomis was locked in combat with a burly warrior who was naked bar a leather kilt. He was covered with tattoos, but they did nothing to protect him. Loomis blocked a sword-thrust then ran the man through with a long dagger. As he thrust and slashed, parried and blocked, Rubin wondered at these enemy soldiers who fought so fiercely despite being mostly unarmoured. Did they have some faith that made them fearless, or was it just a pure hatred of the City?

'Rubin!' Loomis shouted. Rubin barely saw the blur of motion to his left but he swerved and felt the heavy swish of a cudgel pass close by his ear. He spun and skewered the wielder before the man could swing again. *They're all so slow,* Rubin thought. *Is this how Marcellus feels in a battle, that all his enemies are sluggish and weak?* He could sense no power within him yet he felt invulnerable, as if his opponents were all in their first fight, green and unskilled. As the long morning passed he killed every man who came against him, his blood thrilling in his veins.

But, for all his efforts and Marcellus' leadership, the City's defenders were losing ground pace by pace. Even Marcellus had been forced to take up his shield and defend himself from the frenzied attacks of swarms of warriors whose only focus was on killing him.

It was around midday when, it seemed, he'd had enough. He ordered the retreat. His troops swiftly backed away, certain of what was to come, and this time Rubin went with them. Marcellus flung his shield at an enemy soldier, bellowing his defiance, and fought on with two swords, the blades whirling so fast they seemed to create an impenetrable barrier around him. When the pain spiked in the base of his skull Rubin watched with dread and fascination.

The tattooed fighters did not run, not this time. They screamed and they writhed, their bodies torn and tormented, but only a handful of them turned tail. And one determined warrior, blood gouting from eyes and ears, in the final agonized moment of his life, lunged forward and plunged his blade deep into Marcellus' side.

Rubin yelled, 'My lord!' and ran to him, reckless of the agony in his head.

Marcellus staggered. He seemed to be held upright only by his armour. His power faded and was gone. Soldiers of both sides raced forward, desperate to be the first to reach him. Rubin outstripped them all and threw himself in front of his lord, his outflung shield deflecting an enemy sword slashing towards Marcellus' neck. He plunged his knife into the attacker's eye, then held off the renewed attack by the enemy as Marcellus sank slowly to his knees. City men lifted their wounded leader and carried him away. His duty to protect his lord for the moment done, Rubin left the fight to others and followed.

Marcellus was hurried to the casualty station, dark blood pumping from his side. His face was deathly pale, as if all his lifeblood were swiftly draining from the deep gash, but his eyes were open, searching the sky.

He was laid on a pallet bed and Rubin helped pull off the gore-drenched armour. A surgeon quickly packed clean cloths into the injury in a bid to staunch the blood, which was frothy with air. Rubin knew this was a bad omen. He watched the flow, willing it to stop, but the cloths turned instantly red, as did those that replaced them. He wished he knew more about Marcellus' capacity to heal himself. Any ordinary soldier would be dead within the hour from a wound this deep, this vital, but Rubin himself had suffered worse and survived in the end.

And so, as the battle raged on mere paces away, Rubin sat by his lord's side and willed him to live.

CHAPTER FORTY-FIVE

As twilight fell on the grasslands beyond the Great North Gate, the gentle light softening the carnage beside the Cairn of Ashes, a lone horse plodded out of the north. The City walls within her sight, the rider stared in dismay at the bodies on the blood-soaked ground in front of her and at the vast army massed at the broken gate in the distance.

Emly slid from the saddle and knelt beside the nearest corpse. The soldier had been slashed across the face, his features impossible to discern. She moved to the next, who had no injury she could see. She felt his bloody hand. It was cold. She walked among the dead, seeing many she recognized, some mutilated, some with no clear cause of death for all were clotted with dry blood. But she knew none of their names and it was only when she found Stern's torn body that she wept. She had thought him long dead at the Vorago and it seemed pitiful to find him here so near the City, defeated so close to home.

Then, through her tears, Emly saw a sprawled figure with an eyepatch. Hurrying over she found it was Casmir. He had a fearful gash in his chest and his skin was cold to the touch, but he was not yet dead, for he opened his one eye when she murmured his name. She jumped up, ran to the horse and grabbed her water skin. But Casmir would not drink, turning his head away.

'Emly,' he whispered. She bent close and his breath was light as down on her face. 'You were always witness to my undoing,' he said, his voice serene.

She did not ask him why he was there, among the heroes of the City.

'Can I do anything, Casmir?' she asked but he moved his head a little to say no. She knew he was beyond help.

'Can I take word to anyone, a wife, a son?' she asked but he made no reply and she realized he was dead.

Then she noticed the jacket he was wearing. It was Evan's, and she had believed it lost on the Vorago battle-field. With difficulty she rolled his body over and stripped it off. She ripped open its silken lining, now stained with blood and mud. Gleaming in the fading light was the Gulon Veil. Her thoughts in turmoil, Emly took it out carefully then held it to her breast. She looked at Casmir. She unfolded the veil and laid it lightly over him. The familiar lacework beasts – her childhood friends – frolicking around it seemed a mockery in this place of slaughter. Emly placed her hands on Casmir's chest and willed his heart to start beating again. She waited, speak-ing under her breath, petitioning the gods of ice and fire to make him live.

But the assassin remained dead and she sat back, defeated. She had been told the veil had virtue to heal, to make the dead live, but she did not know how. Overcome by sorrow, she bowed her head and her tears fell on Casmir's face as she asked the gods to admit him to the Gardens of Stone, though she knew she did not have the right for she was not a soldier.

Eventually she stood and, clutching the veil to her breast, walked to the cairn. It was built of flat stones and was taller than a man, but on a plaque facing west, the direction of last things, words were inscribed. Em did not know what they said, but it seemed important and she vowed to return one day and read the words if she was able. She looked south, to where the City and its battling armies were vanishing into darkness. She knew she had to get away from there and she wondered how far it was along the wall to the next gate and if that was also besieged.

Why was the assassin wearing Evan's jacket? She assumed he had picked it up on the battlefield, scavenging after the fighting was done. Or perhaps Casmir had joined the battle and taken the jacket afterwards. Either way he could have had no idea what treasure he was bringing back to the City.

Surveying the dead warriors, she tried to fix them in her mind's eye, for if she did not remember them, who would? She draped Evan's jacket round her shoulders, stowed the veil in her cloth bag, then clambered back on Patience and turned his head west, following the wall.

It had taken her no more than twelve days to return from the Vorago, Patience eating up the leagues with his remorseless stride. She had seen nobody but the dead. As darkness fell each night she had chosen her place to sleep with care, denying herself a fire for she feared it would bring scavengers or those she dreaded most, Fkeni tribesmen. She could not know that the Fkeni had been annihilated by the enemy army as it made its way south, hunting or trampling over any living thing in its wide, scouring path – animals, birds, plant life and the last few Fkeni, who had fought bravely against overwhelming numbers but whose people were now wiped for ever from the earth.

It was just a day into her journey when Em had found the remains of City soldiers by the trail. They had been torn and gnawed by animals, but she had recognized Quora's body from the beads in her hair and by the Fkeni knife she carried in place of the one she had given Emly. Em had wondered what happened after the battle, and how these three had made it that far and what had stopped them. She had taken their knives, hiding them in her pack as surety for she feared losing the pigsticker above all things, except for the stallion.

After that she had ridden Patience hard, traversing the high mountain pass in a single weary day. She had come across more corpses, including many enemy warriors with their strange tattoos. Most of the bodies had been gnawed and dismembered, but as the days passed more of the corpses she saw were intact and she knew she must be closing on the army, and the City.

When she arrived at the Narrows she had feared herself defeated for she could not imagine crossing the wide water alone. She remembered the day, years ago it seemed, when she had crossed it in the other direction, riding atop the warhorse while Evan swam beside them. She had wept that night, wondering if she would ever get home and what she would find when she got there.

The crossing had been terrifying and she feared for them both as Patience was swept far out of their way by the strength of the water. But the big beast had an indomitable spirit and eventually he gained the far shore, exhausted and shaken by his struggle. That was three days ago and she had spent the long days and nights since resting the horse and idling on the bank of the water watching the birds and animals creeping back now the vast army had passed.

Once they were in sight of the City, Emly had wondered again if she'd been right to return and abandon Evan to the mercies of the strange woman Selene. But then she had found the veil, and finding it convinced her she was doing the right thing. She now believed Evan had been wrong to steal it, for ill luck had plagued the City since its departure. She could only return the Gulon Veil to the empress and throw herself on Archange's mercy.

As she slept that night, tucked in a grassy dell, her dreams haunted by corpses, a man walked into her camp. Patience gave a snort of recognition and the man patted his neck and whispered words of calm. He looked down at the sleeping girl and marvelled at her persistence. And he wondered if the plague would take her once she found her way into the City. He thought it probably would, for he was sure the blood of the Serafim ran strongly in her. Would she survive it? Perhaps. Would she go on if she knew about it? Probably.

When Emly awoke it was still dark. The chill air made her shiver as she quickly saddled Patience, and as the first fingers of dawn touched the land they set off along the wall again heading, though she did not know it, towards the sea. She wondered that this stretch of the wall was so quiet, deserted except for wild beasts and birds, while the gate behind her was under siege. Em had no idea of the geography of the City. The only map she had ever seen was in the throne room of the White Palace and she did not recognize it for what it was for she could not read. Despite a life spent within the City she did not understand the scale of it, the hundreds of leagues of mighty walls stretching from the heaving streets of the south to the empty lands of the north, from the Seagate all the way to the Wayfarers Gate. She guessed only that if she followed the wall she would eventually find another gate to enter by and she hoped the next would not have an enemy army camped outside.

It was midday and Patience was dawdling a little in

the sunshine when Em heard the beat of galloping hooves behind them. Panic clutching her throat, she kicked the warhorse into a run. Leaning forward in the saddle she yelled at him, urging him on, terrified of being captured by the enemy army, or worse, Fkeni.

'Emly!' a voice bellowed above the pounding hooves, and in her terror she closed her ears. Then she glanced over her shoulder and saw it was a single horseman and that Patience was drawing away from him. Her initial panic subsiding a little, she realized it was in fact a familiar figure riding a familiar horse. Relief washed through her and she reined Patience in and waited, trembling still, as they came alongside. She was more surprised to see Blackbird than his rider. The two horses nuzzled each other.

'Where did you come from?' she asked Stalker, thinking how true he was to his name.

'I've been on your trail for a day or so, since you crossed the Narrows,' he told her, grinning. She smiled back, her heart lifting. He was the first living person she had seen for many days and he was a reassuring sight, his mount bristling with weapons and with a brace of rabbits slung from the saddle. 'I hoped to stop you entering the City,' he explained.

'Why?' she asked him, her mind full of questions, the least of these being why he was always dogging her steps.

'There is plague inside. Best avoid it and take a wide circle round to the coast,' he waved one arm north, 'and go to the port of Adrastto. You'll be safe there. Have you got coin?'

'Plague?' It was a dread word, yet it seemed distant and irrelevant to Emly. 'But I must get to the White Palace,' she argued. 'I must see the empress.'

He snorted. 'When last I saw you, lass, you were fleeing that woman.'

She ducked her head, reluctant to tell him the truth. 'Nevertheless I must go.'

He watched her, grey eyes thoughtful, but she remained silent. Then he looked around and heeled Blackbird towards a small copse of trees. She followed and they both dismounted. Em eased off her boots and wriggled her toes in the sunshine while Stalker swigged from a water skin.

'How far is it to the next gate?' she asked him.

'The next is the Wayfarers Gate, the last before the sea. You could be there by sunset, but you'd be mad to go inside. The plague is a terrible thing. Carry on to the coast, then head north to Adrastto.'

She thought about it. She knew she should trust Stalker, for he had fought beside Evan and her lover respected him; besides, he had saved her life, but the big man's habit of suddenly appearing from nowhere then vanishing again had made her wary.

'Why are you so determined to return?' He asked it gently and the kindness in his voice went to her heart like an arrow.

'I will tell you the whole truth,' she offered, 'if, in return, you tell me one true thing.'

Stalker laughed shortly, but his voice was cool when he said, 'This is not a game, girl.'

'Yet each time I see you I feel I'm a small part in one,' she retorted.

He nodded his big head. 'Ay, I suppose you're right, in a way, but it's not *my* game. So tell me.' He looked at her, waiting.

She confessed, 'I stole something from the empress and now I must return it. It is important, so, even though there is plague, I must get to the palace.'

He frowned, his brows bristling, his eyes dark. 'You are speaking of the Gulon Veil.' She nodded. She was no longer surprised by what Stalker knew.

'I will take it for you,' he offered. His voice was casual but his pale eyes bored into her, heavy with intent. 'I'm going south anyway. I will ride around the enemy army. I can get the veil to the empress more quickly than you, even if you could survive the journey. Now, where is it?'

He rapped the last words out, like one used to being obeyed. She suddenly felt afraid. He was much stronger than her and could wrest the veil from her in a heartbeat if he chose.

'You could not get into the palace,' she argued, knowing she was only delaying the inevitable. 'I can. The gates would open to me. I can walk straight into the empress's presence.'

'And be executed in a heartbeat. She's an unforgiving woman.'

She bowed her head in acceptance. 'Perhaps that is what I deserve. I betrayed her kindness to me: I stole from her and ran away.'

Suddenly the tension in him faded and he smiled. He leaned back on the grass and sniffed the air, looking around at the grassy plain and the sky and the grey line of the wall disappearing into the distance. He turned his gaze back on her and his eyes were kind, and his voice was gentle as he spoke.

'I'm sorry, lass. I would not wish to alarm you.' He shrugged. 'I was curious to see the thing. It is famous and very rare and I've heard it spoken of all my life.'

At these reasonable words Emly's fears floated away and she marvelled that she could be so suspicious. Stalker was her friend. He had saved her life more than once.

She stood and pulled the veil from her bag. It was crumpled and looked like nothing but an old rag. She handed it to him. He held it to his heart, just as she had done the day before. Then he opened it out on the grass and ran a brawny hand over it. The veil started to gleam, the creases smoothing out until it was as she remembered it, smooth and silken, shining under the morning sun. As his hand touched each lacework animal its dull colours shone and sparkled. Em watched, marvelling anew at its beauty.

'It is a rare thing,' Stalker repeated. His voice held neither awe nor reverence, only the careful calculation of a man with much to gain, or lose.

'I tried . . .' she hesitated to confide in him but wanted to make up for her grudging manner. 'I tried to save a man, yesterday, by the cairn north of the gate.' She pointed back the way she'd come. 'There was a battle there. Stern was killed, and many others. I tried to save a soldier who'd just died. I thought the veil could make him live again.'

'It could. But you cannot bid it. For you it is just a pretty piece of cloth.'

He folded it. She held out her hands for it and he paused, then gave it to her. It felt oddly heavy in her lap.

'Can only Archange use it?'

'And other Serafim.'

Faltering, she asked, 'Are . . . are you a Serafim?'

He laughed and the sun shone a little more brightly. 'No, I'm not, lass.'

'Then – and this is the one true thing I ask,' she said, 'who are you?'

Stalker lifted his ginger head, scenting the air. 'I must ride,' he declared.

'One true thing,' Em urged. She put her hand on his sleeve. He looked at it, sighed and looked south again, as if eager to be off. But he said, 'My name is Stalker.'

She waited patiently. Layers of silence formed around them. Finally, as she knew he would, he spoke.

'Have you heard the rich and powerful speak of reflections?' he asked. His voice was distant.

Emly remembered Archange telling her of such things. The old emperor created replicas of himself, and these were called reflections. Evan had called them walking corpses. Em thought they had all been destroyed in the fall of the Red Palace. She shivered and nodded uncertainly, frowning.

Stalker looked into her eyes. 'I am one of them.'

She smiled a little, thinking he was teasing. This was her friend Stalker, a living man who bled and snored and pissed like any other. She had imagined reflections as ghouls of the night, dim replicas of people, walking in a half-life of malice and shame. Then she recognized the truth in his eyes, and his overwhelming sadness.

He looked south again, as if drawn by an invisible thread. 'My lord,' he went on, 'created me to do his will.' She realized he was confessing to her, perhaps relieving himself of some of the secret burden he bore.

'Who is he, your lord?' she whispered.

'His name is Hammarskjald and he is responsible for this fearful army which is even now attacking the City, ready to kill and pillage all within.' He looked into her stricken face. 'He burns with hatred for the City and he has waited many centuries for the right time to destroy it. That time is now.'

'But why? Why does he hate the City so?'

Stalker sighed then laughed shortly, more like his old self. 'Most people do, lass. There is much to hate. But he has a long-held feud with its overlords. He was one of them once but they banished him and then, when he vexed them still, they tried to kill him.'

'Why?'

'They all had their reasons. They called him a criminal, though their own crimes are monstrous. And he is a terrible man, even by the standards of the

Serafim. But he is old and wily and will die hard. He plans to destroy the City with plague and with the sword, and pull down the White Palace.'

'Pull down the palace!' Emly was appalled. 'Can he do all that?'

Stalker nodded. 'He is well on his way to it. The old emperor is dead. The City is vulnerable thanks to the endless grudge between Archange and Marcellus. The Serafim have always squabbled among themselves. The two of them have formed an alliance now they know who they're facing, but it is too late. Much too late.'

'Why did Archange hate him so much, this man?'

'It is hard to follow a feud that has formed and festered over centuries. But there is one dispute between them which diminishes all the rest. Archange had two daughters.' He pulled on his braids as she'd seen him do before when thinking. 'Both were abused, cruelly treated by the old emperor Araeon, an evil man the City is well rid of. One of the daughters lost her wits. The other, well, she fled the world of men and she suffers still.'

'And what does Hammarskjald have to do with that?'

'He tried to help them, the daughters, and later their own two daughters, poor lost creatures.'

'And she hates him for that?' Emly asked, baffled.

'Ay, she professed other reasons to revile him, but that was at the root of it. He reminds her that she failed to save them herself.'

'What happened to them?'

'The elder disappeared into the Halls. They say she still walks there in the deepest dark. I have been down there myself searching for her, but I believe now she is dead. The other you have met. She found sanctuary in the lost city of the Vorago and has found a kind of peace there.'

'Selene?'

He nodded. 'She is Archange's younger daughter but she is deeply troubled in her mind. Do not betray her sanctuary to the empress if you return to the palace.'

Em, musing over what he had said, asked, 'What woman would not try to save her own daughters?'

He shook his head. 'It is not as simple as it seems. Age-old grievances, and debts paid and owed over a millennium have kept an uneasy balance of power among the Serafim. And Archange fled the City for a very long time and that was her choice. But for this crime Hammarskjald blamed her and she has never forgiven him for that.'

'And you are his . . . ally?'

He bowed his head. 'I do his bidding. I can do no other.'

'Yet you fought for the City, with Evan and Stern and the others?'

He grinned. 'I have a long leash and I like a good scrap. And I always root for the underdog who battles to his last breath. Besides, I am hard to kill too.'

He looked south again as if alert to a distant summons. 'I have followed my own path for many years. But I always knew he would eventually pull on the leash and I must follow him. That time has come.' He paused. 'If you ever see me again, girl, run away.'

He said the words so casually she barely took them in. She frowned.

Leaning forward, stretching out one strong hand, he said, 'You see, the final thing my lord needs to ensure the City's destruction is the Gulon Veil.'

Gripping the veil, Emly rolled away from him and leaped to her feet. He stood quickly. She ran to Patience and leaped into the saddle. Limping on his game ankle Stalker made a grab for her stirrup. She kicked him hard in the face and felt the crunch of bone. He lost his grip, cursing. She seized Blackbird's reins and urged Patience into a gallop.

As she fled she heard a bellowing roar behind her. But whether it was of frustration or triumph she could not tell.

Emly arrived at the Wayfarers Gate before dusk, exhausted from riding but fearful of entering the City. Stalker's words whirled round her head and she wondered what to believe. Was there really plague inside or was he trying to stop her entering with the veil? Had he lied to her before, manoeuvring her towards the sanctuary of the Vorago to keep her from returning? But that was before she had found the veil. Perhaps he was truly trying to keep her safe? There was too much she didn't know, but the loss of Stalker as an ally was a crushing blow.

Her mind was as tired as her body and she sat passively on the warhorse and let him plod up to the gates. The gateway was built of rich red stone, a massive arch which dwarfed the horses and riders milling at its foot. To Em's surprise the gates were wide open and troopers in their hundreds, armed and armoured, seemed on the verge of departing. She made her way through them, her progress watched by stern and unfriendly eyes. She feared they were judging her – a girl alone, dirty and barefoot, riding a warhorse through their ranks. She urged Patience on and he shouldered past, Blackbird following behind, until the press of riders thinned out.

'Can we help you, girl? You look lost.'

A stocky infantryman, red-faced and fair bursting out of his uniform, stood in her path.

Em sat up, looking around her, alert to danger. 'Who is commander here?' she asked.

A woman soldier, sharp-faced, came up beside the man. She asked, 'What do you want of him?'

Em hesitated. 'City soldiers,' she told them, 'lie dead near the cairn at the next gate.' She pointed. 'Someone needs to know.'

She fell silent as the pair stared at her. The man looked at the woman and said, 'I'll go.'

He disappeared into the melee and the woman looked up again at Em. Concern in her voice, she said, 'You look exhausted, girl. Climb down and rest. Have you eaten?'

Em shook her head, biting her lip to stop it trembling. The soldier's kind words had gone straight to her heart. 'I must go on. I have to get to the White Palace.'

The woman looked astonished. 'What do you want to go there for? It'll take you days, even on that big beast.'

Her partner came back accompanied by a tall captain with a face of stone and deep, hooded eyes. Em repeated to him what she'd told the pair and the officer snapped, 'How do you know that, girl?'

'Because I was there.'

'At the Great North Gate? You saw the battle?'

'No, I arrived after it was over. They were all dead.'

The captain stared at her, clearly disbelieving. Then he focused on the two horses. 'Get down, girl. We need your mounts.'

'But they're mine,' she argued, hearing the tired whine in her voice.

He looked her up and down, and she was conscious of her bedraggled clothes and bare feet. 'Stole them, I'd wager,' he concluded. He made a grab for the stallion's bridle but Patience, startled, reared and the officer flinched.

'Get those horses,' he ordered the two soldiers, who

glanced at each other and stepped forward without haste.

Em found anger rising in her, fighting back against her fatigue. 'I have to get to the White Palace,' she told him and the officer snorted his disbelief. 'But you can take this one.' She was reluctant to hand over Blackbird, but could not justify keeping him if the cavalry was in need. She leaned over and lifted Stalker's water skins and pack off the beast and slung them on her own saddle, then untied Blackbird's tether.

The stout soldier took it and nodded to her, but the captain spluttered, 'You do not bargain with the army, girl. Climb down now or you'll be arrested.'

She turned Patience's head away and kicked him into a trot. She heard the captain shouting at her, but within moments his words were lost in the clamour of troopers and their mounts.

Emly let the horse wander under the starlit sky. She needed to sleep and eat, but she could not leave Patience and she had no coin. She had rarely been in the streets of the City alone and had no idea where to go. The Wayfarers Gate was an armed camp, seething with soldiers. Though it was nearly night there were street vendors shouting their wares, children crying and squealing, and carts loaded with barrels or crates or sacks of grain making their way with difficulty through the crowded thoroughfares. The carters yelled at one another and their donkeys brayed and the bells on the nearby temple added to the cacophony. Everyone looked as if they had something to do, even the children, and Emly seemed to be the only one who did not. She kept looking south, to her destination. The Shield of Freedom was barely visible now.

The horse wandered on and came to a line of hospital tents. Many were painted with the ominous red eye – the symbol of pestilence – and Emly knew then that

Stalker had told her the truth. The crowds thinned out here and she halted. A hand touched her ankle. She started, realizing she had drifted off in the saddle, and gripped the reins.

'It's all right, girl. It's only us.' It was the two soldiers again. Racked with nerves, Em was on the verge of kicking Patience on his way, but the big man held out his palms and stepped back. 'We won't harm you and we won't take your horse,' he assured her. Emly relaxed a little, though she still held tight to the reins, as he introduced himself as Thorum and his partner as his wife Wren. They offered her some of their bread and water. She accepted, but wondered why they were being so kind.

'We had a friend,' Thorum told her as she ate, still seated high above them. 'She went to the White Palace back in the summer and we haven't heard from her since. Her name is Mavalla. She was injured and alone. If you see her tell her we're with the Fighting Forty-seventh. We march on the Great North Gate with the dawn, if she wants to join us.'

'I will tell her if I see her,' Em said. She hoped they would not ask her why she was going to the Shield, and they didn't.

'How do you plan to get there?' Wren asked, peering up at her.

It seemed a foolish question. 'I can see it,' Em said, pointing south. 'You can see it from everywhere in the City in daytime.' Even in the twilight they could see lights twinkling on its flanks.

'But it is a long ride and the City is a perilous place,' the woman said. 'Plague is rife. And the captain won't be the only one looking for a good horse.'

'I will get there,' Em said stoutly. Stalker's last words to her had convinced her she must return the veil, and as soon as possible.

'Ride the wall,' Thorum suggested.

'The wall?' Emly looked up at the massive stone battlements. She wondered if he was joking. 'Can you get a horse up there?'

'All the Great Gates,' the soldier explained, 'have ramps or flights of shallow steps so you can ride up on to them. You'd be able to follow the wall all the way to the Paradise Gate then cut across to the mountain from there.'

'Won't they stop me?' she asked, doubtful of the idea.

'The walls aren't manned,' he told her, 'apart from bands of watchmen. All able-bodied soldiers have been ordered to the gates where the enemy are trying to break in.' Thorum chuckled. 'You could probably ride all the way to the Seagate. I've heard that's the way imperial messengers go.' He looked to Wren for agreement and she nodded.

'It will be dangerous,' she added, 'but not so dangerous as riding through the City streets, a lone girl on a valuable horse.'

'Thank you,' Emly said, suddenly energized by the plan. She grabbed the reins, eager to be off. But Thorum laid a hand on her stirrup.

'Don't start now!' he said, concern in his voice. 'It's dark and you need rest.'

'I'm running out of time,' Emly told him. She felt a gathering menace at her back, forcing her onward. She thought of something Evan would say, *I'll sleep when I'm dead.*

'I need to get there as soon as I can,' she told them. 'I have to get to the empress.'

The two soldiers stared at her, no doubt thinking her deluded, but Thorum pointed to his right. 'The eastward steps are along there past that white temple.' He grabbed the rein before she could ride off. 'The wall passes over the minor gates,' he explained, looking hard at her to see she understood, 'but when you reach the Great Gates – the Great North, Araby and Paradise – you'll need to ride down off the wall. And you'll have to be careful,' he said, eyeing the long knife at Em's side, 'for there could be fighting at any of them. But it should be a fast ride to the Shield from the Paradise Gate.'

She nodded her thanks to them both and urged the warhorse forward. Rat's feet of panic skittered up her spine. If Stalker was right and Hammarskjald could somehow use the veil against the City, she had to return it into Archange's safekeeping, but she feared she might be too late.

CHAPTER FORTY-SIX

PATIENCE RACED EASTWARD UNDER THE STARS, HIS BIG iron hooves striking sparks from the cold stone. It was as if he knew where he was going and he seemed as eager as Emly to get there. On the first stretch of their journey, back east to the Great North Gate, they had passed only one band of soldiers who yelled at them to stop but scattered as the great warhorse thundered by. Though tired and hungry Em felt safe up on the broad, empty wall. They were passing only empty fields to their right, and to their left the parapet protected them from any enemy outside.

She heard and smelled the battle at the Great North Gate long before she could see it. She eased the horse to a trot and approached with trepidation. Stopping for a moment to look over the parapet, she could see the dark stain of the enemy army crawling like black maggots round the base of the wall and the broken gate. She rode on. Soon the wall-top was crowded, defended by City bowmen loosing a stream of arrows down into the attackers. The stones of the wall were slick with blood, and dead and injured archers lay under the parapet. Some stretched out their hands for aid, pleading for water, but Emly hardened her heart and rode by with eyes averted.

She found the steps leading downward and at the top she reined in, transfixed by the battle below. Now she was close up she could see the massive Great North Gate had splintered. Thousands of enemy soldiers had poured through, to be met by City warriors. The sound of clashing weapons was deafening and the screams of agony and stench of blood made her feel sick.

Patience stepped from foot to foot, anxious to be off. She steered him down the steps. She had planned to follow a wide circle around the fighting, but once she was down in the seething City again she soon found herself lost. It was chaos. All around her was a press of soldiers, hemming her in on all sides. Soldiers were marching towards the battle and struggling away from it. Some were on stretchers, although many of the most grievously wounded had been left to find the casualty stations alone. There was a fire somewhere and choking smoke drifted over them. Patience shook his head, his eyes wild, but she urged him on. A dozen times Em was tempted to jump down and help a soldier, blinded or crippled by hideous injuries. But she fixed her eyes on the eastward wall and reminded herself of her duty. There were more plague tents here, scores of them, and she found herself breathing lightly, fearing the miasma of sickness would enter her body.

A hard hand grabbed her foot. 'Here, girl! Give me that horse!'

A wounded man, his face masked in blood, pulled on her bare ankle, trying to dislodge her. She dragged out the pigsticker and jabbed it into the back of his hand. He fell away, howling. She kicked Patience on, looking desperately for the steps. She could see the wall leading east and south but there seemed no way up on to it.

Then she noticed two men in uniform pointing at her, talking. They started pushing through the crowd, eyes fixed on her. If they reached her there was nothing she could do to stop them pulling her from the saddle. She smacked Patience on the rump, shouting at him to move on. He started shouldering his way through the press, his great bulk making a path away from the two men. An injured soldier went down under his hooves. Tearfully Em closed her ears to his cries and urged the stallion forward.

With a gasp of relief she spotted the ramp leading upwards on the eastern side of the gate and urged the warhorse towards it. The mob around her thinned, then she was free and she kicked the horse up the shallow steps, sucking fresher air into her chest.

At the top she looked back once, troubled. She knew little about the strategies of warfare, yet any fool could see the enemy was winning.

The lift-shafts inside the Shield of Freedom were a feat of engineering which only the Serafim, at the height of their arrogance, could have achieved or even considered. There had been seven major shafts, including the one from the Lake of Tears at the base of the mountain to the Serafia at its peak, and a handful of minor ones plus myriad maintenance tunnels. But when something isn't used for a hundred years, or two hundred, or three, it is reasonable to close it off, board it up, brick it up, then, of course, forget it.

The lifts' cylindrical cages and the hauling machinery at the head of each shaft had long since fallen, dropping one by one in a meteoric shower of rust and dust. Only the last remained, at the top of the highest shaft. It floated in the dark waiting, shuddering from time to time as if it knew its inevitable fate. It was the haunt of spiders and beetles and moths, yet the white-eared bats which swarmed through the mountain declined to roost there as if they knew such a nesting-place would be perilous.

When the soldiers came, hunting the assassins who had killed Dol Salida and Dashoul, they had peered into the lone cage to ensure it was empty. They hadn't ventured inside. No one with any sense would step into the thing, which seemed ready to plummet at any moment. And it was a long way down.

Before midnight on the night after the new moon, there was a soft flurry of moths around the cage and Fin Gilshenan, sole survivor of the intruders, squeezed down from where, nestled in the narrow space between the top of the cage and the roof of the shaft, he had been hiding recovering from injury. He was about to embark on his final mission.

He lowered himself into the cage, which trembled a little, and stepped out on to the rock platform. He lit a lantern. His eyes smarting from the unaccustomed light, he reached up and carefully slid down from the top of the lift a long wooden box. He opened it, revealing variously coloured waxed tubes. He picked out two green ones then pushed the box back out of sight. Grabbing the lantern, he set off.

As he limped towards his destination his injured thigh gained strength and mobility with movement. While the deep knife-wound had healed sufficiently for him to complete his task, it had drained some of his certainty. One green flare – that was all he needed, he told himself angrily. An earlier Fin would have trusted them to work without question. But, like him, they had been lying in a cold, damp place for too long and he wanted to be sure.

He stepped out into the fresh night air and sucked it in. The sky was thick with stars, the moon just a thin sliver, as he had calculated. Inwardly he thanked the unfailing routines of the palace soldiery, who marked the watches, day and night, with the tolling of bells, which had helped him keep count of the days of his long recovery.

He was on one of the highest parts of the mountain, outside the palace walls, facing south to where his lord Hammarskjald would be watching on this starlit night. He pushed the butt-end of the flare into a crack in the rock. Fingers trembling a little he struck a phosphorus stick and set its fire to the fuse. Two long heartbeats of anxiety passed, then with an exhilarating whoosh the flare soared high over his head, showering green sparks, lighting the white walls of the palace with a sickly glow.

Blinded by the flare's brilliance, he squinted towards the southern mountains. Slowly they came into view, silhouetted under the starlit sky. He waited, hardly daring to blink for fear of missing the answering flare. Would it be red or white?

He had last seen his lord more than half a year before when he and his comrades had set out on this mission. His every action since had been centred on this one night. By sending up a single green flare he'd signalled his continued presence but admitted something which shamed him – he had not found the baby as his lord had ordered. He was ready to suffer the consequences when the time came. It would not affect his work tonight, if he received the order to go ahead.

And there was his answer, much closer than he'd expected! A soaring red light climbed into the sky and hung there, spitting sparks. He breathed out his relief and grinned to himself in the darkness. Red for action, he thought. Red for blood.

Emly was crawling up the face of the Shield, desperate to reach something. Her shoulders and knees were on fire, her fingers stiff and numb as she clung to each tiny handhold. Rain drummed on her back and she was drenched through, her clothes dragging her down. With nerveless finger-tips she probed the rock-face above, as she had done a thousand times before, feeling for another handhold. But this time there was none to find. The rock was sheer, implacable. The rain came down harder and threatened to wash her off the mountain. Scarcely able to see, she pulled out the pig-sticker and dug it into a thin line in the sheer surface above her head, banging it in with her fist. Then she levered herself up to find the next hold.

When she reached the top, trembling with exhaustion and weak with relief, she flung one arm over the parapet and, shoulders screaming, rested for a moment. Then she pulled herself up, scrabbling with her toes, and got the other arm up.

She peered over. Waiting for her was a Fkeni warrior, black robes flying, shining sickle in hand. With ruined teeth he grinned at her and sliced the blade towards her face.

Em woke with a start, heart pounding, and nearly slid from the saddle. She shook her head to dispel the shards of nightmare, realizing she had to rest. She had been riding for a night and a day and now it was dark again. She could feel time at her back, urging her on, but she ached all over and she was worried for Patience, who had dropped to a slow trot, his head low. She reined him in and slid off, legs protesting. She hauled down Stalker's pack and found the old, rusty cooking pot she'd seen him use. She unhitched a water skin and filled the pot and put it down for the horse, who eagerly pushed his nose into it and started sucking up water. It was the best she could do; she had no food for him.

She looked about them. Under the myriad stars the land was bright as day, but colourless, eerie. On one side dark fields stretched off into blackness. On the other, over the wall, was empty grassland. Ahead of them the wall went on, ever south, a broad, glinting road. She could hear nothing but the sough of the breeze and the thump of her heart. She closed her eyes and after a while the eager heartbeat slowed. The silent stillness was comforting. Trusting Patience would not wander, Emly lay down on the hard stones of the wall, laid her head on her old cloth bag, and slept.

Elated by the order to proceed, Fin Gilshenan returned to the lift and climbed gingerly up on top. It shuddered again. This would be the last time he would have to seek sanctuary there. By dawn his perilous hideout would lie in smithereens far below.

From its hiding place he pulled down a second, larger box. It was heavy and difficult to manage on his own. That had not been the plan, after all. But he manhandled it down then dragged it out on to the area in front of the lift-shaft. He stood, catching his breath, looking back at the open cage hanging hollowly in the darkness like a devouring mouth.

He crouched and opened the box, its hinges grating loudly in the silence, and took out the sticks of explosive, tied in bundles. He had been told exactly where to place each one and the order in which to light the fuses. They were long fuses. He did not plan to die this night. He took one bundle out. Here, above the central shaft, it would be enough to bring down the main bulk of the palace when it exploded. He secured the rest in his backpack, then, grunting with effort, he set off.

He could follow the shafts and tunnels blindfold. The ways he used into and out of the palace were still unknown to its soldiery, though his lord knew them all. It was easy to evade the few palace guards that remained, and he eyed them with contempt from the darkness as they stomped by with loud boots and louder voices.

One bundle of explosive he tucked between the joists supporting the soldiers' quarters, and one on the roof above. *Always disable the soldiers first.* Then another on the roof of the throne room. This was only symbolic, his lord had told him, but it would be a fine symbol.

One he hid under the wall leading to the empress's apartments. The final bundle was placed to bring down the white gates of the palace, symbolic again, but the shattered timber and rock would trap anyone trying to flee. The White Palace would collapse, destroying the last centre of power in the City.

When his lord arrived with the conquering forces there would be only bodies to greet him. And Fin Gilshenan, his loyal servant.

The Shield of Freedom loomed huge to Emly's right. She had passed the Araby Gate without incident and now the Paradise Gate must, she hoped, be within reach. Beyond the battlements all was calm, just rolling grassland all the way to the mountains on the horizon. She had seen no sign of the enemy since they left the Great North Gate. The City looked peaceful too. They were passing above houses and streets. Though it was barely dawn people, horses, carts and carriages all seemed to be going about their daily business, apparently unmoved by the terror at the Great Gates. She wondered if they even knew about it. She remembered the empress telling her that the City was so vast that when the southern districts were flooded then invaded almost a year ago, people in the north hadn't known about it for days.

She leaned forward to pat Patience's neck. She knew the big warhorse could travel all day, but he had not eaten since before they entered the City. Once they came down from the wall she must find sustenance for them both. She wondered what would become of him when they reached the palace. Would he be sent off to die in the war? Was that his destiny?

The sun was still below the horizon when she saw they were nearing the gate. Sounds of battle reached her ears and dread gathered in her belly. She reined in and looked over the battlements. The enemy army was a dark blur on the grasslands. She wondered if they had broken through, as they had at the Great North Gate. As she rode closer she could see tall wooden towers standing close to the wall. She frowned, wondering what they were. In her tiredness she could only guess. Were they trying to reach the top of the wall? But they were too far away. In her muddled mind Emly could make no sense of it.

Her eyes were gritty and she had to keep reminding herself to hold on tightly. If she fell asleep would Patience know where to go on his own? She saw men running along the wall towards her, shouting and waving their arms. She kicked Patience into a canter. The soldiers grabbed at the reins but she passed them and rode on.

Something hit her hard in her side. Shocked and confused, she looked down and saw a feathered shaft sticking out of her. She wondered what it was. It was far too short to be an arrow. Then she felt herself falling, falling. Something hard smashed into her and she was claimed by the darkness.

The first two explosions brought down the soldiers' quarters and woke everyone in the palace – those who still lived. Valla was thrown to the floor of her small storeroom and, in pitch blackness, body battered and mind bruised, she scrambled into her clothes. She had no idea what had happened, but her only concern was the empress. She opened the storeroom door and was hit by a wave of hot, acrid dust. Coughing and choking, she hurried in the direction of Archange's apartments. Feeling her way, she stumbled over debris and bodies. She could hear the screams and moans of the injured. Something brushed her leg; she felt the gulon's slick flank press against her and heard it cough.

The next blast knocked her feet from under her. Struggling up, she saw part of the roof had come down. Dawn light glinted above but she could not see where she was. She peered through the flying dust but recognized nothing. Then she saw the gulon, waiting for her by a dark hole in the rubble. It padded back and forth impatiently. It seemed to know where it wanted to go and she could only follow it, hoping it would lead her to the empress. It scampered ahead and she followed cautiously, climbing over fallen roof beams, squeezing through narrow gaps in collapsed walls. She saw no one, and she feared she might be the only soldier left alive.

As the dust began to clear and she regained her sense of direction, she stopped, looking around. The gulon was going the wrong way. It was heading downward. 'Stop!' she ordered. The gulon halted then started pacing back and forth again. Valla was gripped by indecision. She needed to get to the empress but could find no way upwards. Another explosion rocked them and Valla crouched and covered her head as more debris and dust rained down. *What is happening?* she wondered. *Is it the cannon Marcellus spoke of?*

The gulon whined and, knowing no better, she followed it. It had led her truly before.

They worked their way through the broken palace, lit occasionally by shafts of dusty light, until they reached the mouth of a dark corridor. The gulon dived in without pause. Valla looked around, trying to work out where they were. There was less damage here and she realized they had reached one of the secret tunnels inside the mountain. Flickering torches still rested on wall brackets. She grabbed one and plunged in after the gulon. It led her along narrow paths, down steps, then up again into a wide cave. Valla raised the torch and looked around. It had been hewn out of rough rock, but the floor on which they stood was smooth. To one side was an open metal cage, big enough to hold several men, suspended from the gloomy ceiling. It hung above a hole, a great gash in the rock. Valla stepped to the lip of the abyss and looked down. Cool, dank air rose from below. She had heard about these shafts. They were very ancient and no one knew what they were for. The gulon scampered into the hanging cage, making it creak and sway slightly. The beast scrambled up the rocky wall behind it, sniffing. She wondered what it could smell.

Then it snarled and Valla whirled round, drawing her sword. A small man, slender and straight, stepped out of the darkness. His skin was deathly pale and he wore a heavy bandage around one thigh, dark with old blood. He held a single lighted phosphorus stick. As she watched him, bemused, he bent down and, keeping his eyes on her, set light to something at his feet. It fizzed and seemed to crawl across the floor. She wondered what it was.

The man drew two daggers and bowed to her slightly. Valla wanted to smile, but she knew any opponent must be taken seriously, however harmless-looking. He darted in.

He was skilled, far more skilled than she'd anticipated. He was lightning fast and his technique was flawless. But she was the one with the sword and it took her only a few moments to disarm him, then slash his throat. He staggered back, blood gushing, eyes wide. He backed into the open cage and stood there holding his neck, dark blood spurting through his fingers. Then the fifth explosion sounded and the reverberation from the blast shook the cave, showering down rocks. The small man slumped to his knees. There was a frozen moment. Then the cage, freed at last to die, plummeted suddenly into darkness. It made no sound.

Sheathing her sword, Valla saw the cage's fall had trapped the gulon on a narrow ledge on the far wall of the shaft. The beast ran back and forth, its paws pattering, but it could find no way off. It peered down into the shaft then stared at Valla across the abyss, its yellow eyes hectic in the torchlight. It whined.

There was no way she could reach it. She grabbed the torch from the floor and held it high. Looking around she saw a rusty metal pole lying discarded and picked it up. It was heavy but she thrust it across the open shaft and caught its end on the ledge. The gulon sniffed it. She called to the beast, trying to make it run along the pole, but it sat down. Anxious to reach the empress, Valla began to walk away but the gulon howled. She stopped and returned. She could not leave it. Finally it placed one paw on the rusty pole. Valla crouched, holding the end so it would not roll. Suddenly the gulon ran across the precarious bridge. Under the rhythm of its paws the far end of the pole bounced off the ledge. The beast would have pitched into the shaft but, stretching over the abyss, Valla grabbed it by its oily scruff, then by one front leg, and, its back paws scrabbling madly, she lifted it out to safety.

With a nervous spring it pulled away from her and rolled over on the ground, then jumped up and dashed back into the tunnel. Valla smiled.

She hurried over to the flame lit by the little man. It was still fizzing and creeping along a length of cord. She followed the cord and found it led to a bundle of cylinders tied together. Valla wondered what they were. She watched the moving flame then, as it drew close to the bundle, she stamped it out. As an afterthought she kicked the whole contraption down the shaft.

She had turned to follow the gulon when a voice called, 'Valla!' She reached for her sword as a figure hurried into the light pool. It was Thekla, the empress's granddaughter.

'Valla, you must help,' she cried, wringing her hands. 'Help me rescue Archange!'

Guilty that she'd been diverted, Valla sheathed her sword. Thekla gave a cry and bent forward as if in pain.

'What's wrong?' Valla asked her, catching her by the shoulders. 'Are you injured?' She did not see the thin dagger Thekla pulled from the folds of her skirts. The woman, a surgeon after all, stabbed her unerringly through the heart. Valla had no time to commend herself to Aduara. She was dead before she hit the floor. Thekla wiped her blade on the soldier's jacket and sheathed it. Then, crouching down, she rolled the body to the edge of the lift-shaft and dropped it over.

Fighting Knife was a mountain woman whose tribe, along with the Tanaree and Tuomi, had survived for millennia in the high peaks beyond the City's plains. They called themselves simply Fsaan, the People. Once they had been a terrible foe. Their focus, their vigour, their sole appetite was hunting their enemies. But they had been conquered and enslaved and then, when the war pressed on the City's resources, abandoned; and the few remaining pockets of the People lived a frugal, fragile existence deep in the Blacktree Mountains.

Despite her name, Fighting Knife was a goat-herder, as her forefathers had been for as long as the oldest of old ones could remember. Her knife was used to cut the necks of her animals, when needed, not those of her enemies. But she was a fierce creature, and she had needed all the strength and ferocity she could muster when, in winter two years before, the last few People, starved from their homes and forced to flee the City's blood-soaked armies, had made their way down from the peaks to seek succour in, of all places, the City.

Each day Fighting Knife fought for her family in any way she could. She stole food and clothes in winter, butchered dogs and rats when she had to, and found occasional work, often on her back, but then a woman must use all her resources to survive. She knew her pearl eye, damaged when she was an infant, frightened City folk for they were ignorant and stupid. The People knew the pearl eye was a sign of mystical wisdom. Some days, if there was a chance of work, she wore a patch to cover it and sometimes she thought she would be better off without it altogether, for a missing eye or leg or arm was a commonplace in this war-tired place.

Now she sat on the wall north of the Paradise Gate, far from the fighting, counting her takings. She looked at the eastern mountains, clothed thickly with tall trees, and, in memory, smelled the thick pungent sap and felt the springy mattress of needles under her bare feet. Her gods lived in the clouds that brought life-giving rain, in the sun which brought growth, and in blood which brought life. She had not forgotten them though she had walked away from their land, a decision she daily regretted.

She had been eyeing the rider coming towards her, thinking it a rare thing to see a horse on the walls, and, as it passed her, rarer still to see a woman on horseback.

As she watched, thinking how reckless the rider was to venture so close to the enemy's high towers, as if in answer the horsewoman jerked, then slumped in the saddle. The big stallion faltered to a halt paces from where Fighting Knife sat. The rider fell off like a sack of laundry. The horse trotted on, then stopped, uncertain.

Fighting Knife stood and went over to her, blade in hand, though the woman looked dead and, besides, harmless. But someone who owned such a horse might own other things of value. She ran her hands over the body, looking for coin, but there was nothing. The woman, just a girl really, smelled of sweat and horses and fear. Her feet were bare like a pauper's, like Fighting Knife's own feet. The arrow had plunged deep into her side.

Then the rider opened her eyes. 'Help me,' she whispered.

Fighting Knife could do nothing. She looked at the blood pooling on the stones. A wound of that sort was always fatal. There were many worse deaths. The girl spoke again and Fighting Knife bent close.

'The veil,' the girl breathed, 'to the empress.' Her face was pale as ice and her dark eyes were pleading.

Her words meant nothing and Fighting Knife stood up. Perhaps she could catch the horse . . . The girl grabbed feebly at the hem of her skirt. 'Please.'

The woman crouched down again. 'What you want?' she asked reluctantly, for dying wishes were sacred.

'There's a veil, in my bag, it belongs to the empress,' the girl told her haltingly, her eyes wide with pain and shock, her breathing agonized. 'Take the horse. You must. Must. Please.' Then her eyes closed and she said no more.

Fighting Knife looked at the mountain where the empress lived. It was a long way. She eyed the horse and it eyed her back. She scrambled to her feet and walked towards it. It backed away. She put out one hand and made friendly noises as if it were one of her goats. She knew nothing about horses. One hand outstretched she walked up to the beast, which was trembling, poised for flight, and gently unhooked a battered cloth bag from its saddle. The stallion snorted and trotted away. Fighting Knife rummaged in the bag. Dirty old clothes. And at the bottom a shawl or scarf.

She pulled it out. It was a bedraggled piece of cloth, grey and creased. She was about to drop it and walk away when a gleam of morning light caught her eye. She held it up and the sun came out at that moment and caught the warp and woof of it and she saw golden lights and intricate threadwork, then animals prancing in a circle, a dog, a horse, a fish. It was a marvellous thing and worth money, she guessed, eyes narrowing. Perhaps the empress would pay for it. The woman was said to be a shaman and might be grateful to Fighting Knife.

Pushing the cloth into her own bag she set off. When she looked back she saw the big horse had returned to nuzzle the dead girl.

CHAPTER FORTY-SEVEN

'WHY MUST YOU GO TO THE WHITE PALACE, LORD?' Rubin asked in the early hours of that morning as he helped Marcellus don his riding leathers. Though his wound clearly pained him and blood still seeped through the dressings, he had declared himself fit to ride. He was leaving the defence of the Adamantine Breach in the hands of Langham Vares and Darius to head for the Shield of Freedom.

Marcellus scowled, his face livid in the half-light of daybreak. 'Do not question me, boy!' he snarled.

Rubin held his tongue and closed the lord's soft leather jerkin over his blood-stained shirt and tied its straps.

After a baleful silence Marcellus sighed. 'Fate is dragging me there,' he confessed, his face troubled. Beneath his eyes the skin looked dark and bruised. 'I feel it in my bones and I am helpless against it.' He rolled his shoulders, trying to loosen sinews which would be sorely tested by the ride.

But the battle for the City is here, Rubin thought. *What can be more fateful than this time, this place?*

As if he had spoken the thought, Marcellus replied, 'The Serafia is barely defended now. I fear Hammarskjald covets Rafe's son and hopes to keep me distracted here while he steals it.'

'The baby? Why?' This was the first time Marcellus had mentioned the child. He had asked Rubin nothing of Fiorentina's deliverance from the wreck of the Red Palace except the assurance that she still lived.

'Because it is the offspring of a reflection, something which has never been seen before.' Marcellus paused in thought. Every line on his face seemed deeply scored, his skin drawn tightly against his skull. 'Some fear it will prove a monster. But I believe it will be more powerful than any of us.'

'Hammarskjald plans to kill it?' *Who would be the monster then?*

Marcellus shook his head slowly. 'Perhaps,' he said. 'The wheel of history is turning and is crushing all our past certainties. If I knew what was in that man's mind we would not be where we are now.' He picked up his sword-belt. 'Let's ride.'

Almost from the outset of their journey Marcellus' temper shortened. Rubin glanced at him from time to time, for his face was ashen and slick with sweat. But any suggestion that he pause to rest was angrily rebuffed and Marcellus pushed them on.

When, with the sunrise, explosions ripped through the White Palace and echoed across the City, the horses started and reared. Their riders struggled to control them. Marcellus spoke softly to his mount and the beast settled. They all looked up at the peak but it was shrouded in cloud. Marcellus pressed on.

The garrison town at the base of the mountain appeared abandoned. Rubin halted his mount and stood in the stirrups, looking around, shocked at the change in so few days. The wooden shacks looked deserted, the paddocks lay empty and wild dogs slunk in the shadows. And the great bronze gates lay wide open, unmanned. Marcellus said nothing but his face was dark as he rode through and ascended the Shell Path. At the top the gates of the White Palace lay broken as if by a giant hammer-strike, and beyond Rubin could make out only ruins. Dust hung thickly in the still air and through it he could see dead or injured soldiers laid out in the great courtyard. Nothing stirred. He wondered what had caused such devastation and if anyone could have survived. He thought of Valla and Elija and was filled with fear.

As they trotted their horses into the courtyard Rubin heard orders bellowed within and armed guards came running through the swirling dust to challenge them. They were blood-stained and dirty; some carried injuries, and their eyes were red and raw, but they lined up across the riders' path ready to defend the broken palace.

'What happened here?' Marcellus demanded, drawing rein and sitting up straight for the first time in hours. He eyed the defenders one by one, then barked, 'Laudric! You know me.'

'Yes, lord,' replied a burly, thick-bearded soldier, stepping forward. 'It was around dawn, lord. We heard loud thunderclaps, then there was a monstrous earthquake.' He looked at his comrades for support. 'We fear the gods are angry.'

Marcellus snorted. 'Why are the bronze gates undefended?'

'The guards down there deserted like dogs.' Laudric coughed then spat on the ground. 'It was two days ago; the people of the base town started fleeing, the whores and the pedlars. They'd heard rumours that the Paradise Gate had been breached and they ran from fear of the enemy army and the plague they bring. The gate guards, they disappeared the next night.'

'Cowards!' Marcellus growled. 'Were they hunted down?'

'No, lord, we don't have the numbers. We were

ordered to stay and guard the empress.' He cleared his throat of dust. 'Lord, we have been ordered—' he began, his face reddening. He grasped his sword-hilt and glanced at his comrades again. 'We have been ordered to arrest you, lord.'

Marcellus laughed shortly, though there was little humour in the sound. 'City soldiers desert the Shield and go unpunished – but you have orders to arrest its most loyal son?'

But before Laudric could reply, Marcellus held up his hand. He smiled and lowered his voice, the tone becoming warm and gracious.

'Laudric, you have served the City for a lifetime.' The man's eyes were fixed on his lord's. 'You fought in the ranks of the Fourteenth Serpentine, as did your father Arrian and your grandfather Beran, whom they called Bloodhand. There was a day, on the field of Saris, when I led the Fourteenth. Remember?' Laudric nodded and his hand dropped from his sword.

'Do you really want it to come to this, on this day of days when the City's future is on the brink? Do you really want a fight between your men and mine?'

'No, lord.'

Marcellus waved his hand and the dazed, battered guards shuffled to one side, doubtless relieved. He kicked his horse on and the beast pushed past. As they crossed the courtyard, the mounts snorting and blowing, Rubin could see that the palace's outer buildings were in ruins but the main body still stood, though badly damaged. Walls were cracked and canted, the graceful bridges and balconies had fallen, as had some of the roofs, it seemed, for piles of broken beams and shattered tiles lay in their path. There had been a fire too, for some of the stone walls were blackened and smoke mingled in the air with the dust. Soldiers were clambering over the debris, heaving up timbers and levering stones. As the riders watched a body was dragged from the ruins, but it was crushed and lifeless.

'What has done this?' Rubin asked, but Marcellus made no reply.

The horses could go no further and the men were forced to dismount. In front of them was a mound of debris, the remains of the soldiers' barracks. There was no way past it other than over the top, yet the rubble was still shifting treacherously. As they watched, a chunk of stone the size of a small house toppled over on one side, crashing into a hefty roof beam which rolled, picking up other material, starting a landslip which slid off the mountain, the sound of its crash echoing from the rocks below. Soldiers climbing the pile froze as it fell then stolidly resumed their work for, it seemed, there was no other option.

Marcellus appeared undeterred. He was looking high above the rubble and Rubin followed his gaze. On the far side he could make out a wide staircase climbing into the centre of the palace.

'Bring the casket!' Marcellus ordered, and Rubin took from his saddle the pack holding the white, wooden box he had been entrusted with. He wondered again what it was for, why so precious that his lord wanted it with him in this place of devastation. He slung the pack on his back.

Marcellus' urgent need to get into the palace was palpable and he started climbing the mound of debris, his men following his lead. It was hard going, even for the able, for stones shifted as the men scrambled over them and it was impossible not to breathe in the thick dust. Rubin's heart was in his mouth as they edged under a tottering wall, then over piles of broken beams which seemed ready to give way beneath them. By the time they were halfway to the top Rubin could tell

Marcellus' strength was failing. His face was grey and clammy and his breath rasped in his chest. He was moving forward only with an effort of will. His men, infected by his urgency, kept pressing ahead, then had to stop to wait for him. Rubin knew how cruel that must be to his pride. As Marcellus neared the top of the shifting debris a stone rolled under his boot and he fell awkwardly to one knee, starting a small avalanche. He remained motionless and took a breath, then another. The captain of his guard, who had been shadowing him closely, placed one hand under his lord's elbow, to steady him or help him rise. Marcellus swung on him, cursing him viciously, and the man stepped back, his face stone.

Fuelled by his anger Marcellus climbed on. They reached the staircase with relief, but then realized it was blocked further up where a wall had smashed down on to it. They had to climb again to get round this obstacle.

Inside the palace was worse, if anything, for in the dismal, dusty stillness they could hear the pleas and groans of men and women crushed by fallen walls. There was little chance of freeing them. Rubin guessed it would take many strong men to shift the great chunks of marble and alabaster. A handful of survivors, both soldiers and servants, struggled this way and that, carrying water and stretchers and medical equipment to those they could help.

At last they found themselves in a wide corridor, largely undamaged, which it seemed was becoming a centre of the rescue operation. Dead or wounded soldiers lay on the floor and propped against the walls, all coated in thick dust. The only difference Rubin could see between the quick and the dead was that those clinging to life still bled. Rubin bent to scrutinize each as he passed, dreading he'd find Valla dead or dying. He lingered to help an injured man, his legs crushed, who pleaded with him for water.

'Rubin!' Marcellus growled, and he closed his mind to the soldier's plight and sped on.

To everyone's relief the choking dust thinned higher up and they came out into open, fresher air. Rubin craned his neck upwards. Above them, black against the sky, was the curved lip of some great structure. He had no idea what it was. Following Marcellus' slow bootsteps, he climbed the last few stairs and found himself on the edge of an immense circular platform. He stared around, trying to make sense of what he saw. Over the black and white chequered floor lay a thick layer of what looked like ice. It was cool up there, and silent, and beyond the edge of the platform was nothing but grey cloud. Rubin shivered. They seemed to be at the top of the world.

He looked at Marcellus, who said curtly, 'The throne room,' and Rubin was surprised to see a sheen of satisfaction in his eyes as he surveyed the devastation.

He realized the walls of the great chamber had collapsed, leaving just a short section still standing to their left. To their right a score of palace guards flanked a high white throne on the very edge of the floor. And there, wrapped in shawls and seated on rich cushions, was Archange, clad all in black, her white hair loose. Just one woman attended her, dressed in a gold gown. Rubin examined the soldiers' faces to find Valla, but he could not see her. He'd been told she was always at the empress's side, so why was she not there now? He searched each face again, hoping.

Marcellus stepped forward. The ice crunched under his boots and Rubin realized it was a million shards of broken glass, glinting and winking in the weak light.

Marcellus and Archange gazed at each other across the floor. There was no birdsong, no sound from the broken palace beneath them, not even the faintest sigh of breeze. The grey mist muffled everything beyond the floor. Somewhere in the distance a dog barked once and was silenced.

Marcellus spoke up. 'Well, Archange,' he cried, 'what a mess this is.' His voice was clear and strong and only Rubin and his men could see the glint of wet crimson across his jacket.

The empress remained mute, unmoved, so after a moment Marcellus continued. 'I have come for the Gulon Veil,' he told her, and he beckoned Rubin who stepped forward with the casket. It was cunningly made of shining white wood, its lid secured by a tiny gold catch.

Archange said nothing, but a deep voice rich with amusement boomed, 'She doesn't have it, you fool!'

Only then did Rubin notice the big man sitting cross-legged at the base of the remaining throne-room wall. He stood gracefully, though he was not young, and picked up the sword lying beside him.

'Hammarskjald!' Marcellus exclaimed, as if greeting a long-lost friend. 'I'd a hunch you'd be here! Is this ruination your doing?'

'It is,' the man's voice rumbled. He sheathed the sword as if, for all the armed men before him, he would have no use for it. He wore the ragbag uniform of a mercenary and his wild ginger-grey hair and beard were knotted in unkempt braids. Tall and broad-shouldered, he stood at ease in the throne room. As if he owned it.

So this is Hammarskjald, Rubin thought, leader of the enemy army. What arrogance must he have to stand here alone? The soldiers, even Marcellus himself in his weakened state, seemed diminished by the man's presence. Rubin wondered if this man shared Marcellus' skill in butchery and he shuddered, feeling the draining of spirit which comes with the onset of dread. He feared he was about to witness another show of carnage.

'And the plague I hear about?' Marcellus asked in his familiar, genial way. 'That has your bloody fingerprints all over it.' He looked relaxed in the presence of his enemy, as if they were discussing the merits of a thoroughbred or the price of timber. You would never know, Rubin thought, that he was gravely wounded, perhaps at the end of his strength.

'Ay,' replied Hammarskjald. 'It is.'

'You must tell me about it some time. Meanwhile,' Marcellus said, with a calculating glance at the empress and back, 'do *you* have the Gulon Veil?'

'I do not,' Hammarskjald replied, and he strode along the very lip of the floor, glancing down into the mist. 'No one does,' he said, kicking a chunk of glass off the edge and listening to it fall.

Rubin's eyes followed him, captivated by the man's aura of invulnerability. He dragged his gaze away and saw all the men-at-arms were watching Hammarskjald too. They knew where the power lay. Looking at Hammarskjald again, at the massive, muscular shoulders, the braided hair and beard, it slowly dawned on Rubin that he had seen him somewhere before.

Hammarskjald turned back to Marcellus as if he'd momentarily forgotten he was there. 'The veil was stolen by a renegade soldier and went north with Marcus' army. It vanished at the Vorago. There was a great victory there.' He paused, then added with a feral smile, 'For my army, of course.'

'Then why are you here, Hammar? Just to gloat?' Marcellus asked and now Rubin could hear the strain in his voice behind the affable manner and wondered what it cost him to maintain the illusion of strength. 'You must know you will never leave this mountain alive.' At his words his men drew their swords.

Hammarskjald ignored them, answering, 'I am here for the child.' Turning to the empress, he demanded, 'Hand the brat over, Archange, and I vow that my army and I will walk away and leave the City. That is all I want. The future of the City and everyone in it in exchange for one infant.'

At last Archange stirred. As if the discussion hadn't happened, or wasn't of relevance to her, she commented, 'You are injured, Marcellus.' Her voice was husky and to Rubin she sounded frail. Rubin wondered why she would point this out, for here Marcellus was her ally. Wasn't he?

Marcellus shrugged it off. 'A graze only.'

Hammarskjald strode to the centre of the floor, kicking glass shards like autumn leaves. He looked intently at Marcellus, as if weighing his strength, then his gaze lingered briefly on Rubin and Rubin felt a flicker of recognition. Then he remembered. The legendary Hammarskjald was the man with the ruined ankle he'd met in the sewers on the Day of Summoning. A man he feared he had abandoned to his death. Was he the same? How could he be? They had met in semi-darkness and the words they exchanged were few, but Rubin remembered the injured man's apparent lack of concern at his plight, and his satisfaction at the news that the Red Palace was in ruins. *'Good,'* he'd said. *'Who builds a palace on top of a river? The poor fools.'*

'Where is it, woman?' Hammarskjald asked the empress. 'My agents have scoured this palace and the child is not here. Where have you stowed them, the boy and its mother? They are somewhere on this accursed mountain.' His tone was threatening, but Archange seemed not to hear and busied herself pulling her shawls around her against the morning air. Rubin shivered in sympathy, from fear or from cold, he could not tell.

He looked at the three arch-enemies – Marcellus and Hammarskjald, confident and relaxed, and Archange, indifferent. He knew each was playing a part, for the onlookers and for each other, but he suspected that deep down each was relishing it. And he realized that, though the City's future hung in the balance, this game between them was a familiar one – they had played it before in other times and places, though the odds and the prizes had changed over the centuries. Today they were wagering the lives of all the City's people for the possession of a child and, what, a piece of cloth? None of them had the veil, if Hammarskjald's words could be trusted, but who had the baby, Marcellus or Archange?

Hammarskjald stared at the empress for a long moment, then, it seemed, decided to alter the odds. 'Thekla!' he called.

The woman at Archange's side left the empress and glided across the floor. Rubin saw it was the sharp-tongued surgeon he'd met in a hospital while searching for Valla. She had discarded her bundled clothes of grey and now wore a slender golden gown, incongruous amongst the grubby, weary soldiers in the broken throne room. The empress watched, her expression unreadable, as a player she believed was her ally moved across to her opponent.

'She would not tell me, my love,' Thekla said to Hammarskjald and her voice was the chirrup of bird-song after a long, dark night. 'The old hag claims not to know about the reflection's get. I've been trying to wheedle it out of her.' She cast a scornful look at the empress. 'But she is stubborn and suspicious.'

Hammarskjald took her hand and brought it to his lips. They were an ill-matched pair, he in his dirty, ragbag clothes, she in a sheath of silk seeded with pearls which gleamed in the flashing lights from the shattered glass. She had clearly dressed carefully for this day, for this man, as though the death and ruination about her were of less importance than her appearance.

'What happened here?' Hammarskjald asked her. 'Fin Gilshenan failed. Much of the palace still stands.'

'He was thwarted by a soldier,' Thekla told him. 'She killed him before he could complete his task.'

'Then it's as well he's dead,' he replied, 'or I'd have disembowelled him myself.'

Watching them together, Marcellus shook his head and chuckled. 'What is it about these Vincerus women, Hammar? You can't leave them alone, even after all this time. They will be your downfall, mark my words. None of them was ever of any worth, except Saroyan. She was the only smart one among them.'

Thekla turned on him, her beautiful voice now dripping venom. 'Yet you had her put to death! You will pay for that!' she spat. 'Your death song will be endless.'

Marcellus shrugged. 'See? All mad as a bag of cats,' he commented, looking around. 'She will creep up on you one night and stab you in the back,' he predicted to Hammarskjald. 'Or worse.' He winked.

Is this what it is to be a Serafim? thought Rubin. *To boast and strut like street merchants while beneath them loyal soldiers lie crushed and bleeding and throughout the City people are dying in agony? Is this all their great power is reduced to?* Since he had first heard the word 'Serafim' on his father's lips, and understood the inheritance he carried, Rubin had squirrelled away all the information he could find on those mysterious beings. He had plagued his mother and tutors with questions, had gleaned clues and abstruse references from books, and chipped away shards of information from the granite of his father's disinterest. Marcellus had satisfied many of his questions, but he was tight-lipped on where his people came from and the nature of their powers.

Now Rubin stood among them, and he found he had nothing but contempt for them. He had been appalled by Marcellus' slaughter of the enemy, but had accepted it as vile necessity. But this was worse. For the first time he was seeing how Marcellus conducted himself when among his peers, and for the first time he looked at his lord and felt shame.

Marcellus turned to Archange. 'You must be getting old, cousin, if you let that rabid polecat under your guard.'

Thekla lunged at him with a scream of fury and Hammarskjald took two lightning paces and grabbed her wrist. Marcellus' men leaped in front of him but he rapped out an order and they backed off. Hammarskjald whispered to his woman, holding her tight to him, one hand at her waist. She nodded, then favoured Marcellus with a chilling smile.

'So,' Marcellus concluded, clapping his gauntleted hands together. He seemed invigorated by the atmosphere of malice and hatred. He looked from the big man to the silent empress and back. 'It seems we are at a stalemate here.'

Stalemate, Rubin thought, *in a game for supremacy while thousands suffer.*

'Not at all,' Hammarskjald replied. 'Within days my army will have conquered the City and brought a deadly plague to everyone within its walls.' He paused to let them absorb his words. 'Only I can stop them. Will you really doom the entire City for the sake of a single child?'

Archange cleared her throat and addressed him for the first time. 'Would *you* condemn so many people to a terrible death,' she retorted, 'for the sake of a single child?'

As the silence lengthened, Rubin tried to understand. The Serafim lived very long lives – he had learned that much – though no one could say *how* long for no Serafim was known to have died of old age, or so Marcellus had asserted. But in a long life, with godlike powers you can use to acquire anything you want, what still holds value for you? And who do you compare your successes with, other than those diminishing few who are like you? So down the years the Serafim had quarrelled over lands and armies, boundaries and castles, gold and concubines, and over the Gulon Veil. *This is all about which of the three can win advantage over his peers*, he thought. *Hammarskjald is using the might of tens of thousands of warriors to threaten the City of Gold in the hope of getting his hands on Fiorentina's baby, an infant, a wild and reckless throw to win an unknown quantity who might not be a Serafim, who might not even have survived the trauma of birth.*

Rubin could no longer stay quiet. He needed to do something to break the impasse. Though fearful, he strode forward and offered, 'I will go with you, lord. Take me instead of the child.'

Hammarskjald stared at him without expression, but his pale eyes darkened.

Rubin felt Marcellus' hand grasp his shoulder. 'Don't be a fool, boy!' he warned, but Rubin ignored him and forged on, knowing the die was cast. 'I am the son of a Serafim and of two Families,' he declared. 'Use me for whatever fell purpose you have planned for the child.'

'You are Indaro's brother?' Hammarskjald's deep voice rumbled.

For all his fear, Rubin felt a trickle of black amusement. Would he always be known as Indaro's brother, Reeve's son? He nodded.

Hammarskjald threw back his head and laughed and his merriment rang out across the City. As if in answer the morning sun at last burned through the cloud and lit up the field of play.

'You are an arrogant pup!' Hammarskjald cried. 'I do not want *any* Serafim – I have seen more than enough of them over the centuries. But the newborn is a first. It is unique, incomparable! You are just one in a failing line of dullards.'

Humiliated and angered by the man's contempt, Rubin reached inside himself for the power that lay there. Whether it responded to his fear or to his anger he didn't know, but at his thought it flowered in his belly.

Quick as a flash, before Rubin knew what was happening, Hammarskjald's eyes darkened to black and he trapped the younger man in his gaze. Rubin was held transfixed, unable to move a muscle, as he was hit by a blast of cold, burning energy which ripped the clothes from his body, then the skin from his flesh. He screamed in agony and horror. Hammarskjald released his grip on him and Rubin was flung across the chequered floor, sliding on the ice to the very edge. In a wild insanity of pain and fear he scrabbled with bloody fingers for purchase but there was none to be found and he screamed again in terror as his naked, skinned body shot out over the edge and plunged—

He blinked.

'And why a plague?' Marcellus was asking Hammarskjald, seeming genuinely interested. 'It seems a blunt weapon of choice.'

Rubin stood trembling, panic skittering around in his mind. He stared down at himself, at his travel-worn clothes and old boots. He clutched the carved white box to his chest like a shield, trying to calm the terrified pounding of his heart. Like someone jerked from a nightmare, he struggled to separate the real world from dreams. No one was paying him any attention; all eyes were on Hammarskjald.

'It is not just any plague,' Hammarskjald boasted. 'It

is engineered to afflict only people with our blood running in their veins. Serafim blood. Alien blood. And after a thousand years of your stewardship that amounts to most of the City's accursed population.' He spat the words with contempt. 'Anyone else exposed will become a carrier but will not sicken. Which is why,' he explained, 'my soldiers are spreading it without falling victim themselves. In a matter of days your, and my, blood will be wiped from the City, from the planet. And good riddance.' He looked round at them all, gloating in his achievement. His eyes lingered on Rubin and his eyes gleamed.

Marcellus' face was serious now, all amiability vanished. 'But you have ensured your own immunity, I'll wager?' he sneered.

'Even you, Marcellus, must admit that after all this time you have only distorted this world's history with your meddling.' Hammarskjald's voice darkened. 'This plague is a cure for all that, though a harsh one. It will wipe out everyone who has ever been subject to our taint.'

'Is it always fatal?'

'No, but it will make this City a necropolis for generations to come.' At this Rubin saw Thekla gaze up at her lord, eyes shining with adoration, and he wondered if either of them was sane.

Marcellus paced forward and his guard moved with him. 'Then why do you need the child?' he asked. 'To dissect it, Doctor Hammarskjald? To find out how a despised reflection can sire a living child? Is that what has really brought you from your bolthole? To discover how you can breed a new race of Serafim, subject to your will, to replace the old ones who proved so obstinate?'

But Hammarskjald would not be drawn. He looked around at his audience. 'Now,' he said, 'a decision. It is simple and I'll wait no longer. Give me the child. If not I will walk away from here and the City will die in agony.'

'You will not walk away, Hammarskjald!' A new voice rang clearly in the sunlight. 'You will die today in this place. That I promise you.'

Rubin swung to look as, with a crunch of boots on glass, a tall, rangy soldier leaped up on to the throne-room floor, sword in hand. He was fair, with cold pale eyes, and the burst of fresh energy he brought with him sliced like a shining blade through the Serafim's twisted war of words.

'Who is this?' Rubin whispered to his lord.

Marcellus' eyes narrowed. 'His name is Evan Broglanh,' he said.

Broglanh was a gregarious man. He enjoyed the company of soldiers, and of women, though not necessarily at the same time. He felt most alive in the uproar of battle, in the clamour of a crowded inn or at a riotous horse-race. He had spent little of his life alone and was unused to it. He was neither comfortable with his own thoughts nor wanted to be.

But on his sea journey back to the City from the Vorago he had had plenty of time to ponder, about Thekla and Selene and Archange, and the past choices he had made, and he was forced to face how wrong he had been. And he realized finally that he had been played for a fool.

He had been smitten by Thekla from the first, felled by blind lust as only a young infantryman can be when offered the solace of a beautiful woman who treats him like a lord. That she was granddaughter to Archange, who had taken a keen interest in him since his childhood, he thought only fortuitous. Just as he considered it merely a lucky accident that his long-held ambition to kill the emperor fitted neatly with Archange's plans for the City.

And so whenever he could return to the safety of the City from the blood-drenched fields of battle, he would speed to Thekla's home and she was always there, warm and inviting. That she was a surgeon who should have been tending the injuries of the fallen did not occur to him. Caught like a fish on the hook of his desire for her, he believed his soldierly charms were all that wedded her to him.

After Archange had become empress Thekla confided to him, for the first time, her growing anxiety for her grandmother. *I fear Archange is fated to follow Araeon*, she had told him as they lay in her bed. *As she ages and weakens I'm afraid she will seek the succour of the veil, to strengthen her power and people the palace with undead reflections, as Araeon did. Power always corrupts and she already has more power than any one woman should.* Those huge worried eyes, gazing into his, sucked him in and drank him down, convincing him it would be better for the City if the veil were to vanish for good. Broglanh was not aware of Archange's knotty, ambiguous relationships with her daughters and granddaughters. And if he had been, he wouldn't have cared.

So Thekla had concocted a plan and he had fallen in with it. They had agreed he would steal the veil and take it and Emly to the Petrassi port of Arocir. There Thekla would eventually join him, they would send Em to a place of safety and the pair would flee with the veil to somewhere it would never be found.

We should destroy it, Broglanh had argued, a worm of concern burrowing into his mind. She had agreed, but told him, *It is hard to damage. It cannot be burned or torn. It must be taken apart piece by tiny piece. It is intricate work and I can only do it if we are far from danger.*

Unlike Emly, Broglanh had a clear understanding of

geography. He could visualize the map of the known world and knew the quickest way home from the Vorago was by sea. So after leaving Selene he had walked, for only a short time each day as he gained in strength, then for longer, out from the mouth of the valley and east along the coast to the nearest fishing village. There he had found a fisherman who agreed to take him south to the Seagate.

But his satisfaction at arriving at the City's harbour had turned to dismay when he saw the multitudes trying to leave. The Seagate was a camp of desperate refugees, all frantic to escape the invading army and, he learned, the plague the enemy was carrying. Getting into the harbour, heaving with people, was almost impossible from land. Fares for transport by boat to the Wester Isles and beyond were sky-high. As Broglanh walked the Seagate, speaking to soldiers and traders and seamen, he learned that the City was under siege on three sides and that two of the Great Gates were expected to fall any day. He purchased a mount easily, for horses were two a pente when everyone was riding into the harbour and no one was riding out.

So when, early that morning, he heard the explosions on the Shield, and looked up towards the White Palace with alarm, he was almost there. As he rode through the broken gates, gazing round at the destruction, soldiers turned to look at him. He knew they recognized him, but they were too busy treating the wounded to care. In the courtyard he dismounted and tethered the horse then strode towards the ruins. He scarcely noticed the small woman, dark-skinned and wearing a black hat decorated with the gaudy ribbons of a prostitute.

'Lord!' she cried. 'Lord!' She grabbed his sleeve and he shook her off.

'Be off with you!' a soldier told her, hurrying over. 'I've told you before! Be off!'

'Lord!' she persisted, scurrying alongside Broglanh as he crossed the courtyard. She dug in her canvas bag and pulled out a grimy rag and tried to show it to him.

'I don't—' he began, thinking her a pedlar. Then he saw what she was holding and stopped, dumbstruck. The Gulon Veil! He took it from her reverently, feeling its familiar silken folds. But how had it returned here from the Vorago? For a moment he thought Emly must have brought it, but no, he'd lost it on the battlefield.

'Where did you get this?' he demanded.

'Girl,' the woman cried. 'Girl dying.'

He grabbed her by the shoulder. 'Where?' he demanded. The whore was tiny, her head on a level with his chest, and she cried out in fear. 'Where is she?' he asked again, shaking her.

'Dying! She say,' she touched her mouth to make it clear, 'say, give empress.' She pointed at the veil and nodded, staring hard at him, willing him to understand.

'Where is she, woman?'

The woman flung her arm towards the east. 'Wall,' she said.

Broglanh looked where she was pointing, racked with uncertainty. His heart screamed at him to ride to Emly and save her if he could. But it might take all day, if he found her at all, if the whore could be trusted. Meanwhile he had the Gulon Veil right there in his hands, delivered there by a turn of fate he did not understand. He knew he had to seek the empress first and, if she lived, return it to her.

'Stay here! Understand? Stay here!' he yelled at the woman and she flinched. 'Understand?'

He grabbed her canvas bag, ignoring her wail of complaint, and stuffed the veil inside. Then he turned to the guard, who had been watching wide-eyed. 'Do you know who I am?' he barked. The man nodded vigorously. 'Bring her food and water and make sure she stays here,' Broglanh ordered. 'If you lose her the empress will roast your balls on a stick!'

Broglanh climbed up through the ruins. He clambered over the soldiers' quarters and saw the handful of warriors, bloodied and covered with dust, labouring to dig their fellows out. He decided to make his way towards the west, where the empress's apartments lay, but was soon thwarted by a high wall on the verge of collapse. He skirted round it, found a hole in the broken stonework beyond and scrambled through. Then he stopped and looked around, trying to work out where he was. He recognized the flight of marble steps leading towards the throne room and raced up them, but they were blocked halfway up by more ruin, more rubble. As he climbed around the blockage he saw with a shock that the throne room's walls had collapsed, the great glass dome vanished.

Then he heard Thekla's sweet voice above him and he halted, thrown into uncertainty. He had convinced himself on the voyage that she had planned his death and Emly's and the downfall of the empress. How she, and her mother Selene, fitted in with Hammarskjald he was still unsure, but he was certain now her motives were base. Yet the smoky notes of her voice instantly evoked the touch of her skin, the scent of her body, the heat of her desire. He stood gripped with indecision. But as he listened longer and heard her words of bile and spite a chill coursed through him and he knew he had been right in his suspicions. Then he heard a familiar deep voice threaten the destruction of the City and he drew his sword.

He bounded up to the throne-room floor and was struck by the atmosphere of hatred and malice swirling there. His gaze took in Archange, hunched on the

Immortal Throne, her bodyguard around her, her pale thin hands clutching a black shawl. On the other side of the floor the big man who looked so like Stalker but who he now knew was Hammarskjald had his arm around Thekla's waist. She was clad in gold and pearls but he understood now that her heart was black with corruption.

He turned to the third group, eight armed men standing apart from the empress. What was their role in this? Then he recognized Marcellus and all breath left him. Marcellus? Alive? But, he told himself, Marcellus was executed by Fell Aron Lee on the Day of Summoning. They had discussed it, brothers in arms, after the fall of the Red Palace. Fell told him he'd severed Marcellus' head from his neck and thrown it from the battlements. Marcellus was dead. Broglanh's thoughts spun. *What in the name of all the gods*, he asked himself, *has happened since I left?*

All this took two beats of his heart, then with an effort of will he pushed the conundrum aside. He had only one job here. 'You will not walk away, Hammarskjald,' he told the man. 'You will die today in this place. That I promise you.'

Thekla darted across the floor towards him, eyes wide. 'Evan!'

Cold rage rose within him and he flicked up his sword and stopped her with the point to her breast. It was all he could do not to pierce her through. 'One step further and I will stick your heart, woman,' he snarled.

She looked into his face and saw the fury there. She fell to her knees. 'Evan,' she implored, 'hear me. You are my one true love. This man—'

As if she were not there, Broglanh turned to Hammarskjald and raised his voice. 'You told me that next time we met you would kill me.'

The big man nodded.

'So,' said Broglanh, 'try.'

Hammarskjald laughed. 'Lad, I am sorely tempted. I like a good scrap, as you know well. And it would be a rare battle.' His hunger was transparent. 'People who saw it would remember it all their lives.' He sighed. 'But I must decline.'

'You made a vow,' argued Broglanh. He knew he could appeal to the man's pride.

'But,' said Hammarskjald, glancing across the floor, 'above all I am a practical man and you have powerful allies who are even more eager than you are to see me dead.'

'What,' Broglanh asked scornfully, looking about him, 'two old people and a handful of soldiers?'

Hammarskjald chuckled. 'Those two old people are no older than me and they have some power, failing though it is.'

Marcellus stepped forward. Broglanh, with his practised soldier's eye, noticed the slight hitch in his gait which spoke of an injury. 'I enjoy a fair fight as well as the next man,' Marcellus announced. 'Fight away. I'll not interfere. Nor will Archange.' He cast a look at her and the empress nodded. He stepped back.

There was a moment's silence and Broglanh quelled the urgency in his heart and allowed a bored, contemptuous smile to slide across his face.

'Ay,' said Hammarskjald, his decision made. He unsheathed his great sword. Broglanh had seen it many times before – or one very like it – bathed in blood, cutting and killing the enemy. Now it was clean and bright and sharp. But he felt no fear, only scorn. The big man was proud as a rooster and it would be his undoing.

He dropped the bag concealing the veil at the edge of the floor, his sword-belt with it. The two men moved to the centre of the throne room and stood lightly, watching one another. Broglanh felt the glass slide under his boots, a treacherous surface to fight on for both of them.

'First I'll disable you, then I'll skin you alive,' Hammarskjald told him, his voice no longer hiding the anger he felt.

Broglanh rolled his shoulders. 'Don't go to any trouble on my account.'

He'd been five years old when first given a sword and since then he had fought with every type of blade made by man. He had learned to slice and hack in the heat of battle, when all around was anguish and death, and he had been taught the subtle art of fencing with épée and sabre. He had killed many, many men and women. He had battled in helm and heavy armour, in the cold of winter and in the dry desert heat. Now he was dressed lightly, in clothes he had lived in for half a year, worn, dirty and blood-stained, but which fitted him like skin. And he was stronger than he had ever been, thanks partly to the big man facing him. The mountain air filled his heart and he knew with complete certainty that if any warrior in the world could kill Hammarskjald it was he. But it had to be quick, for he suspected the big man could fight all day, and the next, and never flag.

He darted forward, narrowing all his strength and focus into a lunge for the heart. The attack was parried with ease and he barely escaped the murderous riposte which sliced his worn shirt. Hammarskjald kept coming with terrifying speed, his blade like flickering lightning seeking a way past his defence. Broglanh parried and blocked, knowing he had never faced a faster opponent. He felt himself tense as he fought, his blade slowing fractionally.

A watcher might think they were evenly matched, for

they circled and clashed and circled, neither giving a pace. But Broglanh was defending with all the skills he possessed. He was constantly within a hair's-breadth of death.

Yet he held his focus and watched his opponent for the smallest advantage. Stalker, he knew, had an injured ankle, the left. Hammarskjald forced him back in a frenzy of blows, the last of which nicked his shoulder, drawing blood. Heart hammering, Broglanh took the chance to spring backwards a few steps, moving lightly on the shifting floor. Hammarskjald followed, quick as a cat, and Broglanh saw that he too favoured the left leg. It was as if the two men, Stalker and Hammarskjald, shared the injury in some way. Broglanh did not understand it, but he could take advantage of it.

He drew his long knife and Hammarskjald grinned. *Say something*, Broglanh willed him silently. *Sneer at me, then you won't feel able to draw your second blade.*

'You are a good enough fighter,' Hammarskjald told him, 'but you need all the blades you can carry against such as me.'

Broglanh smiled.

Hammarskjald attacked, but instead of backing away Broglanh sprang forward and to his right, then dived and rolled past his opponent's flank. Hammarskjald pivoted on his left foot, moving his sword from right hand to left, ready to slam it into Broglanh's back before he could recover. But as the big man spun on his heel the glass shifted under him a fraction and he twisted to recover his balance. His sword missed Broglanh, who spun and slammed his knife up to the hilt into the man's side. He dragged it out and bounced back, watching.

It was as if nothing had happened. Hammarskjald regained his balance and, taking a lightning stride, lanced his sword at Broglanh's heart at full stretch.

Broglanh swayed but the blade sliced along his ribs. He spun away, ignoring the pain. Then he saw that the wound to Hammarskjald's side, a wound that would have floored any other opponent, had slowed the big man a tad. A bloody stain was crawling through the cloth of his shirt. Broglanh sprang forward and stabbed like lightning at the man's left arm, piercing deep into the bicep. Hammarskjald hesitated.

'Finish him!' he heard Marcellus growl.

Hammarskjald grinned and took the sword in his right hand. 'I can fight as well with either, boy,' he said.

Broglanh felt time slow. His blood was pounding in his ears. He took a deep breath of mountain air, feeling its virtue run through him. Then he darted forward and thrust at Hammarskjald's heart. The big man's sword flashed up, knocking Broglanh's aside. He lunged at Broglanh, but again the soldier sidestepped and parried the blow, before whipping around and slamming his knife into Hammarskjald's ribs for a second time. Hammarskjald bellowed like an ox and grabbed Broglanh by the shirt. They both fell to the floor, but it was Broglanh who scrambled up.

He wrenched his knife from Hammarskjald's side and watched the crimson blood gush, then, standing above him, he plunged his sword through the man's heart until the point ground into the marble floor beneath. Hammarskjald gasped, eyes rolling. Broglanh stood, watching the flow of blood from the two wounds. It slowed but didn't stop. Wanting to be sure, he crouched and grabbed the ginger head and twisted it brutally, snapping the neck, feeling it crunch. Distantly he heard Thekla cry out. He stood up, chest heaving. He looked into the man's face. Hammarskjald blinked.

Broglanh ran to the tribeswoman's bag and pulled out the Gulon Veil. He heard gasps from around the floor. He bunched the thing up and thrust it in front of Hammarskjald's eyes.

'I had it all the time, big man,' he said. 'You were so easily fooled!'

He waited, and at last Hammarskjald's eyes glazed over. Broglanh stood there still, watching, his sword ready.

Marcellus walked up beside him. 'He's dead, soldier,' he confirmed.

'Fell thought you were dead once,' Broglanh replied, his eyes fixed on the body.

Marcellus chuckled, but his voice sounded deathly tired. 'That was just a reflection.'

Broglanh closed his eyes, felt the heat on the back of the lids. He thought of Stalker, wondering briefly who it was he had killed. 'Perhaps this is a reflection too.'

'No,' Marcellus said. 'It is not.' Broglanh turned to look at him and saw satisfaction in the man's face.

'*Did* you have it all the time?' Marcellus asked him, nodding at the veil clutched in Broglanh's fist.

'No,' he confessed. 'I lost it. A valiant girl brought it back to the City.'

Then he walked across the blood-stained floor to Archange. As he knelt before her the pain in his shoulder and ribs cut into him and his knee almost gave way under him. He closed his eyes for a moment and the ground beneath him lurched. He sucked in a breath, willing away the pain and weariness, for he was not finished yet.

'My lady, you have my sword and my life.' Offering her the veil he looked at her properly for the first time. He thought she had aged, shrunk, since last he saw her in the summer.

'I should have you hanged, drawn and quartered,' she said mildly, taking the veil and clutching it to her. 'Where is Emly?' she asked.

'Dead, I fear.' The words clanged like a death-knell. Now the fight was over, the Gulon Veil back where it belonged, he was gnawed by dread. Was Emly truly dead? Had she succeeded in returning the veil to the City – the gods only knew how – only to die in the attempt?

The sound of sobbing came to his ears and he looked round. Thekla had thrown herself across Hammarskjald's body. Broglanh turned back to Archange, who was watching her, her face unreadable. She gestured to one of the guards to take Thekla away.

'I'm getting old,' she confessed to her lieutenant. 'I knew he had an agent in the palace, but I never suspected it was her.'

Broglanh no longer cared. 'Lady, with respect,' he said, desperate to depart, 'I must find Emly and bring her back to the palace, alive or dead. I vow I will surrender myself afterwards.'

She nodded and he stood and fled the floor.

Far to the south, at the Adamantine Breach, Darius Hex watched with black despair as the enemy hordes poured through the City's defences. His spine broken, his legs useless, he lay in agony, unable to do anything about it.

The Nighthawks had fought a valiant fight. They had battled steadfastly, their numbers slowly dwindling until they were too few to make a difference. Then Darius had ordered them to abandon their mounts and stand with the surviving defenders, who still held the breach despite terrible losses. Langham Vares was dead and Darius found himself commander of the embattled army.

He had been felled early that morning, as the sun rose behind a dismal mist. Though overwhelmed by the sheer weight of numbers he had fought on with sword and shield until an axeman had found his unprotected back. The man had been killed by Darius' comrades, but the commander knew he would never stand again. At his order they had dragged him to the top of the broken wall overlooking the battle where he lay, in torment of body and heart. He was armed with a knife which he would use on any enemy soldier who came within reach, and maybe on himself in the end.

He had watched as the enemy army struck again and again, waves of warriors, careless of death it seemed, exultant in the victory they could see ahead. They were led by a tall, broad-shouldered man with braided hair and beard. Though he was not young, the warrior seemed invincible and Darius' soldiers were defenceless against his mighty sword. He was bellowing his battle cry and, amid the horror, he almost seemed to be enjoying himself.

Then, his sword raised for a killing blow, he seemed to pause. Darius lifted a bloody hand to wipe his eyes. The big man stood motionless for a moment, and it was as if the whole world had stopped turning. Then three City soldiers lanced their blades into him and he fell, disappearing among the horde.

But Darius was sure he was dead before they struck.

CHAPTER FORTY-EIGHT

RUBIN LOOKED AT MARCELLUS, WHO STOOD STARING out over the City, and wondered what he was thinking. In the past hours he had been diminished in Rubin's eyes. He had been found wanting, squabbling with his peers and playing petty games for advantage whilst down in the streets honourable soldiers died. And as a warrior of legend he had been forced to stand and watch as two stronger men battled for the future of the City. Rubin wondered if Marcellus was capable any longer of feeling shame.

He followed his lord's gaze and saw smoke rising in the south. They had only left the fighting there early that morning but it seemed like a year ago. He glanced up at the sun and saw it had passed its zenith and was starting its fall into the west. It had been a long day and it was far from over. Hammarskjald's death, though so crucial here on the mountain, would make little difference down in the City. Tomorrow, or later this day if the empress decreed it, they would have to return to the battle.

Rubin heard the shuffle of boots and turned to see an old soldier, his face bruised and bloody, his arm in a stained sling, hurrying across the throne-room floor. He stared in bewilderment at Hammarskjald's body as he passed, then he addressed Archange.

'Lady,' he said, bowing stiffly, 'my apologies. The roof of my quarters—'

'What news, Eufara?' she snapped.

'Only terrible news, empress. The Great North Gate and the Paradise Gate have both been overrun. The Adamantine Breach too; the defenders were overwhelmed. The enemy are loose in our streets, killing and burning.' He coughed dust from his throat. 'I have ordered the bronze gates reinforced. All available soldiers, every man and woman who can stand and hold a weapon, have been sent to defend them. I will go myself and—'

'No,' the empress ordered. 'I want you here.'

The old man bowed his head.

Appalled, Rubin urged Marcellus, 'We must go down and defend the gates. The enemy could be here by tonight!'

His lord did not reply immediately, then he looked slowly round and Rubin saw he was not downhearted. His face was grave but the fire of resolution blazed in his eyes. 'No, boy,' Marcellus declared, 'there is another way.' Turning to the empress, he cried, 'Archange! We can still save the City if we use the veil. You can no longer deny it!'

Perched on the edge of her throne, she peered at him, eyes sheened with distrust. To Rubin's surprise she rapped out a few words in a language he had never heard before, and Marcellus replied in the same. Then Archange sat back and sighed.

'Very well,' she said, reverting to the City tongue, 'if there is nothing else for it. Though I believe it hopeless. And there must be five of us to even attempt it.'

'The Gaetas claim to possess the arcane skills we need,' Marcellus told her. 'What have you done with Jona?'

Archange did not answer but she beckoned Eufara

and at her word he sent two of his men running off. 'I have sent for Giulia too,' she informed Marcellus. 'She will make up the five if you're committed to this desperate course.'

'I don't understand,' Rubin confessed, looking between the two of them. 'Are you talking about this?' He pointed to the bedraggled cloth the tall warrior had given Archange, which she held clutched in her lap.

'*This* is the Gulon Veil,' she told him, holding it up. Its folds smoothed out as sunlight lit the delicate lacework and the dull grey gleamed silver. 'It is very old, as old as we are, and was once used to heal the sick and injured.'

'But it has a greater, protective power,' Marcellus added. 'Five of us – five Serafim – might shield the City using its power. Its designers intended that in times of greatest danger—'

Rubin interrupted. 'Then what are you waiting for? Why are you just talking about it? People are dying down there!'

'Silence, boy!' Archange snapped. 'You don't know what you're talking about!'

All Rubin's weariness, his disgust at their feuding, his humiliation at Hammarskjald's hands and his fear for the City rose up in an explosion of rage. He roared at the empress, 'Don't call me boy!'

The power and authority of his voice rolled through the air and armoured soldiers recoiled as if struck by a hammer-blow.

Archange nodded in mute acquiescence. 'This is not something we do lightly,' she explained, her voice persuasive. 'The veil might . . . *might*,' she emphasized, her eyes on Marcellus, 'protect those with Serafim blood, but it is designed to cure disease and it will identify those without our blood as infected. It will destroy them all, invaders and anyone else. Are you prepared for that?'

'But that would mean killing our own citizens!'

Marcellus shook his head. 'Our blood is strong, Rubin. That is why people of the City live so much longer than anyone else in this world, why they are so hard to kill. Over the centuries the fittest – descendants of the Serafim – have survived and flourished. This plague of Hammarskjald's is so deadly precisely *because* most City people have our blood in their veins.'

'But,' the empress added, 'we would be attempting something which has never been tried before, and the veil is ancient now and damaged.' She clasped it to her breast as if loath to be parted from it again.

Rubin asked, 'Why hasn't it been tried?' He was thinking of the long war against the Blues.

'Because its designers required that five Families of the seven agree to deploy such a potent force,' Marcellus explained. 'That consensus has not been seen in a thousand years.'

'And because for centuries the emperor kept it for himself, as his own personal plaything,' Archange added, pursing her lips with distaste.

In his heart Rubin felt hope flare, not only that the City might be rescued, but that the Serafim – himself included – might ally for a common good for the first time in a millennium. He felt he was at the fulcrum around which history was moving.

A guard clambered up on to the floor, prodding a shackled prisoner ahead of him at sword-point. The newcomer was dark and slender, his face cut and bruised. Blood crusted his clothes. As his shackles were unhinged, he looked at Hammarskjald's body and his eyes flickered around those present, seeking answers.

'Jona,' the empress said stiffly, 'it seems you were not, as I assumed, acting for Hammarskjald.' From Archange this was tantamount to an apology.

'No, woman,' Marcellus declared, 'he has always

been *my* agent.' With a glimmer of his previous good humour, he added, 'It seems you have poor judgement when it comes to picking allies.'

He turned to the newcomer. 'The Gaetas profess to know the mystery of wielding the veil,' he said. 'The City is overwhelmed by invaders and by plague. If ever it were needed it is now.'

'It's never been done,' said Jona, frowning, looking around at them. 'And we would need five Families of Serafim. Five different sources of *einai*—'

Marcellus interrupted, addressing the empress again in that alien tongue. She nodded.

'I have sent for Giulia,' she told Jona, 'and this is Reeve's son Rubin.' The three Serafim turned their dark gaze on him and he sensed the power in them like a brewing storm. He hoped he was equal to whatever would be asked of him.

'I need the casket,' Jona said, nodding towards the box Rubin was still holding, and he handed it over. Jona looked at it intently, running his hands over its gleaming wood.

The second guard returned and spoke to Eufara.

'Empress, the lady Giulia has gone!' the old man reported. 'Her servants say she departed the Khan Palace before dawn.'

'Alone?' she demanded.

'No, lady, with the boy Elija, and a woman and baby.'

Marcellus cursed long and fluently, then glared at Jona who was examining the casket as if unwilling to meet his eye. Archange looked between them, her eyes glinting with, what? Curiosity? Amusement? Rubin felt strong undercurrents shifting among the three. There was a great deal here he still did not understand.

'Is this the baby Hammarskjald wanted?' he asked. 'Fiorentina's child?'

Marcellus nodded distractedly, his normal poise rattled. Rubin wondered why. If the City fell, then even the Khan Palace would eventually be overwhelmed. Surely Giulia was taking mother and child to a place of safety?

Impatience spilling over, he put speculation behind him and raised his voice again. 'Each moment we waste, people are dying! I'm tired of hearing you talk. Now is the time to act!' he urged. 'Giulia may be gone, but whether we are five or four we must try. We are the City's only hope!'

A day before, even hours before, he would not have dared speak to them like that. But he had learned a great deal about the Serafim and his respect for them had been fatally undermined. He glared round at the three, daring them to disagree. Anger flickered across Marcellus' face at his words, but he nodded. Jona followed his lead.

The empress sighed and said, 'Very well. We will attempt it, though I fear the consequences for us all.'

Broglanh raced from the throne room and down through the palace, barging past the soldiers clearing passageways and stairs. He had already forgotten the greatest sword-fight of his life. His only thought was for Emly. The whore had told him she was dead, but he had to see for himself. He knew Archange had the power to heal her, if only he could find Em and bring her to the palace. He leaped down a last flight of steps and out into the courtyard. It was deserted save for bodies laid in rows.

'Evan!'

In spite of himself, he turned when he heard her voice.

She came to him forlorn and dishevelled, her glorious hair dusty, her gown in disarray. She walked across the courtyard, holding her hands prayerfully at her breast.

He watched her as she approached, searching inside himself for emotions. But he felt no more for her than he might for a thieving whore who had rifled his pockets as he lay in a drunken stupor.

Thekla walked across the stones barefoot, face cast down, then she gazed up at him and he was transfixed. She was magnificent. His heart yearned for her. She was not the wrongdoer but the victim. Hammarskjald had seduced her, abused her and betrayed her. For long heartbeats he was held in her thrall.

'Please . . . Evan.'

She gripped the bloodied knife she'd hidden between her palms and thrust it at his neck. She was quick but he was quicker. He snatched it from her, cutting her hand deeply, and the blood flew. She gasped, the picture of a woman hurt, her eyes huge with dismay. But now he saw clearly through her duplicity.

Broglanh grabbed her black curls, wrenched her head back and punched her. She fell to the ground but was up again like a cat. Blood on her mouth, she screamed her hatred at him. She lunged forward and tried to gouge his eyes. He grabbed her arm, but she bit deeply into his hand and he let go with a curse.

She was panting, her face contorted, eyes crazed with hatred. 'I'll kill you!' she screeched, her voice thick with fury. She tried to smash a knee into his groin then got her fingers to his throat. He caught hold of her wrists, ripping her hands away. Screaming with frustration, she whipped her head round and sank her teeth into his neck.

Broglanh threw her from him as he would a poisonous snake and she fell to all fours. He drew his sword.

'My love!' she cried, rising to her knees. She spread her arms, a heroine waiting for the sword to her heart.

He paused a breath, then stepped forward and sliced her throat.

He turned away, ignoring the sounds of her death throes . . . and spotted the little tribeswoman standing in the shadow of a broken wall, her hands at her mouth as if stifling a scream, eyes horrified. She tried to run but he caught her in three long strides.

'I won't hurt you,' he told her, then realized he was yelling. He was trembling with the strain of staying calm, but he managed to lower his voice. 'Tell me. Where is the girl who had the veil?'

The woman stared at him. Did she understand? He let go and stepped back, sheathing his sword. 'I won't hurt you,' he said again, softly. 'Tell me where she is. Please.'

She spoke haltingly and he listened, trying to make sense of what she said. He looked around the courtyard then saw a cavalryman he knew entering the broken gates leading a train of horses. Dragging the woman along, Broglanh ran to him.

'Amalric! Mount up and follow me!' he ordered. 'And bring her with you!'

Then he ran for his horse.

The empress and Marcellus ordered their guards from the floor, forbidding them to return unless expressly ordered. The last to leave, with a show of reluctance, was the old general. As he disappeared from view Jona Lee Gaeta knelt and opened the white casket, laying the hinged lid flat on the floor. The box appeared empty, but its inside gleamed palely like mother-of-pearl. He took a deep breath and held his hands above it. Rubin saw his lips move. Slowly the emptiness within the box thickened until it was filled by a roiling silver-grey mist. Jona looked up at the empress. She hesitated before handing him the folded veil. Jona held it for a few heartbeats, face solemn, then laid it reverently over the open casket. He stood up. After examining each of the others in turn, as if gauging their resolve, he turned his eyes back to the veil.

Rubin felt feverish with anticipation, his joints weak and heart racing. Within himself he could detect no morsel of the power Marcellus called *einai*. The three Serafim were standing around the Gulon Veil, looking down, silent and grave. Rubin did the same. For long moments nothing happened, then almost imperceptibly the threads of the veil began to brighten as though each was saturating with energy. Its folds stirred into movement and it slowly unfurled of its own accord, like an animal roused from sleep. Rubin stared, mesmerized, as the veil stretched out, expanding, shimmering. It flowed sinuously across the floor, its curled edges pushing aside the shards of the throne room's glass roof. The watchers stepped back to give it room to grow.

Rubin was transfixed, but he was merely a spectator, uninvolved. He closed his eyes and it was then he felt the *einai* stir. It swelled quickly, racing through his sinews and nerves. It was much stronger than before and a spasm of dread made his eyes open again. The veil was floating just above the floor, shining, throbbing with light and power. Jona raised his hands and it rose, until it was above their heads and still growing, blotting out the sun. Its silvery ripples were like a brewing storm, a roiling thunderhead, heavy with fate on this bright day. Jona stretched out his arms and the veil spread yet further, thinned, dissolving into a pearly radiance.

Rubin shut his eyes again and, with an effort of will, surrendered himself to the power.

He sensed he was floating in the sky high above the Shield. He was part of the veil and it part of him. He could feel its silken strands running through his veins, tugging on his sinews, sliding round his heart. Bathed in its luminescence, he felt safe in its strength. It was bliss. Distantly he was aware of the others, motes on the edge of vision. In a flood of understanding, he knew what he must do: free his *einai*, let it flow and blend with that of the other Serafim in the medium of the veil. He thought it and it was so. As their powers merged he recognized each of the three like different coloured threads in the veil itself. He could taste their colours, touch their scents, see their sounds, hear their textures.

Gates flew open in his mind and memories began to flood in, faster and faster, crowding in until his brain felt like a water skin filled to bursting. In that broken, dizzying kaleidoscope of impressions he learned everything about the three Serafim – their births and lives and loves, their ambitions, frustrations and failures. He experienced their birth-shock and battle wounds, the ecstasy of love and the potency of hate. He felt the terrible ennui of lives lived too long yet unfulfilled.

And buried deep within the avalanche of borrowed memories he glimpsed visions of the world Marcellus and Archange and others of the First had fled – a world of wonders unknown to him yet clothed in stone, stinking, dying, a glittering sarcophagus.

Broglanh rode from the palace, heading for the Paradise Gate. He whipped the horse on, yelling at anyone in his way. His eyes were fixed on the distant Paradise Tower, willing it to get closer.

Thoughts of Emly filled his head. Since the first day he had met her, battling against all odds to save her father from the inferno of the House of Glass, she had never been less than brave and true, despite everything she had been through. Those long summer days, as they travelled together with the Khan army, had been some of the happiest of his life. As he journeyed ever further from Thekla's thrall he had been beset by misgivings about their scheme to steal the veil, but his misplaced faith in her had lingered – a thin, overstretched thread – until he met Hammarskjald and her mad mother in the Vorago valley.

He was tormented by the knowledge that he had betrayed Emly just as he had betrayed the City, snatching away the veil when it was most needed. Now he had returned it to its owner and by killing Hammarskjald had, he hoped, made some restitution to the empress and the City. But if Emly were to die, if she was already dead, it would be his fault and his burden and he could not live with it.

He kicked the horse on, leaning forward in the saddle, checking behind to ensure Amalric was following. As the beast halved the distance to the wall they began racing past streams of women and children and old folk, their goods piled on carts or donkeys or their backs, trudging down the road away from the Great Gate, away from the invading army and its terrible contagion. Injured warriors walked among the refugees, but many lay by the roadside unable to go further. The stench of blood and death hung, tangible, in the air.

As he approached Paradise and its warren of lanes and twittens Broglanh recalled the whore's directions and steered the lathered horse towards the northbound wall, staying clear of the battling armies. He tried to ignore the sound of sword on sword, metal on flesh, though his heart and gut responded. He kicked the animal on.

At last the wall came into plain sight. Reining in and standing in the stirrups, careless of stray arrows, he searched for the steps going north. He spotted them, and the City fighters battling to defend them. He urged the horse round the rear of the fighting, vowing to himself that if Emly were truly dead then he would return here and end his life with honour. How much time had passed since she was injured? Far too long, he feared. He told himself not to hope.

At last the horse broke free of the throng and Broglanh urged it up the steps, then kicked it into a gallop along the top of the wall, heading north. The sounds of battle began to diminish behind him. Then, with a jarring clash of hope and dread, Broglanh spotted his own big warhorse on the wall ahead. The beast was rearing and lashing out with his hooves at anyone who came near. There was no sign of his rider. A band of civilians, ignoring the battle for the City so close by, had gathered to watch. Someone had managed to get a rope round the stallion's neck, but it had broken and the end bounced and flew as the horse struck out.

Broglanh threw himself off his lathered mount, enraged that these people could turn their backs on the battle being waged on their behalf to watch a dancing horse. He bellowed at them as he barged through and they fell back like the sheep they were. He stopped and called to the stallion. Patience's ears flicked, and he abandoned his vigil to trot calmly over. Broglanh patted his neck.

Then he saw her, a small pile of rags huddled against the parapet. His heart slowed and stuttered, and the rest of the world – the gaping crowd, the distant battle – vanished. All he could hear was the beat of his heart and the dry rasp of his breath.

She had curled up with her back to the world. He knelt down and gently turned her over, light as a bird. Her hands were thick with blood, which lay in a sticky pool beneath her. His breath stopped. So much blood, such a small body. He took her in his arms and looked into her face, pale as water under the dirt, willing her to live. He pushed her hair back and touched her cheek.

The skin was cold. He laid his ear against her breast and listened. He could hear nothing. And tears, unknown to him since childhood, flowed down his face.

After a while he became aware of the tribeswoman crouching beside him. 'Dead,' she said with certainty. 'Dead now.'

Fighting Knife, moved by the warrior's fierce devotion, laid her hand on the girl's head and prayed to the god of the Fsaan, whose will was always a mystery but whose mercy was eternal, to let the girl live. Behind her the crowd, suddenly respectful, sank as one to their knees and began to petition their own deities.

High above the mountain the veil floated and span. Drifting in its threads, heedless now of the City and its distress, Rubin experienced the ages-long lives of the Serafim as if they were his own. At last he understood. He knew what they were. And he was amazed.

Only distantly was he conscious of the Gulon Veil. Alive and eager, it continued to expand, as it had been designed to, its farthest edges racing towards the walls of the City to form a vast dome encompassing all the savagery within.

Then, like silver, incandescent rain, it descended.

At the Great North Gate the brutal hand-to-hand combat faltered and stopped as warriors of both armies gazed up in terror and awe.

A curtain of bright light was descending from the sky, roaring towards them like a sheet of flame. As it touched the top of the Great North Tower the stones crackled and sparked fire. It sank to the battlements, and the soldiers, defenders and attackers alike, scattered in panic.

Valla's old comrades Thorum and Wren, soldiers of

the Fighting Forty-seventh, ran for their lives, then, seeing they could not outpace the threat, threw themselves under a fallen stone arch. But they could not escape. Silver motes of light swirled all around and there was nowhere to hide.

Thorum, believing death was about to snatch them, took Wren's rough, blood-stained hand in his. 'You are my life,' he told her. 'My wife, my sister and my comrade.'

They flinched as the sparks touched them, but it felt like cool rain on a hot afternoon. The pains of their wounds drifted away and they gazed at each other in wonder. They crawled out of their hiding-place and looked around.

All the invaders, high on the wall and in the streets, scorched, flared briefly then charred like moths at a flame.

Darius Hex was sunk in despair. He could not bear to watch as the enemy hordes continued to pour into the City through the Adamantine Breach, trampling the dead and dying in the ditch, clambering over the bodies on the earthwork and overwhelming the last gallant defenders. A strong man, he had begged his gods for release but they had not answered his pleas.

Then there was a moment of quiet, of calm. The din of battle ceased and he opened his eyes and looked up, hoping to see the Gardens of Stone but fearing it would be the blade that would end him. The sky seemed full of light and he blinked the sweat from his eyes. He pulled himself up to sitting, the agony of his shattered spine making him cry out. The battlefield seemed glazed with burnished silver. The fighting had stopped, for the enemy soldiers all lay dead, their bodies burned and contorted as if by a great fire. City warriors stumbled around, disorientated, bewildered.

Darius realized his pain had vanished, as if it had never been. *Am I dead?* he thought. *Or is this a dream?* He found he could move his legs and he climbed shakily to his feet, dazed and mystified, then gazed out over the hushed City.

Evan Broglanh did not see the silver veil descending from the sky. He did not hear the cries of fear and awe all around him. His gaze was fixed on Emly's face as he willed her to live.

He had killed and killed over twenty long years – hundreds of warriors sacrificed in the name of the gods of ice and fire.

And when Emly opened her eyes and smiled up at him he believed, and for ever would believe throughout their long lives together, that for once the gods had shown mercy on their most faithful servant.

CHAPTER FORTY-NINE

RAPT IN THE VEIL'S EMBRACE, RUBIN WALKED LIKE A ghost among the Serafim's thousand-year memories, pulling together the myriad scraps of recall and emotion, living their successes and losses as his own. He marvelled at the pioneers' courage and the wild ambition of their task, and wept for their ultimate tragedy.

For the Serafim were Mankind's last, best hope of averting extinction.

Oblivion would be slow in coming, long predicted, but Man's greed and arrogance, and his insatiable curiosity, would in the remote future inexorably drive this planet's resources to the brink of collapse. Then the iron rules of entropy would set in, making extinction inevitable. Cruelly, Earth's last survivors would know by then that they stood alone in the cosmos, a bizarre aberration in an otherwise sterile universe. And that their planet's death would end that brief, improbable experiment – life.

In pioneering craft, the building of which would exhaust the darkening planet's last resources, three teams of voyagers would be flung into the past to pivotal points in Man's history. These travellers were human, but they were bred to be the best, the strongest and longest-lived. They possessed special Gifts, some shared, some individual, all enhanced. Their goal, to protect and guide the primitive people they found and, maybe, alter their narrative enough to save the future world and life itself. One of those teams was named Serafim.

Personalities filled Rubin's mind. Araeon, wise leader, whose strength and resourcefulness kept them alive in an alien world where so many perished. Marcellus, ever-faithful, the studious recorder of the team who in time became its legendary warlord. Archange and Hammarskjald. Sikander Khan. Donal Broglanh. And many others. Rubin knew them all, and their darkest secrets were laid open to him.

In the beginning the travellers had struggled to survive in this hostile world, and were united by the trials they faced. The brutish tribes they encountered would not be taught, or guided, or even helped. The wildlife was vicious and even the land, as if disturbed by their anachronistic presence, was torn by violent earth tremors. But as their footing became secure and the humble foundations of what would become the City were dug, schisms began to form between those of the team who chose to watch and record and subtly guide the primitives, and those who would force change upon them. There was conflict among the Serafim, then treachery and murder.

Most of them abandoned the City within a century, despondent that their high ideals had been so distorted; they tried to return to their home and their fate remained unknown. Those who stayed – who formed the noble Families Khan and Sarkoy, Vincerus, Guillaume, Gaeta, Kerr and Broglanh – stubbornly refused to accept failure. They were determined to force this world to their will. They targeted the primitives' first sparks of scientific progress, for rampant technology driven by the pursuit of profit and the needs of the military would, in time, be the most obvious engine of planet failure. Thus, as any innovation might start the wheel of history rolling towards catastrophic collapse, Araeon decreed that all inventions be suppressed as they emerged. His acolytes roamed far and wide seeking them out – the printing press, magnifying lenses, gunpowder, the steam pump – and their creators were discouraged or killed.

But for all their resourcefulness and resolve the Serafim could only completely control the City, and the rest of the world raced towards its destiny despite them. Finally the City stood alone, a pariah ruled, in the world's eyes, by evil magics.

Even the loftiest ambitions become corrupted by time and circumstance. Over the course of a millennium the Serafim, who wished to be wise and benevolent teachers, instead became rulers, dictators, tyrannical gods.

Rubin, basking in the deep vaults of memory, became aware that the *einai* was pulling away from him, slowly at first, then with shocking speed. The veil's threads, tender and warm before, now cut and tore. Furious, he suspected duplicity by the other Serafim. Then he realized his foe was the veil itself, now huge, ungovernable, writhing like a muscular serpent. He fought it as it sought to draw his power from him. He felt the fear, then desperation, of the other three as the Gulon Veil absorbed their *einai* like a parched desert sucking up rain. Rubin strove with all his youthful strength. And with a terrible wrench to his mind and soul he pulled himself free. His body collapsed on the throne-room floor and lay as if dead.

Within, his mind was still trapped, fracturing. Wild thoughts and images tortured him; alien memories he could not understand were trying to tear his grip from reality. Though free of the veil, he was locked into the footprints of the Serafim in a world of stone and metal, both rich and barren, flying through their skies in flimsy craft. He breathed their foul air, staring up at a starless sky. His mind tried again and again to flee from the maelstrom of terrifying memories, but each time it was like waking from a nightmare to find the dreams were real and the monsters were about to devour you. He struggled to recall the narrative of his own life but could remember nothing of himself, not even his name. He was sinking in a terrifying morass of other people's experiences and could find no way out.

Who am I? he asked himself. *What is my name?* He tried desperately to remember, but was buffeted and torn by older, stronger minds than his, clamouring phantoms vying for dominance.

He was striding the corridors of the Red Palace, uncomfortable in new ox-blood armour, furious and frustrated at being out-thought by lesser men. His bodyguard clattered behind him and senior officers scurried at his side proffering advice that was all too little, too late. He stopped at the top of the Pomegranate Stair and, his face stone, half-listened to their lacklustre words. All the while he wondered who was really responsible for this invasion of the Red Palace – Hayden Weaver and his brother had neither the cunning nor the imagination, Saroyan not the courage . . .

His eyes caught a movement in the gloom and he saw young Rubin Guillaume climb into sight on the stairs, his face suddenly aglow at the sight of his lord. Marcellus nodded to him, thinking angrily: Why don't I see this transparent devotion on the faces of my own men?

Rubin Guillaume. There was a swirling, vertiginous change of perspective as Rubin recognized himself in Marcellus' recollections. *Rubin.* He grasped Rubin's memories and saw flashing visions – Indaro's face as she turned to smile at him, the darkness and stench of the Halls, Valla fighting one-armed to save him. Dragging his mind from the morass of memory, he passed out.

When he awoke in his own body, his own mind, he groaned in agony. The brutal marble beneath him was an instrument of torture after the bliss of the veil. He pulled himself up on one elbow, the joint screaming, then rolled on to his back. Every muscle ached. Even his bones hurt.

Cautiously he tried to bring to mind the fixed points of his life and, with relief, remembered the grey house on the Salient, gulls crying on the salty air. He recalled the long afternoons spent with Marcellus as his lord charmed him with tales of war and wonder. He saw Captain Starky's pale face loom out of the gloom and felt the hard corners of carved knucklebones in his hand. Though alien thoughts still screeched and clamoured for his attention, Rubin felt he could control them.

Then, with a sense of dread, he thought back to the Serafim and all he had learned about them. He remembered everything they had been through, how they had tried and why they had failed, and grief for their lost humanity overwhelmed his heart. For a long time he was becalmed in a sea of misery.

The pains from his exhausted body eventually roused him. Still confused, Rubin tried to recall what he had been doing before the terrible onslaught on his mind. Then it came back to him – the invasion of the City, the four of them deploying the veil – and he opened his eyes. High above the Gulon Veil shimmered.

He rolled over and climbed wearily to his feet then turned in a circle, gazing out over the City. The veil's pearly dome encompassed everything from the Seagate in the south to the Great North Wall, from the Salient to the Paradise Tower. Beyond its gleam he could see the sun was just starting to set. Though he had experienced other men's lives over centuries, little time seemed to have passed there on the mountain.

He looked at the floor. Marcellus lay sprawled on his back among the glass and blood and Rubin knelt by his side ready to wake him, then froze in shock. His lord's face was a skull, the eyes lost in shadow, the skin frail and white as bone. Fearfully Rubin touched his shoulder. 'Lord!' he whispered.

Relief coursed through him as the eyelids flickered. Rubin stood and turned to the others. The empress lay back on the Immortal Throne, eyes open but unseeing. Jona was motionless on the floor. Both had aged. With a stab of dread, Rubin examined his own hands. They trembled a little but seemed the same – no wrinkled skin, no blemishes of old age.

He gently helped Archange to sit. She felt as delicate as swansdown, her clothes hanging on fragile bone.

'It has done for us.' Marcellus' voice trembled. Rubin hurried back to him and supported his lord as he stood, clutching his side where the wound was bleeding again. 'We succeeded,' Marcellus grunted, gazing at his hands, the hands of an old man. 'I felt the invaders burn. But the veil sucked us dry in the process. We did not foresee that.'

Jona too climbed slowly to his feet. His black hair had turned iron-grey but he appeared less damaged than the empress or Marcellus. 'Four of us were not strong enough to control it,' he sighed. 'If Giulia—'

'We have sacrificed a great deal,' Marcellus interrupted. 'But we will have to live or die with it.' He looked Rubin up and down, frowning. 'Your youth seems to have protected you.'

Although he would never admit it to Marcellus,

Rubin felt satisfied by the outcome. He thought the loss of *einai* would prove a good thing for the City. For all the travellers' original high intentions, it had in the end been primarily an arena for them to play out their family rivalries, their petty jealousies and vendettas. Its citizens had been no more than pawns in their power games. Now the last Serafim were fatally weakened, the people might have a chance to rule their own destiny.

'We must go down,' he urged his lord. 'There will be much to do and people will need our help. We have the dead to dispose of, food to gather and distribute, defences to rebuild.'

But he realized he was talking to himself. Marcellus was not listening. He was looking at Archange assessingly.

'You are dying, cousin,' he concluded coldly.

Rubin saw he was right. He had known, even before the veil had snatched her power, that the empress had little time left. Now she clung grimly to the arms of the throne as if clutching at a cliff; her eyes had become lost and childlike, and her mouth moved uncontrollably as if she were trying to speak but could not find the words.

'I could wait for you to die,' Marcellus told her, staring at her as he might an injured dog, wondering if it was worth the effort of killing, 'but that might take days and the City needs a strong leader. And we all know the Immortal Throne is rightfully mine.' He bared his teeth in a death's-head grin.

Rubin stared at him in despair. For all the day's revelations, for all its horrors, had Marcellus learned nothing? He brought to mind the young pioneer his lord had once been. All those high ideals vanished, corrupted into personal ambition. Inwardly, Rubin was racked with sorrow.

Hunched on the throne, Archange muttered, 'You would be emperor?'

'That was Araeon's wish, and it was agreed by all of us long ago,' Marcellus told her. 'You remember as well as I, Archange. And the child changes everything,' he went on. 'A newborn Serafim, sired by a reflection. It could be the first of many. A new race of Serafim, unspoilt by the past, just as Hammarskjald predicted.'

Archange peered at him. Her lips trembled but her words were clear. 'First you call on Araeon, then Hammarskjald, in support,' she croaked. 'What does that say of your ambition?'

'My ambition, as ever, is the future welfare of the City,' he retorted. He looked around at them, smiling, and Jona stepped up to stand beside him.

Archange leaned forward, spitting, 'You are a fool, Marcellus! Like Hammarskjald, your pride was ever your undoing.'

She fixed her gaze on Marcellus and Rubin was startled to feel her power move ominously among them once more. It was much weaker than before, but it was enough to fix Marcellus, already grievously damaged, in its thrall. A spasm of fury crossed his face as he realized, too late, what she was doing. He roared like a baited beast but could not move. Archange's black eyes flashed at Jona. Before Rubin knew what was happening, Jona had pulled a knife and thrust it deep into Marcellus' heart.

Marcellus slumped to his knees, face contorted. With a bellow of pain he gripped the hilt and dragged the blade out, stared at it unbelieving. Casting his eyes up at Jona he choked, 'Traitor!' Then he fell back, blood pumping from his chest in thick, rich spurts. Panic-stricken, Rubin dropped beside him and tried to staunch it, pressing his hands over Marcellus' heart, but it gouted through his fingers, unstoppable.

Gurgling sounds rose from Marcellus' throat as he tried to speak, then blood poured from his mouth. As Rubin watched in anguish, his eyes became dull, the muscles of his face slackened. The blood-flow slowed to a trickle, then stopped.

Rubin sprang up and, raising a bloody hand towards Jona, threw a bolt of power at him. The assassin was flung high into the air then crashed to the floor, sliding on the glassy surface. Helpless under the force of Rubin's wrath, he slithered across the throne room.

Time slowed as Rubin watched, savouring his revenge. Eyes wide with panic, Jona slid to the edge of the mountain-top. He scrabbled for purchase as Rubin had done, if only in his mind, when Hammarskjald tormented him. But as Rubin relived his own terror and saw it reflected in Jona's agonized face he stayed his hand at the last moment. He stopped the assassin's slide on the very brink of the abyss, leaving him frozen, suspended over the drop.

Rubin turned back to Marcellus' body and, stunned by shock and grief, sank to his knees, tears flooding his face.

As if from a great distance he heard Archange's words of venom. 'Jona was never a traitor!' she told the dead man, her voice slurring, indistinct. 'He was always loyal to me! Only your colossal ego let you think he was ever your man.' She seemed oblivious of Marcellus' death.

'He's dead,' Rubin told her through his tears, but she couldn't hear him.

'I warned you I would pay you back for Saroyan's death!' she slurred.

'He's dead,' Rubin repeated, raising his head. 'He can't hear you.'

Grief and fury vying within, he sprang up and strode towards the throne. The empress cringed before him and he witnessed the play of emotions over her ancient face. Fear battled there with triumph, and confusion. And cunning.

'You can heal me, boy,' she muttered slyly. 'Yours is the power now.' She clutched at his hand and he drew away, repulsed. Her gaze, once so terrible, wandered as if she was forgetting her words as she spoke them. Rubin guessed she had used her last morsel of power to destroy Marcellus and she would, as his lord had predicted, soon be dead.

He turned his back on her and considered Marcellus' body, wondering: *Can I heal him? Can I bring him back? And if I can, should I?* He was gripped by indecision, mystified by the power he now seemed to control. Then, miserably, he thought the unthinkable. *Will the world be a better place without Marcellus in it?*

He knelt by his lord's side and laid the body out, the arms across the chest. He gently closed the dead eyes. In his mind he said goodbye, for he could not utter the words aloud. Then he stood and went over to where Jona still lay, half off the edge of the floor, unable to move. The man watched him come, fear in his eyes.

'Have you always been Archange's man?' Rubin asked him without emotion.

Despite his plight, Jona spoke defiantly. 'Since I was old enough to make a choice.'

Rubin bent down and grabbed his hand, then, releasing him from his thrall, helped the man to safety. Jona tried to stand but his legs gave way and he sat down. After a moment Rubin joined him and they sat side by side on the edge of the blood-stained floor watching the sun go down over the City.

'Why did you not kill me?' Jona asked after a while, his black eyes curious.

Because treachery and loyalty are two sides of the same coin, Rubin thought. *And I would have done as much at one time. I would have killed Archange if Marcellus had ordered it.* And there had been enough death.

But he said simply, 'My father once told me loyalty was the most important virtue.' He did not add, '*but you should choose its recipient with care.*'

He heard the stealthy steps of soldiers behind them and, without turning to look, he flung them away from him. He heard them crash to the floor, rolling, their armour and weapons clattering on the black and white marble.

Jona watched with interest. 'It seems you have gained the power we lost,' he commented.

Rubin shrugged. 'I don't know what happened. I didn't ask for this.'

'So you will be emperor now.'

Rubin gazed at him. *What is it about these people?* he wondered. *So obsessed with power and its uses.*

And yet . . . should he take the throne? With so many dead and Archange dying, who would then deny him? The remaining armies would fall into line once they had a taste of what he could do. He would be a wise, benevolent ruler and make up for some of the Serafim's transgressions.

He thought about it for half a heartbeat then shook his head. 'The City doesn't need another emperor,' he said, 'it needs to be healed and rebuilt by those who define its heart – its people.' People like Elija and Emly, and Valla, he thought.

Though the enemy hordes were destroyed, the City was maimed and suffering. There would be a great deal to do. He *could* use his power to mend and restore. But he knew that was how the Serafim had become corrupted, first dictating the end they desired then shaping measures to suit it. *No,* he thought, *I will leave the resurrection of the City to its people. They must make their own future, for good or ill.* Instead he would seek out

Fiorentina and her son and ensure their safety – fulfilling the duty placed on him by Marcellus so long ago. And he would send word to Indaro that she could come home now. The bleakness in his heart lifted a little at the thought.

But first he had to find Valla.

'They were men and women of honour, the First Serafim,' Jona was musing, watching the horizon where the sun had left a stain of rose and gold. 'They wanted to save their world. Everything they did was with that in mind.'

Rubin realized they must have shared experiences in the veil trance.

'But they had an impossible task,' he replied. 'They did not know for sure how their world had gone so wrong, and could only guess how to fix it.'

From the vaults of memory he heard Marcellus' voice – a young Marcellus, not yet sullied by power and failed dreams. '*We don't know what we're doing*,' he'd said once in a fit of candour. '*We're blind men using cudgels to perform brain surgery.*' He smiled. Marcellus would never be truly gone while Rubin held his memories.

He turned to look at his lord's body. Soldiers were now swarming the floor, though they eyed Rubin with fear and gave him and Jona a wide berth. Some raised Marcellus up and carried him away. Others attended the empress, who seemed unconscious or dead – Rubin couldn't tell which and he didn't much care.

'Why did Archange and Araeon hate each other so?' Jona asked, following his gaze. 'She never told me, though it was that hatred which brought us to where we are today.'

Rubin thought he was both right and wrong. If Archange had not conspired against Araeon then the City would not have been so weakened that Hammarskjald felt able to make his play. Yet . . . if Marcellus had been less loyal to the emperor they would not, maybe, have become enmeshed in the long, draining war. Besides, others shared the blame, Rubin knew now, and most of them were long dead. It took many people to destroy a City, or a world.

He tapped the memories crowding his brain. 'Something happened before they even reached here, the First Serafim,' he recalled. 'They planned to secure their position by increasing their number. But their offspring were few and far between and when they did quicken they usually died at birth or in their first days. Some believed,' he said, remembering, 'that the journey back through the centuries had been an insult to Nature, and that barrenness was her revenge.'

'But they had plenty of time,' Jona pondered. 'With such long lives women had centuries in which to bear children.'

'Yes, and slowly their numbers increased but they never flourished. Which is why they began breeding with the primitives. That had never been the intention, in fact Araeon had forbidden it. But—' Rubin stopped and shrugged. He'd learned a great deal that day, but Jona was still hundreds of years older than him and there was nothing Rubin could tell him about forbidden love.

Instead he said, 'Araeon began to lose his sanity a very long time ago. A strong leader and an arrogant man, he desperately wanted Sarkoy sons. But they didn't happen. That is probably when he started abusing the Gulon Veil, creating reflections in the dark depths of the Red Palace. He hoped to create a female version of himself to mate with and produce offspring.'

Rubin felt no revulsion at this, no judgement. *To know all is to understand all*, he thought. But Jona's face darkened. Rubin thought of his ancient mother Sciorra, imprisoned in the Iron Palace, and her grisly obsession. Her distorted reflections were all despatched, under Jona's orders, as soon as they drew breath. *Will such madness seize us all if we live that long?* he thought. He shuddered with foreboding.

Then, 'In the end Araeon did what seemed both obvious and inevitable,' he went on. 'He wed his sister. By then few recalled that Araeon and Archange were brother and sister, and those who did didn't care. Yet still they had no sons. Rather they had two daughters and in his corruption Araeon abused them vilely, as he did his daughters' daughters. Later Archange may have regretted her deeds, for she adopted the Vincerus name for herself and her girls. Marcellus conspired in the charade; at the time it suited him to have her beholden to him.'

But he had seen her black heart. She had wed Araeon with the calculated intention of founding a dynasty. And their daughters, Selene and Eithne, were damaged from birth. They shared Archange's capacity for hate, though not her strength. Thekla, also spawned by the emperor, was as corrupt as he was, though she hid it behind her mask of beauty.

Rubin got slowly to his feet, the weight of the world on his shoulders, and looked about him. The soldiers had departed. Only Hammarskjald's body, in a circle of dry blood, had been left for the carrion birds. He gazed up. Crimson eagles were circling beneath the dome.

He said, 'Fixing your heart on one goal, however well-intentioned, will always open you to corruption.' Jona caught his eye and nodded. Both knew it was a warning.

Rubin looked at his hands, sticky with Marcellus' blood. He blinked and they were clean. Then he made his way back across the floor towards the ruined stairway, planning to seek out Valla. Suddenly he stopped and turned. There in the gathering darkness on the edge of the floor stood the Immortal Throne, silent and implacable. He walked over to it and looked at it closely for the first time. He touched its smooth warmth, closed his eyes and listened to the white alabaster. What was it telling him?

Stepping back, he drew just the smallest drop of *einai* from the deep well he had to command, and hurled the great alabaster throne backward. It flew off the mountain then crashed down, smashing on the rocks below into bone-white rubble and dust.

EPILOGUE

THE PATCHWORK GULON PADDED THROUGH THE RUINS of the White Palace and down the long tunnels beneath, searching. Time had no meaning for the creature and it was scrupulous in its investigation of every chamber, every courtyard and corridor, working its way down through the layers of the mountain, undeterred by time or by infirmity.

When it found her at last, broken and long dead, lying in pitch-blackness at the root of the mountain, a place which would not be rediscovered by men for many centuries, it sniffed her ice-blonde hair and her black and silver uniform and realized at last that this was just a rotting corpse, no longer of use even as food.

It sat on its haunches and waited for a while, scratching occasionally. Then, undeterred, it followed the demands of its loyal little heart and padded away, hot on the trail of *the woman*.

'This is the grand style of storytelling. Gemmell's triumph is creating men and women so real that their trials are agony and their triumph is glorious'
CONN IGGULDEN

DAVID GEMMELL

His bestselling epic trilogy re-imagining of the story of Troy

TROY: LORD OF THE SILVER BOW

Three lives will change the destiny of nations. Helikaon, the prince haunted by a traumatic childhood. The priestess Andromache, whose spirit and ferocity threatens the might of kings. And Argurios, the legendary warrior – cloaked in loneliness and driven by revenge.

In Troy they find a city torn apart by rivalries. And beyond its fabled walls blood-hungry enemies eye its riches and plot its downfall.

It is a time of bravery and betrayal, a time of bloodshed and fear. *A time for heroes . . .*

TROY: SHIELD OF THUNDER

War is looming. The kings of the Great Green gather, each nurturing dark plans of conquest and plunder.

Into this maelstrom come three travellers: Piria, a priestess with a terrible secret; the legendary warrior Kalliades, and his friend Banokles, whose destiny will be forged in the battles to come.

Together they journey to the fabled city of Troy, where a darkness is falling that will eclipse the stories of mortals for centuries to come.

And written with Stella Gemmell

TROY: FALL OF KINGS

Darkness falls and the Ancient World is divided.
On the killing fields outside Troy, forces loyal to the Mykene King gather. Among them is Odysseus, fabled storyteller and reluctant ally to the Mykene, who will soon face his former friends in combat.

Within the city's walls, the ailing Trojan king has pinned his hope on two great warriors: his favourite son Hektor, and Helikaon – who will avenge the death of his wife at Mykene hands.

War has been declared – a war fought by heroes whose fame will echo down the centuries . . .

Includes a tribute to David Gemmell's life and work by Conn Iggulden.

Available in paperback and ebook